This is th   which cor
of George Warleggan and his beautiful wife,
Elizabeth, and of the enmity between the two
households. It also introduces us to several
new characters, including Demelza's brothers,
Sam and Drake Carne, and Elizabeth's niece,
Morwenna, who falls in love with the one man
she cannot marry. Later Ross undertakes a
daring cross-channel raid to France to save
his friend Dwight Enys from a prison camp.

But above all the book is dominated by the
personal antipathy between Ross and George,
as both look back on their rivalry for Elizabeth's love . . .

WINSTON GRAHAM

The Black Moon

A Novel of Cornwall
1794–5

Collins
FONTANA BOOKS

First published in 1973 by William Collins Sons & Co Ltd
First issued in Fontana Books 1975
Eighth Impression October 1977

Copyright © Winston Graham, 1973

Made and printed in Great Britain by
William Collins Sons & Co Ltd Glasgow

For Marjory

Charles Vivian Raffe POLDARK (1667-1708)
m. Anna Maria Trenwith [of Trenwith] (1680-1758)

Agatha Mary

Claude Henry (1698-1748)
m. Matilda Ellen Peter (1699-1756)

Mary Ellen } died
Robert } young

Maria (1717-79)
m. Alfred Rupert Johns (1719-81)

Charles William (1719-86)
m. Verity Michell (1740-73)

Joshua (1724-83)
m. Grace Vennor (1740-70)

Rev. William Alfred Johns (1744-)
m. Dorothy Grenville

many children

Verity (1758-)
m. Andrew Blamey (1748-)

Francis (1760-92)
m. Elizabeth Chynoweth (1764-)

Charles } died
Claude } young
Robert }

Claude-Anthony
(1764-71)

Ross Vennor (1760-)
m. Demelza Carne (1770-)

Andrew (1793-)

Geoffrey Charles
(1784-)

Julia (1788-90)

Jeremy (1791-)

Jonathan CHYNOWETH [of Cusgarne] (1690-1750)
m. Anne Tregear (1693-1760)

Jonathan (1710-77)
m. Elizabeth Lanyon (1716-50)

   Jonathan (1737-)
   m. Joan Le Grice (1730-)

   Elizabeth (1764-)
   m. (1) Francis Poldark.
   (2) George Warleggan

Robert (1712-40)
m. Ursula Venning (1720-88)

   Hubert (1750-93)
   m. Amelia Tregellas (1751-)

     Morwenna (1776-)
     Garlanda (1778-)
     Carenza (1780-)
     Rowella (1781-)

Luke WARLEGGAN (1715-)
m. Bethia Kemp (1716-44)

   Nicholas [of Cardew] (1735-)
   m. Mary Lashbrook (1732-)

     George (1759-)
     m. Elizabeth Poldark (1764-)
     (née Chynoweth)

      Valentine (1794-)

Cary Warleggan (1740-)

Tom CARNE (1740-94)
m. Demelza Lyon (1752-77)

   Demelza (1770-)
   Luke (1771-)
   Samuel (1772-)
   William (1773-)
   John (1774-)
   Robert (1775-)
   Drake (1776-)

A preface to a novel – at least, a newly published novel – savours of pretensions, but in this case a word or two of explanation does seem essential.

Many years ago I wrote four novels about the Poldark family and eighteenth-century Cornwall. But after finishing them the modern world, and particularly the techniques of suspense, came to interest me more. Although thinking vaguely that some time in the future it might be enjoyable to pick up the Poldarks again, I gradually drifted further and further away from them in mood and in style. One does not grow older without development and change. Eventually the idea of writing another book about them came to be something not really open to serious consideration.

But sometimes the totally unexpected occurs, and one day last year, for no discoverable reason, it became necessary for me to see what happened to these people after Christmas night, 1793. I became very preoccupied with finding out, and it appeared to me, rightly or wrongly, that to return to an old mood was as much of a challenge as creating a new one. *The Black Moon* is the result.

But do not expect it to 'solve' everything, to tie up loose ends or to leave no new ones trailing. That isn't the way it happened at all.

BOOK ONE

CHAPTER ONE

Elizabeth Warleggan was delivered of the first child of her new marriage at Trenwith House in the middle of February, 1794. It was an occasion of some tension and anxiety.

Throughout it had been understood and agreed between Elizabeth and her new husband that the confinement should take place at their town house, where the best medical attention was available; but Truro had been pestilential for months, first with summer cholera which had persisted right through to Christmas, and then more lately with influenza and measles. There had seemed no hurry. Dr Behenna, who rode out weekly to see his patient, assured them that there was no hurry.

And so possibly there would not have been, but on the evening of the thirteenth, which was a Thursday, Elizabeth slipped and fell while going to her room. The fine stone staircase leading up from the great hall ran into a typically dark Tudor corridor from which the two main bedrooms of the house were reached by a flight of five more steps. Elizabeth caught her foot in the rough edge of the top stair and fell to the bottom. No one saw her, though two of the servants heard her cry out and the noise of her fall; and one of them, hurrying along the corridor with a warming pan, came upon her mistress lying like a broken flower across the bottom step.

Immediately the house was in panic. George, fetched from the winter parlour, came heart in mouth, picked up his fainting wife and carried her to bed. As Dr Dwight Enys was still at sea, the only medical man within easy reach was old Thomas Choake, so he was summoned for lack of a better, while another servant was sent galloping to fetch Dr Behenna.

Except for a bruised elbow and a turned ankle, Elizabeth at first seemed no worse, and after a generous bleeding she was given a warm cordial and settled off to sleep. George disliked almost everything about Choake: his pompous conceit, his boasted prowess in the hunting field, his neck-or-nothing surgery, his simpering wife, and his Whig opinions; but he

11

made the best of it, gave the old man supper and suggested he should stay the night. Choake, who had not been inside the house since Francis Poldark died, stiffly agreed.

It was a grey meal. Mrs Chynoweth, Elizabeth's mother, in spite of her blind eye, lame leg and stumbling tongue, had refused food and insisted on staying in her daughter's room to be there if she woke; so only old Jonathan Chynoweth joined the other two men at the table. Talk was of the war with France, which Choake, following his hero Fox, opposed, of Edward Pellew's exploits at sea, of the Duke of York's inept display in Flanders, of the reign of terror in Lyons, of the scarcity of corn, of the rising price of tin and copper. George despised both the men he sat with and was mainly silent listening to them wrangling, Choake's hoarse growl, Chynoweth's throaty tenor. For a time in his mind the anxiety had passed. Elizabeth had shaken herself, nothing more. But she must not be so abominably careless of herself. Often recently she had done what George considered foolhardy, reckless things, while carrying this precious burden, this first fruit of their marriage. One perhaps expected her to be depressed, temperamental, given to quick tears. One did not expect her to risk her life attempting to ride a horse which had been long in the stable and was unreliable at the best of times. One did not expect to find her lifting heavy books on to a high shelf. One did not expect . . .

It was a new side to her personality. George was always discovering new sides to her; some fascinated, some, like this, disturbed. From the first moment he set eyes on her so many years ago, he had always wanted her, but perhaps wanted her most as a collector, as a connoisseur wants the most beautiful thing he has ever seen. Since their marriage possession had familiarized but not spoiled the image. On the contrary, he had come to know her for the first time. If real love was in his nature, then he loved his wife.

On these calm reflections, breaking them up like a stone cast in a pool, interrupting the two stupid old men and their ill-informed chatter, came a servant to say that the mistress was awake again and had a bad pain.

Dr Behenna arrived at midnight, having left his Truro patients to the blundering mercies of his assistant. Choake did not offer to leave, and George let him stay. His fee was unimportant.

Daniel Behenna was a youngish man, still the right side of

forty, stout, short and authoritative, and had come to Truro only a few years ago. George Warleggan was a fairly shrewd judge, and he perceived that the wide demand for Dr Behenna's services in and around Truro might, at least in part, be a matter of personality and address. Nevertheless, he had had some startling successes with his new methods, and, above all, he had studied midwifery under one of the most distinguished of London physicians. He seemed far to be preferred to any other doctor within a day's ride.

After a short examination of the patient, he came out and told George that Mrs Warleggan's pains were certainly birth pangs. He described these as 'wandering' but otherwise normal. Quite clearly the child was now going to be premature, but it was still alive. Mrs Warleggan was standing the pains well and, although there would clearly be a greater risk now, he had every reason to be confident of the outcome.

At noon on the following day, in the worst of George's anxiety, his parents turned up, having nearly wrecked their coach traversing the winter tracks. They had been staying in town when the news reached them. Nicholas Warleggan said they felt it their duty to be with him at such a time. Trenwith, apart from its few splendid entertaining rooms, was not a big house by Elizabethan standards, and the secondary bedrooms were small and dark. George was barely polite to his parents and sent them off with a servant to settle in a cold room as best they could.

Elizabeth continued to have severe spasmodic pains, but at lengthy intervals, and the presentation, said Dr Behenna, although normal was far too slow. He took tea with the family at five and quoted from Galen, Hippocrates and Simon of Athens. The third stage of pregnancy had, he said, now begun, but if there was no issue shortly he had decided to use forceps since, he said, the mere irritation of these when applied to the child would be likely to stimulate the labour pains and provoke a natural birth.

But providence was on the mother's side, and at six the pains became more frequent without stimulation. At a quarter after eight she was delivered of a baby boy, alive and well. There was a total eclipse of the moon at the time.

A little later George was allowed up to see his wife and son. Elizabeth lay in bed like a clipped angel, her fair hair streaming across the pillow, her face limp and linen-pale but her eyes – for the first time for weeks – smiling. Until then George

13

had not realized how long it had been. He bent and kissed her damp forehead and then went across to peer at the wisp of humanity lying red-faced and trussed like a mummy in its cradle. His son. The fortune whose foundations Nicholas Warleggan had laid thirty-five years ago when he began tin smelting in the Idless valley had developed and multiplied until it included commercial, mining and banking interests which stretched as far as Plymouth and Barnstaple. George in the last ten years had been responsible for much of the later expansion. The child born today, if he survived the hazards of infancy, would inherit it all.

George knew well enough that his marriage to Elizabeth Poldark had been a great disappointment to his parents. Nicholas had married Mary Lashbrook, a miller's daughter with a nest-egg and no education – even today it showed plainly – but they had had very different ambitions for their son. *He* had had the education, *he* had the money, *he* was able to mix in circles completely closed to Nicholas as a young man – not entirely open to Nicholas even now. They had invited rich and eligible girls to their country seat at Cardew; they had risked snubs by holding parties for the titled and the well connected at their town house in Truro. They had asked questions and waited anxiously for the right name to drop from his lips, as they felt sure in the end it must. He had a strong personal eye to social advancement. A title would have been all. Even a small title. 'Mr George and the Hon. Mrs Mary Warleggan.' How nice even that would have sounded. Instead, after remaining unmarried until he was thirty, the age of discretion surely for a man who had been discreet even as a youth; now a clever, calculating, able man with his every thought turned towards power and advancement, he had chosen to marry the delicate, impoverished widow of Francis Poldark.

Not, of course, that Elizabeth's pedigree was anything but impeccably ancient and carried a considerable prestige in the county. In the ninth century one, John Trevelizek, had given a third of his land to his younger son, who took the name of Chynoweth, which meant New House. The elder son had died without issue, so that all had come to the younger. This first known Chynoweth had died in AD 889. It was doubtful if the King of England could go back so far. But George knew how his father felt. The stock was *exhausted*: look only at Elizabeth's father to see that. And in spite of their long lineage the Chynoweths had never done much more than survive. They had never attained distinction, nor even achieved the only worthwhile alternative available to mediocrity, the wealthy marriage. The nearest to eminence was an ancestor who had been a squire to Piers Gaveston, and that was not altogether a notable recommendation. Although always known to the great families of Cornwall, they had never had any personal or family link with them.

But Elizabeth was beautiful; and she had never seemed more so than now. Visited at discreet intervals by her various relations and friends, she looked as lovely, as frail and as unspotted by life as if she were twenty, not thirty, and as if this were her first marriage and her first confinement, not her second time round.

Among Elizabeth's first visitors was of course her father-in-law, and after he had kissed her and asked after her condition and admired his grandson, Nicholas Warleggan closed the heavy oak door of the bedroom behind him, carefully descended the almost-fatal five stairs, and walked heavily along the floor-creaking corridor to the main staircase and the great windowed hall. Perhaps, he thought, he should not be too unsatisfied. Here at least was the succession he had desired. His daughter-in-law had done all that could be asked of her. And perhaps the Warleggans now no longer needed, and in the future still less would need, powerful family connections. They need not woo the titled families of Cornwall: the families soon enough would be glad to accept them. They were strong enough in their own right. George's marriage to Elizabeth was already proving something of an asset – for she was definitely one of *them* – and a title might come their way by some other means: a seat in Parliament, large monetary gifts to one or other of the borough mongers . . . This war would certainly help. Those middlemen owning and marketing the commodities could not fail to prosper. Banking facilities would be in ever greater demand. The price of tin had risen £5 a ton last week.

As he came to the bottom step Nicholas Warleggan reflected that, as an additional bonus to her patrician breeding, Elizabeth had brought this house into the family, the Poldark family house, begun in 1509, not completed until 1531, and since then scarcely touched until George undertook his repairs and renovations of last summer.

The turns and twists of life led to some strange results.

Nicholas's first visit here eleven years ago had been to the reception and banquet following Elizabeth Chynoweth's marriage to the son of the house. Then the Poldarks, though impoverished enough, had seemed as securely settled here as they had been for the past hundred years, and the Trenwiths for another century and a half before them. Old Charles William had been alive, belching and stertorous but active enough, head of the house, of the district, of the clan, to be succeeded by Francis when the time came, a young and virile twenty-two – who was to guess at his untimely death? – then came daughter Verity, a plain little thing who'd later made a poor marriage and lived now in Falmouth. Besides this there were the cousins: William Alfred, that thin sanctimonious clergyman and his brood, now gone to a living in Devon. And Ross Poldark, who unfortunately was still around, and prospering by all accounts, not yet having fallen down a mineshaft or been imprisoned for debt or transported for inciting to riot, as he so well deserved. Sometimes the wicked and the arrogant flourished, against all reasonable probability.

As Nicholas Warleggan walked across to the splendid window one of George's new footmen came in to snuff the candles which had recently been lighted. The sky was still bright outside, with a frosty look against the butter-yellow of the candles. It had been a mild month, altogether a mild winter – fortunate for the many destitute, though not good for general health. Influenza, they said, was carried by the heavy clouds and spread by the humidity; it needed a cold snap to clear it away.

The fire hissed with new wood thrown on around a massive elm log which had been carried in yesterday. The footman finished his task and went silently out, leaving Nicholas Warleggan alone. That other time, that first time, eleven years ago, this fine hall had been far from silent. He remembered then how envious he had been of this house. Shortly afterwards he had bought one twice its size – Cardew, towards the other coast, in its own deer park, all in Palladian fashion and finished to the most modern style. Compared to it, this place was provincial and old-fashioned. Stonework showed inside everywhere, there was far too much black oak panelling in the bedrooms, many of the floorboards creaked and some of them had worm, the close-stools stank and were out of date compared to the *chaises-perchées* of Cardew, bedroom windows were ill-fitting and let in draughts. But it had style.

Apart from the satisfaction that it had always belonged to the Poldarks.

Nicholas remembered too at that wedding how grey-faced and haggard young Ross Poldark had looked. George had known him before, but it was *his* first sight of the fellow, and he had wondered at his sour look, his lidded eyes and high cheek bones, his disfiguring scar – until George told him. They had *all* wanted Elizabeth, it seemed: Ross, Francis and George. Ross had thought himself enfeoffed, but Francis had moved in while his cousin was in America. Three young fools all at loggerheads, all for a pretty face. What else was there about this girl to make her so desirable? Nicholas shrugged and took a poker to stir the fire. The *delicacy*, he supposed, the frailty, the lovely ethereal quality; all men wanted to nurture, to protect, to be the strong man caring for the beautiful helpless woman, potential Launcelots looking for a Guinevere. Strange that his own son, so sane, so logical, in many ways almost too calculating, should have been one of them!

As he pushed at the fire one of the smaller logs fell out with a clatter, brightly burning and smoking at one end, and Nicholas stooped to pick up the tongs. As he did so something moved in the chair beside the fire. He started up sharply and dropped the poker. The chair had been in the half shadow but now he saw someone was sitting in it.

'Who's that?' said a thin voice, sexless in its age. 'Be that you, George? These damned servants . . .'

Agatha Poldark. Aside from young Geoffrey Charles, the child of Elizabeth's first marriage, who hardly yet counted, Agatha was the only Poldark left in the house. To all the Warleggans she was affrontful, a haggard hunk of gristle and bone, properly long since dead. Nowadays she even smelt of the grave, but in spite of everything an activating spirit moved in her. Nicholas's wife, Mary, who to the family's annoyance was a prey to every superstition, regarded the old lady with real dread as if she were somehow animated by the protesting ghosts of generations of long-dead Poldarks wishing ill upon the interlopers. Agatha in this house was the snag in the silk, the fly in the ointment, the stone over which everyone sooner or later stumbled and fell. It was said that she would be ninety-nine in August. A year or so ago it had looked as if she were taking permanently to her bed, so that at the worst then she could have been quietly ignored by everyone except the maid appointed to look after her;

17

but since Elizabeth's marriage, and especially when she learned that a new child was on the way, she had recovered a spark of combative vitality and was apt to be found tottering about the house at the most unsuitable times.

'Oh, 'tis George's father . . .' A tear escaped from one eye, lodged in the nearest furrow and began slowly to work its way down towards the whiskery chin. This was no sign of emotion. 'Been up to see the chibby, have you? Regular little spud, he be. A Chynoweth through an' through.'

A black kitten moved on her lap. This was Smollet, which she had found somewhere a few months ago and made peculiarly her own. Now they were inseparable. Agatha never stirred without the kitten, and Smollet, all red tongue and yellow eyes, could hardly ever be persuaded to leave her. Geoffrey Charles, with a small boy's glee, always called the cat 'Smell-it'.

Nicholas knew that Agatha only said what she had said to annoy him, yet was annoyed by it nevertheless. He was further irritated that he could not reply to her in suitable terms, for she was very deaf and, unless one shouted in her ear – and such nearness was offensive – no communication was possible. So she could go on talking, making outrageous remarks, without fear of contradiction. George had told him that the only way of annoying her was to turn one's back and walk away while she was speaking, but Nicholas was damned if he was going to be driven away from the fire by this repulsive old woman.

He put the log back, but inefficiently, so that an end of it sent a thin spiral of smoke up into the room. He would have rung for a servant to correct this, but he let it smoke in the hope that it would irritate Agatha's chest.

'That surgeon,' said Agatha. 'Great numbskull of a fellow, tying up the poor little crim so tight against the convulsions. There's better ways than that to protect against convulsions. I'd have'n freed this eve if I had the ordering of it.'

'You do not have the ordering of it,' said Mr Warleggan.
'Eh, what's that? What's that you say? Speak up!'

He might have shouted something in return, but a door opened then and George came in. At times, perhaps most when not in company and therefore both were relaxed, the similarity between the two men was marked. A little shorter than his tall father, George had the same heavy build, the same strong neck, the same deliberate in-toed walk. They were both good-looking men in their formidable way. George's

18

face was the broader, with the bottom lip drawn up in the middle and jutting to create shadow. There were small lumps on his forehead between the eyebrows. If his hair had been cut in short tight curls he would have looked like the Emperor Vespasian.

'A pretty sight,' he said, as he neared the fire. 'My own father in conversation with the original Witch of Endor. How does it go? "I saw Gods ascending out of the earth. An old man cometh up and he is covered with a mantle." '

Mr Warleggan at last put the poker back. 'You should not let your mother hear you speak in that way. She has no fancy for supernatural talk even in jest.'

'I'm not sure it is in jest,' said George. 'In better days this old twitching decayed carcase would have been helped on its way by a suitable ducking or a witch's bridle. We should not have to suffer it in a civilized household.'

The kitten, to Agatha's pleasure, had arched its back and spat at the new arrival.

'Well, George,' she said. 'I trust you feel a bigger man now you're father of an eight-month brat. What's he to be called, eh? There's too many Georges about, with all these kings. I mind the time . . .' She coughed. 'Fire's smeeching. Mr Warleggan's scat it all asunder.'

'If I were you I should have the creature confined to her room,' Nicholas said. 'She should be guarded there.'

'If I had my way,' George said, 'she would be thrown on the midden tomorrow – and perhaps others with her.'

'Well, whose way do you have?' asked Nicholas, knowing very well.

George looked at him speculatively. 'The way of a man in possession of a fair city. When the citadel has been won the stews can wait awhile.'

'You could name him Robert,' came the thin voice from the armchair. 'Him with the crooked back. First of the name that we know. Or Ross. What'd you say to Ross?' The wheezing which broke out might have been caused by the smoke but more probably it was the result of an old frame trying to accommodate malicious laughter.

George turned his back and strolled to the window and looked out. Although the hall was warm near the fire, cold airs stirred as soon as one moved out of its range. 'I trust,' he said, 'that soon this old creature will swell up into a great tumour and burst.'

'Amen . . . But touching on names, George. I conject

19

that you and Elizabeth will already have some thoughts on the matter. We own some good ones within the family – '

'I have already decided. I decided before he was born.'

'Before he was born? Oh, but how could you do that? If it were a girl – '

'This accident to Elizabeth,' said George. 'It might have been fatal to them both, but now it has not been so I feel some heavy finger of providence in it – as if it were pointing a time and a place and date. Having regard to the date, as soon as I knew the child would be born on that day, I chose the name. If it were a girl, the same.'

Mr Warleggan waited. 'What is it, then?'

'Valentine.'

'Or Joshua,' said Aunt Agatha. 'We've had three in the family to my knowledge, though the last was a bad boy if ever there was one.'

Nicholas hopefully watched the thin smoke from the fire curling round the old woman's chair. 'Valentine. Valentine Warleggan. It matches well, is easy on the tongue. But there is no one in either family of that name.'

'There will be nobody in either family like my son. History does not have to repeat itself.'

'Yes, yes. I will ask your mother how it appeals to her. Is this Elizabeth's choice too?'

'Elizabeth does not know it yet.'

Nicholas raised his eyebrows. 'But you are sure she will like it?'

'I am sure she will agree. We are in accord in so many things, many more than I expected. She will agree that this union of her and me is a rare one – the oldest gentry and the newest – and that the fruit of such a union should not look to the past but to the future. A quite new name is what we must have.'

Nicholas coughed and moved out of range of the smoke. 'You will not get away from the name Warleggan, George.'

'I shall never have the least desire to get away from it, Father. Already it is respected – and feared.'

'As you say . . . The respect is what we must build on, the fear is what we must dissipate.'

'Uncle Cary would not agree.'

'You pay too much attention to Cary. What was your business with him last week?'

'Routine affairs. But I believe you draw too fine a line, Father, between respect and fear. One merges with the other and back again. You cannot separate two emotions of such similar colour.'

'Probity in business induces the first.'

'And improbity the second? Oh, come –'

'Not improbity, perhaps, but the misuse of power. In a moment you will be telling me I read you a lecture. But Cary and I have never seen eye to eye on this. I ask you, whose name do you wish your son to bear?'

'Yours and mine,' said George evenly. 'That is the one he will bear. And where I have walked on your shoulders, he shall walk on mine.'

Nicholas went back to the fire and replaced the smoking log where the smoke could go up the chimney.

'That's better, my son,' said Agatha, waking from a doze. 'You don't want the fire floshed all about the hearth.'

'God alive, I believe that old woman's stench has drifted over here!' In irritation George went over and pulled the tasselled bell. Mr Warleggan continued to cough. The smoke, although now dispersing, had settled on his chest and he could not clear it. Without speaking they waited until the servant came.

'Fetch the Harry brothers,' George said.

'Yes, sir.'

'Take a glass of canary,' George said to his father.

'Thank you, no. It's of no moment . . .'

He spat in the hearth.

'Comfrey and liquorice,' said Aunt Agatha. 'I had a sister died of the lungs, and naught would soothe her but comfrey and liquorice.'

Presently Harry Harry hulked in the doorway, followed by his younger brother Tom. 'Sur?'

George said: 'Remove Miss Poldark to her room. When you are there ring for Miss Pipe and tell her that Miss Poldark is not to come down again today.'

The two big men brought up a smaller chair and lifted Aunt Agatha protesting into it. Clutching the mewing kitten to her breast, she croaked: 'There be one thing amiss with your little son, George. Good seldom comes to a child born under a black moon. I only know two and they both came to bad ends!'

Nicholas Warleggan's face was purple. His son went across to the table, poured wine into a glass and brought it impatiently back.

'No . . . it is the . . . Oh, well, a sip will help perhaps.'

'Elizabeth'll hear 'bout this!' said Aunt Agatha. 'Carried out of me own hall like a spar o' driftwood . . . Ninety year I known this hall. Ninety year . . .' Her frail complaints disappeared behind Tom Harry's broad back as she was carried up the stairs.

'We should have had Elizabeth at Cardew for the lying in,' said Mr Warleggan between coughs and sips, 'then we should have been spared these irritations.'

'I think it not inappropriate that our first child should have been born here.'

'But shall you stay? I mean to make it your home?'

A wary look crossed George's face. 'I am not sure. We have not yet decided. This has *been* Elizabeth's home, you understand. I do not fancy selling it. Nor do I fancy maintaining it solely for the convenience of the Chynoweths and the residue of the Poldarks. And I have already spent money, as you can see.'

'Indeed.' Nicholas wiped his eyes and put away his handkerchief. He eyed his son. 'There is one other Poldark to be considered, George.'

'Geoffrey Charles? Yes. I have nothing against him. I have promised to Elizabeth that his education shall be as expensive as she desires.'

'It is not just that. It is the fact of his being so firmly attached to his mother's apron strings. I hope your son – this new baby – will distract Elizabeth from her preoccupation with him, but it would seem necessary – '

'I know exactly what would seem necessary, Father. Give me leave to manage my own household.'

'I'm sorry. I had thought simply to suggest . . .'

George frowned down at a stain on his cuff. The matter of Geoffrey Charles's future had been one of the few points of difference with Elizabeth these last months.

'Geoffrey Charles is to have a governess.'

'Ah . . . Good . . . But at ten – '

'He would be better with a tutor or to go away. I agree. Some good school near London. Or Bath. That we – have not been able to arrange yet.'

'Ah.'

After a pause, while Nicholas read between the lines, George added. 'For a year or so, at least until he is eleven, he will stay here. We have found a suitable person to look after him.'

'A local person?'

22

'Bodmin. You will remember the Reverend Hubert Chynoweth, who was the Dean there. He was Jonathan's cousin.'

'Did he die?'

'Last year. Like all the Chynoweths he had no private
money, and his family is poorly off. The eldest girl is seventeen. She is genteel – like all the Chynoweths – and has had
some education. It will please Elizabeth to receive her.'

Mr Warleggan grunted. 'I would have thought there were
enough Chynoweths about the place. But if it suits you . . .
You've seen her?'

'Elizabeth knew her as a child. But a dean's daughter as a
governess should be no social detriment.'

'Yes, I see that. And she will know how to behave. The
question is whether she will be able to make Master Geoffrey
Charles behave. He has been greatly spoiled and needs a firm
hand.'

'That in due course he shall have,' George said. 'This is an
interim measure. An experiment. We must see how it works.'

Mr Warleggan mopped his forehead with his handkerchief.
'My cough has gone now that old woman has gone. D'you
know I believe she wished it on me.'

'Oh, nonsense.'

'What was that – what was that she said about the child
being born under a black moon?'

'There was an eclipse on Friday, a total eclipse, at the
time of his birth. You didn't notice?'

'No. I was too preoccupied.'

'So was I. But the Sherborne paper mentioned it. And
I did notice the animals, and some of the servants, were
restless.'

'Your mother is coming down for supper?'

'I assume so. We shall go in in ten minutes.'

'Then . . .' Nicholas Warleggan shrugged uncomfortably.
'If I were you, do not mention that old woman's nonsense
to her.'

'I had no intention of doing so.'

'Well, you know how she is – a little wayward in matters of
superstition. She has always paid too much attention to
signs and portents. It is better not to worry her with such
things.'

CHAPTER TWO

In the mid morning of a windy March day two young men were tramping along the mule track which led past the engine house and the derelict buildings of Grambler Mine. It was a day of lowering clouds and flurries of rain, the wind westerly, booming and blundering. Glimpses of the sea showed it to be licked white and untidy; where there were rocks a mist of spray drifted.

A dozen or so cottages straggled beside the mine. These were still occupied though in poor repair; the mine buildings themselves – those not built of stone – were already in ruin; but much of the headgear and the three engine houses remained. Grambler – on which the prosperity of the senior Poldarks had depended, to say nothing of three hundred miners and spallers and bal-maidens – had been closed now for six years and the prospects of its ever opening again were remote. It was a depressing sight.

''Tis the same all the way, Drake,' said the elder one. 'One mine smoking twixt here and Illuggan. It is a dire picture. But we must not sink into the sin of ingratitude. A merciful God has ordained it so for our chastisement.'

'We're on the right way?' asked Drake. 'I never been afore. Did I come? I don't mind it.'

'No, you was too small.'

'How much farther then?'

'Three or four mile. I don't recollect too well.'

They turned and went on, both tall young men not immediately recognizable as brothers. Sam, the elder by four years, looked more than twenty-two. He had big shoulders, an ungainly walk, a thin, deeply furrowed face, which looked sombre as if it bore all the sorrows of the world, until he smiled, when the sorrowful lines broke up into benign and affable creases. Drake was equally tall but of slighter build and notably good-looking, with a fine skin unmarked by the pox; a mischievous face; he looked as if he enjoyed poking fun. It was a propensity he had had to keep on a leash when in the vicinity of his father. They were both poorly but respectably dressed – in dark blue barragan trousers with low quartered shoes, waistcoats and jackets over coarse shirts. Sam wore an old hat, Drake a pink striped neckcloth. Both carried small bundles and sticks.

They crossed the Mellingey stream by a footbridge that nearly gave way under them, then climbed to a coppice of pine trees, with beyond it the next ruined mine, Wheal Maiden, which had been silent half a century and looked it. Stones lay where they had fallen. Anything of use had long since been carried away. The rooks rose and made a commotion at being disturbed.

But now in the shallow valley they were entering they could see smoke. On a quiet day they would have seen it earlier. Both walked a little slower as they neared the end of their journey, as if hesitant to end it. As they went down the high hedged lane they could peer between the ferns and the brambles, the hawthorn and the wild nut trees, and could see the engine house – not a new one, it looked as if it had been rebuilt – but the headgear was all new, the huts that clustered around were new and in obvious use; the Mellingey stream, which curled back into this valley, had been dammed and they could hear the thump and clatter of the water-driven tin stamps; all the noises had been held back by the wind; a dozen women worked on a washing floor; farther down the water activated a sweep which rotated awkwardly round and round helping to separate the ore. A train of mules with panniers on were being driven up the opposite slope of the valley. At the foot of the valley, with a small lawn and a few bushes only separating it from all the industry, was a low granite-built house, part slate roof, part thatch, bigger and grander than a farm house, with its outbuildings, its squat chimneys, its straggling wing and its mullioned windows, yet hardly of the distinction to be called a gentleman's residence. Behind the house the land rose again in a ploughed field running up to a headland; beyond scrubland to the right was a beach with a scarf of slaty sea.

'Twasn't no lie,' said Drake.

'Reckon you're right. It look different from when I came afore.'

'This work is all new?'

''S I reckon. Nanfan said it had not been started more'n two year.'

Drake ran a hand through his shock of black hair. ''Tis a handsome house. 'Though not near so great as Tehidy.'

'The Poldarks is small gentry, not big.'

'Big enough for we,' said Drake with a nervous laugh.

'All men are alike in the sight of the eternal Jehovah,' said Sam.

'Mebbe so, but it isn't Jehovah we got to deal with.'

'No, brother. But all people are set at liberty by the blood of Christ.'

They went on and recrossed the stream and came up to the house. Disturbed, some seagulls blew up from the lawn like white clothes flapping in the wind.

The two young men were saved the necessity of knocking because the front door opened and a small plump brown-haired middle-aged woman came out carrying a basket. When she saw them she stopped and rubbed her free hand down her apron.

'Yes?'

'If ye please, ma'am,' said Sam. 'We'd like to see your mistress.'

'Just tell her two friends has called.'

'Friends?' Jane Gimlett eyed them and hesitated, but she was not sufficiently the well-trained servant to stare them down. 'Wait here,' she said, and turned back into the house. She found her mistress in the kitchen bathing one of Jeremy's knees where he had scuffed it climbing a wall. A large hairy dog of anonymous breed lay at her feet. 'There's two young men at the door, ma'am, want to see ee. Miners or the like, I'd say.'

'Miners? From our mine?'

'Nay. Strangers. From a distance, I'd say.'

Demelza looped up a curl of hair and straightened. 'Stay there, my handsome,' she said to Jeremy, and walked along the passage to the front door, frowning in the brighter light. At first she did not recognize either of them.

'We came to see ye, sister,' said Sam. 'Tis six years since we met. D'you recall me? I'm Sam, the second one. I mind you well. This is Drake, the youngest. He were seven when you left home.'

'Judas!' said Demelza. 'How you've both grown!'

Ross had been up at Wheal Grace with Captain Henshawe and the two engineers who had built the engine. They had been over to check a fault which had developed in the pump rod, and the engine had been stopped for half a day until they came; so the opportunity had been taken to carry out the monthly cleaning of the boiler.

It was in a thoughtful but cheerful mood that Ross started

back to the house. The mine, he thought, had now reached the limits of its foreseeable expansion. It employed thirty tributers, twenty-five tut-men, six binders and timbermen, and about forty workers of one sort and another above ground. The engine was now working at near its comfortable capacity, and the water it pumped up from sixty fathoms was ingeniously channelled into a wooden trough which worked a small water-wheel at surface which itself worked a secondary and much smaller pump. The water then flowed down a ten-fathom adit until it worked a second water-wheel built sixty feet below the level of the first wheel and about thirty feet below the level of the sloping ground, where it ran on down the adit to come out at the washing floor built just above Demelza's garden. A fair amount of the mined ore was still sent to be crushed and washed at the tin stamps of Sawle Combe, for there was not enough room for more stamps in this valley without destroying it as a place to live.

Further extension of the mine looked uneconomic. To build another engine or to attempt to work this one harder would be self-defeating. Coal cost 18s a ton free on board, and even the war had not yet raised the price of tin to a level where a fair return was assured. One of the contributing causes of this was a swing in fashion away from the use of pewter to the use of cloam and china. It was a nation-wide change of habit and had come at just the wrong time.

Nevertheless, because the lodes were so rich and, in spite of their depth, so accessible, this mine was paying where so many others were failing or had failed. Great concerns like United Mines had been losing £11,000 a year before they closed. Wheal Grace, small as it was, was rich beyond his hopes and in six months had eaten up his many debts like a benevolent Lucullus. Two months' profit had paid off the whole of his £1,400 debt to Caroline Penvenen; in another two months he had discharged his debts to Pascoe's Bank and swept away all his lesser dues; by May he could repay the twenty-year-old mortgage which Harris Pascoe personally held. Soon there would be money on deposit in the bank, or to invest in five per cents, or to keep in bags under the bed, or to spend on whatever they wanted most.

It was a heady brew. Neither he nor Demelza had become acclimatized yet; they behaved as if the last ton of ore might be raised this afternoon. A week ago he had taken Demelza down the mine and shown her the two rich and expanding floors; supposedly it had been to convince her; in

27

fact, though he saw them daily, it was as much to convince himself. He felt he needed the reassurance of her conviction too.

With the mine being so close to the house he went home most days for dinner, which was usually about 2 p.m. It was now barely 1, but he had some mine figures he would work out in the library. Since the reconciliation of Christmas he had spent as much time at home as possible; it was another form of reassurance. They had all but lost each other – she had been prepared to go, had been on her way out of the house. Now it seemed incredible that they had been so near to parting. The warmth of their reconciliation had been full of passion, had brought them closer in some ways than they had ever been before, all defences down. Yet it had been a slightly feverish warmth – and still was – as if their relationship were recovering from a near-mortal wound and they were trying to reassure themselves. The quieter levels of absolute trust which had existed before had not yet been regained.

And tempering their delight and relief at the success of the mine was the knowledge of the alien presence at Trenwith House only four miles away. Often they would forget it; then it would recur like an undulant pain, so that temporarily they were at a distance from each other again. The birth and christening of Valentine Warleggan was the latest thorn in the flesh. Neither said what was uppermost in their minds; it could never be uttered by anyone. But Caroline Penvenen had written to Demelza:

'Such disappointment not to see you there, though to tell the truth I had hardly expected it, knowing the deep and abiding love Ross and George have for each other. I do not remember ever having been inside Trenwith before; it's a fine house. The brat is dark, but I think favours Elizabeth; a well formed and quite handsome child, as children go. (I never really care for them until they are about three years old. Dwight will have to arrange it for me somehow!) A big assemblage for the Christening – I did not know there were so many Warleggans, and one or two of the older ones a small matter unsavoury. Also as much of the near-by county as would turn out on a cold day.' She had gone into details of those present.

'Uncle Ray not able to go with me, alas too weak. He misses Dwight's ministrations. The last letter from Dwight

28

was two weeks gone, aboard the *Travail*; but that itself was two weeks old when received, so in knowledge of his whereabouts I am already a month out of date. I fume at this like a love-lorn maiden in a tower, feeling it the worse for the knowledge that but for me he would not be in the Navy at all. I wish someone would *stop* this war . . .'

Although the letter had been written in all friendship, Ross would have been glad not to have received it. It lit the scene and revived memories of the house and the people he knew so well. The one person Caroline did not mention in the letter was Elizabeth herself. She did not of course know half the story, but clearly she knew enough to exercise tact in a letter to Demelza. He could not and would not have gone to the christening had they been invited; but it irked him more than he had ever thought probable that he was debarred from the family home, from calling on old Agatha, from seeing his nephew, from viewing the renovations and repairs that were taking place. He had seen enough when he made his last uninvited call at Christmas to know that the house was already changing its character, was taking on an alien personality.

As he passed the window of the parlour he glanced in and saw his wife seated in conversation with two strange young men.

He turned at once and went into them.

Jeremy wriggled off her knee and ran to him crying: 'Papa! Papa!' He picked him up and hugged him and set him down while the two young men stood awkwardly, not quite sure what to do with their hands. Demelza was wearing the bodice of fine white poplin she had made out of two of Ross's shirts and decorated with lace from an old shawl; a cream linen skirt, a green apron; a bunch of keys dangled from her waist. They had not yet found the opportunity to replenish her wardrobe.

'Do you remember my brothers, Ross?' Demelza said. 'This is Samuel, the second oldest, and Drake, the youngest. They have walked over from Illuggan to see us.'

A hesitation. 'Well,' said Ross. 'It has been a long time.' They shook hands, but guardedly, without warmth.

'Six year,' said Sam. 'Or thereabout. Since I were here, that is. Drake hasn't been afore. Drake was too young to come then.'

'Tis a tidy stroll for a little one even now,' said Drake.

Demelza said: 'I believe your legs are longer than Sam's.'

'We've all got long legs, sister,' said Sam soberly. 'Tis something our mother give us. And you the same, no doubt, if the truth be seen.'

Ross said: 'Have you been offered something to drink? Geneva? Or a cordial?'

'Thank ye. Sister did ask. But later maybe, a glass of milk. We don't touch spirits.'

'Ah,' said Ross. 'Well, sit down.' He glanced at Demelza and hesitated whether to leave them, but her lifted eyebrow invited him to stay. So he sat too.

'Tis not that we mind drink in others,' Drake explained, lightening his brother's tone. 'But we better prefer not to take it ourselves.'

'How is your father?' Ross asked, with a natural association of ideas.

'The most high God was pleased to take'n to Himself last month,' Sam said. 'Father died well prepared for his meeting wi' his blessed Saviour. We come to tell sister. That and other things.'

'Oh,' said Ross. 'I'm sorry.' He looked again at Demelza to see how this news had affected her, and he saw not at all. 'How – what was amiss?'

'He died of the pox. He hadn't never had it, and it came sudden and he was buried within the week.'

Ross decided that the elder brother's voice, though fervent, was not charged with emotion. Filial love had been a duty, not a choice.

'We all had it when we was young,' said Drake. 'It marked us but little. Did you have it, sister?'

'Nay,' said Demelza, 'but I nursed you through it. Three of you at one time, and Father stone drunk every night.'

There was a pause. Sam sighed. 'Well, give him his due, those days has been past these purty many year. Not since he wed again did he ever touch liquor.'

'And Step-Mother Nellie?' said Demelza. 'She is well?'

'Bravish. Luke is wed and from home. William and John and Bobby have followed father and would be down mine, but the mine is closed. There's rare poverty in Illuggan.'

'Not merely in Illuggan,' said Ross.

'True 'nough, brother,' agreed Sam. 'Round Illuggan and Camborne way, when I were a little tacker there was upwards of five-and-forty engines working. Day and night. Day and night. Now there's four. Dolcoath's gone, and North Downs,

Wheal Towan, Poldice, Wheal Damsel, Wheal Unity. I could read ye a list so long as my arm!'

'And what do you do?' asked Ross.

'I'm a tributer like the rest,' said Sam. 'When I can lease a pitch. But the Lord in his great mercy have seen fit to afflict me too. Drake here were apprenticed to a wheelwright for seven year. He d'work on and off, but most lately there has been naught for he neither.'

Ross began to suspect the purpose of their visit but refrained from saying so. 'You are both – of the Methodist connexion?' he asked.

Sam nodded his head. 'We both have a new spirit and walk in the path of Christ, following his statutes.'

'I thought you were the one that *hadn't* seen the light,' Demelza said. 'Yes ago, when Father came once asking me to go home, he said all were converted but you, Samuel.'

Sam looked embarrassed, ran a hand over his lined young face. 'That is so, sister. You've a rare memory. I lived without God amidst innumerable sins and provocations for upwards of twenty year. I existed in the gall of bitterness and in the bond of iniquity. But at last God pardoned all my sins and set my soul at liberty.'

'And now,' said Drake, 'Sam has found salvation more stronger than the rest of us.'

Ross glanced at the other boy. There was a suggestion of irony in the tone but none in the pale composed face. This one had a look of Demelza; the colouring, the eyes, the clarity of skin. Perhaps too in a sense of humour. 'You're not so sure for yourself?' he asked.

Drake smiled. 'Upon times I d'fall from grace.'

'Don't we all,' said Ross.

'You're of the connexion too, brother?' Sam said eagerly.

'No, no,' Ross said. 'It was meant as a general comment on life, no more.'

Jeremy ran back and pulled at his mother's skirt. 'Can I go now, Mama?' he asked. 'Can I g'n play with Garrick?'

'Yes. But mind for yourself. No more walls till that has healed.'

When he had gone Sam said: 'You 'ave others, sister?'

'No, the only one. We lost a girl.' Demelza smoothed her skirt. 'And Father and the widow? They have others, I recollect?'

'A little cheeil rising five, named Flotina. Three others was all called to God.'

'God has a lot to answer for,' said Ross.

There was an embarrassed silence. In the end neither boy rose to the bait, as their father would certainly have done. Demelza said: 'What time did you leave home this morning?'

'Left home? Soon after cocklight. We took but one wrong turn and was sent back by gamekeepers. I was in the error for I thought twas the way we had come last time.'

'You possibly had,' Ross said. 'But there are new owners at Trenwith who are blocking paths that have been rights of way for generations.'

'It is too far to walk back today,' Demelza said. 'You must stay over.'

'Well, thank ye, sister.' Samuel cleared his throat. 'I' fact, sister – and brother too – we was come to ask a favour of ye. In Illuggan there's many as has not tasted flesh meat in three months. We d'live on barley bread and weak tea – and pilchards when they can be got. That's not to complain, mind. Merciful Jesus saves us from any hunger of the soul. We are refreshed by the clear fount of His eternal love. But many die of want and disease, and have fallen asleep in their sins.'

He dried up and grimaced. 'Go on,' Ross said quietly.

'Well, here, brother, we hear tell there's work. Word reached us last month that your mine was doing bravely. It was said as you'd took on twenty new hands last month and twenty the month afore. Me and Drake. I'm so good a tributer as you'll find, though I says it myself. Drake's a handy man, handy at all manner of things, aside from the turning of a wheel. We come to see if there's work for us here.'

Jeremy had just taken Garrick into the garden, and Garrick was bouncing around him and barking. Jeremy was the only one now who could make Garrick behave like a puppy. Ross bit at his finger and looked across at Demelza. She had her hands folded in her lap, her eyes demurely down. This did not at all disguise from him the fact that a lot would be going on in her head and that she would have a number of precise and coherent views on the subject of this request. But she was giving him no inclination of what they were. This presumably meant that she wanted him to make up his mind.

All very well, but it directly concerned her. This was a difficult request for him to refuse: relationship, need on their part, prosperity on his. But Demelza had had to fight to get away from her family – chiefly her father. She was still remembered everywhere, no doubt, as a miner's daughter; but as his wife she had been accepted in most society over these last four years. Now that they had money they could progress further. Good clothes, some jewellery, a renovated home. They could entertain and be entertained. She would not be human if, after years of near poverty, she did not now have ambition. Did she at this stage want to be trammelled wilth two brothers living near-by, working men, poorly spoken, claiming relationship and privileges which would embarrass her and everyone else? Not merely would this raise contacts with the people who worked for them: the miners, the engine men, the streamers, the blowers, the bal-boys and bal-maidens, the farm labourers, the cottagers, the house servants. At the moment, although it was known she was one of them, it was accepted that she was Mistress Poldark. The present relationship with everyone was a singularly good one; there was real liking and friendship but also real respect. How might it be altered by the arrival of the two Carnes? And these two might be followed by three or four others. What if they married round here? Would it suit Demelza to have a brood of mining in-laws, necessarily poor, necessarily ill-found, naturally claiming something different from the rest? Particularly the women. Women didn't have the same tact and sense of position as men.

He said: 'This is a small mine. We do not employ above a hundred, counting all both above and below grass. Our prosperity is of very recent growth. Nine months ago I was in Truro arranging for the sale of the engine and headgear of our mine to the venturers of Wheal Radiant. Now we have found tin in such quanity that, even at the uneconomic price of tin today, we are making a substantial profit. All the signs are that the two lodes are widening and deepening as we advance. There is at least two years' work ahead for all. Beyond that I cannot say. But with the price of tin so low, with the margins of profit so narrow, it is comon sense not to expand more. First, because the more tin there is on the market the less it will fetch. Second, because the longer the war lasts the more likely there is to be need of metals, and the more chance then of a rise in price. So we have had to turn many people away when they came to seek for work.'

He paused and looked at the two young men. He wasn't

sure how much they would grasp of this, but they seemed to be following well enough.

Sam said: 'We would not wish for to take other men's work.'

'I think,' said Ross, 'it is something on which I shall have to consult Captain Henshawe. This I can best do in the morning. Therefore I'd suggest that you spend the night here. I think we can put you up either in the house or in the barn.'

'Thank you, brother.'

'Captain Henshawe has all the hiring of the workmen, and I shall know better when I have spoken to him. And in the meantime we will give you dinner.'

'Thank you, brother.'

Demelza stirred, to push her hair from her brow. 'I think,' she said, 'Samuel and Drake, that it is proper for you to call me sister. But I think it is proper that you should call my husband Captain Poldark.'

Sam's face broke up into its smile. 'That, sister, we'll gladly do. I ask your pardon, but tis more in the way of the Methodist connexion to call all men brother. Tis a manner o' speaking.'

Ross pursed his lips. 'So be it,' he said at length. 'I will see Captain Henshawe in the morning. But you understand it is not a promise of work, only a promise to consult with him.'

'Thank ye,' said Sam.

'Thank you, cap'n,' said Drake.

Demelza got up. 'I will tell Jane we shall be two more to dinner.'

'Thank ye, sister,' said Sam. 'But d'ye follow twas not for that that we come.'

'I understand.'

Ross told the young men to sit down again and then followed Demelza out. As he caught her up in the passage he pinched her bottom and she gave a muffled squeak.

'No indication,' he said. 'I have no idea whether you want me to give them work or not.'

'It is your mine, Ross.'

'But it is your choice.'

'Then the answer is, yes, of course I do.'

That night in bed Ross said: 'I have had word with Henshawe and we can fix them up. That's if they are willing to

34

take what we give them. I don't want to increase the number of tributers, and I can't take men off their pitches; but there's room for one extra tut-worker, and Drake can be employed in the engine house if he so chooses.'

'Thank you, Ross.'

'But you realize that these young men may possibly prove an embarrassment to you.'

'In what way?'

Ross explained some of the ways.

'Well, yes, that may be so,' she said. 'So I shall have to suffer it, shan't I. And so will you.'

'Not to the same extent. Anyway it is your decision. I must say you gave me as much idea of your feelings this afternoon as when we are playing whist and you forget what is trumps.'

'When have I done that? Ever only once!' She sat up against the pillow, leaning her elbow on it, and looked at him. 'Seriously, Ross, although I'm your wife and share everything, this is still *your* property, *your* mine, *your* people. So if you say you do not want these young men, well, send them off without thinking of the relationship! It is your *right* to be able to do so, and if you do I'll not complain of it.'

'But for your choice they will stay?'

'Yes, for my choice they will stay.'

'Enough. No more need be said.'

'A little more need be said, Ross; for you cannot expect me to maintain my dignity in the house if you pinch me the way you did this afternoon when we were scarcely out of their sight!'

'All ladies of quality must learn to suffer this,' Ross said. 'But they show this quality by suffering it in silence.'

A ribald reply came to Demelza's lips but she suppressed it. It was in the quick thrust and counter-thrust of joking that the chasms could still appear. Probably Ross sensed this, for he knew that with no holds barred it was practically impossible to get the better of his wife. He put his hand on her knee under her night-shift and let it close quietly there.

'Where shall you lodge them?' Demelza asked.

'I was thinking of Mellin. Now that old Joe Triggs has gone Aunt Betsy has a room. It would help her too.'

She said ruminatively: 'I think I might've recognized Sam, but d'you know I should never have thought it was Drake.'

'He's somewhat like you, isn't he?' Ross said.

'What?'

'Well, the colouring. The shape of face. And a look in his eye.'

'What sort of a look?'

'You ought to know . . . Difficult. Hard to handle.'

Demelza withdrew her knee. 'I knew there was some ill word coming.'

Ross put his hand on her other knee. 'I prefer this one. This one has the scar on it where you fell out of the elm tree when you were fifteen.'

'No. I only scratched my legs then. This was when I pulled the cupboard on top of myself.'

'You see. Exactly what I meant. Difficult. Hard to handle.'

'And getting battered an' worn.'

'Not to notice. Blemishes on the beauty of a person one loves are like grace notes adding something to a piece of music.'

'Judas,' said Demelza. 'What a pretty speech. You'd best go to sleep or I shall begin to think you're serious.'

'Pretty speeches,' said Ross, 'should always be taken serious.'

'That I will do, Ross. And thank you. And I promise not to remind you of it in the harsh light of day.'

They lay quiet for a time. Ross was feeling sleepy and he allowed his mind to drift away over the comfortable, satisfactory things in his life – not the exacerbations of their Warleggan neighbours, not thoughts of Elizabeth and her child, not apprehensions about the progress of the war; but the success of the mine, the freedom from the load of debt, the warmth of his affection for his wife and child. So far they had done little to add to their house servants; and in the excitement of the mining success the farm had been neglected. Ross began to think of the hay prospects and of ploughing the Long Field, of walking bare-foot across the firm sands of Hendrawna Beach; the prospective rebuilding of the library; shopping in Truro, taking Demelza further afield. When Demelza said:

'Touching on children, Ross . . .'

'What children?'

'Ours. I think it probable that before the year is out I shall be adding to the livestock.'

'What?' He came back from his comfortable dream. 'What's this? Are you sure?'

'Not sure. But I've missed this month and as you know I'm regular as the moon. Last time you blamed me for not telling you soon enough, so I thought this time I'd best alert you right away.'

'Good God,' said Ross. 'I somehow hadn't expected that!'

'Well,' said Demelza, 'it would be a small matter surprising if I hadn't. Since Christmas it's been nothing else, has it.'

'Did you want it to be anything else?'

'No, thank you. But it would be surprising if something like this hadn't happened.'

'Yes. I suppose you're right.'

There was silence. 'Are you upset?' she asked.

'Not upset. But not altogether delighted. Oh, not for the same reasons as last time: I'd be happy to have more children. It is just the hazards that present themselves both for you and for the child. The world so constantly presses upon one, with every form of risk, that now, just for a while, having just this moment escaped the burden of poverty and the threat of debt, I would have liked a year or two accepting no more hostages to fate.'

'Just by living we are all – what you call it – hostages to fate.'

'Of course. Mine is the coward's attitude. But I'm not so much a coward for myself as for those I care about.'

Demelza wriggled down a bit. 'Maybe it will be a false alarm. But anyway don't worry for me. It was all right both times before.'

'When will it be?'

'About November, I suspect.'

'D'you remember the storm that blew up at the time of Julia's birth? I think it is the fiercest storm I ever saw. When I went for old Choake it was almost impossible to stand.'

'And he was no use when he came. Mrs Zacky did it all. I'd better trust her any day.'

'I'm told Elizabeth had this new man, Behenna, from Truro. I believe he's lately out of London and has good ideas.'

The brief silence that followed was customary at the mention of Elizabeth's name. It was not deliberate on either side, but the conversation seemed to wilt of its own accord.

'If I have to have a man I'd better prefer Dwight. By November he should be back.'

'I'd not bank on it. I do not see an end to the war yet.'

'I must go and see Caroline very soon. We've not done so much for her as we should.'

'It is what I was thinking walking back from the mine today. But I don't want you jogging over there now. It is a long trip –'

'Oh, Judas, I may jog for months yet, Ross, and come to no harm! If she will not leave her uncle, one or both of us must go and see her. It must be frustrating not even to be able to speak to him of her concern for Dwight.'

'Ten minutes ago,' Ross said, 'I was drifting off into pleasant dreams. Now I am wide awake, all the comfortable cocoon I was spinning around myself torn asunder by a simple announcement. It is not that I am lacking in happiness for what you tell me but only that I now lack the simple complacency that makes for sleep.'

'Do you need to sleep?' Demelza asked.

'. . . . No. Not yet.'

He moved his head and laid his face against hers, and they lay breathing quietly together for a few seconds.

He said: 'I hope it is a girl. But not like you. One of you is more than enough.'

CHAPTER THREE

A tall man of about forty with a long, distinguished face rode up to the door of Killewarren, dismounted and pulled the bell. He was dressed in a brown nankeen riding suit which had been cut by an expensive tailor, highly polished brown boots so dark as to be almost black, and a black silk cravat. The points of his collar stood up at each side of his face. He was clean shaven and his hair, dark but greying at the temples, was his own.

When the manservant came he asked for Mr Ray Penvenen.

'Well, sur, master is that poorly,' said the servant. 'If you'll come this way, sur. Who shall I say's called?'

'Mr Unwin Trevaunance.'

He was shown into the big living-room on the first floor with its faded plush velvet curtains, its good but shabby furniture, its threadbare Turkey rugs. Since he came here last, about four years ago, it had all gone further downhill. The mirror above the fireplace had mildew at one corner. A piece of the heavy flock paper was curling away from the wall. He wrinkled his nose in distaste, ran a finger along the mantelpiece and then examined his finger for dust. He decided not to sit down.

After about five minutes Caroline Penvenen came in. To his annoyance she was carrying her little pug-dog, which gave a short growl ending in a yap when it recognized the visitor.

'Unwin!' said Caroline. 'This is a surprise! So Horace remembers you too! Don't worry, darling, I'll not let the big man eat you. I saw you at the Warleggan christening but we did not seem to meet.'

'As you say.' Unwin bowed his big head over her hand, which could only be extended a little way because of the dog. 'I saw that your uncle was not there and was told that he was unwell. I thought I might be permitted to call to see him. I trust he is better. '

'Not at all better, I fear. But thank you for your kind inquiry. I will tell him you have called.'

'He is not to be seen?'

She shook her head. 'The doctor said not. And in faith I would think the strain of it would tire him too much.'

'Who is your doctor?'

'Dr Sylvane of Blackwater.'

'I don't know him. But then I am seldom in Cornwall. He is . . . efficacious?'

'What a long word. I do not know the answer to that, Unwin. Uncle Ray grows steadily worse; but that may be the progress of the disease which no doctor may be able to stem, however efficacious.'

Unwin glanced out of the window. Rain was lashing on it. 'A heavy shower. An April shower. I must ask the shelter of your house until it is past.'

'That with pleasure. Will you take some refreshment? We have some good French brandy, recently run in. Or ale? Or canary?'

'Thank you, brandy, if it is not too much trouble.'

Caroline pulled the bell and gave the order when the servant came. Unwin was eyeing her with undisguised interest. He decided she had not improved in looks since he had first met her, a tall, wayward, red-haired beauty of eighteen, at her Uncle William's home in Oxfordshire. A beauty who was also heiress to two elderly, wealthy and cheeseparing bachelors. What could be better? He had followed her to Cornwall, and after eighteen months of sporadic courtship had thought her safely landed, when instead she had suddenly cut loose and refused to have anything more to do with him. Since then there had been a rumour of her engagement to Lord Coniston, but that too had come to nothing. Unwin thought he knew the reason for all this. It was partly the cause of his coming today. But she was not as attractive as she had been. Her tall slender figure had become angular, her skin less fresh-looking. At twenty-two she was still a beauty; and wherever she went her height and colouring would mark her out; but it pleased him that he could detect a going-off. Perhaps in the end she would become a trifle less wayward and headstrong.

When the brandy came Unwin sipped it and munched a biscuit. 'Um. Very good. So the war has not interfered with the traffic across the Channel.'

'No, from all accounts it appears to have increased it.'

'Fewer men to guard the coasts, eh? But it is a serious matter to trade with an enemy. There is all the possibilities of spying, of selling information, of helping to weaken a blockade. It's something Pitt should know about.'

She let Horace slip from her knees, and he rolled fatly on the floor. He lay there wheezing and gasping with a suspicious, bloodshot, white-cornered eye on Unwin. 'Your career prospers, I hope?'

'Indeed. My seat was finally confirmed this year and my rival dislodged. Now I am promised an under-secretaryship shortly. I would like it – and shall probably get it – in finance. Finding the money to prosecute this war is one of the most vital of the problems we have to deal with.'

'Fighting it is also vital, I should have thought,' said Caroline.

'That also I may yet do. We are very short of men. I wonder Ross Poldark does not think of returning to the 62nd Foot.'

'You should ask him.'

He looked out of the window again. 'Tell me, Caroline. Your uncle. I trust you don't – this doctor does not forecast a fatal termination?'

'Dr Sylvane will never forecast that while a patient has one breath left or a toe that will twitch when you touch it; but I must confess I am not hopeful.'

'If or when this happens, what shall you do? Return to London? You could hardly remain here alone.'

'Why not? I don't know. I prefer to live from day to day.'

'Of course . . . I often wonder what would have happened if you had not quarrelled with me that evening in May two years ago.'

Caroline smiled. 'Well, then I should have been your wife, Unwin. That is not difficult to see. But I should not have been a good wife for you.'

'Permit me to have my own opinion on that. I think, I even venture to think that you might yourself have been happier. I am not an ogre. Most people think me personable enough. And I have some importance in the world. You could have had a full life, and a most interesting one. Even if you did not love me I believe it would have been a splendid alliance. Far better than the life you are now leading, here, alone, far from your London and Oxfordshire friends . . .'

'And nursing a sick old man?' said Caroline. 'Oh, yes, I should have had a different life. And so would you. But this is true of all decisions. If I go riding tomorrow I am not sitting by the fire. If you had not come to see Uncle Ray this morning you would not run the risk of being soaked on the way home. We make our choice. Isn't that what parsons mean when they talk of Free Will?'

Unwin's bottom lip jutted. He did not admire this sort of flippancy. 'True, my dear. But all decisions are not irrevocable. If you felt so inclined the option is still open. '

Horace, stirred by his mistress's foot, rolled over again and yapped once. Thereafter there was silence, except for the patter of rain and a drip somewhere where water was coming through the roof.

'To marry you, Unwin? What makes you think I may have changed?'

'I don't assume so. But we are both older. What we said in heat two years ago was not necessarily final. In the meantime you have not married, I have not married. It could still be.'

Caroline smoothed the Mechlin lace at her wrists. Her fine eyes looked misty for a moment, and he thought she was going to yield. Then she vigorously shook her head. 'Thank you, no, Unwin, it could not be. For me it could not be. When we parted that May evening after your brother's reception I perhaps expressed myself a little forcibly, a thought – unflatteringly. If you wish to excuse me for that you may put it down to my temperament and my youth. But – the decision has not changed. I couldn't marry you. I'm

41

sorry. But thank you for the compliment of asking me again.'

Unwin took a sip of his brandy. He stretched his long legs and stared at a splash of mud on his shining boots. He swallowed the other half of the biscuit. 'Well . . . so, that is your choice. I'll not presume to argue with it. But perhaps we might agree that until one of us marries another the door is not altogether closed. If at any time you should change your mind and I should not be in Cornwall, John will know my address.'

'Thank you, Unwin.' She was going to tell him that nothing would ever induce her to write, but a maturer appreciation of other people's feelings kept her silent. 'And I'll tell my uncle you called.'

It had just stopped raining, and a rent in the cloud cover showed the blue skin of the sky. But drops were still lining up on the window sash.

Unwin said: 'I thought that young doctor attended your uncle. What was his name? Enys. Dwight Enys.'

Caroline wondered whether the question was loaded. It was impossible to tell how far gossip had travelled, how far her name had ever been linked with Dwight's outside a small closed circle. 'Dr Enys is one of those who have already gone to fight. He joined the Navy at Christmas, as a surgeon, of course, and he is now on patrol duty with the Western Squadron. My uncle greatly misses his medical care.'

'Indeed. I hope he was not involved in the fighting of last week.'

'What fighting? I had not heard.'

'I was in Falmouth yesterday, and all the talk was of it. Ned Pellew's squadron. They say the battle lasted eleven hours and took place in a furious gale. A great man, Sir Edward. We need more like him.'

Horace was snuffling and snoring now as if suddenly asleep. After a moment Caroline said: 'One receives all news so late here. Do tell me more details if you have them.'

'Details? Oh, of this naval affair. Well, they were scant enough. Pellow was commanding the *Arethusa,* I believe, and two other ships, and they sighted and attacked a French ship of the line and a French frigate. I do not know how they compare as to size, but I imagine the French ship of the line was very much the largest of the vessels engaged. The outcome was a desperate battle in which both French ships were driven ashore and ended as total wrecks. We lost

42

one of our ships.'

'Lost? Sunk, do you mean?'

'Driven ashore in the gale like the Frenchies. The *Arethusa* and the other frigate came safely away. The whole town was full of it yesterday. Every ale house was crammed with common people drinking Ned Pellew's health.'

'I have several friends,' Caroline said, 'in the Western Squadron, and one or two I believe were on the *Arethusa* or her accompanying ships. Do you know the names of the accompanying ships?'

Unwin finished his brandy. 'I heard. They were mentioned more than once. But it is hard to remember. The name of one ship is so much like another.'

The sun was out now, shining on wet slate and bough and flagstone. Under them, in the stable directly below this room, they heard a horse whinny and snort.

'Wait,' said Unwin. 'I have it. One was the *Travail,* under Captain Harrington; the other was the *Mermaid,* but I don't recall the captain's name. Banks, was it? I'm not sure.'

'And which was wrecked?'

'The *Travail,* I think. Yes, that must be it, because Harrington was killed in the action, and *Mermaid* hazarded herself trying to pick up survivors . . . My dear Caroline; was there someone well known to you on board? I trust I have not upset you?'

'No, no,' said Caroline thoughtfully, after a long moment. 'I believe it was just someone walking over my grave.'

In her small porticoed house at the end of the main street of Falmouth overlooking the open mouth of the bay, Verity Blamey, née Poldark, was putting her child to bed when there was a knock at her front door. The sun had recently dipped and flared behind the land and a night wrack of cloud had gathered over St Mawes. The water had lost all its colour and glittered like a tarnished pewter dish. Lights were beginning to wink in windows and at mastheads.

Mrs Stevens had popped out to see a neighbour, so Verity was alone in the house. Before going downstairs she peered through the parlour window and saw that her caller was a tall young woman leading a horse. She thought she recognized the colour of the hair. She went down and opened the door.

'Mrs Andrew Blamey?'

'Miss Penvenen, isn't it? What is wrong? Are you unwell?'

'May I come in? My horse will be safe here?'

'Yes, yes. Do come in, please.'

The tall girl followed Verity up the stairs and into the parlour. There were pink spots in her cheeks which made Verity think at first that she had an inflammatory fever.

'We've not met,' said Caroline bluntly and without preliminary. 'All these years. Although we have so many friends. I need help. So I thought I would come to you. Isn't that strange?'

'Of course not. You have been such a friend to Ross. Anything I can do. First sit down, and then some refreshment.'

'No.' Caroline stood by the window holding her riding crop. 'What I want to know – I don't know if you can help me. I have just ridden from Killewarren.'

'From Killewarren? Unaccompanied?'

'Oh, that.' She dismissed it. '*Have* we ever met? Officially, I mean. You seemed to know who I was.'

'I have seen you twice. The first time was in Bodmin four years ago.'

'But you know of me, as I know of you. Ross will have talked of me and of my friendship with Dwight Enys.'

'Yes. Oh, yes.'

'Has he told you that at Christmas I became engaged to marry Dwight?'

Verity buttoned the neck of her plain linen frock. She did not know quite what distressed Caroline but the sudden arrival of this brightly coloured, elegant young woman made her feel dowdy, as if a butterfly had come in and was beating its wings beside a brown moth. She knew Caroline's reputation for unconventional behaviour, for dramatic actions, and she wondered in what way she was to be concerned in this latest move.

'I have not seen Ross or any others of the family since Christmas. Demelza has written twice but she did not say anything.'

'Well, it was to be kept secret from my uncle who does not approve – and who is mortally sick. It was to be kept from him until Dwight came home and we were to see him together. Because of me, because of the – difficulties which arose, Dwight joined the Navy.' Caroline seemed out of breath.

Verity went to a sidetable and picked up a decanter. Liquid bobbled in a glass, which Caroline took with a nod, though she still did not drink.

Verity said: 'I knew he was in the Navy. Not the reason.'

'He sailed just after Christmas, and I have had two letters from him. He is in the Channel patrol, part of the Western Squadron under Sir Edward Pellew. He is in a frigate under Sir Edward Pellew.'

Verity stared at her. 'Yes? Oh . . . Do you mean he has been in this latest action?'

'I do not know for sure. But someone called on me this morning. I was told of the action. I was told that one English ship was sunk. Do you know its name?'

'I think . . . Wait a minute – I have a news sheet.' Verity went across the room and fumbled among some woollen things. 'This is it. Yes, the *Travail.*' She looked up. 'It was lost off the French coast. Miss Penvenen, don't tell me that . . .'

Caroline sat down on the nearest chair, and a little brandy spilled on the carpet. Verity ran to her, put her arm round her.

'Well, my dear,' Caroline said, 'it is very embarrassing for me, I assure you, for I have only known you five minutes, but I feel rather sick.'

'Do you know I do not believe I was meant to be a sailor's wife. You must know more of it than I, Verity, how one should behave.'

'Drink this. Just a little. It will do you good.'

'Yet I was never one to collapse as a blushing maiden. My old nurse did not encourage it. "Young ladies," she used to say, "is meant to be strong, not grow up like lent lilies." So I rarely if ever faint as a pastime.'

'Put your head back now. You will be better soon.'

'Oh, I am better. Who am I to complain? It is the others who are not better.'

'The ship was wrecked, not sunk by the French. It all took place in a gale. There will have been many survivors.'

Caroline lay back for a while, drawing in slow breaths. 'Do you know, all the way across here, I was saying, that stupid man Unwin Trevaunance has made a mistake! When I get there I shall find that I am being deceived by this irritating custom of the Admiralty for naming so many ships so nearly alike. It will not be just that one. It will not be the *Travail.* I will find it is the *Turmoil* or the *Terror* or the *Trident.* All the way here I kept saying to myself . . .'

45

'You should not be too upset, my dear. Anything may have happened. He might be safe and well.'

'I thought, I must go and see Ross's cousin. I will pay her a social call. There is really no one else. Of course I could have gone to Susan Pellew herself; we have met once; or to Mary Trefusis, or to one of the other people whom I have some acquaintance with; but it seemed – I felt it more natural to call upon Ross's cousin whom I had never met!'

'It was right. How I wish Andrew were here . . . And James, Andrew's son, is at sea too. But I must think . . .'

'Are there no details in the news sheet?'

'Nothing. Just repeating a dispatch from Captain Pellew, who is still at sea. It simply says about the *Travail* that she took the ground in the – in the Bay of Audierne and that the *Mermaid* when attempting rescue work narrowly escaped shipwreck herself.'

'Where can we ask – Is there anyone who will know more?'

'That is what I have been thinking. I think the news was brought in by a naval sloop. Because of Andrew I am well known in the Packet Office. Ben Pender is usually there until eight. If anyone would know, he would. I'll come with you, of course. I think I hear Mrs Stevens has returned, so I can leave little Andrew with her. Do you feel able, to walk?'

'Oh, yes. Oh, yes. My knees are growing stronger minute by minute.'

'It is a quarter of a mile down the street. I'll get my cape. You will, of course, stay the night.'

'I don't think I can. My uncle is ill. When I heard this news I went in to him, told him what I was going to do. I fear it upset him for, although he knew no more than I told him, my somewhat obvious desire to know the truth about Dwight must have given my feelings away. When I have what news there is I can ride back.'

'Three hours in the dark? There are too many starving men abroad. You *must* stay. I'll tell Mrs Stevens to prepare a room.'

Ten minutes later they went out and made their way over the cobbles and the mud and threaded among the people crowding the narrow street. Shops were still open, the ale houses busy, drunks lay in corners, children played and screamed, blind men and lame men begged, old soldiers stood and gossiped, sailors three abreast sang lewd songs, house-holders stood at open doors, dogs barked and fought and seagulls screamed over all. It was a fine evening and warm for April after the rain. But for Caroline it was a scene without savour, without warmth, without light. These were not human beings who crowded around her but grey and white shadows impeding her progress towards an inevitable end.

At the packet office Ben Pender, a tired little man in an old-fashioned wig and snuff-brown suit, was talking to a packet captain in blue and braid, who at once got up and bowed over Verity's hand. Verity introduced them to Caroline and explained her mission.

The captain said: 'Unfortunately, ma'am, we only have the message passed on by the sloop, which came in with the news and left by the next tide. Pellew and his ships are still at sea. But here the message is in full – for what it is. Sir Edward Pellew reports having first sighted the two Frenchmen, the *Héros* and the *Palmier,* the *Héros* being a 74-gun two decker, at 3 p.m. on Thursday afternoon in thick weather some fifty leagues south-west of Ushant. The wind was blowing hard from the westward and sail was made in chase. At three quarters past five the *Nymphe* and the *Travail* came up with the French ships.' He looked at the paper Ben Pender had put before him and hooked a pair of spectacles round his ears. 'According to this account a running fight then took place lasting about ten hours in a steadily increasing gale, first under lowering clouds and rain, then with furious squally showers by the light of a half moon. During this the *Mermaid* also became engaged and the five ships drifted towards the French coast. By the time the Brest peninsula was sighted in the half dark the *Héros* was disabled and the *Palmier,* the *Nymphe* and the *Travail* had suffered considerable damage. Both Frenchmen tried to make the Brest estuary but in their damaged condition could not do so. The *Palmier* struck a rock by the Isle de Sein and sank, the *Héros* drifted into the Bay of Audierne and ran aground in heavy seas. The *Travail* also could not withstand the force of the gale and was wrecked near the *Héros.* The *Nymphe,* though almost in shoal water, succeeded in weathering the Pointe de Penmarche and making the open sea. The *Mermaid,* which had suffered the least of the five ships, attempted to close in to help the wrecked ships but was forced to turn away to save herself. Casualties in the *Nymphe* were sixteen killed and fifty-seven wounded. In the *Mermaid* five killed and thirty-five wounded. Captain Harrington of the *Travail* was killed early in the action.' The captain unlatched his spectacles from behind his ears. 'That is the end of the dispatch, ma'am.'

A clerk came in with a lighted lantern to add to the one on the desk. It helped to show up the charts, the drawings of ships, the yellow bills of lading, the scales, the inkpot and quill, the mahogany furnishings, the brass rails, the tiled floor.

Caroline said: 'Did you see anyone from the sloop; personally, I mean?'

'I had some words with the captain. But you'll understand he was not in the action. He simply bore the tidings.'

'Did you – discuss the *Travail* at all?'

The captain hesitated. 'A few words, ma'am. But from my own experience I can tell you that survival in a shipwreck is much a matter of good or ill fortune. If the frigate came in upon a beach there must be a very good chance of a large number being saved. That I'm afraid we shall not be likely to know for a little while, for such survivors as there are will necessarily be prisoners of the French.'

CHAPTER FOUR

May came in windy and wet, and stayed so. It seemed long years to Demelza since they had had one of those idyllic Mays of brilliant sunshine and gentle breezes when the whole peninsula had swum out into the calm blue sea of summer, when the flowers had bloomed unharassed and the warmth of the day had been on your back wherever you went. Last year had been the same as this; rain and wind almost all the time, with a break in the middle of dull quiet cool weather – the time she had gone to Werry House to the ball. (A vile memory – she could not bear to think of it.) The May before there had been that party at the Trevaunances at which everyone had expected Unwin to announce his engagement to Caroline Penvenen, and he had not done so. All the time then the weather had been grey and cold.

The year before that Ross and Francis had taken the decision to reopen Wheal Grace, and Ross had met George Warleggan at the Red Lion Hotel and they had had words and Ross had thrown George over the banisters . . . And she had been carrying Jeremy . . . She remembered the endless blustering winds.

Now she was pregnant again, though so far she had no difficulty in keeping the fact a secret from everyone but Ross. And now they were passing rich and could afford as much coal on the fires as they pleased. And the old gaunt library where she had first learned to play a few notes on the spinet was going to be repaired. And her younger brother, Drake, was to work on it, being a handy man with his plane and saw. And Sam was down the mine—not as a tributer but as a tutworker: that was to say he broke the ground at so much a fathom: he stood neither to gain nor lose by the quality of the ground he spent. It was not so profitable as tributing but neither was it so much a gamble, and it was a livelihood, steady work for steady pay. One could feed one's body and have time to consider one's soul.

Sam and Drake, offered a room in old Aunt Betsy Triggs', had asked instead if they might repair and occupy Reath Cottage just over the hill—the little cob-walled cottage Mark Daniel had built with his own hands for his pretty young wife—before he killed her with the same hands a few months later. The roof had long since fallen in, and much of the rest, built in such haste, had not stood the test of wind and weather. The people of Mellin and Marasanvose would not go near the place after dusk: they said that the little moonflower face of Keren could be seen any time lolling out of the window, its tongue swollen and its bloodshot eyes staring. But the Carnes were made of sterner stuff. As Sam put it, no hurt or harm could come to the souls of men who had been saved from the toils of Satan by the perfect love of Jesus.

So in their spare time they hammered and sawed and patched and chiselled, and the stuff that came out of the old library was often useful to Drake to carry across to their cottage. That their choice of a cottage of their own, however ruinous, in preference to a share with Aunt Betsy had any secondary intent did not occur to Demelza until early in May when she heard that Sam was hoping to extend the lower room of Reath Cottage, and that he had already held a small prayer meeting there.

Indeed, Samuel considered that there was no time to waste. Methodism in most counties went up and down in popularity and enthusiasm with the years; but this was especially so in Cornwall where the population was more volatile in temperament and the distances always furthest from the enlightened control and guidance of its founders. The great Wesley himself while still alive had scarcely ever dared to leave his Cornish converts alone for more than a year at a time. Although there were strong and earnest groups in some of the towns and villages who never wavered in their faith and their prayer, there was constant backsliding in other parts and a falling from grace. Sawle with Grambler had long since fallen from grace, as indeed had all the surrounding district as far as St Michael one way and St Ann's the other.

Sam found it a sad and a barren sight. There was a small meeting house at Grambler which had been put up by subscription and by the miners themselves in the prosperous sixties, but since the mine closed and the people had drifted away the meeting house was neglected and in bad repair. Some still kept to the old principles, without however meeting together or renewing their faith in communal prayer.

Sam met with resentment here and there, for a stranger from as far afield as Illuggan was no better than a foreigner; and the general feeling was that the only way such an intruder could be tolerated was by his being seen and not heard. Sam was not content to be quiet, and sour looks came his way; but his relationship with the Poldarks saved him from worse trouble. So the little nucleus of the converted who in the years of neglect had not lost grace altogether began to meet each Sunday evening in Reath Cottage. Sunday morning or afternoon Sam led them to church, proper.

There were four churches within walking distance. St Sawle, Grambler-with-Sawle, was the nearest, then came St Minver, Marasanvose. A little further off were St Ann's, at St Ann's, and St Paul's on the way to St Michael. But in the bad storm of May, '88, the roof of St Paul's had fallen in, and no one had had money to repair it, so services had been indefinitely suspended. At St Ann's, the vicar lived in London and had never yet visited the church, so that services were held there at rare intervals, when a locum could be found. Parishioners wishing to get married could seldom have the banns called, so they had to afford to buy licences or do without the blessings of the church, and parents had to carry their children to Sawle for christening.

St Sawle, Gramble-with-Sawle, with its two chancels, its leaky roofs, its side-slanting tower and over-filled graveyard, was looked after by the Reverend Clarence Odgers, a cleric who received £40 a year from the incumbent, who lived in Penzance. Odgers, having a wife and a brood of children to keep, eked out his living by growing vegetables and fruit. The church was neglected but had a fair congregation, a noisy rather than tuneful choir and, of course, the patronage of Trenwith House.

The nearest big house to St Minver, Marasanvose, was Werry House, but the Bodrugans only went to church twice a year, and the vicar, Mr Faber, doubled with another church near Ladock and was a fox-hunting man. St Minver was a small church, and the first time Sam and Drake went there were only five others in the congregation. Of these, two were men who talked all through about the price of corn; of the three women, two were mending shirts and the third, who was the caretaker, was asleep. After the service there was a christening to be done, and the caretaker had forgotten to get water for the font, so the vicar spat in his hand and anointed the child with his spittle in the name of Christ. Sam and Drake came out in time to see him mount his broad old mare and clatter off down the rocky track.

So when the little nucleus of Methodists began to accept him as their leader, Sam took them to Sawle Church as the best of the four. Besides, Drake always seemed to want to go there.

For two weeks the brothers had been foraging for a new central beam to support their repaired roof and to carry the extra weight of slate, put on in place of thatch. Possibly the weak pit-prop which had been used for the central beam would bow no further; but one couldn't be sure, and sometimes it gave an ominous crack.

In the last week in May Pally Rogers told Sam that a fine piece of ship's timber had washed in at St Ann's and been taken possession of by one of the seine boats there. So the next time Drake had a few hours free and Sam was up from his core they walked over to look at it. It was not a mast but a cross-beam: eighteen feet or so in length and very nearly a foot square. For use in the cottage it was four feet too long but otherwise perfect. The seiners wanted seven shillings for it. After some bargaining they settled for five.

For two shillings more, the seiners said, they would row it round and deposit it on Hendrawna Beach. The brothers politely refused. They left a deposit of three shillings and

51

said they would come for it on the morrow, which was the last day of the month and a Saturday. Sam was on the night core and Drake was able to get off at three in the afternoon, so they were in St Ann's well before five. Within half an hour they had paid the difference and had started back.

This week the weather had at last relented and the sun was hot as they climbed the long hill out of the village. The great beam had not yet fully dried out and it soon began to feel like lead. It was going to be a long and trying walk. By the time they had done two miles Drake, who was not yet as strong as his brother, began to wish they had paid the extra two shillings to have the beam 'delivered'. They had all night to carry it in, but the difficulty if they stopped to rest was getting the beam back on their shoulders again. They could only stop where there was a convenient wall or support on which to rest the beam waist high.

They were now on the same path they had taken from Illuggan in March, and they presently came to the fork in the track where in March they had attempted to cross some fields and been turned back with ugly words by the War-leggan gamekeepers. They had never attempted to cross the fields since but both were well aware from later experience that the way through the fields and the two small woods beyond cut at least a mile off their journey. They stopped for a minute. There was no one in sight. You could not see Trenwith House or any of its buildings. There was a barn of some sort in the next field.

'I say risk it,' said Drake. 'They can't be everywhere all the time.' So they crossed the field, which was grazing land, though not even cattle were to be seen this evening.

The second field was barley, and the old right of way ran across the middle of it towards the wood on the other side. The barley had been sown to ignore the old path, but in the main had not grown thickly over it, as if even ploughing had not destroyed the impress of years. They went through the middle, waiting every moment for the angry shout, even the shot.

It did not come. They lifted themselves over the broken stile into the wood.

From here it should be easier. They were not sure how far it was yet on private land, but they knew the path came out at the first cottages of Grambler village, and that could not be far. The whole of the wood which they now entered, which was perhaps half an acre in extent, was azure with bluebells. The young elm and sycamore leaves were bursting out in a brilliant pale green through which the slanting sunlight dappled the ground. Halfway was a clearing where a tree had recently fallen and only a few sprouting saplings grew. The caterpillar ends of bracken were thrusting up among the bluebells. The fallen tree and an old stone wall would provide a resting place for the beam.

'Let's stop for a while,' said Drake. 'My shoulder's fair crackin'.'

'Not for long,' said Sam. 'I'd be easier out o' here.' But he lowered the beam, took the piece of sacking off his shoulder and began to massage it.

They squatted a few minutes in sweating satisfaction. A thrush came down near them, balancing his fan of a tail, then chattered affrightedly and flew off. Some small animal, probably a squirrel, moved in the undergrowth but did not show itself. Overhead the sky was high and brilliant, as if it had never been exposed to the sun before.

'Phew! I've no sprawl to move yet,' Drake said. 'I reckon we shall've earned this piece o' driftwood by the time we get him home.'

'Hush!' said Sam. 'There's someone abroad.'

They listened. At first there was no sound, then quite close someone was talking. The young men dived for cover. In the following pause a blackbird began to sing, his clear pellucid song taking no account of anything but the summer's evening. Then he too fluttered away as a rustling increased and there was the clack of a heel against stone.

Two people came into the clearing. One was a fair-haired boy of ten or eleven, the other a tall dark girl in a plain blue dress with muslin fichu and a straw hat in her hand. Held in the other arm was a sheaf of bluebells.

'Oh,' said the boy in a clear voice. 'Someone has cut a tree down! No, it has fallen! I wonder if they know . . . But what is this strange piece of wood?'

The girl fished in a pocket of her frock and took out a pair of steel-rimmed spectacles, which she put on to stare at the beam. 'It looks like a piece from a barn – or a ship. Someone must have brought it here. Recently too, for the bluebells have all been stepped on.'

She turned and peered around. Drake made a movement to show himself but Sam caught his arm. But the damage had been done: the young boy's sharp eyes had seen the yellow of Sam's kerchief.

'Who is it? Who's there? Come out! Show yourselves!' Although he spoke in a commanding tone the boy was nervous and took a step away as he spoke.

They came slowly out, dusting the broken twigs and bracken from their clothes, rubbing their hands down the side of their trousers.

'Day to you,' said Drake, as ever politely pleasant in a crisis. 'Sorry if we startled you. We thought to rest awhile and had no wish to disturb no one.'

'Who are you?' said the boy. 'This is private property! Are you my uncle's men?'

'No, sur,' said Drake. 'Leastwise, thinkin' ye mean Mr Warleggan. No, sur. We was just carren this piece of timber from St Ann's over to Mellin. Tis all of six mile and we thought to lay our burden down for a few minutes, for the beam is some heavy. I trust we done no wrong.'

'You're trespassing,' said the boy. 'This is our land! Do you know what the penalties are for trespass?' The girl put her hand on the boy's arm but he shook it off.

'Beg pardon, sur, but we thought this was a right o' way. We seen the stile and years ago when we come this way there was naught to let or hinder us.' Drake turned his open smiling face to the girl. 'We intended no wrong, ma'am. Perhaps you'll kindly explain to young Mr Warleggan that we 'ad no thought to trespass on private land –'

'My name is not Warleggan,' said the boy.

'Beg your pardon again. We thought as this was Warleggan land –'

'This is Poldark land and my name is Poldark,' said the boy. 'However, it is true that until a year ago village people were allowed to go this way, though never by right. It was only that my family had long been indulgent in such matters.'

'Mr Poldark,' said Drake. 'If your name's Mr Poldark, young sur, then maybe you'll see fit to overlook this mistake, because we're related to Captain Ross Poldark, who, twouldn't be fanciful to suppose, may be related to you.'

The boy looked at their working clothes. He had a high fresh colour and a natural arrogance of manner inherited from his father. He was tall for his age and rather plump; a good-looking boy but with a restive air.

'Related to my *uncle*, Captain Ross Poldark? In what way related?'

'Cap'n Poldark's wife, Mistress Demelza Poldark, is our sister.'

54

This was a statement rather beyond Geoffrey Charles's knowledge to refute, but he looked sceptical. 'Where do you come from?'

'Illuggan.'

'That's far away, isn't it?'

'Twelve mile maybe. But we don't live there now. We d'live at Nampara. That is, at Reath, just over the hill from Nampara. I'm working in the house for Cap'n Poldark, carpenter and the like. My brother Sam is down mine.'

The boy shrugged. '*Mon Dieu. C'est incroyable.*'

'Please?'

'So perhaps it was my uncle who sent you to get this beam?'

Drake hesitated but Sam, who until now had let his younger and more charming brother do all the talking, interposed to remove the easy temptation. 'I'm sorry, no. Your uncle didn't know nothing of this. But d'ye see, with the assistance and to the greater glory of God, we been building up an old cottage. We been working on it two month or more and wanted a long beam fourteen, fifteen foot long for to carry the roof. And this was washed in at St Ann's and we bought him and was carren home.'

'Excuse the question, ma'am,' Drake said. 'But I b'lieve I see you at Grambler church most Sundays?'

She had taken off her spectacles again, and looked at him coldly with her soft, short-sighted beautiful eyes, 'That may be so.'

But Drake, however deferential, was hard to put down. 'No offence meant, ma'am. None at all.'

She inclined her head.

'In the second pew from the front,' he said, 'right-hand side. You have a rare handsome hymn book wi' a gold cross on him and gold edges to the leaves.'

The girl put down her sheaf of bluebells. 'Geoffrey Charles, as it was customary in the old days to come through this wood . . .'

But Geoffrey Charles was looking at the beam. 'It is off a ship, isn't it? See, here is a hole that must have had a metal rod through it. And the corner has been chiselled away. But all that will surely weaken it as a beam, won't it?'

'We reckon to cut that end off,' said Drake. 'We only d'want fourteen feet and this is nigh on eighteen.'

'So why did you not saw it off before you left St Ann's? It would have made it that much less heavy to carry.' The

55

boy chuckled at his own astuteness.

'Yes, but maybe we can find a use for the stump. Good oak be hard to come by. Where you've paid for him all ye don't like to take only the part.'

'Is it very heavy?' The boy put his shoulder under the end that rested on the fallen tree and lifted. He went red in the face. *Mon Dieu, vous avez raison –'*

'Geoffrey!' said the girl starting forward. 'You will hurt yourself!'

'That I will not,' said Geoffrey, letting the end down again. 'But it is heavy as lead! Have you already borne it more than two miles? Try it, Morwenna, just try it!'

Morwenna said slowly: 'It is only two fields after this wood to the public way again. You will see the old path still marked. But when you go do not loiter.'

'Thank you, ma'am,' said Sam. 'We're in your debt for that.'

Her dark sober glance went over the two young men. 'I think there will be two men in the furthest field now milking the cows. If you were to wait a half-hour they would then be gone and you would run less risk of being stopped.'

'Thank you, ma'am. That's a kind thought. We're doubly in your debt.'

'But before we go let us see you lift it!' cried Geoffrey Charles. 'I cannot imagine you carrying it three miles more!'

The two brothers exchanged glances. 'Aye, we'll do that,' said Sam.

So, watched by the young woman and the young boy, they heaved it upon their shoulders. Geoffrey Charles nodded his approval. Then they lowered their burden again.

Geoffrey Charles, his earlier hostility gone, wanted to stay on, but Morwenna took him by the arm. 'Come, your mother will wonder what has become of us. We shall be late for supper.'

Smiling, Drake picked up the bluebells for her and put them into her arms. Geoffrey Charles said: 'I have not seen my Uncle Ross for some time. Pray give him my respects.'

Both the brothers bowed and then stood together watching Geoffrey Charles and his governess return through the trees the way they had come.

Morwenna Chynoweth said: 'I think, Geoffrey, it might be advisable that we should say nothing of having met those young men.'

'But why? They were doing no harm.'

'Your Uncle George is strict about trespass. One should not want to get them into trouble.'

'Agreed.' He chuckled. 'But they are strong! One day when I grow up I hope I shall be as strong.'

'You will. If you eat well and go to bed early.'

'Oh, that old tale; You know, Wenna, I wonder if there was a word of truth in their story of being related to Uncle Ross. Mama has told me that Aunt Demelza was low born, but I had not realized as low as that. It may well have been a fable to enlist our sympathy.'

'I have seen them in church,' said Morwenna. 'I remember seeing them; but Captain Poldark comes so seldom that I have no way of knowing if they were in his pew. I think they sat at the back.'

'The younger one is funny, isn't he? Such a funny smile. I wonder what their names are. I must ask Mama some time about Aunt Demelza.'

'If you ask your mother about them she is sure to discover our secret.'

'Yes . . . Yes, I am not good at keeping a secret, am I? So I will leave it a few days . . . Or why do you not ask? You are so much cleverer than me!'

By now they had reached the far side of the next field and the gate which led into the garden of Trenwith. The chimneys and gables of the house were to be seen among its surrounding trees. As Morwenna lifted the latch of the gate they heard footsteps behind. It was Drake halfway across the field running and leaping among the grass and stones to overtake them.

He came up smiling and gasping for breath. In his hands was a large bunch of bluebells, much larger than the one Morwenna carried. He handed them to her.

'All that time you wasted talking to we. You might've picked as many more as I've picked as many more. Thank ye, and good eve to you.'

They stood and watched him trot back. Morwenna looked around to see if there was anyone about who might have observed him. Among the bluebells were pink ragged robin and white milkmaid. Having regard to the speed with which it had been done it was a pretty bouquet. Morwenna knew from his eyes that it was meant as a bouquet. She resented the impertinence, coming as it did from one of his station. But he had gone running and hopping back into the wood.

CHAPTER FIVE

Ross went to see Caroline Penvenen on Whit Tuesday, the 10th of June. He had shopping to do and business in Truro and suggested that Demelza should come as far as Killewarren with him, spend a few hours with Caroline and then make a leisurely return home. Demelza refused.

'For one thing, I'm queasy. It won't last long, if I mind the other times; but just now I'm queasy, and riding behind you don't make it better. Also I would have to borrow a mine pony.'

When he reached Killewarren and was shown into the parlour Caroline was already waiting for him, and he explained Demelza's absence, though not the reason for her indisposition. (It was one of the few morbid quirks in Demelza's character, he thought, this desire always to hide her pregnancies from people until the last moment possible.)

Caroline said: 'But even for you, there was no need . . .'

'Need enough. I presume you have no further news?'

'I have written to the Admiralty twice but they say they have no information yet.'

'No information about Dwight or about the *Travail*?'

'About the *Travail*, I gather. Here is the last letter. One of the petty humiliations of this matter is that I have no official status. I am not his wife, nor his sister, nor his cousin, nor his ox nor his ass nor anything that is his. I still avoid telling people of our engagement, since it could so easy come back to Uncle Ray.'

He thought how drawn and thin she looked in her long dark frock: the tall bright sunflower had suddenly faded.

'Are you eating anything, Caroline?'

She looked up. 'Am I allowed no secrets?'

'And now that hunting is over, do you have any change of company or scene? Do you go out?'

'The most excellent company in the world is my horse.'

'You do not ride to us.'

'I do not like to be from home more than two or three hours.'

'My dear, I know it's easy to advise, but even if the worst were true, you have your own life to consider.'

'Why?'

He got up from the chair he had just taken and put the letter on the bureau. 'Oh, I am the last one to chide you, being of a somewhat melancholic temperament myself. Demelza is the one to advise: whatever her circumstances I believe she would find ten good reasons for living and for appreciating her existence. But even I must urge you . . .' He stopped.

'Yes, Ross,' she said smiling sweetly at him. 'Even you must urge me – to do what?'

'Not to despair.'

She shrugged. 'Of course I dramatize the situation. It is an old failing of mine. But you will understand that for one of my temperament the waiting *and* the inaction is – a little trying. This doctor is a fool, but if I can judge the signs right Uncle Ray cannot live many weeks longer. *So* I am bound by some sort of blood tie not to let him die without at least one friendly face by his bed. *So* I cannot go to Plymouth, to London, wherever one does go to *press* for news of Dwight . . .'

'What use would it be? If the Admiralty does not know, who can know? Only the French. In the case of officers it is usual – it *has* been usual – to exchange them quite quickly. Certainly their names should soon come through. But the revolution is now so out of hand . . .'

'The *Mercury* says that Danton is dead.'

'Oh, yes, a month or more ago. He at least was a great man. Now we are left with the rats.'

'It says Saint-Just and Robespierre are supreme.'

'No one is supreme for more than a day. The fault it seems in any revolution is that it must always run downhill. Victory is always for the extremists. There is always someone to say that the party in power is not ardent enough.'

'There must be an end somewhere.'

'It must end in some form of oligarchy, but these people are not strong enough. Who controls the army will ultimately control France.'

He stood staring out of the window at the bright day, his eyes concentrated on things that were not seen. The way his hair grew now you could hardly see the old scar. She watched him quietly. She sometimes thought she had more understanding, more fellow feeling towards him than towards Dwight, whom she consumedly loved. Ross was obstinate, like herself, the non-conformer, the near-rebel,

59

the believer in his own judgment even when his judgment went against the observed facts, a man who always kicked out at and resented the malignant irrelevances of fate.

'And in the meantime?'

'In the meantime the guillotine works day and night. Last week a Duke and two Marshals of France, all over eighty; Malesherbes the lawyer, together with his wife, his brother, his children and his grandchildren; an establishment of nuns, tied together and heaped in carts; the King's sister, Elizabeth; girls for singing an impudent song; boys for being the sons of their fathers. They're killing more women and children now because there are not enough men left.'

Caroline got up, went to the sideboard, poured herself a glass of brandy. 'And you tell me to hope for Dwight's survival. What chance would there be for him among such a rabble even if he reached the shore?'

'Oh, there is all the difference. An enemy – even an Englishman – would never be half so bitterly hated as one of their own kind with aristocratic blood or a different view of government. And these – these revolutionary excesses chiefly affect Paris and the larger cities of France. I would not think the treatment of an English officer shipwrecked on the Brittany coast would differ materially from that accorded a French officer shipwrecked in Cornwall.'

She sipped her drink and looked at him over the rim of her glass. 'Oh, don't think I am taking to the bottle. If I choose a solvent for my present anxiety, it will not be in the lees of liquor.'

'I was not thinking that.'

'You still believe the war will be long?'

'Well . . . one tends to underestimate the effect on a French general of knowing that retreat for him means the guillotine.

'You know more than I can glean from reading the papers, Ross.'

His eyes were lidded; then he looked up and smiled. 'As you know – to your cost – I have contacts with gentlemen in the Trade. Now that prosperity has come I no longer take any part in it myself – surprising how *respectable* one grows with money in the purse – but my old colleagues are still about. I talk with them sometimes. They bring back news . . .'

'Might they have news before anyone else of this ship-wreck?'

The question surprised him; stupidly it had not occurred to

him where her thoughts were leading.

'Roscoff and the other Brittany ports are some way from where this – the *Travail* went ashore. I have no idea of distances there, but I will ask. Two or three of the men I know speak serviceable French. If there is a hope of finding out anything of value I will go myself.'

She put her drink down, moistened her lips. The spirit was bringing colour to her face. 'There is no need to put yourself at risk, but I thought – '

'Little enough risk. But first I will find out when the next run is due and ask someone to make inquiries. There is no need to wait for a St Ann's boat if one is not going soon. I have friends at Looe also.'

'Try both,' said Caroline.

Ross was to spend the night at the Pascoes' and was to dine with Harris Pascoe at three. He found his old friend in very good spirits. Passing through the bank with its two clerks busy with customers, they went into the dining-room behind and ate alone.

Harris said: 'You will be delighted with the war news, Ross. Perhaps you have already heard it in town?'

'No, I have only seen Barbary, who was much concerned for the safety of one of his ships which is overdue with timber, and perhaps he was too worried to take heed of it.'

'He should not be, for it will directly concern him. Howe has won a f-famous victory off Ushant. He caught the French fleet under Admiral – I do not recollect his name – the French fleet being the larger, and in a day-long battle has cut it to pieces! Seven French ships of the line destroyed or captured and of the rest many seriously damaged and all put to flight! It is one of the greatest victories in history and should bring this detestable régime to its knees! The blockade will now be complete!'

They drank to the victory, and ate hashed mutton and a roasted goose followed by strawberries with a good French wine and a crusted port. Ross asked if Harris's daughter was away.

'Not away, but staying with her aunt for a day or two. You have heard that happy news also?'

'No?'

'She is engaged to be married – to your c-cousin St John Peter. I wonder you have not heard; though in fact the engagement was only made public at the beginning of this month. We plan an October wedding. It is a very happy time for Joan – and for me also, although I shall greatly miss her. But it is time I had grandsons, and, although my sons are hardly yet fledged, Joan is twenty-nine.' Harris chewed reflectively and took a small bone out of his mouth. 'I had thought, I had feared . . . You remember her attachment for young Dr Enys. It came to nothing – I believe he is n-now at sea – but I feared that having committed herself, as it were, to him, she might miss marriage altogether. She does not easily change allegiances. Of course she has known St John – as I have known him – for many years; but it never occurred to me, as perhaps it did not occur to her, that any attachment might develop. I am happy also that through this marriage the Pascoes and the Poldarks will be brought a little nearer together. It's a very favourable outcome.'

Ross murmured his congratulations. Perhaps Harris Pascoe detected some reservation in his guest's good wishes, for he said: 'Oh, I know St John Peter has not been the most industrious or studious of young men. But it is not an uncommon pattern when one inherits a small estate quite young . . .' The banker stopped, for he perceived that he might be on delicate ground.

'It is a very familiar pattern,' Ross said. 'One inherits the traditions of a gentleman, the pride of a squire, a dislike of work and a contempt for trade; all of which might be tolerable if the estate were not too small to live off and already heavily mortgaged by one's father.'

'I was not attempting to draw a p-parallel, Ross. In any case you made no bones about abandoning such a tradition and the outcome happily is now in no doubt. I have hopes, with Joan's steadying influence and the ambition which may come of fathering a family, that St John will find a new incentive in life. He is only twenty-seven.'

That made him at least two years younger than his bride, even if one did not suspect her of having forgotten a year or two.

'Oh, I think St John has much to commend him. He is a cheerful, gay fellow and very good company. We have never been close, but of course the cousinship is somewhat removed – I do not quite know how to estimate these relationships. I believe that although his estate is much reduced the young man has a couple of sinecures which help him to remain both solvent and a gentleman.' Ross caught Harris Pascoe's eye and laughed. 'Oh, I beg your pardon, Harris. I did not intend to sound so sour. I am very happy both for you and Joan. And, in so far as our ties may be strengthened by this marriage, I am happy for that also.'

They talked of other things. Banking business was booming, for the war had created a mood of expansion which at times was feverish. Although the mining world and Cornish industries were still depressed, money over the country as a whole had become cheap and had led to new enterprises springing up which hoped to profit from war conditions.

Ross said: 'With whom does St John Peter bank?' Knowing already.

'Warleggan's. He is very friendly with them. George has helped him in a number of ways; and of course I do not take exception to that. The community should not be expected to divide itself up into camps. It would be the worst thing.'

'I agree. But willy nilly, Harris, you I suspect are in mine.'

'Yes. I do not admire the Warleggans or their business methods. Honesty is not a set of rules, it is a standard of ethics. By the first criterion they are honest, by the second not. But – they exist. And I suspect – I fear – that as men like them prosper, more and more such will come to the top. Well, we can't alter the world, we can only adapt ourselves to it. As for my future son-in-law, it should not matter that he banks elsewhere, th-though I shall hope that when he marries he will move. I am settling a substantial sum on Joan.'

'Naturally.'

'This of course is between ourselves. It would be – unhelpful if it got out.'

'Oh?'

'Well, you know, the stability of a bank depends on the good standing of its partners. Since it is not a joint stock company, no one is really certain of the depths of its purse. When my father died there was a startling increase in the business we did, because men reasoned that the son of a man who left so substantial a fortune must be rich enough to be safe!'

'I had no idea.'

'Similarly if men knew I had settled any substantial part of my fortune on Joan, it would leave them feeling less secure of the amount I had left to meet all the contingencies of trade.'

Ross shook his head. 'Harris, it is not really for me to suggest; but I wonder if there might be something to be said for offering St John Paul a modest interest in your bank – in some form of junior partnership? It would be a way of safeguarding Joan's future and his.'

Harris refilled both glasses. 'It did occur to me. Indeed, I came halfway round to the matter when St John was dining with us last week. I gather from what he said that he would be only too happy to accept such an interest if he were to take no active part. Like Spry, for instance. But he gave me the impression that he would not wish to be concerned in any way with the day-by-day running of the bank or in fact to have his name prominently associated with banking and usury.'

Ross shifted uneasily in his chair. He wondered if this dichotomy of attitude was likely to prove the basis for a happy marriage. 'I always find,' he said, 'that the lesser the gentry the greater the pretensions. No doubt the years will bring him wisdom.'

'. . . Th-these are our first strawberries. With this cold spring they have been slow to ripen. And your own affairs? All is still prospering?'

'We shall have a fine show of tin at the next Coinage. I have been wondering how this new money coming in might be put to use; a man who depends on a single venture is more vulnerable to cold winds than one who spreads his interests.'

'I would certainly not advise investment in another mine. This time you have triumphed against all odds . . . You have heard of course the rumour about the other mine you started?'

'What? Wheal Leisure? No.'

'It is said that the champion lode, that of red copper, is no longer answering well. It is running thin and threatening to die.'

'I hadn't heard that. And since it is almost on my doorstep I think it passing strange I should not have.' Ross stared at his friend. 'Harris, you always surprise me: you have the gossip of the county at your fingertips.'

'I hope it *is* gossip, for the sake of the ventures.' Pascoe spoke a little stiffly.

'Gossip was the wrong word. But the reason I tend to discount this news is that Will Henshawe is captain there and a venturer. As you know, he is captain of Grace too and one of my oldest friends. I should have expected him to have told me if the lode were dying.'

'No doubt.' Pascoe took off his spectacles and polished them on his napkin.

Some drunken men were shouting outside. There was a scuffle and a sound of blows and someone ran off shouting.

Ross said: 'No, I had not thought of any further adventure in mining. But there are other outlets for investment. The foundries, shipbuilding, the roads . . .'

'I will keep a l-look out, Ross. But at the moment, with your prosperity so young, perhaps it is not an unwise thing to keep your money safe at a bank as you are doing now. It is easy to withdraw, instantly usable at need. In another year perhaps you will have a greater surplus.'

'In six months I shall have a greater surplus,' Ross said. 'Don't forget, except for Henshawe's small stake, I own the mine entirely.'

'Perhaps I am always a trifle the pessimist,' said Pascoe, putting back his spectacles. 'But maybe that is one of the necessary characteristics of a b-banker. I do not like this war and what it is doing to us, even though it may bring a temporary prosperity. In order to destroy this system which we so much detest we are creating conditions over here which run contrary to our dearest p-principles. This new move of Pitt's, the suspension of the Habeas Corpus Act, strikes at the heart of our freedom. Imprisonment without trial – it is going back two hundred years! And this huge army we are raising; it is not a *levée en masse* like France's, but the m-methods of raising it are as unsavoury. Kidnapping, debauchery, bribery, any way of enlisting men. And Pitt is borrowing, borrowing at exorbitant rates to finance the war – taxes are heavy, I know, but more taxes would be better. As it is, he is mortgaging the future. I don't like a policy which, whatever its intentions, b-bears hardest on the poor.'

Ross said: 'You know you are speaking to the converted or perhaps you would not be speaking at all. But I have changed my views a small matter in the last two years. At first Burke's thunderings failed to impress me. But one by one I have watched them come true. This is an evil that we face. When I fought in America I remained unconvinced half the time of what I was fighting for. I would fight much more readily this time.'

'I trust you don't intend to.'

Ross was silent. 'I am thirty-four, and I have a wife and

a – child to consider.' He had been about to say children. 'We are forming a local branch of the Volunteers. What little I remember of soldiering may be useful there. But of course it depends how things develop. England may soon be fighting alone.'

'I pray God not.'

'Well, I don't know. Sometimes this country is at its best when alone. The history of our unsuccessful wars are the history of our coalitions.'

They got up, and the maid came in to clear. A small fire burned in the grate and Harris warmed his hands before it. When the maid had gone, Ross said: 'It would be a strange quirk of fate if Wheal Leisure were to become less profitable now, George Warleggan having gone to such lengths to possess it. If it were not for the other venturers I should be vastly amused.'

The next morning, having made his purchases, Ross strolled down to the river behind the old town hall where the Whitsun market was held. There were many things he needed for the farm, chiefly livestock, so much of which had been sold to realize a few miserable pounds two and a half years ago. Of course it would all be put right some day, and some day soon. But one could not buy really good stock in bulk and in a hurry. One built up a farm lovingly, as he had done until the winter of 1790. He had no intention of buying any cattle or pigs today without even Cobbledick to drive them home; but a horse for Demelza to replace Caerhays was an urgent need, and if anything really suitable should be about he might take it.

The really suitable presented itself quite early in his stroll. This Whitsun fair was not as big as the Redruth fair held every Easter Tuesday, where on one occasion Ross had picked up something of considerable significance in his life, but it filled the fields running down to the river. Stalls and compounds straggled across six or seven acres of trampled muddy grass. Men already lay drunk outside beer tents; half-naked urchins tumbled and fought for scraps whenever a scrap was thrown; farmers in leggings haggled over the price of sheep and the quality of grain; thin muddy-flanked cows chewed slowly and waited their fate unaware; a ring was being prepared for the afternoon's wrestling; a bull snorted and stamped in protest against the stout rope holding him; beggars without legs, beggars without noses, beggars holding out withered hands: these would probably be driven out of the town before nightfall; the usual sideshows: the flame-eaters, the pig with six legs, the fortune tellers and the fat woman. Fortunately it was a fine day, but every footstep ploughed deeper into the mud.

Ross was among the stalls where some old clothes and second-hand shoes and wigs were for sale, when a harsh voice behind him said:

'Well, my grandfather's ghost, if it ain't the young Cap'n himself! It's you, my son. There couldn't be no other!'

He turned. 'Tholly?' He could not believe his eyes. 'But I supposed you dead!'

A heavy man with the square shoulders of an asthmatic; stooping, forty-six years of age, dressed in a fustian long coat, primrose yellow waistcoat, dark green corduroy trousers, a green silk neckcloth. A flat nose, dark hair grizzling, ice-grey eyes, beside one of which, puckering it like an inefficient seamstress, ran a scar which made Ross's look no more than a cat's scratch. In place of his left hand was a steel hook more suitable to a butcher's shop.

'Dead I been – or near it – oft enough, but come up smiling. It's been a long time. Thirteen – fourteen year?'

'Eighty-one,' said Ross. 'Thirteen. It seems a century. I knew only that you'd gone to sea. You've been away all this time?'

'Till last year. Then I lost this.' He lifted his hook. 'So they'd have me no longer. Old Tholly was done for, by God. I been back in the country a year, though not recent in these parts. Can I sell ye a bull pup? I breed 'em for baiting. That and all else I can lay hands on. Young Cap'n, by God. Your father be dead, I suppose?'

'Eleven years.'

They talked for a few minutes, and then Ross took the other man to a nearby tent and they drank Geneva and sat on a bench. Mixed feelings for Ross. Bartholomew Tregirls came of a world he had forgotten, or at least of a world which rarely came to mind. The days of his youth seemed to belong to some other person. The dividing line was his time in America. They had been the formative years. He had gone out a wild youth and came back a mature man. Although he no more conformed when he came back than before he went out, his youthful scrapes now seemed ridiculous, frivolous, childish, without good cause except the waywardness of a spoilt boy. In those early days Bartholomew Tregirls, in age

67

halfway between himself and his father, had been the high priest of mischief, off with old Joshua on wild jaunts in which Ross was allowed no part or playing ringleader to the boy when they came home. After his wife died Joshua had been bereft for two years, then he had broken out into all his worst habits, and no woman who lifted an eye to him had been safe. Tregirls, a big handsome young man then, already asthmatic but with all the nervous vitality of the kind, had been his partner. It was an outraged father in St Michael who had attacked him with a meat knife and nearly put his eye out. But his spoiled looks hadn't affected his appeal for women, and he had gone on until, involved in a robbery which, if he had been caught, would have carried the death penalty, he had slipped away one night, leaving his wife and two young children destitute.

An age had passed. Ross had some affection for this big powerful man sitting beside him, but an ambiguous feeling of distaste at being reminded of his existence. And the years had changed Tholly – changed him in fact and also in the eye of the beholder. He looked seedy, battered, and reduced in size and importance.

'You're wed, my son, I s'pose? Wed long since, I s'pose, with a growing family? How's the old place? D'ye still go line fishing? D'ye still wrestle? D'ye still run over to Guernsey for a drop of spirit? How's the rest of 'em? Be Jud still alive? Jud and that great cow Prudie?'

'Yes, they're still alive, though they've left me, live now in Grambler. Yes, I'm married, with one son. No, I wrestle no longer, have not done for ten years – except now and then in anger.'

Tholly laughed loudly and then caught his breath. 'God damn my chest, tis playing me up this morn. Oh, I wrestled regular till last year when I lost me arm . . . Got me bones still with me.' He rattled a linen bag dangling from his waist and looked at Ross smiling. 'I hear that Agnes be dead. D'you hear aught of Lobb or Emma?'

His children. 'They're both near by. Lobb is a tin streamer in Sawle Combe. Emma is a kitchen maid at the Choakes'. Agnes lived but three years after you left.'

'Poor soul. She was ever a patient palched little wranny, and by God, young Cap'n, she had to be patient with me!'

Even the phrases were out of a long-dead life. Long before Ross had ever fought with the 62nd Foot he had been known as 'Young Cap'n' to a select few, to distinguish him from

'Old Cap'n', his father. Joshua's title had not been earned by any military service but by his having opened Wheal Grace; thus he had become a mining captain, something of more importance than a military title to the Cornish mind.

'Some day I'll go see them,' said Tholly. 'Do they take for me or for she, d'ye reckon?'

'Lobb is like his mother. Emma I'd say more like you. A tall good-looking girl. Twenty she'll be now? Or twenty-one?'

'Nineteen. Lobb'll be twenty-five. Either of them wed?'

'Lobb is. I do not know his wife but they have five children. Emma is not yet, so far as I know.'

In the silence that fell again between them the two bells of St Mary's church began to ring. The cadence floated over the little town, over the murmuring muttering fields of the fair-ground, not wholly chiming but coming of a more leisurely, more gracious and more melodic world. The shrill cries of urchins, the lowing of a cow, the distant shout of a showman, were overborne by the drifting sound of the church bells.

'Some day I'll come and see you, my son,' Tregirls said. He smiled through a shambles of decayed teeth. 'If so be as I be welcome. Since I left the sea I've not had the luck of all the world. I buy and sell and make do. Can I not sell ye something now? Something to take home to the little wife?'

'Is that your stall? What do you have?'

'Everything you've the mind to conjure of. I'll sell ye anything ye want save maybe this.' He lifted his hook. 'That I use on the women now. I put it round their little necks so's they cannot wriggle away.'

'The same old Tholly. Well, I want no bull-pups. It is not a sport I enjoy. I had an eye open for a likely horse, but I am in no hurry about it –'

Tholly Tregirls thumped down his mug. 'I have the very thing for ye, my boy.' He moved his hook to pat Ross's arm with it and then refrained. 'There's two splendid mares behind the stall, and one could be yours at the right price. The better-most be a fine young skewbald no more'n three year old and scarce broke. Judith is her name. Let me show you. Let me show you. Though you'll pardon me if we keep our voices lowered, as I hold no licence for the trade.'

Judith was thin and ill-kempt, though an attempt had been made by some nefarious means to give a gloss to her coat.

Skewbald was an exaggeration, for she was brown, with only three insignificant white patches. She had bruises on her knees and a rolling eye. However, she suffered Ross to examine her teeth without a protest.

'This is not a horse, it's a pony,' said Ross.

'Ah, she'll grow yet awhile. She's of fine stock, I can tell ye that, young Cap'n.'

She had a gentle mouth, that was one thing, and her rolling eye might be nerves rather than ill-temper.

Ross released her mouth. 'Women you can deceive me on, Tholly, but not horses. She is six or seven years old if she's a day. Look at those central incisors. You should know better than to cheat an old friend.'

Tregirls hunched his shoulders and coughed loudly into the air. 'You was ever one with an eye, my boy, whether for women *or* horses. I'd be glad to welcome ye in partnership . . . But thirty-five guineas and you can have her. I'll make nothing on that – indeed will lose on it – but I'm short of cash, and will make the sacrifice for old times' sake.'

'Increase the sacrifice a small matter and I might be interested.'

As they wrangled it occurred to Ross that by buying from this man he was likely getting a bad bargain. Many things might be wrong, all sorts of tricks being played. But under-mining his good sense was the comfortable feeling that this amount of money no longer mattered to him. He was helping an old friend; if the worst happened it could not be a total loss; the mare could be used as a mine pony.

So the bargaining was only half-hearted on his side, and presently twenty-six guineas changed hands. Bartholomew Tregirls appeared impervious to any change that had occur-red in the younger man in thirteen years: he was ready to resume precisely the same old relationship, avuncular, the dominant character of the two. Ross did not undeceive him. Tregirls was no fool and would learn or be taught if the occasion came. But this was a chance encounter that might never be repeated, a brush between two people – some-time friends who had long since gone their own way. Ross did not think Tregirls would return to his old haunts. He had not been popular in the villages, particularly among the married men.

CHAPTER SIX

Although she had never lived farther than twelve miles from
the sea, Morwenna Chynoweth had seldom visited it and had
certainly not been aware of its presence as she was at Trenwith. Her father, a serious man of a Puritan turn of mind
with a consequent leaning towards the lower church, had not
taken his religion lightly and he did not consider jaunts to
the seaside appropriate for even his youngest children. As
for the eldest daughter, she was too busy helping her mother
about the house, with the other children or with social and
charitable works, to have time for riding for pleasure or visiting friends. Four times in her early teens she had gone with
her father when he had preached at sea-coast parishes, but on
these occasions she had had little chance to enjoy or admire
the coast.

Here it was different. A girl as serious in some ways as
her father, with religious ideals and a strong sense of duty,
she had come to this appointment sorrowing as much at the
parting as her sorrowing family but resolved to be everything a worthy governess should. However, in spite of the
loss of prestige in her new position, she found she was
beginning to enjoy herself much more than in her old life.
Geoffrey Charles was wayward and intelligent, but it was
no harder controlling or teaching him than it had been her
own . sisters; Mr Warleggan, if a little frightening, was
gracious enough in his impersonal way; Cousin Elizabeth
had been kindness itself and went out of her way to alleviate
any feelings of a discomfort or shame she might feel in
her new position; and there were servants all the time
to do the really menial work. Furthermore, not for pleasure
but in the interests of her duty, she could take Geoffrey
Charles any number of fascinating trips – into the countryside, on the cliffs, along the beaches. And she had a pony
always available.

They were little more than a mile from the sea at Trenwith, but where Trenwith land abutted on the sea it was all
sharp raw cliffs with one or two seaweedy coves only
accessible by narrow and dangerous paths. A mile to the
left (if you were looking out to sea) the land dropped towards

Trevaunance Cove with the village of St Ann's beyond. A mile or a little more to the right was Sawle village with its shingly inlet which rose again in a short sharp cliff before reaching the property of Captain Ross Poldark. There was fine sand at Trevaunance and at Sawle when the tide went out; there were tantalizing glimpses of untouched golden sand in mainly inaccessible points; but by far the best sand and the best beach anywhere was Hendrawna, just beyond Captain Ross Poldark's land and almost into Treneglos property; four miles odd if you went direct, five or six if you skirted round.

Morwenna had not yet learned the causes of the estrangement between the two houses but she knew of its existence. That is to say, the Ross Poldarks were seldom mentioned; and on the one occasion when Geoffrey Charles had brought up the name in company he was effectively squashed. She could not tell quite where the point of enmity existed, what injury, real or fancied, had been committed and on whom and how. When the subject was approached, George was suddenly dangerous, touchy, given to sarcasm; but it was not directed at all against Elizabeth. She was equally touchy, cold; they saw eye to eye in their dislike. It was a strange situation to Morwenna who, whatever the shortcomings of her home life, had always been on terms of immediate and loving friendship with every cousin she ever met. Clearly the Ross Poldarks had done something unforgivable. It was difficult to imagine what. Naturally she was curious; but she shied away from asking the one person likely to tell her. She felt no repugnance for Aunt Agatha; too often she had been in the company of very old and dying people; but she could not bring herself to shout the questions into the whiskery ear; it was a confidence to be sought in a murmur, not shouted like a naval broadside.

No actual prohibition from Elizabeth that their walks were not to come near Nampara land, but Morwenna felt she would be erring in the spirit of her instructions if she took Geoffrey Charles there; so whenever they went on Hendrawna it was by making a detour, leaving their ponies tethered to a granite post in the sandhills and coming on the beach where the undulant sandhills gave way to a buttress of low cliff on which the mine, Wheal Leisure, was working. Where they came out they could just see the chimneys of Nampara House about a mile and a half away.

Late June set fair, with easterly airs so light that they

were only just perceptible. Morwenna and Geoffrey Charles went quite often to this beach – with, of course, a groom; but him they left with the ponies. Geoffrey Charles had discovered the joys of paddling, and they would both walk along, thrushing their feet through the water as it licked its slow way in. They would occasionally meet people, who would give them good afternoon as they passed; scavengers looking for anything of possible value that the tide might bring in: women bent double in premature age, ragged ex-miners with ominous coughs, underfed waifs, mothers with a straggle of children at their heels; now and then a working miner down from the mine taking a quiet stroll or emptying refuse for the tide to eat. But the numbers of such were few, especially on calmer days when the sea was too quiet to bring anything in. The groom did not like letting them go off alone, but, as Geoffrey Charles rightly said, the horses were a far more valuable property to steal than they were, and anyway from where Keigwin stood he could usually keep them in sight. Once to begin with they had galloped on the beach, but getting the ponies on the beach and off again at this point was a hazardous process with a steep little drop to negotiate.

On a Wednesday at the beginning of July they saw a man coming towards them and Geoffrey Charles recognized him as one of the youths they had surprised carrying the ship's timber across their land. As they came nearer he too recognized them and came trotting across the damp sand towards them and touched his hand to his head.

'Why, Master Geoffrey. And Miss Chynoweth. This is a rare surprise! Day to ee both. Proper weather this, eh?' They exchanged a few words, then he said: 'Going for a stroll? Might I walk along with ee for a few paces?'

He fell in without waiting for their consent. He was bareheaded and barefoot, drill trousers rolled up above the knee and tied there with hemp. Morwenna knew she should not tolerate his free and easy manner, but there seemed no actual lack of respect, and with Geoffrey Charles so clearly welcoming it was difficult for her.

'Oft times I d'come on this beach for a stroll just so soon as I may get an hour off. The finest beach ever I been on. I've not seen you before. Ride over or walk, did you? Maybe you know it all far better'n me.'

Geoffrey Charles wanted to know about the building of the cottage, whether the beam had fitted and how they had secured it. Construction of any sort fascinated him. Drake tried to explain the problems they had had to face. Mr Geoffrey must come and see it some time. It was back over the hill only a mile or so from here. If Miss Chynoweth would not mind. Geoffrey Charles said of course he would come and of course Miss Chynoweth would not mind.

Drake said then: 'Have ye seen the Holy Well? But then you will've. I'm the stranger on the scene . . .'

Geoffrey Charles had heard of a holy well but had not been to it.

'Well, tis better part of a half-mile along here over along towards the Dark Cliffs. Ten minutes and you'll be there. See that there buttress of cliff standing out?' He moved nearer to Morwenna and pointed it out to her.

'Yes, I see. But it is too far for today.'

'Oh, no,' said Geoffrey Charles. 'We've only been on the beach ten minutes, Wenna! We haven't even paddled yet. We can do it easily. Keigwin will not mind. I'll run and tell him what we are going to do.'

'I don't think your mother would wish us to wander so far from him—'

'I'll see ee come to no harm, Miss Chynoweth,' said Drake, looking at her in respectful admiration. 'Twill take little or no time if Master Geoffrey would like it, and tis hard to find the well without someone to guide you the way.'

Geoffrey Charles went rushing off to tell the groom and the two young adults began walking slowly towards the cliffs.

'I hear tell you've not been in this here parts much longer than brother and me, Miss Chynoweth.'

'About four months.'

'Tis almost the very same. My name's Drake Carne, Miss Chynoweth. I hope you'll excuse the liberty of me suggesting to walk with you . . .'

Morwenna inclined her head.

'You've not, I s'pose, met my sister yet, Mrs Ross Poldark?'

'No . . .'

'You don't b'lieve she's my sister?'

'Oh, yes . . .'

'She's a rare sweet soul. Brave and clever. I'd like for you to meet her.'

'I don't often come this way, except riding with Geoffrey Charles.'

'Well, he's her nephew, like. By marriage. And she's not

seen him for over three years.'

She said: 'I do not think the feeling between the two houses is of the best. As a newcomer it is not my place to ask why. But until it improves I cannot bring Geoffrey Charles to Nampara. Indeed, I am not sure whether his mother would approve of his walking on this beach.'

'Don't tell her, please.'

'Why not?'

'Then I should never – we shouldn't – it is the best beach around.'

Morwenna looked at him with her dark serious eyes. It was a pity that in a man of her own class all he had said could be considered gracious and polite, whereas from such as him, it could only be an impertinence. It was a pity that he was the most beautiful young man she had ever seen. 'If you will show us this well, Mr Carne; that I'm sure will be a kindness.'

Geoffrey Charles caught them up, panting, and ran right past them. Then he stood, hands on hips as they caught him up. 'I wish I was dressed like you, Drake. That's your name, isn't it. I wish I was dressed like you. These clothes, I'm always afraid of soiling them. They are suitable for a party, not for a country tramp.'

'They're suitable for your station, Mr Geoffrey,' Drake said. 'But if you d'take care you'll not hurt them. Tidn more'n a short climb.'

'A climb?' said Morwenna. 'You did not say that.'

'Well, tis scarce above thirty feet, and that some easy.'

Cliffs and sandhills faced the sea at intervals towards the end of Hendrawna Beach, and they passed two bluffs of rock before Drake stopped. 'I'd best lead the way,' he said. 'Then if Miss Chynoweth could follow me I'd be at hand to give her a help up; while Mr Geoffrey, you will be behind her to help her too if need be.'

They went up. It was, as Drake had said, an easy climb, and Morwenna could have been up like a cat if she had not been impeded by her skirt and her determination not to lift it. So she had to take Drake's hand twice, and on consideration this was perhaps a worse choice. His hand was warm and hers cold. There was some frightening transmission between them.

At the top he took them across a small green platform to a cliff of overhanging rock. Raised a foot from the ground by its rocky sides was a pool of water about four feet across.

'This is it,' said Drake. ''Tis fresh water – taste – though so near the sea, and they d'say twas consecrated by St Sawle more'n a thousand year gone and twas used by all the early Christian pilgrims walking 'long the coast from one monastery to the next. Taste, tis pure water.'

'You know all this – so soon,' said Morwenna.

'Old Jope Ishbel told me – he as works at Wheal Leisure. He d'know all there is to know. But, mind, I had to come and find 'n for myself.'

'It's lovely water,' said Geoffrey Charles. 'Taste it, Wenna.' She tasted. 'Um.'

'It is a wishing well too, or so they d'say. What you must do, Jope Ishbel says, is put the first finger of your right hand deep in the water and make three crosses with it, saying "Father, Son, Holy Spirit" and then you get your wishes granted.'

'It's sacrilegious,' said Morwenna.

'Oh, no. Oh no tis not, begging your pardon, Miss Chynoweth. It's a holy place just so much as a church. Don't we ask for things in church? I do. You do, Master Geoffrey.'

'Yes, yes, surely, I shall wish. Show me. Do you say it aloud?'

'Only the prayer, not the wish. See, this way.' Drake rolled up his sleeve, dipped his finger and hand into the well, glanced quickly at Morwenna. Then he made his three crosses, saying 'Father, Son, Holy Spirit', hastily withdrew his hand but did not shake the drops off it. 'You must let it dry,' he said.

Geoffrey Charles, much intrigued, soon followed, and then pestered Morwenna to do the same. At first she refused but presently gave way. With the boy and the young man watching, she took off a small garnet ring and put it on a stone, then slid the sleeve of her riding jacket up till her wrist and slender forearm were bare to the elbow. She put in her hand, finger extended, thought a moment, then made the three crosses and muttered the prayer. As she leaned over, her hair fell about her face, showing through it gleams of cheek and curve of ear.

'No, not yet!' said Geoffrey Charles, as she straightened up and moved to pull her sleeve. 'You must let it dry!'

They all stood in silence. The sea was quiet too, and the only sound was the breeze stirring the grasses on the cliff edge and a lark trilling in the high sky.

'How foolish we must all look,' said Morwenna quietly,

slipping her ring back. 'I am sure the old monks would not consider us suitable pilgrims, making our flippant wishes at this well.'

'Mine was not flippant,' said Drake.

'Nor mine!' said Geoffrey Charles. 'It is hardly flippant to ask for –' He stopped just in time, and they all laughed.

As they came to the descent Drake said: 'Half a mile on, near the Dark Cliffs, there is some handsome great caves. One's called the Abbey. Tis just like a great church inside: arches, pillars, naves. One day I'd dearly like to show them to ee, if so be as you'd be interested.'

'Oh, yes!' said Geoffrey Charles. 'We would, wouldn't we, Morwenna. When could we go? When?'

'It is not the sort of thing you could do without your mother's permission.'

'Tis a lot easier than this here,' Drake said. 'No climbing. You just walk in off the sand. But if you could name a day I'd bring candles, for with candles you can see the more.'

'Oh, Wenna!' said Geoffrey Charles. 'We must!'

'Perhaps *you* can persuade your mother,' Morwenna said obliquely. 'You know how much she will do for you.'

They began the descent, which was not quite so easy for a woman shod for riding.

'D'you know why they are called the Dark Cliffs?' Drake said, stopping halfway. 'A simple answer: because they are always dark. See, even now with the sun full on 'em they're black as night. 'Vyou ever been that far, Mr Geoffrey?'

'No. We've never been this far before.'

'*I've* never been that far neither. Not yet. Come, Miss Chynoweth, you must leave me help you. '

'No, thank you.'

'You must. Tisn't safe else.'

'I can manage.'

'Please . . .' He took her arm and hand like a precious treasure newly gained.

The library had always been held in particular affection by Demelza. When first in this house as a child servant she had spent hours of her time in it, exploring the broken-down room and the treasure-trove of its mildewed contents. Since then much of the detritus of twenty-five years had been thrown away or given away, and the better pieces had been repaired and brought into the house. At the far end was a trapdoor leading down into a larger cavity built for purposes

Demelza preferred not to remember. Apart from the walls there was not much of the room worth saving. The roof would have to be demolished, all the window frames knocked out, the floor renewed, for there was rot in it all over.

Ross's first idea, born when prosperity was only just sprouting, had been to incorporate the library into the living space of the house for the first time. (Never completed, it had never been anything but a lumber room at best.) But as his financial condition became more assured so his sights were raised. The rooms he had seen in the house in London when he had visited Caroline Penvenen, the improvements at Trenwith, an occasional elegant room in one of the town houses of Truro, had all inspired him with ideas to build and decorate at least one room at Nampara, and that the largest, in a manner suitable to a more gracious way of living. So it had been planned to lay an oak polished floor, put up a good plaster ceiling, and perhaps have walls of light pine panelling. But the prospect of another child caused a further reassessment. There were six bedrooms at present; little enough if four servants slept in. Jeremy would soon need one of his own. There had never been a way into the library except by going out of doors or through Joshua's old bedroom with the box bed. Why could they not turn Joshua's bedroom on the ground floor into a dining-room, and raise the library up a floor to the same level as the rest of the house, building two larger bedrooms above it, and make a way to them through the lumber room and the apple cupboard which were now above Joshua's bedroom?

Lack of skilled, or even semi-skilled, craftsmen would be one of the obstacles to such an undertaking. Nampara House, when Joshua put it up, had been built to a utilitarian design, and the men who worked on it were as rough-hewn as the house they built. If the house had mellowed in thirty-five years the quality of the available workers had not changed. Plasterers would probably have to be brought from Bath or Exeter. Carpenters to put up a new roof were easily found but not to make a handsome door or mantelshelf. Stone masons could build a wall to last for ever but few around could work the resistant granite or ornament the slate.

Drake had worked at the mine for his first weeks but had soon been moved to begin some preliminary dismantling of the library, and he soon showed that he was the best carpenter around, even though it was not his trade.

One day when Ross was away and Demelza had come into

the library in search of a dust sheet, Drake said to her:
'Sister, do you never have no trade with the folk of Tren-with?'

She said: 'No, Drake.' Just that and no more.

'Mr Francis, who died, he were Cap'n Ross's cousin. That correct?'

'That is correct.'

'Was they not partial to each other?'

'They had disagreements. But they were good friends in the last years of Francis's life.'

'I've asked you 'bout Geoffrey Charles before. Do you not wish ever to see him?'

'I'd be glad to see him, but his mother and his step-father would not want him to see us.'

Drake took two nails from between his strong teeth and put them on the bench. 'Is there not too much ill will in the world, sister? Don't you think so?'

'That I do. But you may take it from me, Drake, that this is an ill will that no Christian prayers will blow away. I don't wish to explain it to you the more, but that is the way of it.'

'Can I ask, is the ill will on your side or on their side?'

'Both.'

She had found her dust sheet and was now looking through some old cost books. There was a certain set to her chin.

He said: 'Sam wishes you would turn to Christ, sister.'

She frowned at the book and pushed back her curl of hair. 'Sam wishes a lot.'

'Do you not ever have ardent longings to find your Saviour?'

'I am not learned in these things.'

'Well no more're we . . .'

'But you think you know?'

''Tisn't the question of learning. Tis the question of feeling you're dead in sin and in the bonds of iniquity, and seeking the forgiveness of God.'

She looked up, her eyes at their most direct. She had not heard *him* speak like this before. 'And you have had that?'

'I b'lieve so. Sam have had it more so.'

'Sam,' she said, 'has had everything more so. He reminds me of Father.'

'Oh, but he's not like Father. Father was a — was a bull. He'd fight for Christ in just the same way as he'd fight when he were drunk. Sam's gentle. He's a born Christian, Demelza.'

It was not often he used her name. She smiled. 'Perhaps I was not born one. Maybe that's what's wrong. I go to church once a year with Captain Poldark. Christmas Day we go together and take communion. Rest of the time I try to behave as a Christian should. Maybe there's one neighbour we can't love as ourselves, but most of the others we try to live with peaceable and kindly. I think maybe the trouble with me – or is it the trouble with you? . . .'

'What?'

'I'm not convinced of that much *sin*, brother. Oh, I know I could do better, this way, that way, the other way. And of course I don't love God enough. I'm – earthy. I don't look at a figure on a cross, I look at the things round me. *Those* are what I love: my husband, my child, my dog, my garden, my spinet, my bedroom, my home. Earthy. You see. But I have love overflowing for all those. Those are more important to me than a Man sitting on a throne in Heaven. I hope if I explain it to Him when I see Him, He'll come round to see it my way . . .'

'But don't you see, Christ is among us all the time. Love him first and all the rest will be made over again.'

She was silent. 'I don't think I want it all made over again, Drake. I think I want it just as it is.'

Drake sighed. 'Oh, well, I promised Sam I'd try.'

'You promised . . .' She laughed. 'So that explains it all! It is not you speaking at all but *Sam*. I might have guessed!'

Drake picked up his hammer and stared at it in frustration. '*No*. No, sister, tisn't true. I'm saved and in grace just same as him. But he's the more convinced in trying to save others. And he thought – we thought . . .' He picked up a nail and hammered it home.

'And you thought your sister was utterly in the dark and estranged from God? Isn't that what you call it?'

'Well, it come natural, don't it, to think of folk close home. And Sam d'know that I'm more with ee than he is. And he thinks ye've more of a taking for me than for him . . .'

'If you put nails in like that you'll have to draw them out again. And that'll split the wood . . .' She turned a page of the cost book. 'I'm sorry, brother. You should first try to convert Captain Poldark.'

'I'd dare not try,' said Drake.

'No more would I,' said Demelza. 'But for all that, don't tell me he's not a good man!'

80

Drake perceived he could do no more. 'Pity, a rare pity. This library . . .'

'What of it?'

'Sam were thinking. Only just thinking. That as the Society grew this'd be a handsome place for our meetings.'

Joe Nanfan had come into the library carrying a deal plank. Since he was injured in the mine collapse of last year he had taken to carpentering and was learning fast.

Demelza let out a long pent breath. 'I think I believe you *both* take after Father.'

Drake smiled uncertainly at her as she got up and left.

Later that evening, Ross still being away, Drake came to her in the garden.

'Excuse me, sister, if I were taking liberties this forenoon. I trust you think no worse of we.'

Demelza said: 'I couldn't but think worse of someone who wants to use our new room as a meeting house.'

They both laughed. 'But serious,' he said.

'Serious,' she said, 'you've a beguiling way, Drake. I tremble for the young women around here.'

His face changed. 'Well, maybe yes, maybe no. I fear tis not all so simple as that . . . Sister, I have another favour to ask of ee, and this is my own and maybe I shouldn't ask this neither . . .'

'I'm sure you should not,' Demelza said. 'And I'm sure you will.'

'Well . . . I can read if I go slow and careful; but we've only one bible betwixt the both of us, and Sam d'have it all the time. He d'read to me out of it, but that don't help *my* reading. And I can't write. Mind, I can pen my name but naught else. I want the practice.'

'You need another book? That you can have with pleasure, though our selection is small. Another bible?'

'Well, sister, if there be another book I'd better prefer that, seeing as we have the one bible already. Some good book, mebbe, as will help to improve me in two ways at the same time, like. And also,' he added as Demelza was about to speak. 'If I practise to write I would dearly like for you to help me. See what I d'write, tell me where I go wrong. You know. For mebbe ten minutes a day, no more.'

She considered a hollyhock which needed staking already, otherwise the next wind would flatten it. Hollyhocks were really unsuitable for this coast, and she would have given them up long ago if she had not loved them so much. One needed sturdier things, lower growing. Anyway, she was coming reluctanatly to acknowledge that this was essentially a garden which did well only in the spring. Daffodils, primroses, tulips, they were always splendid; but the soil was so light that any heat in summer quickly dried it out, and the plants lacked food.

'Sam cannot do this for you?'

'Sam is not overmuch betterer'n me. Now I seen that notice that you penned for the workmen 'bout them keeping off from walking on your garden, and that's bravely writ. You must've writ a lot, sister. You must've practised at it.'

'I started writing when I was your age, Drake. No, a year younger. That's seven years since. It takes time.'

'I've time.'

'My writing,' she said. 'You should see some of the documents done by the law, done by clerks and the like. *That's* writing. Mine looks like a spider with a broken leg.'

'I just want to be able to make my wishes known.'

'I think you do that quite well now,' she said, stooping to grasp a weed. She tugged, but the head came away in her fingers, leaving the root.

He said: 'Here,' and bent beside her, dug his long fingers into the sandy soil and came out with the root. 'What shall I do with'n?'

'That heap over there. Thank you, brother.' She straightened up, and the breeze blew her hair back from her forehead. 'Very well, Drake, I'll help you. Always provided you do not try too hard to convert me.'

He patted her hand. 'Thank ee, sister. That's brave and fine. You're a real Christian.'

CHAPTER SEVEN

Ross had been two nights in Looe, staying with his old friend Harry Blewett. Over a late supper he told Demelza that Blewett's boat yard was booming, and that he was still willing to offer Ross a share in the business. Such money as Ross put in would be used to extend the yard, which at present was strained to capacity.

Demelza said: 'What if the war is over soon?'

'A good yard, well run, can hardly fail to remain a going

concern. The need for boats may not be so great if the war ends, but the need will not altogether disappear, the way a lode of tin or copper can.'

She helped him to more chine of mutton. 'And . . . the other thing?'

'They have made only one run since early June, but two of their men then inquired on my behalf. So far nothing. The Breton fishermen, they say, move about from port to port but they seldom journey inland and they have no knowledge of prisons or camps or of any prisoners of war. I have offered fifty guineas for definite information that can be confirmed about the English ship *Travail* and possible survivors. They are going over next week if the weather is favourable.'

'And from St Ann's?'

'Will Nanfan has found out nothing about Dwight, but he did hear that English prisoners in Brest had been ill-treated by the rabble, stoned in the streets and put in abominable jails. These he thought were captured merchant seamen; and of course naval officers would get preferential treatment.'

'You will not tell Caroline this?'

'Certainly not.'

She picked up his plate. 'Pudding? Or jelly? Or gooseberry tart?'

'Tart, if you have made it and not Jane. Thank you.' He watched her get up and cut the tart. The coming child had done nothing yet to alter her figure; she still had the same leggy grace, the same look of youthful intent. 'While I was in Looe I met two French émigrés, both aristocrats, a M. du Corbin and a Comte de Maresi. I asked du Corbin what was most likely to happen if Dwight had survived the wreck. But I think du Corbin is still living in a chivalrous time. He asserts that all officers captured are automatically exchanged or released on parole and that therefore, as we have heard nothing, Dwight is dead. What I don't think he realizes is that, even in the year and a half since he left, conditions in France have run down. Communications are distintegrating and until some order is restored no one really can control procedures which used to be taken as a matter of course.'

She sat down and watched him cat. She sat with one elbow on the table, the other smoothing the cloth. 'I have a fear that if you hear nothing soon you may go over to ask questions yourself.'

'The risk would be small if I did. Neither government has yet made any attempt to stop the trade.'

'It is not just "governments", as you call them. It is people. We are at war. Some may forget it if it lines their pockets, but others will remember. Hatred will grow week by week. See what Will says about the crowds in Brest. You might be attacked at sea – or captured and taken prisoner yourself – or stabbed in the back. That is one risk. The other is being caught landing back in England. We have had one bitter narrow escape. Twould be too much to expect another.'

He smiled. 'What a lot of hazards you see! I suppose you have forgotten what I said to you when you told me you were with child. And do you know what you replied? "Just by living we are all hostages to fate."'

'It is not the same thing, Ross. Women – whether high or low – it is their natural lot, their destiny to bear children. I have had two. Why should the third be any different? But men are not – it is not their natural destiny to travel overseas and risk their lives in an enemy country.'

'Not for a friend?'

'Ah. I know. I know . . .' She puckered her brows. 'You make me sound mean. Why do you make me sound mean, Ross? But others can do what you can do. Employ them. We have money enough – that is the way to use it.'

Services at Sawle Church were held at eleven in the morning on the first and third Sundays in the month and at two in the afternoon on the other Sundays. On these occasions Mr Clarence Odgers said prayers and preached, and the choir and musicians sawed away at a few psalms and hymns, helped by the sparse congregation. Old Charles Poldark had liked an evening service starting about five or six, so of course it had been arranged to suit him; but a couple of years after he died, with the rest of the Poldarks taking so little interest in the church, a more convenient time had been reverted to. Then when Francis died there had only been Elizabeth, with her small son, and such had been the claims on her time and energies that all the old customs had fallen away; in particular, and most to be regretted on Mr Odgers's part, the weekly obligation of the big house to feed the curate. Attempts by Mr Odgers to induce Ross Poldark to take over this and other devoirs had signally failed.

But now that the house belonged to the Warleggans a new

régime had come in, and Mr Odgers was pleased to see the new squire in church every Sunday he was in residence, together with such other members of his household as he thought fit to bring. There were no signs yet of a reversion to the old custom of victualling the needy cleric; but help of an even more valuable kind – in the form of actual *money* – had occasionally come Mr Odgers's way; and this was so unprecedented that the little man was only too anxious to make any alterations in the shape, time or condition of the service that Mr Warleggan might desire.

In his heart, or on his knees, Odgers had to confess that things were not quite the same with Mr Warleggan as with Charles or Francis Poldark. None of the Poldarks had been as regular in attendance as Mr Warleggan was proving. Old Charles had been difficult with his sudden likes and dislikes and his constant belchings, and young Francis had sometimes been bitter and sardonic. But they treated him as one of themselves. Or almost one of themselves. It was 'Lost your place this morning, did you, Odgers? Thought I was asleep, didn't you, but that goes to show I was not. Aarf! Not that I blame you with all these damned Hebrew names.' Or Francis would say: 'Damn me, Odgers, that fellow Permewan with his bass viol; I've never heard a worse noise from a sow in farrow. Could we not ask him to take some water with his gin?' Mr Warleggan was different. Mr Warleggan would call him up to the house and would say: 'If you cannot get a sufficiency of bellringers, Odgers, I will send two of my men. See that they are properly rung next Sunday.' Or: 'I notice some of the congregation do not rise when we come into church. Will you kindly see in future that all do so.' It was not just what was said but how it was said – none of this man-to-man familiarity which, while never bridging the gap in social station, helped to disguise it. Rather a cold over-politeness which was more suitable between master and employee.

As to the second request, Mr Odgers had entered no comment upon it when it was made. There had been a time, when Odgers had first taken up the curacy, when it had been the custom for most of the congregation not merely to rise when the Poldarks entered but to *wait outside* until they came and then follow them in. It had all been very free and easy but it had been taken as a natural part of village life. 'Afternoon, Mrs Kimber,' Charles would say, as he passed, 'hope you are better,' and 'Av'noon, sur, nicely, sur, naow, thank ee,' Mrs

Kimber would reply, with perhaps a bob or a curtsey if she felt like it; and in they would all go. But this custom had gradually ceased during Francis's brief tenure, particularly after Verity left. There wasn't much point, for instance, in waiting outside if no Poldark ever turned up. When Francis died it had all gone from bad to worse; the congregation had fallen off and those left had become unruly; no one cared about the church any more.

Now someone cared but in a different way. The congregation had to be brought under a new discipline, and not one which had ceased altogether to be a discipline and become a casual, time-sanctified habit. Trenwith servants and those depending in some degree on Trenwith for trade or patronage presented no problem. But there were a number of independent-minded souls whom Mr Odgers would have to work on.

To begin with he went about it by posting himself and his eldest son, who performed the duties of verger, at the church door a few minutes before the start of the service. Then, as soon as the Warleggans were seen approaching, his son was sent hurriedly into the church to stop the congregation chattering and make them rise while Odgers walked down to the lychgate to greet the arriving party.

George, however, made it all much more difficult by frequently arriving late. The Poldarks, to give them their due, had never been three or four minutes out at most. If they were delayed or unable to come Charles would send Tabb or Bartle telling Odgers to start without them. So it had been the customary thing not to start until they came; it had again been part of the natural order of the day. But George and his party were sometimes ten minutes late, and then the congregation became very restive.

Normally between twenty and thirty villagers would come to the service, with a few extra in the choir. (Dr Choake, who was vicar's warden, would attend with his wife regularly on the first Sunday in the month, Captain Henshawe, the people's warden, somewhat less often, and the Poldarks from Nampara once a year.) But of late these basic numbers had been swollen by the attendance of a solid block of men and women, some twelve to eighteen strong, who filed in led by a man called Samuel Carne, and seated themselves in the back five rows by the font. Odgers knew them to be Methodists, a sect that he hated but could do little to check. Although they came to church, as now, they really had little respect for its authority and still less for its ordained ministers. But their behaviour in Sawle Church was exemplary, and he could do nothing to turn them out.

Too exemplary. It showed up the behaviour of the other parishioners, who were wont to chat and gossip among themselves and had grown accustomed to doing so right through the service until Mr Warleggan stopped that too.

On the second Sunday in August, the service being at two, Sam Carne led his flock into church about five minutes before the hour, and as usual, after a short prayer, they all settled back quietly into their seats to wait for the service to begin. The rest of the congregation was at its noisiest, and they cast unfriendly looks at the Methodists and tittered among themselves, thinking pretentious the reverent manner of the people in the back rows. Unknown to Mr Odgers, George was entertaining friends, and, although they would not begin dinner until after the service, they had been drinking tea and practising archery and generally enjoying the summery day, so that it was fifteen minutes after two before eight of them appeared at the gate. They were George and Elizabeth, Geoffrey Charles and Morwenna, St John Peter and Joan Pascoe, Unwin Trevaunance and a Miss Barbary, the daughter of Alfred Barbary. Mr Odgers hurried down to greet them and was nodded to by some and smiled at by others as they went past.

Then George said, half stopping: 'Has the service begun?'

'No, Mr Warleggan, we are all ready to begin –'

'That singing . . .'

Mr Odgers pushed at his horsehair wig. 'It is none of my doing, but certain members of the congregation while away the time singing a hymn of their own devising. I have sent John in to stop them. It will cease in a moment.'

They waited and listened. 'Egad,' said St John Peter, 'it sounds like a Methody hymn.'

'It will stop in a minute,' said Mr Odgers. 'It will cease in a moment.'

'But why should we wait?' Elizabeth asked good-humouredly. 'Is that not what churches are for? Perhaps if we hurry we can join them.' She squeezed George's arm. 'Come, dear.'

He had looked annoyed when the singing did not stop; but Elizabeth's words cooled him off, and he made a little disclaiming gesture to his guests and went on.

As he came into the church the Methodists had reached the last verse, and the sight of him, plus an inability to remember all the words, almost silenced them. But a few, led by Pally Rogers and Will Nanfan and Beth Daniell, all of whom resented certain fences that had been erected during the last few months and who had nothing to fear from George Warleggan or his family, sang out more loudly than ever to make up for the loss of other voices, and the last verse followed George and his party emphatically all the way to the pew.

> 'A rest where all our soul's desire
> Is fixed on things above;
> Where fear and sin and grief expire
> Cast out by perfect love.'

There they subsided. The rest of the congregation had duti-fully risen at the arrival of the Trenwith party. The Wesleyans had not.

Mr Odgers moved into his stall and coughed and cleared his throat.

'Let us pray,' he began.

Sam Carne was on night core that week, and when he came up it was raining so he hunched his shoulders against the weather and began to walk over the brow of the hill towards Reath Cottage. As he got near he saw a small damp figure standing by a horse just near the bed of the dry stream below the cottage. It was the Reverend Clarence Odgers.

'Why, sur, good morning to ye. Was you looking for we? I think brother's gone work. But twill be drier inside. Come you in.'

Sam had no doubt as to the subject of Odgers's visit. He led the way into the dark little cottage, and after a moment's hostile hesitation, Odgers followed. He looked about at the oblong room with its crude chairs, many of them knocked together out of driftwood or pieces of timber from the mine. On a table at the end a bible lay open, and Odgers noticed with distaste that the chairs were arranged in three rows facing the table. On a wooden board on the wall was written, 'Be ye saved in Christ'.

Sam towered over the little parson. 'Do ee sit down, sur. I be that pleased to welcome another man of God into our home.'

The phrase was not well judged to start the conversation

on a happy note. Odgers said: 'This is not a parochial call, Carne. I think that is your name. I believe you are a new-comer in this district.'

'Six months gone the Lord directed our steps into this parish, brother and me. We d'love and worship Christ every Sabbath in your church regular.' Sam's sad young face creased into a smile.

'Yes,' said Odgers. 'Well, yes, so you do.' He was not by nature a belligerent man, having had neither the money nor the breeding necessary to nurture arrogance; but he had received his instruction. 'I have seen you there, you and your friends, and it was about this that I come to speak to you. Yesterday before the service you sang – you sang and chanted for ten minutes in a way that was unbecoming to the dignity of the church and to my position as a clerk in holy orders. You – you and your group – arrive every week, sit together and behave as if you were holding a private service within a service!'

'Ah? Twas not our intention, sur. We come together – as you d'say – and sit together and sing together, to bear wit-ness to our conversion to the gospel of Christ, to show as we have been saved by the blood of the Lamb. We all –'

'You speak of conversion to the gospel of Christ, yet you and all your sect have repeatedly sought to undermine the *church* of Christ, have you not, to subvert its holy doctrines and to set up rival and revolutionary practices. There can be little doubt that you and your sort set out to overthrow law and order and the proper teaching of God in his ordained and consecrated houses!'

Mr Odgers had begun weakly but had gathered strength as he went on. George's prejudices had set fire to his own. He put his fingers through the buttons of his waistcoat and took a deep breath to continue, when Sam interrupted him.

'Now, sur, you're being very hot 'bout we, but what you d'say edn true – not the truth as it is in Jesus. Never by no thought, word or deed do we nor any of our like seek to over-throw holy doctrines – we seek to embrace them where they been all but forgot! By true repentance and acknowledg-ment of our sins we discover God's mercies as manifested in Christ Jesus. Which be *open to all* – every man jack of us who can come down on his knees and confess his faults! So he can lay hold of His blessing. You can, just so much as any one of us!'

'You dare to say that to me! I who by the laying on of hands have been granted the authority and grace of Apostolic succession –'

'Mebbe. I don't know nothing 'bout that. But we overthrow no holy doctrines. All we d'ask is for all sinners to think on their sins and to flee from the wrath to come. We attend church, regular, seeking forgiveness and salvation in Christ. Tell us, sur, what there be wrong in that. We obey the precepts laid down by our honoured father, Mr Wesley, and by –'

'Ah!' said Mr Odgers, pouncing. 'Ah! There you have it. You elevate this man, this renegade preacher, and claim an authority for him that overrides the authority of the Anglican church! This is just what I say: you claim to be independent of truly consecrated governance! When you come to church –'

'Ere,' said Sam, getting warm himself. 'Sur,' he added as an afterthought. 'And what do we find when we d'come church, now? Eh? Tis more like a market place'n a house of God. Folk chattering 'bout the price of tin. Folk saying eggs is going to be scarce come winter. Little childer active like twas a bear garden. Womenfolk gossiping, menfolk bawling crost the aisle. Tis no decent or seemly way to behave. Tis as if Satan have crept into the holy place and made it his own!'

'Satan has indeed crept in!' declared Mr Odgers. 'But not in those who dutifully accept the teachings of the English church. It is in persons such as yourself who seek to overthrow due authority both in the church and in the nation! There is little to choose between rebellious sects such as yours with your independent classes and your love feasts and your presumption of – of religious enlightenment and those Jacobin clubs which teach the ignorant rabble first equality and impertinence and disrespect for their superiors and then vile revolution which in the end denies Christ and brings all humanity down to the level of the gutter and the sewer!'

The argument continued for a time, each getting more heated but less coherent, until Odgers stalked out of the house slamming the door behind him. Perhaps Sam did not improve things by reopening the door and offering to help Mr Odgers climb on his borrowed horse, help which was first angrily refused and then as angrily accepted. As the horse turned for home with Mr Odgers only half in control of it, Sam

said: 'I shall pray for ee, sur, every day of my life!' Then
he stood in the rain, hands on hips, until the little man disappeared over the hill. His face had been hot and angry, but
as it cooled the lines relaxed and he smiled at his tensed hands
and relaxed them too. It was not the way to behave for
someone who had found Salvation.

Odgers had ended by forbidding them the church. Sam
did not know the law but he doubted whether anyone could
legally do this. There had been similar trouble once over at
Illuggan. But it would be hard to continue to worship at a
church in face of such hostility on the part of the parson.
It could of course be done. It was the privilege of the fol-
lower of Christ to face persecution. But the parson's name
and authority still stood for something in the eyes of many
of his flock, and some would not like to go and defy him.
That meant St Ermyn's at Marasanvose. You could not miss
church altogether.

Drake, he knew, would be upset. Drake, for some reason,
always specially looked forward to his visits to Sawle Church
and disliked St Ermyn's. Sam shrugged. Well, there would be
a prayer meeting tomorrow night. No doubt the older members of his group would have something to say.

CHAPTER EIGHT

Ross saw Henshawe almost every day, but it was two months
before he brought up the gossip about Wheal Leisure of which
Harris Pascoe had told him in June. By now rumours were
rife in the neighbourhood but so far Henshawe had not said
anything.

Mid-August was three months since the last 'setting day' at
Wheal Grace; that was when the tributers had last bargained
for pitches in the mine, agreeing to raise ore to the surface
by their own labours and at their own expense – saving only
overhead costs such as pumping water, etc. – in return for a
proportion of the value of the ore raised. This in some mines
was held as a quarterly or two monthly auction, so that
the miners could bid against each other; but Ross did not
like this for it often led to bad blood among the miners
themselves, two men with a specially profitable pitch being
subject to the undercutting bids of their neighbours. Setting

for the next three months was therefore conducted between Ross and Henshawe and the men concerned quietly and peaceably over a table, others being called in only if the men in possession could not come to an agreement with the owner and captain. In fact, there were no disputes this time. Most of the tributers had worked on a 12s 6d in the £ share until Christmas and had made a fat killing with the mine becoming profitable from October. Since then there had been three setting days, and twice the miners' profit percentage had been reduced, as was the custom, so that now the bargains struck ranged from 4s 6d to 6s 6d in the £. Henshawe was for pressing for a further reduction but Ross said no, let them take their profits. He was doing handsomely, and there was no reason why the tributers should not also do well. Besides, in an area where there was so much distress, even a few people with good money in their pockets spread their prosperity abroad.

When the last of the tributers were gone the two men sat together for ten minutes going over the books, and then Ross put his question. Henshawe looked up from the pipe he was lighting and turned to study the flame of the taper before he blew it out.

'Oh, tis true enough. The main lode has dwindled to a mere line. We've tried all ways to come upon good ground again but there's been no fortune so far.'

'And the other lodes?'

'Oh, fair enough but small, as you know. And the quality's not there. Twas the red copper that brought in the profits. Mind you, at present we can just keep going. It is turning over, keeping men employed. At the last accounting we still showed a narrow profit.'

'Ah,' said Ross. 'This was what I heard as rumour.'

'I thought you would be sure to know. Tis all about. Leastwise in this district. It is useless to hide it.'

'But you were so asked?'

'Yes.' Henshawe stretched his big booted foot, rubbed some of the sandy clay off it with the other boot. 'I was perplexed whether or no I should tell you, but when something be decided at one mine, then I reckon you must abide by what has been agreed. But the next ticketing will show it all.'

'What is the share holding now?'

'Mr George Warleggan has taken over Mr Coke's ninety.

All 'long, of course, Coke was naught but a figurehead. Mr Cary Warleggan has bought in Mr Pearce's thirty. The others are not changed.'

'So they own the half. It is an interesting situation, Henshawe. But for the fact that my friends own the other half I would be greatly diverted.'

'And most of your friends still work in it,' said Henshawe.

'Yes. I am glad it is still in profit.'

Next day by hand Ross received a letter which was an invitation to dinner at a house a few miles outside Truro. It was from a man called Ralph-Allen Daniell, whom he had met only a few times in all. Once when he was struggling to maintain the existence of the Carnmore Copper Company, Daniell had offered him some disinterested assistance in obtaining parts for the smelting works. And then little over a month ago, at the last tin ticketing, Daniell had been one of a group with him coming out of the Red Lion together, and afterwards they had walked through the streets talking.

Daniell was a very rich merchant, middle-aged, comfortable, well thought of, who had had no need to align himself with anyone, since his interests were wide enough to guarantee his independence and his innate caution saw no virtue in taking sides. He was a great-nephew of Ralph Allen, the innkeeper's lad from St Blazey who had gone up country to make his fortune and become a philanthropist in Bath. Daniell had ambitions to copy his namesake: he had already given a number of benefactions to charities in Cornwall and recently he had bought 500 acres on the banks of the Fal and was building a mansion there. The invitation was to dinner at the new house. Ross suspected that this was probably one of a series of receptions Daniell was giving to show it off.

The invitation was shown to Demelza.

'It is our first for months!' she said. 'What a pity; I would have liked to have gone.'

'And why should you not go?'

'I cannot appear in company with a great swollen belly.'

'Your belly is scarcely larger than usual; and I should know. I would deny even a lynx-eyed old woman to detect anything when you're dressed.'

'But it is altering daily now, Ross. This is not until the 28th. By then I shall look like Dr Choake.'

He fought down a laugh. 'In any event what does it matter who knows? I am not ashamed of my wife's pregnancy.'

'I am not ashamed but I don't like to parade it in front of other folk – especially smart folk.' She picked up the invitation. 'Where is this Trelissick?'

'About four miles from Truro, I should imagine.'

'It is a long way to ride.'

'Ah, in that case I understand. Then I shall refuse for us both.'

'Why both? You can go.'

'I don't go to social occasions without my wife.'

'But it might be good – it must be good for you to be more among your own kind.'

'My own kind are here all around me.'

'You know what I mean.'

'Well, it is neither of us or both.'

She said after a moment: 'As for the riding, that is nothing. I used to ride bare ridged before Julia was born – that was when you were not about. But I do not fancy going into – into that sort of company feeling fudgy faced and pudding paunched.'

'Let us look at the map,' Ross said. 'I think we could ride across the moors to Killewarren, take a cup of chocolate with Caroline, and then go on to the Fal from there. I believe the house is near King Harry Ferry. Then in returning we could sleep in Truro and do some shopping and come home comfortable the next day.'

She went to the mirror and looked at herself sideways. 'Well, we have not been from home since little Andrew Blamey's christening. It would be nice to have a jant.'

'Jaunt,' Ross gently corrected her.

'I better prefer to call it a jant,' Demelza said.

They left home before eight on the 28th. It was a perfect day for such an outing: warm without great heat, mixed sun and cloud, with shadows drifting gently over the countryside, moved by a tolerant breeze. Even the barren land of the north coast looked full and heavy today, and as they rode south so the trees and the vegetation and the ripeness grew.

Demelza had been relieved to find she could still get into the blue riding habit made by Mistress Trelask seven years ago, and she wore the blue tricorn hat with the white feather in it ordered for her by Verity at the same time. She rode

Darkie, who now at about sixteen years old was too reliable to jolt her rider even if a badger ran across her path. Ross was quite content to follow on Judith, who was proving a fair investment although still too restive to trust with a pregnant lady.

They reached Killewarren about ten-thirty, but when they were shown into the parlour they were astonished to find not only Caroline but Ray Penvenen, crouched in a velvet smoking jacket sizes too big for him, with a rug around his shoulders before a coal fire. Mr Penvenen had not been good-looking in the prime of life: sandy-haired, undersized, his lashless eyes always red-rimmed, a sharp mobile nose, indrawn lips, his hands warty and seldom still. Now he resembled a mummified caricature of himself. The skin of his face was so sallow and brown that he might have been a half-caste, all his flesh had fallen away, the eyes were sunken and dull. One felt he would look exactly the same when he was dead.

Yet he knew Ross and acknowledged Demelza and was not short of dry whispered conversation. So what should have been a pleasant meeting with Caroline over a cup of chocolate became an occasion of forced and stilted talk in an over-hot and stuffy room.

They stayed just twenty minutes and then took their leave. But after they had come downstairs Caroline drew them into a small sitting-room by the front door. She said: 'Last week I took a whole day off and went to see Susan Pellew at Treverry. I told her the truth about myself and Dr Enys and asked her what news her husband had given her of the battle. She was kind enough to give me his letter to her about this, and I said I would faithfully return it in a week or so. I'm sure she will not mind if you read it, if you have the time.'

Ross and Demelza read it together standing by the window. 'Dearest heart,' it began, 'you will ere now have received news of the successful action which we fought against the French on the 21st and 22nd last. A full report has gone to the Admiralty, and you may know many details, yet I feel I should give you what information I have with my own pen.

'On the Monday afternoon aboard the *Nymphe* we were about fifty leagues off Ushant and beating into a south-westerly wind when a sail was discovered to the north-west of us and we gave chase. At first we supposed the stranger to be a frigate, for the weather was so thick that it did not suffer us to get a good view of her for upwards of an hour. Then we saw her to have no poop and could clearly make her out as a French two-decker. With her was a frigate as yet barely visible but closing the distance. The French clearly desired not to come to action but we bent all sail in pursuit. I had with me the *Travail* and the *Mermaid,* though the latter had fallen behind and was only just in sight. The wind by now had increased to a gale, and the sea was fast rising. At half past four the larger enemy carried away her fore and main topmasts in a squall and so we were able to come up with her and see she was the *Héros,* commanded, I found later, by Commodore, *ci-devant* Baron, Lacrosse. The frigate was the *Palmier,* I do not yet know her captain. At three quarters after five we shortened sail to close-reefed topsails and poured in our first broadside as we crossed the stern of the *Héros.* The enemy returned it from some of the upper deck guns and by showers of musketry from a company of troops, of whom I believe there were some two hundred on board. So close were we that some of our crew tore away the enemy's ensign which had become entangled with our rigging. We then tried to pass ahead and gain a position on the enemy's bow, but the *Héros* avoided this and attempted but without success to lay herself on board, actually grazing the *Nymphe*'s spanker-boom in doing so.

'Thereupon began a long and bitter fight between our frigate and this French ship of the line. A half league away the *Travail* and the *Palmier* were similarly engaged, and I grieve to have to tell you that early in that encounter my dear friend and comrade Captain Ernest Harrington was struck in the chest and thigh with musket balls, and expired shortly thereafter. He will be much missed, for a finer man never breathed. The command of the *Travail* was taken over by Lieutenant Williams, who handled his ship throughout the action with great skill and courage.

'The gale and the action continued all night with a very heavy sea, and the violent motion of the ships made the labour of the crews most excessive. On our *Nymphe* the men were often up to their middle in water, and some of our guns broke their breechings four times. But all did their duty nobly. The *Mermaid,* by having come later on the scene, suffered less extensively than we did; but the *Travail* continuing her engagement with the smaller French ship, was in worse case than either, her masts and rigging being very much damaged, her mizzen topmast being shot away, as was also her gaff, spanker-boom and main topsail yard. This we were able to see as these engaged ships drifted more closely to our own. We could also see that she was answering sluggishly and lying heavily as if there were some feet of water in her hold.

'At four o'clock in the morning one of our sailors spied the French coast, and immediately the tacks were hauled aboard and we broke off the action, wearing to the northward. Night signals of danger were sent to both the *Mermaid* and the *Travail*. As we bore away the *Héros* discharged a final and most destructive broadside into us, the three lower masts being all wounded and the larboard main topmast shrouds shot right away. It then required great activity and coolness to save the topmast which if lost would surely have meant the loss of our ship.

'By now all five ships were drifting rapidly towards the French shore, close in with the surf, a heavy gale dead on shore and a tremendous sea rolling in. We were carrying four feet water in our hold, and to beat off the land would have been a difficult undertaking even for an unwounded ship. We saw the *Palmier* strike and heel over and the *Héros* drifting unmanageably towards the beach. The *Travail* with all her principal sails shot away was in like case, but the *Mermaid* hazarded herself for some time trying to get a rope aboard. For our part we were in such grave danger that we could only stand to the south until we saw breakers on the lee bow and then wear ship in eighteen fathoms and stand to the north until land was again seen close ahead on the weather bow with breakers under the lee.

'By now we had almost given ourselves up for lost, and I thought much of you and of my dear children, consigning my own body and soul to God; but by some miracle the masts and rigging which had suffered so much hurt withstood the full fury of the gale and after working and tacking for five hours more we passed a mile to windward of the Penmarche and gained the open sea.

'We had seen the *Héros* lying on her broadside in the surf and the *Travail* a half mile further on in like state, but could not raise a finger to help. I know not the loss on the *Travail* or how many of her brave men got ashore. But a Cornish fishing smack with whom we had communication said that three days later there were men still on the *Héros* and still unable to be rescued because of the heavy seas.

'My love, I have written much of this, but know you that I am thirsty for news of home and hope you will write again soon. Your last letter . . .'

As they rode away Demelza said: 'That house. That terrible old man. It is too bad, Ross. She looks old herself.'

'I know it is too bad.'

After the woods around Killewarren they again climbed up to moorland, with the track bare and stony, abounding with gorse bushes and heather and at times so overgrown that it was difficult to follow. It was a desolate area, worse than the north coast, windswept and treeless. There was a squat cottage here and there, a mule working a windlass, a tethered goat. They disturbed a hare, a fox, and two wizened half-naked children, all of whom ran away with the same speed and anxiety. Then over the spur of the land they rode down into trees again. Here and there the track became so deep set between hedges that one rode almost through a tunnel.

Demelza said: 'Let me ride Judith for a change. I am sure I can manage her. She is really very docile.'

'Be content where you are.'

'Oh, I am content enough. And comfortable enough. But you don't look right on her. Your legs are too long.'

'If you attend the way you are going you will not need to be concerned for my legs.'

They crossed the turnpike road and reined up for a few minutes while Ross made sure of his direction.

Demelza said: 'That letter. I do not think if I was Caroline that I should be at all comforted by it. In so long a battle there must have been many killed. And then to be wrecked in such a storm.'

'So far as the battle is concerned a surgeon should be less at risk, since his place is between decks attending to the wounded. But Dwight may not have kept his place, being the man he was – or is. Still, I would have thought the shipwreck the worst of it . . . This way. The other track will lead us too far south.'

They went on. His choice was the right one. After another couple of miles they began to descend a narrow valley which led to glimpses of the blue river: then they turned in at some fine new entrance gates and discovered a large square mansion built of brick and stone, with tall windows looking over slanting sun-shot meadows towards the Fal.

Demelza said: 'Do you know this is the first time I have not been nervous, Ross. Going into company like this.'

'You're growing up.'

'No, I think it is carrying your child that makes the difference. I feel with him to help me I am somehow more confident.'

Ross said: 'In that case I think it is going to be a she.'

Ralph-Allen Daniell said: 'Of course I shall not live to see it, but these trees we have planted in the meadows will break up the prospect and give it an added elegance. At the present it is all a trifle new and un-mellow. We plan gardens before the house and a folly in the wood to your right.'

'However unimproved you may think it,' Ross said, 'the prospect is one of the finest. What is that path?'

'It leads down to the boathouse. The advantage of living on a river is that one has a broad highway at one's disposal. On a fine day now I would not think of riding to Truro or to Falmouth; and several great houses are within a few minutes' rowing.'

'You make my thoughts of improvement seem miserable.'

'To Nampara? I have never been there. It is near Werry House?'

'A few miles. It was built by my father while my mother was alive. Then when she died he lost interest and it was never quite completed. Since then there has been no money for maintenance, let alone improvement.'

'That has changed now, I gather.'

'Modestly speaking. But of course the house is small by any standards. To give it any of the elegance of this house we should have to pull it down and begin again.'

'You're too kind. But in a few years, who knows, you may have that choice. The Bassets have built Tehidy on the proceeds of their mines. As indeed the Pendarves and many others.'

They were standing on the terrace looking down towards the river; and just then they were called in to dinner. It was rather a grand affair, grander than Ross had associated with Ralph-Allen Daniell, and quite the smartest dinner-party Demelza had ever been to. She was more than ever glad that she had brought her best day frock to wear. The principal guests appeared to be a Viscount and Viscountess Valletort, who were English in spite of their name. With them were four French émigrés, a Viscomte de Sombreuil, the Comte de Maresi (whom Ross had met briefly in Looe), a Mlle de la Blache and a Mme Guise. Others in the party were Ross's cousin, St John Peter, a Lieutenant Carruthers, Miss Robartes, who was an old friend of Verity's, and Sir John Trevaunance – Unwin having returned to London. Both St John Peter and Lieutenant Carruthers had danced attendance on Demelza at one of the earliest balls, and this made her feel more at home in the distinguished company.

It was a young party, for apart from the host and hostess and Sir John Trevaunance, everyone was under forty. Lord Valletort was about Ross's age, and his wife a year or two younger. She was very pretty but quite the thinnest young woman Demelza had ever seen. Yet she contrived not to look frail. It was as if she had been specially bred tall and thin-boned to mother aristocrats. The four French people were a little overdressed for a country dinner-party – although in Demelza's opinion underdressed would have better fitted Mme Guise. She had startling black hair and wore a gown of white lace over an astonishingly décolleté under-bodice. It was very hard for the men not to look through the lace. Mlle de la Blache was about twenty years old and altogether more dignified.

As for the two Frenchmen, Demelza thought they were probably the handsomest men she had ever seen. De Sombreuil was in his middle twenties, tall, slim, dashing, with a presence and a manner that impressed without any sense of display. De Maresi, whom she had the ordeal of sitting next to all through the long dinner, was about ten years older, short, slim, dashing, if anything even more handsome, but altogether more aware of his looks. The ordeal for Demelza lay in the fact that de Maresi spoke English fluently but with so strong a French accent that often it was just as if he were talking in his own language. He smelt so strongly of scent that he spoiled the flavours of the dinner, and had an arrogance which might, Demelza thought, go some way to explaining the French Revolution.

Her other companion at the meal was Sir John Trevaunance, an old friend ever since she had cured his cow, red-faced and of a jovial disposition so long as money wasn't involved.

They ate and they drank and they ate. Boiled cod with

100

fried soles and oyster sauce; roast beef and orange pudding; wild duck with asparagus and mushrooms; fricandeau of veal with sage stuffing and high sauce. After this there were syllabubs, jellies, apricot tarts, lemon puddings and sweet pies. And madeira and claret and Rhine wine and port and brandy. The French count addressed most of his early conversations to his other partner, Mrs Daniell, leaving Demelza free to talk to Sir John about his cattle. A nice homely unexacting conversation which suited her well. But presently de Maresi turned his brilliant eyes on her and made a speech that she found completely unintelligible.

'Please?' she said.

He began again, ending: '. . . and vy is ver burtiful.'

'Yes,' said Demelza experimentally, passing a tip of tongue over her lips.

This agreement pleased him and he continued speaking. In the next sentences she caught words that sounded like: 'English fass, Cornish fass, rainy vezzer, complexeeon.'

She did not answer this but, assuming some compliment, smiled at him brilliantly.

He said: 'Assfor zis sayings sat ser English vomens is cold, eaten my experiences sat all. Ivor deenform you, M'dame – I haf not catch your nom – satin twelerfth mont my experiences hafperswarded me to serve you oak ontraire. Tooser mans français ser womens anglaise is hart to begin puteesy after. Toonot lie to me, M'dame, I beg you, vortis no good.'

'What we use,' said Demelza, 'as I have been saying to Sir John, is tar water, for it is good for anaemia and the consumptions both in animals and in human folk. Where I lived when I was little there was a man who, when he felt the consumptions coming on, would jump in a cold pond up to his neck; then he would take a half-pint of gin and sleep for three hours and be greatly recovered.'

'M'dame,' said de Maresi, 'pressey no more. A woman hoodisombles vis so grandsharm riv-eels so clear where her tort sardir-ected, so pressey no more. Allas, I leave vis ser Valletorts of terdinay. So ser rendezvous vilbyard to orange today. Put latter in ser vick I haf ser two day clear, anve could learn more feach osser in ser ways most delicieuse.'

'Talking of the things,' said Demelza, 'that I think you are talking of, is it true or but a rumour that the Prince of Wales is tiring of Mrs Fitzherbert and that he is being pressed into a marriage with a princess from Brunswick? Do you know any of these things, sir?'

'Luckit zese ands,' said the count, spreading them among his lace cuffs. 'Vorkas not been a part. Put *many* vomens. Seez are smooth for ser smoothness say *car*-ess. For your smoothness, M'dame. I sink you are ver smooth. I see ser skeen vyor preasts's like satin. You af serlong slim legs; sat I *op*-serve ven you climb ser steps. Sis vilbe sermost appy momen ven I am free to deescofer you.'

'I think, sir,' said Demelza, 'that your apricot tart is about to be laced viz cream and rum, and you would do well to discover wezzer you can attempt zat. For my part I am full up and can do no more. Nor can I talk no more the way you talk, for I trust it means nothing at all.'

'Hoho! I shall show you sat! Pressey veshall meet in Friday, so I shall show you sat!'

So the conversation ran on and so dinner ran on until four-thirty. When at last it was over the ladies left the men to their brandy and port.

Talk at the littered table was desultory and sleepy now, for everyone had eaten and drunk too much. But after a while it sparked into life again, and the subject, inevitably, was the war. Charles, Viscomte de Sombreuil, had lost his father and his elder brother two months ago on the guillotine, and now was head of the family. Charles had been out of France for two years, fighting the Revolutionaries in Germany and Holland, but now he was in England to press for a British-aided French landing in Brittany to raise the Royalist flag. A Breton called the Comte de Puisaye had also arrived in England, and by telling of the sufferings of the Bretons and the passionate Royalist feeling that existed there, had caught the ear of the British government. Thousands of Bretons (or Chouans, as they were called when in revolt) were only waiting for a landing. Indeed, the whole country was sick of murder and excess, and it would rise tomorrow if there were half a chance of overthrowing the Jacobins.

De Maresi, however fascinated he might be by a woman's skin, was equally fervent for such a counter-revolt. What they wanted, he said, was not British soldiers but British armaments, British gold and British sea-power to help to land a French force and so put the next surviving Bourbon back upon the throne of France. This, he said, was no charity they were asking. A successful counter-revolution now, while the forces of the Jacobins were in such disarray, would in the long run save countless British lives and hundreds of millions of British pounds. It would bring the war to an end not by conquest, which might take a decade, if it occurred at all, but by an internal uprising which could see peace within the year.

Lord Valletort strongly agreed with this, as indeed did most of the others, and talk hinged not so much on the desirability of restoring the Royalists as on its practicability and what force, what expenditure of arms and money, would launch it with a fair chance of success. At one point Ross wondered if perhaps those present were to be canvassed as to what contribution they could make in money or help, but this speculation proved unfounded. He agreed with most of what had been said and only wondered whether the difficulties of establishing such a counter-revolution were not being minimized.

Presently, when they rose and were going out to join the ladies, Ross had his first chance of conversation with his foppish, good-looking cousin, who had been the most silent during the recent discussion; not, Ross was sure, from being in any sense overawed but because he was too tipsy to keep awake.

'It's a year or more since we met. How are your parents, St John?'

'Oh, Ross! Ho, Ross! Well, Ross! Mother puts a bold front upon a timid disposition, that she does. I believe she is always waiting for some fell disease to strike her, d'you know. Like an old ewe with neck meekly bowed waiting for the axe. Father. As for my saintly father, Ross, well. Father is lame with a gouty ulcer on the ankle that won't heal and makes him deuced tetchy, d'you know . . .' St John yawned enormously. 'And you, Cousin Ross? I hear your mine prospers at last. Damn me.'

'Everyone hears it. Fortunately it is true.'

'I was at the old home early this month – stayed the night. They have done big things. Big things. If you give Smelter George his due, Ross, he is never tight with his money and he knows how to use it. Elizabeth looks well, considering her narrow squeak of February.'

'Narrow squeak?'

'Well, this falling downstairs while she was in pup. Not the most excellent of . , .' St John yawned again. 'What did you say?'

'I said nothing.'

'Damn me, I thought you did. When one yawns one's

ears block up. Not the most excellent of behaviour when eight months forward. Howbeit, the new babe is none the worse – no cross eyes or spavin legs. We saw him and he looked none the worse for his unceremonious arrival. None the worse at all. By the bye, cousin, I think that that damned Frenchie has his eye on Demelza, so you had best watch out for her. Before ever you know it he'll be boarding her. You watch.'

'Oh?' said Ross. 'I think Demelza knows what to do with grappling irons . . . But I believe we should congratulate you – on your engagement. Joan is not here today?'

St John hiccupped. 'Damn me, no. She was not asked.' He shrugged. 'She will be when she is married to me. She will be.' He moved off.

Ross stared after the handsome young man, the mop of fair hair, the stooping figure. It was all very well, but somehow he never quite got on with the fellow. Today the bluntness of those last few sentences irritated him. If one were about to marry a banker's daughter, one might well be aware of her inferior status, but presumably one loved the girl, or her money made up. In either event one did not accept invitations without her or, if questioned, reply in that fashion. Maybe it was a mistake to take too seriously what was said in one's cups. But *in vino veritas*.

After tea there was music. Lord Valletort, it seemed, was fond of opera, and to please him Ralph-Allen Daniell had brought together three musicians who sang arias from Mozart and Monteverdi. Having considerably over-eaten, been stripped naked by de Maresi's knowing stares, and made moderately intelligent conversation while the women were alone, Demelza sat in some discomfort, enjoying the music but longing to walk in the garden and praying to God that no one would ask her to perform today.

They did not. This was a professional entertainment, if not a very good one, and it stopped prompt at seven, when the Valletorts and the four French aristocrats rose to leave. Demelza thought they should be going too, but most of the others stayed on, and Mrs Daniell invited her and Miss Robartes to walk down as far as the river with her. Ross had disappeared indoors again, Lieutenant Carruthers and St John Peter were practising archery, Sir John Trevaunance had not yet wakened from the sleep into which the music had lulled him, so she picked up a scarf to put round her hair and followed Mrs Daniell.

Ross was in fact in Ralph-Allen Daniell's study, having been invited there to examine the plans of the house and some of the building and decorating costs which Daniell thought might be helpful to him in his reconstruction of Nampara.

They studied them together for ten minutes, and then Daniell said: 'There is one other small matter that I would like to raise with you, Captain Poldark, while we have a minute alone. It is something that I and one or two of my colleagues have been considering during the last few months. That is the matter of your becoming a Justice of the Peace.'

Ross had felt that the invitation to see the plans had been a little contrived, but he had not supposed this was at the end of it.

'Oh, indeed?'

They looked at each other across the table. Ralph-Allen Daniell was a big man and stout, dressed even today almost as plainly as a Quaker, and sober in his manner. When he smiled, as he did now, it expressed friendship but not levity.

'Ever since your cousin Francis died there has been a vacancy in that district for a magistrate. When your uncle died Mr Francis Poldark wanted to refuse the office, saying he was too poor, but we prevailed on him that it was his duty to serve. There has been a Poldark in such a position for more than a hundred years. It seems a pity to break the tradition.'

Ross sat down and crossed his legs. Wine and food always paled his face instead of flushing it.

Daniell said: 'There is in fact a shortage of a first-rate man in that district. Old Horace Treneglos is really too infirm and too deaf to serve, but we know he does not wish his son to be made a Justice while he lives. Hugh Bodrugan is erratic in his appearances and in his judgments. Ray Penvenen, we understand, is dying. Trevaunance, of course, is good.'

'It's a sorry lot, I agree,' Ross said.

'Now that you have become captain of the Volunteers in your area, now that you have more freedom and more leisure from the daily routines of the mine, particularly now that the French war is entering on a more bitter phase, we badly need someone of your name and position and character to hold a responsible place and discharge a justice's duty.'

Ross was silent. He knew of the suggestions which had

been in the air when Francis died. But he had hardly taken them seriously, had not responded to them and they had soon died away. Like Mr Odgers's expectations of a Sunday meal. He said: 'Nowadays there is of course this unrest in England too. The spread of revolutionary ideas.'

'Well, yes. Yes indeed. We need strong leaders at a time such as this.'

'Mr Daniell, I wonder if you have not forgotten that – let us see, how long is it? – that only four years ago I was on trial in Bodmin before Mr Justice Lister and a jury of twelve on a charge of inciting peaceable citizens to riot and furthermore did commit riot contrary to the laws of the land. That, I believe, was the beginning of the indictment, but there were other charges to follow.'

Daniell had coloured. 'On all of which charges you were acquitted.'

'True. Though if I remember aright the judge in discharging me said the jury's verdict owed little to logic and much to mercy.'

'I do not know anything of that, Captain Poldark, but the fact remains that you left the court without a stain on your character.'

'Yes. I suppose you could say that.'

'You suppose you could say that. Such charges therefore could hardly be held against you.'

'No. But I would also remind you that two years before that I forced my way into Launceston gaol and took out a servant of mine who was serving a sentence there.'

'I had heard something of it. Was not the man dying?'

'As it happens, yes. But it can hardly commend me to my own class as a suitable person to enforce the law.'

Daniel took out his tortoiseshell snuff-box and offered it to Ross. Ross smiled and shook his head. Daniell said: 'If you look about you, Captain Poldark, you will find scarce anyone who has not at some time kicked over the traces when he was young. It is not a condition peculiar to yourself. Look into the behaviour of most of your neighbours and you will find few who do not have some youthful misdeed to account for.'

'Oh, indeed. And not only youthful. But you would urge me to take this position on the principle that a reformed sinner makes the best parson?'

'I would not have put it that way.'

Ross nursed his knee and stared out at the bright day.

'What is the name of these windows? Venetian, is it?'

'Yes.'

'The house is quite notably light. One of the lightest I have ever been in.'

'You have an ancient name, very much respected in the county. Until your nephew and your own son grow up there is no one at all to represent it except yourself.'

'My father was never a justice.'

'No. But then his elder brother Charles was alive.'

It was not only that, thought Ross.

'Education and experience are also of particular value in administering the country,' said Daniell. 'This was where old Horace Treneglos was valuable, being a Greek scholar, and where John Trevaunance is especially useful, having read some law at Cambridge when a young man. Your wide experience will contribute to the efficiency and competence of the bench.'

'This is an idea put forward by you personally, Mr Daniell?'

'No, no, by a number of us. It was agreed. There will be no obstacle, I can assure you. People thought it was time.'

Ross uncrossed his legs and stood up. He said: 'I envy you all these books. I see you have Tom Paine's *The Rights of Man*. A forbidden book?'

'Not when I bought it. I should incur a penalty if I sold it today. Have you read it?'

'Yes. I do not find it quite as revolutionary as some would make out.'

'Well . . . It depends how one views it. Pensions for the old at fifty? Education of the poor? A tax on incomes amounting to confiscation of all above £23,000? Some would call that revolutionary enough.'

'As you say, it depends how one views it. Of course it is outrageously radical. But Paine to me is a visionary who has set his sights too high, not a revolutionary in the most aggressive sense, not a true admirer – though he affects to be – of what the French Revolution has done. It is not the possession of private property that he is decrying but the unrestricted use of it for selfish ends. I am told that Pitt sympathizes secretly with much that he has written.'

'The essence being that at this time one's sympathies should remain secret,' said Daniel dryly. 'Do you know if he is still alive?'

'Who, Paine? God knows. No one knows who is alive

or dead in France today.'

There was silence.

Ross said: 'I fear I must refuse.'

Daniell closed the snuff-box and dabbled his nose with a fine but plain cambric handkerchief. Outside some doves were cooing. It was a pleasant sound coming through the open window on the warm August afternoon.

Ross said: 'I appreciate your thought and the thought of your friends in inviting me; and in refusing I trust I shall not incur a risk of being considered either ungracious or sanctimonious. But I cannot bring myself to judge my fellow men.'

'One simply interprets the laws of the land.'

'Yes, but that involves passing judgment. And although I now try to abide by the law, and hope to continue to do so, there have been occasions in the past when I have challenged its validity – and there may be occasions in the future when I shall do so again. Not perhaps on my own behalf. I do not personally expect to be without a roof, or to work in life-destroying conditions, or to become crippled with phthisis at thirty, or to see my wife starve or my children crawling naked on the floor of a hut. I do not expect to be subjected to the temptation of stealing firewood to keep warm or a hare to warm my family's belly. But often in these cases the law makes no allowances for the circumstances in which the crime was committed. It did not where my servant was concerned, and so he went to prison for two years and there died. I am no revolutionary in the Jacobin sense. I believe in the laws of property. I do not like thieves. But the sentences are too severe. If a man came before me accused of trespass and trapping rabbits on someone's property, I would be unable to avoid asking myself if, in his circumstances, I should not have done the same. And if I should have done the same, how can I condemn him?'

'All justice is not blind and brutal.'

'By no means.'

'You would not presumably feel this way about a man who kills another, or who rapes a girl, or who sets fire to a hayrick – '

'Certainly I do not, but they are matters more often dealt with by the higher courts.'

'So for the smaller offences which came before you you could perhaps temper justice with leniency.'

'And fight all my fellows on the bench? Could I see eye

to eye with Hugh Bodrugan on sentencing a poacher? It would be the start of another civil war!'

Daniell bit his lip and looked up at the tall rather gaunt man by his bookcase. 'Serving as a magistrate, as you'll appreciate, is not all sitting in judgment on one's fellows. A magistrate wields power in the country both for good and ill. He has much to do with rates and taxes and the uses they are put to. Building roads, repairing bridges, dredging canals. Much of the administration of the country. An energetic man such as yourself would have many opportunities for service. It would be a pity to turn down the opportunity of doing so much good for fear of doing a little harm.'

Ross shook his head and smiled. 'You argue very graciously, Mr Daniell. I wish I could be as gracious in my refusal. If I thought that the men with whom I would be sharing the bench were in any way like-minded or even open to argument I might think otherwise. If the laws of the land were becoming more liberal and more lenient I would be happy to try to interpret them. But just now, under the threat of what happened in France, we are going ever backwards. The very talk of leniency, of liberal ideas, of reform, of bettering the conditions of the poor, is tantamount to treason. One is stamped a Jacobin and condemned as a traitor. Last week a man was hanged in London for taking £1.15.0 out of a shop. Now there is imprisonment without trial. If we speak too forthright in public, none of us is free of the risk. Oh, I know,' he went on, as Daniell was about to speak, 'I know very well the excuse, and in some measure I understand it and condone it. But already it has gone too far, further I think than is justified by the public good or in consideration of public safety. In order to defeat a tyranny overseas I believe we are in danger of creating a tyranny ourselves. Do you not see that, holding these opinions as I do, it would be a grave mistake on my part to accept your offer?'

Daniell sighed and stood up. 'I understand your reasons. I still think they are not adequate reasons. It is for men of liberal ideas to try to interpret the law and to help to run the country, not to withdraw and leave it to the harsher spirits. These emergencies will pass. The good governance of the country must continue. However, so be it. Shall we rejoin the ladies? I see them coming up from the river.'

They walked out together, through the hall and on to the terrace. No one was there yet, except a servant setting another table for tea. In this river valley they were sheltered from the wind, and a great peace brooded over the scene. The three women made a colourful splash of heliotrope, ochre and rose-pink against the green background. Demelza had taken off her jacket, and her silk blouse glinted in the sun.

'Of course you know,' said Ralph-Allen Daniell. 'Or perhaps you do not. Perhaps it is something I should say at this stage . . . tell you. Since the need for a new man in your district is really somewhat urgent, a new man will be found. Certainly the other name will now go up. That is if, as I assume, you are quite adamant in your decision . . .' He waited but Ross did not speak. 'We shall have to offer this seat on the bench elsewhere, and the most obvious, indeed the only other candidate of appropriate standing, is George Warleggan.'

Demelza waved her scarf. Ross did not wave back.

'An admirable choice,' he said, his voice betraying only a little of his feelings. 'Warleggan has all the qualities that I lack.'

'And lacks many of the qualities that you have. I think it a pity, Captain Poldark . . . Well, my dears, did you enjoy your stroll?'

They stayed until nine, drinking tea and munching biscuits and sweet cakes and talking amiably of this and that. Daniell offered them a bed, apologizing for not having included this in his invitation, but they politely refused, and after a pleasant leave-taking rode back up the valley and joined the turn-pike road to Truro. They were in the Red Lion Inn by eleven, where Gimlett had already arrived bearing clean sheets and to make sure the room was clean and properly prepared for them and that there was adequate service and accommodation for their horses. Except for ticketings, it was the first time Ross had been in the inn since the occasion of his brawl with George three years ago, when in a last flicker of anger he had pushed the innkeeper to the ground as well; but the little man was clearly pleased to see his important client and to let bygones be bygones. Ross tried to be as gracious as he could over their light supper, but he was somehow now quite in the mood to unbend convincingly. Demelza, who had thoroughly enjoyed her day, could not understand him, and it was not until they were alone together in the bedroom that he told her of the offer Ralph-Allen Daniell had made and of his reply.

'Oh, Ross,' she said.

'What do you mean? Oh, Ross!'

'Well, I know how you feel and I'm glad that's how you feel; but it do seem such a pity.'

'A pity that I have these feelings?'

'No. A pity that you had to refuse because of them. I think . . . tis wrong that you should not mix more with your own folk and – and be a person of importance among them. This was a chance to be . . . I want you to have the respect you are entitled to.'

'Which you think I now don't receive. Thank you.'

'Ross, don't get teasy with me. I am sorry if what I've said is not pleasing to you. Of course whatever you think is best for yourself, I accept that. But a person has a rightful place in the world, and yours is – is in some such position. You are by birth a squire and – and seeing to the law is what squires do. It grieves me that you had to refuse.'

'You'd think better of me if I were some pot-bellied liver-grown stinking old lecher like your bed-friend Hugh Bodrugan who drinks himself under the table six times weekly and has a ready hand for any woman's skirt or blouse which happens to be conveniently within reach. You'd admire my position in the world then? You'd think this showed me to be a person of importance?'

'No, Ross, it would not; and you know I did not mean that. And you know too that Hugh Bodrugan has never been my bedfellow. Nor has my skirt or blouse ever been conveniently in reach for him.'

'Would you like me to be a hypocrite, fawning on people who have power so that a little may come my way? So that I may strut and crow on my own little dung-hill? Would you like me to be pompous, arrogant, blown up with my own conceit, seeing myself as a little god dispensing judgment on other lesser creatures? Would you like – '

'Please, Ross, unfasten this button. My blouse has been tight all day. I think, I believe I shall not be able to wear it again until after November.'

He looked at the back of her neck, at the wisps of hair curling on the pale skin. He undid the three buttons and turned in furious irritation away. They spoke no more until they were both undressed and in bed. Ross put out two candles and left one burning. It was smoky, and the smoke curled upwards like a wisp of her hair. He tried to control his unreasoning resentment.

111

'So you think I did wrong,' he said.

'How can I say? How can it be wrong to do what you believe is right?'

He had not told her of the man likely to be appointed in his place.

'It was a splendid party,' she said. 'But that Frenchman . . .'

'Ralph-Allen Daniell is to be High Sheriff of Cornwall next year. Did you not hear them say it at the dinner table?'

'No. What is that? It sounds that impressive.'

'Maybe they were vetting us – seeing how you could behave and that I did not wear a tricolour as a cravat. Valletort is the Lord Lieutenant's son, you know. Old Mount Edgcumbe. Did you like him?'

'I hardly spoke to him – I liked his wife. If that is high society, then I think I liked it, Ross. Better than what I've seen before.'

'Yes, it is a cut above the Assembly Ball. There is a stage at which the possession of money justifies itself by enabling its possesor to become urbane, cultured, refined and elegant. When this happens there is probably no better society in the world.'

'I hope . . .'

'What?'

'That we shall be in it again sometime.'

'I do not imagine my refusal of this office will endear me to them. Those we met today are the progressives, who in better times would be the reformers, who pride themselves on openness of mind. But I suspect that at this juncture even they will tend to reason that who is not for them is against them. It is a tendency in time of stress and war. At present the landed gentry of England are seeing bloody revolution behind every drawn shutter.'

'Oh, well . . .' She gave a little philosophic shrug. '. . . we have so much to be thankful for. It is not important. You have brought the list of what we are going to buy tomorrow?'

'Yes. It is a foot long.'

'Good. Then let us think of that. Good night, Ross.'

'Good night.'

He snuffed out the final candle. The only light then was from the lantern in the passage slanting in under the ill-fitting door. From downstairs came a loud murmur, occasionally interspersed by shouts, from the tap-room.

They both lay quiet, thinking their own thoughts. And both knew that, however much they bought tomorrow, however extravagant in their purchases they became, the events of today had taken the savour out of it.

CHAPTER NINE

George received the invitation in September by letter, and, after a suitable delay, replied saying he would be pleased to accept the Lord Chancellor's appointment.

He had hoped for something like this but had thought it probable that he would have to wait until either Horace Treneglos or Ray Penvenen died. He had only been living at Trenwith a year; nor was he permanently in residence, though he had stayed deliberately longer here than convenience dictated. He had wanted to be accepted in the district, but often he had fancied himself cold-shouldered by people like the Bodrugans and the Trevaunances. This appointment was an important evidence of acceptance. Money talked. Money would soon talk before breeding.

It was the more pleasing because three years ago his father had tried to get him elected a Capital Burgess of the city of Truro and had failed. His father was both a burgess and a magistrate, and had been of real value to the town; he had also been a constant, ready and vocal supporter of Viscount Falmouth, in everything that that gentleman projected; but when George's name came up to fill a vacancy his lordship had put someone else forward, and that was that. However hard the Warleggans tried to be nice to the Boscawens, the Boscawens were never quite nice enough in return. The reason was perfectly clear, though the Warleggans only partly perceived it. Lord Falmouth controlled the borough and the corporation. As an aristocrat with enormous landed possessions he was used to the deference of people like Hick and Cardew and the other members of the corporation. Such men did not presume to friendship. But it was not so easy to extend the same sort of patronage to a man who owned five hundred acres and a house nearly as big as Tregothnan, as well as the biggest house in Truro, and had such substantial banking, smelting and mining interests as to put him among the richest in the county. So Lord Fal-

113

mouth had decided that one Warleggan on the corporation was sufficient for the time being.

This success in a country district, therefore, where prejudices and cliquishness among the older families were at their strongest, was a signal advance. And it owed nothing to his commercial power in Truro. It warmed him through.

Of course he hid his pleasure from Elizabeth, telling her casually at supper one night, saying he had quite forgotten to mention it before.

She said: 'Oh, I'm glad. Francis used to complain of it as a nuisance, but I used to think an interest in other people's affairs took him out of his own.'

Her tone, as casual as his but genuinely so, nettled him. Naturally to her and her like it did come as a matter of course. Jonathan had become a magistrate when his father died: there was no achievement in it, it was simply the boring duty of a gentleman.

'Yes, well, they will have to do with me when I am here. They must know we shall be in Truro a large part of the winter.'

'Have you yet settled on a date to return?'

'We have nothing social until the 5th October. I would have thought the end of this month, if that is convenient to you.'

'I shall be glad of the change.'

'Why?'

'Why?' She looked up at him. 'Should I not be? The weather has broken and shows no sign of picking up. Last year, being with child, I was not able to enjoy things in a normal way. Now I look forward to seeing my friends – and yours – the concerts, the card parties, the balls. It is a change of scene.'

He bent to his meal again, satisfied by what she said. Ever since they married he had felt some reluctance in her to stay at Trenwith, and he had often wondered if there were more behind it than he knew. Of course before they married he had promised her a life at Cardew, but when it came to the point his father had not been prepared to vacate the house. In his effort to convince her that marriage to him offered everything she wanted, George had been guilty of one or two exaggerations, of which this was the greatest. Elizabeth had tried to hide her disappointment, but it was more evident now since Valentine was born. George always suspected that this desire to leave Trenwith was in fact a desire to put more distance between herself and Ross Poldark.

This was their only meal alone. Two years of marriage had seen subtle changes in the relationship which the birth of Valentine had accentuated. George had deeply desired only one woman in his life, and his achievement of this end had brought him immense gratification. He had taken Elizabeth with all the passion in his nature, and to his particular delight had found her responding in a similar way; for he was not to know that there was more reactive anger than genuine passion in the response. The immediate consequence was that both put out more emotion than it would have been their normal nature to do, and fusion was exceptional for them both. But Elizabeth's early pregnancy had been an excuse to descend from these summits, and they had never been scaled again. George in his nature was cold, and Elizabeth no longer had to prove anything to herself. Since Valentine's birth she had not refused him, but it was a proposal and an acquiescence, not a mutual need.

They were both aware of this. George knew what happened to some women temporarily after they had borne a child. He knew how it had been between her and Francis after the birth of Geoffrey Charles. That it had not been so after the birth of Valentine gave him satisfaction. In any case for the time being he was content. The possession of Elizabeth was almost enough on any terms. The emotional demands upon himself were the less. And Elizabeth was content with this damping down of a relationship she was not sure she had ever wanted.

But in spite of this cooling in a physical sense, there was little lack of amity in their daily dealings. From the very first days of their marriage George had been gratified by the degree to which Elizabeth was prepared to identify her interests with his – even in her hostility towards the Poldarks of Nampara. When he married her he had thought her as frail and beautiful as a butterfly; marrying her ministered to his protective as well as his possessive instincts. But while he still saw her as both physically frail and beautiful, he had found her possessed of a good brain, a common sense as level as his own, an ability to manage a household without his assistance and an interest in his career which never failed to surprise him. It was not an accident that she had survived for nearly two years as a widow and run this big house with no help, no man and no money.

The only point at issue between them of late had been, as usual Geoffrey Charles. Elizabeth expected him to spend the autumn with them in Truro, but George argued that if he were likely to go away to school in a year or so it would be better for him to learn to be without his mother for periods of time. Leaving him at Trenwith in the charge of his governess and his uncle and aunt would be a gentle way of severing the tie. Personally Elizabeth saw no reason to sever the tie as yet – she saw no reason in fact why he should ever go away to school – but after a good deal of rather tight argument, in which much was felt but little said, she eventually yielded.

So Geoffrey Charles was to stay. After supper that night Elizabeth came on Morwenna sewing in the winter parlour.

'Oh, Morwenna, there is something I had intended to have mentioned to you. It is true, is it, that you have been riding on Hendrawna Beach?'

The girl put down the needle work she was doing. She needed no glasses for this close work. 'Yes. Did Geoffrey Charles tell you?'

'He did not volunteer the information. I found sand in his pocket and asked him.'

'Yes,' said Morwenna. 'We have been several times. Was that wrong?'

'Not wrong. But straying further afield than I have the fancy for you doing.'

'I'm sorry. It is in fact less far than we ride the other way. But if you do not wish us to, we need not go there again.'

'How do you get on? Do you go through Nampara land?'

'No. I thought from what you said you'd not like us to do that, so we go round by Marasanvose and through the sandhills which I believe belong to Mr Treneglos.'

'Keigwin goes with you?'

'Oh, yes. Though sometimes Geoffrey Charles has a fancy to walk and then we walk on alone.'

'He is a strong-willed boy. You must not let him get the upper hand of you.'

Morwenna smiled. 'I do not think he does, Elizabeth. But he is not so much strong-willed as – persuasive.'

Elizabeth smiled too and put a hand to turn the handle of her old spinning-wheel. She had not used it for over a year.

Morwenna said: 'There is a holy well among the low

cliffs about a half way along the beach. If you have not seen it . . .'

'I have not seen it.'

'Geoffrey Charles would greatly wish to take you there, I know. And beyond that are some caves which are quite fantastical. It is like going into a great abbey. But all dripping water. Very eerie and strange. Why do you not ride with us one day, Elizabeth?'

Morwenna's eyes had an unusual brilliance, Elizabeth thought. Perhaps it was some trick of the candlelight.

She said: 'Some day, perhaps. Next summer. But now the days are drawing in and there is the risk of strong tides I would feel better pleased if you did not go on another beach this year.'

'We are very careful.'

'I would prefer you not to have to take that sort of care.'

'Very well, Elizabeth. Geoffrey Charles will be greatly disappointed, but whatever you say, of course, we will do.'

There was something vaguely combative in the words which contrasted with Morwenna's normal quietness of tone. Elizabeth's sharp perception picked it up, but she did not feel there was anything she could really query. Geoffrey Charles, she thought, had also been secretive. If necessary she would get the secret out of him.

Morwenna turned again to her needlework. Very eerie and fantastical: that was what the day had been. A meeting with Drake at ten – he had somehow got off work – a brilliant morning with clouds building up for afternoon rain; a mile walk along the shining ochre sand – soft today from some freak of the tide so that their footsteps were left in a deep track behind them; Geoffrey Charles running to and from the edge of the water laughing with delight at its lick on his bare feet; the two young adults walking more gravely and talking together, laughing together sometimes at Geoffrey Charles as if seeking excuse and common ground for expressing their pleasure at being alive and in each other's company; their approach to the great caves, not so long since vacated by the sea and still a-drip with water; the wide pool at the mouth of them, and Geoffrey Charles pulling up his trousers as far as he could and splashing through it; of Drake's offering to carry her and her refusal, instead going behind a rock and taking off boots and stockings, then walking skirt-held through graspingly cold water over the knees and safely to the other side; the scraping of tinder to make a light, the

117

smoking tallow candles on old miners' hats Drake had brought for them, the exploration through slithering seaweed and among driftwood and the flotsam of the tide ever further and deeper into the echoing reaches of the caves. She was always afraid of enclosed places, and this was no exception; and she was afraid of the great white surf roaring not so far away lest the tide might turn treacherously and cut them off. But the fear added to the excitement and was bearable because it could be shared among them, and particularly with him. It was not a situation, her attraction for this rough young carpenter, that she could accept or be content with in rational moments; but nothing, no prohibition of class or creed, could have prevented her absorbed enjoyment of the morning.

Elizabeth had said something.

'I'm sorry. I was dreaming. Excuse me.'

'As the autumn comes on, I would advise you not go far afield, even with Keigwin as your escort. The village folk are law-abiding, and in any case know you and respect you; but the harvest has failed and that must lead to more poverty and distress. And the further you stray the more likely it would be that some harm would befall you. Indeed, as the bad weather comes it would be safer not to take Geoffrey Charles out of the grounds at all. Remember, this is his first year of comparative freedom, and we should not overdo it.'

They had not overdone it, surely, that morning, though the morning had not ended with the exploration of the caves. After they had come out into the air again the sun had been a hot eye burning them, the sky a meridian blue, with a ridge of cloud creeping up from the north as black as a black sheep's fleece; and Drake had stripped to his trousers and gone jumping into the heavy waves that rumbled on the sand. Not to be outdone, Geoffrey Charles, ignoring Morwenna's protests, had stripped himself of everything and gone in naked. Morwenna had followed to the edge and had stood there watching them while the bubbling froth swirled and ebbed about her legs. Afterwards they had lain drying behind a rock in the hot sun, Geoffrey Charles for decency's sake covered by his undershirt. Had they overdone it? Was such exquisite pleasure forbidden and wrong?

'Morwenna!' said Elizabeth sharply.

'I am indeed sorry, Elizabeth; I was thinking. Forgive me again.'

'I was saying that I hope while I am away that you will

118

keep him closely to his studies. In a year or so Mr War-leggan is determined to send him away to school, perhaps to Bristol, or even as far as London. It is essential therefore that he keeps attentive to his work, particularly to his Latin.'

'I will do my best to keep him at his studies,' said Mor-wenna.

Will Nanfan was a big man with fair hair greying and thinning, who kept some sheep on his smallholding and eked out a living by this and other means. He was an uncle of Jinny Carter and the husband of the tall blonde Char, whom Jud Paynter had once lusted after. He called to see Ross one evening with news of a contact he had made in Roscoff, one Jacques Clisson, a merchant who travelled the peninsula buying up lace and silk gloves to bring to the port for sale to the English traders. He knew as much about affairs, said Nanfan, as anyone you could find who would be prepared to open his mouth for money. According to Clisson there were six or seven hundred English in prison in Brest, and a few at Pontivy and La Force, but by far the largest number were at a place called Camp-air – though in the queer French lingo it was spelt Q-u-i-m-p-e-r. There there were three or four thousand English, of all sorts and conditions, women and children, merchant seamen, matelots, officers, the sick and the well, in one enormous convent, which had been turned into a prison. According to Trencrom's map, which Nanfan had brought along, Quimper was only a few miles from the Bay of Audierne where the *Travail* had foundered, so the chances were that if there were any survivors they would have been taken there.

Nanfan had asked Clisson what information he could get about names of ships, prisoners, and officers in particular, and had offered fifty guineas for a full list of the names of officers saved from the *Travail* – if any. Clisson had said he would do what he could, but that it was dangerous work and might take time.

Ross straightened up from the map. 'Did this man give any idea of how the prisoners were being treated?'

'Not well. Bad, i' fact. Jacques says tedn the ordinary folk, tes the rabble that's got the upper hand. Among that sort there's little decency left.'

'How do you meet Clisson if you have no date fixed for your next run?'

'He belong to be in Roscoff every mid-week. Thursday to

Monday he's on his travels. Comes home Monday night wi'
'is horse and his pack'orse and the stuff he's bought for
England.'

'Does he speak English?'

'Oh, yes. Else I wouldn't understand'n.'

'I picked up a smattering of French when I was a boy,
Will, going over with my father; but I would hardly think I
know a word now. Do you remember my father?'

Nanfan smiled. 'Oh, yes, sur, I mind him well. I mind
seeing your mother once too, though that were long ago, when
I was no more'n a tacker. She were riding a horse alongside
of your father. She were tall. And thin, like – or thin then
– wi' long dark hair.'

'Yes,' said Ross. 'Yes. She had long dark hair . . .' For a
moment he was a child of nine again and a part of her
sickness and her pain. It was terrible the darkness then, and
the crying woman, and the unguents and the balm and the
scurrying feet. Illness and sad smells and an old nurse and
the parchment colour of his father's face. Smoke casting a
shadow, and the shadow was disease and death. He blinked
and shook the image away. Now it was twenty-five years later
and his wife and child bloomed and the corroding worm
had gone from the house.

He said: 'In those early days when I went across with my
father as a boy, ours as you know was not organized as a
business: we sailed to Guernsey only to stock up our own
cellars with brandy and rum and tea . . . Even then the
British government was trying to put a stop to the trade at
Guernsey. Roscoff is much the same run, I suppose?'

'No different. But Roscoff is rare and prosperous. Two new
hostelries they're building; and there is English, Dutch, French
merchants there, all doing a fine trade.'

'Not interfered with even by the Revolutionaries?'

'Not even by the Revolutionaries. Ye can stroll around in
the town wi'out let or hindrance; but I reckon if ye was
to stray far beyond its boundaries, then you'd be picked up
soon 'nough.'

Will began to roll up the map. It made a crackling sound
in the silent room. 'Mind, tis a bit edgy in Roscoff. Everyone
be there for the trade, but everyone d'watch everyone else.
It is spy on spy, as ye might say. Men d'look over their
shoulder at other men. Even women is on the squitch. We
will need to go careful wi' Clisson, for if someone let it be
known as he was having truck wi' the English gentry twould

be simple to denounce him – that's what they call it – denounce him, and he'd be took to Brest and axed.'

Ross nodded. 'So if I went over it would be better if I had some good plain business there, trading or the like, and then meet Clisson by accident?'

'It would be well advised. And clothed like one of us. Ye'd not be amiss then if you've the mind to come.'

'I'll see Mr Trencrom,' Ross said.

CHAPTER TEN

In 1760 when the meeting house at Grambler had been projected, after one of the great Wesleyan revival meetings near, Charles Poldark, then a stout, active, cautiously prosperous man of forty-one, had been approached to give a piece of land on which the little house could be built. Although disliking Methodism as he disliked any deviation from the norm, and distrusting it as in a sense a rival to the authority of the squire, he was prevailed upon by his new wife, then only just twenty and already the mother of his two children, to allow them a corner of land abutting on the straggling village of Sawle. Young Mrs Charles, although never admitting it to her husband, had as a girl heard Wesley preach, and had come near conversion herself.

Charles, always cautious, would not give the land but leased it on a three lives basis. However, on the bottom of the lease he wrote that 'A new lease on a further three lives shall be granted free at the discretion of my successors'.

By the time the last of the three men died on whom the original lease had been based, it was 1790, and Methodism in Grambler had fallen as low as Bodmin church spire; but Will Nanfan's father, then still alive and one of the original founder-members of the Society, had remembered enough to take two other elders and call on Francis and ask for a renewal of the lease. Francis, preoccupied and unbusinesslike, had simply waved a hand at them and said: 'Forget it: the property is yours.' After due thanks, old Nanfan had mumbled something about a deed and Francis had said, 'Of course. I'll see to it.' He never had, but as he was so young there had seemed no need to press it.

Tankard, George Warleggan's solicitor, had been out from

121

Truro weekly since he took up residence, establishing just where the boundaries of the Poldark property began and ended, looking through old mining leases and generally tidying up the neglect of years. When any questions of rights came up, George had instructed that wherever there was doubt this should be firmly resolved but that Tankard was to err on the side of generosity. George had no desire to establish himself in the neighbourhood as a severe landlord, and indeed no need. He always paid his servants and his employees well; much above the average for the day: it cost so little extra, and for it he demanded and received good service with no nonsense and no sentiment involved. But he did dislike vague agreements, loose ends, untidy clauses, things understood rather than written down. He had a formidable, tidy and efficient mind and it did not appreciate inefficiency in others.

Often the cases were simple enough to decide without reference back, but one afternoon before he left to return to Truro Tankard said: 'That Meeting House, Mr Warleggan, just on the edge of the village. Last week I saw they was repairing the roof, so I looked up the documents that you have here and I found they was operating on an expired lease. This forenoon I called round to see them. There was the three of them there and I pointed out the situation anent the lease, whereupon the eldest of them, a man called Nanfan, said that when the lease expired four years ago the land had been gifted to them by Mr Francis Poldark. I asked them for the relevant deed, but Nanfan said this had been a verbal gift. Mr Francis Poldark had simply said: "You may have the land," and left it at that. Of the three men present on that occasion, two of them, including this Nanfan's father, have since died, so there be only one witness to the event. I said as I would refer the matter back to you.'

George looked at the map on the wall of his study which showed the boundaries and details of the estate. 'That it? Yes. They even call it Meeting House Lane, I see. Well, it has been sanctified by time, I suppose. Draw up a formal deed of gift. Find someone responsible on the other side to sign it. Let it be done properly.'

'Very good. I'll attend to that next week.'

'But a moment . . . These are the dissenters who have been annoying us in church, aren't they? Odgers, this grub of a parson we have here, has been doing battle with them. He has forbidden them the church, and now he says they attend service at Marasanvose and hold meetings in Grambler while the church service is on. Our church was three parts empty last Sunday.'

Tankard waited obediently halfway to the door.

George tapped the map. 'Leave it. Let it lie in abeyance until next week. In the meantime I will see Odgers and get his views.'

Two weeks later George went to Truro, partly on business, partly to see that their town house would be in all ways ready to receive them. Elizabeth stayed behind, attending to all the minor businesses which require thought when one is moving for several months. In the evening about six a deputation of three men called to see her.

It was not a convenient time: she had been busy all day and had had words with her mother, who was at her most tiresome. The elderly gentlefolk who had been engaged to look after the Chynoweths had left in July, and had not been replaced. So exacting was Mr Chynoweth that only the most needy would stay in such a situation and so far she had turned down three new pairs of applicants. It meant more work for the ordinary servants and more responsibility for Elizabeth. Also today little Valentine had been sickly and fretful and she hoped he was not sickening for something. Yet she had lived in the district ten years, knew everyone in the village, and could not bring herself to turn them away without seeing her.

In fact, only two came into the parlour; Tom Harry, who escorted them, thought three was a crowd, so the youngest member of the party, Drake Carne, had been told to wait in the kitchen. Of the two who came Elizabeth knew only one, the big middle-aged, highly respected Will Nanfan, whose smallholding ran beside a corner of the estate; the other was a younger man, tall, tow-headed with a thin lined face that belied his youth.

They stood awkwardly before her – it was difficult dealing with a woman but it seemed their only chance – they did not know what to do with their feet or their hands until Elizabeth, smiling, told them to sit down. Then with some hand-twisting and throat-clearing they told her their tale. When it was done and she had all the information they could give her, she said:

'You must appreciate that it is very difficult for me to interfere. I leave all the management of the property to my

123

husband, Mr Warleggan, whom you should have seen instead. It would have been far better, because he could have given you a considered answer.'

'We did ask for him last week, but Mr Tankard d'say he is too busy to see us.'

'Well, he is a busy man. I'll tell him you've called; but if this is his decision and not just the lawyer's then I cannot promise to alter it.'

'We thought,' said Nanfan, 'as Mr Francis had give the land to us. Perhaps you could put it to Mr Warleggan that – well, it's fair and proper for we to keep it. If Mr Francis Poldark hadn't said as we could have it –'

'Are you sure he said that? Could there have been some misunderstanding?'

'Oh, no, ma'am, my father were quite sartin. And old Jope Ishbel d'say the same. Besides, in the first lease Mr Joshua Poldark say it is to be renewed.'

'At the discretion of his heirs – is that it?'

'. . . Well, yes, ma'am.'

'Yes, ma'am,' put in Sam Carne quietly. 'And the heir is Mr Geoffrey Charles Poldark, ma'am. And he be under age . . .'

Elizabeth looked at the stranger. 'Are you an attorney?' Knowing well he was not.

'Oh, no, ma'am. A simple sinner seeking divine grace.'

'Well, you are right. My son is only ten. I and my husband are his legal guardians. Whatever we decide we decide on his behalf.'

'Yes, ma'am. And we ask your kind help. For in the saving of our house you will be doing God's handiwork and saving what were put up to the glory of King Jesus.'

Elizabeth half smiled. 'I think there are some who would dispute that.'

'There are always folk as malign us, ma'am. Each day we joyfully ask God for His forgiveness of them.'

'I trust,' said Elizabeth, 'that you will not have to ask His forgiveness of us.'

'I trust not, ma'am, for twould be a sore blow to our connexion to lose this house when we have done no hurt nor harm to any man. Thirty-five years agone divine Jehovah put it into the minds of His faithful and penitent servants to build Him this house, and this they did with their own hands. Ever since then it have been used for naught but the cleansing of the spirit and the holy worship of Christ.'

'Is not the church the proper place for such worship?'

'Indeed, yes, ma'am, but we must all lovingly witness to God in our daily lives, and a meeting place, where folk who has found salvation may mingle with they as is seeking it, is also a proper place to worship, saving your pardon. We go to church reg'lar – all our society d'go to church reg'lar. Many, many of them go to church who'd never be seen in one else. We're all humble, rejoicing servants of the Lord.'

Elizabeth closed her book, and her fingers played with the fringe on the marker. She was tired and wanted to end the interview. Will Nanfan she liked and respected, though she knew he had had one or two brushes with George's servants in parish matters. The young man she was not so sure of. The respectfulness of his tones did not hide a certain combativeness in his nature. She felt he would argue till sunrise if need be, and that his conviction was so burning that in argument he might forget the difference in their stations. This was one of the great problems of Methodists: the converted felt themselves above earthly class distinctions. Christ was their master, and their only one. At the throne of the Heavenly Grace all men were equal; and all women too: Elizabeth Warleggan and Char Nanfan and whatever little miner's daughter this thin blond man was married to. In principle no doubt it was what one accepted in one's Christian faith; in practice it did not work out.

Yet she was not an ill-natured woman and she saw the justice of their appeal. She said: 'Well, as I have told you, it is my husband who makes those decisions, but I will undertake to see him when he returns next week and to put your case before him. I will explain to him that you see this as a firm promise made to you by my late husband, Mr Francis Poldark, and ask him to reconsider his decision in that light. I can do no more, but I will see that it is attended to as soon as Mr Warleggan comes home.'

'Thank ee, ma'am,' said Will Nanfan.

'Thank ee, ma'am,' said Sam Carne. 'And may our divine Saviour go with you.'

It was rather as if, Elizabeth thought, he was a priest and she a member of his congregation.

In the kitchen Drake hung about under the glowering eye of Harry Harry, the elder of the two brothers.

It was a fine big room this kitchen, down three steps from the rest of the house, with a stone-flagged uneven floor and heavy beams across the ceiling, from which hung down on hooks a sheaf of fine smoked hams that made Drake's mouth water. For so big a room it was ill-lit, with a single window set high in one wall; but the top of the split door beside it leading to the yard was open and admitted more light. A fireplace almost filled one wall, and an enormous black kettle was suspended from an iron hook above the fire. In the other corner by the door was a hand pump with a wooden bucket under it.

Presently Harry decided that the young man could exist without his surveillance and went off, so Drake wandered to the door and watched another man outside filling a bucket with fine coal. Behind him a young voice said:

'Why, Drake! Is it not Drake! What are you doing here?'

Geoffrey Charles was smiling all over his face, which was shiny and polished as if just washed.

'Mr Geoffrey.' Drake put his finger to his lips. In a lowered voice: 'I'm here wi' Brother and Will Nanfan, calling upon Mrs Warleggan, your good mother, on a matter of business.'

Geoffrey Charles laughed but lowered his own voice. 'What is secret? Are you not supposed to be here?'

'Oh, yes. Oh, yes. But tis our other meetings that's secret. So tis best not to know each other, else you might be forbid to see me again.'

'I meet whom I like,' said Geoffrey Charles. But he kept his voice lowered. 'We have not seen you since the day in the caves. The weather has been so bad that we have scarce been out riding. And then most days you are at work.'

'True 'nough. How is Miss Morwenna?'

'Brave. She is washing just now, so I have been turned out. Look, my mother and Uncle George are going to spend the autumn in Truro. It should be easier to meet when they are gone. Can I send a message? Excuse me, can you read?'

'Read 'nough,' said Drake. 'But maybe they will not want you meet me.'

'If they don't know they can't say, can they?' Geoffrey Charles took Drake's hand. 'Let me show you the house. This time of day there is no one about.'

'No, thank ee. Twould not do. Another time maybe.'

'You promised sometime we could go hunting for tadpoles, Drake. Remember that? When we were coming back across the beach you said so. When could we go?'

'Tis the wrong time of year. You d'know that.'

126

Geoffrey Charles stood on one leg and then on the other. 'Yes, I suppose I do. But that is the trouble – before, before, when Papa was alive, the big pond at the other side of the house had lovely toads. And not *ordinary* toads, Aunt Agatha says. She says my great-grandfather brought them specially from Hampshire, years and years and years and years ago, and they've been here ever since. They had yellow lines down their back, and they didn't hop, they *ran*. It was such fun to see them. And they would make such a noise croaking in the evening. *Croak! Croak!* Like that. Aunt Agatha's very cross that they've gone. And in the spring there were tadpoles and minnows and water-beetles, and the cows would go splashing in. But since Mama married Uncle George it has all been cleaned out, and the toads have been killed, and the cows are not allowed in any more. It is *ornamental*, they say. They have put flowers round it and water-lilies at one end, and they have put stones in the bottom to stop the mud.'

'So what would ye do if you had tadpoles and toads, Mr Geoffrey? How could you keep'n?'

'Oh, in jars in the stables. There's jars and jars all empty in there. And maybe,' Geoffrey giggled, 'maybe when they grew into toads I'd put them back in the pond just to hear them croak.'

'Look ee,' said Drake quietly. 'I reckon twould be best if we was not seen talking now. You run 'long and keep quiet 'bout we have met before. Then sometime in a week or so when I get a day off I can leave ee know and, if Miss Morwenna will allow, we could maybe go over all together to the pools behind Marasanvose and I can show ee where the frogs and toads d'live.'

'When my mother and uncle have gone, Drake, if I ask you to come to the house, will you come?'

'I don't b'lieve twould do. Who is here?'

'Wenna, of course. And then my grandfather and grandmother. And Aunt Agatha, who is really my great-great-aunt and nearly a hundred years old. That is all. Will you come?'

'I'll think on it, boy. You're a good friend but we must not hurt other folk. Now go now, else there may be trouble.'

When George came home Valentine was still unwell, and it looked as if they would have to delay their departure for a few days. Elizabeth forgot about her visitors until the Wednesday when, after a month of rain, the weather relented and they were able to walk in the garden together in the warm sun. It was a rare occurrence for George to walk anywhere. For exercise he would go off riding, usually with Garth or Tankard or Blencowe. He scarcely ever appeared to take an interest in the garden, though sometimes he would surprise her by a remark that showed he had noticed more than she supposed. His real interest was in large-scale planning. He wanted to widen the drive and build new gateposts and have a fine pair of wrought-iron gates; and he intended to push down two old Cornish walls in order to extend and improve the vista from the back of the house. On the whole his taste was good, though it leaned towards formality; wild gardens, herbaceous borders, rustic fences hung with climbing plants, these had no appeal for him at all. In the flower garden he preferred the flowers that were neat of habit, and in the beds he liked them set in rows or squares.

Now Elizabeth told him of the deputation that had called on her.

He was silent until she had finished and swished at some tall leaves with his cane. 'Curse their impudence,' was his first comment. 'I do not appreciate visitors who sneak in when my back is turned.'

'I think they tried to see you, and Tankard turned them away. And no doubt they supposed I should have a softer heart.'

'And have you?'

'Well, I suppose so. Although I do not think I altogether trust Methodism. It is in some way subversive. But we shall not stamp it out by claiming back the land. And if Francis promised it to them . . .'

'We have only their word for that.'

'I do not think Will Nanfan would lie. Nor the other man. Give them credit where it is due, their peculiar mania imposes a strict code.'

They walked on as far as the threshold of the herb garden. George said: 'Subversive is the word you used, and that is exactly right. All such closed societies are subversive even when they are disguised under religious blankets. They are seedbeds for radicalism, and often Jacobinism – which, as we know too well, seeks to overthrow the state and put in its place bloody tyrants such as you see in France. All these groups at heart have the same objective, whether they are called Wesleyan Methodist Societies, or Corresponding Societies, or Foxites. And if they seek to create revolution, then they are traitors and must be treated as such. I think we should not be doing our duty at this time if we permitted them to remain.'

Elizabeth said: 'I do not think this piece of garden has ever looked the same since Verity left. She spent so many loving hours over it that it was always tidy and sweet smelling. And *useful*. Now the cooks pick leaves and trample other plants down in so doing, and the weeds have got out of hand.'

'It is the next thing that shall be done.'

'Well, if it is done I wish to superintend it, otherwise so much of value will be thrown away.'

They turned and began to walk back to the house, George hunching his shoulders in that way that always suggested the bull.

'Who was the other man who came with Nanfan? Did you know him?'

'A stranger. Young, big, spoke like a miner. He was fair, with a lined face.'

'That would be one of Demelza Poldark's brothers.'

Elizabeth stiffened. George with cool curiosity noticed the involuntary movement.

'I did not know she had any.'

'But you do not remember – the day of that child's christening, the one that died? The father turned up unexpectedly with a brood of brats trailing behind him and quite spoiled the day for the proud mother.'

'Yes. Yes, I do now. I had almost forgot.'

'The father crossed a course with John Treneglos. He objected to the area of bosom that Ruth Treneglos exposed!'

Elizabeth frowned. 'But do you know her brothers are here now?'

'Tankard told me. They have come over, the two of them, from Illuggan. No doubt the living is softer under the wing of their brother-in-law.'

'He is – this one is not at all like his sister.'

'Except perhaps in presumption.'

They passed by the pond. In spite of the rivulet of fresh water running through it and efforts to clean out the bottom, the water was still opaque where the movement of the stream disturbed the sandy mud; but the general effect on this lovely autumn day was pleasing to them both. The water winked and glinted, and the big slate stones brought from Delabole ringed the side and made walking beside it a pleasure instead of something which could only be essayed in overshoes.

'I am also told,' George said, 'that the two Carne brothers are quite the ringleaders in this Methodist revival which is going on. Before they came the sect was dormant, but since they came it has been much in evidence again. They are all tarred with the same brush. Though in truth I do not think Demelza has any religious ardour in her. She has probably caught her atheism from Ross.'

They scarcely ever spoke the name, either of them, Elizabeth because she could not bear to, George because he was still afraid of Elizabeth's reaction. Sooner or later, he felt uneasily certain, Elizabeth, who in most cases had such strong and secure loyalties, would leap to his defence. So far she had not. Not once since their marriage had she done so. It was still a surprise, because all through their long acquaintance, before marriage, especially when he was trying to win her round after his estrangement from Francis, he had had to glove his tongue at mention of Ross. He could never show his bitterness, his dislike. But about the time of the marriage Elizabeth had, as it were, changed sides. His only course was to accept that when she married him she had moved her loyalty, her friendship, her trust. With her it was a case of 'Thy people shall be my people, and thy God shall be my God.' Yet even now, after fifteen months of married life, he was still apprehensive that an incautious word should provoke the reaction that it would have done two years ago.

It did not this time. All Elizabeth said: 'Yes, I remember the family now. Did the mother not come as well?'

CHAPTER ELEVEN

In the middle of September Demelza gave up the struggle to hide her pregnancy from the gaze of the world and resigned herself to two months of discomfort and ungainliness. Ross, to her surprise, never seemed to mind these times, but she minded them for herself. She was happy for the future and looked forward to meeting the baby when it was born, but she always disliked looking matronly and hated to be even mildly inactive.

The bad feeling between Ross and Tom Choake had more

recently subsided, and they were talking again. It was an uneasy peace but a civil one, so Choake was retained once again for this confinement, he being clearly more skilled than the other ignorant quacks who served the villages round. But at Demelza's request Mrs Zacky Martin, in whom she had greater personal faith, was engaged as a nurse to assist him.

In early October Drake told her the news about the Meeting House, and she passed it on to Ross. It was evening, Jeremy was in bed, and they were sitting beside a fire of cherrywood which had burned brightly when lit an hour ago but now was sulky though pleasantly odorous.

Ross said: 'The trouble with George is that he never surprises me. In the end he always fulfils my worst expectations. I should have thought, since he was doing his best to curry favour in the district, that he would not want unpopularity in this way.'

'Unpopularity with some, popularity with others.'

'Yes, I think you are right. The more he appears a defender of the established church, a supporter of orthodoxy, an enemy of faction, the more he commends himself to most of our friends and neighbours.'

'And of course he is going back to Truro for the winter.'

'Yes. If he had to turn them out, for his own peculiar reasons, this was the time to do it. By next spring it will be at least part forgotten.'

Demelza turned over Jeremy's trousers to see her repair the better. They were still very small in size, but very soon she would be dealing with an even smaller. Her eyes flickered up to Ross, who had taken a spill from the fire and was lighting his long-stemmed pipe; went on to look around the room and enjoy the improvements they had brought to it within a year. The new clock, the rich cream curtains of silk paduasoy, the table with the pedestal legs, the Turkey rugs; the writing desk and chair bought after their visit to the Daniells.

There was still much needed, but at present further expenditure waited on the rebuilding and decorating of the library. Spurred by such splendid examples as Trelissick, Ross was hoping to put up something which was far better than anything his father had built but which would not be altogether unsuitable as an addition to the older building. He had borrowed a couple of books and they had spent long evenings studying and discussing them. He had got a man called

Boase, a draughtsman in Truro, to draw up a plan and sketch of the wing, how it was to be built and how finished.

She said: 'I suppose they will have to meet somewhere.'

'Who?'

'The Methodists.'

'They can use Reath Cottage.'

'It is very small. You cannot get above fifteen in there. I think they are hoping to build another one somewhere.'

'They would do well this winter to concentrate on physical survival.' Ross stirred a log with his foot, but it still refused to burn. 'The pilchard catch was poor for the third year running. The harvest is the worst most men can remember. With much of our own corn ruined, and shut off as we are now from European supply, there is likely to be something of a famine, with famine prices everywhere.'

Demelza said: 'They have asked me. Sam and Drake have asked me if they can have a corner of our land to build on.'

Ross stared. 'Oh, *no* . . . Demelza, this is too much! Why should they come to me? I have no interest in their sect!'

'Nor I. I suppose it is because I am their sister and you are –'

'Confound your brothers!'

'Yes, Ross.' She rocked gently backwards and forwards in her chair. 'Unfortunately it is not just my brothers but many of your old friends too. Will and Char Nanfan. Paul and Beth Daniel. Zacky Martin –'

'Not Zacky. He knows better –'

'Well, Mrs Zacky anyhow. Jud Paynter –'

'A lot we owe that seedy old scoundrel –'

'Then there's Fred Pendarves and Jope Ishbel and quite a number of others. They look to you as their friend in a peculiar sort of way.'

'But at heart I like Methodism little better than George! It is a damned nuisance and I never know what will emerge from it . . .'

Demelza said: 'Well, now at last I have a solution. When you and George next meet and are growling at each other like two bulldogs waiting to tear each other's throats, I shall mention Methodism, and you will have a subject you can happily agree on! At least some good has come of our evening's talk.'

Ross looked at her and they both laughed. 'All very well,' he said, frowning through his laughter, 'all very well, but it is an awkward favour to be asked.'

'I don't ask it. But they have, Ross, and I honestly did not know what to say or what you would say.'

His pipe had gone out and he lit it again. This was a whole-time operation and nothing was said until it was completed.

'I suppose I have nothing really against the Wesleyans,' he said. 'And I know I should examine my prejudices from time to time to see if they should not be abandoned. But for one thing I mistrust folk who are always bringing God or Christ into their conversations. If it is not an actual blasphemy it is at least a presumption. It smacks of self-conceit, doesn't it?'

'Perhaps if you –'

'Oh, they always claim to be humble, I grant you; but their humility does not show in their opinions. They may be fully conscious of their own sins, but they always are more concerned with other people's. In their own view they have found salvation, and unless the rest of us follow in their path we are damned . . . I remember Francis making a delicious speech to your father on these matters at Julia's christening, but I can't recollect the words . . .'

Demelza put down the tiny pair of trousers and picked up a sock. 'What *are* your religious views, Ross? Do you have any? I wish I knew.'

'Oh – practically none, my love.' He stared into the sulky fire. 'I imbibed from my father a sceptical attitude to all religions; he considered them foolish fairy-tales. But I don't go so far as that. I have little use for religion as it is practised, or for astrology, or for belief in witchcraft or omens of good or ill-luck. I think they all stem from some insufficiency in men's minds, perhaps from a lack of a willingness to feel themselves utterly alone. But now and then I feel that there is something beyond the material world, something we all feel intimations of but cannot explain. Underneath the religious vision there is the harsh fundamental reality of all our lives, because we know we must live and die as the animals we are. But sometimes I suspect that under that harsh reality there is a further vision, still deeper based, that comes nearer to true reality than the reality we know.'

'Hm,' said Demelza, rocking gently. 'I am not sure that I know what you mean but I think I do.'

'When you are fully conversant with it,' Ross said, 'pray explain it to me.'

She laughed.

'My political views,' he said, 'are similarly substantial. This

133

war is bringing out all the contradictions in them. I have always urged reform, even to the lengths of being considered a traitor to my birth and situation. I saw much that was good in this revolution in France; but as it has gone on I am as eager to fight it and destroy it as any man . . .' He blew out a thin trail of smoke. 'Perhaps it is in my nature to be contrary, for I always see the opposite side from that of the company I am in. Even though I did not like the American war I went to fight the Americans!'

Silence fell. He said: 'But confound it, I do not want them on my land! Why should I have them? This is largely the fault of your overgrown brothers. Before they came everybody lived in peace and the two religions dozed comfortably together!'

'It is likely true, Ross, and I am sorry. In fact, Samuel proposed I should ask you if they could put up a house on the rising ground by Wheal Maiden, which would only be on the very verge of our land, and so that they could use the stone from the old engine house. There's a lot of it scattered around, and they say they will clear it up and use the chippings to make the track firmer so that the mud does not settle there in the wet weather.'

He did not reply, and she went on, 'But do not think I am persuading you. I promised to tell you what I have asked, and that I have now done. It is all one to me.' She looked down at herself. 'Or maybe I should say all two to me.'

'How is Our Friend? I do not ask often because I know you do not like to be asked.'

'Brave, though a shade bowerly. I would be more happy if another matter was settled.'

'What is that?'

'Whether you will be attending your cousin's wedding to Joan Pascoe next week.'

He stared at her. 'But you are not going; you said you could not. What difference does it make whether I go?'

'Because of where you will be if you do not.'

He said: 'I don't understand. Who told you anything about it?'

'Oh, Ross, I have my own spy system in this house.'

He shifted. 'It was only decided yesterday. I have been intending to tell you but have been too much the coward.'

'When do you go, then?'

'Sunday if the weather holds. It may be their last full crossing of the winter. Mr Trencrom is being more careful

134

of his boat than he was a few years ago. Lord, I remember how cold it was on the Scillies, waiting to meet Mark Daniell!'

'I wish you was only going there.'

'It is safe enough in Roscoff. Possibly I may stay a week and return in a Mevagissey or Looe boat.' He explained about Jacques Clisson.

Demelza said: 'I shall not rest easy while you are there. You know that. And neither will he – or she.'

'I know that too. I'll not stay an hour longer than necessary. But you must, please, be prepared for an absence of ten days.'

Demelza put down her sock and wrapped up the sewing in a linen cloth.

'I think I will go to bed, Ross. Our Friend always wakes so early in the morning.'

Sunday was fine and relatively still, and Ross left the house soon after midday. He took with him some food, a flask of brandy, a heavy cloak, a short knife in a leather sheath, and two hundred guineas in two pouches about his waist. He took dinner with Mr Trencrom and joined Will Nanfan and the *One and All* before dark. Farrell, the skipper, and all the men were known to Ross.

October when the big tides run is not the best time to navigate the north coast of Cornwall, but tonight the sea was quiet and they made fair weather of it to the Land's End and back along the southern tip to Newlyn. The wind was fitful and unreliable but never altogether dropped, and by dark the following day they were off Roscoff, having seen nothing larger all the way than a single ketch and a group of Breton fishing boats.

He met Jacques Clisson with Will Nanfan in a tavern called *Le Coq Rouge* in a steep cobbled street leading down from the church, and he knew at once that Clisson was a spy. He could not have said precisely why. The Breton was a stout blond little man of about forty in a blue seaman's jersey and a round black cap, clean shaven except for long sideboards, good teeth showing in a charming, ready smile, blue eyes clear and candid. A man not to be trusted. But after twenty minutes Ross amended his first judgment. A man perhaps to be trusted so far as a specific mission went, and so long as he was paid and so long as no one offered him a better price for some contrary act. Such men exist in all countries and prosper in times of war and especially in neutral or international ports where the combatants can meet without fighting. They have their value and they have their price, and they have their own code.

He said: 'The prison of Quimper is in a disused convent, monsieur. That is to say, all convent are disused in France today, you will understand . . . Although the most prisoners are English, there are also the Portuguese and Spanish and Dutch and German. The number are very great and the food are very small. There are large number of sick and wounded.' Clisson shrugged. 'I believe conditions vary from prison to prison. The commandant at this one is a onetime butcher from Puteaux and he is very strong for the revolution . . . As of course we all are, monsieur, I hasten to add!' Clisson glanced behind him. 'We all are. But in different ways . . . The gaolers come in the main from the slums of Rouen and Brest. It is not a good situation.'

'How can you get me the names of those in the prison?'

'It is difficult. In a camp of forty men, perhaps. But in a camp of four thousand . . .'

'They must be divided, the civilians perhaps from the combatants, the officers from the ranks. And money talks.'

'Money talk, but so does Mme La Guillotine.'

'Do you know any of the guards?'

'One does not *know,* one talks *with.* One exchanges words over a glass. The name of prisoner are sometimes mentioned.'

'What names?'

'Oh . . . I have heard no one from the *Travail.* I have never heard of the *Travail* . . . Captain Bligh is a prisoner there off the *Alexander,* Captain – Kiltoe, I think it is – off the *Espion,* Captain Robinson off the *Thames.* And among the civilian, Lady Ann Fitzroy, who is taken on a passage from Lisbon. These are talked of, and others.'

'Do you not perhaps know one guard better than the rest?'

The Breton lifted his beret and scratched at his fair hair with a bent forefinger. 'There is one I could speak to. He is not a guard. But he is a clerk who works in the prison.'

'Who would know what we want to know?'

'Possibly. Last time I drop a word about survivor from the frigate *Travail,* which is wreck in the Bay of Audierne in April. He is cautious, reluctant to say. But he does give it as his view that there has been survivors who are intern there.'

Ross sipped his drink. 'For fifty guineas do you think he would provide you with the names?'

'For whom, monsieur?'

'For him. And fifty for you.'

'I have already been promised that much.'

Ross glanced at Will Nanfan who was idly rubbing his thumb around the edge of his glass. Will did not look up. He wondered if this were the moment to break and to suggest another meeting later. He sensed some resistance in the French man, as if he were slightly offended at being pressed too hard. But all his own instincts were against further delay.

'Then a hundred for you and fifty for him.'

Clisson smiled politely. 'I would need one hundred now. Fifty for me to prove an earnest, fifty to give him if he is able to do what we ask.'

Ross motioned to the waiter to refill their glasses.

'I agree to that. But I shall wait here in Roscoff until you have the information.'

'Aw, monsieur, I cannot promise it soon. My friend cannot perform the miracle.'

'I shall wait.'

Clisson stared at Ross. 'It is not always safe to stay. You will understand that what goes on in this port is tolerated – one turns the blind eye – but the Committee of Public Safety does not sleep. You, monsieur, if I may say so, do not look the fisherman – nor even quite the smuggler. It would be a risk.'

'For one week?'

'Can you find business here?'

'I can make some.'

The waiter came and bobbled cognac into the three glasses and went away.

'The matter is not without risk to me also. It is not good that I shall be seen talking to a strange Englishman – and then re-meeting him so soon. Go home, monsieur, and I shall find a means of communicating with you, without fail.'

'One week. With twenty-five guineas extra if you have the names for me by then.'

Clisson raised his glass and across the rim of it he met Ross's gaze with sincerity and total candour.

'To your good health, monsieur, and to your preservation.'

Mr Trencrom had given Ross the name of a Scottish merchant called Douglas Craig, who owned a store in the port, and with whom he could affect to do business for an hour or so each day. After the *One and All* left on the Wednesday, he put up at a hostelry called the *Fleur de Lys* and did not venture out of doors in the daytime except for his morning visit to Craig.

Roscoff reminded him of a Cornish fishing village, Mousehole or Mevagissey, in the shape of its harbour and in the little granite and slate cottages climbing the hillsides around, with the water lapping and the wind pushing and the gulls for ever screaming overhead. But it was altogether a more prosperous community. The Bretons were better and more brightly dressed, both men and women, with waistcoats and coats, frocks and shawls of clear scarlet, violet and grass green. They crowded the streets, talking, arguing and bargaining loudly, especially in the mornings when most of the business was done. In the evenings for an hour or more after dusk the little town hummed with talk, and to go into the streets then was like entering a dark garden when the honey bees were still out.

English ships put in twice during the week he was there, and when they did there was noise and bustle which went on into the small hours. There were two organized brothels, apart from the unofficial houses, and these did a smart trade. English was the universally understood language, and he had little opportunity to practise his French.

Douglas Craig was a man of forty, who said he had been living in Roscoff since he moved there from Guernsey twelve years ago. The war had not interfered with him, except that he had to report monthly to the local gendarmerie, as had all other aliens. 'I do not mind telling you, Captain Poldark, that at the first, when news of the bloody doings in Paris reached us, I was much of a mind to drop everything and go. Nightly I waited for the tramp of feet outside my door, but trade was so good that I stayed on, cursing myself for my courage in doing so. Some left, but after a few months they came back, walked around, talked to their friends and settled in again. So we go on, from hand to mouth, as it were. I pray the war will stop tomorrow; but while it goes on and while we are unmolested business has never been better. Like so many things in life it is a question of weighing the risks against the rewards. At present, just at present, and crossing my fingers and touching wood, the rewards are still uppermost. But go carefully, I advise you. Attract no more attention than you can help.'

All went well until the Saturday. On Saturday morning just as he was about to set out to see Craig he was attended on in the inn by three men, two of them gendarmes with muskets. The third man, who addressed him, was about fifty, short and stocky with a pockmarked face to which either dirt or some skin ailment gave a dark blotchy hue. He was not quite in uniform and not quite in civilian clothes. He wore the familiar black tricorn hat with a rosette on the front brim, a high stock coming up to his lower lip and stained with food and grease, a waistcoat striped horizontally, with enormous lapels, a green tail coat and tight trousers of a dirty grey.

Ross understood the first question barked at him, but wisely decided to know no French. Thereupon the questions came in a guttural English which he could just understand.

Name, address, age, occupation, business here?

Ross Poldark of Nampara in the county of Cornwall. Thirty-five. Importer of wines and spirits, representing Mr Hubert Trencrom of St Ann's whose partner he was.

Date of arrival, ship of arrival, business done and with whom, date of departure, reason for staying?

Twenty-second *Vendémiaire,* the cutter, the *One and All,* owned by the said Mr Trencrom, business done with Mr Douglas Craig, likely to be leaving on the thirtieth, but it depended on return of cutter. He had stayed to clear up various outstanding matters with Mr Craig, namely, a balancing of the accounts, the question of the new levy on spirits, the supply of barrels from Guernsey and a general wish to expand trade.

Papers proving all this? Ross went for his bag and produced the papers Trencrom had given him and those he had been able to get from Craig. It was a considerable sheaf, and the pock-marked *agent* took out a quizzing glass to look at them. The quizzing glass was of gold, inlaid with brilliants, and had clearly belonged to someone else.

The *agent* after two or three long minutes thrust the papers back. He had eyes of a pale bottle green.

'You will submit to a search.'

Ross submitted to a search. It was perhaps fortunate that all but twenty of his remaining hundred guineas had been deposited with Douglas Craig.

Presently he began to dress again. The *agent* stared out of the window and one of the gendarmes shuffled his feet.

The *agent* said: 'Foreign nationals, enemies of the Republic, landing on the sacred soil of France, are subject to summary arrest. They are then brought before the National Tribunal for sentence.'

Ross fastened the buttons on his shirt sleeves. 'I am not an enemy of France. Only a business man trying to conduct a trade which it is to the benefit of France to continue.'

'It is not to the benefit of France to permit spies to come ashore and live openly in their ports and villages.'

'I am not a spy, and the Republic needs English gold. I and my friends bring gold to this port and to others like it. The intake every week of the year is very substantial. If I were arrested it would gravely deter others from coming, for I have not stirred beyond the port of Roscoff and have made no attempt to act in any way contrary to commercial practice.'

'You act entirely against the law in spending a single night on French soil without reporting to the gendarmerie.'

Ross put on his coat and replaced the small personal items taken from the pockets. 'Forgive me, monsieur, if I erred in this way. I assumed, however wrongly, that this port was exceptional in the privileges it provided for the free flow of commerce from one country to another, and that therefore that the spirit of the law should be observed rather than the letter.'

The *agent* lifted his chin irritably above his dirty cravat. 'Even for foreign *neutrals,* the penalty for a first offence such as yours is a fine of twenty guineas. For a second such offence it is arrest.'

'Would it not be possible on this occasion to treat me as a foreign neutral and allow me to pay the fine?'

'It would be possible' – the man's eyes flickered to Ross's purse – 'on condition that you left Roscoff immediately.'

'I am waiting for the return of the cutter. It is promised for Monday night.'

'That will not do. There is a vessel in now, the *May Queen.* She will leave tomorrow night. You must board her immediately and leave with her. If you are found ashore after midnight tonight you will be arrested.'

Ross said: 'The *May Queen,* I think, comes from the Isle of Wight. That is two hundred miles from my home. Perhaps the next – '

'It is your own concern, monsieur. Mine only is that you leave here.'

'Perhaps an offer of another twenty guineas . . .'

'Would lead to your arrest for attempting to suborn an officer of the Republic. Now, monsieur, I will trouble you for the fine and an undertaking to leave . . .'

CHAPTER TWELVE

Ross boarded the *May Queen* just before dark that evening. Its master, a man called Greenway, was helpful enough in offering a passage home but was not amenable to the suggestion that he should find an excuse to remain in Roscoff another day. The French were funny these times. You could never be sure how they would jump. And in any event Captain Poldark would do well for his own sake to be out at sea by Sunday night.

Captain Poldark was not at all pleased at the idea of being out at sea by Sunday night, so Greenway made another suggestion. Almost certainly some other vessel would arrive in Roscoff tomorrow before they left. If Captain Poldark was determined against his best interests to stay, then they could ferry him over to the new arrival, which would be sure to stay in port twenty-four hours buying stock and loading up.

So it happened that just after dark on Sunday Ross was transferred to the *Edward,* a two-masted lugger from Cawsand, and he remained on board all through a blustery Monday, with only the company in the cramped quarters under the foredeck of a cat and a parrot.

It had not escaped him that the arrival of the *agent* and the two gendarmes might have been sparked off by Jacques Clisson, as a convenient way of pocketing a hundred guineas and perhaps making something extra as an informer for the French. It would be a way of scaring him off back to England, with a day of reckoning for Clisson too far off for him to worry about. Tonight would show, for he had arranged to meet Clisson at the same tavern at eight. One wondered how quickly news travelled round the port, whether Clisson would in any case learn that he had left and not turn up.

At seven-thirty, when he had just been estimating the distance to swim ashore, the tiny coracle of a ship's boat arrived as promised, and a young Devon lad rowed him to the harbour side. Disbursement of another guinea ensured that the boy would stay with the boat, just in case there was need of a hurried exit.

It was three ill-lit busy streets to *Le Coq Rouge*. Ross had borrowed a scarf from the skipper of the *Edward* and with this round his head and a stoop of the shoulders he hoped to be unrecognized as he eased his way through the crowds. The tavern was a greater risk, but he pushed aside a blind man importuning at the door and went quietly in. It was more than half full, and the light here was poor also, but he soon saw that Clisson was not there. It wanted five minutes to eight.

He sat in a corner and ordered a drink and waited. It was all a gamble, he thought, a gamble on his judgment of the amount of surveillance likely to be kept, a gamble on his estimate of another man's character, an estimate swinging to belief in Clisson after the deep suspicions of the first encounter. At half-past eight he ordered another drink and wondered if he could find out where Clisson lived. Five minutes later Clisson walked in.

His little round bland face was creased in a scowl as he peered about the low flickering room. He saw Ross and pushed through and sat beside him.

'They told me you had left. I came only on the chance, just to be sure. It is bad for me to meet you here.'

If he was playing fair Clisson was probably as anxious to see him as he was to see the Breton. Another seventy-five guineas was at stake.

'I shall be glad to leave,' Ross said.

'So I would advise you to if *they* are interested in you. But first, well, I have been successful. I have a full list. You have the money?'

'Here.'

Clisson held out his hand. Ross hesitated and then passed the purse. Clisson weighed it in his hand, and then opened it to see the colour of the gold. 'Enough. I will take the amount as correct. Here is the list.'

A dirty piece of thin parchment. A great many names, seventy or eighty, some so badly written as to be barely readable. His finger went down the column. 'Lieutenant Archer, the *Travail*.' He had almost missed it, for the writer had a peculiar way of making a 't'. So *some* had been saved. He checked his haste, went carefully on. 'Mr Williams (acting captain), the *Travail*. Mr Armitage, Lieutenant, the

Espion. Captain Kiltoe, the *Espion,* Captain Porter, master, the *Thames,* Mr Rudge, midshipman, the *Travail,* Mr Garfield, master, the *Alexander,* Mr Spade, Lieutenant, the *Alexander,* Mr Enys, surgeon lieutenant, the *Travail,* Mr Parks, midshipman, the *Travail –*'

He had gone on and missed it. He peered closely at the name to make sure there was no mistake. Then he took a thin sheet of paper out of his tobacco pouch with a list of officers from the *Travail.* All the others were on it – Archer, Williams, Rudge, Parks, and a half-dozen more. And Enys. So he was alive. There could be no mistake. There could be no cheating over this. So the time and money had not been spent in vain.

'Thank you,' he said.

'Monsieur.'

'Now I must go.'

'And quickly. But I will go first. Forgive me if I do not see you back to your ship.'

While Ross was away Demelza had a caller. If not precisely from Banbury Cross, the visitor nevertheless rode an excellent white hunter and was in essence a fine lady, though the anxieties of the last months had tarnished her brilliance. Demelza at the time was baking bread. This she always did herself and would never leave to Jane Gimlett, who had a heavy hand. The bread was just beginning to plum when someone rat-tatted on the front door. Jane came back and told her it was Miss Caroline Penvenen.

'Oh, Judas. Well, ask her into the parlour to wait, will you, Jane. Tell her what I am doing, and will see her in a moment.'

While the woman was gone Demelza rubbed her floury hands and arms on a towel and went to look at her hair in the cracked mirror by the larder door. She set it to rights as best she could and undid her apron. Then she went into the parlour.

Caroline was standing by the window looking taller than ever in a grey waisted riding habit and small fur hat. The bright light silhouetted her figure but concealed her expression as she turned.

'Demelza, I am renowned for arriving at inopportune moments. I hope you are well.'

'Yes, well, but just at this minute, as Jane will have said . . . But stay. Stay to dinner. If you can excuse me for the next quarter of an hour . . .'

They had kissed, but a little uncertain of each other.

Caroline held Demelza at arm's length before releasing her. 'I could hardly have told even now. How long is it?'

'About six weeks, I suppose.' Suddenly her mind jumped on. 'You have news of Ross?'

'Oh, no. You will have the first news, my dear. I came only to see you.'

'Well, make yourself comfortable. Sit down and rest. Is your horse seen to? . . . Oh, what a fine horse! Is he your own?'

'I have had him two years – since my twenty-first birthday. But look, must I be punished for coming at this wrong time by being made to sit here like a naughty girl? May I not keep you company?'

'Well . . . baking bread is tedious, and the kitchen will be overwarm for you after your ride and –'

'Would you believe it, I have not seen bread made since I used to steal into the kitchen in my mother's house. But perhaps it would embarrass you if I came?'

This was precisely what it would do, but Demelza had to protest it would not, so presently they went together into the kitchen, to Jane Gimlett's manifest confusion, for she clearly thought that whatever Mrs Poldark chose to do in her own home was her own business but that this was certainly no place for a lady of Miss Penvenen's birth and breeding. In the end she dropped a basin and knocked over a stool when bending to pick it up, so Demelza sent her off to do something in the still room, promising to recall her when the fire wanted taking out of the oven.

'Where is Jeremy?' Caroline asked, perching on the stool that had now been set upright again. 'He is well?'

'Yes, thank you. Though he is always ailing little things. He is not at all like Julia, my first child, who never ailed one day all her life until she caught the morbid sore throat that killed her. You'll stay to dinner?'

'I would like to, but thank you, Uncle Ray has taken the fancy for me to dine in his room. Although he eats little himself he seems to like the sight of another doing what he cannot.'

'Is there any change?'

'Nothing for the better,' Caroline said lightly. 'But he simply will not allow himself to die. I had never realized before what tenacity we Penvenens had!'

144

Demelza took out as much of the dough as she could lift in her hands and put it on the board. 'It is hardly to be wondered at that you're so thin. Surely he will not mind if you stay out one day?'

Caroline tapped her boot. 'It is very odd – you know that old saying about blood being thicker than water? Well . . . I was thrown upon my uncles when I was ten years old, and I do not think in the years they had legal charge of me that I could claim to have been an obedient or grateful niece. Indeed, I should not be surprised if they both wear a few grey hairs the more for having had this care thrust upon them. But . . . when one of them is ill, and sick to death – indeed, certainly doomed to death by the sugar sickness – then I am surprised to find myself drawn into defending him against these unfair attacks. It is like a husband and wife quarrelling, when, against an assault from outside, they patch up their differences and stand shoulder to shoulder. So . . . I am standing shoulder to shoulder with Uncle Ray – so far as I can, that is – which is difficult physically since he now never stands at all.'

'Did your father and mother die young?' Demelza asked. 'Ross has never told me.'

'Ross does not know. Yes, my father was the youngest of three brothers, of whom Ray is the eldest. When my father was twenty-eight he financed an expedition to discover the sources of the Nile. He never came back. My mother married again but died when I was ten. My step-father is still alive and is a member of the Middle Temple, but I have not seen him for many years and he has never shown an interest in me. So the two staid old bachelors adopted me and spoiled me and gave me the promise of a considerable inheritance, which has made me the object of various fortune hunters, such as Unwin Trevaunance.'

It was the first time these two women had talked alone, and they were still not at ease. Demelza was conscious of her homely clothes, her homely occupation, her ungainly appearance, while this elegant red-haired girl sat on a stool and tapped her riding boot and watched her. Nowadays she seldom felt conscious of her humble origin when dealing with people, she had been Mrs Ross Poldark for seven years and that was enough. But Caroline was a rather special case: someone for whom she could only feel friendship and gratitude but someone almost of her own age whose upbringing had been a world away from hers, who did not soil her hands with

145

work one day in the year and who always talked so casually even when serious. Someone, moreover, for whom Ross at this moment was risking his life and liberty.

'Why do you knead each lump so long?' Caroline asked.

'Because if I don't the bread will have holes in it. We eat a lot of bread. There are five loaves here and a little over. Perhaps if I made you a small one with this smaller piece you would like to take it back with you?'

'Thank you. It's my birthday, so I shall look on it as a present.'

'Oh, it is not good enough for that! Happy returns! I wish . . .'

'What do you wish?'

'I was thinking out loud. I'm sorry . . . I wish that Ross could come back today with the news we both seek.'

'Do not be sorry for saying that.'

'I'm not sorry for wishing it, but I am superstitious. It appears to me it is something we should not talk about.'

'Well, that may be so . . . But sometimes I think while I am cooped up in that old house that I must talk to someone about it or I shall go out of my mind. Demelza, I am sorry to have brought this anxiety on you.'

Demelza began to lift the round masses of kneaded dough on to a metal tray. 'Ross tells me there is little risk.'

'But it must give you anxiety, his being in France at this time. I think I should tell you that it is not at my request that he has gone.'

'I don't suppose it is. Even though you have good right to request it.'

'No . . . No one could ever have that right.'

This part done, Demelza stood back and rubbed her hands down her apron and then with the back of her wrist pushed the dank hair away from her eyes. 'He has been gone a week and four days. If all goes as planned he should be home soon.'

'I dread his coming.'

'Let us go back into a more comfortable place. There is nothing more I can do here for ten minutes or so.'

They went back and chatted for a time. The thing Caroline most needed was to talk, and to talk specially of Dwight, which she now did in her helplessly flippant way, apologizing every now and then for boring her listener with such a tedious recital. Presently they went back into the kitchen together and Demelza went under the arch of the stove, opened the

146

iron door of the oven and raked out the white hot remnants of the gorse. Then Caroline lifted the other end of the heavy tray and they slid it into the oven. On this came Jeremy crying out for food, and in the end Caroline was persuaded to stay to dinner with them after all.

Demelza was glad of this, for she had had enough lonely meals since Ross left, and she was also glad of Jeremy's noisy presence, for as usual he talked all through the meal. This kept conversation on a suitably unemotional level and also seemed to divert Caroline, who was not used to small boys.

When it was over Jeremy sped off and Caroline rose to go. 'No, no, thank you, my dear, for your consideration, but Uncle Ray will already be in a relapse after missing me for so long. It will take me until I don't know what time to get home, and I must fly at once.'

'I'll tell Gimlett to bring your horse.'

'I'm sure I have wearied you with all this talk. But, you know, at Killewarren, I cannot behave openly at all. I cannot fret except in my own room. If Dwight is dead I am not even his widow. I am nothing. Which is perhaps what I rightly deserve to be.'

Demelza kissed her. 'Let us wait and hope.'

A few minutes later Caroline was riding her white horse over the stream and up the valley. Just before she disappeared among the straggling trees she turned and raised her hand. Demelza waved back and then went in.

Betsy Maria Martin had already cleared the table. Demelza went into the kitchen to inspect the bread and to receive Jane's scoldings for having raked out the oven herself. Then she returned to the parlour and sat for a few minutes at her spinet. She still took lessons from Mrs Kemp but she had reached a stage at which she was making little progress. At first it had seemed so easy: she had been able to conjure tunes out of the spinet without any tuition at all; but as the music that Mrs Kemp gave her became more advanced so the effort to conquer it seemed to take some of the pleasure out of the playing. So now very often when she needed relaxation she shirked the new pieces and played the old, most of which never staled. Nor did Ross tire of them. Sometimes too she sang a little.

The trouble with music was that in some ways it was too nostalgic. If for fun she even sang now: 'There was an old couple and they was poor', it brought up so many almost

147

lost feelings of the heart that it nearly moved her to tears. If she sang, 'I d'pluck a fair rose for my love', it conjured up early memories of Trenwith House and that first Christmas time. And so on. Music, she thought, perhaps could be a continuing process, like life, a shedding of one skin as fast as another grew. Instead every tune seemed to exist with its notes firmly rooted in an event or an emotion or a period of time.

So, it was necessary to take trouble and put the old out of one's mind and concentrate on the new. Mrs Kemp had brought her a piece in May by an Italian, but she had not yet begun to master it. The left hand would not quite ever get the notes right. *That* was her problem, she decided, it was not lack of application but lack of talent, lack of the sheer ability to use her fingers right.

A footstep sounded behind her and Jane Gimlett said: 'Captain Poldark is home, ma'am.'

She leapt off the piano stool. 'What? Where? Have you seen him?'

'Make one move,' said Ross, appearing in the doorway, 'and *phit,* yer dead.'

'Ross, my dear, my dear!' She was in his arms and kissing him.

'Did I not tell you there was no risk?'

'Oh, you're back! Safely back!' She clung to him.

'Can you find some dinner for me? I am ravenous hungry.' He kissed her several times more, on the lips, the cheeks, the eyes, as if his hunger was not all culinary. Jane Gimlett discreetly disappeared.

'And Dwight? What news have you? Is there any?'

'Dwight is alive and a prisoner. That is all I know –'

Demelza let out a crow of delight. 'You have told Caroline?'

'No, I came straight home, of course. I will tell her –'

'But she left not an hour since! Which way did you come?'

'From Truro. She has been here? We must just have missed. I came to Cawsand on Tuesday and from there by pilchard driver direct to Truro. There I hired an old lame horse that reminded me of Darkie and have come limping home. I left him at the other side of the stream to surprise you, but then at the last moment thought I must not surprise you, so I stole into the kitchen and flushed out Jane to break the news. I believe my coming back has upset you more than my going away.'

'It has not at all upset me like your going away. He is

really alive? You have proof, Ross?'

'Proof enough. No details. Only evidence that he is a prisoner of war at a place called Quimper. I do not think conditions there are good, but he is *alive*. I must tell Caroline soon.'

'Ross, you must tell her now! If you rode after her you might catch her before ever she reaches home!'

'So I must be turned out of my house again so soon as I have returned, eh? Here I am, with a cavernous belly, weary and saddle sore, and you ask me –'

'I will tell Gimlett to saddle Darkie. She has had little enough of exercise, and while that is done I will cut you a slice of pig and some new baked bread and a pat of butter and you may eat it before you leave! –'

'This is a splendidly generous womanly welcome,' said Ross. 'And you're no fatter for my absence! I hope you have not been starving my child.'

'Yes, I have, and rightly so, and will starve you in an equally good cause. Oh, Ross, I am so glad! It will make Caroline over again.'

'And not displeased for Dwight too,' said Ross, 'though as I have said conditions in the camp are bad and must temper our relief.'

'I have a feeling now in my bones that all will be well. Ross, go you and tell Gimlett; I will cut you a plate of food.'

So then for ten minutes the house was all noise and bustle, and Jeremy came chattering in, and Ross patted him absentmindedly with one hand while gulping food with the other, and very soon Darkie was at the door and Ross on it, and a touch of Demelza's hand and he was off in pursuit of Caroline up the valley while the wind ruffled the horse's tail and the early dusk closed in around them all.

BOOK TWO

CHAPTER ONE

Demelza's child was born on the 20th November and was a girl. This time Dr Thomas Choake contrived to be present and to deliver the child safely. They would have done better without him, but at least he did not kill her or the child or permanently maim either of them with medical refinements. A seven-pound child and very healthy. After five days had gone and there was no sign of the dreaded child-bed fever, Ross began to breathe freely and to take pleasure in this new member of his family.

They named her Clowance.

The following week Raymond Richard Eveleigh Penvenen, Esq., of Killewarren, finally gave up the unequal struggle to survive against an opponent who offered him no mercy, no quarter and no hope, and died quietly in his bed with Caroline his niece sitting beside him. There was a considerable turn-out of the county for his funeral on December 1st. His brother William could not get down from Oxford as he was confined to his room with gout, so Ross walked with Caroline behind the bier. Mr Nicholas Warleggan attended, but not his son.

On the Sunday afternoon, which was the 7th, Drake Carne called at Trenwith House with a bunch of primroses he had picked, and was admitted and spent two hours with Morwenna and Geoffrey Charles.

This Sunday visit was nothing unusual. The first time he had come at Geoffrey Charles's command, nervous and expecting to be ordered out by some relative or person in authority. No one had said anything. Except for a couple of servants he had seen no one else. Then he had repeated the visit at Geoffrey Charles's request. Then he had taken to calling casually every Sunday about teatime and slipping away again just before supper. The friendship had ripened rapidly. It was 'Geoffrey' and 'Drake' now, though still – just – 'Miss Morwenna'. Geoffrey Charles had never had a friend like this before and he loved being treated as a grown-up and learning the things Drake taught him. He had even picked up some of Drake's accent, and Morwenna was constantly correcting him. As for Drake, he had a natural warmth and, being the youngest of five brothers, had never had someone younger than himself to talk to. It was a mutual attraction without ulterior motives, although the ulterior motive was there too.

Often she took part in the game or the exercise or the talk or whatever happened to spring out of the visit. Sometimes she withdrew and watched the tow-headed handsome boy and the dark-haired handsome young man, as it were from a distance, even if the distance in measurable assessment was only two yards. Sometimes she was unexpectedly drawn in and Geoffrey Charles excluded – though he did not notice it – and she and Drake exchanged glances in which emotion, or something, had unexpectedly gathered, and then she was afraid. At heart she knew that she was behaving in a way Elizabeth would have emphatically condemned, just by admitting this young man, because he was a common carpenter and wheelwright, aside altogether from the added bar of his being Mrs Demelza Poldark's brother. But something stronger than fear of disapproval prevented her from making the decisive move to break the friendship. She did not examine her motives clearly or her feelings either but drifted on a tide of pleasurable recollection and anticipation between one meeting and the next.

On this Sunday she had to tell Drake that this meeting must be the last for some time. On the fourteenth they were both leaving, along with Mr and Mrs Chynoweth, to spend Christmas in Truro and at Cardew, and it would probably be the end of January before they returned.

'Oh,' said Drake, all the fun going out of him, 'that's a pity, that is. I shall miss ye both. Tis a real pity. All good things d'come to an end, I suppose, but – '

'We shall be back,' said Geoffrey Charles. 'It is only for a month or so.'

'But I reckon, then I reckon the others'll be back too, and that'll stop us meeting sure enough.'

It had been a dark afternoon and the candles had been lighted early. The three were in the small room behind the winter parlour, where they often met and where they were unlikely to be disturbed. Morwenna had taken the bunch of primroses and was arranging them in a shallow pewter cup.

'You're clever to have found so many. This mild weather has encouraged them, but there are none in the garden.'

'These was in the wood where we first met. I'll mind that day all my life, that day that we first met. Twas like no other I ever known.'

Morwenna looked up from the flowers. The light from the candles illuminated her short-sighted eyes. 'I shall remember it too.'

'Come,' said Geoffrey Charles, 'let us take him round the house! You have never seen the entire house, have ye, Drake; and since it will be mine some day it is right that I shall be able to show it to you.'

Drake said: 'I can just say, Miss Morwenna, I just say as it has been a grand new thing for me. I never known anyone like you – like you before. I give years of my life just – just –'

'It is a good evening to show you,' said Geoffrey Charles, 'for my grandfather and grandmother are both confined to their chamber with rheumy chills and there is no one else about. You have not ever been to my bedroom, Drake. There are drawings there that I would like to show you. I did them last year when I was laid up with the measles. And I have some stones from the old mine, Grambler, that closed down years ago . . .'

Morwenna said: 'I think we have done wrong to meet as we have, Drake. There cannot be anything but – distress at the end of it for either of us – for any of us.'

'My room is right at the back,' said Geoffrey Charles, 'that little turret room that you can see if you look at the house from near the pond. If we go through the hall I can lead you up the spiral staircase to the minstrel gallery and then through to my room.'

'Never wrong, Morwenna,' Drake said. 'I'll never own it said that twas wrong to meet as we have done. Of course I know I have no right, no proper right . . .'

'It is not that, Drake. Of course it is not wrong in that sense, but you know how it is in this world –'

'Must we be of this world?'

'Well, yes, for we cannot escape it. For if we even tried . . .'

'Come along,' said Geoffrey Charles, tugging his arm. 'Come, Wenna, I command you.'

Preoccupied with emotions which were passing over the boy's head, they allowed him to dictate their next move. At the door Geoffrey Charles said: 'Oh, we had best take a candle, for the upstairs will not be lighted,' and picked up a bronze candlestick with a wide base to prevent drips from falling.

They passed through the big parlour, with Elizabeth's spinning-wheel in the corner and her harp beside her favourite chair. Although for a while they had been taken away she had had them brought back to their old positions. Through into the hall. A sconce of candles had been lit here but only faintly illuminated the great room. The fire had been allowed to die down so that a single log smouldered like a half-extinct volcano. Morwenna pulled her shawl about her shoulders.

'These are all my ancestors,' said Geoffrey Charles. 'See this one, this is Anna-Maria Trenwith, who married the first Poldark. And this is my great-uncle Joshua as a boy, and that is his favourite dog. And this is my grandmother, who died when she was thirty-three. My Aunt Verity was named after her. It is a shame my Aunt Verity never had her portrait done. And this is my great-grandfather, my great-aunt Agatha's father. Oh, there were lots more here until two years ago, but when Mama married Uncle George he had many of them taken away. Uncle George is always for tidying up.'

'Like clearing the toads out of the pond,' said Drake.

Geoffrey Charles giggled. 'Oh, he hated *them*. But I don't think he hates my ancestors. It is just that he has left only the best.'

They went round the room, looking at the things the boy was pointing out. Then he led them to the narrow door in the panelling and they followed him up the spiral stone staircase to the minstrel gallery. They stood, hands on the stone balustrade, looking down into the shadowy hall.

'It has never been used since I was born,' said Geoffrey Charles, 'nor before, for years and years. My grandfather didn't like music. But when I grow up and get rich I shall have a ball here and the musicians will sit up here playing for the dancers.'

Drake said to the girl: 'Will ye write?'

'But we are only to be away for a short time.'

'Tisn't that. It is like the end. You've said so yourself . . .'

'We shall be back,' said Geoffrey Charles. 'So don't worry about that. Now, follow me.'

He opened another scarcely visible door and they squeezed through and came out on to a narrow landing.

'Geoffrey,' said Morwenna. 'I think we should go down. Drake will play that game –'

'You go if you wish to. I want him to see my drawings, and they're all pinned up on the walls. This way. Quiet now, for my old aunt is in the next room, and although she is very deaf she can always hear a loose floorboard.'

The boy's room was up three steps at the end of the corridor. Elizabeth had given him this after George had complained that his old room was too close to theirs. It was a turret room with stone mullioned windows looking three ways and therefore exciting for a boy. It also had the largest fireplace on the first floor, and this fire was kept in constantly from October to May, so that Geoffrey Charles could occupy himself in comfort. Tacked to the walls were a number of bold drawings of horses and dogs and cats which he had done over the last two years.

When they got in they found that the fire was out, and Morwenna exclaimed at the slackness of the servants. George and Elizabeth had taken half the staff with them to Truro, and those left were trading on the lack of personal control. Morwenna bent over the dead embers and drew them together and tried to blow some life in them, while Geoffrey Charles showed off his pictures. Then suddenly the room was in darkness as Geoffrey Charles knocked over his candle.

'Oh, God's life!' said the boy. 'Now we are in trouble. *Mon Dieu*, Drake! Sorry, Wenna. Is there a light from the fire? There's no tinder, I know, for I took it downstairs.'

He came to crouch beside Morwenna, but there was hardly a spark. 'Wait here,' he said. 'I'll rush down to the hall. It will take no more than a minute.'

'Geoffrey, I'll go,' said Morwenna standing up. but by then he was out of the door and pattering off down the passage.

They stood in silence listening to him until his footsteps died. Morwenna put her hand on the mantelpiece.

'He's very wilful. I have tried to discipline him but he has been spoiled so long.'

'Not spoiled,' said Drake. 'Betterer that way than cowed and timid. He's a real boy. I'm dearly fond of'n.'

'I know you are.'

'Nor not just of him neither.'

She did not speak.

'Are ee cold, Morwenna?'

'No.'

'I thought you shrimmed.'

He put his hand on hers. Until now it had been their only contact, rarely made even then, and then in the most apparently accidental way. Never before deliberate like this. She tried to withdraw her hand, but his hold was firm. It was quite dark, and darkness and desperation gave him courage. He lifted the hand and kissed it. The fingers stirred and then were still. Then with his heart thumping as if it would burst he turned her hand up and kissed the inside of each finger in turn. It was an unusual gesture for a rough young man, but again the dark, in which he could only see the silhouette of her hair and face, salved embarrassment and released him from ordinary prohibitions.

She said: 'Don't, Drake.'

He released her hand and she let it fall to her side, but still she did not move away. So they stood facing each other in the complete silence of the old house. There were ten people in it besides themselves, but there might have been no one. She stood there slim and taut and tall like a wand. And like a wand she seemed to sway slightly in the dark.

He committed the offence of touching her, of putting his hands on her shoulders. It was the first woman he had touched in that way, and his emotion was too pure for desire, too reverent for possession, but each was implicit at a further remove.

'Morwenna,' he said, the words coming through lips hardly able to form them.

'Don't, Drake,' she said, and might have been drowning. And in fact, emotionally, was.

He said: 'You are going away from me. Ye cann't go away from me like this.'

He bent his head and put his lips against hers. Her lips were cool and a little dry, like petals just unfurling from the bud. Complete chastity and complete sexuality coexisted in them.

When they separated it was with a sense of a return to self-consciousness after an experience that transcended self. She moved back, gripped the mantelshelf, lowered her head; he made no overt move at all, stood there rock-like, rooted in his own emotions. So a relationship was sealed that had no business to begin and no authority to continue; and silence lay between them until the padding of feet outside told them that Geoffrey Charles was returning with a light.

By a coincidence of time Morwenna Chynoweth's future was just then under discussion at another and altogether different place. In the Great House in Truro supper was taken later than in the country, and the interval between six and nine, on the rare occasions when there was no tea party or card party or conversazione to attend, was when George and Elizabeth sat together in the large drawing-room upstairs and talked of their everyday affairs. George had completed his business for the day, Elizabeth had long since finished her few household duties, and the nurse, Polly Odgers, was in charge of Valentine; so they were quite alone. George's business affairs ran smoothly, the house almost ordered itself, so there was less for each to do than in the country: more time for social occasions, and more need of them.

When they were alone and unoccupied long silences were apt to fall which, while being in no sense inimical, were not entirely restful. Elizabeth found that George did not read much, while Francis had always been reading. Although her married life with Francis had not been a happy one – certainly not as successful as her life with George – it had been more relaxed. When they had been sitting together in a room alone she could forget Francis's presence. She could never altogether forget George's. He often watched her, and when she glanced up and did not catch his eyes she fancied he had that moment looked away. She could not make out whether he was still in that condition of savouring a pride of possession – it seemed like it; had she been a more conceited woman she would have been satisfied it was that. But sometimes, when she did catch his glance, there seemed to be an element of suspicion in it.

She was sure it was not a suspicion of real ill – but rather of something to do with her happiness, her contentment, particularly as to her contentment with him. He knew that, for all her modesty, she had a kind of assurance he could never equal, because never since she was a child had her confidence in herself been questioned in this respect. If she met a duke he would instantly recognize her for what she was, and in a few moments they would be chatting together as equals. Therefore, *could* she be happy with a rich parvenu? Did she not resent a connection with trade which advertised itself by having part of the ground floor of their house used as an office and a bank? *Was* she not bored with his company? *Did* she not find his manners lacking, his conversation banal, his clothes wrongly worn, his relatives uncongenial? This feeling did not make for repose, for ease of manner, for complete relaxation. Elizabeth had not been married to him long before she realized how very jealous he was – not merely of Ross, though of him most of all, but of any personable man. So she watched her behaviour with other men – who not unnaturally, because of her looks, made much of her – and she watched, slightly, her tongue lest she should give him unwitting offence.

This evening George had been out for a while, and when he came back they talked of a reception and ball they were planning for New Year's Eve. This was impracticable at the Great House which, in spite of its pretentious name, was only so called in comparison with its neighbours. The Assembly Rooms, where all dances in Turo were held, was the obvious place; but George hankered to hold it at Cardew, where there was room enough and of course all the added prestige of such an event being held in one's own home – or one's father's home. But there was clearly a risk. Winter in Cornwall seldom struck before mid-January, but rain was the perpetual hazard of the autumn months, and although Cardew was only five miles, and only just off the turnpike road to Falmouth, rain could turn the rutted road into a quagmire of mud which on the night might deter any but the strongest in leg and heart.

Of course most of Cornish dancing society *was* strong in leg and heart; but it did add an extra hazard to the success of such an occasion. The time for country balls was mid-summer; winter was the time of the town. Elizabeth had preferred the town, if only because it would enable her to invite a number of her old friends whom she'd seen more of this winter than ever since her first marriage but who lacked transport or the money to hire it or for one reason or another would not get out to Cardew however fine the night. But she had not insisted. On all matters except those on which she felt very strongly she let George have his way. And so it was fixed for Cardew, a band had been engaged, and a number of notables had been invited who had not been present before. In this George was making capital out of Elizabeth's name and hoping they would come. The Bassets and the St Aubyns – like the Boscawens – though meeting him occasionally in the way of business or at the house of a common friend, had so far avoided accepting his personal hospitality . . .

The composition of the company, as to age, had to be discussed. George's main interest was in older people, for social reasons and to show off his house; but it was necessary to leaven this with a sprinkling of the unmarried and the post-adolescent, not only to bear their larger share of the dancing but to give the party a zest that it might otherwise lack. George was against having many of the really young. Never having been young himself, in the sense of being frivolous, scatter-brained, enthusiastic or jolly, he had little patience with such excesses in others, and he felt it a mistake to lower the tone of the evening by encouraging it at Cardew. The young, anyway, unless they were titled or came as the children of older people, lent little distinction in proportion to their noise. Besides, although the older Warleggans and the older Chynoweths would be there to greet people of their own age, no one at Cardew would represent the early twenties or the under-twenties.

'Well,' said Elizabeth. 'We are not yet quite old ourselves. Are we? Are we, George?'

'Not old, certainly, but – '

'And Morwenna will be there. Can she not easily look after the girls?'

There was a thoughtful pause, while they listened to the apprentices who were making a noise putting up the shutters of the saddler's shop opposite. Elizabeth was still not sure whether George really approved of Morwenna. He was unfailingly polite to her, but Elizabeth, skilled as she was becoming in reading his far from communicative face, thought him extra guarded in Morwenna's presence. It was as if he thought, here is another of them, another of the Chynoweths, highly bred in spite of her modest looks, listening with sharp ears and downcast eyes for some error of taste that I may make, showing up my vulgar origins. One is enough; one is my wife. Must there be two?

'I have been thinking of Morwenna,' George said, stretching his strong legs in his fashionable but uncomfortable chair.

When it was clear that he intended to add nothing more, Elizabeth said: 'And what have you been thinking of her? Does she not please you?'

'Do you think the experiment has succeeded?' When he met Elizabeth's eyes he said: 'I mean, do you think she has

158

been successful as a governess for Geoffrey Charles?'

'Yes. I think so. Indeed. Do you not?'

'I think she is a woman and would be suitable to teach a girl. A boy needs a man.'

'Well . . . that may be true. In the long run that may be true. But I think he is very happy with her. Indeed sometimes I feel jealous, for I believe he has been happier this last summer than I have ever in my life seen him. He made little demur at being left behind.'

'And his studies?'

'Summer is not the best time for learning. We shall know better when he comes next week. But on the whole I would have thought there was good progress. Perhaps that is saying little, since before he depended on me for what he could learn!'

'No mother could have done more. Few would have done as much. But I think if he is to go away to school he will need a man's care. In any case, Morwenna's stay with us was agreed only for a year, wasn't it?'

Elizabeth said: 'I feel sure she would be very upset to be sent home in March.'

'Of course there is no hurry. At least not that sort of hurry. And I was not thinking necessarily that she would need be sent home.'

'Do you mean she would stay with us as an additional companion to me – and you would engage someone else for Geoffrey Charles?'

'That might be so. But my mind was running more on the thought that she is now of marriageable age. She is well-bred, well-mannered, and not at all uncomely. Some useful marriage might be found.'

Elizabeth's mind went quickly over this; what he said came as a complete surprise to her; she had had no idea he had ever considered such a thing, or could be bothered to consider such a thing. She looked at him with slight suspicion, but he was idly tapping at his snuff-box.

'I have no doubt she will marry in due course, George. She's – as you say she is not uncomely, and she has a gentle and sweet nature. But I think you have forgot the big stumbling stone – she has no money.'

'No I had not forgot that. But there are some who would be glad of a young wife. Older men, I mean. Widowers and the like. Or some young men would be glad enough to ally themselves with us if only by marriage.'

159

'Well . . . no doubt it will happen in due course, and without our assistance.'

'In certain circumstances,' said George, putting his snuff-box away without having taken any, 'our assistance could be had. I would be prepared to give her a small marriage dowry – that is if she were to marry someone of our choice.'

Elizabeth smiled. 'You surprise me, my dear! I had not thought of you as an arranger of marriages, especially on behalf of my little cousin! In twenty years, perhaps, we shall be considering other and more important marriage prospects – for Valentine; but until – '

'Ah, well, that is a long road ahead. And your cousin is not little, by the way. She is tall and, properly dressed, would draw a few eyes. I see no reason why if a suitable marriage were arranged it would not turn out to everyone's benefit.'

The general direction of George's thinking, instead of being mysterious, was now perfectly plain to Elizabeth.

'Had you a suitable marriage in view?'

'No. Oh, no, I had not got as far as that.'

'But you have thoughts.'

'Well, the choice is not extensive, is it? It is limited, as I said, to an older man seeking a fresh young wife or a younger man of good birth but little fortune.'

'So surely some names will have come to your mind. Should we not make a list?'

'No, we should not. You find this amusing?'

'I do a little. I think Morwenna would be flattered to know you spare her so much attention. And now you cannot leave me in this suspense.'

He looked at her, not liking to be laughed at. 'One idly turns thoughts over. No more. One I had considered was John Trevaunance.'

Elizabeth stared at him. The laughter had quite gone from her eyes. 'Sir *John*! But . . . what gave you such an idea? A confirmed bachelor. And he is *old*. He must be sixty!'

'Fifty-eight. I asked him in September.'

'Do you mean you have *discussed* this with him?'

'Indeed not,' said George restively. 'Of course not. But did you notice the day he came to dinner he appeared to pay special attention to Geoffrey Charles after, while the others were at tea? It occurred to me that it was not likely to be Geoffrey Charles of whom he was taking this sudden notice.'

'Now you mention it . . . But why should it not be

Geoffrey Charles?'

'Because they have several times met before without any such interest. This was the first time the boy had a governess.'

Elizabeth got up and went to the window to give herself time to think. She drew back the lace curtain and looked out at a farmer's gig lurching over the cobbles below.

'I do not believe Morwenna would tolerate such an idea.'

'She would if it were put to her as her duty. And to be Lady Trevaunance would be a big enticement. Mind you I know nothing certain of his thoughts; but if at this ball he were to show her some preference I think it would not be unseemly to make him a proposal. He cannot relish leaving his possessions to his spendthrift brother. She could bear him a son. Also, he is a kindly man but acquisitive of money, and his affairs have not been going too well since the failure of the copper smelting scheme. For such a marriage I would be prepared to be exceptionally generous . . . And, of course, the thought of an eighteen-year-old girl can be a considerable attraction to an old man.'

Elizabeth shivered. 'And your other thoughts?'

'I did think once of Sir Hugh Bodrugan, who is a year younger than Sir John, but I am not so greatly taken with an alliance between his family and ours, and as he is such a lecher I did not think you would like him for your cousin.'

'I certainly would not!'

'Then there is his nephew, Robert Bodrugan, who presumably one day will inherit whatever is left of that estate. But at present he is penniless, and one does not know how the money is left. Constance Bodrugan is still a young woman.'

Elizabeth let the curtain fall. 'Go on.'

'I think I tire you.'

'On the contrary.'

'Well, who knows what is bred of idle speculation? . . . There is Frederick Treneglos. He is twenty-three and had more than a little time for your cousin at that same party. It's a good family – nearly as old as yours – but he is a younger son, and the Navy is a dubious paymaster. A few make rich prizes but the most remain poor.'

'I think I would like him better than any of the others so far. He is young – and boisterous – and has enthusiasm.'

'I also noticed at that party,' said George, 'that he had more than a little time for you.'

'Well . . . he has manners. Which cannot be said of all

the young. Yes, I like him. Are there others on your list?'

'You still find this a jest?'

'Far from it. But I must have some concern for Morwenna's happiness. That must be of account too.'

'Morwenna's happiness must be our chief concern. The only other two I have considered are both widowers. One is Ephraim Hick . . .'

'You mean William Hick.'

'No, Ephraim, the father. William is married.'

'But Ephraim is a *drunkard*! He is never sober after midday any day of his life!'

'But he is rich. And I do not like William Hick. It would be agreeable to see his father spawn another family and deprive William of his expectations. And Ephraim will not live long. As a rich widow Morwenna would be a far more valuable prize than she is today.'

Elizabeth looked at him. As usual when thinking he sat quite still, his shoulders a little hunched, the big hands clasped together. She wondered why she was not more afraid of him.

'And the last choice?'

'Oh there may be others. You may well think of others. The last I had in mind was Osborne Whitworth. He is young, a cleric, which might please your cousin –'

'He is married, with two young children!'

'His wife died in childbirth last week. You will notice I have added him to our list of guests. By the end of this month he should be sufficiently out of mourning to accompany his mother. I believe he is just thirty, and as you know recently installed at St Margaret's, Truro. With two young children to manage and considerably in debt, he must seek another marriage soon. One which provided him with a dean's daughter and at the same time cancelled his debts would I think attract him not a little.'

'But what,' said Elizabeth curiously, 'attracts you?'

George got up and stood a moment, idly turning the money in his fob. 'The Whitworths were nothing, Sir Augustus a highly ineffectual judge. But Lady Whitworth was a Godolphin.'

So that was it. An alliance with a family now in decline but itself allied with half a dozen of the great families of England, and in particular the Marlboroughs.

'Yes,' said Elizabeth presently. 'Yes.' She came back from the window and patted George's shoulder lightly as she passed. 'It is all a very interesting speculation, my dear, and I am still surprised that your thoughts should have gone so far. For my part I still think of Morwenna as a child hardly old enough for ideas of matrimony. I still think it premature. I am sure she is very happy with us and would like to continue with us for a while. Let us make haste slowly, shall we?'

'There is no haste,' said George. 'But I do not think the question should be shelved.'

CHAPTER TWO

The great frost came down on Christmas Eve. Before that the month had been mild but very wet. Ceaseless rain had flattened alike the sea and the fields and the smoke from the mine chimneys; rivulets had formed in fields and the Mellingey had been in swollen spate, the roads and tracks were quagmires. George had sent his coach to fetch the two elderly Chynoweths, and five times there and five times on the way back the coach was bogged down in mud and had to be dragged out. In order to lighten the load the day being temporarily dry, Morwenna and Geoffrey Charles followed on horseback.

Ross and Demelza had intended holding a christening party for Clowance over the Christmas period; but it had failed on a matter of numbers. Verity and Andrew Blamey had been asked, but young Andrew was teething, Verity wrote, and, dearly as she would have loved to see them, she felt she could not risk such a journey. Caroline promised to come and spend a few days, but somehow there was no one else intimate enough to ask. Both of them shied away, and always would again, from the celebrations and the double christening they had given Julia. It had been an ill-omen for her.

On the 23rd the rain stopped, and Caroline arrived in bright afternoon sunshine. But it was a curious sunshine, with something aged and sinister about it, as if it belonged to a world which was slipping away, was leaving them behind. As the day waned the light lost its last warmth and the sun became a disc of brass, contaminating the sea with its base metal light and flinging shadows of cobalt grey among the cliffs and the sandhills. The ceaseless wind had dropped: boughs and twig and every blade of grass were still.

'I believe we are in for a change,' Caroline said as she dismounted. She kissed Demelza, and then turned her cheek expectantly for Ross to kiss. 'It is time. We have been hock deep in mud at Killewarren ever since the funeral.'

'It is a change,' said Ross, having liked the taste of her skin. 'But I think it will be a cold change.'

'But you are slim, Demelza! I thought one stayed plump for months after bearing a child!'

'I was a podge. It has not all gone, I believe.'

'Enough has gone,' Ross said. 'It does not suit – you – to be thin.' He had been going to say, it does not suit a woman, but stopped in time.

As they went in the manservant who had come with Caroline untied the valise strapped to his horse and Gimlett took her cloak and fur and crop. Soon she was inside and sipping tea while Ross stabbed at the fire to make it blaze and Demelza tied a bib under Jeremy's chin and Ena Daniell brought in the hot scones.

'When am I to be allowed to see my new goddaughter? It is not seemly to have me here without her knowing of it. Has she been warned?'

'Soon,' said Demelza. 'Soon. You will see her when she wakes. Which usually is regular at seven. How well you look, Caroline!'

'Thank you. I'm better. Thanks to this man . . . Not that I do not wake up in the nights and wonder about my erring fiancé, wonder what he sleeps on and if he has any comforts in his internment and if he ever thinks of me and if and when he will be released . . . But I am – no longer alone in the world – you know? you know how it is? – even now that my uncle has gone I am yet no longer alone.'

'We know how it is,' Demelza said.

'Since Uncle Ray died I have hardly had a minute; I have been striving to get some order in his estate; but as soon as Christmas is over I shall go to London and see the Admiralty and ask what chances there are of a ransom. If the French no longer exchange prisoners they will surely take notice of money.'

They supped late, Demelza played a little, cool airs stole in the parlour and they all went early to bed. The next morning was fine and equally still but now cold. There had been no frost in the night, but each hour that passed saw a slow ebbing of the temperature. By midday the grass was crunching underfoot, and Drake and the other two men working on the library were blowing their hands with smoky breath. At three o'clock Ross sent them home. Then he walked up to the mine. Night cloud was drifting up from the north. All was quiet in the engine house except for the regular clank of the pump rods, the clicking of the valve gear, the hiss of steam. It was warm inside after the cold of the evening; two lanterns reflected light off the great brass cylinder, the shining piston rod. Ross had a few words with the younger Curnow before he left. A sudden glare lit the darkening scene as the firedoor of the boiler was opened for two men to shovel in coal – everything glowed, brittle and orange and etched sharp; then it shut again and the cold dark of the afternoon had crept closer in the interval.

In the house an enormous fire had been built to ward off the draughts. It was the customary night for the choir of Sawle Church to come carol singing. Demelza remembered when they had come on the Christmas before Julia's death; she had been alone and Ross had returned later to tell her of the failure of the copper smelting venture. Tonight she had mince tarts and ginger wine all ready in the kitchen but they did not come. About nine, which was their usual time, she looked out to see if she could see anything of them, and what she saw made her call Ross and Caroline to the window. The ground outside was being covered, very quietly but very efficiently, with enormous feathers of snow.

It snowed till eleven, then stopped, but was snowing again before they went to bed, and by morning three inches had fallen and the sun was out. The garden had been turned into a dazzling feathery forest. Icicles hung and glittered from window-sills and gates. The valley and all the mine buildings were smothered in fine snow which blew to powder in an icy breeze. But did not melt. So near the tempering sea, snow, rare anyhow, almost always disappeared or began to disappear the day it fell. Not so now. When he went out with John Gimlett to see to the cows, Ross realized that all was not over yet, for clouds were assembling again, elbowing each other, leaden yellow across the north-west dome of the sky.

The christening was to be at eleven. Ross tested the ground and found it not too slippery, so they decided to proceed with it. Caroline was prevailed on to let her groom walk ahead of her holding the bridle; next came John Gimlett holding the bridle of old sure-footed Darkie, which carried Demelza with Clowance; then Ross on a skittish and temperamental Judith, with Jeremy in front of him; and following on foot a string of servants and friends: Jane Gimlett, Jinny and Whitehead Scobie, a brood of Daniells and Martins and, inevitably, hoping for something, Viguses. Others joined in on the way or were waiting at the church: Captain Henshawe and his wife, the Carne brothers, the Nanfans, the Choakes, and of course, a little late and a little drunk, the Paynters. Scuffling through the snow, shivering in the biting wind, they assembled in the icy church and the Rev. Mr Odgers, looking as pinched and shrivelled as one of his vegetables that had been left out all night, stuttered through the service.

The godparents were Caroline, Verity, for whom Demelza stood proxy, and Sam Carne. The last named had caused some argument among the parents. 'Damn me,' Ross had protested. 'He's no doubt a worthy young man, and being your brother is the more to be commended, but I don't want to turn the child into a Methody!' 'No, Ross, no more don't I. But I think Verity is like to be far away and Caroline, even if she weds Dwight and stays on at Killewarren, is not, as she admits herself, of a religious turn of mind – while Samuel is.' 'By God, he is! One is never for a moment allowed to forget it!' 'But that is just the way Methodists talk, Ross. I think he is a good man nevertheless, and he is much beholden to us. I think if anything happened to us he would devote his life to her.' 'God forbid,' said Ross. 'What hazards parents sometimes prepare for their children!'

Nevertheless he gave way, as he had more or less given way on the matter of allowing a new preaching house to be built out of the ruins of Wheal Grace; that is to say, he had told Demelza it could be built but not yet permitted her to tell her brothers. He thought it could all well wait until the spring, when problems of mere survival would not be so acute. In the meantime the old meeting house at Grambler had been forcibly closed this month, and such furnishings as it still possessed – benches, a small lectern, two lamps, two bibles, some hymn sheets and some wall texts – were sharing Will Nanfan's barn with his cow, his sheep and his chickens.

At the end of the service Mr Odgers, having had to break a crust of ice on the font to damp his fingers, quietly put his prayer book down and fainted right away, overcome by the cold. His wife screamed that he was dead, that she was a poor miserable deserted widow with seven children still to feed; but a few minutes of Dr Choake's ministrations together with, and more importantly, a flask of brandy that Ross was carrying, brought life and tears to the eyes of the little man, and presently he was able to limp away on the arm of his sorrowing and lamenting wife.

Jud Paynter, who was in one of his awkward moods, saw an ill-omen in this and chewed it over between his gums and his two teeth in spite of all Prudie's efforts to muzzle him.

'Tedn right,' he said. 'Tedn proper. Givin' a cheeil a name like that! Clarence is fur a boy, not a cheeil. Tedn sense. Tedn 'uman. Theare's a bad omen to 'n, I tell ee.'

'Giss along, you great lug,' Prudie hissed, shoving him to be quiet with her elbow. 'Clowance, not Clarence. Skeet out yer ear'ole.'

'I'm earin' just so much as you! An' tis all wrong! All *wrong,* I tell ee! For there's the passon flat on 'is tiddies to prove 'n. Clarence indeed! What they'm *thinkin' of* . . . Poor little quab. She'll scarce see the new year in, I reckon.'

'You'll not see the new year in nor yet the old year out if you don't shut that gurt opening in yer face,' Prudie hissed, dragging him towards the church door.

'Clarence!' said Jud, disappearing reluctantly. 'Gor damme, tis fit to sink ee, what folks'll do to their own kith an' kine. Leave me be, you dirty ole sprousen! . . .' His compliments faded.

The rest of the company had seen fit to ignore this muttered disturbance. Demelza was wrapping a warm shawl more tightly round her precious new daughter, Caroline was wondering how she might dispose of the musty prayer book she had been lent, Zacky Martin was blowing on his fingers, and Polly Choake was trying to see her reflection in a brass memorial plate. Ross went to meet Dr Choake, who had just seen Odgers off by the vestry door.

'Tell me, Choake, how is my aunt? My great-aunt, that is. Have you been to see her recently?'

Choake looked at Ross suspiciously from under hairy eyebrows. 'Miss Poldark? Miss Agatha Poldark? We attended upon her in the middle of this month. We found her little changed. Of course our condition is one of age rather than of gouty disease. Effete matter riots in the sanguinaceous system and oppresses the vital members. We eat but little, we move but little. Yet the living spark remains.'

'Who is attending on her? Is she not almost alone in the house now?'

Choake began to draw on his grey woollen gloves. 'I could not say. On our last visit the Chynoweths had not left. But Miss Poldark has a proficient maid who understands the rudiments of nursing. If there were any change we should be sent for.'

At the door of the church Ross looked up at the sky. The dying sun had now been overtaken by its funeral pall of cloud; and since they went inside the whole scene had become appallingly cold and depressing. An idle, absent-minded flake was already drifting down from a sky which looked loaded with snow.

He said to Demelza: 'Can you take the children home? If there be any risk of slipping, tell Gimlett to carry Clowance. I am worried about Agatha alone in that house and have a mind to call while I am so near. It may be a day or so before it is possible again.'

'I would like you to see her,' Demelza said. 'But I would not like you to see her today. I do not want to mend your bruises and broken teeth on another Christmas Day.'

'Oh, little risk of that. And there were no teeth broke, only loosened . . . George is from home, and servants could not deter me.'

'I believe the Harry brothers are still there. They know you – have fought with you before.'

'They cannot deny me sight of my aunt.'

Demelza grimaced her doubts. 'I don't know . . .' Then she had an idea. 'But why do you not take Caroline? She is welcome at the house. And they could hardly refuse you entry if she were there.'

'You hear, Caroline?' Ross said. 'Would you not prefer to go straight back to a roaring fire?'

'Since Demelza permits it, I would rather be your roaring guardian.'

'Well, then.' He put his hand round Demelza's arm, squeezing it gently and looking down at his tiny daughter, who had borne her ordeal with little complaint. 'Give such good people as come back with you a strong tot of rum and some of your splendid cake. We shall be home to dinner.'

'Your breath,' said Demelza, 'looks like the engine at Wheal Grace. I never recollect it so cold, and I am afraid for Clowance. Help me up, Ross, and let us go.'

Trenwith House looked empty and lifeless as Ross went up the three steps and pulled at the bell. The whole countryside was a leaden monochrome. A thin column of smoke rose into the air from a back chimney of the house and was dissipated by the breeze. Two choughs stood on the roof of an outhouse, and a seagull planed across the clouds looking for food.

A red-faced maid Ross did not know came to the door and reluctantly allowed them into the hall, then fled to find a senior servant. There was no fire in the hall. Except for the protection from the wind, it was scarcely less icy here than outside. Caroline drew her fur cloak around her and shivered.

'It is not quite the scene I saw here when Elizabeth's boy was christened.'

Ross did not answer. As always this place was full of memories, one laid upon another, yet each one individually separate and vivid – and now void.

A woman came in wiping her hands down a dirty apron. She was fat, and everything about her was short, especially her legs. She was more like a big dwarf than a small woman. Half obsequious, half resentful, she said her name was Lucy Pipe and she was Miss Poldark's maid and what could she do for them? Ross told her.

'There now. I dare say now. But d'you see Miss Poldark be sleepin' and be not to be disturbed. I dare say twould be mortal bad for she to be woke up now – '

'You dare say what you please,' Ross interrupted. 'Will you lead the way or shall we go alone?'

'Well, tis not for me to stand in your way, sur, but – '

Ross went slowly up the stairs, examining the portraits as he went and wondering what had happened to those no longer considered worthy of wall room. At Nampara they were notably short of ancestors. Perhaps Elizabeth would part with some of them . . .

At the door of the bedroom Lucy Pipe inserted herself in front of Ross. Her breath smelt of spirits, and her skin, on closer viewing, was erupting with a skin affection. The roots of her thick black hair were choked with dandruff.

'There now. Let me see now sur. I'll go see Miss Poldark, see if she be asleep. I'll go see. Eh? I'll go see.'

She disappeared inside. Ross leaned against the wall and

exchanged glances with Caroline, who was tapping her riding whip into her other gloved hand. After a few moments Caroline said: 'Oh, I know her sort, she will be tidying up. Let us go in.'

As they entered the woman was pushing an unemptied chamber pan under the bed, while Aunt Agatha, a lace cap awry on top of a wig that was awry, was clutching at the bed curtains and muttering feeble curses. A black cat, half grown, stretched itself on her bed. In spite of her age her eyesight had remained remarkably good, and she recognized her visitor.

'Why, Ross, ain't it? Why, damme, boy.' She scowled at the straightening figure of her maid and aimed a feeble blow at her backside. 'Damme, ye should've telt me who twas! Skulking away like that! Real skulk she be . . . Why, Ross, come to wish me the Christmas wishes, eh? God bless ee, boy!'

Ross put his cheek against the whiskery cheek of the old woman. He felt he was touching something out of a lost age, an age already dead but for her. Essentially a warm man but seldom a sentimental one, he felt a tug of emotion at kissing this stinking old woman, because here was the one contact that remained with a lost childhood. Both his parents long dead, his uncle and aunt dead, Francis dead, Verity seldom seen, here was the only one who remembered with him that time of stability, of thoughtless youth, of prosperity, of an unchanging family inheritance and tradition, the one link that remained between him and this house and all it had once meant to him.

Aunt Agatha pushed him sharply away and said: 'Now, this be not your wife, Ross. Where's my little bud? Where's my little blossom? Don't ee be telling me as you're following your father! Leastwise Joshua stopped his whoring while Grace were alive!'

So Caroline had to be introduced and explained away at the top of his voice while Lucy Pipe folded a towel and clattered dirty crockery in a corner and the cat eyed the intruders jealously and the captive blackbird twittered in its cage. Now that he had time Ross could take in the untidiness of the room, the foul smell, the dirt, the curtain with a ring off, the miserable fire.

It was surprising how much Aunt Agatha could still take in if you bawled directly into her ear. It was simply that no one could really take the trouble of getting to close quarters with her. It was of course something of an ordeal. Now she learned for the first time of Ross's new daughter, of the prosperity of his mine, of the alterations planned at Nampara, of Dwight's captivity in France, of Ray Penvenen's death.

In the middle of this Ross glanced at his tall companion who had perched on the edge of a chair and was examining distastefully some nostrums on the table beside her. 'I am sorry for this, Caroline. The air in here is very sour. Why do you not sit downstairs?'

She shrugged. 'You forget, my dear. I am no stranger to the sick room. Your old aunt is little more noisome than my old uncle was.'

They had been talking five more minutes and Agatha was launched on a stream of complaints when Ross came to a decision which had been formulating in his mind ever since he came into this neglected room. He stayed the old woman with a hand on her skeletal arm. She looked up, munching on toothless jaws, eyes alert, the inevitable tear trickling down the ravines of her right cheek.

'Agatha,' Ross said. 'You can hear me well?'

'Yes, boy. There's little I can't hear when folk speak plain.'

'Then let me speak plain. You shall come home with us. Our house is not so grand as this, but you will be with your own people. Come to live with us. We have a comfortable room. Bring this maid if you so wish: we can accommodate her as well. You are old and it is not right you should be among strangers.'

Lucy Pipe folded the last towel and noisily poured some water out of a pitcher into a bowl, splashing the water on the threadbare carpet. Then she filled a kettle and shoved it on the sulky fire.

Agatha's face twitched and she munched away for a minute more. Then she grasped Ross's hand. 'Nay, my son, that I couldn't do . . . That what you said? That what you meant – come live wi' you at Nampara?'

'That is what I meant.'

'Nay, boy. Lord damn me if tis not brave and fine to think on it, but, nay, I could not. An' *would* not. Nay, Ross, boy. I've lived in this house ever since I noozled the nepple, an' that's ninety and nine year, and no one shall put me out till my pass comes. Cheil, girl, woman and old body . . . I been here nigh on a century, and no whipper-snapper and

171

upstart from Truro shall fooch me forth! *Why,* what would my *father* say!'

'It is good to have courage,' Ross shouted. 'But it is also good to understand the changes that time has brought! You are alone – the last Poldark here – dependent on undependable servants. Look at this woman, this lazy slattern – no doubt she tends you in her way, but she does not care, she has no concern for you –'

'There now, sur. Tis not fitty nor proper to say no such thing –'

'Hold your tongue, woman, or I'll nip it out . . . Agatha, hink before you so quickly decide. I cannot come here when George is at home for he protects the house with his bullies. Elizabeth, no doubt, cares for you, but there is no one else. If you will not decide to live with us permanently, give us the pleasure of coming for Christmas – and stay until George and Elizabeth return. Do you not lack for company here? Are you not very much alone?'

'Oh, aye. Oh, aye, alone . . .' Her claw patted his sleeve. 'But at my age, wherever you live, you be alone . . .'

'Alone, I grant. But need you be lonely also?'

'Nay. Tis true.' She nodded. 'Ever since your uncle went – an' more since Francis was took – I been lonely. They don't *talk* to me, Ross. No one do *talk* to me. Alone. All on my own. But not so much alone as I shall be in a year or two.' She gave a gulp of self-pity which ended in a cackle of laughter. 'Till then I mean to stay where I belong to be. Miss Poldark of Trenwith. Though I be sick and weary and all scrump with the cold, I mean to stay till my hundredth birthday next year. And to *torment* George, Ross. I real torment him. He hate me dearly and I hate him, and tis a rare pleasure to get him all riffled up with anger like a ram's cat. Why, if I left this house I'd not live the month. Not even wi' all your care – and your docy little bud to tend me. Nay, God bless ye, boy. And God bless ye, ye thin rake of a gel. Back to your childer, and leave me be!'

They stayed another ten minutes, and Agatha had a drawer opened and brought to her, and took out a small painted cameo, which was to be given to little Clowance; but she would not be moved from her decision. Acknowledging her to be probably right but exasperated nevertheless by her obstinacy, Ross turned suddenly at his most venomous on Lucy Pipe.

'*You,* slut. You're paid, housed, fed: see to it you discharge your duties! A word from me to Mrs Warleggan will have you turned out of the house. *And* I'll do it – for I'll come by surprise again, as this time. When I come I want this room *clean* – d'you hear, *clean!* – that curtain mended, the glass shining, Miss Poldark's ornaments and possessions disinterred from these layers of dust. I want a *good bright* fire – no sulky coal and no sulky maids, else out you go! No unemptied night trays thrust under the bed; the close stool properly *cleaned,* Miss Poldark's night rail washed, and *all other linen! D'you hear me!*'

'Yes, sur,' said Lucy Pipe, obsequious and resentful with the same glance. 'I dare say as I can do what you d'say, but oft times – '

'Save your breath. And get off your fat rump and *work!*' Ross looked at Caroline. 'Shall we leave?'

After a last Christmas kiss they went, out into the cold and draughty corridor, back the way they had come. Both were relieved to be out, to be breathing an air not tainted with putrefaction. They did not speak, but when they reached the hall Ross said: 'Wait. There is one more thing . . .'

Caroline followed him through two doors and along a narrow corridor to another door, which he flung open. They were looking down into the kitchen. In the big dark room two lanterns were already burning, and a great fire raged in the hearth. There were some Christmas decorations, and about the kitchen five servants lolled in various postures. At sight of him they stopped a song they were half through, and three of them – the three women – got to their feet, uncertain who he was but aware that he represented some authority they were not expecting.

Ross entered no further than the steps.

He said: 'I came to call on you at my cousin's request to make sure that all was well in her absence. What do you think I should report to her?'

None of them spoke, but one put down his cup and another hiccupped and wiped her nose on her sleeve.

'That you are all drunk and unable to attend upon your proper duties? Do you think I should say that?' He glanced at Caroline behind him. 'Do *you* think I should say that? . . . It is Christmas. Perhaps I should turn a blind eye to harmless rejoicing. But how can it be harmless when a sick old lady upstairs lies unattended. *You!*' One man jumped as Ross looked at him. 'Answer me!'

'Well, sur . . .' The man stuttered and shuffled and rubbed

his hands down the sides of his breeches. 'Well, sur, tis not our work to tend on Miss Poldark. See –'

'Listen,' Ross said. 'It is not my concern what is or is not your work. There is one lady in this house who must receive your full attention *at all times*. Miss Poldark is your mistress while the rest of the family is away. She is old and infirm, but she knows well what goes on. And I shall know well what goes on through her. So care for your step. I mind not how you neglect the house so long as she is well attended. When she rings a bell, *two* of you go to see her *at all times*! She must be waited on and her every request obeyed. Else you will all be discharged. *Understand!*'

'Yes, sur.' 'Aye, sur.' One after another answered, muttering, murmuring, resentful but scared. After a moment's more looking round Ross turned to Caroline. 'Now, let us go now.' At that moment another man came into the kitchen. It was Tom Harry.

'Ah,' said Ross. 'So you are here.'

Harry had stopped in the doorway. He was carrying a jar of rum. 'What do you want?'

'I was instructing the other servants on their business. They must take greater care of Miss Poldark, or they will be discharged.'

'I'll thank ye to git out.' The man spoke truculently, but he was less confident without his employer beside him.

'Heed what I say, Harry. It's for your own good.'

'You've no business comin' yur interfering.'

'It's Christmas, and I come only to warn you, as I did last year. But if you wish to dispute the matter you must say so.'

Harry blinked. 'I'll thank ye to git out.'

'Remember what I said. I shall be back a week from today with a horse whip, to be used where it seems necessary. I want Miss Poldark differently attended to. See to if you value your own good health.'

They went out then. Judith whinnied at the sight of her master. Ross helped Caroline to mount, then climbed up himself and they crunched slowly down the drive together. It was now beginning to snow in earnest, and they had left it late enough.

As they came to the gate, which Ross held open for her, Caroline said: 'How I love a strong man!'

He blew out a breath. 'Your jest is well deserved.'

'Sometimes truth is spoken in jest.'

'Ah, yes, but that is only by accident.'

'Not at all by accident in this case.'

He smiled at her. 'I cannot believe that so civilized and refined a woman as yourself can really appreciate our rough country ways.'

'That shows how little you know me,' said Caroline.

They rode off through the feathering snow.

CHAPTER THREE

Six inches had fallen before midnight. By then the stars were out but it was freezing hard. An icy wind moved over the land as if it had come straight from Golgotha.

They were late to bed, being reluctant to tear themselves away from the raging fire that Ross had built. In the end the whole of the back of the fireplace glowed red, and they had to retreat further and further from it, scorched to their faces but always assailed by the cold airs behind. Upstairs warming pans had been in the beds, fires were burning, coal buckets were full, logs were stacked for the long night, but still they stayed down, clinging to the extra glow and companionship of the parlour, the light of the candles, the pleasant desultory talk.

At length Caroline got up and stretched. 'I must go or I shall nod off here. Don't disturb yourselves! This candle will escort me. I'll lie deep under the blankets and think of others less fortunate. Indeed, though not a praying woman, as you know, I may try to find words to say something special for one particular man and trust this weather is not spreading over France as well. Good night! Good night!'

When she had gone Ross said: 'We should go too,' and both settled back in their chairs and laughed. 'But we should,' he insisted. 'Clowance is still an early waker, even now that she is born, and I do not suppose she will be at all deterred by the snow.'

'Do you think Caroline mean what she say?' Demelza asked. 'About her house. About making it a centre for French émigrés?'

'Caroline always means what she says. Though I don't think her invitations will be open and indiscriminate. There is a lot of talk of this counter-revolution in France, and it's clearly her intention to foster that in any way she can.'

'And how can she?'

'Emigrés usually lack money. Also sometimes with the best will in the world on both sides, they outstay their welcome at one house or another. Two of those we met at Trelissick, the Comte de Maresi and Mme Guise, have been staying at Tehidy now for five months and they and their hosts would I'm sure be not unwilling to make a change. There are others like them.'

'Are they in this – what do you call it? – counter-revolution?'

'De Sombreuil is one of the prime movers. He and de Maresi, and a man called the Comte de Puisaye and a General d'Hervilly. There are constant messengers passing to and fro between England and Brittany.'

'But what do they hope they can do?'

'Half of France, the saner half, is sickened by the excesses of the revolution. All sensible men want a return to stable government, and many see a restoration of a Bourbon as king the only way of achieving it.'

'Is he in England too?'

'Who?'

'The – Bourbon.'

'The Comte de Provence. No, he is in Bremen at present. But he would come to England when the time was ripe. The idea would be to make a landing in Brittany and proclaim him king. The Bretons are much disaffected and would rise in his support.'

'Do you think it might succeed?'

'It was first talked of to me at Trelissick in July. At that time I thought the plans too vague. But they appear, from what Caroline says, to have made practical progress since then.'

'But why is Caroline concerning herself in this? Because of Dwight?'

'Well, Dwight is in Brittany, and perhaps she thinks of his release coming this way. But chiefly I believe it is because with Dwight a prisoner she cannot bear inactivity. Of course she is going to London in the new year to see if she can free him by paying a ransom; but I think the Admiralty will warn her against this because, once the ransom was agreed and paid, there would be no one to be trusted to see that their side of the bargain was kept. It would be likely to be expensive and useless, and I know she suspects this. Therefore, to help to plan an uprising in Brittany, working to overthrow the revolutionaries, is the best way of using up her energies and absorbing some of her anxiety.'

Demelza was silent for a while, staring unwinking into the brazen embers of the fire. 'D'you know, Ross, I believe Caroline is more than half in love with you.'

Ross fingered the hair covering his scar. 'I believe I am more than half in love with Caroline, but not in the way you mean.'

'What other way is there?'

'The way of friendship – companionship. We accord so well. But on my side it is quite different from what I feel for you, from what I once felt, may have felt . . .'

'For Elizabeth,' said Demelza, bringing it into the open.

'Well, yes. But as for Caroline, do not think there is in my feeling for her any rivalry with my feeling for you. Nor do I suppose for a moment that there is any comparison between her liking for me and her love for Dwight. It is a peculiar thing, but there it is.'

' "Things" can ripen suddenly and very rapid. That is surprising too.'

'Not in any way that can be a danger to a happily married man.'

'There is always a danger. Especially when the wife has not been able to be a wife – or look a wife – for a while.'

'How better could you be my wife than by bringing me another daughter?'

'That is a very – worthy sentiment Ross.'

'Worthy! Good God, is that how you see it? What a perverse creature you are! There is nothing worthy about it. And I promise you that when you don't look like a wife to me I'll tell you.'

Demelza pushed off her slippers and moved her toes about. 'Well, perhaps wife is the wrong word – perhaps I used it wrong. You see, Ross, in every right marriage, in every good marriage a woman has to be three things, don't she? She's got to be a wife and look after a man's comforts in the way a man should be looked after. Then she's got to bear his children and get all swelled up like a summer pumpkin, and then often-times *feed* them after and *smell* of babies and have them crawling all about her . . . But then, third, she has also to try and be his mistress at the same time; someone he is still "interested" in; someone he *wants,* not just the person who happens to be there and convenient;

someone a bit *mysterious*, like that woman he saw riding to hounds yesterday, someone whose knee or – or shoulder he wouldn't instantly recognize if he saw it beside him in bed. It's – it's *impossible*.'

Ross laughed. 'Surely it applies also in the opposite way. What does a woman expect of her husband – '

'Not near so much. It's not as impossible.'

'But to some extent. Well, I'm not going to reassure you, if that's what you want, for if you are not reassured by now, no pretty speeches I can offer you will make the difference.'

'No, I am never reassured – '

'And why should *I* be? You only have to crook your finger and the men come running. Your past is littered with their importunings.'

'I believe,' said Demelza, 'that you must be feeling guilty, for you are accusing me of what never happened. You always accuse me when you feel guilty yourself.'

'D'you remember,' Ross said sleepily, 'what happened a year ago yesterday? We began to talk about our love for each other, and the principles of fidelity and I don't know what else; and at the end of it you were going to leave me. Remember? You had got as far as the saddle, and if a barrel of beer had not fomented at the wrong time we might not be living together at this moment.'

'I always thought that that beer had a taste to it.'

But his half jesting warning had silenced her.

After a minute or so she said: 'I'm grateful to Caroline for going with you to Trenwith today; and as it turned out her absence made it easier for me. The folk who came back are not quite as comfortable with Caroline as they are with us.'

'I was surprised to find them all gone.'

'Well, it was such a bad day they wished to be home before it grew worse. And Sam was holding a meeting for some of them.'

'What you have saddled that poor child with!'

'But he is a kind man, Ross, though you may jest. Last eve in Grambler he found old Widow Clegwidden crawling back to her shack on all fours trying to carry a bucket of water. She's so bad in the legs with rheumatics that she cannot stand, and she has a quarter mile to go to the pump. He says he will go every eve and do that for her when he comes off core.'

'There will be plenty of opportunity for it,' Ross said, 'if this weather lasts. Coal is up this month to forty-five shillings a chaldron. Potatoes are up from four shillings to five shillings a hundredweight. There is a great scarcity of barley for making bread. Eggs are five for two pence, butter a shilling a pound. What can a labourer buy on eight shillings a week?'

'Could we not do more for folk ourselves?'

'Well, those working on our mine are not hard hit, but it gives us no excuse for living in a blinkered world. I had thought to approach some of the other landowners and suggest we might help in some more concerted form. But of course I know what their answers will be – that they already contribute to need through the Poor's Rate. They also help such deserving cases as are near home. They do not they would say, wish to encourage idleness and sloth.'

'But is it idleness they would encourage?'

'No, it is famine and disease they would *dis*courage, if they would look at it right. In normal times it may be in the main the widows, the orphans, the infirm and the old who need the Poor's Rate; but now it is also the able-bodied and the industrious, because even those who are in work cannot earn enough to keep themselves.'

Demelza said: 'Perhaps Caroline would help to bring the others together. After all she is a landowner now.'

'But not noticeably more sympathetic towards the poor than the others. She lacks Dwight's influence on her.'

'You talk to her, Ross. I believe you could persaude her.'

He raised a cynical eyebrow. 'We'll see. But you over rate my influence.'

Demelza put on one of her slippers and stirred the other with her toe.

Ross said: 'I'll take a last look round at the animals. It's four hours since Moses Vigus left them and I never trust him too far . . . We could take more help on the farm. That is one way – one practical way to give work.'

'Ross' she said 'there is one other thing I should perhaps tell you before you go. Sam told me in confidence and asked me not to tell you but I said we did not have secrets from each other . . .'

He nodded. 'That is a good beginning. Is he still fretting about his preaching house?'

'No. I have hinted – just hinted that in the spring you may favourably consider that. No . . . He is a small matter concerned over Drake.'

'Over Drake?'

'It seems Drake has been seeing a lot of Geoffrey Charles. They have struck up a great friendship and Drake has been visiting Trenwith regularly – that is until Geoffrey Charles left.'

'How did they meet? But what is wrong in it – except for . . ?'

'His friendship is not only for Geoffrey Charles. He has discovered also a great attachment for Geoffrey Charles's governess Morwenna Chynoweth.'

Ross stood up and stretched. The candles flickered lazily. 'Elizabeth's cousin? Have I ever seen her?'

'She was at church when we went at Michaelmas. She is tall and dark and sometimes wears spectacles.'

'But how has this come about? One does not suppose there is any contact between Drake and such as she.'

'They met out of doors and a friendship has followed. Sam says that although Drake tries to hide it he is quite infatuated. I do not think Elizabeth or anyone else knows of the friendship. Now of course they have all gone to Truro for Christmas but they are expected back next month. Sam is worried because he believes it will take Drake out of the connexion.'

'That might be the least of his anxieties.'

'I know.'

It was very quiet in the house. Even the sea was quiet. After the constant winds one noticed it, the stillness, the silences of snow.

'How old is she, this girl?'

'Seventeen or eighteen.'

'And is she – has she become fond of Drake?'

'I suspicion so, from what Sam says.'

Ross made an irritable gesture. 'Why do they not all move away, the whole damned lot of 'em! There is this constant embarrassment of enmity. I do not suppose John Trevaunance or Horace Treneglos would welcome an attachment between Drake and a niece of theirs but at least we could meet and discuss it together in a reasonable manner. But between George and us – and indeed between Elizabeth and us now – everything is poisoned. Clearly Drake cannot have any hope of prospering his suit there.'

'I do not know what he can hope himself.'

'Sometimes infatuation sees no further than the next day.'

'Sam says Drake will take no guidance from him in this,

and he asked me what he should do.'

'What can any of us do? I can discharge him and send him home to Illuggan, if you wish, but why should I penalize him for what is not really a concern of ours?'

'It may become a concern of ours, that's what I'm afraid for.'

'D'you want me to dismiss him?'

'Judas, no. But it's a small matter worrying. I would not want for him to get at cross with George and George's gamekeepers.'

'What is this girl like, do you know? Has she a mind of her own? If Elizabeth gets to know, and forbids the friendship, as she will, do you think this girl will defy her?'

'I know no more than you.'

'A pest on your brothers,' Ross said. 'I believe they were sent here specially to become a nuisance to us. We should have hardened our hearts at the beginning and sent them back where they belong.'

The weather did not relent. There was little more snow after that night, but what fell stayed on the ground. All England, all Europe was in a winter's grip. In Demelza's bedroom the water in a hand basin, brought up overnight, was frozen solid each morning, and on the third morning the basin cracked. Downstairs in the parlour, even though the fire burned all night, the frost spun spiders' webs on the inside of the windows, and this was not gone by two in the afternoon.

In Cumberland all the great lakes froze, and the Thames began to mist and choke. By the New Year ice floes were cutting hawsers and damaging vessels in the river, and a week later it froze at Battersea Bridge and at Shadwell to permit people to cross the river on foot. Preparations were put in hand for one of the great fairs. But it never came, for a sudden brief thaw in the middle of the month made the ice unsafe without actually moving it.

In Cornwall the rime did not leave the trees for days, and after brief sun at the end of December a darkness settled over the county like a half twilight, with an endless east wind which pierced everything in its path. A man and a woman were frozen to death at St Ann's – both far gone in drink trying to keep out the cold. A gravel pit on the Bodrugan estate was found to have ice on it fourteen inches thick; and even the Bodrugan chamber pot had a solid crust each morning. Sir John Trevaunance's thermometer hanging on the wall of his house several nights showed nineteen degrees of frost. To his annoyance he found when the rain came that he could not measure it because the frost had burst his gauge. The ground, even where it was blown free of snow, was too hard to turn up or to permit anything to come through. As he complained bitterly later in the month, a man might bleed to death at the nose for want of nettle-tops to bruise for a styptic.

In Flanders a French army, ill-conditioned and half-clad and as covered in itch and vermin as its commander, General Pichegru, was suddenly galvanized by an order to advance across the frozen Maas – which bore even the weight of cannon – and outflanked and surprised the English and Dutch and drove them before it. As one river after another solidified before the advancing army the retreat became a rout, and in every town that opened its gates to the French there were crowds to greet them as friends and liberators. On the 20th January Amsterdam fell. The sea was dotted with escaping ships crammed with fugitives and their possessions; but the Dutch fleet, anchored near the island of Texel, left it too late to move and were frozen in, whereupon the French cavalry galloped across the icy wastes of the Zuider Zee, dragging their cannon behind them. Then might have taken place a battle unique in the history of the world, between mounted hussars and warships frozen in snow like encrusted fortresses. But the Dutch, perceiving their own disadvantage, gave up without a fight. By the end of the month French control of Holland was complete.

If the weather helped the French with their plans to conquer the Netherlands, it hindered George Warleggan in his plans to conquer Cornish society. On the 31st December a partial thaw briefly set in, bringing with it hail and water snow. Even the hardiest members of Cornish society, inured as they were to privations in the pursuit of pleasure, hesitated before a journey of several miles over roads which one of them described as having the consistency of hasty pudding. Those influential and superior people who had been invited to spend the night at Cardew and had not liked to refuse because of Elizabeth, now gratefully accepted the excuse and sent soaking messengers to present their apologies.

It was a disastrous evening. The band arrived in the forenoon, but one of the musicians slipped at the front door and so badly sprained his ankle that he could only take to a bed. Enormous quantities of food were being prepared by the resident servants, but the extra helpers who had been engaged did not turn up until after the guests, and some food and drink, which had been coming from outside, did not arrive at all. The house, normally in Elizabeth's opinion so warm and draught-proof after Cusgarne and Trenwith, tonight seemed enormous and cold and echoing, partly because it was vulnerable to a south-east wind, partly because so much furniture had been moved and cleared away to make room for the hundred and twenty guests, partly because by midnight only thirty-two had turned up and were quite dwarfed by the preparations made to receive them. To George's quiet fury, those thirty-two were the youngest and halest but least influential of his friends or sons of his friends, and the noise they made, though necessary in all that emptiness, jarred on him unbearably.

Nevertheless, having long guarded his looks and his tongue in public, he showed only an agreeable face; and for his own pride he would not vent his chagrin on Elizabeth or the servants. Instead he decided to turn the evening to whatever profit he could.

Among the younger people who had come tonight, three had been named by him in his talk of Morwenna's future. The older ones anyway had been ruled out by Elizabeth's clear opposition. On Ephraim Hick and Hugh Bodrugan he had accepted her veto; her objection to John Trevaunance, except on a score of age, was less easy to understand. But it eventually began to dawn on George that, whatever other pros and cons there could be for such a marriage, Elizabeth would not be happy to see her young cousin become Lady Trevaunance and living as Lady Trevaunance as a near neighbour. It was an objection which had not at first occurred to him but once made, in however oblique a form, was one of which he immediately saw the point.

In any event Sir John was not here tonight, and had not even sent an apology. Robert Bodrugan was here, and Frederick Treneglos, and Osborne Whitworth. Having less than he expected to occupy his time, George was more able to observe their behaviour to Morwenna and Morwenna's to them. And the behaviour of one or two other young dogs who came sniffing around.

At his suggestion Elizabeth had had a new white frock made for Morwenna, and he found himself pleased with the result. Her dark brown hair and rather dark skin and large startled short-sighted brown eyes were well set off by the white satin. So was her figure. A man singularly untroubled in the ordinary way by sexual fancies, he could not prevent his eyes from dwelling upon the slim statuesqueness of her body and considering what it would look like unclothed.

It was a thought possibly not entirely absent from the eyes of the younger men in the room, and while the girl was too quiet and too shy ever to become the focus of attention, she did not lack for partners or interest. It seemed to George that she had bloomed overnight, and he wondered if possibly he had set his sights high enough in considering her matrimonial prospects, if perhaps with further grooming and careful training she might not catch the eye of someone still more elevated – a younger Boscawen, for example, or even a Mount Edgcumbe. It was a dizzy thought.

But probably a vain one. She had no money and, even if all else went well, there would be opposition from the families. The Boscawens in particular, though so wealthy themselves, were noted for their marriages to more money. George, though ready to further a favourable alliance, could not produce the sort of dowry that would turn Morwenna into an heiress.

So of the possible suitors there? Robert Bodrugan showed no interest at all and was lavishing attentions on the notorious Betty Devoran, Lord Devoran's stocky-legged niece, who was meeting him more than halfway. Frederick Treneglos, after an initial sortie, had joined a noisy group of young men at the door who were agitating for group dances and round dances instead of the more formal dances on the programme. Only the Rev. William Osborne Whitworth was among the constant visitors to Morwenna's corner. Not that personal preference was all, as George well knew. The proposition could be put to any of them as a practical deal, and it would be the subject of sober study as a suitable or unsuitable bargain. But a marked preference helped. And on the whole, of the available choices George somewhat favoured young Whitworth. First, he was a clergyman, and who better to marry a dean's daughter? Second, he was a widower with two young children, whose need of a new wife must be urgent. (George noted that his recent bereavement had not prevented his appearance in a brilliant green cut-away coat and lemon yellow gloves.) Third, he was short of money. And fourth, his mother – who had not braved the weather tonight – was a Godolphin.

As for Morwenna, she saw this tall, loud-voiced, affected young clergyman as only a partner to step with on the floor and listen to afterward. She was enjoying the dance and the unexpected attentions of a number of young men. But it was a superficial enjoyment, as her whole existence in Truro had been superficial this Christmas time. It was as if her life was split horizontally, the upper surface part being concerned with the pleasant enough day-to-day routine of rising and eating and companioning Geoffrey Charles and ploughing through the snow to St Mary's Church and drinking tea and working on a sampler and helping Elizabeth at a whist party and climbing the circling top stairs to bed in a tiny cold room on the top floor. Below that life, in the lower half of her life, were sick-sweet memories – of a boy's dark eyes and too pale skin, of his rough-gentle hands on her shoulders, of his lips, as unpractised and as full of promise as her own. Day by day, hour by hour, she lived the times again when they had met and what they had done and what they had said to each other.

It was an uneasy dream, for she knew it had no validity for her. Though better spoken than some, his thick Cornish accent and primitive sense of grammar belonged to the lower classes. His rough clothes, his rough mode of life, his lack of education, even his Methodism, marked him off as someone not to be considered as a suitable companion for her. She knew that her mother and sisters would be just as shocked as Elizabeth if they ever got to know that she was even meeting him, and that they would all feel she had betrayed her trust by permitting a friendship between him and Geoffrey Charles. That anything more could develop from it would be unthinkable. She often went cold at the fear of discovery. But deep under that, like some strong slow-moving current of the blood carrying all obstacles before it, was a heart-lurching knowledge that only what had happened between her and Drake was real. As real as illness, as real as health, as real as life and as real as death. All else was vanity.

So she slept and woke and slept and woke and performed her duties and lived her life; and when a good-looking young man led her out on the floor for a gavotte – whose steps she hardly knew – she accepted his attentions and his hand with a dazed, half-blind innocence. And when a big young man with a clerical collar but no other evidences of holy intent stood beside her chair for twenty minutes and boomed

185

away about the war and the weather and the education of children she nodded and murmured, 'indeed, yes,' at suitable moments and looked at him with a mental as well as a physical myopia.

The New Year was duly celebrated, and dancing went on until two. Because of the weather conditions George offered open house to all who cared to stay the night, and all accepted. The idea of going out into a wet howling easterly gale with inches of mud and slush underfoot and crusty snowdrifts in ditches four feet deep was enough to deter the bravest. And the idea of sharing beds and bedrooms was exciting and had hopeful implications, most of which, mainly because of the excessive number of people about, were not realized. But no one ever quite knew what happened to Robert Bodrugan and Betty Devoran; and the youngest unmarried Teague girl, Joan, out without her mother for the first time, somehow escaped the surveillance of her sister, Ruth Treneglos, and had some very formative experiences with Nicholas, the eldest Cardew.

George went some way to be pleasant to Ossie Whitworth, and before he left invited him to call on them in the new year in Truro. Somehow in the course of the casual conversation the name of Miss Chynoweth happened to occur, and the Reverend Osborne, whose sensibilities were not entirely dulled by his conceit, raised an eyebrow. He knew better than to pursue the subject at this juncture, but the seed had been planted. In a few days' time he decided he would call on the ladies and take tea. Then before matters proceeded any further, there would have to be an interview with Mr Warleggan. It would be a delicate interview in which the two men had to hint at subjects not fitted to the tenderer ears of women.

CHAPTER FOUR

Weekly Ross ploughed through the snow and ice to see Aunt Agatha. With no Caroline to offer him the protection of her presence – she had gone home on the 29th – he yet continued to go and come away without offering or receiving violence. Lacking George's presence, the servants were intimidated by his; and in the main Tom Harry avoided him. (Harry, the nastier of the two, had followed his master to Truro.) So each week he climbed to the over crowded, noisome room and sat a half-hour with the old lady, listening to her complaints and trying to sift the real from the imaginary, stroking Smollett, feeding crumbs to her blackbird, joining her in anathemas on the weather and keeping Lucy Pipe on her mettle for fear of being discharged. So whenever he went, and he kept his visits to irregular times, the fire was roaring in the chimney, the bedlinen was clean, and Agatha and the room moderately tidy. Even the smell had become tolerable.

Usually he found the old lady pretty alert, but her moods greatly varied. Sometimes she was pathetic and on one occasion said tearfully to him: 'Ross, ye know, I cann't understand why I be still *alive*. I b'lieve God's forgot all about me!' But the very next visit she was furious at some neglect she had suffered and exclaimed, 'Damn the woman! I tell ye, she did it deliberate. It might've *killed* me!'

Sickness began to sweep the district. There were many deaths, mainly among the children, and mainly from bronchial influenza and malnutrition. Jud Paynter, who had recently taken over the duties of gravedigger, complained the ground was so hard that he 'had to teel 'em like taties'. One day at the end of January when Ross was up at the mine, Henshawe followed him in to the draughty little office which had been built near the engine house to accommodate what had originally been located in the library.

'I think I should tell you, sur. Since you complained last time you was not told.'

'About what?'

''Bout Wheel Leisure. You said last time as you'd heard rumour that the main lode was failing when you was in to Truro; and I didn't tell you because –'

'Yes, yes. I don't complain. I see your difficulty and respect you for it.'

'Well, yes, sur, that's as maybe. But news gets out, and I don't like for you to get news second hand and think, what didn't Will Henshawe tell me' bout that?'

'So? What are you trying to tell me now? Has the lode been rediscovered?'

'It was our quarterly meeting yesterday, held at Mingoose, for Mr Horace Treneglos is not hale enough to go out this weather.' Henshawe bit nervously at his thumbnail. 'Twas a poorly attended meeting, for Mr Pearce's clerk represented Mrs Trenwith, and the Warleggans sent their

187

lawyer Mr Tankard to speak for them.'

'Well, I hope you still showed a profit.'

'Yes, sur, we did, though twas only just the right side the ledger. But that's not what I wanted to tell you. Twas decided to close the mine down.'

Ross stood up. '*What?*'

Henshawe nodded, his eyes as cold as the day. 'Warleggan's man had come with his instructions, and that's what he says and that's what is decided.'

'But what a monstrous thing! At this juncture, with such – But you say you are still in profit?'

'Just. Tankard says that is the time to close. With the red copper exhausted we'd be hard set to show a profit through this year, and he says close *before* the loss begins. And he carried the day.'

'But how? The Warleggans control only a half of the shares. You told me so yourself a few months back. Has there been some –'

'Renfrew voted with them.'

'Renfrew? But he . . .'

'Is a mine chandler, sur. He depend at St Ann's for all his trade with the Warleggan mines there. You could hardly blame him if he went along with them if they let him know twas expected of him. Mind, I'm not saying they did – but usually the mine chandlers be the last for voting to see a mine closed, seeing as they profit from the supply.'

'Merciful God,' Ross said. 'I could wring their necks! This will mean throwing upon the parish sixty or seventy folk: thirty-five to forty families will be affected, among them some of my own friends. When we started Wheal Leisure most of my neighbours went to it, and I was glad to offer them that employment; so that, as you know, for Wheal Grace we took on mainly Sawle and Grambler men. Now I cannot turn *them* out to make room for those laid off at Leisure! Nor can I – nor can I suddenly double the work-force and the output at Grace just to accommodate them! One day I believe I will kill George!'

'Do not say it, sur, even in idle anger,' said Henshawe. 'It is, we all know, the worst time possible for such a closure. But . . . it is the way of the world. Folk will be in greater distress – but they will bear it – as they always do. After all, no one's a miner who don't expect this may happen. Mines are always opening and closing. See how near we were at Grace last year. It could have happened the other way.'

Ross's anger seemed too great to be contained within the small low office. His head, though twelve inches from the beams, looked as if it might push them off. 'It could have happened but it did not! What is insufferable here is that Leisure was still solvent! Not a penny of anyone's money was being lost. It is like an attempt to hit at me through these miners and village folk! It is as if the Warleggans had said: He's prosperous now – so let him have starvation on his own doorstep – let pestilence and privation kill the women and children off all around him! We can't destroy his own mine but we can destroy his neighbours!'

Henshawe was biting again at his thumbnail. 'I had to tell you, sur, but I knew twould be a blow. I hoped you'd not take it so personal, for it may not be personal. After all, Mr Warleggan is living in this district now and I think he seek to be popular. So it cann't be to his advantage to be thought to be cutting off the livelihood of all those folk. I don't *b'lieve* tis personal to you. I think it is just – business.'

'May such business rot in his throat.'

'Aye and amen. But it is the new kind of business, sur. I seen it before, and no doubt we'll see it again. We'll all lose the blown-up value of our shares – the Warleggans just so much as any. Indeed, Mr Cary Warleggan, who but recent bought out Mr Pearce's share, will stand to lose most, for all the rest of us have done handsome-handsome out of the money we put in. Mr Treneglos, myself, Mrs Trenwith, Mr Renfrew: all told it cost us less than £100 each, and we've got that back twenty-fold and more. Mr Pearce must be laughing to have made the same and to have sold his shares so recent . . . No, sur.' Henshawe laid a hesitant hand – small and white for so large a man – on Ross's sleeve. 'No, sur, it be all justified in the name of business. I talked to Tankard after, and I believe he is telling truth. So long as Leisure produced red copper and showed a real profit, the Warleggans would have kept it going. So soon as the red copper ran away, and it became just a mine showing little profit and adding copper to the market, it was bad in their books. By just producing copper it was competing with their other three mines and forcing down the price they could go for the copper raised from them!'

'I would like to take George down a mine,' said Ross. 'I wonder if he has ever been down one. Do you think you could arrange it?'

Henshawe said: 'I beg you, sur, to say nothing of this t'anyone, for twill not be public for a month or more. But I felt I had to tell you. I'd like your word.'

January ended and February came in with the winds and the frosts unchanging. Caroline, unable to journey to London except by sea – which was something even she did not care to face – instead took up the cause of the poor as Demelza, and more particularly Ross, had asked her. Accompanied by a groom, she slipped and slithered on her white horse from one big house to another, cajoling, bullying, or enticing its owner to contribute to a subscription she was raising for the labouring poor and the starving miners. She started the fund with twenty guineas herself, and Ross gave the same. She considered that everyone of their standing should be expected to contribute no less; but she had hard work in some of the houses. Sir John Trevaunance, who did not like her very much since she had refused Unwin, argued that he was already giving corn to his own workmen at a reduced price and had been doing so for three months – why should he be expected to contribute a second time? He offered £2. Caroline refused it and sat on. When she had been there three hours she rose and said, well, perhaps tomorrow he would feel better disposed: she would call back tomorrow. Sir John increased his subscription to £10. Caroline accepted this but said she would call for the other half next month.

Old Horace Treneglos was willing but his son John laughed in her face and said he hadn't that much ready cash in the world. Caroline then said she would send a cart over and take the contents of one of his barns. In the end they found fifteen guineas. Sir Hugh Bodrugan happened to be in a good mood and gave her twenty without argument. There was no one at Trenwith, so she wrote a letter to George and sent it in by groom. The groom came back with twenty-five guineas. Caroline thought, five guineas extra to be at the top of the list? Then she started on the smaller fry, from whom she could expect less. But like an Irish priest who knows what every member of the congregation can afford, she set a figure, with the help of her bailiff, Myners, before she called at each house. In this way she surprised £10 out of Mr Trencrom before he could formulate the proper excuses.

The object of this subscription was not charity as such,

but to buy the contents of a corn ship which was due in St Ann's shortly and sell the contents to the miners and their families at a reduced price. Only in the direst cases was the corn to be given, for the Poor Rate was supposed to keep everyone above starvation level.

At the end of January Aunt Agatha told Ross that Elizabeth had written to say they would not be back just yet as Valentine was unwell, and they could not move while the bad weather lasted. Nor did Geoffrey Charles and Morwenna and the older Chynoweths return.

On February the 16th Demelza was feeding the birds in her frozen garden – those which had not died of the cold being tame that they would take bread from her hand – and she came on a first snowdrop opening its white star through the crusty earth. She at once ran in to tell Ross – but it was the only sign. The east wind blew an eternal grey cloud over the land, and the land shivered and crouched. Sam, though preoccupied with the number of souls he had to save, found himself forced to consider their bodies as well. Works, he knew, did not go before faith, but necessity sometimes drove him to act as if they did.

One casualty was Nick Vigus, surprisingly, for he had cheated his way through life so successfully that one wondered he could not lie his way out of the pneumonia which attacked him. But even Dr Choake's ministrations, costing 1s 6d a visit, did not help him, and, no cleverer than the rest when his time came, he died quietly in the night; and Jud had the privilege of digging the hole to contain his old friend and companion in wickedness. Vigus left a widow, a son, three daughters, and two daughters by his eldest daughter. They were soon on parish relief.

Wheal Leisure closed on the 25th of February. On the following day Ross took on twenty more hands. It was a measure of charity which he explained to Demelza he felt he had to afford. Not to bring up more ore from the floors of tin at present being worked but to explore the ground further, chiefly in the direction of old Wheal Maiden.

'If I mine more now I defeat my object. But our margin of profit will permit this extra expenditure, and who knows, one may be discovering some new lode for the future? It simply means that our costs will rise relative to what we raise.'

That same week the ship with the corn came in, and the contents were brought ashore and sold off the following

Sunday morning and each succeeding Sunday from the parish schoolroom of St Ann's. The price for wheat was set at 14s a bushel and barley at 7s a bushel, this being about half the price they were fetching in Truro market. Distribution and sale were conducted in a most orderly fashion, the queue forming about two hours before the sale began. The sale was conducted by the parish overseers, but Caroline or one or other of the main contributors was there each week in case of dispute over price or quantity.

Having seen the scheme launched, Caroline at last went off to London; but not before she had held a meeting at her house for the French émigrés. She invited both Ross and Demelza, but Demelza could not go, Jeremy having caught the prevailing influenza and being dangerous feverish. Demelza missed Dwight almost as much as Caroline did. The heavy-handed, stertorous Dr Choake with his liking for the knife always scared her, especially when directed towards one of her children. Jeremy hated him, ever since he had stripped him naked and lugged him down the bed by his ankles to get a better look at him. It was a long way from Dr Dwight Enys, who came and sat by the bed and quietly talked and sympathetically asked questions and then gently examined, and all the time, with eyes that were weighing and assessing, was reaching a conclusion and a diagnosis.

Nor was it only Demelza who missed him. Typhus first showed itself in the Poor Houses which were situated between Grambler and Sawle, and there it stayed for a month or more; but everyone knew that, once fledged, it would move and spread in its own ill time. Smallpox of course was endemic but on the increase. Choake was shocked that Jeremy had not yet been inoculated and wanted to do it at once; but Demelza, who knew that the surgeon always cut the patient's arm to the bone, postponed the evil day and said she would consider it and privately prayed for the return of Dwight.

Drake heard twice from Geoffrey Charles, childish letters saying little, and almost nothing of Morwenna. They told of Geoffrey Charles's doings and of Geoffrey Charles's undying affection for Drake and each promised an early return. The second letter said they had been further delayed because of Valentine's illness, but that he and Morwenna would definitely be back at Trenwith by March the 6th.

On March the 5th it began to snow again.

Valentine's illness was a serious one. As he approached his

first birthday his appetite fell off and he was troubled with vomiting and diarrhoea. Then he began to sweat heavily in his sleep and kick off his blankets even on the coldest of nights, and Polly Odgers was kept awake continually covering him. When Dr Behenna found the child's bones to be very tender and the wrists and ankles to be swollen, he recognized the onset of the common and disabling disease.

Rickets was a frequent ailment of childhood, but one from which the Poldark family had been singularly free. Aunt Agatha, when she heard of it in the letter from Elizabeth, pronounced that there was 'poor blood on both sides'. It was very worrying for the Warleggans, for to them Valentine was the crown prince, and it would be humiliating if the child who was to inherit all they had were to grow up deformed or handicapped.

Daniel Behenna, riding the cobbled sickly streets of Truro like a demi-god, pronouncing his judgments with the confidence and certitude that all men needed, called each day to see his little patient, and very shortly decided on the best treatment, indeed the only treatment for such a case. At six in the evening, which was Valentine's normal bed-time, he called and opened a vein in both of Valentine's ears between the junctures. He mixed the blood thus obtained with twice the amount of aqua-vitae – the alchemic name for unrefined alcohol – and with this mixture he bathed the neck, sides and chest of the child. Then he took a green ointment of his own preparation, heated it in a spoon and rubbed it briskly and very hot into the screaming boy's wrists and ankles where the bones were at their most tender. This went on for ten nights, during which the child was not allowed to leave his bed or to have his night shift changed. At the end of that time he was fitted with splints to both legs and both arms.

It was a remedy to which Valentine did not respond. He developed a high fever and at times seemed on the point of death. Another doctor was called, who endorsed the treatment so far given but thought more extensive bleeding and a purge should now follow. Also a flannel wet with hot spirits should be applied regularly to the child's feet. A week later the anxious parents called in Dr Pryce of Redruth, who being in fact more a mine surgeon than a general physician had had long experience with rachitic illness. He thought the boy should be released from his splints, kept quiet and warm, entertained in bed but restrained from standing and given as much warm milk as he could be persuaded to drink. A few days later recovery was on the way.

Through all this, although both parents were equally distracted, George had continued to discharge his business and to further his own ideas for the future.

In one respect George had been quite wrong about Ossie Whitworth. Being of non-genteel birth himself, he had supposed that any conversation between himself and the young clergyman on the matter of a marriage settlement must necessarily be discreetly approached and discursively conducted. Not at all. Not for the first or indeed the last time, George learned that the higher you were born the more you were inclined to call a spade a spade.

George had been thinking of a dowry of £2000. When the figure at last came to be dropped into the conversation Ossie spurned it. He had, he said, debts of over £1000. To live at St Margaret's, Truro, in any style at all, meant looking for a sum which would enable him when it was invested to enjoy an added income of around £300 a year. If with Morwenna he received only what would amount to £1000 clear of debt he could do virtually nothing at all. Carefully put about, it might bring him £70 a year, but that would scarcely double his income from the living.

Plain speaking now clearly being the order of the day, George politely asked him what figure he had in mind. Osborne said not less than £6000. George was now beginning rather to dislike this conceited young man. Only the thought of his mother's connections kept George's tongue in check, however, this did not restrain him from pointing out the facts of the case as he saw them. In the first place, Morwenna was eighteen, the daughter of a dean, and came of one of the very oldest families in the country. Further, she was devout, healthy, of a good temper, particularly fond of motherless children – of whom Mr Whitworth would no doubt remember he had two – a good manager in the house and very comely to look at. In the second place he, Mr Warleggan, only acted towards her *in loco parentis* and had nothing to gain in promoting her welfare except a desire to please his wife and a genuine affection for a very good girl. There was no reason why he should lay out any money at all, but he was prepared to give the girl a dowry of £2000. For that sum, which was no mean sum these days, there would be plenty of young men available. If Mr Whitworth felt that elsewhere, somewhere near at hand, he would find a pretty young lady with £6000 of her own who was prepared to link her destinies with a debt-ridden and almost penniless clergyman, then of course he was entirely free to seek her out.

But of course, George said, there was no hurry at all. Perhaps Mr Whitworth would care to go home and think it over.

This was in late January. Osborne went home and discussed it all with his mother, as George knew he would. He left it ten days, as a matter of tactics, and then called again. He said he had given their talk the fullest consideration and he had returned only because his devotion to Morwenna was unchanged. He felt that to obtain such a lovely and loving wife he would accept £4000. This, after all was discharged, would only bring him in an income of about £200 a year, and could Mr Warleggan, or still more Mrs Warleggan, be happy at the thought of their cousin, however happily married, subsisting on less? George said he too had had time to think the matter over and had of course discussed it with his wife. But, conditions being what they were, business bad, war problems rife, mining in the depths of depression and no settled future to be seen, he felt he could not increase his offer beyond £2500. To that he said he would add as a special concession £250 to cover the repairs that he learned would be desirable at the vicarage.

The Reverend Osborne Whitworth went away again and returned towards the end of February. The bargaining was hard and bitter and eventually agreement was reached. Morwenna was to take with her £3000. Neither of the contestants was entirely unsatisfied. Ossie had an income of £100 a year from his mother, unmentioned in these negotiations. With this and his stipend and the new increment, his total income would now be upwards of £300, and with this he would become a man who could hold up his head in any company. And as for George, he had brought another useful blood link into the pattern he was weaving.

The other party involved in all these discussions was so far entirely ignorant of their existence. To her it was not specially significant that the Rev. Mr Whitworth had called four times at the house since Christmas and that he had twice taken tea with her and Elizabeth. To Elizabeth was given the task of enlightening her.

It was not a privilege she welcomed. She felt that as George had made all the running, indeed, all the arrangements, he might just as well complete the operation. George thought otherwise. This part was a woman's task. All the difficult negotiation was past; this had been his problem and his responsibility. Now the pleasant outcome could be left to his wife. No woman, certainly no penniless girl, could be anything but overjoyed at the news that she was to be made an heiress and was to become the wife of the town's most eligible young clergyman.

Elizabeth put it off for two days, pleading Valentine's illness as an excuse; but a note from Ossie saying he hoped to attend upon them on the morrow, forced her hand. He could hardly be expected to come into a company where his bride-to-be did not yet know of his intentions.

It was evening before she could find the right opportunity, and even then she had to follow Morwenna into the tiny music room on the first floor and to shut the door behind her as if about to impart some dreadful secret.

It was clear from Morwenna's face in the flickering candlelight that the news was indeed a shock to her, and not, as George predicted, a pleasant shock.

Taller than Elizabeth, she stood absolutely still in her dove grey velvet frock listening as if frozen, not a finger moving, only a muscle in her cheek beginning to twitch as Elizabeth went on with the story. She heard it all out and did not speak. Because of the silence which fell at the end of each sentence, Elizabeth found herself saying more than she had any real need – emphasizing the good looks of her future husband, the excellence of the match, the sudden change which would come over Morwenna's situation, how she was to be transformed from a governess into a prominent lady of the town, of George's excessive goodness and generosity in making such a match possible. So she went on until she saw Morwenna's tears begin to fall. Then she stopped.

'Does all our thought for you displease you, my dear?'

Morwenna choked, and put up the back of her hand to her eyes. The tears did not stop, they fell on her hand, through her fingers, dripped on her frock and thence to the floor. Elizabeth sat on the stool by the harpsichord and idly turned a piece of music, waiting for the initial distress to pass. It did not pass. Morwenna just stood there silently weeping.

'Come, my dear,' Elizabeth said, impatience creeping into her voice, not because she felt impatient but to hide the sympathy that she felt she should not show.

Morwenna said at last: 'I do not care for him; how can he care for me? We have exchanged as much intimate talk together as would two whist players of an afternoon. What can he know of me or I of him?'

'He knows enough to wish to make you his wife.'

'But I do not *wish* to be his wife! I do not wish to be anyone's wife as yet. Have I not pleased you? Are you displeased with my behaviour as a governess to Geoffrey Charles?'

'Far from it. If we had been displeased with you, do you think Mr Warleggan would have made this tremendous gesture on your behalf?'

There was a long silence Morwenna looked round through her tears to find somewhere to sit down. She groped and discovered a chair, her hands trembling as she lowered herself upon the seat.

'You are – very generous, Elizabeth. So is he. But I had no idea, no notion.'

'I appreciate it must have come as something of a shock to you. But I hope, after you have reflected on it for a while, that you will not think it too unpleasant a shock. Osborne is, after all, in holy orders. Your life with him will be all it was in your father's house but greatly improved as to your personal position. We shall still – '

'Does my mother know?' Morwenna asked wildly. 'I could not possibly accept without her permission! If she – '

'I wrote to her yesterday, my dear. I do not think she can possibly be anything but delighted with such a match. For an elder daughter, of good birth, but without money – '

'I am sure my mother would be quite delighted with the match if she thought Mr Whitworth and I loved each other. Did you tell her that we loved each other?'

'I do not think I used those words, Morwenna, for that is something you must tell her yourself. I told her that an engagement between you and Mr Whitworth would be announced shortly; I told her of Mr Warleggan's great generosity towards you, and I told her of Mr Whitworth's birth, youth and good looks, and of his really excellent prospects in the church. No doubt you will be writing to her soon yourself. You do write weekly, don't you?'

'And if I tell her – if when I write I tell her that I don't know Mr Whitworth, that I certainly don't love him and scarcely even like him; what will she say then? Will she still be delighted, Elizabeth? Will she still wish me to marry him?'

Elizabeth played two or three thoughtful notes on the

197

harpsichord. It needed tuning. No one ever played it. It had been bought by Mr Nicholas Warleggan to furnish the house, but no one had ever played it.

'My dear, pray think this over before you say anything more, certainly before you write to your mother. I think she would be greatly upset if, having learned from me of your splendid match, she then heard from you that you were not contented in it. She will wish you to be happy, as we all do; but she would be grievously disappointed if she thought you were finding fault with such a match because of a false and romantic idea of what a marriage ought to be.'

'Is it false to have a romantic idea of marriage, Elizabeth? Is it wrong to feel that there should be love in marriage? Tell me, Elizabeth, tell me about your first marriage? How old were you then – eighteen, nineteen? Did you not love Mr Poldark? Did you not know him well and exchange loving confidences before ever the match was made? Or was it all arranged, as this has been arranged, without your consultation?'

Elizabeth waited until Morwenna had blown her nose and wiped her eyes. 'Perhaps it is unfair to you, my dear, that we should try to put an old head on young shoulders. It is natural to expect romance. But it is not something on which a successful marriage can be based. In this you must accept the guidance of –'

'Did you? Did you not marry for love?'

Elizabeth raised a hand. 'Very well. I will tell you, since you demand to know. I married for what I thought was love, and it did not last for a twelvemonth. Nay, not for one whole year. After that we tolerated each other. Perhaps it was no better and no worse than most other marriages. But the fact that we thought ourselves in love with each other did not contribute one way or the other to the outcome. Now I have married Mr Warleggan, and although this was somewhat more matter-of-fact in origin, it is proving altogether more successful . . . Is that what you wanted to know?'

'It is not what I wanted to hear,' said Morwenna.

Elizabeth got up and put a hand on her young cousin's shoulder. 'The French have a saying – is it the French? I don't know, I believe so – there is a saying that you do not put a boiling kettle upon the fire. You put cold water in the kettle and allow it to warm. So with marriage. In marriage you and Osborne Whitworth may come to love each other far more than if you had loved each other at the start. One expects less, one discovers more. Instead of demanding perfection we demand nothing and so often receive much.'

Morwenna wiped her eyes again and then the backs of her hands. 'I do not know what to *say*, Elizabeth. It has – come as a *great* shock, a very great shock. Of course I am not unappreciative of your thought. I know you and Mr Warleggan mean it only in kindness. But I – I cannot see myself . . . I cannot feel that this is my . . . Indeed, the more I think of it –'

Elizabeth kissed her forehead, which was cold and clammy with shock. 'Say nothing more now. Sleep on it. It will all look different in the morning. Indeed you may find yourself quite excited at the prospects that are now open to you. I'm sure your mother will be. Such a match for you is more than in ordinary circumstances she can have hoped for.'

She left the girl sitting alone with a single candle flickering in the small draughty music room. She had tried all along to keep her own voice detached, the conversation on a cool unemotional level. She felt she had succeeded, but it was not without cost to herself. She would have liked to have talked to the girl on her own terms, asked her what her feelings really were about her future husband, tried to console her and encourage her in quite a different way, not as an older relative but as another woman and a friend. But all along Elizabeth knew herself to be George's wife. She had had a task to carry out, and she had dutifully performed it. It would have been disloyal to George to have talked to the girl in any way that might have encouraged her to thoughts of disobedience.

Besides, if confidences had once begun, she knew she might sooner or later have found herself ranged against him.

The early snow of March melted and was succeeded by a cold thaw. Gales and sleet followed, with floods such as had not been equalled in the memory of man. The Severn burst its banks at Shrewsbury and carried away bridges, the Lee overflowed the Essex Flat, all the Fens were under water and many of the inland banks swept away, the Thames rushed through London and submerged so much of it that inhabitants at Stratford and Bow lived in their upper rooms and used rowing boats in the streets. Vessels were wrecked all round the coasts, but this time unfortunately none cast itself upon the hospitable shores of Grambler and Sawle.

In Holland the French were triumphant, and the British

government sent transports to the Weser to evacuate the remnants of their army, an army which, let down by its allies, its commissariat, its medical supplies and its own officers, had lost 6,000 dead in a week, mainly from typhus and the cold. Frederick William of Prussia had already made peace with his adversaries, and there would be barely time to get the remnants of the Expeditionary Force home. The remaining countries of northern and central Europe were preparing to make the best peace they could with the new dynamic that the French brought. Virtually the war was over. But Pitt said: 'It matters little whether the disasters which have arisen are to be ascribed to the weakness of Generals, the intrigues of camps or the jealousies of Cabinets; the fact is that they exist, and that we must anew commence the salvation of Europe.'

One person who was happy amid these disasters, who came back from London by stages, the coach slithering and sliding and lurching among the thaws of early March, was Caroline. A first prisoner-of-war list had been received by the Admiralty on which the name of Surgeon-Lieutenant Dwight Enys was officially recorded. What, however, was more to the point was a three-page letter in the same mail bag from Dwight himself. Demelza was in her garden on the 11th of March, staring with particular pleasure at a crocus which had decided to rear its canary yellow head before the last frost was out of the ground, when Caroline arrived, and she knew at once by the look of her that she brought good news. Ross happened to be near by, and they went in out of the wind and read the letter together in the parlour.

'1st February, 1794/5

'Caroline, My Love,.

'I am writing this altogether unsure whether it will reach you and confident only that, now I have paper and pen, I must do so in the hope and prayer that our gaolers will be as good as their Word and let this letter pass.

'Where am I to begin? All these months I have so often composed letters to you in my heart, but, now the opportunity comes at last, I am tongue-tied. Let me say then first, that I am safe and not unwell, though our treatment has been far from what one would have expected from a civilized Nation. I do not even know how long you had to wait before you were appraised of the fact that I was a prisoner. If you have written to me, I have received nothing.

All communication with the central government has broken down, and internment camps and prisons, it seems to me, are administered locally according to the whims of the Commandant.

'Well, that is, I suppose, one of the fortunes of war – or of this war. At least we have been kept alive, after a fashion. It seems like ten times ten months since our battle with the French all through the afternoon and on all through that night with a great gale blowing and the sea roaring. You will, I am sure, have heard Enough of this Engagement; and my part in it you will be able to picture without the Necessity of lurid description. For more than three quarters of the time I was working in a cleared space between decks with my apprentice, Jackland, and by the light of a sharply swinging lantern. Such help as I could give to the wounded was so rough and ready as to be a nightmare of slap-dash surgery. Oftentimes I was thrown upon the patient or he upon me, so that the dripping knife I used as much endangered one as the other. But by two in the morning the water had rendered my makeshift hospital untenable, and all came on deck to await the end.

'Yet it was another two hours before we struck. I do not remember if I told you that of our total complement of near 320 less than 50 were volunteers. About a half of the total were Pressed men, some with no previous sea experience at all; there were another 50 who were Debtors and minor Felons who had been given the choice between a prison sentence and serving at sea; about 25 foreigners, Dutch, Spanish, Scandinavian, who had been swept up by the gangs of Plymouth; and the same number of boys: urchins, orphans and the like. This crew for ten hours had fought a continuous battle with an enemy and with mountainous seas, and you would have thought that the prospect of Ship-wreck would have turned them into a panic-stricken rabble. Yet after we had struck the utmost calm and discipline reigned among the men. For nearly four more hours they worked at the construction of Rafts and life lines, and only six attempted to desert and were drowned. In those four hours, under the confident and firm hand of Lieutenant Williams, they ferried ashore first the wounded, then in gradual order and by a strict rotation all the crew, and so at last the officers. I was fortunate to be sent first with the wounded, of whom two died on the beach, but of the entire crew only three, aside from the six deserters, were lost to the sea.

'Very soon we were surrounded and escorted inland by French armed Police and lodged in a school before being marched to our present Prison the following evening, so I saw little of the plight of the *Héros*; but she had thirty English prisoners on board whom I have since met and treated, and they tell me that she struck in a less favourable situation than we did, that complete panic thereupon reigned Aboard, and that it was four days before the last was brought ashore, leaving many dead aboard from their privations and the sea around littered with corpses. Near four hundred perished from this Vessel alone.

'Well, we have been in this Prison ever since, and 1 at least have been fortunate in that I have never had cause to be idle. With three surgeons only among many thousand, and the usual outcrop of bilious fevers and scrofulous conditions resulting from bad food and close confinement, we have none of us lacked for Occupation. So far there seems to have been no talk of parole or repatriation or Exchange. None of the senior officers has been freed or ransomed or exchanged; and there are in the prison English ladies, one at least titled, the like of whom you would consider the French would have no purpose in retaining, but here they still remain.

'My own Caroline, this is no love-letter, as you will by now have seen. If this reaches you it will at least give an Account of what has happened through this long Year. I can only say that amid all the trials of this present time you are never absent from my thought, that the locket you gave me is always warm against my Heart, and that, however long this separation continues, it cannot alter my love for you and my devotion.

'Good night, Caroline, my love.

'Your devoted,

Dwight.'

'I have left word with the Admiralty,' said Caroline, 'regarding a ransom. But at present they do not advise it;' she lifted an ironical eyebrow at Ross; 'as foreseen by you. They are trying to arrange exchanges, but up to now they have not been successful with prisoners held in Brittany.'

'Now that the French are so victorious against other countries,' Ross said, 'it may be that they will be able to turn

202

their attention to controlling their own.'

Nevertheless he did not privately rejoice as much as Caroline and Demelza were doing. The Admiralty list and the letter only confirmed what he had discovered from Clisson six months ago. In the meantime, and quite recently, he had received reports from Brittany of the conditions of the prisoner-of-war camps at Quiberon and elsewhere along the coast. Even if one allowed for a measure of exaggeration, the accounts were horrifying. So, while he showed a pleased face to the two women and joined with them in speculating on Dwight's release, he felt that the chances of their seeing the young surgeon home alive and well were not more than even, and that the urgency to arrange an exchange or a ransom was greater than either of them realized.

CHAPTER FIVE

Ross continued his weekly visits to Agatha until early April. Then one day when he called on her she said:

'They be back.'

'Who? George?' Ross said, startled in spite of himself, for the boldest of us likes to be prepared within himself for trouble.

'Nay. The Chynoweths – the old folk. And Geoffrey Charles and his governess.'

Ross found time to admire her reference to the old folk.

'And George and Elizabeth?'

'Next week or the week after, they say. But they said they'd be home for Easter, and now that's by.'

Ross put his head near to the whiskery old face and shouted: 'You know that when he returns my visits to you must necessarily cease.'

'Aye. Shame on him. Cess to him. Shite take him.' Agatha stroked her black cat while uttering these curses. Ross thought that an earlier generation would have greatly feared her. 'Ross, boy, I've a thing to say afore ye go. Mind you the tenth of August?'

'The tenth? I do not recall it. Oh . . . but it is your birthday . . .'

Agatha's mouth quivered above her purple gums. 'My hundredth. That's what I been living for. No Poldark hasn't ever reached it afore. Nor none beyond ninety, so far as I know. There was Rebecca, Charles Vivian's sister, but she died of a bursten and rupture well afore her ninety-first. And she were the eldest by long strides. Till me. And now Agatha Poldark's going on for a hundred! Four months more, that's all I got to stay. Think on that!'

Ross made appropriate noises. The old woman's mouth was working with excitement as if she were going to have a fit.

'So . . . my son. On the 10th August I be going to have a party. Eh? Eh? What's that you say? A *party*! Twill cost no money to that tight-fisted gale that Elizabeth's wed. I've got *money*. Not much, mind, but more'n enough for that . . . My father left me a little nest egg in three per cents an' it's been adding on ever since. I give some to Francis last week but there's still some left.' She gasped and rested a minute, trying to get her generations right and resting and gathering her strength for the next effort. Her whiskers seemed to bristle. 'George can't stop me. Twould get all about the county that he'd stopped me. I'll have all my friends – them I've not seen for years and years. And I'll have the neighbours, all the neighbours, and – and a big cake. You and your little bud'll be invited. And that tall long lean thin red-haired sprig of a gel you brought here Christmas. And your childer – I want to see your childer afore I die. So mind that. Mind August tenth!'

Ross patted her head. It was the longest speech he remembered from Aunt Agatha. 'I'll remember. We shall come. Now rest or you will tire yourself. See, the weather's relenting at last, and in another week or so it will be warm enough for you to get out in the garden.'

On his way downstairs he met a girl he had not seen before.

'Miss Chynoweth?'

Morwenna had a rather unusual short-stepped tripping walk, which probably came from being unable to see very far ahead of her. She peered up at him.

'Mr Pol – Captain Poldark, is it?'

'You are just from Truro, I believe?'

'We came on Tuesday. Just after the holiday.'

So this was the girl Drake had a taking for. Not pretty. But demure. And fine eyes. But they were a little swollen.

'You are all well in Truro?'

'Some have had influenza. And baby Valentine has been

dangerously ill in rickets but is better. Thank you.'

Had she been fretting for Drake? 'I have just been visiting Miss Agatha Poldark. She keeps in fair fettle, considering her age.'

'Yes. I thought she looked better than when we left. She has stood the weather uncommon well.'

'While you have all been away,' Ross said, 'I have visited her weekly. The servants were becoming idle and neglectful. Such a visit was necessary as there was no one of her family left behind.'

Morwenna nodded but did not speak.

'Now you are back I must discontinue these calls. As you will know, Mr Warleggan does not welcome me here. So this will be my last visit. Can I rely on you to see that Miss Poldark is well cared for until Mr and Mrs Warleggan return?'

She flushed very easily. 'Of course, sir. And Mr Chynoweth is about. We shall make sure that she is not neglected.'

'Or left entirely alone.'

'Or left entirely alone.'

'Thank you.' He took her hand. It was cool and clammy. She was not at all like Elizabeth. No poise. None of that delicate patrician beauty.

'Good-bye, Miss Chynoweth.'

She answered him very quietly and watched him go.

It had been a desperate two weeks. Her first refusal to accept the arranged marriage had taken place with Elizabeth only on the morning following the evening when she was first told of it. Dry-eyed now, she had argued as rationally as she knew how. Deeply appreciative of their thoughts for her future . . . great opportunity, she knew . . . position in society . . but marriage was something she was not yet prepared for. In one year, two years perhaps, even if then so favourable a match was not forthcoming. She was happy with them; indeed she might never marry; she had thought often of going into a convent. At present she wished more than anything to stay with Geoffrey Charles. It seemed vitally important to her that she should finish her task with him before even thinking of anything else.

She detected in Elizabeth's eyes for the first time a flicker of sympathy – though it might have been there before, it had not shown. The meeting ended in a deadlock but with just a gleam of hope.

Not so her interview with George that evening. In twelve months they had had few direct personal conversations with each other, and this was like no other that had preceded it. Although Elizabeth was present she took virtually no part. He did not storm, he was not even angry – she would almost have preferred it had he been so. He just casually, politely but authoritatively, swept her objection aside. He might have been her father announcing that he had found her a place in a school and she was to start next month. That she preferred to stay at home and play with the baby was understandable enough, but that was not how the world went on. It was necessary to grow up.

She found herself arguing against something that in George's eyes had already happened. She had been given in marriage. Her place in the school was booked. Tears, fears, some distress was natural. It would pass. Mr Osborne Whitworth was calling at four tomorrow and would take tea with her alone.

Panic nearly led her into complete defiance; but on the brink she was intimidated by George's authority. He was thirty-five, rich, influential and an altogether formidable personality. She was only just eighteen, scared of him, and a long way from home. She tried instead to hedge. She knew, she said, nothing yet of what her mother would say, and after all it was her mother whose word carried the most weight with her. In any case, whatever her mother said, she needed *time*. She needed a month, two months, three months perhaps. Time to adjust herself to thoughts of marriage. Time for this, that and the other: she invented excuses, some of them reasonable, others that would not bear examination.

George did not bother to examine them. He was content enough that he had made the first breach, that she had made the first concession. Thereafter it would all follow as it had been planned. His only concession to the objections was to call the Rev. Mr Whitworth into his office for five minutes when he came to take tea the following day and to warn him that his bride-to-be was a little high-strung and should be given time to adjust herself.

Ossie was not nervous. Neither was he at all high-strung. A sturdy young man, with heavy legs that might have belonged to a sailor, he was well aware of his good looks, his good birth, his good voice and his wide knowledge of the most fashionable clothes for men. His appointment to the church had only marginally curbed the last of these attributes, and not at all the first three. His experience of women had been not unextensive but had been mainly confined to the jelly houses of Oxford and to his first wife, on whom he had bestowed his attentions twice weekly until she died of it. Since Truro was a small place and his face and his cloth already too well known, he had need of another wife for more personal reasons than the care of his two motherless children.

From the start he had found Morwenna a pleasant person to lead out on to the floor for a gavotte, and to sit in a drawing-room with and be handed cakes. He did not in fact care all that much for her face – though he admitted that her modest expression was very suitable for a cleric's wife. But her body was a different matter. For some days now he had been thinking carefully of the swell of her breasts under the prim grey muslin blouse, of the slimness of her waist, of her long young legs, of her surprisingly small, slippered feet. He had an odd partiality for women's feet. The thought of the possession of all this, the exclusive and personal possession of all this, had recently interfered with the concentration of his prayers. But of course he had not allowed such thoughts to gain any hold until he was sure also of the personal possession of £3000.

He felt now that marriage to this young woman at an early date was necessary to clear his mind of the sick fancies circulating there.

But the meeting with his affianced bride did not go off quite so well as he had expected it to. Once he had her alone, which privilege was allowed him immediately after tea, he continued his monopoly of the conversation, at first on a casual note, telling her in detail of a hand of whist he had played the night before. If his partner had not led the king of spades on the second round he would scarce have known which way to look for it, but thereafter, by drawing trumps, they had made twelve tricks between them – and their opponents had held ace, king of hearts and ace of diamonds. He had cleared £18 on the evening, and none so down in the mouth as Willie Hick, who never could bear to be the loser!

Ossie laughed long at the memory and, to be polite, Morwenna briefly joined in. Did Miss Chynoweth play whist, he asked? Miss Chynoweth did not. This depressed him a moment, but then, recollecting the object of his call, he resumed on a lower and more romantic note. He told

Morwenna that she must overcome her surprise that he had noted her in the way he had, but that in fact ever since he set eyes on her at the Cardew ball he had been determined to make her his own. Unlike Sam Carne, Osborne Whitworth seldom introduced God into his daily conversation, but at this point he stated that he felt God had guided him to accept Mr Warleggan's invitation to the ball when all his normal instincts, as a recently bereaved husband and father, had urged him to refuse. 'Desolate as I then was,' he said, 'I felt you had been sent into my life to comfort me, to console me, to be my new helpmeet and my wife, and to be the mother, the new mother, for Sarah and Anne. It was a happy day for me when I found my sentiments returned. You will find the vicarage warm and comfortable. A little neglected – there is dry rot in two rooms and one of the chimneys needs renewal – but now we shall soon put that right.'

While saying this he had been standing with his back to the fire, hands behind his back and the tails of his cut-away silk coat hanging forward over his arms. His violet gloves were on the table beside him. Morwenna struggled to find something to say. Her impulse was to burst into tears and run from the room; but she had been treated so much as a child in her arguments with George and Elizabeth that she would not now on any account act like one. Instead, without looking at him, she muttered something to the effect that she was not at all sure that his sentiments *were* returned. It was the nearest she could get, she found, to an outright rejection. Being a modest girl, in whom further modesty had been instilled as a Christian virtue by both her father and her mother, she found herself complimented against her will by his proposal; and although she was adamantly against it, she racked her brains as to how she could convince Ossie that she was not for him, without hurting his feelings.

It didn't work. Ossie so far unbent from his position as master of their future destinies as to take her hand and kiss it. 'It is a natural feeling, Miss Chynoweth – Morwenna – it is a natural feeling. All women – all good women, that is – come to marriage with some hesitation and shyness. But the sentiment will *be* returned, I do assure you. Not only am I a clerk in holy orders, I am a man of feeling. You have nothing to fear from me. Our love will grow together. I shall tend it and *see* that it grows.'

Morwenna withdrew her hand. During this avowal she had

glanced up at her suitor's face and seen a momentary expression in his eyes that a more experienced woman would have recognised as lust. She saw it only briefly and as something rather startling and dislikeable. Stumbling and embarrassed, she began again. Part hostile towards him, part apologetic, she told him that she did not in fact return his sentiments at all, and that she feared she might never do so. Then, seeing his face again and aware that she had at least partly conveyed her meaning to him through the thick haze of his conceit, she timidly compromised and said that more than anything she needed time. It was the old plea, that which she had put forward to George. Time, to her, meant everything. She felt if the momentum of the marriage arrangement could only be arrested, then it might creak to a halt in due course of its own accord. To put off, in her weak position, to postpone was all.

So Osborne went away, a dissatisfied and somewhat offended man. He did not, of course, take the refusal too seriously; he only blamed George and Elizabeth for not having sufficiently prepared the ground. He knew that it would all come right in the end. But he was aware, dimly aware, that there was a core of resolve in this slim, shy girl, and that it had to be tactfully overcome before a wedding day could be fixed. For the moment he would have to be content with his sick fancies.

Thereafter another terrible week for Morwenna. A letter came from her mother to Elizabeth saying how delighted she was at the news. The two elder Chynoweths, appraised of the situation late in the day – as they were about most things – approved the match and added their congratulations on its arrangement. The only grain of comfort was that her mother wrote in her letter that she had not received her usual letter from her daughter that week and was awaiting it.

The decision to let her return to Trenwith with Mr and Mrs Jonathan Chynoweth and Geoffrey Charles was taken late one evening. Elizabeth said to George: 'Why not let her go? Perhaps she has been too close-confined here since Christmas. It cannot surely affect the match for a few weeks. After all Osborne has only been a widower since the beginning of December.' And George had agreed. He did not want to drive the girl into some act of outright despair; absence from William Osborne might make the heart grow fonder. But in fact he was thinking more of Osborne's heart than the girl's. He perceived that the bait of £3000 was becoming no less important because it could not yet be swallowed; and he also saw that Mr Whitworth's eyes followed the girl about wherever she went. For his own part, Conan Godolphin, Ossie's uncle, had been in the news at court, so George was more than ever attached to the match. On neither side was it likely to cool, or be allowed to cool by the other.

Back in Trenwith, away from the now oppressive presence of George and Elizabeth, Morwenna felt as if she were starting a new life – or at least re-entering an old one. Freedom to breathe, freedom to think again without thinking of her suitor, freedom to ride and walk and read and talk: for the moment she was able to banish the threat of a loveless marriage, to banish the threat even of making a decision. Here she wrote a long letter to her mother explaining everything – or nearly everything – and asking that she might come home for a week before anything was finally decided.

She kept carefully to the grounds of Trenwith, avoiding any contact or thought of contact with a young man whom she knew she should not see again. Any decision about Osborne Whitworth must be made without regard to a chance friendship which had grown up here in the autumn months of last year – for she knew that, whatever else, *that* held no future for her. Geoffrey Charles, of course, as soon as he returned was clamant to go and seek out Drake; but she made one excuse after another to put him off, and then on the third day fate came to her aid, for the boy jumped off his pony and cut his ankle badly on a stone.

Thereafter she walked and rode alone for a space. She went about her ordinary business, teaching Geoffrey Charles, sitting reading to him, visiting Aunt Agatha – a little more often as a result of her meeting with Ross – seeing to her aunt and uncle, sitting alone after they had gone to bed wondering what she should do with her life and fearing a tap at the window, a low whistle in the dark.

It came on Sunday about the usual time. She saw him first walking up the drive – in broad daylight – without any kind of concealment, walking up in his Sunday clothes, his dark barragan trousers, his green velvet jacket, his pink striped neckcloth. He came on, tall, shabby, lithe, walking straight up to the front door as if he had been invited.

Heart thumping, mouth dry, she met him at the door. She was anxious lest he should pull at the bell and draw a servant, now far more concerned that this visit should be a secret than she had ever been before. He had come to the side door most of those dark afternoons of November and December; he had come at Geoffrey Charles's invitation; he was of a low class but respectable; if Geoffrey Charles chose to invite him there was really no reason why he should not do so; his relationship with Demelza Poldark made him at once both more and less *persona grata*. Any blame attaching to her, Morwenna, in the friendship could charitably be put down to inexperience on her part.

Now it was no longer so. Osborne Whitworth's proposal had jolted her out of her young girl's day-dreams, her excuse for irresponsibility. In three months she had grown up.

'Drake!' she said, and cleared her throat. 'We did not expect you tonight!'

He looked at her face eagerly, attentively, his own face alight with pleasure, but curious, searching, wanting to renew his recollection of her, only half taking in her unwelcoming expression.

'Miss Morwenna . . .'

'Have you come to see Geoffrey Charles?' she asked. 'Unfortunately he has cut his ankle bad. I do not think –'

'I know,' he said. 'They told me. That's why I come.'

She knew that she should shut the door on him but lacked the courage to do it without a few words of excuse. Then a noise from the direction of the stables made her aware again of how visible they were here, and she drew back and let him in, shut the big door, stood with her back against the door.

'Miss Morwenna, tis a brave sight to see ye. Is the boy abed? Can I go up?'

'I do not think . . .'

He stopped. 'What do you not think?'

She stumbled over the words, not meeting his gaze. 'Of course he would like to see you, but I know his mother would not approve . . . Since we went away . . .'

His own face had fallen. He was still watching her closely. 'But she an't back yet.'

'No . . . no . . . Go on up.'

She followed him up the stairs, along the narrow dark passage to the turret room. When he saw who came in, Geoffrey Charles let out a whoop of delight and put his arms round Drake and gave him a great hug. So they sat for half an hour, talking, chattering, laughing and forgetting the unforgettable, ignoring what could not be ignored. In this company Morwenna's studied calm, her controlled detachment did not survive long. Soon she was laughing and talking with the other two. The release, the relief, was the breath of life to her.

Geoffrey Charles showed Drake his new drawings, and Drake told them about how they were beginning to clear the land at Wheal Maiden to put up a new meeting house there. 'Ye know, by that chimney on the hill afore ye go down to Nampara proper.' Most of the time he appeared to be talking to Geoffrey Charles, but most of the time his eyes strayed to Morwenna's face, searching and searching. And most of the time she kept her eyes averted; but just once and again she glanced up, and then they looked at each other. And they looked at each other.

Talking of what had gone was good, but shadows crept on to the edges of their sentences as Geoffrey Charles made plans for the coming summer. Drake was to show him where the toads lived over at Marasanvose, so that he could bring some back with him and keep them in the stables. Drake must take them both again to the Abbey caves. Drake must show them his own cottage and the plans for the new library at Nampara. And he, Geoffrey Charles, would show Drake where the choughs nested on the cliff edge, also the rocks where samphire grew and was gathered by the village children, and where two had fallen to their deaths.

At length Drake rose to go. Geoffrey Charles's wound had been well bound by Dr Choake and he was not supposed to leave his room for another week, so they could make no plans to meet out of doors, but Drake promised he would come again on Sunday next at the same time. If Mr and Mrs Warleggan returned before then word would be sent to him not to come. Geoffrey Charles kept him another ten minutes and still called repeatedly after him as he left the room.

'I'll see you out,' Morwenna said.

So they went downstairs together and in silence. There had been flecks of snow in the wind again today, and the sky was as grey as their thoughts. For all laughter had gone from them when they left the room. As they reached the hall Drake said: 'Can ee spare me a minute?'

She nodded and led the way through the big parlour to the little sitting room beyond. It was the shabby little room where they had met all through the winter, and it had become almost a private sitting room for the girl and the boy since she came to the house. It was one on which George had not yet turned his renovating attention. The dusty curtains were of a heavy blue velvet and pulled together on rings gone rusty with the salt air. The old turkey carpet showed its threads by the door and in front of the fireplace. The furniture was the jetsam of other rooms, a table or a chair put here when it was replaced elsewhere. Yet it was comfortable; a bright fire burned; a newspaper lay open on the table beside ink and quill; pairs of stockings of Geoffrey Charles's hung over a chair back waiting to be darned; miniatures of Morwenna's father and mother stood on the mantelshelf.

He said: 'You don't want for me to come here no longer?'

He was standing with his back to the door as if guarding it. She went across and crouched by the fire.

'That would be better for us both,' she said.

'Why? What's changed? What's changed ee, Morwenna?'

She stirred the fire with an iron poker too big for the grate. 'Nothing has changed. It is just better that we should no longer meet.'

'And – and Geoffrey Charles? Am I to see naught of he?'

'I will . . . explain to him that it is better this way. I think soon, perhaps, he will be going away to school, and then it will be easy to forget.'

'Twill not be easy fur me to forget.'

'No.' She nodded, still crouching, her back curved like a bow and as taut. 'It will not be easy for you.'

'And you? For you, Morwenna. What 'bout that?'

'Oh,' she said. 'It will be easy for me. I shall go away too.'

He came slowly over and stood by the mantelshelf, awkward, clumsy, his carefree, independent, boy's face constricted into new lines. 'That edn true. Tell me it edn true.'

She stood up and moved away. Once before they had stood too close by a fire. 'Of course it is true. This casual . . . acquaintance should never have begun. I am afraid I allowed Geoffrey Charles to get out of hand.'

'Mebbe you allowed me to – to get out of hand.'

'Yes,' she said indistinctly, 'Yes, I did. It was not at all proper. Please forgive me for having allowed it to happen, and now go.'

There was a long silence between them. She thought, if he doesn't go, if he doesn't go soon . . .

He said: 'Morwenna, I'll go if you'll look at me when you tell me.' He had come up behind her again.

She looked out on the courtyard of the house. The grass

was now cut, the edges tidy, the old pump removed and a modern marble statue put in its place, but she saw none of this. Another impediment was at present added to her shortness of sight.

'These months,' said Drake. 'These months I've thought of naught else. Working, eating, praying, sleeping, ye've never been absent. You're everything in the world. Day and night. Sun and moon. Wi'out you tis nothing, nothing.'

'I think,' she said, 'that you should go.'

'Tell me, then. Look at me and tell me to go.'

'I have told you.'

'But not looking at me, so that I can see the truth in your eyes.'

'The truth . . . Oh, what is that? I am just saying that you should leave me.'

'And I cann't believe the words till I know what's in your heart.'

She half choked. 'The heart, Drake? Do you suppose that this has anything to do with the *heart*? That is not the way the world works. But because we are in the world – *of* it – we have to keep to its – its rules and laws. If you don't know that already, you must learn.'

'That's not what I'm waiting t'learn.'

'It is all I can tell you.'

'No . . . That's not all, Morwenna. Just – just look at me. Just show me your heart and tell me to go.'

She hesitated and then turned, her eyes blind with tears.

'Don't go, Drake . . . At least, not just yet. Oh, Drake . . . *please* don't go.'

CHAPTER SIX

By the spring most of the larger houses were distributing corn, but their own supplies were scarcely more than enough for their own needs. Nor was it available to buy, even to people with the money to pay for it, for with the European ports closed against them, the ships could not import the grain. In London the death rate was higher than in any year since the Great Plague of 130 years ago. Many were ill in Sawle and Grambler of a strange digestive complaint that could have derived from an exclusive diet of underbaked barley bread and weak tea. Typhus still spread a little but something seemed to hold its hand, as if waiting for the better weather.

Undeterred by all the distress and by other calls on their time, Sam and Drake Carne and a dozen other men, in such little spare daylight as they had, had begun to clear a site at Wheal Maiden. Every day Ross regretted that he had encouraged them, but every day he had to admit a grudging admiration of their determination. A roster was kept and each man worked his specified number of hours. Sometimes passing by he heard them singing hymns as they worked. Sometimes the women worked. Sam had even succeeded in recruiting a few of the destitute miners from Wheal Leisure to give him a hand. Payment was in Heaven, except for the occasional cup of tea.

One day Ross had gone to see Caroline, who was now supporting six French émigrés at Killewarren, and Demelza had been trying to sow some hollyhock seeds, to replace those which had not survived the winter. Sir John Trevaunance had advised her that these were best started in boxes of sandy soil and planted out later. She was not far from the lilac tree beside the front door when she saw a man coming down the valley on a pony which was several sizes too small for him. As he clattered across the stream he took off a battered hat and raised it to her. She saw that his other hand – the hand which held the reins – was an iron hook.

'Morning, Mrs. Morning, Ma'am.' He was not quite sure of her position. 'Be you Mrs Poldark?'

'Yes.'

'The Cap'n's wife?'

She nodded. He smiled, showing a mouthful of decayed teeth, and stepped down. It was no more than a step. He was a very big man, middle-aged, hawk-faced despite a flattened nose. He had probably been handsome once, before the great disfiguring scar.

'Be the Young Cap'n in?'

'Do you mean Captain Ross Poldark? No, he's from home.'

'Ah . . . Well I'm glad to meet ye, ma'am. Me name's Bartholomew Tregirls. The cap'n will've spoke of me.'

She said, yes, yes, Ross had, but privately she could not remember much. An old companion of some sort who had sold them the pony . . .

Tholly soon enlightened her. Close friend of the old captain, Cap'n Joshua, friend and companion of Cap'n Ross when he was but a tacker; many's the wild time they'd had together: line fishing, wrestling, rum-running, chasing the girls, gambling; all innocent, mind, but wild, wild in a sort of way. Towering over her – and she was not short – he told her this, while his ice-grey, canny eyes summed her up in a half-respectful, half-impudent fashion. Probably he had heard of her origins and was trying to discover from the expressions on her face whether Ross had married a saucy piece who would give as good as she got and would be out for a lark herself, or an ambitious climber who would be so careful of her new position that she would try to freeze his reminiscences to death.

Demelza nodded and smiled and said, yes, and no, and indeed, and fancy; while she made her own assessment. Then she invited him in to take tea. He was pleased at this, if not by the beverage offered, and followed her in and sat like a bear in the parlour, looked at askance by Jane Gimlett who brought in the tea. But he was still not quite sure where he stood, because his hostess did not quite fit into either of the expected patterns.

For her part Demelza summed him up as a dangerous man – because he looked to her like a man whose regard for person, law or property was conditioned only by his personal need. He looked a pirate.

Tregirls hitched up his green breeches, took up the cup and its saucer, and looked at them as if they were curiosities from another world and he wasn't sure whether to bite them. Then he took a gulp of the contents.

'I warned Cap'n Ross as I might come around these parts again, these parts being me own parts as you might say; born and bred in St Ann's; and I've two children in the neighbourhood, I thought t'see something of 'em now I'm off of the sea for good. Lobb, my eldest, and Emma, my youngest. Not as there ain't others about too, but I don't acknowledge they.' He set the cup down with a clack.

'Ross will be that sorry to have missed you,' Demelza said.

'Oh, I'll call 'gain, if you'll allow. I'm not to be far away, and tis more or less permanent, I conject. I'm staying with Sally Chill-Off.'

'With who?'

'You know, her as keeps the kiddley in Sawle. Don't say you don't know the Widow Tregothnan.'

'Oh, yes . . . we used to have – perhaps you remember Jud Paynter?'

'Jud? That I do. Walks like a gelded bulldog –'

'Well, he is there most nights when he has the money. I wonder you have not seen him.'

'I only been there three days, mistress. Jud!' Tholly leaned back and stretched out one leg. 'That bring back the memories. My grandfather's ghost, it do! And Prudie! Great lump of caff she were. Like a house. They played the old Cap'n up, I tell ye. The worms not got her neither?'

'Not neither,' said Demelza, sipping her tea.

'I'll never know where Jud picked her up. Came back one day wi' she riding on a pony. The old Cap'n took her in. More'n I'd've done. Great cab of a woman.' A hint of old strife moved in his voice.

'She's no smaller,' said Demelza.

Tregirls hunched his shoulders and coughed. He said: 'I got tissick. It come on sudden and as sudden go.' As he shifted in his seat, a thin bag round his waist rattled, and he grimaced and grinned. 'Know what that be, ma'am? Bones of me arm and hand. Carry 'em everywhere, even in the bed. I been at sea eight year – two year a prisoner of the French – fightin' here, fightin' there. Killed more than I can count. And not a splinter, not a scratch. But this – ye see this?' He indicated the puckered scar. 'Done by a jealous father, just over the hill. And this –' He held up the iron hook. 'Crushed by a gangway, in port. Just coming alongside and they ran the gangway out, and my arm were in the way. Dangling it was when they pulled me clear. Surgeon had it off in a twink. Saw, saw through the bone; then the tar barrel. No time even to be properly drunk. Makes me sweat o'nights even now.'

'It makes me sweat too,' said Demelza politely.

Tregirls threw back his head and laughed. 'Well, thank ye, mistress, for the kind thought. And why do I keep 'em? Ye don't ask me what most folk ask me, why do I keep 'em?'

'Why do you keep them?'

'Ah, tis too late now to ask that question! But I'll tell ye, whether or no.' He hunched his shoulders against the next cough. 'I'm not a praying man, not by no means. I says "God bless" when I wakes up and "Amen" when I lies down, that be all. But I reckon there's somethin' to it, and I reckon at the Last Trump, I'll be in me grave, and they'll jerk me out like I was a stranded fish, and what'll I do if all me bones is not complete? Think you I want to go up to Heaven – or even down to Hell – with a hook for a hand? No, ma'am, not me, ma'am; so I carries the bones along wherever I goes,

217

and I reckon they'll be buried with me. When will Cap'n Ross be home?'

'Not until after dinner.'

He got slowly up, bending his head like a man used to low ceilings. His whole frame seemed to dominate the room. 'Thank ye, ma'am. Tell the young Cap'n I'll be back, mebbe tomorrow, mebbe in a day or two.'

'I will.'

She followed him to the door, where he blinked in the watery sunlight. His pouch rattled again. ''Twas done less'n two year gone, but the bones've cleaned up like they was new. Stank a bit at first, but that's all gone. Like to see them, would you?'

'Next time,' Demelza said.

He grinned at her, showing his ravaged teeth. 'That were a fine horse I sold you.'

'Pony.'

'Well, call it what ye will, Cap'n Poldark got it dirt cheap. Would ye be having a fancy to buy a bull-pup? Finest pedigree. Finest for bull baiting. Three months old. Or a ferret? You need one.'

'I'll ask Captain Poldark,' she said.

He strode over his small, ill-kept pony, put on his hat, took it off again to her, and then kicked the animal with one heel and they began to proceed slowly up the valley.

Demelza watched him until he was out of sight. Then she went in. Jane Gimlett was clearing the tea.

'Who were that, ma'am?' she said. 'If tis not rude t'ask.'

'A sort of a ghost,' said Demelza. 'I think . . . A sort of a ghost.'

Ross said: 'My ivers.' An expression she had only heard Prudie use before. 'What did he want?'

'To see you. Chiefly, I believe. Perhaps also to see me.'

'You?'

'Well, yes. To see what the Young Cap'n had married.'

He laughed. 'Likely enough. I do not suppose he went away with a negative impression.'

'I don't know rightly what that means, Ross.'

'Well, are you ever negative?'

'I felt a small matter so this morning.'

'Did you like him?'

She said quietly: 'My husband's friends are mine.'

'That was not what I asked.'

'You see? I am being negative.'

'Not a bit. You're being evasive, which is quite different.'

She thought about it. 'Ross, last year two people came out of my past. This year, if one comes out of yours . . .'

'Let's hope he is not going to be as much trouble to us as Sam and Drake! . . . But it is typical of him that he has found a berth with Sally Chill-Off. I wondered, when I saw him last and he said he wanted to come home . . . But to find a warm widow who has been a widow too long, and one with a beer shop where he can make himself doubly useful – that is the perfect solution!'

'And he is breeding bull-pups and ferrets and who knows what else besides.'

'I believe you do not like him after all,' Ross said, teasing her.

'I do not think I altogether like having old bones rattled in my face to see if I will shiver.'

'It is his way.'

'With women?'

'Perhaps. He has had many, and that as often as not blunts a man's perceptions for women, for particular women, for the exceptional woman anyway. What did you talk of, when you had exhausted such raillery?'

'His children. He has not seen them for I don't know how many years.'

'I do. It is thirteen. They were brought up in the poorhouse.'

'He said his daughter worked for the surgeon.'

'Yes, she's a kitchen maid at Choake's. She's like him, tall and bold and good-looking. The rumour is that she has had one man after another; but I suppose she must somehow continue to keep it circumspect, as Polly Choake would not have her in the house if it were done too blatant. The boy is like his mother, small and quiet, married, with a brood of children; he works a tin stamp in Sawle Combe. When he left the poor house he was apprenticed to Jose, the farmer; but when he was seventeen he was convicted with another lad of stealing apples from Mr Trencrom's orchard and sent to Bodmin for a month's hard labour. But working on the treadmill ruptured him and so he has not been good for heavy work – '

'Ruptured him?'

'Yes. It is necessary on the wheel, you know, to take fifty steps a minute, and three hours a day, which is the usual, imposes a strain. It is not an uncommon thing to happen. But Lobb Tregirls has always since looked a man with a grudge against life, and I cannot see him welcoming his father back after so many years of neglect.'

A screech owl was squealing by the stream in the evening rain. Ross said: 'Did Tregirls say he had been a prisoner of the French? I wonder if he speaks the language.'

'He only tried his own on me – which in a way, Ross, was sufficient. But why do you ask?'

'This venture.'

'Ah . . . what has been decided?'

'How did you know anything had been?'

'By the length of time you were there. And by your face when you came home.'

He laughed briefly. 'More by the second than the first, I would suppose. Talk is cheap, and there has been enough of it these last months.'

'But now it is to mean something?'

'It would seem so. The Government has agreed to finance the expedition and to provide it with transports and a covering force of British warships. The French when landed will be under Comte Joseph de Puisaye as we expected. We do not know exactly when as yet but it will be during the light weather and when there is a best chance of calm seas.'

'But why do you ask about Tregirls?'

'Well, when the expedition lands, if it is successful, a few English may go ashore.'

'I trust – I hope you are not going to become involved.'

He loosened his stock, pulling at it with a finger against his neck.

'In all honesty, love, I had no thought to be. Not personally. Certainly not at first . . .'

'You have a wife and two children.'

'Yes, oh, yes. I am not unmindful. But let me repeat – there is no English army going, nor any intention of sending one. Five or six thousand French will land, with naval support, and some marines to strengthen them in the early stages. Then great quantities of munitions will be put ashore to supply the Royalists who will flock to join the invaders. *If* the landing establishes itself then some English may be of help in maintaining supplies, establishing a commissariat ashore, or maintaining communications with England. But this is not what might influence me in a choice. Quimper, where Dwight is interned, is only perhaps two score miles from where the landing is likely to be made. When the Royalist army takes Quimper Dwight will be released. It would be of value to him – perhaps more than value – if some of his own people were on hand at the time.'

Demelza put a paper quill in the fire and from it began to light the candles. In the kitchen Jeremy was crying, but for once the sound did not send her hurrying out.

'And if the landing fail?'

'If it fails it will not be likely to fail before Quimper is reached. Believe me, it is vital that that prison be sprung.'

'You do not think even if they are left alone that the prisoners will be – what is the word?'

'Repatriated. Yes, it may be. Those who are left alive.'

Light grew reluctantly. Demelza went to pull the curtains, and he helped her with them. This year even the birds had been reluctant to begin their song. In the wet, chill evening light, the lights of the engine house up the valley were remote and unreal. She pulled the last curtain.

Ross said: 'Have you warned Drake about his friendship with Miss Chynoweth?'

'No. Objections don't often stop love affairs, Ross.'

'I know. But I believe George and Elizabeth are due back this week. I am anxious that there should be no renewal of the quarrel between the houses.'

'I will ask Sam,' she said. 'This week I'll ask him if they are still seeing each other.'

Betsy Maria Martin came in to light the candles but, finding this done, prepared to withdraw. 'What is amiss with Master Jeremy?' Demelza asked.

'If ee plaise, ma'am. He wouldn' eat 'is bread'n milk, and Mrs Gimlett were tryin' to best him and he woudn' be bested, so he duffs 'is spoon in the bowl and splutters milk all 'bout the kitchen, so Mrs Gimlett, she gives he a tap wi' 'er hand and he didn' like'n.'

'No, he wouldn't,' said Demelza. 'Thank you, Betsy.'

The little girl left.

Demelza said: 'What did you mean, Ross, those that are left alive?'

'What? Oh, in the prison . . . Well, as I told you.'

'Perhaps you have not told me quite all.'

'I have heard twice more but have not harrowed you with the details – nor especially Caroline.'

'Well, tell me now.'

He stared at her. 'There was a Dutchman – released in

February, I think because France and the Netherlands are no longer at war. He spent six months at Quimper, and saw many English brought in. One seaman was shot for trying to peer through a hole in the gate of the prison, and his body was left there for two days. The prisoners live on black bread and water, and although there is ample water in the well they are allowed only to visit it twice a day and for long had no receptacles to store it in. Many had been marched almost naked from where they were landed, after having been stripped of their belongings and beaten. Any serious misdemeanour is punished by death, and any general disorder in the camp means neither food nor water for all for thirty hours. No medical supplies, of course, and no blankets. Officers treated worse than the other ranks because they represent the ruling class in England. A French peasant woman, who though pregnant, attempted to pass a bowl of soup to some prisoners was bayoneted in the belly by the guard. The guard was afterwards congratulated by his commanding officer for this act. It is a long story and there is much more. Typhus, influenza, scorbutic fever and most diseases rampant. Dwight will be busy, if he still survives.'

Demelza knelt on the green velvet sofa beside Ross and pushed back her hair to look at him. 'He had survived until February.'

'Yes. He had survived until February.'

A rising wind was now blowing the rain against the windows. Water gurgled in one of the new gutters.

She said: 'I do not understand, Ross. What is it that gets into men? Is it the French who are special savages?'

'No. Though they have a history of civil war and bitterness such as we have been lucky enough to avoid.'

'Yes, well . . . but if you look around at men. And I mean women too, of course. If you look around at them, most are not, do not seem, wicked. Folk round here live hard, work hard, are – *rough*. Only a lucky few have the time, the leisure to enjoy life. But all the others, all of them, they do not seem evil. I have not been brought up delicate but I have seen only a little evil. Scarcely – '

'Such as being beaten every night with a belt by your drunken father.'

'Yes, well.' She paused, put out of her stride. 'But that is in drink . . .'

'Or seeing the boys tie Garrick's tail to the tail of a cat for the sport.'

222

'Yes. But that is – they were young, deserved a beating. But I still don't know where the evil comes from that makes men bestial to others like you have told. And her one of his own folk! I shall *never* understand it, Ross.'

He put his hand up to her neck and moved his fingers where the wisps of black hair curled. 'Perhaps it is because you have so little evil in yourself.'

'No, no. I do not think so. That is not what I meant at all. I do not believe ordinary men *have* this evil. Perhaps it is like a fever that blows in the air, like cholera, like the plague; it blows in the air and settles on men – or a town – or a nation – and everyone in it, or nearly everyone, falls a victim.'

He kissed her. 'It is as good an explanation as any I know.'

She withdrew her face an inch to study his expression. 'Do not be amused at me, Ross.'

'I am not amused in the way you suspect. Not in any superior way, believe me. These days I often have a struggle not to feel *inferior* to you, that is in your judgment of human beings.'

'I don't think I have any judgment, at least not to be proud of. But perhaps I am nearer the earth than you. Like Garrick, I can smell a friend.'

'Or an enemy?'

'Sometimes.'

'And Tholly Tregirls?'

'Oh, not an enemy.' She frowned. 'Perhaps a dangerous friend.'

'In what way dangerous? One who could lead me back into my old bad habits?'

'If you went back to your old bad habits, as you call them, you would be the leader, not the one who is led. No, I meant . . . Your loyalties are so strong – maybe too strong. Once a person is your friend he – he is almost above criticism.'

'Perhaps that is a form of egoism.'

'I don't think I know what that means . . .'

'Egoism is thinking a lot of oneself and therefore of one's own opinions. Whether one's opinion is of politics or religion or wine, or just a friend, to the egoist it is equally above dispute.'

She straightened her legs and sat beside him. 'You confuse me, Ross. I only meant that your friendships have caused you trouble in the past and Tholly Tregirls might become dangerous if he fell into trouble here and you was drawn in.'

'Like Jim Carter, eh? And Mark Danielle? And now Dwight Enys?'

She nodded. 'Except that they was all – worth more, I think, than Tholly Tregirls.'

'That is a nice pink bow on your blouse. Is it new?'

'The blouse is new. It has been made by Mrs Trelask.'

'Good. Good . . . Anyway you are a fine one to talk of friendship! As for Tholly, well, let us see what time brings before worrying about him.'

'Oh, him I am not worrying about.'

'It is this enterprise – and Dwight – that frets you?'

'Yes.'

'You would like me to leave it alone?'

She said: 'These candles are all burning crooked. There is still a draught in the room.'

'We need curtains over the door.'

There was silence. She said: 'You have had two reports from Quimper? What was the second one?'

'Only last week. A young midshipman from the frigate *Castor* wrote to his mother in St Austell. It reached her recently and is dated a month later than the letter Caroline had from Dwight.'

'And it is bad?'

'He says he is the only midshipman left alive of the four who were captured, and that he is near a skeleton and has lost all his hair from illness. He says – and I do not remember the precise words but I cannot ever forget the sense – that it makes one's heart ache to see our men, without money, without clothes, worn down by sickness and emaciated to the last degree, fighting over the body of a dead dog which they sometimes pick up and devour with the most voracious appetites. The head and pluck of such a dog, he says, will fetch thirty sous any day among his starving compatriots.'

Demelza got up.

'I think Clowance has wakened,' she said. 'I think I can hear her.'

Ross did not move while she walked round the setttee. There she stopped and rested her chin on his head.

'When is the landing to be made?'

'Sometime in June we think.'

'Pray that it prosper.'

CHAPTER SEVEN

George Warleggan was not an impatient man, nor one given to displays of ill-temper if things did not go all his way; and he returned to Trenwith in a fair enough mood. The New Year's Ball had been a fiasco, and some probably laughed about it behind their hands; and the minor matter of the Chynoweth-Whitworth match was held up because of the girl's girlish obstinacy; and his father was smarting – and therefore he was smarting – under another snub from the Boscawens. But there was much to please him also. Most important of all, Dr Behenna's heroic treatment – or Dr Pryce's less heroic sequel – had had its effect, and Valentine was well on in his recovery. Behenna was absolutely certain that if there were any deformity at all it would be so slight as to be unnoticeable.

And Osborne and his mother had accepted an invitation to spend a week at Trenwith in early July, and George felt that after a week in Osborne's company Morwenna would not be able to resist the gentle but firm pressure from all sides. And Warleggan interests, stimulated by a war economy, were prospering as never before. And he had made an important new friend at a dinner at Pendarves last week. And his country house, when he returned to it, looked more distinguished than ever. And next Friday he was to take his place on the bench for the first time.

True enough, the journey here had been very tiresome. The rain, so much a part of a normal Cornish spring (and summer and autumn and winter), had fallen incessantly all day, and once they were off the road the going had become such that twice he had suggested to Elizabeth they should take to the horses and ride on. But Elizabeth, although sick with the pitching and lurching of the coach, had refused to leave Valentine in the sole care of Polly Odgers; and so at last they had got through.

By then it was dark, and then, again like a Cornish spring (and summer and autumn and winter), the weather had suddenly relented and they had reached the house as the clouds cleared and a ravishing full moon rose. The wind had dropped, an owl hooted, the ornamental pond glittered, and the sharp roofs of the house threw Gothic shadows over drive and lawn and bush. And welcoming candles glimmered in the windows.

So Elizabeth had retired to bed and he had supped with the elder Chynoweths, who were not as tiresome as usual, and then he had seen Tom Harry and two of the other senior servants and had received an account of the winter happenings and had himself retired to bed before ten and had slept dreamlessly until six.

When he woke he felt fresh and vigorous and splendidly rested. Elizabeth was still asleep, her beautiful arms thrown in fragile abandon across the pale silk quilted counterpane, so he thought he would steal out without waking her and have his horse got ready for an early ride about the estate. He lay for a few minutes more, drowsily contemplating the blue sky visible between the partly drawn curtains, then slipped out and put on his green frogged dressing coat. He stole into his dressing-room, used the *chaise-percée* he had had installed, and then rang for his valet. It was a truly beautiful morning, even though there might be rain again before the end of the day. Perfect at present for a canter, the air so washed and clear after the muggy cold of Truro . . .

A sound came to his ears. It was a sound he peculiarly disliked, and one he had not expected to hear on his property again. It was particularly annoying after all that had been done last year and the instructions he had left behind. So when his valet came he did not ask for washing water but snapped: 'I want to see Tom Harry.'

The servant, hearing razors in his master's voice, hurriedly left, and in about three minutes there was a tap at the door and Tom Harry, wiping the back of his hand across his mouth, came in. 'Sur?'

'Come here.'

Harry came to stand beside him. 'Sur?'

'Listen. What do you hear?'

Harry listened: 'I don't rightly –'

'Quiet! Listen! There!'

'Frogs? Down thur? My life, I cann't believe'n! Twas –'

'This lake was cleaned last year. Why are they here now?'

'Sur, I dunno! Honest, sur, tis the biggest surprise to me! We was on the look out for 'em in March. You know how they do be'ave, sur.'

'You told me last year. They go away.'

'Yes, sur. D'rectly they've mated and left their spawn

226

be'ind, off they d'go an' live in the fields, specially down by the stream. When we cleared 'em last year, sur, twas summer and we could only clear out the spawn and the tadpoles and the young frogs and toads. No more'n that. Tis not possible to find all the old 'uns – '

'So? What happened in March?'

'Sur, we was on the look-out. Soon as they come back, soon as we 'eard one we catched'n. A score or more we catched. Three times through March. But there's been naught since then. Me and Bilco, we been down most every eve, so there'd be none when you comed, sur. I'll swear there's been no sign for all of this month!'

'I hope,' said George, 'you have performed the other tasks I set you better than this one. Go with Bilco and now clean up that pool.'

'Yes, sur! Right away, sur! I'm that sorry, sur! I just dunno 'ow t's come 'bout.'

When Geoffrey Charles heard of the invasion he let out wild hoots of laughter and went hobbling down to the pool to watch Tom Harry and Paul Bilco bleakly wading about in it looking for the creatures. They had their terriers with them, but neither terrier would go near the toads after first catching one and then rapidly letting it go again: the poison under the skin was more than they could face. Geoffrey Charles, after a brief angry word from George, moderated his laughter indoors, and his attempts to draw Morwenna into the joke brought from her a scarlet-faced refusal to follow his line of thought.

Every now and then throughout the day shouts and running feet and the crack of sticks could be heard. Aunt Agatha, up for a few minutes in the morning, somehow got wind of the work and tottered to a vantage point at a window where she was heard cursing the men and encouraging the toads. For most of the day it rather spoiled George's temper, and the servants whenever possible kept out of his way. Geoffrey Charles would like to have joined in Aunt Agatha's anathemas but did not dare. Every now and then the laughter bubbled in him like an underground spring.

The boy's ankle would not heal. A part of the original wound had skinned over, but a sore place had broken out just above it, and Dr Choake's unguents and ointments had successfully prevented nature from taking its course. The patient had been bled, given severe clysters, kept closely confined to his bed for two weeks and then, when that failed, advised to exercise himself and get about with a stick as much as he could. This advice he gladly accepted, for the ankle sore was only painful when it was touched, and he limped around everywhere, talking, talking, accepting Morwenna's teaching with an ill grace and generally proving himself difficult to control.

George watched all this with a dispassionate eye. Morwenna's halting refusal of Osborne Whitworth had not caused any change in his attitude towards her. It was courteous, slightly without warmth – as it had always been – but not at all unfriendly. He usually got his way, and he had no wish to be thought unreasonable, particularly by Elizabeth. So for the moment nothing more was said. But, unknown to George, much more since Morwenna returned to Trenwith had been done. In three weeks there had been three meetings with Drake, who visited Geoffrey Charles each Sunday and, because he was laid up, had seen her for half an hour alone each evening in the back parlour afterwards.

They had been tense, deeply emotional meetings which had matured their relationship as in a forcing house. She had said nothing to him of any rival, partly because rival was the wrong word. How could Drake be a contestant for her hand? And how could Osborne be a contestant for her love? But in those encounters, conscious of the imminent threat to their meetings, yet unable to escape or to resist the discovery of her own feelings, she had followed her impulses or allowed them freer play than she would ever have done, or could in her right mind have conceived of doing, if Drake had been a young man courting her in a conventional way. To receive a young man and sit with him, unknown to her elders, was compromising to her position and her honour, were he never so eligible. But what she was experiencing in these encounters were fiercely uncompromising emotions which she could hardly begin to control. Was marriage to a man she did not even like, a giving of her body in a manner she did not altogether understand, a sharing of unthinkable intimacy, was that *right* because money and position were suitable and her elders had arranged it? Was marriage to – or at least love for – a clean-limbed, upright, good-living young workman, *wrong* because of a lack of money and a barrier of position and education? Was love wrong, *this* sort of love, this heady, rich, sick-sweet encounter; did it have to be stopped for ever?

At their second meeting they had sat together on the shabby couch and had talked of nothing for perhaps five minutes, and then he had begun to kiss her hand, and afterwards her mouth. The kisses were still chaste, but chastity drowned in the emotions they aroused. They sat on the settee together – out of breath, dizzy, drunk, happy and sad; and lost.

After he had gone she realized that whatever she felt about marriage to Mr Whitworth was no excuse for allowing anyone else this freedom. She had not been brought up in a religious household for nothing, and she had prayed a good deal while in Truro. Chiefly it had been for strength to resist the family pressure; and she wondered guiltily now whether in fact her prayers had been not so much for guidance as for support in a decision she had reached without God's help. She needed strength of another kind now, strength to resist the temptation of the flesh – for that presumably was what it was – strength to keep a balance, strength to be able to continue to resist a marriage that she did not want without giving way to a misalliance which could only lead to disaster.

On all this had come at last a letter from her mother, long, wise, reasoned, but not comforting. Of course she must not marry someone she did not desire to marry. Certainly she must not marry in haste. But . . . and then came the buts. The Dean had died almost penniless. Mrs Chynoweth, through the kindness of a brother, was not destitute, but she had three other daughters to bring up. None of them would have a position. All the girls would have to seek employment as governesses or teachers of some sort. They would be fortunate if they could find so delightfully pleasant a post as hers. And without money their marriageable prospects were not high. Being a governess all one's life was not a future she would *desire* for any of her daughters. But in *her* case, Morwenna's case, the prospect was completely changed. Through the munificence of Mr Warleggan, she was offered a substantial dowry. With it came marriage to a rising young clergyman – of the same persuasion in the church too – not himself penniless and with expectations of more when his mother died, and of good family too. With that marriage came a good vicarage in the most fashionable town in the county, position, a home, children, all, one would think, that a young woman could desire. Such would be her circumstances that it might even be possible in time to have one of her sisters there to care for *her* children. She must think long before refusing all this, and she must pray, as they all would pray, for her guidance.

In the meantime, Mrs Chynoweth ended, she was writing by this post to Elizabeth counselling gentle treatment for her daughter and suggesting a two months' delay before she was asked finally to make up her mind.

So the third meeting with Drake, and a more successful attempt on her part to keep it on an even keel. Wholly successful at first, so that he was hurt and dismayed. But it did not last. In her heart something said: 'If I am to lose this, is it not excusable to indulge it while I may?'

George had returned on the Tuesday, and the toads were cleared throughout Wednesday. Tom Harry said over and over again to George and to everyone else who would listen that he couldn't understand there being so many. George grunted and made no other reply, but he woke in a peace on Thursday and Friday and Saturday mornings. On the Sunday they were back again.

Now a rare anger came upon him and he would have had Tom Harry and Paul Bilco thrashed, had Tom's elder brother not come to him with a special plea and a possible explanation.

'These're not the toads we got rid of last year, sur. These're ordinary toads such as live in the ponds of Marasanvose.'

'So?' said George impatiently.

'So maybe they've walked. Frogs and toads is queer critters. They've spawned here for upwards of 'alf a century. Or else . . . Or else they've been brought yur for devilment.'

George looked at his servant, who was uneasily trying not to look at George.

'Why should anyone wish to do that?'

Harry did not know. It was not his place to furnish explanations. But George had no difficulty in answering his own question. A meeting house taken over for a store shed and its members turned out? A mine closed down and families existing off parish relief? Paths through his estate closed and fences erected? Any or all of these might give rise to a childish wish for reprisal.

'How far is it from Marasanvose?'

'Upwards of three mile to the nearest pond.'

'Could they walk that far?'

'Well, sur, I b'lieve they could, but I don't b'lieve they 'ave.'

George watched the dismal efforts of his servants fishing in the pool again. 'I want a watch kept, Harry,' he said. 'From dusk to dawn. Since it is their responsibility, let Tom and Bilco keep it.'

'Yes, sur. Beg pardon, sur, but if tis some loustering 'ooligans at fault, they'll not prob'ly be back afore next Tuesday or Wednesday. They'll leave a day or so till the next time – just the way they 'ave this.'

'Let a watch be kept every night until they do come. It will do your brother good to stay awake more than is his custom.'

'Yes, sur. Very good, sur.'

So another day passed just like the Wednesday. It was a rare sunny and fresh spring day, but there was little pleasure in the household. Geoffrey Charles got into trouble for constantly leaving the room and hobbling up to his bedroom. He made the plea of a slight stomach ache, which alarmed his mother, but in fact the only cause of his stomach ache was suppressed laughter. Since Morwenna refused to share his suspicions he would have adored to share them with Aunt Agatha, but he quailed at the thought of shouting them into her ear with Lucy Pipe possibly near by.

It was unfortunate that on the same day George should learn of Ross's weekly visits to the house. Elizabeth had heard of them the first day she was back but had thought it more discreet not to inform him. Since he returned George had not seen Aunt Agatha. But this sunny Sunday she was tempted to totter downstairs on Lucy Pipe's arm and she was in the big parlour alone when George passed through it after having been down at the pool seeing how many toads his gamekeepers had caught.

Thereafter ensued a conversation, or perhaps more truly a monologue, which resulted in Elizabeth's being confronted by her husband in a state of white-faced anger.

'Did you know Ross Poldark had been coming here regularly while we have been away?'

She flushed. 'I heard from Lucy. I thought no good would come of making an issue of it.'

'Do you mean by telling me?'

'Yes. It is done. We can take no steps to prevent it now.'

'The impudent, arrogant . . . *Coming* here, when he knows

231

he is not wanted – *forcing* his way in, tramping over my property, wandering about the house, making free of it, ordering and bullying my servants, observing what has been done here, no doubt looking in our desks and sitting in our chairs and – and using the house as if it were his own. By God! It is beyond bearing!'

Elizabeth bent over her child, affecting to study his sleeping face. 'My dear . . .'

'Yes?'

'I share your irritation, and understand it, though I feel it perhaps less acutely. He had no right to enter this house without your permission. But unfortunately we gave him an excuse – no more, but it was an excuse – by leaving Aunt Agatha unattended –'

'There were servants! She has her own maid –'

'If you will let me finish, I was going to say, unattended by any relative or friend. Of course she had servants and a personal maid, and that should have been sufficient, but you do see, don't you, that this offered him just the opportunity to behave in the high-handed fashion that is his wont. Also, without justification, he regards this as his family house because it was his grandfather's and he spent much time here as a boy. He knows it intimately – I believe better than I do – and I have no doubt that if he had been refused admittance at the front door he would have found his way in by some other means. You will remember how he came upon us once.'

'Are you saying that even now, even when we are in residence, I have no means of keeping him out?'

'I do not think he will attempt to come. Not if he is wise. Not if he meant what he said last year. But I think if Agatha lives another year we must make other plans for her. He mustn't be granted the excuse.'

George too looked at his child. Since his illness Valentine had put on weight and, sleeping, looked quite beautiful. Like one of those angels George had seen on the painted ceiling of a mansion in Greenwich. The chubby hands clasped, the lips pursed to blow Gabriel's trumpet. He was dark-haired like his father, but very fair of face, the fine curling hair framed ear and eye and nape. As always this sight gave George pleasure and a sense of achievement. It damped down but could not altogether quell the double angers of the day. He had spoken out against Ross more vehemently than he had ever done before in their married life, and, although he

232

could not quarrel with Elizabeth's sentiments, he would have liked to quarrel with her coolness.

'If Agatha lives another year! No doubt you will be fully aware of what she is planning for August!'

The sleeping child stirred, and Elizabeth pulled up the blanket. 'She told me. I suppose it is natural to wish for such a celebration.'

'In our house. With our servants!'

'It is her house, George. Before me, before you, before Ross. She says she will pay the—'

'Oh, pay! That is the least of it. You must be aware that ever since I came here, since long before we married, she has conducted a personal feud against me. She hates me and my family and resents my possession of what she considers the Poldark house. Yet now she is claiming the right to celebrate her hundredth birthday here, using the house as if it were her own and inviting all her stinking and decrepit friends!'

Elizabeth smiled. 'My dear, all her stinking and decrepit friends are long since dead and gone. Those she would invite are likely to be elderly people of the country whom we know too.'

'And Ross Poldark?'

'Ross Poldark?'

'She has just told me that she intends to ask him to her party.'

Elizabeth put her hands on the side of the cot. 'Oh, dear.'

'And his wife. And his two children.'

Valentine began to stir and woke. The voices had roused him. It was in fact time he was up and fed, but Dr Behenna had advised them to let him sleep on just as long as he could, and had added a little diluted tincture of opium to his nightly medicine to make his advice more effective.

'I don't think he would come,' Elizabeth said.

'You underestimate him.'

She shook her head. 'No. I don't think he will come—not and bring Demelza.'

'Why not? It will give him the opportunity he wishes to add to his recent insult.'

She sighed. 'Perhaps we ought to see it as a chance to mend the old feud.'

He watched her carefully. 'Do you wish that?' It was a very important question to him.

Valentine opened his eyes and saw them looking at him

and suddenly smiled. The illusion of angelic innocence was quite gone. George picked him up at once and held out one of his fingers for the chubby hand to grasp.

Elizabeth said: 'I would be happier if I never saw them again. I would be happier if I were not living so close to them. But if Agatha wishes it, they surely must be invited. And if they come, we surely must attempt to hide our dislike and let the occasion pass as it may. The feud two years ago was the talk of the county. A superficial reconciliation will at least still the remnants of that talk.'

'And that is what you wish?'

'I don't say that it is what I wish. But we cannot deny Agatha her birthday party. It would get about everywhere that we had refused her, and do us more harm than half a dozen feuds.'

Later that morning after his ride, during which, accompanied by Tankard, he visited a number of the outlying hamlets and distributed a little judicious charity, George came back and saw four men still searching with their nets in the pond. A thought came to him. Ross Poldark had frequently been to the house this winter. He had frequently talked to old Agatha up in her room. When the pool was first being cleared of toads Agatha had complained that they were a special kind brought here by her father from Hampshire and that it was disgraceful to have them killed. During her communings with Ross this winter she might well have complained to him. Might he not perhaps be responsible for this wanton and childish practical joke?

It did not seem quite in his line; yet the more George thought about it, the more the events seemed to link together. Who else could know of his personal aversion? Who else, among the village people, would know or care about the clearing of the pool? Who else, certainly, would have the mind to think this thing out, to bring the toads back to the pool especially to greet his return. Although it was a ludicrously childish joke, it showed a degree of thought and ingenuity. And malice.

Round at the stables he sent for Harry Harry.

'Sur?'

'Look now. I want those two men who are going to guard the pool at night reinforced. I want five men. And I want you to be among them.'

'Me, sur? Yes, sur.'

'Understand? Five of you. Every night for the next week.

From dusk till dawn. Cancel your day duties altogether. I want you all to be fresh and alert for a whole night's watch.'

'Yes, sur.'

'And, Harry. If you catch someone and he offers any resistance do not deal with him lightly. Remember he is trespassing, poaching and resisting arrest. A bloodied head and a few broken bones will not be out of keeping at all.'

'No, sur. Rely on me, sur.'

'But . . . try not to rouse the house. We do not wish to upset the ladies.'

CHAPTER EIGHT

There had been a moon last week, but now it rose too late to be of use in the early part of the night. But there were a few stars about in a patchy, windy sky. It was light enough for the purpose and perhaps safer than moving among the high shadows cast by the moon.

Drake slept early and woke about ten just as his brother was soundly in his first sleep. It was difficult to quarrel with Sam, and indeed there had been no real quarrel between them from the beginning of this affair. Only grief. Only sadness. Only regret, that Sam's own brother, whose uttermost acceptance of Christ had seemed so sure, so rooted in his heart and in his soul, should have allowed his conviction to wear away until he was in the very valley of the shadow.

For a time Sam had prayed with him and argued with him, explaining that his heart was like a garden from which the tree of evil had long been cut down. But the stump remained, and that stump, though lightly strewn with the earth of repentance, could send out, and clearly had sent out, strong and sinful shoots which threatened to choke and kill the flowers of the spirit. Let Drake beware. Let him pluck it out in time lest the deadly remains of his carnal mind become rampant and he be lost for ever to Satan and the Pit.

Drake's arguments in this case were that he did not feel his actions were in sin. That he was meeting a young woman of another religious way of thinking was perhaps unfortunate; but if it ever went beyond that, who knew but that she might in time be converted? Marriage was not sin. Wedlock was not sin. Love was not sin. That he was meeting a young woman of a completely different class and in a situation which made marriage almost impossible, was still more unfortunate. But it was innocent. (Or almost innocent.) That because of this preoccupation he was taking a too carnal view of life he was prepared to admit. But he was not prepared to admit, as Sam argued, that this life was only a preparation for the next. Drake loved this life; he loved everything about it: the sunsets, the moonrises, the ruffled golden glow on ripe corn, the ink-black sheen of a blue-bottle's wings, the taste of fresh spring water, lying down and stretching on your back when you were tired, getting up in the morning with a whole new day ahead, eating fresh-baked bread, feeling the cold sea rushing round your legs, roasting a potato in the embers of a fire and peeling it and eating it while it was still too hot to hold, walking on a cliff, lying in the sun, turning a good piece of wood, beating the sparks from iron. He could have listed fifty more pleasures.

And among the things he loved was a girl, and this was the greatest love of all. There were many aspects of the affair which were unfortunate, but he felt no sin. Paradise might hold greater glories but he could not imagine them.

So Sam and Drake had agreed to differ. When he was home Drake still participated in the full life of the circle; he still did his weekly volunteer work on the foundations for the new meeting house on the hill; he still prayed with Sam nightly. But Sam had given up trying to control Drake's movements at other times; and when he chose to rise in the early hours of the night and absent himself from the cottage Sam did not comment. He could not believe real evil of his brother; and indeed from Drake's face in the morning Sam thought he could judge that the devil had not got him in too tight a grip.

This was the third time Drake had been out. It was the sort of high-spirited joke that appealed to him. George War-leggan, whom he had never spoken to and only seen in church, had become something of a dragon figure. This was the only way in which he could attempt to spear the dragon.

Drake had first thought to do it only once. He had borrowed two fish jousting baskets from old Betsy Triggs and a piece of pilchard net from a man in Sawle. With the latter and with the help of a pole and a couple of pieces of wood, he had made a sort of coarse shrimping net. Thereafter it was easy. The frogs and toads were mating late this year and the three connecting ponds at Marasanvose were alive with them. He caught a couple of dozen and put twelve in each basket and tied a piece of sacking over the top. Then up and away. He was back in his bed in little more than two hours.

He had thought it fun and hoped it would work. The toads might well not like their move and be off back to their old haunts by morning. But the Trenwith pond had been their natural home, and he thought they would not object. Of course he knew he was taking a risk, and a risk out of proportion to the laughter and the satisfaction to be found in it. Trespass was a serious crime, particularly trespass at night. But he knew the Trenwith grounds well by now, having explored them both to and from his Sunday visits to the house. Although tall, he was a quick and quiet mover, and he felt sure he could outwit any clumsy keeper who did happen to be abroad. The risk of dogs was small, for George did not like dogs. There were only a couple of terriers belonging to the Harrys, and they seemed to be shut up most of the time.

On the Wednesday he wondered if his visit had been noticed, but on the Friday, returning to their cottage, he found a note waiting for him from Geoffrey Charles. Presumably it had been delivered by one of the house servants.

'Dearest Drake,

'I was so *excited* on Wensday! Toads were in the pool and Uncle George was besides himself with *fury*! Was it you? I *larfed* so much I was sent to my room. Tom and Paul have been in dire trouble for not clearing the pond. They were in it all day, catching the Toads. They have catched them all I believe. Dearest Drake, when can we meet and go to Marasanvose?

Love, Geoffrey Charles.'

In another hand, scribbled hastily underneath. 'If it were you, you *should* not have done it. M.'

So on the Saturday night he did it again. There seemed little more risk, for clearly the gamekeepers were getting the blame, and Geoffrey Charles was getting the fun. This time, although darker than the Tuesday, the moon had risen before he reached the Trenwith pool, and Drake

237

proceeded with a good deal of caution. But no one saw him come and go, and his second legacy of toads was left for Geoffrey Charles's diversion.

So it might have ended, with no further letter to spur him or to warn him. But things got out, as they always will when villagers are employed at a house. Polly Odgers talked to her father, Lucy Pipe talked to her brother. Char Nanfan had the story from Beth Bate, whose husband, Saul Bate, was a gardener at the house. There were whispers and speculation. The country folk had no belief in an invasion of toads from the outer fields. These were Marasanvose toads, and they hadn't hopped there on their own four legs. It was a joke and a good joke, and what made it more interesting was that nobody knew Who. There was talk and laughter about toads and frogs raining out of a clear sky, and how Mr Warleggan had best open up one of his mills for making them into meat for his kitchen. And so on.

And therefore, Drake felt, it was worth doing just once more.

The frogs and toads were in full voice tonight. This sort of weather suited them: fresh and damp though still chilly. Drake set down his two baskets and went about his task. He hardly had to get his feet wet. They croaked and bubbled and snored all around him in the half dark, and although silent at his approach were easily caught as they hopped away. As before he was careful not to net all the noisiest ones, otherwise he would have a bag of males who, finding themselves bereft of their opposite numbers, would see no cause to continue their love songs.

When they were full he tied a piece of hessian over the tops of the baskets, then hid the net in the fork of a tree and began his laden walk. His captives, quietly tumbled together in the bottoms of the baskets, were themselves quiet.

It was nearly three miles to Trenwith land, and he edged himself over the gate not far from the copse where he had first spoken to Morwenna and Geoffrey Charles. Now he went more carefully, avoiding dead sticks and watching for the unexplained shadow. He thought it likely that someone would be watching tonight; but if they did it would be near the fringes of the pool.

The pool itself was bordered on two sides by lawns, on a third by a piece of open land well trodden by cattle in the old days; and with the farm buildings near. The fourth, where the pool was at its narrowest and where the tiny stream that fed it trickled in a narrow pebbled gulley, was grown about with hawthorn, gorse and a few wind-harried pines; and it was from this angle that he had approached before to let his captives plop gently one by one into the freedom of the reedy grass at the pond's edge. This time he took the precaution of setting his baskets down about thirty yards back against the side of an isolated shed and making a preliminary circuit.

It was after midnight and the house was in darkness except for a single gleam in an upper room that Drake had not seen used before. He made his way to the left and saw that there were no lights at the side of the house or over the stables where the servants slept. A thin dry night-wind rustled the grasses, a wind still without comfort to the struggling spring. The rain of yesterday made the going soft and spongy, so that there was less chance of stepping on a brittle twig. In the far distance the sea reverberated.

He saw the first man almost at once: a figure leaning against the nearest stable door. The man was too far away to be at his most effective, but had probably retreated there to get out of the chill wind. It wouldn't be difficult to deposit the frogs without disturbing him. But did gamekeepers keep watch alone? Usually, like pigeons, they came in pairs.

The second man might be more conscientious than his companion. Or each might be taking it in turn to keep the closer watch. Now if one sheltered by the stable door, the other would be likely to be somewhere in his range of vision, so that a pre-arranged signal . . . Drake went carefully over the few places of concealment that were available. Tree, wall, bush, stone pillar, tree, tree, cart, wall, shed, bush, ah . . . He saw him. The other man was sitting quite near the pool, so that his head was not above the level of the bush that hid him. He had been very still, and it was only a momentary movement of his head that betrayed him.

This was going to be more difficult. He could not possibly put the toads in the lake without being seen. All he could now do would be to approach under cover of the bushes and slip them quietly into the stream, hoping they would in the natural course of things make their way to the pool by following the stream down.

Drake turned sharply and bumped into a man.

'Got you!' growled a voice, and a hand grasped at his arm.

That sharp movement, which had been made without any

239

apprehension of danger, just saved him from immediate capture. He wrenched his arm away, coat sleeve tearing; a great stick whistled past his ear to glance off his forearms, clattered into the wall. He ducked and fell, scrambled on hands and knees, half running, half falling towards the house. Another man suddenly in his way; he swerved just in time. The place alive with men. Gamekeepers, he saw rather late, did not always hunt only in pairs.

He was now in the main drive, plain for all to see; they were converging on him from different sides. He turned at right angles, darted for the low wall beyond the flower beds. Two of the men ran to cut him off, but fear and his long legs beat them: he was over the wall and in open country, running for his life across the first of two fields that led to the copse where he had first met Morwenna. They had no dogs; for that he had to be thankful.

But he was not out of the wood yet – nor even in it – for another figure broke into the field from the direction of the main drive – on horseback, and riding to cut him off from his best way of escape. Drake veered for the far corner where the ground fell sharply away. Here was the ruin of an old windmill, long untended and scarred sometime by fire. Lack of shelter anywhere in this direction, but temporarily, after he had scrambled over the low stone wall he was approaching, he would not be seen. The windmill ruin an obvious hiding place, but beyond it the land undulated away towards St Ann's, fenced off for the first time in living memory, ploughed and sown with spring wheat.

This old Cornish wall was not more than three feet high; it ran in broken patches back towards the farm buildings. He somehow fell over it, turned right, and scrambled along on hands and knees, cutting them on stones and sharp stumps of cut-back gorse. It was a frenzied crawl, which had to be not only rapid but quiet. Had the horseman jumped the wall his efforts would have failed. But the man clearly did not like putting his pony at it in the dark; he jumped off and then climbed over the wall, followed by two running panting men who had now caught him up.

As they came over Drake lay flat among the gorse and the stones, rationing his breathless lungs, only now conscious of the pain in his forearm where he had been struck.

'This way, I reckon . . .'

'Bastard's in mill, I don't wonder . . .'

240

'We'd best split.'

'Got a knife 'as 'e? Rats when they're cornered.'

'Tom, take the mill. And you, Jack. I'll ride down, see whether there's sign or sight . . .'

They were splitting, but only into two. They'd no fancy for a fight in the ruin, one against one. A respite. But only for a couple of minutes.

While their feet were clattering he moved. It was just luck: he could not see which way their faces were turned. But no shout came.

He went on, bent double now. He was trying to work out how many men were out. Five or six at least. Three were temporarily accounted for. But almost certainly the horse rider when he could find no trace of him towards the copse would realize he could not have gone so far and come back. Where were the others? Still by the house?

Temporarily silence had fallen on the scene. As his lungs slowed, his arm throbbed more. He reached the end of the wall. If he cut away from here and reached the stables there were, as far as he remembered, two orchards behind the house, then another couple of fields climbing to the moorland which gave on to the cliffs.

He stared at the dark stables. A horse whinnied and an owl fluttered from one of the roofs, otherwise quiet. If they were waiting for him they were waiting for him. In a few minutes the other men would be back. He glanced behind. The horseman was not yet on his tail. He looked up at the house. From here he could not see whether the single light still glimmered. Which was Morwenna's room? He had never seen it, never knew where she slept. Geoffrey Charles's looked over the back of the house. Strange, his friendship with the boy – never just a cloak for the other thing.

He moved, but not now towards the stables. At the front of the house the light had gone out. He slid across towards the pond, target for a musket or another pursuit. But they were all away, chasing him in another direction.

Past the pool and up the stream. His two baskets were where he had left them, but there was movement inside. The inhabitants were losing their fear and becoming restless. He picked up the baskets and carried them to the pool, removed the hessian, plopped the toads into the shallow water at the edge. One croaked almost as soon as it was set free.

With a basket on each arm he began cautiously a half-circuit of the house, and having completed it he moved off towards the cliffs.

By morning his forearm was black, but he went in to the library as usual and managed somehow to carry on. There was in fact little to do now until Ross came to some decision. When the roof was taken off it had been discovered, contrary to all expectation, that although the walls of the library were granite-faced they were in fact not solid granite at all but were made of rubble stone. This was wall building of a more primitive kind: stones built up into a rough double wall about two feet six inches apart, mortared over and the space between filled with anything that came to hand: stone chippings, clay, subsoil and the attle from the local mine. The result was strong enough but there was some hesitation as to whether to use it to support a second storey. It had been irritating to Ross to discover that the engine house of Wheal Maiden had been built of the best granite . . .

However, Drake was able to employ himself and would have passed unnoticed if it had not happened to be the day for his once-weekly lesson in reading and writing. Though he managed the first half successfully, the second half defeated him.

'You're holding your arm too stiff,' said Demelza. 'Is your arm stiff? What have you been doing?'

'I slipped and fell,' he said. ''Tis nothing but a bruise, but it d'make it hard to form the letters.'

'Let me see.' She waved aside his protests and made him take his jacket off. 'Oh . . . Well, that is a rare old bruise to get from a fall. Let me . . . it is not broke?'

'Ugh . . . No. Just a bruise. It is just coming out, that's why tis so dark coloured.'

'You should bind it up. Else you'll scrow the skin, and if it breaks you'll have a sore place. I'll find a piece of cloth and some basil ointment.'

When it was done she said: 'Well, you cannot write today. We shall have to do some more reading.'

They spent the weekly hour of study in the parlour, and it was a time they had both come to find pleasure in. During the winter months brother and sister had come closer together. Often they saw things in the same way. Though men in those districts matured early, he was still in some respects very young. His fresh, carefree male vitality appealed to her. She hated the thought of his coming up against the Warleggans in a fruitless and unequal struggle yet had never said anything, for it seemed to her so futile. Now, quite on impulse, she broke her silence. It was too late. But it always had been too late.

'Are you still seeing Morwenna Chynoweth?'

He looked up, startled. 'Who told you?'

'Sam.'

'Oh . . . Sam.' He breathed out his relief, then his face closed up. 'Yes.'

She waited but he did not speak. He had picked up the book he had been reading earlier and was paging through it. She said: 'It is a pity it has happened.'

'Maybe . . . Maybe that's what most folk would say.'

'Drake, I don't believe any good can come of it.'

'What's good?' he said. 'I wonder sometimes.'

'Good for either of you. Is she fond of you?'

'Oh, yes.'

She said: 'I've often thought to say something. But though I'm your sister perhaps it isn't for me to interfere.'

'Not yours. Not Sam's.'

'But don't take it amiss.'

'No, I'd not do that. You wish well.'

'I wish well. But I wish much it had been someone from some other household. Who knows, some accommodation might have been come to. But – not with the Warleggans.'

'Morwenna is not a Warleggan. No more 'm I a Poldark.'

'But related, that's the misfortune.'

'Feuds are wicked things, sister. I do not know the rights nor wrongs of this one, but they should play no part in the life of someone dedicated to Christ.'

'Yet Sam himself feels this – this friendship is an unfortunate one.'

'He d'think it unfortunate because he believe it to be carnal and so thrusts God into second place. And he d'think it unfortunate because Morwenna aren't of the connexion and not saved and therefore might lead me away.'

'And might she?'

Drake shook his head. 'We've scarce thought o' that. But there be more'n one way of serving God. I d'believe two people – a man and a woman – in perfect harmony can give more to the world and to God than either of 'em can do separate.'

Demelza looked at him with a gentle eye. What he said was so much in line with her beliefs and with her experience that she had no amendment to make.

'Morwenna Chynoweth is a dean's daughter. Would she be willing . . . can she accept a life . . .'

'Oh, don't ask me, sister. Tis more'n I yet know. I know I have naught t'offer her – naught. Tis a hard bitter thing for me. As yet – so far – we can plan no more'n the next meeting. And oft-times not even that. What should be so good betwixt us – God given, I b'lieve – is all stained up wi' forethoughts and afterthoughts and the prohibitions of this world . . .'

He had got up, still holding the book, walked to the window.

Demelza said: 'Only one other thing, Drake. If you meet, we cannot stop you. It is between the both of you and no other. But where you meet, that is another thing. It should not be on the Trenwith estate now Mr Warleggan is back. He has many servants, and violence has twice been offered to Captain Poldark when he has gone there. If Mr Warleggan knew you were coming to meet his cousin, then you might get even bigger bruises than the one now on your arm.'

Drake half turned. 'What happened to Captain Poldark?'

'He – returned the violence. I do not think there was a victor, but blood was shed.'

'I'll bet twas . . .'

Demelza had come up behind him and took his sound arm. 'If I do not want it for my husband, neither do I want it for my brother. And you would not be in so strong a position as he was to resist . . . So have a care, for my sake – and perhaps for Morwenna's . . . Now, what page had we reached? Twenty-two, wasn't it? We had just turned over.'

Drake walked back to Reath Cottage about four. Demelza said he could not work with one arm and must go home and rest it. But his body was without rest or wish for rest, so he thought he would make a pot of tea and then go for a long walk across the beach. He had been so preoccupied with other things that he had not even put his feet in the sea since last November. Sam would not be home from the mine until late.

He scraped a light and put it to a few sticks piled in the hearth. Mark Daniell when he built this cottage had not had much skill in design, nor even care for it, so that the single fireplace and chimney was so sited that when the fire was lit in the winter it seemed to create extra draughts from

244

every direction: door, window and roof. If in the interests of warmth and comfort one gradually stopped up the draughts, a point was reached when the warmth in the house suddenly increased. It was at this point that the fire always began to smoke.

There was a pitcher half full of water that Drake had drawn from the well in Mellin that morning, and he eked two cupfuls carefully into a pan and put it on the crackling sticks. Just then someone knocked on the open door, and he turned to see Geoffrey Charles standing there.

The boy ran into his arms. Trying not to wince under his embrace, Drake laughed and hugged him in return, his eyes eagerly looking through the doorway for another figure.

'Is this a surprise? Is it, Drake? Were you surprised? I stole out. No one knows. *Mon cher,* I'm near on eleven. Isn't it time I rode abroad –'

'Miss Morwenna?'

'She is helping Mama to make cowslip wine. I ordered Santa to be saddled and Keigwin said, where are you going, shall I ride with you, and I answered, oh no, just so far as the copse near the gates; so then I mounted and just rode through!'

'But did ye know where to find me any'ow? I work – normal days I'm not from work till six –'

'I asked. And I took the chance you might be here. It's luck, you see. My lucky day.'

'Mine,' said Drake. 'Mine to be in to bid ye welcome. I'm making a dish of tea. Join me, will ee?'

The boy said he'd be delighted, and they chattered about this and that while the pan boiled. To cover up his disappointment that his visitor was alone, Drake told him the problems of the draught and the fire and laughed about their efforts in the winter to stay warm and yet continue to breathe. Geoffrey Charles was looking round.

'It is like a chapel, Drake. It is more like a chapel than a house. I do not believe I would like to live in a house arranged this way. But about the fire, why do you not dig up the floor?'

Drake sprinkled a few leaves from a tin box into each cup and poured the hot water on it. 'What then?'

'The ground falls away from the front door, so you could lay a drain pipe all the way to the fireplace. Cover it and beat it down. Then put a grid – a fine grid it would have to be – where you build the fire. Then the air would come in from outside and blow up the chimney. Drake, did you come again last night?'

'Come again? I've no milk, Geoffrey. Will ee drink'n without?'

'There were *more* toads! This morning there were *dozens* more! And making an enormous and extraordinary loud noise! Uncle George was beside himself!'

'That's a rare good idea 'bout the hearth. Are ye going to be an engineer, boy? But all the ash would fall through the grid and block the drain, I reckon. How 'bout that?'

'You'd have to clean it out, like cleaning soot from a chimney. Did you come?'

'I reckoned them clouds was bad last night. I says to myself, I says, afore ever cocklight comes twill be raining toads, and then what'll Master Geoffrey say?'

The boy gurgled with delight, and accepted his cup and stirred it. 'You're teasing me! It *was* you, wasn't it! There was *such* a to-do this morning: servants running, terriers barking, gamekeepers sploshing about in the pond! Oh, it went on for hours! Uncle George was so angry! I went up to my room and hid my face in the pillow with *un access de fou rire*! Dear Drake, how did you manage it without getting caught? I heard that they had been up all night watching for a trespasser – and had near caught one! Did they near catch you? Do you fly in the air? Have you witch's wings?'

But Drake would not be drawn. He did not know how reliable the boy's tongue was, and although he was happy to let Geoffrey Charles suspect what he liked, he was admitting nothing.

'And how is your ankle now? Is it all healed over at last?'

'Not complete; but it is better than when I laid up. Talking of flying in the air, you remember the bow you made me in November, and how you said you would make me a better when you had time, and I said I wished we had a design for a real longbow such as they used at Agincourt? Well, I have it now. It is in a book Uncle George has bought me, and I copied it on this sheet for you to see.'

As they sipped the hot weak tea they spread the paper on the rough table and stared at it together.

'You see,' Geoffrey Charles said, 'I have put in all the measurements and the other details. But first we shall have to find some yew. It says in the book that nothing else will do so well.'

246

'But this is a bow – does it not say tis for a pull of sixty pound? That'd be too much, my son. Ye could not fire it. Perhaps – '

'I'll grow. When I go away to school I should want to take it with me. There is sure to be archery, and it would be grand to arrive with a proper longbow. Nobody else, I'll wager, would have – '

'Twould be better scaled down none the less. Forty pounds would be more'n enough. Did ee say you was going away to school?'

Geoffrey Charles nodded. 'Uncle George is already making inquiries for me. I shall miss you, Drake, but it will be only for a part of the time, and when I come back for the holidays – '

'You'll be too grand to talk to the likes o' me. And what will Miss Morwenna do while you are from home?'

'Oh, I shall not go, I believe, until after Morwenna is wed. And I shall *never* be too grand for the likes of you, Drake, for you're my very best friend. You're my first friend, the first real true friend I ever had. As I grow older I shall be more my own master, and it will be not so much, please Mama this, and please Uncle George that. Then I shall be able to have you much more *closely* as my friend than I can now!'

Drake was folding the drawing the boy had brought. 'Miss Morwenna to be wed? I don't follow. What do ye mean?'

'Oh, it happened while we were in Truro. A clergyman – Ossie Whitworth. I do not very much care for him myself – he reminds me of a pigeon. But it was all fixed up by Mama and Uncle George before we left.'

'And . . . what do Morwenna say?'

'Oh, I believe she does not mind. After all, it is marriage that girls are for. Of course they will live in Truro, so I shall see her from time to time. Drake, do you know of any yew? If I could get some . . .'

'I'll make it for you – sometime . . . When I – when I . . .'

'You may keep this plan. That is why I copied it – '

'Geoffrey, when are they to be wed?'

'Morwenna? Oh, I do not believe there is a day. There was some dispute, I believe. Morwenna did not want it yet. Anyway I am glad because I do not wish to lose her while I am home.' Geoffrey Charles put his cup back on the side. The twigs in the hearth had burnt down, and only a gleam or two showed in the heart of the fire. 'I will ask Uncle George for a piece of yew. He can get anything.'

They went outside and talked in the fitful sunshine. Geoffrey Charles did not notice his friend's silences. At length Drake said: 'You must go, boy; else they'll be sending out a search party and saying I'm a kidnapper. But would ee do something for me? Something special?'

'Of course! *Certainement!* What?'

'I want for you to take a message to Miss Morwenna. Tis something I forgot when last we met up in your room, and now Mr Warleggan's back tis more'n I dare to come to the house. Tis just – just something I forgot tell her when last we met, up in your room.'

While the boy waited outside, throwing stones across the valley to disturb some rooks, Drake went inside and with a pencil borrowed from his visitor tried with trembling fingers to make the letters Demelza had taught him. He scarcely felt the pain in his arm.

'M. Will yow met me at the charch Sundy five a clok. Ile wait. D.'

He had no means of sealing the message, but he tied it with a strip of ribbon off an old shirt of Ross's which had come to him via Demelza. He had no fear that Geoffrey Charles would open it. When he went out again with the pencil and the quill of paper he asked the boy to give it to her when she was alone, and this he promised to do.

Then Geoffrey Charles was mounted on his pony, and Drake grasped the small soft hand and stood watching the boy trot away towards the main track at the Gatehouse. Then he went into the cottage again and knelt before the fire, trying to bring it to life again. He went for some shavings and strips of wood he had brought from his work and fed these to the embers, and presently by blowing on the sticks he brought a flame back licking at the new wood. He stayed there. It was not cold, but he felt cold. There was no need to revive the fire at this time of year and if Sam had seen it he would have said it was wasteful. After March you burned wood only to cook, and as often as not went to the baker's even for that to save your fuel. But Drake was cold. He began to shiver. He felt he needed the fire. He needed it for company as much as for heat. He felt as if the warmth had gone out of the world.

BOOK THREE

CHAPTER ONE

It was the third week in May before Tholly Tregirls called
at Nampara again. Shortly after his visit to Demelza there
had been a row at Sally Chill-Off's kiddley, for which he was
partly responsible. Normal times Sally kept good order, and
the fact that she was a widow always helped. Men regularly
staggered home drunk, but for the most part it was a peaceful procession, and if one or another became aggressive and
sought to pick a quarrel, there were enough responsible ones
to sit on his head or throw him into the ditch outside.

Tholly's arrival changed that. In theory the presence of a
man in the house – and a powerful, tough man – should have
contributed to law and order. But it released the customers
from an unwritten obligation to see to the safety of the
widow. Also, village folk have long memories, and there were
some who remembered Tregirls without warmth or pleasure.

Afterwards no one quite remembered how the trouble
began; but in fact the instigator of it was, of all people, that
Jud Paynter. Under the influence of Sam and his teaching,
Jud's Wesleyanism, which wavered with the years, had suddenly caught fire, and, although he did not allow it to interfere with his drinking habits, he felt himself called to attend
prayer meetings and to imbibe new wisdom weekly.

One trouble with Jud was that anything he learned he felt
powerfully concerned to pass on, and as his voice was always
loudest in a crowd, what he was saying could not altogether
be ignored even in the noisiest company. That night, well
warmed with noggins of beer laced with rum, he had got
himself into a corner in which were also Jacka Hoblyn,
Sid Bunt, Joe Nanfan and two St Ann's men, Kemp and
Collins, and was giving them the benefit of Sam's reading of
the day before, so far as he was able to remember it.

'There were this yur king – gracious know 'ow long ago –
but this yur king in the Good Book – true as I'm telling ee.
Nebranezzar. He d'put up this yur golden image – big, biggerer 'n a house, biggerer 'n a mine chimley – set 'n down in
a plain and says, 'e says, any time I d'blow on my 'arp,

sackcloth, dulcimer and salt box all you lot 'as to flatter down and creep around like bullhorns. And any as don't, any as don't flatter down and worship when you d'hear the trump of the 'arp, sackcloth, dulcimer and salt box, phit, into the burnin' fiery furnace, and yer dead. See? So – '

'Ye got the names all wrong,' said Kemp disagreeably. 'All wrong. I mind when I were in dame school I was telled the story. Nebranezzar indeed! – '

'How long was you in dame school, Tom?' Tholly asked, filling up a glass. 'Long enough to put a knot in the dame's daughter?'

He meant it as a joke, but Kemp was one of those with a memory.

'Then,' persisted Jud, showing his two teeth, 'then up starts three men. Like you, me and Jacka here. Up they stands and they d'say, "King, oh, king, live for ever! But don't 'spect we to crawl around like bullhorns whenever you d'blow on the 'arp, sackcloth, dulcimer and salt box. Because we aren't going to, see? – " '

'And all kinds o' music,' interrupted Kemp. 'That d'come in somewhere. And all kinds o' music.'

'Well, that's what I just said! 'Arp, sackcloth and the rest. That's music, see? Didn't know, I s'pose. But that's music . . .' Jud took a long swig of his laced beer, and his frothy mouth presently appeared over the rim to continue his tale. 'So soon as the king d'hear this . . . So soon as 'e heard – '

'Damme, you're spitting on me!' said Collins, and wiped his face with his sleeve. 'Spraying all over like a wet shower!'

''E d'say to the three – Danged if I mind their names – 'e says, bow down or in the furnace. Bow down when I d'blow the 'arp, sackcloth, dulcimer and salt box, or in the furnace. Frizzle, frizzle, and yer dead – '

''Tis only a tale of old Jews,' said Jacka. 'That's all tis, anyway. Tis naught to do wi' we.'

''Tis out the Good Book!' Jud asserted wildly, nearly upsetting his drink. 'All from the Good Book! Tes out the book o' Job! I d'know, and I tell ee. Tes naught but the merest ignorance to say other – '

'All the Good Book's about Jews,' said Jacka. 'I reckon I don't b'lieve the half of it.'

'Jesus Christ were a Jew,' said Tholly, returning with more drink and picking up the conversation as if he had never left it. 'Maybe we're all Jews, eh? You Tom Kemp, me, the

250

next man. If God's a Jew who wants to be other?'

'Nay, Jesus were a Christian!' shouted several voices.

'If ye all d'want to know the truth,' said Jud, getting up and draining his glass. 'If ye all d'want to know the word o' truth from the Good Book, like I say, like I tell ee, like Gospel, like the word, Jesus Christ were a *Cornishman,* and never say nothing different!'

There was a howl of laughter from those around, and when Jud tried to sit down Collins put his boot there so that Jud jerked up again.

'Go on! Let 'im talk!' shouted Kemp. 'Tis fit to beat you, this is!'

'Course he were a Cornishman!' Jud snarled, his bald head glistening with sweat. 'A St Austell man, that's what 'e were, an' no missment. I tell ee. Born at Bethel, nigh St Austell. I *tell* ee! It all happened around these yur parts. Sermon on the Mount. That's still there, where that was, nigh to Market Jew. St Aubyns d'live there now or some such swells. But tweren't like that in the old days! Tweren't like that 'tall!'

'Aw, giss along!' said Collins. 'Great old may-worm, you. Don't know your backside from your front. Why if I –'

'Jud!' said Kemp, and snickered. 'Jud! There's a fine name for ee. Wonder how ee come by Jud? Think you twas Judas to begin?' He let out a roar of laughter. 'Judas Paynter! Be that it? Judas Paynter!'

Entirely by accident, though it looked by design, Jud brought his glass down with a thump on Kemp's head, then turned and caught his elbow on Joe Nanfan's beer and upset it into Collins's lap. Thereupon he fell across Jacka Hoblyn, upsetting his drink too. In a flood of wasted beer and self-pity, Jacka got up and hit at Jud, who instantly disappeared among their trampling feet, and a fight was on. Tom Kemp, his old grudges simmering against Tholly, with the further insult of being called a Jew, threw the remains of his beer in Tholly's face. Jacka smacked Kemp across the face with the back of his hand, and there followed pandemonium. It was as if the urge to violence had been only just under the surface for most of the evening, and this incident broke the surface up.

In fifteen minutes half the drinking room of the kiddley was wrecked; and when at the end of that time most of them found themselves outside, the drunken fighting went on; and when morning came twelve or fourteen of them were still lying asleep or half-conscious or in a drunken stupor in the road or in the ditch beside the inn, some half-stripped, some lying in their own vomit. It was midday before the last straggler roused himself and crawled away. Jud arived home limping in the middle of the night, and in the morning nursed a bruised nose and a deep sense of injury. During that day he repeated often enough and loud enough for Prudie to hear: 'He *were* a S'n Aus'ell man!'

Later Widow Tregothnan said: 'Twas not all your fault, Tholly, by no means, but you'll get the blame, for in ten year there's been naught so bad, and I don't fancy the complaints.'

'Why,' said Tholly, 'I reckon I only put out four or five wi' my own hands. The rest went peaceable enough.'

'Peaceable? It looks like it. And hands? You mean hand. That there hook is no hand, and some of them you grasped'll feel it. I don't want the magistrates on me. I reckon you'd best move away till the fuss has died over.'

'Move away? But I only just moved in! How long, my dear? I cann't bear to be without you.'

'Give over. A month will do. But mind . . . I'm serious; when you return no more of this, or I'll have to lose you.'

So a month he was away. He took his small under-nourished pony and his six bull-pups and went off to Penzance, where he helped to organize a bull baiting and other activities not smiled on by more respectable citizens. In that time he contrived to sell all his pups at good prices, and to spend the proceeds on good living as he understood it. Nevertheless he returned to Sawle with a new suit and ten guineas in his pocket, though he did not satisfy any of Sally's curiosity as to how he had come by them.

Ross had also been much away these last weeks, and, coming home one day at Bargus Cross where the old disused gibbet stood, he was not altogether pleased to see the tall hunched man waiting for him, with his battered hat, his black woollen cloak, and his long legs dangling on either side of his pony, like a Sancho Panza waiting for a Don Quixote. Having made the comparison Ross hid a smile as he came up. He wondered briefly, with a return of his old self-criticism, whether in fact he did spend part of his own life tilting at windmills.

'I see you coming,' said Tregirls. 'How do, young Cap'n. Can I keep ye company a mile or two?'

'I am taking you out of your way.'

'Far from it. I was thinking of calling 'pon you, but I

been away P'nzance way and I had not been back long.'

'A profitable trip?'

'So-so. I sold all my bull-pups, so if you was wanting one twill be some time afore the next litter.'

'I thought I said no. Did you not see Garrick when you called at Nampara?'

'Garrick?'

'Our dog. He does not take kindly to other dogs.'

They jogged on.

'I seen your lady wife,' said Tholly.

'She told me.'

'We had tea together, me and your lady wife.'

'I'm surprised that you recognized the taste.'

'What of?'

'The tea.'

'Well, twas some strange for me, I must admit.'

'A shock to the system.'

Silence fell for a while.

'I got on famous with your lady wife.'

'That she said also.'

'She said that pony I sold ye was worth its weight. Best animal ever you bought.'

'This,' said Ross, 'is the best animal I ever bought.'

'Oh . . . Well, she's getting on, though, isn't she? Look at her muzzle. Look at her crest. She's going grey. You'll need another soon.'

'Maybe.'

'Leave me know when you do.'

'I hear you have found a cosy berth for yourself at Widow Tregothnan's.'

'We get along. She needed a man.'

'To keep order in her beer shop, no doubt.'

'Oh, that. Twas all a misunderstanding. No harm done. Peaceable as a dovecote now.'

A dove? Ross glanced at his companion. More the carrion crow. 'How are your children?'

'I only seen them last week for the first time. They've no room for me, Cap'n.'

'Does that surprise you?'

'Twas all a long time ago. Forgive and forget, that's my motto. But not they . . . Mind, what a difference betwixt them! Emma d'take after me. Fine strong healthy wench! Personable too.' Tholly licked his lips. 'Aye, personable too. If she warn't me own . . . But Lobb! Poor meader. Just like

253

his mother. No life in 'im. Bent he is, too, bent like a old man. Might be fifty. And his childer! . . . Eldest one is half saved, cann't hardly speak, has fits. And the others, poor palched little things, crouching in the hearth among the cinders, bellies swelled up, legs like spiders. All down-trod, the whole boiling of them.'

From this high ground you could see the sea appearing and disappearing along the edges of the land. You could see the trees around Trenwith and those about Fernmore, the Choakes' place, the drunken spire of Sawle Church, even a distant trail of smoke rising from the one mine working in the district.

'They've made their own life,' said Ross. 'You can hardly expect them to feel a sense of duty towards you.'

Tholly chucked to his pony and dug in his heels. 'I had a thought to help Lobb and his family.'

'Can you help them?'

'I can help them if other folk help me.'

Ah, thought Ross, the catch. One should have expected it.

'In that case charity had better go direct.'

Tregirls hunched up his chest to breathe more easily.

'Charity was not in me mind. Work sometimes, if so be as ye've the work. And when ye need a new nag, when that old mare has had her day, that poor old stumbling mare you're riding, when she's had her day, who better to find yer a new one? I can buy and sell. I know all about women and animals. So – when you have the thought to buy . . . save your own time, young Cap'n, leave it to Tholly, eh? How's that?'

Ross caught the speculative eye of the man beside him and laughed. 'I'll think of it.'

They rode along saying nothing for a while till they came to the fork in the trail where Ross would go on and Tregirls should turn for Sawle.

Ross said as they reined in: 'There is something I could put in your way but I do not know if you would fancy it. Do you speak French?'

'Aye. Rough and ready but plenty of it. Like a native, as you might say.'

'This – this that I might put in your way – there might be some danger in it or then there might not.'

Tholly rattled the bones in his bag. 'That sound like my

young Cap'n. It sound like him and like the Old Cap'n over again.'

'Well, clear your mind, Tholly, it is not. In a few weeks' time I am going to France as part of a French expedition which is expected to land – well, somewhere on the French coast. There will be very few English except English sailors on the ships and English marines, but I am going and thought to take half-dozen men with me who would be under my orders, though I should myself be under orders either from the English commander or directly from the French.'

'I'm your man.'

'Wait. Before you agree too readily let me make other conditions plain. There would be no raiding, no foraging, no stealing French property or taking French women. Anyone found guilty of any such crime would be shot.'

'All proper and above board, eh, Cap'n? But I reckon we're at war with the French!'

'Not when we cooperate with them in a landing. So . . . there would be no pickings for you, Tholly. Indeed, if I found you with any I should feel it my duty to shoot you without delay.'

'So what is there in it?'

'Payment. I'll pay each man who comes. A fixed sum which will be his only reward.'

Bartholomew Tregirls coughed horribly into the cool spring air. 'How much?'

'Twenty guineas.'

The coughing resumed, and when Tholly was able to speak Ross was unable to catch what had been muttered.

'What?'

'I said, make it fifteen, Cap'n, and I'll come.'

It was only that day, his final decision to go; after meetings during the last month at Killewarren, at Tehidy, at Falmouth. The expedition was fully fledged and would sail in three weeks. The main force had been assembled at Southampton: three and a half thousand French in some forty transports; another thousand expected from ports along the coast. Four small ships waited at Falmouth with about two hundred men. The fleet was to be escorted by Admiral Sir Borlase Warren, flying his flag in the 40-gun frigate *Pomone,* with five other warships. Indeed, until it reached its destination, the expedition was to have the company of the whole

Channel Fleet under Lord Bridport, evidence enough that the Cabinet at St James's was giving whole-hearted support. In addition to equipment for those sailing, the transports carried great quantities of arms, ammunition, uniforms and other supplies for the Royalists in France.

The Comte de Puisaye, the giant Breton, was to command, for it was his enthusiasm which had brought the scheme to its present fruition; and the Bourbon princes, though slow or cautious to move themselves, had appointed him Lieutenant General and Commander of the Loyalist armies of France.

Ross had met neither de Puisaye nor the Comte d'Hervilly, who had been colonel of one of the crack French regiments and was to be second-in-command, for they had remained in London; but through Caroline he had maintained his contacts with the handsome young viscount, de Sombreuil, with Mlle de la Blache, to whom de Sombreuil was affianced, with the energetic but somewhat volatile de Maresi, with Mme Guise, who had spent her time in the beds of numerous Cornish gentlemen; and he had met half a dozen others. Of them all he greatly preferred de Sombreuil, who in spite of his brilliance and vitality often seemed to have a shadow on his face. Perhaps it was the shadow of the guillotine which had almost wiped out his family. He told Ross that when peace came Ross must bring his wife and stay with them in their great château near Limoges. It was a genuine friendship and Ross had come to prize it, perhaps particularly because he had relatively few close friends of his own in Cornwall.

In the company of the French he was carried along by their determination and their enthusiasm and their obvious courage. The expedition would not lack for any of these. And reports were mounting – too numerous to be false – of the utter disenchantment of the French people with their present rule of terror. If England suffered harshly from the war and the weather, France fared even worse. Although she was virtual master of Europe, bread queues stretched through every French town. The currency had all but collapsed, so that the peasants would not sell their corn; such control as the Government had hitherto exercised in Paris was breaking down: groups of youths roamed the streets killing and robbing at will; several towns had even dared to elect Royalist mayors. The ordinary decent French no longer yearned for liberty, equality and fraternity, or at least not at the expense of justice, order and food. All this was true;

and Ross was hopeful that this expedition would gain the success it deserved.

It was only at odd times that he felt unsure whether the terrible dynamic of the Revolution had yet expended itself. He knew his own yearnings for a better and more equitable society, and remembered how the original proclamations of the revolutionaries had quickened his heart. Now he was so disillusioned by the anarchy and the tyranny which had followed that he was prepared to fight those same revolutionaries everywhere and anywhere. But he remembered the way in which – only a few months ago – the Dutch towns had welcomed the revolutionaries in. The battle cry might be tarnished and stained, but all the magic had not gone from it. And even though the Dutch might bitterly regret their enthusiasm for this splendid ideal when its practical applications became apparent, and even though the French had had six years to suffer it, the alternative, which was a return to the old régime, could surely offer few attractions. Although de Sombreuil was an exception, the attitude of many of the émigrés Ross had met was that peasants were little better than cattle and should be treated as such. Their attitude even to the English servants of their English hosts was completely without that streak of humanity which marked, in however peculiar a way, the relationship of servant and master in England.

So, in the midst of his enthusiasm and his hope, he doubted. And this was at the base of his decision to go himself and to take a few friends with him. And the men he invited to join him were, apart from the one he had just asked, men who had benefited, or seen their families benefit, from Dr Dwight Enys's ministrations. Jacka Hoblyn, Joe Nanfan, John Bone, Tom Ellery, Wilf Jonas, the miller's son. Will Nanfan he would not ask because he still had a young family by his second wife; Zacky Martin because he had not been well all winter; Paul Daniell because of the old tragedy of Mark and Keren. But this group made six with Tregirls, and it might well be enough. Indeed he might not use any of them.

After he had left Tholly he jogged on until he reached his own land. He was not looking forward to his meeting with Demelza, for now he must tell her of his decision. He knew she would accept it and make the best of it; but he did not like the thought of causing her this worry; and he knew well enough that if things did not go aright with the expedition his secondary plan would lead him into danger. This he was not going to tell her.

But he knew it himself, and he struggled with his own complex feelings as he rode down the valley with the Mellingey stream bubbling and hissing not far away. There had been a real hint of summer in the sun today. The light had been clear and scintillating, the air charged with life and ozone, the sky had looked a million miles high. It was a day that made you feel good to be alive.

Why then choose to risk it all?

First was his heavy obligation to Dwight. That was primary to the decision. But secondary and not to be overlooked was a barely conscious hankering within himself for danger and adventure and the company of men. At home, at the home he was just approaching, he had a wife whose gamin beauty, wit and earthiness he still found totally engaging; and he had a son of four years old, good-looking, sharp with incentive and already full of the most endearing characteristics: and he had a daughter of seven months, dark-haired and dark-eyed like her mother, plump and laughing and contented at being born. All this he put at risk. A chance musket ball would have a broken widow and two fatherless children, and himself written off the page, no longer able to draw breath and life and savour.

Yet, although he could not quite work this out in simple terms in his own mind, the very savour of life, he thought, was itself enhanced if it were not totally taken for granted. Perhaps it was something to do with the whole philosophy of the world into which we were born. If we lived for ever, who would look forward eagerly to tomorrow? If there were no darkness, should we so appreciate the sun? Warmth after cold, food after hunger, drink after thirst, sexual love after the absence of sexual love, the fatherly greeting after being away, the comfort and dryness of home after a ride in the rain, the warmth and peace and security of one's fireside after being among enemies. Unless there were contrast there might be satiety.

He did not suppose that these were original thoughts, but they constituted an element in his decision to go. He knew how quickly Demelza could demolish them if they were put to her. Accepting the first premise, no doubt, she would then go on to point out the fallacy of all the rest. Love is brief, sun is brief, warmth and peace and sexual and parental happiness last but a few years. Few possess them as we now possess them. So savour while we can. They'll go quick enough without inviting the French musket ball to heighten the flavour.

It was practical, and if it came to the argument he would admit she was right. But it never would come to the argument for he never would reveal to her the secondary motivations for his decision. On loyalty to Dwight she would have no answer.

CHAPTER TWO

It had become the custom of the Rev. Clarence Odgers to visit Trenwith House every Saturday morning that the family was at home. He had now given up all hopes of being fed at the house on a Sunday. Although their eldest daughter was employed as Valentine's nurse, George barely acknowledged the existence of a Mrs Odgers or an Odgers family. But Saturday the curate not infrequently was given the inestimable benefit of a small dole of money, and if matters arose concerning the parish they could be discussed then. Further he received his instructions about the morrow, whether Mr and Mrs Warleggan would attend service and if they had any preference for lessons or for hymns.

Today, which was the sixth of June, George received him in his study, a room that old Joshua had made peculiarly his own. George was wearing a cream silk cravat, a long flowered silk morning gown and crimson slippers, and was at his most easeful. One could almost have fallen into the mistake of supposing his affability to be friendliness. It made Mr Odgers's self-appointed task at once easier and more difficult. One broached the subject more readily, but one feared all the more the change of manner which would ensue.

'Mr Warleggan,' he began. 'Mr Warleggan. I trust you will forgive me if I appear to intrude upon the private affairs of your household. It has never been my wish to seem to interfere in anything domestic, or in any aspect of your life which does not have a direct bearing upon the life of the church here in Grambler and Trenwith. But, Mr Warleggan, there is something I feel I ought to tell you. If you already know it, and approve of it, then I trust you will accept my humblest apologies and consider the matter as never having been mentioned.'

George's face had already altered slightly. 'I am in no position to tell you that until I know the subject.'

'The subject, Mr Warleggan. The Subject, Mr Warleggan, is your niece. Beg pardon, your wife's cousin. I refer to Miss Chynoweth. An estimable young lady, I have always thought, a dean's daughter, a young lady of Christian parts, a help in the church; an adornment, if I may say so, Mr Warleggan, too. An adornment . . .'

George bowed his head in acknowledgment.

'Recently she has helped with the choir and has worked a sampler for the lectern. Highly estimable. But – but, oh, dear, Mr Warleggan, she is meeting – did you know? she is meeting a young – a young man – and one of the Wesleyan sect – and utilising our church as a trysting place. I cannot believe that you would wish her to do that! Especially as the young man she is meeting is one of the ringleaders of those rowdies we were able to exclude from the church on your directions. Or at least, on your advice, Mr Warleggan, on your advice. You will remember my calling to visit you last year – it would be towards the end of last summer – and we agreed then that it would be better in the interests of the parish as a whole – '

George held up his hand to arrest the spate. Mr Odgers then obediently sat silent. George sat there for a full minute before he spoke.

'How has she been meeting him and when?'

'In the church on Sunday afternoons, and possibly on other occasions, I don't know.' Mr Odgers chewed on his sparse teeth. 'Because she helps in the church she knows where the key is hid and so can enter it at all times. I chanced upon them two Sundays ago, entering the church from the vestry: they did not see me for I was able to withdraw in time. But twice I have seen them there in the last two weeks.'

'You are sure it was Miss Chynoweth?'

'Oh, yes, certainly Mr Warleggan. I fear so. And the same young man.'

'What same young man?'

'During your absence, Mr Warleggan, I took the opportunity of visiting Miss Agatha Poldark from time to time. She was long an attender at the church, although it was before my day . . . Well, twice in visiting this house, once on arriving, once on leaving it, I have seen the young man, this same young man, approaching the house as if to pay a call – a call upon someone in it. I can only conclude, it seems only reasonable to conclude – '

'Was this before Christmas or more recently?'

'Oh, before. Afterwards the weather was so inclement, one hardly ventured out.'

George got up and went to the window. This window did not look out over the pool, the source of his other vexations. It looked over the tiny courtyard towards the back of the house.

'I was not aware of these meetings, and you are right to have brought them to my notice. It is possible that they have some innocent explanation, and I trust that is so. But innocent or not, they shall be put a stop to.'

'Thank you, Mr Warleggan. I acted for the best in this, with, I believe, your interests and the interests of Miss Chynoweth at heart – '

Scratching under his horse-hair wig, Odgers went on, telling the same story and offering the same comments in different words. Having received a congratulatory pat, he liked it so much that by reiterating the purity of his own motives he sought a repetition of the praise all over again. He did not get it. George, his mind very busy with what he had learned, had neither time nor further attention for the parson, and with a few words and a few nods and grunts he got rid of him.

George went straight to Elizabeth, who had no more knowledge of the matter than he. Their ignorance pointed the gap in communication that existed, the isolation they lived in although surrounded by servants and the rest of the community. For in spite of Drake's and Morwenna's belief to the contrary, a considerable number of people knew of their walking together on the beach, of his calls at the house, of their meeting at the church since. Secrecy might have been possible in a town, it was not possible in the country where observing one's neighbour was one of the few recreations available to all. Had Verity been in the house, or even Francis, someone would have dropped a hint to them as a matter of course. People were afraid to do so to George because they were scared of him, and Elizabeth, though kind enough, had always been remote.

Various servants were summoned, interrogated and sent

about their business. Next Geoffrey Charles, who by turns was gleefully frank, defiant, tearful and defiant again. Finally Morwenna.

She bore her ordeal with thumping heart and choking breath, but outwardly at first meekly calm. Yes, Geoffrey Charles had been seeing this young man, in her company, at intervals since last summer. As he was related to the Poldarks, she had thought there was little harm in it, even though he had had no education and was a tradesman. Geoffrey Charles, as he must already have told them, had taken a very *great* liking to him. Drake – Drake Carne – had been able to teach Geoffrey Charles many sides of country lore that she could not have done herself. She had tried to attend to his formal education, but how to tie knots, how to build fires, how to shoot an arrow: these were skills she did not have. So the friendship had formed and had – continued.

'And *your* friendship, Miss Chynoweth?' George said. 'How do you explain that?'

Morwenna raised frightened eyes to his and then hid them again by looking at her hands.

Her friendship had grown out of the companionate friendship of the three. She had been glad to see Geoffrey Charles so happy and had entered into his happiness. So, without intent, she had allowed the young man to become fond of her – and had become fond of him.

'And you sit there,' said George quietly, 'and tell us that?'

'I am sorry. I know it was unwise. But that is how it happened! I can be no more than truthful with you, Mr Warleggan. For that is just how it occurred. There was never any harm intended or thought – either on his side or on mine.'

'Let us leave his intentions out of it for the moment. Let us consider yours. You came here as governess to my stepson. By doing this you accepted a trust to look after him and teach him in the ways that you know we would wish. Instead, under the pretext of wanting him to be instructed in country lore – and I must say that I can only possibly see it as a pretext – you entangle yourself with this out-of-work miner, this Methodist; you compromise yourself and drag your name – and Geoffrey Charles's with it – through the mire of the village streets for every gossip to sneer at!'

With blind eyes Morwenna looked for help across at

Elizabeth, but Elizabeth was not looking at her at all.

'I well understand now,' George said, still in a low voice, 'why you were reluctant to accept the proper and successful marriage we had arranged for you. Having given yourself to this miner, you felt you could not come to the marriage ceremony with a pure body and a clear heart.'

'I did not "give myself" to this miner, as you call him!' Morwenna said, standing up and the tears now running down her cheeks. 'We talked and – and we became fond of each other . . .'

'You became fond of each other,' said George. 'That is the second time you have used the expression. Well . . . it is a plain declaration, is it not, made apparently without shame or apology! – '

'I have already tried to – '

'Let me finish, please. I wonder what your father would have said had he been alive. I wonder, indeed, what your mother will say, for she certainly must be told. Or your younger sisters, who, I would have thought, looked up to your as a person whose example they should follow. This intrigue, which has been taking place under our roof, is of such a sordid nature that one wonders how much more of it there is yet to be revealed!'

He went on. Elizabeth, while agreeing with his sentiments, felt that he was too outraged and too severe. She could not help but wonder if, having always thought himself inferior to the Chynoweths, he was not now making special use of the opportunity to strike at one who had broken the rules of good behaviour. Here at last was one he was justified in condemning . . . Also, of course, the offence was made much worse because Carne was Ross Poldark's brother-in-law . . . Not yet being able to see into the whole of her husband's mind, it did not occur to her that George had felt a part-suppressed attraction to the girl himself and so discovered some inverted satisfaction in being specially brutal to her because she had let him down.

Presently, seeing Morwenna look as if she was going to faint, Elizabeth made a sharp urgent sign for George to stop.

'One thing is certain,' he said to Elizabeth. 'The marriage with Mr Whitworth cannot take place. I will write to him giving him a full explanation of the reasons, and ask him to postpone his visit to this house until Miss Chynoweth has left. At the end of this month Miss Chynoweth will go back to her mother. I will also make arrangements for Geoffrey Charles to be sent away to school. In the meantime any communication with this man Carne must cease. I know you will see to it, my dear. I can leave it in your hands. You will do all that is best.'

He left the room and the two cousins together.

There was only one thing Elizabeth possibly could do. She no more approved of Morwenna's behaviour than George, but in such circumstances all the disapproval had already been stated. She put her arm round the girl's shoulders and kissed her wet cheeks.

'There, there. Let us sit down and talk it over. Do not break your heart.'

Every crop was a month behind, and most were deficient and poor in quality. Cornish farmers did not lift their early potatoes in bulk so the frosts of early May destroyed many of them and damaged the other early vegetables. The hay was short and weak, and Ross thought he would not be able to cut until the end of July.

Distress, when it comes to the point of starvation, means unrest and rioting. Trouble had broken out up and down the country. With a revolutionary state only a few miles across the Channel, it was a trying time both for the law and for the law-breaker. Attitudes of admonition and of defiance were taken up and, once assumed, had to be maintained in the face of pressures for compromise. Yet by and large an astonishing restraint prevailed. If the rioters invaded a town they did not sack the shops, they organized a distribution of the goods at what seemed to them a fair selling price. At Bath great numbers of women boarded a corn ship in the river, and when the justices read the Riot Act they said they were not rioting, only stopping the export of the corn, and together sang 'God Save the King'.

Yet repressive measures had to follow, and the ringleaders be punished.

In Cornwall serious disturbances had already occurred in four towns. Again a degree of discipline prevailed among the miners; they seized mills and granaries and forced millers and dealers to sell the corn cheap, but they offered no other violence and usually, having got what they came for, dispersed peaceably enough. But many of the Cornish gentry were in high alarm, and a rumour spread that some soldiers, being ordered to fire on rioting tin miners in Truro, had refused to obey the order. This looked like a direct road to the French hell.

In the district of Grambler and St Ann's there were rumblings but so far there had been no explosion. The long light days were a help, for even the brief nights had a luminosity, and the sun hid itself rather than disappeared. Larks sang high, and the lapwings, which had suffered much in the winter, screamed and squirled and tumbled above the oat fields and the wheat. The hedgerows, after having been plastered down under weeks of frozen snow, seemed to flower the more, and bluebell and campion and milkmaid trembled in a patriotic riot of their own. The sea was quiet and brought no pickings. With the warmer weather typhus at last emerged from its quarantine in the poor house and spread among the mining families. It was high time Dr Enys was back.

Yet in spite of all, the building of the new Meeting House went on. Characteristically, Ross thought, Sam had planned his new house considerably larger than the old. As for the library, after consultation with a couple of builders and with old Horace Treneglos, who was knowledgeable about such things, Ross had decided to proceed with the existing walls. Mingoose, Treneglos said, was entirely built of rubble stone and granite stone and had stood for long enough. But chief reassurance came when Ross decided the two miserably inadequate windows at the end, facing south-west, should be blocked up and a larger one made. Cutting a new hole in the wall removed any doubt as to its strength and fitness to carry another storey.

In June there was a big revival at Gwennap. It had begun at Redruth where eight people almost together suddenly found peace with God. The night following many more were powerfully seized with a conviction of their sins and, after much wrestling and importuning in prayer, had found their Saviour. One of these was a Gwennap man, and he, bearing the glad tidings home, started an even bigger revival, central chiefly on the Gwennap Pit where Wesley had often preached. This great bowl, which some thought to be ancient, had in fact been caused by the subsidence of a large area of the mine workings just below the surface, and it now formed a natural amphitheatre which the Greeks would have loved and which John Wesley had turned to a good account.

The district surrounding, one of the biggest mining areas in the county, contained within a square mile or so, Wheal Unity, Treskerby, Wheal Damsel and Tresavean – all now

265

derelict – and the unemployment and the poverty were therefore intense. But in this district instead of turning to riot they turned to God. Favoured by fine weather and light nights, the revival continued for a week, during which more than five thousand of the ignorant confessed their sins and united themselves into a religious society which rose above the cares and privations of this world and found solace in Christ and the promise of eternal life. Sam, hearing of it on the second day, went to Captain Henshawe, asked permission to absent himself and walked the twelve miles to Gwennap to participate in the religious experience. He tried his hardest to persuade Drake to accompany him, but Drake was in such a state of emotional and physical turmoil that for the moment the spiritual life did not appeal. Sam went on his way rejoicing in the glory of God and in His goodness in opening men's hearts, but sorrowing that his beloved brother should be in such a gall of bitterness that he could not be with him at this precious time.

At Trenwith George no longer insisted that Morwenna should be sent home immediately, but it was understood that she should return to Bodmin early in September when Geoffrey Charles went to school. George had been making inquiries for twelve months about schools, and now, with his usual ability to turn a set-back to good account, he was able to use the recent trouble as a lever to persuade Elizabeth into agreement. Geoffrey Charles was clearly out of hand at home. Look at the hysterical way he had behaved when they told him he must no longer see this young miner, Drake Carne. It seemed likely now that even a male tutor would be unable to control him. A boarding school was the right and only solution.

'Harrow is the school for Geoffrey Charles,' George said. 'I know the journey will be expensive and tedious, but the policy of the governors, declared most recently, is precisely what I think we both want. They say – you see in this printed letter – that whatever the intentions of the founders may have been, "the school is not now generally adapted for persons of low condition but better suited to those of a higher class". This is what we want for Geoffrey Charles, that he should mix with people of his own station and higher. All the other schools I have been considering lately, Eton, Westminster, Winchester, still have a policy of admitting the sons of tradesmen.'

Elizabeth said: 'The journeys there and back will take

nearly two weeks from his holidays. And it will be a big cost for his small means.'

'You know that I long ago undertook the expense of his education. I am told that boarding, books and teaching fees will amount to about thirty pounds a year and clothes another twenty-five. Travel will add to the cost; but he is the heir to this house and estate, and as such should have the best. As *your son* he should have the best.'

Elizabeth smiled as George patted her hand. She knew his remark to be complimentary with a purpose; she knew his desire to weaken the bond between mother and son.

Elizabeth had not yet the detachment – perhaps never would have – to recognize how much Geoffrey Charles had developed since he had attained greater freedom from her. At times she had had her own tinges of jealousy at seeing him so happy in the company of Morwenna; but she would gladly have accepted that as a permanence rather than lose him altogether, as she felt she was going to, to a rough male world which in the process of knocking him into shape would no doubt knock him about so much that he would come home a different boy.

But those happy times were behind.

As George seemed in a warmer mood than of late she broached a subject which she had wanted to mention for some days but which she knew would irritate him afresh. 'Aunt Agatha has made out a list of invitations.' She offered him a sheet of paper on which it looked as if an inky fly had struggled in its death throes. 'Some of this she has writ herself, some Geoffrey Charles has put down at her request. I confess I do not know the half of the people she has named.'

'Nor would wish to.' George took the paper between finger and thumb as if it had come from the bed of a fever patient. 'I really do not see that we are compelled to do this at all. The nearer it comes the more nauseating it appears.'

'Not compelled – not physically. But morally are we not?'

'I do not see it. God's life, I do not see it. What are all those names crossed out?'

'They are all dead. I consulted Mr Odgers and old Agnes in Sawle, who used to work for the Poldarks many years ago. They are people Aunt Agatha no doubt still believes to be alive.'

George handed the paper back. 'Should we not better

have the birthday party in the churchyard? Then all the graves would jump open when we cut the cake.'

Elizabeth shivered. 'Some of these names, of course, we know well and are people we should welcome here in any case. The Trenegloses, the Bodrugans, the Trevaunances. Some of these others are no doubt too old to come or too far away. I do not think it will be a big party altogether. Perhaps twenty or thirty.'

'There must be a hundred names there!'

'Oh, yes, but most will not come.'

'I am not – Elizabeth, if I have to put up with the invasion of my house – our house – by a swarm of unsavoury people to satisfy the last feeble egoism of an old woman – I am not – we are not – offering them hospitality overnight! I will not have our house filled with doddering skeletons, scme of whom no doubt will be incontinent and others feeble-minded; they shall not be put up in our house, not even to maintain a pretence of approving of this ghastly celebration. No, Elizabeth, make that clear from the beginning; tell that old woman if you can get anything into her head, that we will not do that and she cannot compel us!'

'I think,' said Elizabeth pacifically, 'I believe Agatha is making plans for the reception to end about six. So most will have ample time to return – that is, those who have the health and the means to get here.'

George considered this for a few moments, turning the money in his fob. 'So the old woman has ideas as to the sort of reception we are supposed to give her?'

'She is paying for it all, my dear. Remember that. It is the house in which she was born. Forgive me if I remind you of this – of course you know, but . . . you see, she feels she is entitled to it. Just as, say, if your father were forty years older and still living at Cardew. So she – makes plans, and expects us to arrange it in the way she wants – assuming that what she wants is reasonable.'

'And is it?'

'I think so. I have been up in her room quite a little –'

'May God preserve you.'

'And so we have discussed it together. She wants – she would like to invite her guests to breakfast at two o'clock. She will hope to be down to receive them, and this will be served in the big parlour and the winter dining room. Nothing elaborate – hot chocolate or brandy wine to drink, with biscuit-cakes and ginger bread and the like. Then we thought

268

if the day was fine the company could walk round the garden for an hour or more. Some would no doubt stay and chat to Agatha – others could admire what we had done to improve the house and grounds.'

She paused, letting this sink in. If she could get George's active support, or at least soften his opposition, it would make the day easier for her.

'We thought then a cold collation in the dining hall. Agatha wanted a full dinner but I have persuaded her out of it. She will sit at the head of the table, but the others will eat and sit as they desire. Hot soups, of course, but otherwise the more easily prepared things: roasted tongue, cold mutton, chicken pie, pigeons. Asparagus if we can get some, with pickled eggs. Syllabubs and fruit tarts. Then the cake. After the meal we will cut the cake and drink her health. I feel it will all pass very pleasantly.'

George licked his lips. 'And then?'

'And then I daresay Aunt Agatha will feel she has had her day. No doubt she will be worn out with all the excitement. She will stay down until six, she says, but we shall see. At any rate we will serve tea at about six, and I shall hope all have gone home by seven.'

'Amen,' said George. 'But why do we have to make these preparations in June when this lamentable anniversary does not occur until August?'

'I thought I should just mention it to you, my dear, to keep you appraised. You know you do not like arrangements to be made without your knowledge and consent. Aunt Agatha wants the invitations sent out as soon as possible. She is living for this day, and naturally all her thoughts are on it.'

There were crosses to be borne in having married into the Poldark household, and this, the heaviest of them, could not, George felt, in the nature of things have to be borne much longer. So he muttered something in sulky acquiescence and turned away.

CHAPTER THREE

Sam had spent a glorious week at Gwennap, and only when the fervour had begun to die down did he return home. It was a fine day for his walk, and such was his happiness, such was his joy at what the Lord had accomplished in so short a time, that several times on the way he shouted aloud. People far distant, working fields away, lifted their heads and stared after him; gnarled old men, girls in straw bonnets, urchins grubbing among the stubble for gleanings. They thought him mad.

But there was no madness in him, only a sweet joy at being united with Christ. He had seen such wonders at Gwennap as could only have occurred if the spirit of the Lord moved powerfully over the land. And they were not finished yet. Of that he was convinced. It had died down at Gwennap, perhaps temporarily, perhaps, having done its work, for a long time. But once ignited the power and the grace of the Holy Spirit was like a bush fire. It smouldered and seemed to go out, then suddenly it would spring up in another place. The great spiritual revival had begun this time in Redruth and moved after a few days to Gwennap; from there it might suddenly shift to St Austell or Penzance. It might even smoulder and blaze up in the little coastal villages of Grambler and Sawle. Who knew? Who knew what a single vile unworthy creature such as himself, if imbued with faith and in bond with the heavenly Bridegroom, could do?

As he neared home he perceived that his faith all the while had been too little, that he must not only exhort more urgently himself but that he must persuade his little flock to do the same. If only Drake was free of the powerful suggestions of the Devil and could lay hold once again of the full beauty of the blessing, no one knew – or only One knew – what they might accomplish together. He resolved that he must first look into his own heart and discover what carnal weakness lay there which might have prevented him from exerting a sufficient influence on Drake such as would bring him back to a full sensibility of the spiritual life. In some way the error might still be in him. Only prayer – only long hours on his knees before his Maker – would open the doors of self-knowledge. If he could but persuade Drake to share them. Then, who knew how many more they could persuade to share them? Faith could work miracles. Faith *did* work miracles. He had seen it demonstrated before his own wondering eyes all this week.

But sometimes the carnal world grips too cruelly even for a man like Sam to ignore. Whatever sanctification he carried in his heart, the press of material and spiritual evil was to come upon him that day and make his mind a captive to it and drive out, at least for a time, his thoughts of bringing new life to the villages of Grambler and Sawle. It was well after seven before he reached home. One boot was biting into his toes, and he was thirsty and hungry and tired and he looked forward to breaking bread with Drake and telling him the good news of the salvation of so many souls. But Drake was not in. It had been a beautiful day, but a sort of white-coloured rain was now falling over the sea and the sandhills and would probably spread inland in a few minutes. The sun was half blotted out by the squall, but a golden light was falling over the moors and fields behind.

Sam had taken a long drink of water and had cut himself a piece of bread and a square of cheese when there was a tap at the door and he saw Bob Baragwanath standing there. Bob was Charlie's father, and Sam had prayed with them when Charlie died. Bob was not really bright enough to understand quite all that Sam had done and said, but he had appreciated the gesture.

'Yer bro'er,' he said.

'Yes? Drake? What is it? Did he leave a message?'

'No. No message. Bin took. Bin took in. Hour gone. Took in a hour gone.'

Sam put down his bread. 'What's amiss, Bob? Drake took? Took where?'

'Constable – Constable Vage. Took 'im in a hour gone. Took 'im in the jail. Gone St Ann's to gaol house.'

'Drake? To gaol? What for? Constable Vage? I – Did you *see* it?'

'Ay. Seen it wi' me own eyes. Took in for stealin'! That's what Constable d'say. Stealin'! Took 'im in a hour gone.'

They were finishing supper when Sam arrived. During these radiant light days they dined less heavily than in the winter and so supper became a more important meal. It had been a silent meal, as a number had been of late and as the time

271

for Ross's leaving for France drew near. Demelza was not the one to bear a grudge against him for going, but its imminence cast a cloud over her good spirits. She did not chatter as usual about the garden or give him the benefit of her speculations as to Garrick's thoughts when she took the baby rabbit away from him, or describe to him the actions of a bull-finch as it ate the white pulp out of an empty dandelion seed-pod. She was untalkative, and as by nature Ross did not have much small-talk it had been a silent meal.

On this came her brother to inform them that her other brother had been arrested for stealing.

She got up and stared at him. 'Stealing? Drake? That is impossible, Sam.'

'Yes, sister, tis impossible that he should do it, but not impossible that he should be accused.'

'What do they say he has stolen?'

'Well, tis hard to get the truth, but I seen Art Curnow, who were a witness to his going, and the constable d'say to him that he be accused of stealing a bible – a bible wi' a silver clasp – out of Trenwith House.'

'Trenwith House? But when? He has not been near Trenwith House for weeks and weeks, not since George – not since Mr Warleggan came home.'

'I don't know the truth of 'n, sister, I only d'know what I'm told and that Drake be committed to the gaol house at St Ann's an' locked away like he were a felon.'

Ross also had risen, but he turned away from them to hide the annoyance on his face.

'Who preferred the charge, do you know?'

'Mr Warleggan, I bla'.'

That was it. Mr Warleggan. And since this boy was Demelza's brother he would press it with all the greater relish. And how could he, Ross, avoid being drawn in, and particularly avoid Demelza being embroiled in all this while he was away? Infuriating. More than ever he regretted not having taken a strong line with the boys when they arrived and sent them back to Illuggan where they belonged. At the time he had warned Demelza that at some future date her brothers might embarrass her by marrying locally and perhaps hinder her social ambitions. Never in his worst dreams had he thought of one of them having a love affair with Elizabeth's cousin! And now to be arrested for theft – and theft of a bible of all things!

Yet at this stage he must show none of his annoyance to Demelza. She had enough to put up with with his own delinquencies and peculiarities, his own loyalties and outside friendships and the spirit of restless unease which was sending him on this voyage to France. He could not expect her indulgence of this and not extend a similar indulgence to her.

He said: 'Mr and Mrs Warleggan had been away for a couple of days. Do you think Drake visited Trenwith then?'

'I don't know, Cap'n Poldark. I been away myself on the Lord's business. I come back but this eve.'

'Do you know if Drake has been seeing Miss Chynoweth during these last weeks?'

'He met she two or three times in Sawle church, Sunday af'noons. But then twas all discovered and there were a big upset at Trenwith, beginning of this month. So he's seen naught of 'em since. I b'lieve twas said Miss Chynoweth were going to be sent away.'

'Apparently,' Demelza said, 'George has plans to marry Miss Chynoweth to someone in Truro called Whitworth. The Reverend Whitworth.'

'What, Osborne Whitworth, Judge Whitworth's son?'

'I believe. It was to be a good match for her. So there was special trouble when her friendship with Drake was discovered.'

'A posturing fop. You remember him, of course. He made a fuss of you more than once, but was usually outgunned by Hugh Bodrugan and John Treneglos.'

'I remember him,' Demelza said.

'But who told you this?'

'Drake. Last week. When he came for his writing lesson.'

Ross stared down at his unfinished plate of raspberry tart. 'It does not seem likely that this charge is true, surely?'

'Oh, never!' said Demelza. 'Drake is not a thief.'

'Never!' said Sam.

'Yes, well . . . that's all very well but the charge has been preferred. There must be some grounds, however slight. The tedious part of the matter is that if the Warleggans have got their teeth into this it may be hard to persuade them to let go. Anyone else would be open to reason. Not they. You may regret it yet, Sam, that you are in any way connected with the Poldarks.'

Sam said: 'Maybe if I went to see them myself.'

'Far from it. You would be received ill and fare worse. No,

the first thing is to see Drake and discover his version of the affair. Until we know that we can do nothing.'

There was silence. Sam said: 'I shan't make no rest tonight. But twill be no use going till the morning. I'll go over see him there.'

'No,' Ross said. 'You keep away. We do not want you committed on some other charge. I will see to it myself in the morning. '

'Thank you,' said Demelza.

'Until then it is useless to speculate. The accusation may yet be dropped. We have no means of knowing anything more, so it is best to discuss it no more. I'll ride over first thing.'

'God bless you,' said Sam. 'I shan't make no rest tonight.'

The 'gaol' at St Ann's was in fact not a gaol at all but a lock-up house where malefactors were from time to time confined before being brought up for sentence at the local petty sessions. It was part of the house and shop of Mr Renfrew, the mine chandler, and consisted of an upper room and a lower which were both supposed to be kept free for the full operation of the law, but which Mr Renfrew himself used as part of his storage space. As a result the top room was full of coiled ropes, lanterns, blocks and tackle, hempen candles, picks, fuses and all the other paraphernalia of mining. Below was kept for its proper purpose, though the space was encroached upon by whatever Mr Renfrew deemed would not be damaged by the occasional prisoner or assist in his escape.

On the way there Ross thought over his problem. Pursued by last-minute advice from Demelza, who, although deeply concerned for her brother, was still more deeply concerned that her husband should not repeat any of his gaol-breaking escapades of six years ago, Ross was more occupied over his line of tactics should Drake's explanation prove a reasonable or excusable one. Seven or more years ago, when Jim Carter was had up for poaching, he had gone into Truro, appeared at the Quarter Sessions and made a public appeal for clemency. It had been rudely turned down. From that he had learned his lesson. You did not ask for a reasonable mercy in public, you approached the magistrates privately and asked, as a friendly gesture made to you personally, that they should give the offender another chance. How to work here? He could not ask favours of George Warleggan. Had he been a magistrate himself it would have helped matters along greatly. But he had turned that down. Who ever could have foreseen a case like this?

Mr Renfrew was in and greeted him effusively, puckering his short-sighted eyes in a smile. (Mr Poldark was a customer as well as Mr Warleggan.) The prisoner? Yes, Mr Poldark could see him. Of course. Naturally. The lock-up was not perhaps as clean as he, Mr Renfrew, would have wished, but they had been busy this last week. There were, in fact, two others in at the moment, waiting the next meeting of the magistrates. They had all come in yesterday and, what with one thing and another, one hadn't been able to do all one would have wished. Charged? Oh, one had assaulted Mr Irby in his shop. The other had been drunk and had smashed some windows at the Miner's Arms. They would be charged probably tomorrow. Would Mr Poldark come this way? Mr Poldark went this way.

It was quite a small room with a post in the middle from floor to ceiling, for chaining up fractious prisoners. One corner of the room was full of sacks and a pile of driftwood, otherwise there was nothing but the three men. But the smell was hideous for there was no privy, and the sacking had not been moved for weeks. One man still lay asleep in his own vomit, the other two looked up as the door opened.

Ross put his kerchief to his nose. 'Can you give me five minutes with him outside in your yard? I promise he shall not escape.'

'Well, sir . . . I suppose, if so be as you promise . ˣ ˢ'

'You may watch us from a distance if you like.'

Drake was let out. Blinking in the daylight, he looked uncannily pale from his night indoors. With a twinge of angry irritation Ross saw his likeness again to Demelza.

'Well, boy. You're in trouble. How did this happen?'

'Oh, Cap'n Poldark, tis good of you to come. I didn't know as you'd know. What wi' Sam being from home and—'

'Sam returned last night. He heard and told us. What is it all about?'

'Well, I don't rightly know where to begin. You d'know, I s'pose, that I took up wi' this young lady in Trenwith House. Sister d'know all about it—'

'She told me, yes.'

'Well, twas all forbid when the Warleggans found out I'd been meeting of her in church. So we—so we seen nothing of one another since then. But Geoffrey – Mr Geoffrey Charles – he rebelled against it and he been over to see me more'n once. Ye see – ye see, tesn't only Miss Morwenna – tis he also as I – as we have this friendship, see . . .'

'Yes, I understand that.'

Drake rubbed the stubble on his chin. 'This week Mr and Mrs Warleggan was visitin', and so Mr Geoffrey Charles, he sends me a note saying they'll be from home and can I come see him at the house just the once more, as soon he'll be going 'way school.'

'The young fool,' Ross said. 'He was asking you to run yourself into trouble.'

'Well, mebbe. But I reckoned I could manage it – and I did. I went through the fields – then in at the side door – they was waiting.' Drake's face twitched. 'Morwenna says she is being sent away too, so it's like good-bye for we. We just sit and talk for half an hour and then I says I must be going. So then Morwenna – she give me a scarf – so as I shall mind her – as if ever I could forget! – and Geoffrey, he d'say to me, I must give ee something too, Drake. So I'll give ee my christening bible, he says, and that is what he done. I says, no, I can't take 'n, tis your own, wi' your name letters on the front and – and a clasp, I can't take 'n. But he says, please, please, Drake – you d'know the way he has – so in the end I take 'n. Then I d'leave the house and come home. I don't know whether someone seen me – but just then I don't sort of care. I just come home walking blind, and lays the two presents under the straw of my bed and then I lays on it and . . . well, didn't behave manly . . .'

In a near-by field two men were trying to separate a cow from its calf, and the lowing of one and the bleating of the other echoed up into the cool summer morning.

'What day was this?'

'Tuesday eve.'

'And they came for you yesterday. So in that twenty-four hours the Warleggans presumably returned, someone told them of your visit, and it was discovered that the bible was missing. Who came to your cottage?'

'Constable Vage and a tall thin man with close-fixed eyes. I seen him 'bout the estate . . .'

'Tankard, I expect. Did they charge you?'

'They said they had reason to s'pose I had stole a bible and other pieces from Trenwith and they was goin' to search the cottage. They found the bible were I laid 'n. I'd not even so much as looked at'n since the night before when I laid'n there. Somehow I couldn't abear to.'

Ross stared thoughtfully at the young man. 'Yes, well . . .'

Drake said: 'Tis no consarn of yours, Cap'n Poldark. Nor Sister's. I don't want for to make trouble. When I come up afore the magistrates I sh'll tell the plain truth. Tis all an error, and they'll leave me go. I done naught to be ashamed of.'

'I think you would be advised to accept such help as we can give you, boy. Where there is a conflict of evidence the accused person is not always believed. Especially if one of the magistrates has a score to settle. What size was the bible?'

'Oh . . . not big. This size. But pretty, G.C.P. on the out-side. And a silver locking clasp.'

'You were a fool to take it.'

'Aye, I know that. But at the time he pressed so hard. And I was beside meself – scarce knew what I was about.'

'Losing your girl, eh? Yes, that is hard. But you set your sights too high, Drake.'

'When I met her I wasn't aiming for nothing. B'lieve me. It – just come.'

'Yes . . .' Ross looked across at Renfrew, who was osten-sibly counting some shovels. 'Yes. Well, it is time you went back. Was Miss Chynoweth in the room when Geoffrey Charles gave you the bible?'

Drake thought. 'No. She were gone t'see if it were safe for me t'leave. But she must have seen me carrying it when she came back. I made no secret of carrying it.'

'Hm. But – Geoffrey Charles is quite reliable?'

'Oh, yes! I'd stake my life on that.'

'You may have to,' Ross said dryly. 'Now go in. Renfrew! Your prisoner is ready to return.'

Before Ross left Renfrew told him that the local magistrates were due to meet tomorrow, Friday, at the Miner's Arms in St Ann's. Of course, he said, if it were felt a matter of urgency, one or other of them might hear these three cases today and sentence the men or have them sent off to Truro; but with a normal meeting due tomorrow it was almost certain it would all be postponed until then.

Ross nodded, and thanked Renfrew and mounted and trotted off. He thought Renfrew was right. The only magis-trate who would be likely to disturb his day to dispose of one particular case was George, and Ross felt that George, as a new man, would not wish to appear to be taking too much on himself, particularly as the case involved an alleged theft from his own property. However much he might want to see Drake sentenced, or sent off to await sentence, he would do nothing to offend his fellows on the bench or appear to make free with his new authority.

That left a day. The magistrates met at eleven, so there was rather more than twenty-four hours. How to utilise them? Very well to say, I was stupid last time; this must be quite different. How different? By approaching each magistrate privately and in turn? But who would be at St Ann's tomorrow? Who would turn up? Trevaunance, Bodrugan, Treneglos? Warleggan certainly. And how to approach the others? A theft of a bible with a silver clasp was a serious offence. You could not expect them to regard it lightly. It might well be considered too serious for them to try and the boy would be sent off to the Quarter Sessions. If the bible was considered to be worth more than forty shillings the offence, if proved, could be punishable by death. Ross was not sure what the position of minors was in the courts, whether they could be called and what weight their evidence carried. It would not be impossible for George, if he felt vindictive enough, to strengthen his case by some servant's testimony which would outweigh anything told by Geoffrey Charles.

A nasty problem, and he thought to put it before Demelza and see what her feelings and counsel were. But as he neared home his mood changed and his direction with it. Demelza, for all her good sense and judgment, was out of her depth here. She was personally involved for Drake's safety; she knew nothing of law or the tactics which might be necessary to defeat the charge. Who did? Nobody nearer than Harris Pascoe in Truro – or old Notary Pearce. And their advice? Legal, grey and conformist. He could hear them. Get the case referred to Quarter Sessions. Better likelihood of an unprejudiced trial. More time to prepare a defence and sift the evidence. But when would such a trial take place? Ross was due to leave for Falmouth on Sunday, or at the latest Monday. He might be away a month. Anything he could do before Monday would be nullified if he were not present when the case came up.

He had changed direction as he left Grambler village, and he trotted on past the Gatehouse, skirting his own land and coming down over the sandhills to the sea, very much where Geoffrey Charles and Morwenna had been accustomed to come. No wind, for once, and he hooked the reins of Judith over a convenient post and left her there, to walk on the beach.

As sometimes happens on still mornings, there was a momentous surf. It rode in like line upon line of matchless cavalry immolating itself before an impregnable position. Never ending, as fast as one line died another appearing, it pounded in against the obstructing beach. Here and there, where a rock stuck out, white peacock fans shot into the air and drifted, gradually disintegrating into sun-shot mist. The air drummed with sound and motion. Ross began to walk.

So, purely as a tactic, it might be better to attempt to get this tried tomorrow. But how could he influence the outcome? Whichever way he turned, the figure at the end of the avenue was George.

If this had all happened to John Trevaunance it could have been arranged in an hour. Or any of the others. Even Hugh Bodrugan. A civilized discussion, an agreement to differ as to the facts of the case, an apology and an offer of payment of the value of the bible. The boy's a nuisance; send him away somewhere; then I'll drop the charge. Just that.

But how approach George? And how without the certainty of failure? George might have persuaded himself into sincerely believing Drake a thief; but that belief would be strengthened and reinforced by the knowledge that through this belief he could hit at Demelza and so Ross. To approach him in *any* way would invite humiliation. Elizabeth? But Ross could not approach her, not even, he felt, to save Drake's skin. And anyway she would take her lead from George.

Ross glanced up at the cold squat buildings of Wheal Leisure on the cliff. He had hardly been on the beach since it closed. The weather had been so bad, and he had never wanted to look at the mine and see it silent. His first venture, began eight years ago. It had prospered so well until the Warleggans began to encroach. They encroached on everything. Now even on his wish to live on his own land and to live in peace. It was trying to his new-found resolves. Perhaps this venture he was about to undertake in France was a safety-valve for his underlying instincts to violence. It was better to make war on the French than on one's neighbour.

But what if the neighbour persistently invited war? Did one go on constantly turning the other cheek? Two Christmases ago he had put the alternatives before George and then left him to think them over. Since then they had only glimpsed each other, in church or at official gatherings. They had not exchanged a word. It might now be necessary to exchange another word. How else could one make any progress in this matter?

But how exchange a word without the word becoming war? There was no time for letters, and letters anyway would be futile. He must go and see him. Somehow he must go and see him and have conversation – just as he would have done with Trevaunance or one of the others. See somehow if it could be kept civil. There ought to be a way of solving this in a decent way. If George became uncivil then it would be necessary to review one's position.

By now, almost without intent, he was back opposite where his pony was tethered. He ploughed over the soft sand and she raised her head and whinnied. As he mounted he saw Sam coming towards him.

'I seen your pony, Cap'n Poldark. I seen you ridin' this way. I thought twas your pony. I been wonderin' – waitin' . . . Have ye seen Brother?'

Subduing an impulse to snap at the young man, Ross told him what had passed.

'Blessed be the merciful God!' said Sam. 'So twas all a mistake and tomorrow he'll be free.'

'Continue your prayers,' said Ross, 'for it may not be as easy as that. Go now and tell your sister what I have told you, and explain to her that I have been taking a little time to consider what to do. I have now decided what to do. I shall seek legal advice. This may take me an hour or two, but I should be back for dinner. Tell her that, will you?'

'With joy in my heart,' said Sam. 'I earnestly believe that Drake will soon be at liberty. And I pray when this be all past twill be a liberty not only of the body but of the soul.'

'Let us attend to his body first,' Ross said sourly, and rode on.

He did not under-rate the difficulty of what he was going to do. George might well have him thrown off his land. He might well refuse to see him and then they would be no further ahead.

Ross was not an easily daunted man, once he had made

up his mind, but common sense dictated that he should take some measure to protect himself. And the most obvious measure was a companion.

Zacky Martin was a natural choice, but Zacky was over fifty and had been unwell. Paul Daniell was next, but Paul was one of the extra tut-workers taken on when Wheal Leisure closed and would be underground at Wheal Grace. And Sam would have been worse than useless. One could hardly imagine Tom Harry being a fit subject for conversion.

Ross rode on, past the Gatehouse, through Grambler village past Sawle Church and turned down the track to the village of Sawle. On the left was Widow Tregothnan's kiddley, and outside it, pushing a barrel round the corner of the cottage, was the man he wanted.

'Why, young Cap'n! Welcome! And riding the finest pony in the land! Ain't she a beauty? And wasn't she a bargain! D'you know, Cap'n, any time you want to sell 'er I'll be glad to give you what you gave me. Dirt cheap she was at the price.'

'Have a care,' Ross said, 'lest I take you at your word. I am sure you would not like that. Tholly.'

'Yes?'

'Have you time to ride with me? I need a peaceful body-guard.'

'When, now? Aye, gladly. Let me finish heaving this barrel where Widow Sally d'want it, and I'm your man.'

'Have you a gun?' Ross asked. 'Not to use but for display. So as to keep the proceedings peaceable.'

Tholly grinned. 'That I have. Wait but a jiffy and I'll get it.'

CHAPTER FOUR

They rode up to the door of Trenwith in tattered procession; a disparate yet matching couple: two big men, legs dangling, on two small ponies: the knight-errant and his shabby squire. Don Quixote at least had ridden a horse.

The door was opened by one of the servants Ross had lectured in the kitchen at Christmas. He looked startled at the sight on his steps. Ross told him to tell his master he had called and craved a five-minute interview. The servant shut the door in their faces, and was gone nearly the five minutes that Ross had asked. Then he opened the door a slit to say that his master was not at home to them.

'Go tell your master,' said Ross, 'that I come in peace. I mean no harm to him nor to his house, but I require to speak to him on a matter of urgency and if he refuses to see me I shall not go away.'

The servant, gaped, hesitating.

'Nor,' added Ross, glancing behind at Tholly, 'shall I be made to move.'

Tholly, who had not yet dismounted, hitched the old musket over his shoulder and whistled through his broken teeth.

The servant shut the door again.

They waited. Tholly's bright eyes were going over the dignified façade of the old house, the trim grounds, the well-kept farm buildings, the lawns, the flowers, the ornamental pool. 'Fine property,' he observed, and 'Yes,' Ross answered. 'I mind it when your uncle had it; he left the gardens go.' No communication had passed between them as to the object of this visit.

A brown hare scuttered across one of the fields near by, his white tail bobbing. There were partridges in a neighbouring tree. Tholly licked his lips. 'Well stocked, too.'

The door opened again. 'Master will see you – alone.'

'Wait here, Tholly. If I need you I'll call from a window.'

Tholly grinned and raised his hook. 'If you need me, then I'll come.'

Ross was shown into a small room on the first floor which had been his uncle Charles's study. Not much had been changed in here. George was seated working at a desk. Standing beside the desk was Tankard, tall and squinting. George was in an ankle length flowered dressing coat with frogged buttons up to the throat. He did not look up as Ross was shown in but went on writing. Tankard eyed the visitor warily. The last time they had met in this house he had been forced to take shelter under a table while George and Ross fought out their enmity over his head.

Tankard moistened his lips. 'You wished to see Mr Warleggan?'

Ross ignored him. He raised both arms above his head. 'I come in peace, George. I will undertake to offer you no violence on this visit unless it is first offered to me. But

282

I ask ten minutes of your time.'

George said to Tankard: 'Ask this man his business.'

Ross waved Tankard into silence; then he sat down and crossed his legs. 'My business is with you, George, not with your attorney. I would prefer that it should be private, but if you insist on having your legal adviser with you I cannot prevent you.'

'Say what you have to say.'

'When you have finished writing.'

The quill pen scratched on. Ross picked up a book from a side table and idly flipped through its pages.

The quill pen stopped. 'Well?'

'A young man called Drake Carne has been accused of stealing a bible from this house. He is at present in a noisome cell in St Ann's awaiting a meeting of the magistrates, which I understand will take place tomorrow.'

For the first time George raised his eyes, and they travelled impersonally over Ross's shabby riding clothes. 'That is correct.'

'What perhaps you do not know is that this bible was freely given to Drake Carne by its owner, your step-son, Geoffrey Charles. They were parting after a long friendship – a friendship which had been forbidden by you – and Geoffrey Charles wished Carne to have some memento to remember him by. He pressed it on Carne, who reluctantly accepted it and took it home.'

'That is not what I hear.'

'It happens to be the truth.'

'No doubt it is the version which Carne now hopes the justices will accept.'

'Have you asked Geoffrey Charles about this?'

'The boy is a minor whose emotions are easily played on. No doubt he would say anything now to get his seedy friend out of trouble. But the indisputable facts appear to be that Carne insinuated himself into this house while I was away on Tuesday – against my express orders. In other words he committed the most flagrant and culpable trespass, which in itself is heavily punishable at law; and, once in, played on the boy's emotions to persuade him not to give up their so-called friendship but to maintain it in despite of my veto.' George moved a thumb along the feathers of the pen. 'When Carne failed – for Geoffrey Charles had fully accepted that this friendship must end – he deliberately pocketed the bible and left the house with it, intending to turn it into ready money at the first opportunity. By the merest chance the bible was missed: my wife – whose present it was to her son on his christening – noticed its absence from his bedside and asked him what had become of it. After some severe questioning the whole sordid story came out. But there was no suggestion at all of a gift. It was plain theft. Once this was known, Mr Tankard went with Constable Vage to Carne's cottage on your land and the bible was discovered concealed under his bed. He was caught red-handed and I know the other justices will take the same view.'

Ross was inclined to agree with him. George had worked up a very satisfactory case. The obvious flaws were flaws that he could to some extent control. Tankard shifted from one leg to the other, and Ross wondered how he managed to support himself on such bony shanks.

'I suppose Geoffrey Charles will be called in support of your charge?'

'He is a minor and hysterical for a boy. It would do no good for your – friend.'

'My brother-in-law.'

'Yes, if you care to claim it. Your brother-in-law. I do not know the man, but perhaps he too is of a hysterical nature – these Methodists often are. Possibly he stole the bible out of some urge to avenge himself on those in this house who objected to his friendship. I suspect him now of being responsible for other insolences this summer. But let that pass. It cannot affect the outcome of the case.'

'Young Carne appears to have a very deep attachment for Geoffrey Charles – and Geoffrey Charles for him.'

'He attempted to obtain an influence over an impressionable boy. It was an intolerable presumption.'

'On the grounds of the disparity in station, I presume you mean?'

'Yes.'

'But others have aspired to rise above their class. You did.'

Having said it, Ross regretted having said it, for it made any hope of compromise impossible. Yet had not George indicated already that there was no such hope?

George had gone white. 'Show this so-called gentleman out.'

'A minute. I haven't done yet – '

'Well, I have. You promised no violence and, in so far as I can expect you to abide by anything you say, then I shall expect you to leave without violent resistance.'

'I came,' Ross said, 'in a spirit of conciliation. Unlikely in view of what I have just said; and in that spirit I take it back and ask your pardon. I do not like you, George, and you do not like me! but – however unwillingly – we are related. I did not choose the relationship and you no doubt accepted it with reluctance, but there it is. My cousin's son is your step-son, and he is at the centre of this upset between any two other families in the country I dare swear that they would clear it up amicably enough and with nothing worse than a passing hard word. So I had been hoping that even between us – if not for ourselves then for the sake of our respective wives – there might be a "settlement out of court", so to say, and a lot of unwelcome notoriety avoided.'

'I'm afraid what your wife feels is no concern of mine. You should know that by now.'

Ross kept his temper. 'And Elizabeth? Do you have no concern for her?'

'She has no interest in this matter.'

'She must surely have, for her cousin, Miss Chynoweth, is very much involved.'

George stroked his chin. 'Tankard, go downstairs will you, and tell Mrs Warleggan that I will join her in five minutes. And send the Harry brothers to watch this man's escort. We do not want him wandering about the grounds.'

When the notary had gone George said: 'Since you wish to bring Miss Chynoweth's name into this, I can inform you that that equally will do you and your brother-in-law no good. I will preserve her reputation as far as I can, but not to the extent of withdrawing this charge, so you can dismiss any thought of blackmailing me into silence.'

They sat for a few minutes then. Ross said: 'You hope for a good match for Miss Chynoweth. Isn't that so? Whitworth – though I don't like him – would be a good match for her. Is it worth destroying that arrangement and perhaps ruining her life for the sake of trying to punish a boy who did you no harm except to presume too far?'

'Miss Chynoweth's engagement to Mr Whitworth is already at an end. I felt it my duty to write and tell him that she had compromised herself with another man. Naturally this is a confidential communication which he will respect. But Miss Chynoweth will be sent home to her mother in Bodmin at the end of the summer. I have no further interest in her future. Nor has my wife. We would have nothing to lose by your ungentlemanly disclosures. The only one to lose would be Miss Chynoweth.'

Ross looked down at his boots. A flake of drying mud had fallen on the fading turkey carpet. Shades of Uncle Charles who had so often sat where George was now sitting, stertorous and immense, gently belching as he looked through the primitive accounts of his estate. They used to come up here sometimes as gawky youths, he and Francis, to ask some favour, and Charles would be half asleep, a dog under his feet, a decanter of port at his elbow.

He said: 'Do you remember when I called to see you, you and Elizabeth, at Christmas time, '93? You were at supper one evening and I found my way in and we had a conversation about living in peace. Do you remember I held out certain offers of peace and also some consequences which might accrue if the peace were broken?'

'I am not interested in your threats.'

'They were not intended to be threats, only – promises.'

Silence fell again. It was a long time since the two men had been alone together like this. Always their interchanges, whether in the form of words or blows, had taken place in the company of other people. Ross remembered once when they had come out of a ticketing and walked together down a Truro street, but that was long ago. Alone now, though full of hostility towards each other, they were less at ease. In a sense their enmity had been expressed in attitudes which were easier to maintain in front of others. It was not so much what others expected as what they expected of themselves. But now there was no audience. Dislike might run as deep as the deepest river: it could not surface in the conventional way.

Ross said eventually: 'Let him go, George.'

George shook his head, just once, the cold negative. A Roman emperor refusing to alter a decree.

Ross said: 'Face it – this is a storm in a teacup. If it blows into something more you have as much to lose as I.'

'The boy is charged. You are wasting your breath.'

Ross said: 'I respect your intelligence. I know you would never make the mistake of supposing that, if it comes to a fight, I should be impeded by any principles of general behaviour. You may despise my class but I have always been a renegade from it.'

'So? What of it?'

'I say to you, withdraw the charge. As a magistrate there is no difficulty. Let him go tomorrow and forget the whole thing. It is no victory for either you or me – but just for common sense.'

George shook his head.

Ross said: 'Threats are for bullies; and you would not be one to yield to them, I know. But if the case is heard tomorrow I shall see that a good lawyer is present and that nothing is left undone to make sure that the boy is cleared. Geoffrey Charles will be called.'

'Geoffrey Charles is at Cardew. We sent him there on Wednesday. My parents are taking care of him, as he is in an exhausted state and quite ill. His testimony would be quite unreliable.'

'Miss Chynoweth will also be called. However little Elizabeth now cares about her, she cannot relish the idea of having her reputation quite destroyed in the eyes of your neighbours and fellow justices.'

'She will not feel the more kindly towards you for doing it, Ross; but I cannot stop you if you are so inclined.'

Ross drew a breath and slowly let it out. 'Then so be it. You see . . . I do not have, personally, any big stake in this affair –'

'Then drop it and let the law take its course –'

'But Demelza does, and therefore I am reluctantly but deeply committed. I have been to see Drake Carne and I am convinced that he is speaking the truth when he says that Geoffrey Charles gave him the bible as a gift. Therefore, if this case went against him I would see it as a miscarriage of justice, deliberately engineered by you – and therefore an absolute declaration of the war I have been trying to avoid.'

George turned over a page of the letter he had been writing and flipped the paper, but he did not speak.

'If, therefore, the boy is found guilty and receives sentence you will be forcing me to redeem the promise made to you two years ago – one that I would rather not keep.' Ross paused, wondering how little he could say to convey what he meant. All his instincts were against the explicit confrontation. He said briefly: 'There is much unrest among the miners here.'

'There has been unrest everywhere.'

'So far it has been peaceable here. I think, I believe, that my influence in the district has helped to keep them peaceable. Not yours, George. Certainly not yours. Since Leisure closed you have become the most unpopular man in the district.'

George rose. 'Oh, get out of my house! This drama will not help anyone!'

287

'No, wait. I have nearly finished. I intend no drama; but let me point out what I have told you once before: by coming to live here you have offered some hostages to fate. By almost everything you have done – the closing of the old paths, the fencing of the common ground, the destruction of the Meeting House, and the shutting of Wheal Leisure while it was still in profit – you have built up your unpopularity among the miners and the ordinary folk. Not, I know, among the gentry, whom you are most concerned to please. But among the rest. That unpopularity has no focusing point at present, no nucleus on which to build and grow. If this boy goes to prison, it will provide that nucleus.'

George went to the window and adjusted the hang of the curtain. 'Do not deceive yourself. That sort of mob violence is at an end in the county.'

Ross tapped off some more mud on the carpet. 'It has seldom been that, George, it has seldom been mob *violence*. The riots, if so you can call them, have so far been remarkably peaceable. When the men get what they came for they usually go home. But a mob is a peculiar thing to control, as you well know. These mobs have been made up of desperate and hungry men, not angry and drunken men. Have you ever seen pay day even at my small mine? It is difficult to prevent men with money in their pockets from flocking to the kiddleys and spending it. Usually they get drunk in an orderly fashion and the rowdiness is only temporary. But they could, if so incited, form easily into a drunken mob. Then the riot, if it came and was directed at a particular objective, could be violent and ugly.'

'Threats?' said George. 'Do you call these promises? They are plain threats of the ugliest kind, and you would not dare to carry them out. With your reputation, and with the country in so alarmed a state as to the preservation of law and order, you would hang for it!'

'Well . . .' Ross shrugged. 'So it is a threat. But you have no witness, George. You sent your attorney away too soon. I should try to keep in the background in any rioting which occurred.'

'And let others hang for you? There speaks the chivalrous leader of the poor!'

'In this I am not a chivalrous leader of the poor. I told you. I am not prepared to be a gentleman. In this I am fighting you for the liberty of a foolish boy who by great misfortune happens to be my brother-in-law. That is all.'

George turned and hunched his shoulders. 'You are trying to intimidate me with an idle boast. You would never dare to do it. Never for a moment! Go home to your unlettered wife and occupy yourself with your petty mine and forget these delusions!'

Ross got up too, but the men kept the distance of the room between them. 'I cannot tell you, George, whether it is an idle boast until I try. It is six years since last I incited a mob. Then it was successful. Today it might fail. If it failed, then you would accomplish this – this plot to punish young Carne, and nothing worse would come to you than a few fences torn up and a few trees torn down. But if I succeeded then there might be loss of life among the people of this house as well as among the miners. At the end of one night, who knows? Nothing might be left of this splendid home but a few frightened animals and a burned-out shell.'

They stared at each other.

'You cannot mean that seriously.'

'I have not come here to joke.'

'Then do it,' George said whitely. 'That is all. Just do it.'

'I hope you will not force me to try.'

Someone knocked at the door.

'*Wait*,' said George.

Ross walked half across the room and leaned with his hands forward on the desk. 'I do not suppose you will be frightened by these – promises of mine. That was not the object of them. But weigh the alternatives. Is it worth the risk to exact a petty vengeance? We are both, I think, men of some courage – not easily put down. But there is a difference between us. You have the steadier judgment and the more deliberate view of life. I am the gambler. If you think mine is an idle threat, then ignore it. But to ignore it will be the act of a gambler, not of the balanced person I believe you to be. And I, as a gambler, will feel compelled to cover my stake.'

'Have you now done?'

'Yes, I have now done.'

'Then go.'

'I hope for both our sakes that you'll make the reasoned choice.'

Tankard was at the door but Ross shouldered past him unheeding, along the corridor and down the stairs. A maidservant dodged back into a doorway; no one else about.

Tregirls greeted him with his black-toothed smile. 'Safe

and sound, young Cap'n?'

Ross grunted something unintelligible in reply. As they crunched away down the drive an accumulation of seagulls blew up from a near-by field, littering the sky with their white wings.

He was wet with sweat as the first tension began to drain away. He wondered if George was the same. He did not know if he had done any good by his intervention, but he saw that he might well have done a great deal of harm. If George accepted the challenge, then he was now committed to take it up, with all its incalculable consequences. He knew that although Demelza badly wanted to save Drake, she would never have taken the risk that he was now taking, and if she knew it she would condemn it, and if he saw Drake sentenced and then attempted to fulfil his threats she would be utterly opposed to him.

By making his threats, indeed, he might have played into George's hands. If rioters ran amok and damaged or destroyed the house, George might think this a fair price to pay for having Ross Poldark in the dock once more. For, in fact, how could one lead rioters without betraying one's own hand in it? A few men like this gaunt scarecrow now riding beside him would willingly run amok at his invitation, but could he, in spite of all disclaimers, really see them accused of riot in his place? And forewarned was forearmed. If Drake were sentenced and George expected reprisal he was not without support within his own estate. Half a dozen gamekeepers and servants, resolute and armed with guns, could do much to deter a mob.

The thing was a desperate mess, which he, by this intervention, might have made much worse. It really now depended on his reading of George's character. A cautious, cold man, rich and becoming richer, ambitious to be a real power in the county, ambitious to be popular among people of birth and taste, a man accustomed to use money for his own ends, to make it work for him and indeed to use it to pay off old scores. But not at all a man of violence. To him violence was out of date, something medieval, to be despised. In the modern world one accomplished one's purposes by quite different means. He was not at all a coward but he had a great deal to lose by becoming embroiled in anything so crude and dangerous. One hoped too that he was sufficiently sure of himself not to have to resist a threat, for fear of being thought afraid. One hoped.

But until tomorrow at the earliest one would not know. In the meantime the emergency had to be dealt with in stages. If the charge were not dropped there was just a hope – however remote – of getting it dismissed. That depended on who turned up for the justices' meeting tomorrow and how far they could be influenced by a good defence.

It would be almost unprecedented to defend at all on any such grand scale, but after the fiasco of Jim Carter Ross did not intend to entrust anything to his own powers of persuasion. So a lawyer of some sort must be got, and the nearest was in Truro. Old Nat Pearce was too far gone to be of value, but Harris Pascoe would know if there was a good younger man coming on. He would have to be engaged. And he would have to be seen today.

'Tholly,' Ross said. 'I must ride on from here. I'll pay you for your time when next we meet.'

'Sunday?'

'Eh?'

'Twould be Sunday, you said.'

'Oh . . . yes. I had forgot. It is coming so close.'

Tregirls peered at him. 'No change o'plans, I s'pose?'

'I might postpone it until Monday to leave. It depends. In any event we do not expect to sail until the morning tide of Tuesday.'

'Aye, aye.' Tholly reined in his pony. 'That's what you said. The others will walk? Sooner them than me. I was never much of a walker, young Cap'n. Four legs is always better than two. But twill be good to feel a deck under me feet again. Two year is a long time.'

CHAPTER FIVE

Undisturbed by the events of the past week, untouched by the quarrels within the house and the tensions that existed without, one person at Trenwith sat as at the heart of a cyclonic wind making her own centripetal plans, dictating her needs, muttering over her personal frustrations, preparing her trousseau and planning her day. Aunt Agatha had never been married; now she was making special arrangements to meet her spectral bridegroom who was to come and crown her on August 10th with the laurel wreaths of a hundred years. To meet this occasion in the proper manner she needed just as much attention, just as much personal cosseting as any young bride. And of course she was not getting it.

Lucy Pipe was useless – she could scarcely read, and her writing was worse; furthermore she had no authority in the house. She was a servant and messages sent by her were ignored. For a while the young Chynoweth girl had been helpful but now for two days nothing had been seen of her.

The elder Chynoweths had no attention or concern for anyone but themselves, and anyway Agatha and Mrs Chynoweth had never got on even in the palmy days of twenty years ago.

So – that left Elizabeth; and Elizabeth, though the best of a bad lot, was always busy, always edging away, always promising to come back.

'If the materials be not here soon,' she said, 'there'll be time for naught to be done. When will ye be sending next? That Trelask woman. Thinks she can pick and choose now, I suspicion. All these fashionable folk. No time for us old ones. Why, I mind when she was a little sempstress – would come out and mend your stockings for a penny or two. It won't do. Nothing will come of it.'

'I sent last week,' Elizabeth shouted. 'Last week! They have promised material by Monday. Mistress Trelask's daughter will come with it!'

'Eh? Why not?'

'She will *come with it*! And she will stay until you have chosen and she will *make it up here for the first fitting.*'

'Ah,' said Agatha. 'Ah, yes. But when?'

'Afterwards she will return to Truro and the frock will be completed there. There is still plenty of time!'

'Time. That's what's wrong. There be no time. August'll be here and naught done. Where's your – what's her name – Wenna?'

'Morwenna – is – not – well,' Elizabeth shouted.

'What's amiss with her? And where be my topaz ring?'

'Here. In this drawer! Where you put it!'

'Oh? Yes, well. It won't go on. I telled ye. My knuckles is swelled. It's got to be stretched. '

'That will be done. George will see to that.'

'George will see to naught if he can help it,' said Agatha, with sudden energy. She coughed and wiped the saliva from her mouth with the lace of her nightgown. 'You ask Francis to see to it, me girl. He'll see to it. I'll leave ye this ring when I'm gone.'

'I don't want your ring,' Elizabeth said, but she said it in a voice that would not carry. She was feeling very unwell today. The trouble with Morwenna, and more especially with Geoffrey Charles, had physically upset her, and she had seen her son go off to Cardew yesterday with a white angry face that for the first time had vividly reminded her of Francis. Geoffrey Charles and George had always agreed so well – George in the early days had been specially careful to make a friend of the boy – but this quarrel over the miner had caused a first deep rift between them. Of course at not quite eleven years old Geoffrey Charles was still very much under their influence and subject to their orders, but she hated to see the anger and rebellion in his eyes. It boded ill for the future. One had the unpleasant fear that the relationship between George and Francis, which had begun in close friendship and ended in the bitterest enmity, might be repeated in Francis's son. It was deeply upsetting for Elizabeth, who saw any alienation between her son and her husband as leading to the eventual loss of her son's company and perhaps even his love.

She hated this man who had somehow ingratiated himself with Geoffrey Charles, and she hated Morwenna for having connived at it.

'. . . and I want a new jet choker,' Aunt Agatha was saying. 'Th'old one's all broke to jowds, and I want a real new one. You must send Truro for it . . . Here, where are ye going?'

'*I have to go!* I have to see George! And I have to see how Morwenna is! I will come back!' It was awful, shouting. It gave false emphasis to everything.

'Give her polychrest and rhubarb. That's what I was always give. Sets you right in no time. These girls – no stomach in 'em these days.'

She was still talking as Elizabeth slid out and gratefully took a breath of the fresher air of the passage. And now for the other visit. Again a duty. No pleasure at all. But however foolishly Morwenna had misbehaved, Elizabeth had some continuing responsibility for her welfare too.

She knocked but there was no answer, so she went in. Morwenna started up from the chair in which she had been sitting and dozing. She had not slept in the night and now the warm day had overcome her.

'Please sit down,' Elizabeth said. 'Are you at all better?'

'Thank you, Elizabeth. I – don't really know. I think the – the fever has gone.' Morwenna groped for her spectacles. Her cheeks still showed the evidences of dried tears.

Elizabeth sat down and fingered the keys hanging from her waist. 'I shall be writing today to your mother, asking her to come.'

'I have written to her myself. But it is a pity that she has to come so far. You could have sent me home by coach.'

'We thought it better that we should see her – and explain. After all, perhaps we also are in some measure to blame for all this. If Geoffrey Charles was placed in your charge, your mother similarly placed you in ours. We have to try to explain how we failed – how both failed.'

'It cannot,' said Morwenna, 'explain why someone is to be accused of something he did not do!'

It was rare to hear such passion in her voice. Elizabeth wondered at this young man who could awaken such loyalty, and of such different kind. (Perhaps in a sense the loyalty and the love were not so different: both Geoffrey Charles and Morwenna were in the throes of calf-love.)

Elizabeth said: 'You should try not to upset yourself. Nobody has been punished yet.'

'But he has been arrested! Is that not punishment? And accused of theft! He is in jail awaiting sentence!'

'Who told you this?'

'It –' Morwenna stopped. 'I heard it from someone in this house. Tell me it is not true!'

Elizabeth put a hand to her aching head. 'It will all be decided in a day or two. You must admit that the young man was grossly at fault coming here. He was deliberately trespassing –'

'Geoffrey Charles invited him! He wrote asking him. What else could he do?'

'Oh, do? He could have *refused*, knowing well that he had been forbidden the house. And as for taking the bible –'

'He did not take it, cousin. Geoffrey Charles pressed it on him!'

'Did you see that?'

'No. I had gone out for a moment, but I had just given him a scarf to – to remember me by. When I came back he was holding both together. He did not say anything – he did not explain about the bible – we could not speak. We could not say anything to each other! My throat ached so that I could not swallow. I – I nodded to tell him the way was clear, and he – he just kissed me and left.'

The house martins, sweeping up and down from the eaves, made smears of shadow across the window, twittering and shrilling in the afternoon sunshine.

Elizabeth said: 'My dear, I'm sorry. It has been a great misfortune for you.'

'But why,' Morwenna said, her voice almost gone again, 'why, Elizabeth, do you not accept your son's word? Is that not enough?'

'Of course it will be taken into account when the time comes. Geoffrey Charles has been greatly at fault in all this.'

'But he is not to appear! You have sent him away!'

'He was carefully questioned before he left. Everything he said has been taken careful note of. Have no fear. Everything will be very fully gone into.'

Shortly afterwards Elizabeth escaped and spent a half hour playing with Valentine who, apart from a slight curvature of one leg, had now quite recovered his health.

The maternal instinct was strong in Elizabeth – but for various reasons her new son had taken longer to engage her deepest affections than her old. Geoffrey Charles had always been so close to her that to part with him at all had been agony at first and was scarcely better after two years of enduring it. Valentine had usurped his place without seizing on her love. But as he grew and he began to croon and talk and his dark eyes sparkled with mischief and he pulled at her frock and her hair and her face she began to feel some happiness and contentment at handling his little body and knowing he was hers.

Today she temporarily sank other concerns in this pleasure, and when Polly took him again she was dishevelled in appearance but more relaxed and ordered in her mind than she had been. So after a few minutes in her own room to put on some lip-salve and to dab her cheeks with scented powder, she went down to take tea with George.

Sam was on the night core again. He spent it working, digging, hammering, in a half daze, preoccupied with things that he knew he should not be preoccupied with.

Almost against his will before he came down, and at the little prayer meeting a few of them had had, he had offered up prayers for Drake's safety – his physical safety, at that. To him communion with God was a matter of spiritual welfare, not material. He worked to live and urged all others to do likewise, but that done it should be enough. The perils of this life lay in the temptations of the devil not in the hazards of mining, the risks of disease or the oppression of greedy landowners. What was of overall importance was keeping the well of living water continually springing up within the soul. Faith and hope brought joy beyond the reach of any material ill.

But his brother, not yet twenty years old, was in mortal peril of his life. Men had been hanged for less. It seemed then an occasion when an exception must be made and help asked of a bountiful God to preserve Drake a while longer in this carnal world, if it so pleased Him to extend His mercy. The plea was the more urgent – and the more legitimate – because Drake had so come to live in neglect of his soul that if he were to die now, without grace, he would have little prospect of coming into full communion with God and His blessed spirits hereafter.

So he prayed, and so he went down the bal, and so he worked through eight hours of the night. He and his mate were now shoring up one of the exploratory 60-fathom levels that four other men were driving south from the main lode in the hope of discovering new ground for the future. It was one of Ross's 'investments', a device to employ more men at this time, and so far, like the others, it had yielded nothing of value. Jack Greet, Sam's mate, jokingly remarked they'd be coming up under the new meeting house at Wheal Maiden soon.

When the bells rang at six Sam stretched his long back and put his tools over his shoulders, stooped and crawled his way back to the main shaft, and climbed the three hundred-odd rungs of the various ladders up to grass and blinked in the white mist of the morning. He stayed only long enough to make arrangements for a bible meeting that afternoon, then he walked home over the hill. The cottage was cold and dank, and he lit sticks to make himself tea, cut a hunk of bread and munched it thoughtfully before climbing on to his bed. There he lay for a while with wide-open eyes, thinking of Drake and the last revival, whose blessed infection he had hoped to bring back with him from Gwennap.

Somehow it had a little drained out of him. Somehow Drake's arrest had contaminated his mind and drawn his own soul away from purity and grace. He must examine his own conscience afresh to discover the weakness and the sinfulness within him which had allowed this to happen. Sleep was coming on him now but he would not permit it yet. He climbed off the bed and sank on his knees and stayed there for half an hour, often in silent contemplation but sometimes praying aloud. Then at last, rested in his heart, he lay down and quietly drifted off into a dreamless slumber.

So he slept for three hours and was wakened just before eleven by someone moving quietly about the cottage. He half sat up, rubbing his eyes in the bright light and for a moment wondered if he was now dreaming.

'Drake! Is it you?'

'Yes, brother. I tried not to wake ee.'

Sam rolled out on to the floor and stood up. 'Drake! They've left you free?'

'Yes, brother. They've left me free.'

'Blessed God be thanked! So the justices acknowledged the truth when they heard it. What a mercy God has wrought!'

'Amen to that. But the justices haven't met yet. Twas withdrawn. The charge was withdrawn. The Trenwith folk withdrew the charge. It is all over.'

Sam said: 'I'll make tea. Do you sit down and rest. It has been a sore time.' Drake, he thought, did not look uplifted or elevated for his escape. He was so drawn and his eyes shadowed. He was normally shaved twice a week, but this dark stubble of beard was heavier than it had ever been before.

'How did it happen? Was ye just left to go free by the jailer? Did no one see ee before ee left?'

'I seen no one, Sam. But the jailer told me they'd been around earlier. Cap'n Poldark's had to do wi' this. I know not what, but he helped to turn their minds into leaving me go free. Sam.'

'Yes, brother?'

'When you've made that tea, go you to sleep again. I regret t've waked you. I'll take a bite t'eat and then I'll go down Nampara to see Cap'n Poldark.'

Ross said: 'Well, it is finished. Forget it. Don't waste your breath in thanks. Just avoid any such pitfall in the future.'

'I spoke only truth,' said Drake. 'That bible was truly give to me. But what you done you done t'elp me, and I have to say thank you. And I say'n from my heart.'

They were up in the Long Field. After riding in to St

Ann's at nine to meet the lawyer who was coming from Truro, a nasty but clever young man called Kingsley who was now working in association with Nat Pearce, Ross had discovered that the charge against Drake had been withdrawn. He had therefore paid off Kingsley and, having watched from a distance to see Drake emerge from his foetid charge room, he had turned his mare homewards without having been seen by the boy. He had not spent a restful night, for he had staked what might well have been his whole future and the future happiness and prosperity of his family upon intimidating George; and he felt it too high a price to pay, or to have risked paying, in order to redeem a thoughtless, presumptuous boy from a mess which was at least partly of his own making.

He had resented having to do it, and he had bitterly disliked the necessity of such an interview with George – which had rubbed up all their enmity afresh, like an abrasive stone on a sore place – and, because Drake was Demelza's brother and he was taking these actions for her sake, some of the discomfort, the odium, the displeasure that he felt devolved on her. So having achieved his end and before any relief at the outcome could percolate through, he had ridden straight home, brusquely told her that her brother was free and as brusquely cut short her delighted and loving thanks. Up in the Long Field he went to inspect the hay and to consider whether it should be cut this week or left a while longer. On this arrived Drake, pallid, gaunt, lean, attractively boyish, dislikeable as the cause of all the trouble, hesitating, standing before him, following him awkwardly as he moved about the field.

'I feel I done wrong in this,' said Drake, 'causing trouble betwixt your house and Trenwith. Twas not my wish to do so.'

Evidently he had seen Demelza before he came up here.

'There was trouble before you ever came. The only wrong you did was to allow yourself to become involved with a young woman of an entirely different station in life – and that was more her fault than yours.'

'Oh, no. Twas no fault of hers. Begging your pardon; but she never behaved no way but as a lady should.'

'Perhaps we may have different opinions on that,' Ross said.

'No, Cap'n Poldark. No. Tis hard that she should suffer.'

It was mid-June, Ross thought. Late enough anyhow. But

a week's gentle rain followed by sun would bring the hay up another nine inches. It was miserably short. But once this fine spell broke one might well get three weeks' rain. And wind with it. Then the stuff would be lying all over the place like a drunkard's hair newly roused from sleep.

Sourly he said: 'Well, now you will be able to give your full attention to your religion again. Your brother has been worried. He thought you were backsliding. The meeting house still wants its roof.'

Drake said: 'I'm going away.'

'. . . Oh? Where?'

'I don't rightly know. I been thinking. But I caused trouble here, and twas not seemly of me.'

'Back to Illuggan?'

'No . . .'

'I think your brother will be disappointed. To say nothing of your sister.'

The boy kicked at a stone among the grass. 'I got to go away for a while, Cap'n Poldark. T'ease my own mind.'

'Well, have a care where you go. Work is hard to come by, even for a tradesman, and a parish will not accept you as a charge upon it unless it is your own.'

'Yes, I d'know that.'

'To become a vagrant is a lost life indeed. I saw a group recently being driven up the fore street of Redruth. They had done no ill except that they did not belong to the town and so must be whipped on to the next. And there one may presume they would receive the same treatment.'

'To tell truth,' Drake said, 'I don't think it worry me what do happen. So long as I can forget . . .'

Ross eyed the boy. Dramatics? The agony of shattered calf-love: In a few months he would have forgotten all about it and all the damned trouble he had caused and would be larking and whistling about the place as if nothing had happened.

Possibly. But all first love was not shallow. His own had persisted over many years. Demelza's had never changed. This boy was too like his sister.

He said: 'D'you think this hay should be cut now or wait a couple of weeks?'

'Please?'

'This field. Should it be cut now?'

Drake stared at the field so long that Ross thought he was never going to reply.

'What will you do after?'

'With the field? Use it for grazing.'

'Then there's no haste, is there? Hay don't spoil by being left. Not like corn.'

They began to walk slowly back towards the house.

'I'd best be going,' Drake said as they drew near the gate. 'I don't wish for to be in the way just now.'

'Would you like to come to France with me?' Ross said.

'What?'

'I'm going to France. Would you like to come?'

'To – to France?'

'Yes. There are seven or eight going from this district. We are taking part in a French landing.'

'I – when would you be going?'

'Sunday or Monday. We sail from Falmouth.'

Drake walked along for a time in silence.

'It was just a thought,' said Ross, with a sense of relief. 'Forget it.'

'Yes . . .' said Drake. 'I'd like to come.'

'It will not be a religious experience, I would warn you. The French are very – unconvertible. And so would be most of your companions.'

'Yes,' said Drake. 'I'll come.'

CHAPTER SIX

They sailed from Falmouth on the Tuesday morning tide, in an Admiralty cutter, a yawl and a three-masted lugger, totalling about two hundred men. Of these one hundred and forty were French, the rest crew, or Englishmen like Ross joining the expedition for reasons of conviction, adventure or friendship. They rendezvoused with the main fleet off the Lizard on the Wednesday evening and proceeded south in convoy. De Maresi and de Sombreuil were transferred from the cutter to the flagship *Pomone,* and because of his friendship with them Ross went too. His following remained aboard the *Energetic.*

It had been a curious leave-taking. That from Demelza had been muted – not in any way ungenuine, but set about with so many cross-currents that the main stream of her anxiety was not as clear as it had been last October. For one thing, she was not with child and was able to hide her fears better. For another, his saving of Drake from a prison sentence had created a sort of *quid pro quo* in her emotions. Although he had never told her what he had done or said on his visit to George, she knew he could only have achieved his ends by means of a threat, or bargain, which must have entailed some kind of risk to them all. So it seemed that his having courted one danger on her behalf left him freer to engage in another. Or it left her less able to protest. There was a sense of fatalism in her mind too, in that she perceived more clearly than he thought that she had married a man for whom an occasional adventure came as second nature. She liked the idea of it no more for that but saw it as something unavoidable.

He had said nothing definite about return, for this was clearly out of his hands. He might be away two weeks, or it might be six. But he kissed her cool lips and stroked her face and said he would write if it was to be more than four.

'Very well, Ross,' she said, eyes looking clearly into his. 'I shall be waiting. And Clowance will have two more teeth.'

'Have a good care for them. And for yourself, love. I'll bring you back a special piece of silk.'

'Bring me back yourself.'

So he left. Little had been said against Drake accompanying him, for the alternative seemed to be to allow him to cut adrift from all his friends. But again Demelza felt that, having preserved him from one hazard they were now putting him in the way of another.

A call at Killewarren to say good-bye to Caroline.

She said: 'The female of the species has a quite detestable role to play at these times. She offers her house, her time and her money for the planning of a high adventure, and then when it comes to be implemented she is set aside on a shelf like a dusty ornament and left bobbing away there until it is done.'

'I cannot think you would enjoy bobbing away for two weeks in small boats in the company of four thousand sea-sick men. I suspect the high adventure will be packed into a short space of time and the rest will be dull slogging either at sea or ashore.'

'For a man of good sense, Ross, that is a foolish evasion.'

He smiled and sipped the sherry she had pressed on him. 'Well . . . I cannot alter it for you – and perhaps would not if I could. There is a nasty brutish sweat about war, however it may be dressed up, and I prefer the women I care for to be preserved from it.'

'I prefer the men I care for to be similarly preserved, but one way or another they embroil themselves. I trust this may be the last time.'

'Amen.'

He was turning away, but she said: 'Ross.'

'Yes?'

'I have the discomfortable feeling that it is all my fault.'

'What is?'

'Your going. Dwight's being there: that certainly is. So have a care, please, if not for your own skin then for my conscience.'

'I'll have a special care for your conscience.'

'Thank you.' She put one hand on either side of his face and kissed him on the mouth. It took several seconds. 'Well,' she said, releasing him, 'I have been wanting to do that for a long time.'

'It is a mistake to restrict oneself in one's pleasures,' Ross said. 'One should never risk being thought a Puritan.'

They smiled at each other, and he left.

He also saw Verity before sailing from Falmouth, and they had two meals together talking of old times.

He thought of all these leave-takings and of many other things during that first week on board the *Pomone* – not least of George's capitulation which, while it had greatly relieved him, had at the last rather surprised him. It showed him that his estimate of George's character had been correct; but it also showed George up to be a reasonable man. No doubt he had bowed resentfully to an uncivilized threat, but that he had done so proved him to be a person more easy to endure as a neighbour. Perhaps sooner than one ever supposed it might be possible to come to some accommodation in the district so that they could all live in peace.

The weather was fair that week, with an easterly breeze, and each morning when dawn broke, red-smeared and smoky, a wonderful sight was to be seen. To the south of the *Pomone* the ships of the Channel Fleet rode like great sea birds that had settled on the water but held their wings still unfolded. The *Royal George* and the *Queen Charlotte*, both of 100 guns. The *Queen*, the *London*, the *Prince of Wales*, the *Prince*, the *Barfleur*, the *Prince George*, all 98s. An 80, the *Sans Pareil*, and five 74s, the *Valiant*, the *Orion*, the *Irre-*

sistible, the *Russel* and the *Colossus.* And all around the *Pomone* were the rest of Sir John Borlase Warren's squadron: three line-of-battle ships, five frigates and the forty or fifty sail carrying the French troops and their supplies. It was a great fleet, sufficient to put heart into the faintest doubter.

But there were no pessimists in those early days, and the evening meals in the aft cabin of the *Pomone* were cheerful, noisy, confident, conducted haphazardly in two languages, sometimes both spoken together. Charles de Sombreuil was outstanding in the company both as a conversationalist and as a strategist.

Yet even in those very early days Ross was aware of dissension between the leading Frenchmen. It appeared that the Comte Joseph de Pulsaye had never previously met the Comte d'Hervilly, his second in command. Attempts which had been made to bring them together in London had failed, d'Hervilly always being too busy with his regiment. Seeing them at the same table one realized why. De Puisaye was a huge, stout, powerful man, a Breton himself, and one-time leader of the Chouans, those Bretons who had banded themselves together and carried on a desultory war against the Revolution ever since the King's execution. Though a count himself, his nobility, like his accent, was a provincial one, and he had the further disability in the eyes of many people of having been a Girondist in the early years of the Revolution, before he turned against it. D'Hervilly, on the other hand, was a colonel of one of the best regiments of France, the Royal-Louis. His aristocracy was unimpeachable, his relationship with the exiled Bourbons of the closest, and his contempt for M. de Puisaye and his half-peasant following barely concealed. It was an unfortunate beginning to the adventure.

This division existed even among the troops. The spearheads were the few crack regiments available, made up of the finest fighting soldiers, highly trained and disciplined. But of necessity these were few, and the rest of the soldiers were a motley lot, recruited anywhere and anyhow.

Furthermore, as the fleet drew near its destination and as tactical and strategical discussion begun, it became clear that neither of the leaders had a clear idea of how to exploit any early success which might be theirs. De Puisaye waved a hand and explained that at the very sight of a counter-revolutionary force the whole countryside would rise and they would proceed in triumph to liberate one town after another. Two Chouan officers, who had most recently arrived from Brittany, confirmed that 10,000 armed men were in the hills surrounding the area of Quiberon and Carnac and would join forces with them as soon as they landed. D'Hervilly, who had the responsibility of leading the troops, produced his maps and pointed with his long thin forefinger and asked, where, where, where. At each generalization offered him in reply he shrugged and took a pinch of snuff and looked coldly at his friends.

When they were not far from the French coast, an advance frigate sighted French warships, and the whole of the Channel Fleet wore away to give battle. The weather was changing, the sky smeared and troubled, but for a while the wind dropped. Ross took the opportunity to row across to the *Energetic* to see how his own followers were. He found them occupied rather as he would have expected. Drake had borrowed a bible and was sitting in a coil of rope reading it, with his forefinger keeping him in the words. Bone was mending his shirt; Ellery and Jonas were aft helping with a rope; Hoblyn and Tregirls were playing *tric-trac* while some Frenchmen looked on.

Ross could not stay long, for if the wind picked up he would be likely to be marooned aboard the *Energetic*; but he had a word with each, longest with Drake, who had benefited from his week at sea. As he was about to leave Tholly sidled up to him and said:

'Know what I think, young Cap'n?'

'No. What do you think?'

'That this is a bit o' trouble we're running into. This here. This landing, like.'

'Why do you say that?'

'These Frenchies. I hear 'em talking. They think I don't understand. Some of 'em's prisoners of war. They've been prisoners of war and now they're let loose.'

'D'you mean . . . Released to join this expedition?'

'That's what I do mean. Someone's been round the camps in England asking for volunteers. See? You a Royalist? You want to fight for the new King? You want to overthrow the Republic? If ye do, join our expedition.'

'And? . . .'

Tholly coughed loudly through his horrible teeth. 'What ye'd expect. Tis a fine way to go home. That's what they've said. I've heard 'em whisper, whisper in the dark.'

Ross stared across at the frigate which was his home. One of the sails was lifting.

'You think when they get ashore? . . .'

'Some'll fight, maybe. Some'll not. Some'll just down muskets and away.'

'This may be an isolated case. Have you heard many speak thus?'

'Enough.'

'Ah . . . Well, it will have to be borne in mind.'

'Excuse me, sir,' said the sailor who had come with him. 'I think we'd best go.'

'Yes.' Ross patted Tholly's good arm. 'Be careful you do not win too much money from Jacka. He has a nasty temper when roused.'

They saw no more of the Channel Fleet, but news reached them of a sharp engagement in which three French ships of the line had been captured. They themselves stood on for France and anchored in the lee of the Quiberon peninsula on the Thursday evening following.

It was a part of the coast Ross had never been to before. The bay of Quiberon faced east and was formed by a tongue of land jutting out into the sea towards a considerable island, which was called Belle Isle. This tongue of land, he was told, was six miles long and from one to three miles wide. It protected the bay from all winds except the southeast and made this a stretch of coast ideal for landing troops or supplies.

It looked very peaceful that evening with two or three little villages drowsing in the declining sun and scarcely anyone to be seen. The long unbroken stretch of sand reminded him of Hendrawna Beach, except that the surf was non-existent and the cliffs not so savage. He stood with de Sombreuil and two or three others, watching two French coast pilots approaching the convoy. They were each flying a white flag and as they came nearer they could be heard shouting: *Vive le Roi! Vive le Roi!*

'It is the beginning,' said de Sombreuil, quietly now, his enthusiasm given way to sober emotion. 'There is my land. So I salute it. It is all how you see it, is it not? To a man from the Americas or from some other part this is just — land, landfall. To me it is *France*, my home and my life.'

'Where do we expect to put our men ashore?'

'Over there. At the furthest point from Quiberon. That is

the village – Carnac. We are told all will be ready there to receive us. But two officers were sent ahead in a pinnace – two days ago it will depend on their report.'

Ross could see a familiar figure on board the *Energetic*, which was coming to anchor near. He waved a hand and saw a hooked iron raised in reply. There was much shouting between the pilot boats and the anchored fleet, and presently two men came aboard and went down into the cabin below. They were there half an hour and then reappeared accompanied by the lean austere figure of Colonel d'Hervilly.

'He is going to see for himself,' said de Sombreuil. 'I do not think he is the best man to lead such a mixed company, but one does not question his courage.'

They watched the count being rowed to one of the pilot boats and then the boats put in to the shore. One or two other boats, fishing smacks and the like, began to appear and to circle round the fleet. There was no sign of hostility. The sun went down. Two days of rough weather had followed the calm off Brest, but now it was quiet again. Ross wondered if his hay was yet safely in.

After dark M. d'Hervilly came back and a council of war was held in the captain's cabin of the *Pomone*. Ross was not invited to be present but de Sombreuil kept him well posted. It was a meeting of high words. D'Hervilly had found nothing in Carnac: a few Chouan officers, a few amiable peasants ready to help; no sign of the 10,000 men promised, only assurances that they would come, would flock out of the hills to join the expeditionary force once it had landed. Once it had landed, they promised, everything would follow. But on the evidence of his personal reconnaissance d'Hervilly decided that no landing at all should take place.

For a time nothing would move him. It was entirely against all military sense, he said, and indeed against the instructions of the Court of St James, that he should land a weak force almost devoid of cannon, heavy equipment and horse upon a shore where they would be bound soon to encounter well-organized Republican resistance. All the promises of the Chouans, so persistently repeated in London, had been broken. The landing army might remain here in its convoying ships, or it might return to England; he would not, he declared, leave it to its destruction ashore.

Against this all the persuasions of M. de Puisaye and the other Bretons beat in vain. They swore that half Brittany was already in revolt: it needed only a single light to appear in the Bay of Quiberon for the whole country to burst into flame. They asked him what resistance he had met with in his own landing? He was welcomed as a friend. Then Sir John Borlase Warren, who had hitherto held his peace, tried to move the angry Frenchman. Having built up this invasion force, with all its armaments and provisions, did it not seem, he said, inglorious to return without at least making some attempt? Even if the army landed and things went wrong, it would not have its escape cut off. The fleet would remain to guard the lines of retreat. The French fleet had been severely damaged and driven back into Brest. There was nothing to fear at sea. Re-embarkation was always available.

Then someone at last mentioned courage, and it took English intervention to prevent a duel. Then d'Hervilly abruptly gave way. So be it. He was overruled. They should land tomorrow morning at daybreak. The responsibility for the landing should be his – the responsibility for making the *decision* to land was not. That had to be recorded; then he would consent.

De Sombreuil came up at once and told Ross.

'We shall begin to lower the boats now. The troops are to be issued with thirty cartridges and two flints per man, and provisions for four days – nothing else but the knapsack. They will take their places in the boats all through the night and at dawn will begin to land. Helas! It is the beginning!'

'You agree with de Puisaye?'

'I think de Puisaye is too much wind. But it is the thing to do now. And he is right, I believe, in general. The country will rise, if we are not annihilated first!'

Ross rowed over to the *Energetic,* where boats were already being lowered. After finding a space among them in the dark, he went on deck and had another word with each of his friends. Neither they nor the other English on board were preparing to leave. He had a last word with Drake and told him why this must be an entirely French landing. 'Nor have I,' he added, 'offered you any explanation yet as to why I have brought you and the others.'

'I don't mind,' said Drake. 'At least t'as taken my thoughts away.'

'As to what I intend to do – if anything – it will all depend on the success of the landing. I have no fixed plans. Indeed we may do nothing at all.'

'I don't mind,' said Drake. 'It has taken me away from what I left behind.'

The landing took place in the first light of a blurred and showery dawn.

About three thousand French, who had spent most of the night in the little boats dozing and huddling against the chill wind, went ashore near Carnac. By now their coming was not unexpected and they were greeted by volleys of musket fire from a detachment of Republican soldiers who had been hurried there during the night. A few Royalists fell, but d'Hervilly ordered one of his best regiments to land in a cove behind the enemy and climb the rocks to take them in the rear. This they did with the greatest *élan,* many soldiers not waiting for the boats to ground but leaping into the sea and swimming ashore. After barely an hour's fighting the Republicans, who were outnumbered ten to one, dropped their arms and fled back along a road which led to a town called Auray. The Royalists marched into Carnac in triumph as the sun rose through the misty clouds. Crowds of peasants swarmed around them shouting *'Vive le Roi!'* and waving flags. When d'Hervilly arrived he was mobbed. Now that they were actually ashore, now that a Royalist army was in their midst, people really did begin to come in from the neighbouring villages, rapturous with joy. It looked as if de Puisaye after all had been right. De Puisaye was certain he had been right.

He landed himself at ten o'clock along with most of his staff, and was greeted as a liberating angel. De Sombreuil had been with his regiment since dawn, but Ross was now permitted to land, along with de Maresi and a half dozen British naval officers.

It was a wild scene, for the peasants were bringing out their wine and food to feast their saviours. Many of the less disciplined French soldiers had got no further than the beach, where they had thrown down their arms and sat on boxes surrounded by exultant Chouans, drinking wine out of litre jars and accepting cheese and cake and anything else the grateful villagers offered them. Others were roistering in the little town. It was, thought Ross, the perfect situation for a counter-attack.

Fortunately others thought the same. While the Comte de Puisaye was being received at the *mairie* as if he were Louis XVI returned to life, d'Hervilly was issuing orders for detachments of his best regiments to probe into the countryside for signs of the enemy. He led a company of grenadiers himself, Sombreuil another. Ross would have liked to accompany them, and was not at all at home among all the rejoicing.

He walked down again to the beach and watched the supplies being ferried in. In his enthusiasm de Puisaye had ordered that they should be brought ashore and distributed to the Chouans, who were hungry for arms; but no one was totally in command of the operation and no one had received any orders as to how the distribution should take place. As a result it became a free-for-all. Great boxes were unloaded on the beach and broken open. Some were full of muskets, some of shot, some of clothing, some of medical supplies. An attempt was made by a trio of Chouan officers to keep the distribution orderly, but soon the peasants, with their rooted dislike of waiting in turn for anything, were crowding round seizing at things almost before they were unpacked. In many cases Ross saw women going away with English muskets, others laden with new uniforms issued for troops of the line. Sometimes quarrels broke out and the French fought among themselves. He saw six Chouans dragging away a light cannon, wrenching it up through the soft sand. He saw a man with six muskets, unable to carry them, almost on his knees.

At an early stage he had tried to interfere but had been snarled at for his pains.

Lieutenant McArthur, one of the British officers, said: 'Ye can do naught with them. We must leave them be.'

'Someone must tell de Puisaye before it is too late.'

'Could he stop them, d'ye think?'

'At least he could stop the supplies leaving the ships.'

They went back together and after a struggle were able to force their way into the presence of the General. But all were now being carried along on the crest of a wave. D'Hervilly had sent word that an important fort on their right flank, Fort St Michel, had surrendered without a shot, that he was leaving a company of fifty Chouans in charge and was pressing on further south. De Sombreuil had sent back news that a village called Plouarnel had fallen and that the fleeing Republicans had left behind great supplies of food and ammunition. The whole country was rising, as had been predicted. What did it matter if the supplies being ferried ashore were not all distributed as equally as they should be? Soon there would be plenty for all.

The day passed and night fell. All the commanders of the advance detachments had returned, and at a conference in the *mairie* they showed their dispositions. In spite of the chaos of the day these were as wise as a good general could have wished. Roughly the liberators now occupied an amphitheatre with the beach as a stage. The arc stretched about five miles from tip to tip and bulged about five miles inland. The army was well placed to resist attack and yet still had its back to the sea where its immediate provisions lay and its line of retreat. The Republicans had fought here and there but the resistance had not been prolonged or fanatical. Always they had given way.

'Who commands the Republican army in this area?' Ross asked de Sombreuil before they separated for the night.

De Sombreuil grimaced. 'Lazare Hoche.'

'I do not know the name.'

'You will, I fear, unless we are able to scotch it soon.'

'An able man?'

'Perhaps the best they have. But he is yet young – about my age – twenty-six or twenty-seven. Cunning, fierce, wise. We shall see.'

'What are the plans for tomorrow?'

'None yet. Talk, of a certainty. Dissension, of a certainty. Quarrels – possibly.'

'Should we not first take Quiberon? We need a port. Are there not more supplies to reach us from England?'

'Oh, yes. But Fort Penthièvre which guards the neck of the peninsula, it will not be easy to reduce. The peninsula there is scarce a mile wide and is overlooked by the guns of the fort on all sides. There is no cover for attacking troops, and to take it will cost many lives. As for the rest, already you see there is much suspicion, dislike among the commanders. Who knows what will be happening? At least it begins well. We shall see.'

CHAPTER SEVEN

So day came and it was as de Sombreuil had predicted. Argument, dissension and quarrels. The aristocratic French distrusted the troops they were expected to rely on to guard their flanks; they saw the Chouans as a rabble of unreliable peasants who would fly at the first shot. The Chouans saw these arrogant supercilious noblemen as fops and dandies who were given preference in everything, and returned contempt with contempt. Here and there quarrels broke out where a Frenchman of noble birth had been heard mimicking the accents and manners of the people they were expected to associate with.

Meanwhile supplies continued to be ferried ashore and to be distributed to all who came for them. A man had not even to declare his loyalist sympathies to be issued with a musket and a supply of shot. By the third day the whole of the 80,000 muskets had been landed and distributed.

Yet the enemy scarcely moved and had been seen to evacuate several important positions without a fight. It was very hopeful. A division of the Chouans attacked and captured the valuable town of Auray seven miles inland. It had a good river and could be considered a port for small vessels, though it would not take warships or transports. A detachment of grenadiers advanced beyond it to cut communications with Vannes, a centre of much greater importance. Landevan and Mindon fell.

De Puisaye was again all for advancing, without much thought to the military strategy involved. Although he had been the leader of the Chouans for some time before he went to London, his ideas of warfare were vague and heroic. But d'Hervilly's ideas were as limited as de Puisaye's were expansive. He totally disbelieved that if he advanced on Vannes it would fall. He saw only his own army, deficient in horses, cannon and all the heavy armament necessary for meeting a Republican army if it caught him and brought him to battle.

At last it was decided to attack Fort Penthièvre. Ross discovered that de Sombreuil had not exaggerated its formidable defensive situation; yet this seemed the position that must be secured before anything else was attempted. The plan was that the English would support a landing made on the tip of the peninsula by some of the best of the French regiments, the Hector and the Loyal Emigrants, under de Puisaye himself, while the fleet came in and bombarded the fort at close quarters. At the same time d'Hervilly was to lead the attack from the land side, with the Royal Louis and the Dudresnay regiments. Both attacks were to be supported by large numbers of Chouans. It began at dawn, but to everyone's surprise the resistance was half-hearted, and almost immediately the commandant of the fort offered to parley. D'Hervilly, at considerable risk, went into the fort alone to negotiate, and after long hours of bargaining persuaded the commandant to surrender. It was a great triumph. By this capitulation the whole of the Quiberon peninsula fell into Royalist hands. Even d'Hervilly, greeted now as a hero, permitted himself the luxury of a smile.

But thereafter followed further inactivity, confusion, and divided councils. Even the commissariat broke down. Soldiers at a distance of a few miles from headquarters sent messages complaining that they received no rations until six o'clock in the evening. There was no organization to deal with the simplest administrative problems, and apparently there had been little attempt to create any. No one looked even a few days ahead.

Ross was growing impatient. Privately he thought d'Hervilly's caution in wishing to wait for more heavy guns from England before facing a battle was justifiable in a purely military sense, since once or twice already in small skirmishes the untrained Bretons had shown themselves unreliable. But so far as any advance on Quimper was concerned, he could see it being a matter of weeks at the best. There had been no *universal* rising in the countryside, no momentum of revolt. If they had to fight their way forward league by league, who knew what time it would take? Already he had been from home nearly three weeks, and he had written to Demelza by yesterday's pinnace. But he was doing no personal *good* here. He was not even allowed to fight. And so far his Cornish following had only been allowed ashore twice.

And then came news that General Hoche was at last moving. Here and there the lines of the tenuous perimeter first set up by the Loyalists were being dented by sharp Republican attacks. An army of Chouans between two and three thousand strong was routed by a counter thrust from Hoche's centre; then Auray, so recently captured, fell again; the defenders threw away their arms and fled without a fight. An aristocrat called de Vauban had been commanding them, and at length he rallied them and brought them to a halt, but they could not be persuaded to counter-attack, and he sent back messages of scathing contempt. An infective suspicion pervaded the army. Already on at least two occasions Bartholomew Tregirls's predictions had been fulfilled – soldiers fighting for the King had abruptly changed sides and declared themselves loyal followers of the Republic.

Then, three days later, at one of the stormiest council meetings of all, d'Hervilly announced his decision to withdraw all his best troops from the perimeter defences and to concentrate them within the fifteen or so square miles of the Quiberon peninsula. The outer defences were to be manned by the Chouan irregulars, officered by a few aristocrats such as de Vauban and de Maresi. As a piece of military logic it was again unassailable. Protected on three sides by a British-patrolled sea and on the fourth by Fort Penthièvre, these regular forces were now in a position of great defensive strength. But Ross felt that as a piece of political strategy it would be disastrous. To the thousands of waverers in the province it was notice that they should stay quiet and not raise a Loyalist hand until the struggle proceeded further.

Very quickly it was seen that to the inhabitants of villages such as Carnac, who had greeted the invaders as saviours and had given them all possible aid, it looked like a notice of abandonment and desertion. They had little faith in the irregulars holding out for long against Hoche's seasoned troops, and once these villages were recaptured they would suffer merciless Republican reprisals. So hundreds clamoured and wept as the liberating Loyalists army sullenly assembled to move out, and crowds followed the army carrying their belongings and dragging their children towards La Falaise where the first new defences were about to be set up.

Ross had spent most of the day on the *Energetic* and knew nothing of this, but, landing on the beach near Penthièvre with Bone and Ellery in the evening, he saw the troop movements and heard the laments of the people who followed behind, so he hurried to ask what was amiss. Then he spent a couple of hours walking round the peninsula, as he had come ashore for a purpose. After the fort had fallen many of the ordinary soldiers had been billeted in hamlets along the tongue of land; but these were mainly Chouans, the crack regiments, once the fort fell, being deployed elsewhere. Now the good regiments were being brought in and the Chouans were expected to move out to make way for them. Everywhere were arguments, quarrels, orders and counter-orders, bitter disarray. Even the soldiers near headquarters had not eaten anything since dawn.

After a while the three Englishmen went back to the fort and Ross made an attempt to find someone in authority. But the nearest he got was to enter the large officers' room in the fort and to see the bulky figure of the Comte de Puisaye surrounded by a crowd of protesting Chouans. Any hope Ross had of having a word with him was remote indeed, so he returned to Bone and Ellery and said:

'There is nothing we can do tonight. Let us go back. We shall be safer aboard.'

So through the starless July evening, with the tramp of feet, the rumble of wheels, the chatter of excited French in their ears. Ross did not so much fear for his own safety in this mêlée – at worst he could make himself understood in French and he had the authority of manner to carry it off – but Bone and Ellery who could not speak a word might find themselves attacked as spies; for every man suspected his neighbour.

They had almost reached their boat when a solitary horseman came past them. Even in the dark his figure was hard to mistake and Ross called:

'De Sombreuil!'

The horse was reined in.

'Who is that? Oh . . . it is you, Poldark. What are you doing away from your little ship?'.

'I brought two of my friends to stretch their legs. Have you five minutes?'

'An hour if you wish it – for all the good I do here or elsewhere. Decisions are made. Or do they just grow? It is becoming a *cauchemar*.'

Ross said to Bone: 'Take Ellery to the boat. I will join you in a few minutes.'

De Sombreuil had slid off his horse, was patting its nervous nose. Even though it was only a farm horse it had become infected with the general unrest.

'What effect is this going to have, Charles?' Ross said, pointing at the bobbing lights, the moving columns.

The Frenchman shrugged. 'Oh, I know, I know. Who decides it? Not I. Sometimes I am of the councils, sometimes not. In fact I was away when d'Hervilly forced this decision. Of course we have a battle ahead – of course this I know: the enemy is not far away. By this withdrawing we have established a strong position. Who then moves the first? . . . But it is not all just decided by the battle.'

They stood there for a while unspeaking.

'Charles.'

'Yes, my friend?'

'I am of no value to you here – you know that?'

'Of great value to share a meal, a glass of wine.'

314

'Yes, yes, but you know that I am hamstrung because I am no part of the regular English force and because we English have to tread a tightrope lest *we* appear to be invading France.'

'If you were you would not be my friend.'

'This was understood when I chose to come. But you know my primary purpose in coming. It cannot now be achieved in the foreseeable future.'

'Well . . . the battle is yet to be fought. If we had Hoche on our side I should feel the happier.'

'But – forgive me – although the landing may yet succeed, it cannot succeed as we first thought it might. Do you remember de Maresi at Killewarren rolling up the carpet? So he said the Royalist army would roll across France.'

'Louis is always the one for the gesture splendid.'

'So . . .' Ross took the Frenchman's arm. 'How far shall I be abdicating from such high ambitions by leaving you all here and attempting to achieve my purpose in another way?'

'No, Ross. That is not so. The high ambition was ours, not yours. That I accept, and much else also. I would like you beside me in my regiment in the coming battle; but that not being possible you must consider yourself free to go home.'

'Not home.'

'Not home?'

'Not home.'

'Ah . . . I see.'

There was a crack of a cannon somewhere in the distance towards Sainte Barbe but nothing followed it.

'For this,' said Ross, 'I shall need a boat.'

'You have many.'

'A French boat. A fishing boat. A ketch, a small lugger.'

'Well . . . they are not absent from this coast.'

'I cannot requisition one. But you could.'

De Sombreuil's spurs clinked. 'On what grounds? I should not be happy to do this. Feeling between ourselves and these uneducated peasants is high enough already.'

'Then I may not have one?'

'My friend, I cannot tell you to have one. But I cannot tell you not to have one, can I? In Quiberon, in all these villages, at every quay you will see such boats. There is great confusion at this time. Someone will miss it, of course, but if you are very careful, who will know where it has gone?'

'Well . . . thank you, if I should not be acting against the spirit of our *entente* . . .'

'I do not think so. I do not think so. But it will not be easy. Spy out your ground and let it be at night.'

They walked a few paces and de Sombreuil put his hand on the saddle.

'Also, in this enterprise that you undertake, also have a care. It is not an easy matter that you contemplate.'

'Perhaps it is impossible. I cannot know until I see for myself. In the meantime, my friend . . . If I should not see you again.'

'Again? Ever again?' De Sombreuil laughed. 'In one year or two, you shall come to my château in Limousin where we shall drink better wine than anything you have tasted here! My vineyards, though small, are among the best in France.'

'I did not mean ever again,' Ross said. 'But in this adventure only.'

'Well, yes. Well, yes. But of course it may *be* ever again. This will be a bitter struggle which lies ahead . . . Do you know, it is very strange to lose one's family – slaughtered by these *sansculottes* – and also to lose one's country, one's estates, one's ancestral home. One becomes – isolated from life, and rather careless of it.'

'Do not be careless of it,' Ross said, 'for it is all we have.'

'It is all we have, but in order to tolerate it it must be worth the having. This expedition will decide for me whether it is worth the having . . .'

'And Mlle de la Blache?'

'Ah, yes. As soon as this is over we shall marry. When I can take her back to my home and raise a new family in peace . . .'

It is what I have been doing, thought Ross; but all the same I have left it.

'If you are able to see Mlle de la Blache before I – and that would seem a probability – may I ask it that you should give her this small ring? It was my mother's. I found it in a purse just before I left. It is not valuable.'

Ross accepted the ring, fumbled for his purse, dropped it in.

'With my love,' said de Sombreuil.

'With your love.'

'It is a bauble,' said de Sombreuil. 'I did not know I had kept it.'

'I cannot promise delivery.'

'Who can? You or I? We shall see . . . When are you leaving?'

'Oh, not before tomorrow or the day after. As you say, there are many boats. But also many owners. In any event, if before I leave a battle is joined I shall not go but will wait for the outcome.'

De Sombreuil showed his teeth in the dark. 'No battle will be joined – either tomorrow or the day after, not while d'Hervilly commands. We shall stand and glare at each other, we and the *bleus,* for several more days yet, each waiting for the other to make the fatal move.'

Ross waited his two more days. During this time the Republicans, well appraised of their opponents' withdrawal, quickly occupied Carnac and the other villages, the defending Chouans retreating into the peninsula or escaping by boat, to be picked up by the English. Women and children were with them, bearing with them whatever of their possessions they could carry. It was not a heartening sight. The Republicans in fact came to within musket shot of Fort Penthièvre, and then retreated, like a wave that is temporarily spent. They took up positions on the heights of Sainte Barbe and lit fires all along the coast.

So the two forces glowered at each other. The Comte d'Hervilly at last produced a plan of attack. Spies told him that the opposing army was roughly double in numbers to his own, but, unknown to Hoche, an army of Cohuans was in being at the Republicans' back. D'Hervilly believed that if the two armies attacked Hoche simultaneously they could win a resounding victory. It was certainly a possibility, but no one knew when it would be attempted. Ross could wait no longer. The time for him to leave was ripe. So he literally stole away.

It was a typical Breton fishing boat, a two-masted lugger, very similar to a Cornish boat of the same kind. About forty-five feet in length, with a beam of fourteen, it carried a sail area of probably 1,300 square feet and it would handle well in the ordinary rough winds of the coastal areas for which it had been designed. One could not see it being sensitive to the light airs of a summer night.

Fortunately the night they took it there was a stiff westerly breeze. Tregirls had spotted it two nights previously, and for two nights they studied it. The fishermen had been out as usual with the tides, but this boat had not been used. Tregirls had spent a half day in the village and had discovered that three weeks ago the owner had died and that they were waiting for his brother in Vannes to come and claim it.

It was not easy slipping down in the dark. There were so many soldiers about, so many billeted in the cottages that the tiny harbour never really slept as it would at normal times. Yet the lack of absolute quiet had its own advantages. If seen they were less likely to be challenged. And who exactly was to know what orders or counter-orders had been issued by the high command?

So they moved across the cobbles from one shadow to the next. A dog or two barked and a half-dozen drunks lay like dead on the quay. Then Tregirls was aboard, then Drake, then the others, and finally Ross. No one so far had cried thief. But there were anxious moments yet while the *Sarzeau* was detached from its fellows and quietly pulled and poled towards the harbour mouth. The last corner of the stone jetty loomed over them, then they hoisted one sail and then a second. Still no shouts. As the boat answered her helm Ross began to breathe again.

Of the eight who sailed in the *Sarzeau* that night as the sky misted and cleared and misted again, with light cloud, five knew how to sail a boat: Ross, Tregirls, Bone, Ellery and Nanfan; and this was their type of boat. They had been aboard similar craft on and off through the years since they were children. They carried food enough for about ten days, fishermen's jerseys and a number of the brightly coloured Breton neckerchiefs, so that they would pass at a distance for what they were supposed to be. They also carried three pistols, four muskets and a number of knives.

The wind dropped at dawn and did not get up again with the sun, so they drowsed away part of the day moving slowly towards Groix and the Iles de Glénan. There was no hurry. They could do little before dusk. Ross spent an hour with Tholly looking over a map of the area round Quimper and then he took out the ground-plan of the convent which the Dutch ex-prisoner had drawn for him while at Falmouth. It was a considerable building, or rather series of buildings, situated in extensive grounds.

Ross had not ever quite envisaged this sort of enterprise when they left England. At the worst he had thought that the Royalist landing would create such confusion in the province that by the time he reached Quimper the prisoners might already be beginning to free themselves. Instead the Royalists were shut up in a peninsula fifty miles away and on the defensive. The best he could now hope for was that any Republican troops in the vicinity of Quimper were likely to have been drawn south to help Hoche contain the invasion. But whether the guards at the prison would be lax or on the alert and what degree of surveillance was exercised he had no notion. The Dutchman had given him a good idea of the number and dispositions of the guards. But they would all be armed, and he wondered if he were leading these seven cheerful Cornishmen to their deaths. The one advantage – or one of the very few – was that the prison guards would all be conditioned to look for trouble coming from within – not from outside. If there were such a camp at Truro, Ross thought, no guards there would ever expect Frenchmen to appear from the outside and attack them. The analogy was good, for Quimper was on a river ten or eleven miles from the sea.

Ross was a man of action but also a man of introspection. That part of his character which made him so constantly critical of authority also worked against himself. The same faculty which questioned the rightness of the law and the lawmakers was sharp to keep his own actions under a similar scrutiny. It was a combination of character which acted both as a saving grace and as a hair shirt. So today was not as pleasant for him as for the others, who laughed and joked among themselves, happy to be on the move after so much inactivity.

He watched them and listened to them – even Drake sometimes joining in – and doubted his own decision, on which so much hung. Impatience – a sense of timing – a sense of futility – had moved him to leave the Quiberon expedition while its fate was undecided. For all the brave front that the Royalists put on, there had come to be a smack of failure about the invasion, a feeling of impending doom. All his earlier doubts, submerged in the common enthusiasm, had surfaced as the enthusiasm waned. He did not any longer believe that even de Sombreuil and de Maresi felt it would succeed. They stayed on because they were on French soil, and because they were committed to the Royalist cause and because they were brave men.

Should he, then, have done the same, at least until the thing was decided? Was he a coward, or at least less brave, to be deserting them at this moment while the issue was still in the balance? Once or twice during the day he would have been glad to have accepted that stricture if it could have given him the freedom to turn and tell his followers that after all he had changed his mind and instead of hugging the French coast they were going to sail straight back to Cornwall and their homes and the safety and comfort and routine of their daily lives. This undertaking they were about to engage in was proper perhaps to a hot young fool of twenty-one dreaming his dreams of death or glory; it was not the sort of venture to be led by a successful mine-owner of rising thirty-six with a wife and two children and a position in the county. How George would laugh. Or more probably sneer. And how justified he would be!

They made the coast across the bay about six in the afternoon, and then there was much poring over the chart to decide which was the river entrance they sought. Tregirls had been twice in these waters during his years at sea, and it was his experience that took them towards the village of Benodet at the entrance to the river Odet. An hour later they sailed in through the narrow inlet and into the broader water beyond. It was still full daylight but the fact that they were in a French fishing boat enabled them to pass unchallenged. Twice men called to them from the other boats and Tholly replied with obscenities that seemed to satisfy.

The wind was fitful between the wooded hills, and as these closed in and the river narrowed again it almost failed. But they just kept way on. By now they were approaching steep and wooded cliffs. It was a dubious point how far they should sail in. According to the chart, after passing through this narrow gorge the river broadened again into a placid lake more than half a mile wide. But anywhere now they might be stopped, and still darkness was a way off. Ross raised his eyebrows at Tholly, who was at the tiller, and Tholly shrugged and said:

'It's up to you, cap'n.'

'Then risk it.'

They reached the bay, as it was called on the chart, and the dying sun threw startling shadows and tipped the tree tops with flame. A few cottages glimmered in the evening light. Mainly these were on the eastern bank, so they kept close to the western, which was overgrown and much wilder, with one or two châteaux on rising ground among the trees. They came on a tongue of water running off to the left; it was narrow and greatly overhung but the channel looked deep enough to take them. Ross motioned to Tholly, who put the tiller over. They drifted gently into the creek, sails coming down as quietly as they could be made to.

The inlet was no more than a hundred yards, and towards its end the yellow mud was showing. Two curlews flew across the water, crying out their own names in melancholy fright. Tholly brought the lugger in to the left bank, just before the water began to shoal, and Nanfan tied up to a friendly tree.

'Be it high tide or low tide?' asked Jacka Hoblyn gloomily, staring over the side.

'High, but I don't think yet a flood.'

'Mebbe when we come leave the tide'll be out.'

'It depends when we return,' Ross said. 'We have to take that risk.'

They ate supper of bread and cheese and wine while the birds twittered and the sun sank. Then when dusk had at last fallen Ross led the way along the river bank towards the town.

CHAPTER EIGHT

They found the convent on rising ground north of the town. So far they had not been stopped. The great risk was a patrol. If they were once challenged they were lost, for only Tregirls spoke French well enough to pass a casual word without raising suspicion. But again, equating it with England, Ross thought what patrols would be tramping the streets of a Cornish town?

In sight of the high surrounding wall they squatted and Ross told them quietly of the plan of the building in front of them.

'Behind that high wall is a little town. There is one large building and four smaller ones spread over an area I suppose as big as Grambler Mine. Around it is a park, with trees, wheat fields, a vegetable garden, pasture land and a lake. This is so that the nuns could be self-supporting. Now there are no nuns but little else has changed . . . We have no certainty as to which building Dr Enys will be imprisoned in, but I am told that as a physician one would expect to find him in the main one. Now as to this main building. It is to the left of the gate as you go in, and the door into it is on the left of the building itself. The main gate through that wall has a grille through which callers may be viewed before it is opened. Just beside the gate on the inside a sentry box has been built where two sentries are posted night and day . . .'

He stopped. A cricket was creaking and sawing in the bushes.

'Tell 'em no more, young Cap'n,' Tregirls said. 'Else you'll discourage them.'

'Speak for yerself!' said Jacka Hoblyn. A quarrelsome man, Jacka, whom Ross had always been able to control. But he had not reckoned with the long immurement with Tregirls in the *Energetic*.

Ross said: 'As you go in through the main door you will be in an entrance hall, which leads to a church. This church, which of course has been stripped of its religious emblems, is the biggest room in the building, and sleeps five hundred prisoners every night. But to the right of the entrance hall as you go in is another door leading to a chapter house, which has been turned into a guard room. Here all the rest of the guards will be at night – usually six. They seldom patrol the building since there is hardly a path for them to do so among the sleepers. Beyond the church is a row of cells, a recreation room and a refectory. These of course are no longer used for their original purposes but are simply sleeping and living quarters for the prisoners.'

'That all the guards there is, sur?' asked Ellery.

'No. Another dozen or so live in the laundry which is about three hundred yards from the main building. They are the off duty guards who can be called on in an emergency. But I am told that usually only about half that number is there, since many privately prefer to slip back to their homes for the night.'

'Or to somebody else's,' said Tholly.

'Six – twelve – that's fourteen at the least,' said Drake, 'that's if the alarm be raised. But d'you hope to get in without raising the alarm?'

'We think we may,' said Ross.

It was eleven before they moved. A thin sliver of moon was just setting. The Dutchman thought the guards on the gate were changed at 10 p.m., 6 a.m. and 2 p.m. The wall surrounding the convent was about ten feet high and had been ornamented with steel spikes to discourage climbers. The door in the wall was of oak studded with iron, and the grille slid sideways in it about five feet from the ground. When the knock sounded the guard slid back the grille to see who wanted to come in at this time of night.

'*Quels poissons pêche-t-on ici?*' Tholly snarled in his thick voice. '*Eh? Eh? Voici mon prisonnier! Un Anglais qui s'échappe de votre petite crèche! Je l'ai attrapé près de chez moi!*' He held Bone by the collar and shook him.

'Let me go!' Bone gasped. 'Let me go! Ye're choking me!'

After a long pause bolts slipped back. The guard peered out. '*Qu'y a-t-il? De quoi s'agit-il? Qu' voulez-vous? Je ne sais pas de –*' Tholly struck upwards with his dagger into the guard's stomach.

The man gave a scream which choked itself into a gurgle as blood flooded into his mouth. Bone caught him as he was falling; Tholly went past him to meet the second guard just emerging from their little hut. Ross was close behind him but Tholly was first, striking with his iron hook. The second man collapsed with a monumental clatter of musket, hat, sword, belt, equipment and dead weight. Within a minute all eight of the intruders were within the wall, the door shut behind them, waiting and listening.

After that terrible noise there was silence. The crickets were busy with their dry violin solos all along the foot of this wall. In the great building to their left six lights showed. They waited for more lights to go on. Another building low and squat to the right. Could this be the laundry? It was all in darkness. An owl flitted by.

Ross bent to examine the second Frenchman. 'You've killed him too,' he said to Tholly.

Tregirls hunched his shoulders and coughed. The exertion was bringing on his asthma. 'You don't have the same delicate touch, like. Not with this.' He lifted his hook.

Ross made them wait longer than any of them wanted to. Then they moved across grass and gravel and grass again to the door of the main convent building.

It was a small door, round-topped, oaken and solid but without a grille. A lantern hung in the wall above it but was not lighted. Ross rat-tatted sharply at the door, a loud authoritative rap, and waited. Nothing happened. He tried the ring latch but it would not turn. He rapped again.

Footsteps. A French voice grumbling, muttering to itself, clearly not expecting superior officers but supposing some other guard was being a nuisance. Clack of a key. Screech of a door. A man in shirt sleeves holding a lantern. Ross thrust a pistol into his chest. The man opened his mouth to shout; Ross's raised fingers stopped him; he took a step back; Tholly snatched the lantern as he was about to drop it. Door thumped back with a thud. Then they were in, Nanfan grasping the guard's hands, Bone thrusting wadding in his mouth.

A door ajar at the end of the passage; a slit of light falling on panelled wall and tiled floor. Ross slid towards it, Tholly and Drake behind him. As they reached it a man came out. Ross shoved him reeling back into the room and they followed him. Four other men; three at a table playing cards and an empty chair, money on the table, glasses, a jar. The fourth man was standing by the slit window putting on his tunic.

'Stay,' said Tholly. 'Quiet all. Move and you're dead men.'

Jacka Hoblyn had one of the other pistols, Ellery the third. They were all in the room now, a big room, Nanfan and Bone holding the man they had first captured. Jonas unwound a rope from round his waist and with this they began to tie up the six men. Little was said. The man by the window tried to argue, tried to struggle. It did him no good. But it was a long job, tying and gagging them all. Trying on the nerves. It was a full fifteen minutes before they were all done to Ross's satisfaction. Failure here would mean failure of the whole scheme.

'Now,' he said, and lifted down a bunch of eight big keys from behind the door.

With two lanterns from the room, leaving it in darkness, they went out into the hall, to the further door which led into the church. This was locked and bolted. A key fitted; they slid the bolts very carefully. At this stage essential not to give the impression they were coming to let the prisoners out. If this idea communicated itself there would be a mad rush for the doors and a general alarm.

A vile stench of unwashed bodies, sickness, sweat. The church, which was perhaps two hundred feet long by forty broad, doubled its width at the transept and soared into lofty Gothic arches. They had come in by the west door. All the chairs and ordinary furnishings had gone; the floor was an unmoving, unsavoury carpet of human beings, packed so tight they might have been woven together. Here and there one tossed and moaned; some snored; the vast majority lay quiet, whether asleep or awake, as if they knew that only by remaining quiet could they stay alive. God, thought Ross, am I back in Launceston prison rescuing Jim Carter? Do all men's lives run in cycles?

He stared down at his feet. Twenty men to be called on within a few paces. But which to choose? He saw an eye gleam in the light of the lantern. He stepped across a couple of men.

'Hey, you! Wake a minute. We're new to this camp. Just come. Direct us, will you?'

'God 'elp you, matelot. What's there to direct? There be no room to lie 'ere. More room up by the altar.'

'I was directed to find Dr Enys. Know you where he is?'

'Who? Never heard o' him! Clear out and let me sleep!'

The man had put his head down, but Ross caught his emaciated arm and pulled him up.

'Listen – we have to know!'

'Hark yourself, dog!' Ross's arm was flung off. 'I'll have no man lay 'is 'ands on me. If ye so much as – '

Ross took a firmer grip and shook the man. The man kicked and waked two others lying near. 'There's someone ill!' 'You're English, are you not? What sort of help is this? Listen, I wish to know! Dr Enys! You must all know Dr Enys!'

'Enys?' said one of the other men, sitting up. He was a naked cadaver, but somehow still alive. 'Rot you, Carter, with your evil temper. Who's this? Who are all these? New men? God help ye all! Enys? Yes, we all know Enys.'

'Then where is he? Where does he sleep?'

'Not here, matelot.'

'In this building or another?'

'Oh, this, if you can find 'im. He'll be not far from the infirmary. He never is, I'll say that for 'im. But he don't sleep there. Try one o' the cells this side o' the refectory.'

'Which way?'

'Oh, damn your eyes! Go up to the altar. In the south transept's a door leading to the sacristy. Beyond that's the infirmary and then this row of cells. He's like to be there.'

'Thank you, friend.'

His lantern held high, Ross began to pick his way among the other skeletons sleeping on the floor, Bone bringing up the rear with the second lantern. The procession of men wound its way up the church. It was impossible to do so without waking some of the massed sleepers, for there was no room to step between. Once or twice men in the middle of the croc stumbled in the half dark, and curses followed them. Ross knew well he was leaving curious men behind him as well as wakened ones. New arrivals, he was sure, did not enter unaccompanied by guards and carrying two lanterns, and in the middle of the night.

The door into the sacristy could not be opened for sleeping men. Two had to be pulled to their feet and, more thoroughly awake than the rest, pursued the intruders with questions. One of them was very young, very alert – probably a midshipman – and he was the first to guess that they had no business here. He scrambled to his feet and grasped Drake's arm, but Drake could only shake it off and smile and follow the rest. The boy followed them. In his scarecrow state he looked scarcely older than Geoffrey Charles.

Into the infirmary. Here the stench was doubly vile, but the sick men had little more room to toss and turn. They were in rows like corpses in a casualty station after a battle. At least there was a light: a single candle in a lantern hung so high that no one could reach it. It cast geometric shadows, illuminating one sick and ghastly face, leaving another in shadow. A ragged old man with a black beard was tending a delirious patient. He rose as they came in.

'Who are you? There's no more room in here.'

'I am Captain Poldark. We are seeking Dr Enys.'

'I'm Lieutenant Armitage of the *Espion*. You cannot wake him now. He's been off duty but an hour. I have some little medical knowledge.'

'It is not his medical knowledge we seek. Where does he sleep?'

Armitage looked at them doubtfully.

'What are you here for?' demanded the young midshipman. 'Sir, I think they have no business here!'

'No business with you,' said Ross. 'We seek Dr Enys and mean only his good. I assure you, Lieutenant Armitage. My word as an officer.'

'Look, sir,' said the midshipman, 'this man has a dagger! Why are they here?'

'To slit your throat,' said Tholly, looming behind him, 'if ye need more air than will come through a shut mouth.'

Armitage was staring at Ross. 'Have you broken in?'

'Come with us to Dr Enys and I'll explain.'

Armitage said: 'I cannot leave here. Enwright, take them to Lieutenant Enys.'

'Aye, aye, sir.'

As they left, a sick man was crying out for water, and Armitage went to him. The midshipman led the way into a stone corridor with cells opening off to the left. The cell doors were not shut and at the third Enwright stopped.

'I believe he is here.'

Ross went in. There were eight derelict men in the cell, and he held up the lantern, peering to find his friend. They were all bearded, and he thought there was no one here he sought. Then one at the end stirred and sat up.

'What is it? Do you want me?'

It was a physician's reaction, used to waking to a sick call.

'Yes, Dwight,' said Ross. 'We want you.'

To Ross he was at first unrecognizable, with the heavy beard, black freckled with grey, and the skeletal features. He could hardly have weighed more than seven stone. The skin of his face was disfigured with sores. Deep sunken eyes made him look a man with a short term to his days.

At first he was unbelieving. Then he was doubting. Then at last he was reluctant.

Because he had half expected it Ross was the more urgent. 'Look, Dwight, eight of us have risked our lives for this! You have done your share here. Now you owe a duty to others. If you do not come willingly, you come by force!'

'Oh, it is not that I do not deeply appreciate what you have done. But some of these men in my charge are on the verge of dying—'

'And what of you? How near are you to dying?'

Dwight made a deprecating gesture. 'We all take our chance together. All these men with me in this cell have received a little medical training from me in the last twelve months, but they could not take over—'

'There are no other doctors—no other surgeons?'

'Oh, yes, four. But we all have more than we can do, and—'

'So should we go home without you?'

'Oh, Ross, it is not that. No, no. I thank you more than I can say—'

'Believe me, we are not out of the wood yet, and every moment you argue adds to the danger. But when we are gone these other men can get free if they will. We came this far secretly so as not to create a panic breaking out—'

'And how many of these men will stand a chance of reaching England if they do break out? How many will not be recaptured or die in the attempt to escape?'

'It is up to them to choose. No one forces them to try. But if they have the choice, is it not better to die escaping than die in this stinking hell?'

'Aye,' said one of the others who had awakened. 'Go to, Enys. Do not be a fool. I wish I had your chance!'

'Escape!' shouted young Enwright in the doorway. 'Escape!' His shout died as Ellery thrust a rough hand over his mouth.

Dwight looked round at the men above him. Then he looked at Ross. He licked his sore lips.

'Caroline – is she well?'

'She will not be if you stay here.'

'I am ready. Thompson, I leave you in charge.'

'Aye, aye, sir. Think nothing of it. But if there be half a chance I shall be following you.'

'Keep this young fool here,' Ross said, indicating the struggling Enwright. 'Otherwise he will alert the whole of France.'

He handed the boy over and they backed out of the cell. Dwight he saw was unsteady on his feet.

'Which way?' Dwight said.

'Is there another route to the main door except through the church?'

'Through the cloisters. But they are locked at night.'

'I have keys.' Ross showed him.

'Ah.' Dwight smiled painfully. 'Then I'll lead the way.'

He turned to another door and there stopped. The Cornishmen were in a cluster behind him. Bone holding the second lantern to show the way. Dwight made no move. He was listening.

'I think we are too late,' he said.

'What is it?'

Somewhere someone was shouting, and there was a growing murmur of voices. Then there was a musket shot. Before the echoes had died, the bell in the church began to toll.

The Dutchman who had instructed Ross in the geography of the prison had been wonderfully accurate. His one failure was in his estimate of the time the guards changed. Those at the main gate were changed not at ten o'clock but at midnight.

CHAPTER NINE

'Well,' said Ross quietly. 'Perhaps we have come to join you after all. Is there another way out?'

Dwight said: 'No. Nothing possible. There is an exit from the kitchens but it will be bolted. And the door to the kitchen is locked anyway.'

'That we can probably open.'

'Yes . . . Well, it is a thin chance . . .'

With the noise of wakening men around them and shouts and cries outside, they hurried through another room crowded with men just stirring from sleep. Now they could not wait to tread carefully, and many shouted and cursed as they were trodden on. As he brought up the rear Ross thought his comment about joining these prisoners an optimistic one. With two dead guards to answer for . . .

The kitchen door was at the bottom of five steps. Three keys chosen in urgency failed to turn the lock. A fourth succeeded, and they were in a great vaulted room with a few cooking utensils but bare of food. A well with hanging bucket stood at the end. The remains of a fire still smouldered in the hearth. Dirty pans lay about and the smell of stale soup. A door at the end: four or five ran to try their weight on it: Tregirls took the keys from Ross and thrust them in turn into the hole. The second clicked the heavy tumblers but the door would not budge.

'It is bolted from the outside,' Dwight said.

'Hell and damnation! Twould be impossible to open without a thundering noise!'

'Jacka,' Ross said. 'Take these keys and lock that door we've come through. It will protect our rear for a while.'

While Hoblyn ran to do this the others cast around for something to use as a lever. There was a big poker beside the fire and Ellery and Tholly took it to the door, but there was nowhere to get any purchase. The hinges of the door were this side and Ross thought it would be more profitable to attack them than the solid oak door. But if all the guards were free, with another half-dozen at least from the laundry, there were enough to patrol the grounds, and any violent hammering would immediately bring them to this door to wait for them to emerge. The exercise was self-defeating.

Two windows, small and high. But by breaking the glass you could get at the bars beyond. He put his hands to the glass, pressing it, then he took the kerchief from round his neck, put it between his hands and the glass to try to prevent cutting. He was about to lunge when Drake caught his arm.

'Cap'n Poldark. Look.'

'What?'

'The chimney. I been looking up. Ye can see the sky.'

Ross frowned at him. 'So what of it?'

'I can climb it.'

'How?'

'Tis broad enough. And Jonas has some rope left. I can carry'n up round my waist and lower it down when I get to the top.'

Dwight was beside him. 'The fire is still in, bricks hold the heat. You would burn yourself.'

'Nay, not so bad. I've scraped it to one side already.'

Ross said: 'And if we get up? We are on a roof.'

'Better'n being rats in a trap,' Tregirls said. 'I know these Frenchies if they've found the ones we killed.'

Ross took his scarf from the window. 'You believe you can do it?'

'Yes.'

'Very well. Try, then.' For an unwelcome moment Demelza, climbing trees at Nampara, had looked out at him. While Drake took off his boots and wound what was left of the rope round his waist Ross went to the door of the kitchen and listened at it. Noise and clamour from the main area of the convent. The other prisoners, having once been roused, were likely rioting, trying to get out, and were impeding the guards in their search. But it could only be a matter of minutes.

Ross said to Jackie: 'Put what you can against the door. That table might be some use.'

The fire, after being raked away from the chimney, had had water thrown in it, and dust and smoke filled the kitchen. Drake threw down a pastry board where the fire had been and stepped on it; then held the lantern to see up. There were a few hand holes but no proper spikes for a sweep's boy to climb it, such as there would be in England. He took a breath and began.

In a few steps his hands were blistered and the stockings burned from his feet. Then as the chimney narrowed the worst heat went. The brickwork was rough and gave him hand and foot holds, which he was able to maintain through pressure of his legs and back between one wall and the other.

At the top the chimney narrowed more. He had climbed perhaps twenty feet and had about six to go. The soot was in his eyes and nostrils and hair, but when he looked up the stars were visible through it. He blinked and coughed and groped for his next handhold. It was not there.

Someone called up from below, and he answered that all was well. But all was not yet well. By arching his back, head and buttocks against one wall, he made another dozen inches; then another six, then another. The top was now near. He reached a hand up, fingers clutched at a projection, slipped, held. He let go with his other hand and grasped at the top, swung a second. One foot found a precaution hold where the mortar had fallen away. He kicked a couple of times and was up.

They joined him one by one. Dwight was next to the last, for they had to fasten the rope round his waist and haul him up. Ross completed the group. A thunderous banging had begun on the door into the kitchen just as he left. It might hold three or four minutes.

The chimney stood up four feet above a spire of roof which sloped steeply on either side. But other roofs about them of similar size hid them from the ground except on the north side. This way they could see across to the laundry, where many lights now flickered, and to two other buildings which were coming awake.

Dwight said: 'If we can get across the roof of the refectory, there is a way down there. One roof leads to another and there is not six feet to jump.'

'What do we jump to?'

'The back of the convent. Beyond it is the dairy – a separate building – and after that is pasture for the cows and rising ground to the wall.'

'Can you lead? Bone will help you.'

'I can lead.'

'Take your boots off,' Ross said to the rest. 'And for God's sake no stumbling. If they hear us on the roof we are finished.'

They edged along the steep roof, Dwight and Bone in the lead, Ross and Drake in the rear.

There was an awkward point to be negotiated as they came

on to the refectory roof, for the refectory was a single storey only and it meant a drop of about nine feet. Bone went down first, slithering, with help from above, then Dwight was more gently lowered, and so one by one the others followed. From here they could hear shouts in the grounds, and then another musket shot.

Dwight directed them along the side of a parapet somewhat exposed from below. A few clouds were drifting across the stars, but it was too light for comfort. The roof here was decorated with gargoyles and stone effigies. They crept and slithered among these to another drop upon an almost flat roof, and from there it looked no distance to the ground.

'Can you run?' Ross asked Dwight Enys.

'A short distance.'

'Which way?'

'You see the dairy? Make for that, then across the open field. At the gate at the far side of the field turn south. There's an old orchard. A man got out in the spring by using an apple tree which overhangs the wall.'

'There is no other gate but the front one?'

'Yes, but they are kept permanently padlocked, and those will be the places the guards will first go to.'

Ross turned to the group clustered quietly about them. 'You heard that?' They nodded. 'Well, Bone and Dr Enys will lead the way. Tregirls and I will bring up the rear. But if we are discovered don't bunch together. Scatter and make your way over the wall as best you can. The apple trees are our best hope. If some of us get out and others do not, don't wait about outside – make for the boat and wait there. Do not stay by the boat but in the woods near by. Wait through tomorrow's daylight. If some have not turned up by midnight tomorrow, it will be concluded that they have been captured. Sail as soon as there is enough water. *Now.*'

Bone dropped to the ground and caught Dwight as he fell. They both rolled over in the rank grass. As soon as they had picked themselves up the others followed. They ran across to the shelter of the dairy. As they did so figures appeared round the corner of the house and a musket barked.

Bone and Dwight still ahead, the fugitives left the shadow and ran for the field. At the corner of the dairy Ross grasped Tholly's good arm.

'We've got to give them time.'

They stayed in the shadow. Two men came running, one carrying a musket. Ross hit him with the butt of his pistol.

The other saw Tregirls in time and ducked and swung at Tholly's head with his sword. Tholly parried it with his iron hook; metal on metal sparked. Ross hit his man again as he struggled to rise; turned to where the other two were rolling over in the grass. He groped and clawed, grasped at a French boot, yanked the man upon his face and Tholly dispatched him with the iron hook. He was reaching for his dagger, but Ross stayed him.

They followed after the others. A musket ball cracked past them: it was odd, Ross heard no shot, only the near miss of the ball. They were among a group of cows and temporarily safe. Then out in the open again – over a gate and turning right. Tholly had to stop to get his breath.

'Them cows! That white-faced one. I thought twas a Frenchie!'

Ross was peering. 'I can't see the others.'

Tholly straightened up, and his wheezing breath was noisy. He followed Ross, who kept a pace or two ahead. They moved doubled up towards a clump of trees. A figure loomed.

'I came back,' said Drake. 'I wondered – '

'Listen, boy,' said Tholly, 'you're liable to be mistook. My knife don't know the difference – '

'Where are they?' Ross said.

'Over there. By that tree. Tis an easy climb. Sid and the doctor is near over.'

They pushed their way through nettles and brambles. Whatever else had been attended to since the nuns were thrown out, the apple trees had not. Dark figures clustered together.

'Go on!' Ross said irritably. 'Don't wait!'

Hoblyn went next. His figure was briefly silhouetted against the night sky before he picked a way through the spikes and jumped. Then Jonas, then Ellery. As Ellery stood up to jump a musket barked, somewhere quite close. Tregirls was next, and being short of an arm had to be helped to climb the tree by Joe Nanfan. He got to the top and stood to jump and the musket fired again. So it was not accident or chance. Someone could see them.

'Go on, you fool!' Ross hissed, but Nanfan, having noticed how near the shot was, had ducked back into the tree. There might be more than one shooting but it seemed unlikely, and to hesitate now meant giving him time to recharge his gun.

'No!' Drake hissed. 'Go on!'

Nanfan stood up to jump; the gun fired again; Nanfan lurched, then stepped among the spikes and disappeared over the edge.

'Quick,' Ross said. 'Go quick now!'

Like a cat Drake climbed the tree and was on to the wall. Then he stood up to jump but did not jump; instead stood there several long seconds, swaying back and forth as if hesitating. Ross, half up the tree behind him, cursed and swore at him to jump. Then the musket fired for the fourth time; Drake wobbled forward and jumped; Ross, on his heels, was over the wall without trouble.

They had come over into another orchard; these were small trees; a cider orchard probably; the men were clustered round a figure. Ross thought it was Drake, but Drake came up suddenly out of the long grass.

'It's Joe. He's bad.'

Dwight was on his knees beside Nanfan. It was still too dark to see properly, but the ball had hit Nanfan on the side of the head and taken away part of his ear. The ball was still lodged in his skull. He was not yet dead. His eyes were fluttering.

Dwight said: 'There's nothing I can do. Or anyone.'

'God, we need a light!' Ross said.

'We got to leave him!' said Tregirls. 'Else we'll all be in his shoes.'

'I'll stay,' said Drake. 'You go. I'll join ye if I can.'

'Don't be a fool, boy!' Ross snapped. 'They know how we got over. As soon as that marksman tells the rest . . .'

'I *want* to stay!' Drake said. 'I don't *care!*'

'You came under my orders!' Ross said. 'You'll all go, as arranged. I will stay with Nanfan until he . . .'

'Nay,' said Ellery. 'He's my mate. We've worked together nigh on three year an'–'

'And you take my orders! All of you! We came to–'

'There's no need to stay,' Dwight said quietly, standing up. 'He's dead.'

They made their way through the cider orchard, and through another and another, each one taking them farther from the convent but also farther north and away from the river. Having lost the sound of the pursuers they began to make a detour; but Dwight was now too far gone to walk, and carrying was a slow business. Then Drake began to lag behind. They thought it was his feet, but as a little light grew Ross saw him holding his shoulder and went across and found his sleeve soaked in blood. The marksman had been successful a second time. To score two hits out of four on a starlit night said much for the Frenchman's skill and eyesight.

But it said nothing for their chances of reaching the boat today. By dawn they had worked their way round the town and were on high ground looking down on it. They had moved in the right general direction, anti-clockwise, so that the river was not between them and their boat. When it was known that Drake was wounded Dwight had made a temporary dressing to stop the wound from bleeding; but as soon as day came fully – with fortunately a light mist – and they found themselves in a wood which looked untrodden by man, he roused himself to take a closer look. The ball had gone in above the armpit and had come out under the shoulder blade. The size and position of the exit wound suggested that the ball had carried some splintered bone away with it.

With no water to bathe the wound and no fresh lint to put on it, there was little Dwight could do. With bandages torn from shirts the arm was bound to the chest to prevent further bleeding and to hold the pads in place. Drake had lost a lot of blood. It was a toss-up, Ross thought. Many men had recovered from far worse wounds. Many had succumbed to less.

By the light of day they looked a sorry lot. They were all full of cuts and bruises and were black-faced and smeared with soot from the chimney. Dwight's hands were like an old man's, the skin blotchy and brown; the skin of his face was as blue as skimmed milk, emphasizing the red scorbutic blotches. Even his voice was hoarse and thin. Taken now instantly into his own home, given warm milk and chicken broth and a pint of wine a day, and no doubt he would begin to pick up. But given a day in the open without food, followed by perhaps a week's privation at sea, and his chances looked slim. Ross cursed himself. The death of Nanfan had turned him sick. If he now returned home with Drake and Dwight dead in the boat beside him, would he ever be able to live with himself again?

But now at this moment he had to go on as the leader of this vainglorious enterprise. In a sense he had succeeded in his task, in that Dwight was free; and the loss of one man was not an inordinate loss considering the magnitude of what had been attempted. A captain commanding a platoon would consider his casualties light. But Ross, in spite of his rank, was not quite a captain in an ordinary way and this was not an ordinary platoon. The urgent need now was food and water. On board the boat – if it had not been stolen – were rations enough. But they could hardly march through the countryside and spend the day on the boat or set sail in daylight with ten miles of river to traverse. Their present relative immunity was almost certainly because of the emergency further south. If there were twenty guards left in the whole of Quimper that would be likely to be the maximum – and of those, in view of last night's raid and riot, at least a dozen would be on permanent duty at the camp.

Every man's hand no doubt would be against them, but few such hands would be armed with anything more lethal than a pitchfork. Ellery had dropped his pistol somewhere; they still had the other two.

Below, to the south of them, a chimney smoked among a clump of beeches; in the distance they could see the town, with a gleam of river; over to the west was another farm.

'There's water there,' said Tholly, pointing. 'We can tell by the willows.'

'You cannot get at it without crossing open country.'

'Nay, but it comes from higher up. If I can trace it I may be able to reach it without going down. Then there's cows. You shouldn't never have to go short when there's cows.'

'Take Jonas, then. See what you can find. But no risks. It's better to fast for a day than have them all about our ears.'

They went off at six and were not back until eight. They brought back water in Jonas's hat and milk in Tholly's. It was a ration all round and some extra milk for Dwight.

'Ye get sent t'gaol for this back 'ome,' said Ellery. 'My cousin back in '88, 'e got two months in prison for milkin' a neighbour's cow. Justices said it 'appened too often.'

Through the long morning some of them dozed while the others kept watch. Drake had lost his boots in the escape and had rags round his blistered feet. About noon Jonas went off again, with Ellery this time, and an hour later they came back with two eggs from a moorhen's nest. One of these Dwight took and the other was offered to Drake. But Drake said he was not hungry, so it was kept for Dwight until later in the day.

So daylight dragged endlessly on. They saw a woman come in for the cows, a man stacking a hayrick. A dog barked and ran around, but fortunately they were too far away for it to pick up their scent. They could see the mud in the river and later a sail or two moving as the tide rose. It was a still day, and smoke from the town created a haze over it. A high thin cloud obscured the sun. Ross watched the sky anxiously. A storm would be a disaster, but so would a dead calm.

When they came he had thought if things went well they might not return to their boat in the river but might trek across country to the sea and steal some other fishing boat more suitably situated. If they went back to the *Sarzeau* they were gambling on its not having been taken away, and also on their not walking into a trap with soldiers waiting for them. However there was now no choice. Dwight could never walk eleven miles. Nor Drake.

Later he went to sit beside Drake, who was leaning against a bush nursing his wound and his burns. He thought there was a new colour in Drake's cheeks and he did not like it.

'How is it with you?'

'Nicely, sur, thank ee.'

'Think you you can walk when the time comes?'

'Oh, yes. These cloths are so good as shoes, s'long as I don't step on sharp stones.'

'And your shoulder?'

'He'll be stiff for a while.'

They were silent. Ross thought, if that cursed dog should come up here . . .

He said: 'Last night, what made you hesitate so long on the wall?'

'Did I?'

'You know you did. Turning this way and that.'

'I wa'nt sure where to jump.'

'I think you lie.'

Drake shifted but did not speak.

'Were you trying to get shot?' Ross asked.

'Nay! Ne'er such a fool as that.'

'Then you were trying to draw the next shot – was that it? So that I could get over safely while the musketeer recharged his gun.'

Drake said: 'I'm thirsty. Be there a drain left in that hat?'

Ross brought it to him. 'Listen, boy, when I want heroics performed on my behalf I will ask for them.'

Drake put up his bandaged hand to wipe his lips.

'I was hesitating where to jump,' he said.

337

CHAPTER TEN

They started as soon as the last streaks of daylight left the sky. It was a long and tedious descent, for they had to avoid all buildings, whether out-houses or cottages. Anywhere a labourer might be coming home from his fields, and, although there had been no obvious signs of pursuit today, everyone within twenty miles would have heard by now of the raid. Much would depend on whether there was a company of soldiers left within riding distance; if so, they could be here before morning. To say nothing of *agents* from Brest or Concarneau.

Ross and Tregirls led the way. Both had had professional knowledge of warfare and before leaving the *Sarzeau* had taken careful sights of where they had tied up. An exact point on the banks of a strange river was not the easiest thing to locate in the faintly moon-shot dark.

They had been going for two hours in pairs, with Bone helping Dwight behind the first two, Ellery helping Drake, and Jonas and Hoblyn bringing up the rear; and they were not more than a few hundred yards from the river though somewhat downstream. Ross had just changed direction back towards the town when Tholly held up his hook. Everyone fell silent. The most noise then came from Tholly's breathing, which sounded like a kettle simmering.

Ross took a step back until he was beside Tholly, who raised his good hand and pointed. About them in the evening were all the natural sounds: a bird chattering, a trickle of water, the rustle of leaves, a seagull crying in the distance. But there was no wind to create a rustle of leaves. They waited.

A footstep. Very cautious and coming towards them. The undergrowth was thick here, and it was a matter of luck, or Tholly's sharp hearing, that they had heard the men approaching instead of vice versa. To move at all you had to push aside bracken and bramble and low branches of the trees. They were on a path, but one much overgrown, one that had hardly been used this year. Very cautiously, one by one, they shrunk back into the undergrowth on either side. But the footsteps had halted too. Tholly took out his knife.

Muttered voices. They were going past on a fork in the path so close that they could almost be touched. Someone did touch Ross's shoulder. He looked round angrily. It was Dwight.

'They're English. Two men. I think from the prison.'

The footsteps had stopped again. Dwight's whisper must have been heard.

Ross raised a hand to stop Dwight's movement, but as one of the men broke cover, running away, Dwight said out loud: 'Enys here. Are you from the camp?'

One of the two men had not yet begun to run. His figure moved in the undergrowth towards them. Tholly raised his knife.

'Enys?' said a voice. 'Spade here. Lieutenant Spade. Where are you? Speak up.'

'Here! Stop, Tregirls; these are our friends.'

The one who had begun to run halted. They pushed through the undergrowth and stared at each other in the dark. Two ragged men who might have been street beggars. 'Armitage,' said the other. 'I think we have met before.'

Ross nodded. 'Are you alone? Are others with you?'

'Alone. Maybe a dozen of us got away but we split into twos for safety.'

They had spoken in lowered tones, but Ross held up his hand and the whole group were silent, listening. But now there were no more untoward rustlings.

Ross said: 'What happened in the camp?'

'Did you imprison the guards? The guards at the gate found their friends missing and hurried to release those you had tied up. Then they came into the prison with lanterns, looking for you. That pestilential young Enwright started the panic by rushing into the church screaming "*Escape, Escape!*" But maybe he helped, for it began a rush to the doors which even the guards could not stop. I know not how many men were trampled underfoot, but a couple of dozen of us got as far as the walls and about half over.' Armitage ended: 'I fear I deserted my post in the ward, Enys. But the thought of freedom was too much for me.'

Enys said: 'It was too much for them all.'

After a pause Spade said, 'We have not eaten or drunk all day. Have you anything about you?'

'Nothing. But there may be a boat – the one we came in. There's food and drink there if it has not been taken.'

The group began to move again, two men added to the

number. Ross knew that two more would not increase their chances. Yet to save three good men instead of one perhaps made the enterprise that much more justifiable.

They came near to where the river widened to a lake. The water glimmered and reflected the setting sliver of moon. Ross was relieved to feel a breath of wind on his face.

'It's gone!' said Ellery. 'We left'n just by that there tree!'

'Nay, wait,' said Tholly. 'The tree was not bent so. Ah. That is the one beyond.'

Stumbling now along the grass-grown bank, they peered into the dark. There was nothing there, no masts, no . . . But Tholly broke into a run and raised his hook on high. The lugger was still there, masts sloping, all firmly aground in the mud.

Ross hung back a few moments, restraining Dwight and Drake and Bone, fearing the ambush. But no shot came to disturb the tranquillity of the sleeping woodland, so presently, fatalistically he went forward. If there were soldiers here all was lost. If not, and if none came, they had only to wait a few hours until the water returned.

Below decks in the *Sarzeau* was a fair-sized hold. Aft of the foremast was a compartment to hold spare sails; behind that was the big fish room. Aft of that was a hold for carrying nets and behind that the cabin, with the root of the rear mast piercing it through the middle. The cabin was about ten feet long by eight broad, and into this were carried the two sick men.

Water at least they had now, and bread with a smearing of rancid butter. Everyone ate some, but Ross, feverishly concerned with their good fortune at finding the lugger still there, would have no moving about, no noise of any sort. Until the water came they must lie like the dead.

It came, inch by inch, so slowly at first as to be barely perceptible. It seemed impossible that this great boat would ever be lifted off its side and would ride upright. As they waited the night seemed to darken and every surrounding tree to hide a soldier. When the water was half in, a rowing-boat went down in the main stream, and then up again. Guards on patrol, or someone returning home late from a love tryst? A nightjar in the creek kept up his rough churring noise hour after hour.

The water of course would be nearly two hours later than when they had arrived. Perhaps it would never come. Perhaps the lake only filled to these limits in the spring tides after the new and full moon. So near and yet so far. Perhaps they should have made for the coast after all, carrying their two invalids.

The boat began to straighten. Slowly, as reluctantly as the flow of the tide, slow as dough rising for bread, slow as age, slow as death, the boat came up at last, was riding free.

The minimum number to man her: Tregirls at the wheel, Bone and Ellery to hoist sail, the others below. Thank God for this night breeze.

They cast off. Sluggishly she answered her helm. With his pole Ellery fended off the bank and they were away.

The breeze was fitful. Here in the grip of the land it blew and then dropped – seemed to be picking up from another quarter, dropped again. The sails filled and flapped. Filled and flapped. They made slowly across the lake.

And then to Ross's horror he saw that they were not gaining ground towards the lake's entrance – they were losing it. The inflow of the tide was carrying them in towards the town.

He crawled over to Tregirls.

'Can you bring her up? We're drifting faster than we're sailing.'

'I can see that, Cap'n. But we've all but lost the thrice-damned wind.'

'What d'you think the depth is here? D'you think Ellery could pole?'

'Not against this current.'

Ross put his head in his hands. 'My God! May I burn in hell!'

'Nay, you was not to know. We can anchor, maybe.'

'In the centre of this lake, and a bare two miles from the town quays? Someone will see us soon, if they have not already. Then they can send round to close the Vire-Court gorge against us.'

'Maybe we can come about and make back where we come from. The tide will turn in a couple of hours.'

'No, go on. Make for the other bank. While it is still dark there is little to choose between them, and I believe the water is deeper there.'

They crawled slowly across the current, losing ground all the way. By the time they neared the other bank they had just enough way on for Tholly to bring the lugger up into the tide, and Bone let the anchor go and they lowered the sails. Cautiously Jacka Hoblyn reared his head from the hatch.

'What's amiss?'

'We're too early. Tell the others. We must wait for the tide to turn.'

Silence fell. The water lapped gently round the bows.

Tholly said: 'We're no worse off here than where we was before, Cap'n. Who would have waited?'

'A sailor would,' said Ross. 'Or a man with a brain – any condition of a brain. I deserve to lose.'

'No one deserves to lose,' Tholly said, and wheezed a few times. 'That's not the way things work in this world. Folk don't get their deserts. Fortunate for me, eh, Cap'n?'

'You a praying man?' Ross asked.

'Not much of one. You know I don't.'

'Well pray now.'

Some hours later – or days – or sometime while it was still dark, the wind picked up again and they ventured out into the stream. The wind now was less errant and they found the tide had stopped flowing. They sailed quietly and efficiently towards the narrower water at the south end of the lake.

There would always be a tide through here, except at high and low water, and it had been chance which had brought them through on Wednesday without noticing it. With the sort of wind there was tonight they could never have hoped to get through against the current. Now they made fair progress, probably little faster than a row boat, but steady, creeping between the wooded hills, every minute a minute nearer safety. The sky lightened and darkened as clouds drifted across it. Dawn could not be a long way off.

So the gorge was left behind and they sailed down the broadening river. The square shoulders of a big château peered through the crouching trees. It could not be far now, but there was still that other narrow neck to be negotiated at the mouth near Benodet. Boats might be watching here for any escape. It did not occur to Ross to change the men on deck, any more than he thought of going below himself. It was make or break for them all, and Bone and Ellery were the best men.

Tregirls's breathing kept whistling through his black and broken teeth. Ross looked at him, and thought there could hardly be a better model for a pirate. A week's growth of

342

beard, the great knife scar puckering one leather cheek, grizzled hair blowing in the wind, savage teeth just showing, one hand on the tiller, the hook fixed firmly into the bulwark to give him stability. He had killed two men last night with no more compunction than swatting a fly.

Tholly met Ross's gaze and nodded. 'Dawn's breaking, Cap'n.'

Ross had realized it at the same moment, that he could see his companion's face too well.

'How far would you say? Two miles?'

'Oh, less. Just a little way. See, there's the church on the hill. That was soon after we come in.'

Ross looked at the church and then his eyes were caught by what was astern of him. As the light grew it was possible to see three boats and then a fourth rounding the bend they had just left behind them.

'That little way may yet be too much.'

'What d'ye mean?' Tholly looked behind him and the boat lurched as his hand jumped on the tiller. 'Holy Mary! So we're done! They been following us all the way!'

Two more boats, and now a seventh appeared. They were quite a way behind the *Sarzeau* and as yet well out of musket shot, but they were gaining on her.

'We'd best get the others up!' said Tholly. 'Seven fit men and there's four *fusils* below. They'll not find us easy meat! John! Jim! See if ye can set a jib! Git Jacka up and one of they loots to help! We got to try and crowd on all we –'

Ross was pulling at his arm. 'Tholly! A minute! Wait! Wait!'

The other two men had come to the stern, and Jacka had again put his head out at the sound of the raised voices.

'Well?' said Tholly. 'What is it?'

'Look again,' Ross said. 'Look carefully. Do you think those boats are pursuing us? I don't believe so. I think they are the fishing fleet from Quimper just coming out with the morning tide.'

They sailed on. In all eleven boats were following them, and, knowing the winds and currents better, they were catching them up. But if Ross's assumption were correct, this was an advantage rather than a danger. There were two craft in the narrows at Benodet with sails furled but men about the decks and looking in a state of alert. Both could have caught any lugger built. They made no attempt to stop the *Sarzeau*. It was one of the fishing fleet sailing out on its daily task.

As they reached the mouth of the Odet a choppy sea met them. By now the risk was that some of the fishing fleet, which could hardly have failed to recognize a stranger, should take time off to capture it. The *Sarzeau* was still perhaps a quarter of a mile in the lead as they shortened sail and set a south-westerly course to clear the Penmarche Cape. Anxiously they watched. One by one the other vessels straggled off towards the south-east, and the distance between them grew, and presently they were hull down, and then they had all disappeared.

The long delay waiting for the tide, instead of being the ruin of the escape, had in fact saved them.

So all that day, spirits rising, hearts rising as they left the French coast behind. It seemed improbable now that they would be challenged, for no French warship would be likely to pursue a French lugger, and if an English warship did so they could come to no harm.

They made skilly – slices of bread with hot water poured over them and a chunk of sour butter thrown in with a helping of salt. They had enough food for several days, and with any luck they would make England before it ran short. This diet even began to bring Dwight round, and, sitting as he did in the bows of the lugger with the strong warm wind blowing through his hair, some traces of colour came to his paper cheeks. With Tholly's keenly honed knife he hacked off his beard and scraped the worst stubble from his chin.

Drake, however, was running a high fever. On the second day out he was barely conscious. Dwight wanted to sit with him, but they persuaded him for his own health he must stay on deck, and the patient Bone remained below relieved from time to time by Ellery, who had taken a great fancy to the boy.

When they were in mid-Channel the wind changed and became squally, with a choppy head sea, and for a time they made little progress. Ross went for a while to squat beside Dwight, who still sat on deck – now in the lee of the main hatch.

Ross said: 'This will keep us another day at sea. Having come this far, I am anxious to be home.'

Dwight said: 'And I.'

'You must be.'

'Ross, I don't think I have thanked you at all for doing

344

what you have done, for risking what you have risked. Nor can I ever adequately do so were I to spend a week over it . . .'

'Don't try. It is done.'

'But I must try – however surely I must fail . . . When you came, when you appeared out of the night like an apparition, carrying a lantern and a pistol and with your armed men around you, I believe I was slow to accept my good fortune.'

'Not surprising –'

'Oh, yes, surprising. But, you see, even imprisonment such as that has a routine, and after more than a year of it one becomes dulled, half resigned to the semi-starvation, to the squalor, to the sick and dying men, to the stenches and the suppurating wounds and the fevers and the lack of all medical aid, and one becomes a – a cog in the wheel of the camp, an *important* cog, for even a small knowledge of medicine is priceless. The camp was run by a group of us, some more fortunately circumstanced than others. A few of the civilian prisoners were allowed to retain a little money – unlike the rest of us, who were stripped and robbed of everything as soon as we reached the convent. A Lady Ann Fitzroy, who has but recently been released, was invaluable in the small aids she was able to obtain for us – especially in the baneful winter that has just passed. Men were dying about me all the time; but others with fantastical determination continued to live in spite of all their illnesses and privations. It astonishes me always, this human will to live, even when there seems no single thing left to live for. . . . Well . . .' Dwight dabbed the sores on his lips with a cloth and stared over the pitching sea. '. . . well, a dozen of us ran the camp. Everyone in it was in a sense under our charge: the civilians in one block, the soldiers and sailors in another, the women in a third. We organized our meetings, our lives, we tried to devise recreations for the men, occupations – bricks out of straw, but we did all we could. So it became our lives, our vocations. So when you first came – in the first surprise of the moment – I felt I could hardly leave . . .'

'I understand.'

'But do not think I am in that hypnotized mood any longer. I regret – yes, I still regret that those men, nearly all of them, are still prisoners and in need of the attention I can no longer give them. To me true happiness would have been if we could all have been released together –'

'It was not possible.'

'Oh, I know. We should have needed a ship of the line to come home in . . . But now I am free — now I am really free — it is beyond me to express how I feel. To have the clean air, the sun, the salt on my lips, to know I am not going back to that — that hell. To know that I am among friends, and soon shall see all my old friends. And finally to see Caroline . . . I am near to tears.'

'Yes, well . . .' Affected himself, Ross frowned at the unstable horizon.

'How is she?'

'Well enough since she heard you were alive. Before that she reminded me of a cut flower that has not been put in water.'

'I do not think I can see her like this. I shall take a month first to make an effort to restore myself.'

'I rather suppose she will like to do the restoring.'

'Yes . . . yes. I don't know. I am such a scarecrow.'

They were silent. Lieutenant Spade, late of HMS *Alexander*, was at the tiller and he shifted a point into the wind.

'At least two others are saved with you,' said Ross. 'That is a small bonus. And one or two more may yet win their freedom, I am only in much disquiet about Nanfan. I dread the moment of telling his father.'

'Oh that,' Dwight said, 'I have something to confess. When we left Nanfan he was not dead.'

'Not dead? But —'

'Oh, he was dying. The whole brain was damaged. He could not live an hour. But in that hour, I knew unless I lied to you, one or other would stay with him. Out of loyalty, which could do no good, one or other, probably you, would have lost your life too.'

Ross was silent again, thinking this over. What if Nanfan had regained consciousness? Left alone among enemies to die. And once before, at the time of the mining accident, he had confounded the doctors by recovering.

'There was no chance this time, I assure you,' Dwight said, reading his thoughts. 'With internal injuries one cannot always be sure. But this was plain to see.'

Ross nodded. 'And as to our other casualty?'

'Young Carne? I cannot tell yet. I have no probes, no medical tools. Ball wounds are usually non-toxic, but one cannot tell whether any threads of his shirt or coat were carried in with it. Also one does not know how much the bone has splintered. But that is less important to his survival.'

'Then what are his chances?'

'We should know soon after we land. I do not like this high fever, but it may only be caused by shock. If the wound goes putrid of course there is no hope. One cannot amputate a shoulder.'

The head winds continued to plague them, and for a day they made little progress. For all the sail they saw they might as well have been in mid-Atlantic. Lieutenant Armitage, who was the most knowledgeable of them, estimated that they were about sixty miles north-west of Brest and probably therefore about an equal distance south-west of the Lizard. The wind was north-easterly, and to make the landfall they wanted they had to tack continually into the mouth of the wind. To make *any* landfall, they had to beat into it, for the end of England was not far away, and they did not want to find themselves in the Atlantic. All through the night they kept three men on deck: the rest huddled in the foetid cabin which pitched and shivered and lurched without cease. They were running short of candles, but a last one burned tonight in the lantern; some were seasick and some tried to sleep; Dwight sat up with Drake, who appeared to be sinking. Dwight said he was so used to being up at night and had so recovered from two days' sea air that he could well do this.

After arguing Ross gave in, having himself had only a snatched hour here and there since before they left Quiberon. He fell into an exhausted doze in which he found himself explaining to Demelza how her brother had died on the expedition. 'He was near dead,' he said, 'so we left him. It was every man for himself and there was nothing else to do.' Demelza looked at him and her face became Caroline's. 'At least I've brought home Dwight to you. I lost Joe Nanfan and killed two French guards, and a number of British prisoners-of-war lost their lives, and Drake, Demelza's brother, of course he had to go. But at least I've brought Dwight.' And he turned to show her, and all that was there were two hospital orderlies with a stretcher and on the stretcher was Dwight, and he was dead too. 'At least,' Ross said, 'you will be able to bury him in the family graveyard. That makes it all worth while.'

Towards morning he fought a way out of his nightmare and climbed the heaving ladder to the deck. After the moon had set there had been a couple of hours so black that even the breaking tips of waves seemed to have no incandescence; but now a suspicion of dawn was lightening the east. He took a deep breath. He felt much worse than before he slept. His limbs ached, his tongue tasted of sulphur, his throat was sore and he was beset with the nauseas of seasickness. He crawled along to Lieutenant Spade whose turn it was at the helm.

'Is there sign of a change?'

'Not yet. But I have hopes. It would be very rare for a north-easter to blow longer than this one has. At this time of the year, I mean.'

As dawn broke they saw a three-masted barque on the horizon, but she was making away from them and soon disappeared. Presently Dwight came up.

Ross said: 'Well?'

Dwight shrugged. 'I cannot be sure. He is much quieter. It may be natural sleep or it may be a coma. But I have smelled the bandages hourly, and there is no sign yet of necrosis. By noon we should know more.'

About ten the wind dropped and the lugger wallowed like a shot bird in the choppy sea. Then a breeze sprang up from the west, with increasing cloud and a hint of rain. The sails flapped and filled and the craft heeled to the new wind. The struggle was over and they were bound for home.

At midday during a heavy shower of warm rain Dwight came up to Ross, who was at the tiller.

'I think you will have one man fewer on your conscience, Ross. I think he will recover.'

CHAPTER ELEVEN

They reached Falmouth about seven that evening. By now it was pouring with rain and blowing hard. In spite of a white shirt flapping madly from each masthead they earned two shots from the castle, the last of which was certainly not a blank, before a naval pinnace came alongside to examine their credentials.

In the first dark Verity was called to her door and saw a tall gaunt man standing there. Behind him was a scarecrow supported by a burly servant.

'Ross!' she said. 'Oh, you are back? God be praised! I have worried so much for you! Come in! Pray come in! Come upstairs! Are you victualled? I have ample of cold food, and there's wine . . .'

'You remember Dr Enys, my love?'

'Oh . . . oh, yes!' Verity swallowed. 'So it has been a *success*! I am so happy for you! Pray come in.'

They got Dwight upstairs. It was rather a struggle. When they were sitting down Dwight said:

'I am sorry to be so famine struck, Mrs Blamey . . . They did not give us chicken every day at Quimper . . . Your cousin came and winkled me out, and I believe none too soon if he was to save my good looks. A day or two's home cooking will no doubt make some difference.'

Verity stared at him in the lamplight, then spoke briskly to hide her consternation.

'Chicken! That reminds me. We have chicken bones which will soon make a soup. I will call Martha and put it on the hob. It will soon be hot – '

Ross stayed her as she was about to leave. 'How many bedrooms have you here, Verity?'

'Three apart from our own. Enough to accommodate Dr Enys and yourself and your man – '

'There is more to it than that, my dear. We have another sick man. Drake Carne, Demelza's brother, was wounded and even now is still in danger. If for tonight at least you could give him rest, tomorrow perhaps – '

'Bring him at once and let him stay as long as is necessary. There is nowhere else in Falmouth where he could be cared for. Where is he? Downstairs?'

'Still aboard. I had to see you first – '

'Shame on you! Can you send for him? Where are you moored? Mrs Stevens will go when I have roused her – '

'Bone will go, if you will have him. But I would warn you, he is gravely ill, and if you undertake his care it may be days or even weeks – '

Verity smiled at the stocky man. 'Go, Bone, please. Take no more heed of your master.'

So Ross and Dwight and Drake and Bone slept at the Blameys'. Armitage and Spade found room at the King's Arms; Tregirls and Ellery and Jonas and Hoblyn stayed on board the *Sarzeau*.

In the morning Drake was clear-headed although there was

fever about. Dwight anxiously prospected around the bandages, but the smell of gangrene was still absent. As the improvised wadding had not been disturbed for five days he decided to leave it alone for the time. If the flesh were healthy it might do more harm than good to probe.

Dwight was not fit to travel yet, and not anxious to. If Mrs Blamey would generously accommodate him for another day or so he would stay and rest.

Ross said: 'You must not be afraid of meeting Caroline. You under-rate her if you think she will be put off by your frail appearance.'

'It is not my *frail* appearance. I look as if I have barely recovered from the Black Death.'

'However you look she will want to see you.'

'Well, give me two days. Even to ride a horse is a big undertaking.'

'Never mind a horse; we'll arrange a carriage. Though God help you, a part of the road will barely take four wheels at the same time. But have your two days. Meantime I must send word.'

Ross went down to the boat, expecting that Tholly would be willing to mount his waiting pony and ride to tell Demelza her husband was home and safe but could not come for a few days more. But Tregirls was far from willing. Having helped to bring in a French fishing-boat, there was prize money about, and he was not moving from Falmouth till he got his share. He was not unwilling, however, to loan his pony to Ellery, who left for home that morning bearing the news. Ellery was to call in at Killewarren on the way and tell Caroline to expect Dwight on Wednesday. Ross consigned his interest in the prize money to Tholly, on the understanding that any share coming to him should be divided equally among the others as well. In the meantime, if there were any formalities to be gone through, any papers to be signed, they would find him at Captain Blamey's house.

The other two, rather to his surprise, were equally anxious to remain on board. Jack Hoblyn, who had been the most seasick and the most difficult all the time he was away, was now enjoying the small notoriety and in no hurry to return to his family in Sawle. What had looked so desirable when it seemed about to be withdrawn from him, now, because it had become available again, was less enticing.

That there was so much fuss Ross was surprised, though on reflection he knew he should not have been. Both the lieutenants gave interviews to the press, and these would come out in the *Exeter Chronicle* and the *Sherborne Mercury*. A man followed Ross home asking for details, but he received no encouragement.

On the Monday morning, with the rain still pouring down, Ross went in to see Drake, who was sitting up in bed and, apart from the bandaged shoulder and the plastered fingers, was now looking more substantial than Dwight. Perhaps this too was not surprising. At nineteen, if a man does not die from a wound, he quickly gets better.

'So,' said Ross. 'I thought I might have had to take your sister home some bad news.'

Drake smiled. All the damned family, Ross thought, had this wonderful smile. They had certainly not inherited it from their father. 'No, sur. I eaten two eggs this morning and porridge before. I never was so well cared for.'

'Mrs Blamey is my dearest cousin. She will tend you like a mother; and Dr Enys thinks you need another week of it.'

'I'm sure I'll not need to be s'long as that. But twould be brave to stay. I b'lieve in the three or four days . . .'

'We'll see. Or rather Mrs Blamey will see. Dr Enys does not fancy handing you over to some Falmouth apothecary at this stage, for he feels they would be likely to kill you off. So when he leaves on Wednesday, and I leave with him, there will only be Mrs Blamey to say whether you are well enough, and you must obey her.'

'Whatever you d'say, Cap'n Poldark.'

Ross went to the window. It is a sad truth that when a man falls in love with a girl he does not necessarily admire that girl's brothers and sisters, nor even the man and woman who gave her birth. Indeed, such is human nature, that the more a man loves his wife, the more possessively so, the less he is likely to esteem the womb that produced her, or the other fruits of that womb. Ross's was not a jealous or possessive nature, but ever since the Carne brothers had arrived he had regarded them as a nuisance: first, by their mere arrival and claiming of favours on the grounds of relationship; second, because of their extreme Methodism; and third, and more recently, because of Drake's pestilential involvement with Morwenna Chynoweth. He had risked so much to save this boy – on Demelza's behalf – that he resented the risk and had come near to resenting the boy.

But in the eighteen months he had known the two young men his contacts, his true conversations with them, had been practically nil. Because Demelza stood between them as a link she had also stood between them as a bar. Only on this trip had he had any conversation with Drake as a person. And, reluctantly at first, his feelings had altered.

'There is one thing . . .'

'Sur?'

'Before you came with me on this trip you talked of going away. Somewhere, you did not know where. Before I leave here I want your assurance that you will come to Nampara for a couple of weeks so that we may all consider the situation as it now stands.'

'Right, I promise that, Cap'n Poldark.'

'And if you do not fancy staying with Sam, spend the two weeks with us. It may do you good and help you to recover your balance.'

'Thank ee, Cap'n Poldark. I fancy well staying wi' Sam, but mebbe it would be a comfortable change, like, staying wi' you.'

'And,' Ross said restively, 'do not call me Cap'n Poldark. That was Demelza's prohibition. Call me Ross, if you please.'

Drake considered the back of his brother-in-law. 'I'll call ee Ross when I'm twenty-one, if so be's I may – Cap'n Poldark. Twould be more seemly.'

'Seemly for whom?'

'For all concerned.'

'It is a while off yet.'

'Two year.'

Ross was staring out of the window at a crowd collecting to watch two men fighting in the gutter.

Drake said: 'All the same, I think after I been home for a while I did ought to go. I don't think tis ever in me to settle there again. And, like twas said before, twould be more proper after the trouble I brought. And if ever I'm to forget – or try to forget . . .'

'Morwenna Chynoweth?'

'Yes. Though I doubt I ever can or shall. Tis like a far worse wound than this ball in my shoulder – and there's no healing of it.'

'Time will help.'

'Aye. So everyone d'say.'

'Did she feel as much for you, Drake?'

'Yes . . . there can be no doubting.'

'Perhaps that makes it worse – I don't know. I once went

352

through something similar myself. There's no hell worse to be in.'

'And did ee come through it?'

Ross smiled. 'I fell in love with your sister.'

The fight outside was continuing. The watchers were shouting encouragement.

'That were a good thing t'appen.' Drake shifted painfully in his bed. 'That is, if it has been a good thing for you.'

'The best. But it took a time – a long time – to realize it was not second best.'

'I don't b'lieve there can ever be aught in my life that's not second best now.'

'Your life is long – or should be now; now that you have stopped trying to lose it.'

'I never rightly *tried* to lose it. But mebbe I didn't care s'much as I did ought to have done.'

'I was never so foolhardy as you. I tried drink. But I escaped too little so I abandoned the attempt.'

After a minute Drake said: 'I wish I felt there were something to *do* wi' my life! Even Sam, even thinking of God, don't seem no longer t'elp.'

'The more reason we should all talk it over together: your sister and I, and Sam if you wish it. In this case I believe four heads will be better than one.'

'Thank ee . . . Cap'n Poldark.'

To the disappointment of the onlookers, the fighting couple had at last decided to separate, one nursing a bleeding nose, the other limping and puffing. A horsewoman and a groom clattered over the cobbles through the dispersing crowd and came to a stop at the portico below. It was still raining.

Ross said: 'I do not think you will ever be quite like Sam – to whom Christ and his religion mean all. To me his way of life is not natural, yet I am compelled to a reluctant admiration of it.'

'I wish I could be like he. Twould be no problem then to give up thoughts such as I have had –'

'A moment,' Ross said. 'I fear I must leave you.' He had seen the auburn hair flaunting wetly on the shoulders of the dismounted rider. 'I believe Miss Caroline Penvenen has come to call . . .'

She came in, shaking herself like a tall wet butterfly. Her face was composed, and this morning quite beautiful.

'Well, Captain Poldark, so you are back, I see.' She took

his face again and kissed him on the lips the way she had done before he left, to the disapproval of Mrs Stevens ushering her in. 'As promised. And you have brought me back my erring doctor? Safe? Intact? All of a piece? And willing to fulfil the promises made before he left?'

'Caroline . . . You were to have greeted him on Wednesday! We were coming over and would have been with you –'

'And did you think I would be willing to sit in Killewarren stitching a sampler while everyone was living a high life in Falmouth? You misread my temperament. Where is he? Upstairs?'

'I think in the parlour. But he has only just risen. You must have left early –'

'At dawn –'

'But I must warn you. In my letter I gave you some hint that he is as yet very frail –'

'Verity,' said Caroline, half up the stairs, as the other woman was half down. 'How good to see you again! And in happier circumstances than last time –'

'Caroline! We did not expect you! –'

'So Ross says. But you should have. I have waited at home like a fading spinster too long already –'

'Caroline . . . I have hardly warned him! He is only just from bed and I do not think he feels strong enough to –'

'Not strong enough to see me? Does one need to be strong to confront me? Am I a scaly dragon to be shrunk away from until properly announced?' She kissed Verity and smiled at her, her long hair leaving drips of water on the stair carpet. 'So let us go up, shall we?'

There was no stopping her, so they went up. Dwight was standing defensively at the mantelpiece in front of the small fire that had been lighted against the damp. He turned and looked at her, skin and bone, a haggard, discoloured caricature of what he had once been. He was dressed in a snuff brown suit of Andrew Blamey's which, because it was so much too broad, hung on him as if he were a clothes-rail. He was clean shaven and his hair cut, though it showed its streaks of grey. His face was a little less ghastly than when Ross had first seen it, but it was still paper white, blotchy with sore places and skull-like in its emaciation.

Caroline stood there a second, a gentle smile on her face but without visible change of expression.

'Well, Dwight,' She took off her hat, shook it once and

354

dropped it on a chair. 'So they have dragged you away and you have come to redeem your promises!' She went across and kissed him on the sores on his lips.

'Caroline!' He tried to turn his head away.

She said: 'Good Heaven, so I still have to make all the advancements! D'you know, my dear, I am never allowed to retain any maidenly modesty, for I have to run after you, to seek you out, and even to kiss you without receiving any embrace in return!'

He was looking at her as if unable to believe she was there, as if not crediting that *she* had not changed, grown older, lost any of her freshness or youth.

'Caroline!' he said again.

'All this time,' she said, 'while you were hiding in that prison camp I have been wondering if I would ever be able to bring you to the point of fulfilling your promise. Time and again I have thought, no, he will never do it, I am doomed to be an old maid. Now, when at the last you are in England, I have to ride all morning through the pouring rain to catch you before you slip away again. Look at my habit, it will take a drying and ironing and perhaps will shrink from very saturation. And my hair.' She twisted some of it in her fingers, and more drops fell on the floor. But now it was not only drops from her hair.

'Caroline, my love, my own . . .'

'Ah, hear that, Ross! So he has committed himself at last! I believe we shall have a wedding after all. If we do, it will be the biggest ever in Cornwall. We shall have to hire an Admiralty band and army buglers and the choirs of three churches, all to celebrate that Dr Enys has been caught at last! . . . You see, I am weeping with relief. I am to be saved from the horrors of a spinster's life! But Dr Enys, you notice, is also weeping, and that, I know, is for his lost freedom.'

'Caroline, please,' Ross said, wiping his hand across his own eyes.

'But I shall not desert you, Dwight,' Caroline said, patting his arm. 'I shall stay near by this house until you are fit to travel, and shall take special care to ensure that you do not slip away to sea. And when you are fit to travel, I shall sit beside you in a coach and link your arm so that you are not able to jump out. When shall we be married? Can you name the day to set my heart at rest?'

Dwight said indistinctly: 'I am not fit – like this. You see,

355

I am a little altered, my love.'

'Yes, I observe, and so we must alter you back, mustn't we? We must feed you on mutton broth and calves' liver and raw eggs and canary wine. Then you will have the courage to take me for your lawful wife, just as we arranged in the good old days . . .'

Verity touched her cousin's arm. 'Come, Ross, let us leave them. I do believe they will not fall out . . .'

Dwight again said: *'Caroline* . . .' but this time as if all the cracks in his heart were widening. 'If you will still take me. But I shall need time . . .'

As Ross withdrew Caroline was still weakly talking. It was the one solutive. 'I think it should be an October wedding, don't you? Having seen old Agatha Poldark's centenary out of the way, we must give the county time to recover before its next giddy round! Until then you must come home with me, even to the scandal of the neighbourhood. We will feed you up right away with the best things that we can find. You shall be cosseted and fed and allowed rest and given the best of everything. And if you are not feeling better in a week or two we will send for the doctor . . .'

On the Tuesday Dwight at last took the old bandages from around Drake's arm. There was some bleeding, especially from the larger back wound, but it was a superficial bleeding, and both wounds were already closing up. But on Wednesday Dwight himself was running a fever, so the ordered coach was delayed by a day.

As it happened, the postponement resulted in their hearing news of the Quiberon expedition. A naval cutter arrived at dawn on the Thursday morning. It was a sombre tale.

Extra supplies, and reinforcements of English soldiers from England, sent out under Lord Moira, had been met by the returning fleet of Admiral Warren. Only the day after the *Sarzeau* left, d'Hervilly had launched his offensive against the Republicans massed at Sainte Barbe. But the strong Chouan support promised as an assault from the rear, catching Hoche between two fires, had sputtered out in a few half-hearted sorties, and the Royalists had been left to attack an army twice as numerous as themselves, in good defensive positions and with far more cannon. The pick of the advancing troops had been destroyed by cross-fire from hidden batteries, with something like half their number killed or wounded, and d'Hervilly himself hit and carried uncon scious from the field. He had appointed no deputy, but in default of one de Sombreuil had managed to withdraw the remnants of his army back into Fort Penthièvre.

But shortly after, aided by turncoats within the walls who had told them the passwords, the Republicans had stormed the fort and put the remnants of the Royalist regiments to the sword. Retreating down the peninsula with such forces as he could muster, de Sombreuil had fought a rear-guard action all the way, while his men melted before the enemy, some changing sides, some surrendering, many taking to the small boats and paddling themselves out to the safety of the English fleet. D'Hervilly was already aboard the *Anson*, seriously wounded. The Comte de Puisaye had left for the *Pomone* the day before, on the pretext that he wished to confer with Admiral Warren, and had not returned. De Maresi had taken a *chaloupe* and with ten others had reached the *Energetic*. Almost all the other officers were captured or dead. De Sombreuil alone had held out with eleven hundred men in a mill called St Julien at the extreme end of the peninsula. With the sea on three sides – now too rough for rescue – and the enemy shelling them from the fourth, they had resisted until the last of their ammunition was spent. Then de Sombreuil had parleyed for the lives of his men; this had been granted with honour and he had surrendered.

But since then, news had reached the English that Hoche's undertaking to spare the lives of those who surrendered had been overruled by the Convention under Tallien, and in a holocaust in a field outside Auray over seven hundred men, the flower of the French aristocracy, had been shot to death. Others – the more important – had been summarily executed on the promenade of the Garenne at Vannes – among them the handsome and brave Charles-Eugene-Gabriel, Vicomte de Sombreuil, in the twenty-seventh year of his age. Another of the executed men, the Bishop of Vol, standing beside de Sombreuil, had asked that his mitre should be removed so that he might say a prayer for them all before death. A guard had been about to do this, but de Sombreuil, his hands bound, had taken the mitre off with his teeth, and had declared in a loud voice that his assassins were not worthy to touch a man of God.

So, with a characteristically grand gesture, had died the one man among the French for whom Ross had come to have a deep and abiding affection. And in his purse was a ring. And sometime it must be delivered to Mlle de la Blache, who would now never live in the great château and help to recreate the family that the Revolution had destroyed.

This complete and utter disaster which had befallen the expedition seemed to Ross a shameful thing – he could not get it out of his mind. The road to hell was so often paved with good intentions; but these intentions should have been at least co-ordinated and given into the control of a true leader. All the heady talk throughout the preceding months, all the high courage and the preparations and the hopes; they had never really stood a chance. The British government was as much to blame as the French Royalists. Half measures, and again half measures. And four thousand British troops sailing off to support the landing when the landing had already failed.

His own small success was overshadowed by the greater tragedy, the greater failure. He could have done nothing to meet it if he had stayed behind; but somehow he felt personally culpable for having left. And he knew now, everyone must know now that the war would be bitter and long. With the failure at Quiberon had perished the last hope of a restoration of the monarchy and a reasonable and negotiated settlement. Against the Republicans there was no hope of an honourable peace. For England it was conquer or die.

Yet his own success was real. Overcoming odds whose length he was perhaps only realizing now it was over, he had fulfilled his main purpose in going with de Maresi and de Sombreuil. For the loss of Joe Nanfan, who had never married and who in a sense owed his life to Dwight, he had brought back his friend. It was an achievement that all his sombre regrets could not quite dissipate.

He left Dwight and Caroline at the gates of Killewarren and refused to go in. He felt they should go to their happiness, go to their future home, absolutely alone. It was the beginning of life for them. They needed no third person. Caroline, who had participated so closely in the preparatory stages, might regret just as much as he the failure of the Quiberon invasion, but for her all else was at present overwhelmed by personal happiness. They had several times tried again to thank him and always he had cut them short.

But his excuse that he wanted to be home was only an excuse in part. The five weeks he had been away seemed a year. Well, he did not know so much about seeking adventure the better to appreciate domestic life. He had had adventure enough at Quimper to last him a long time.

In the warmth of his present feelings – fluctuating though they might be between a sense of achievement and a sense of failure – he had thought a good deal about Drake, and wished he could do more for him. During a number of idle hours in Falmouth his mind had not been at all idle. Drake must be given some status, or some way of attaining status. The trouble was he was still so young. At nineteen, what could one do for a boy? Well, he, Ross, had money now. There ought to be something one could do. And George had said Morwenna's marriage to that clerical fop Whitworth was off. So the girl would be returned to her mother in Bodmin. Would any other suitor come hurrying round for a while? It seemed improbable.

Well, if Morwenna was as much in love with Drake as he with her, the chances were she would be faithful to thoughts of him for a year or so.

So might not something in the end be arranged? Drake might only be a wheelwright, but he was brother-in-law to a Poldark. That counted for something. And class, birth, money were not such rigid structures in England as they once had been. The present Archbishop of Canterbury was the son of a glazier. It was this ability to allow a traffic between the classes which had so far saved England from the fate of France. Every man who rose from nothing to be a person of importance in his community was an additional safety valve in the body of society, allowing some of the compressed steam to escape.

And marriages were not always between equals. Thomas Coutts had married his brother's serving maid, and she was now received by Prince Henry of Prussia; one of their daughters was married to Sir Francis Burdett, another affianced to the Earl of Guildford. The barriers in certain circumstances could fall. Why was the impoverished daughter of the late Dean of Bodmin so impossible of attainment by a talented tradesman with wealthy and well-born relatives? The only real bar had been Morwenna's relationship with the house of Warleggan. Let her only remove herself from Trenwith, and Drake from Nampara, and there seemed no real reason why they should not come together again in a year or two.

On this happy thought Ross came through Grambler village, past the last shack, where Jud and Prudie Paynter lived, and had just forded the Mellingey when he beheld a small boy racing towards him from the direction of the old Wheal Maiden mine. For a moment he did not recognize his four-year-old son until he saw a woman also running, coming out of the wind-battered fir trees, and also coming towards him.

He jumped off his horse and Jeremy leapt breathlessly into his arms, squealing his ravished delight. Then Demelza, smiling her most radiant smile; and he knew he was home.

They laughed and talked and chattered up the hill to where the new meeting house had now got the timbers of its roof on, and down the valley to their home, where the library almost had its second storey complete, and they were met at the door by the Gimletts and the Cobbledicks and Betsy Maria Martin and Ena Daniell, and all were waiting to welcome him like a conquering hero. (Another reward for danger, he thought? There you went again. Life was contrast: light made brighter by the shade. But he was content, and would be content for a long time now if the light would but shine.)

Jeremy, Demelza said, had been up by Wheal Maiden nearly all of yesterday, and she or Jane with him, so that nothing was done in the house all day, and at the end of it no father either. Ross apologized and explained the reasons. Over a late dinner he was hardly able to eat for talking, nor talk for eating; and Demelza, incessant in her questions, was also telling him that he had lost pounds in weight and looked as if he had been in a prison camp himself, and when could they go over and see Dwight and Caroline and when was the wedding to be? (God, thought Ross, it does work, and how unfairly; but I want *her*, not any other, not the most beautiful eighteen-year-old damsel born out of a sea-shell, not the most seductive houri of any sultan's harem; I want *her* with her familiar gestures and her shining smile and her scarred knees, and I know she wants me in just that same way, and if there's any happiness more complete than this I don't know it and am not sure I even want it. So you've been away and risked your life, you damned fool, and this is your undeserved reward.)

And did he see, Demelza was asking, knowing his looks and returning them but wanting to keep the conversation casual for at least another hour, did he see that they all had an invitation to Trenwith House for next week for Aunt Agatha's hundredth birthday – all four of them, and would he make an exception and go?

'Of course we'll go,' Ross said. 'Verity has been invited,

360

and Andrew will be home, so they will both be there – and baby Andrew also. I have asked them to spend the night here afterwards.'

'I am surprised that Agatha was permitted to invite us, but perhaps George could not deny her that indulgence.'

'We'll go,' said Ross, 'and perhaps, who knows, it will be the beginning of a better era between the two houses. I had a desperate unpleasant interview with George in the matter of Drake's arrest; but he *did* release him, and whether he bowed to my threats or listened to my reason, at least the outcome is good. So perhaps we may learn to live beside each other with some reduction of enmity. Indeed, no one wishes to be friends, but it is ludicrous that we cannot meet now and then as civilized beings instead of snarling at each other like wild beasts.'

'May it be so,' said Demelza, but a little doubtfully. 'And Drake? You tell me he is quite recovered?'

'From the musket ball? Not altogether. But Dwight thinks him out of danger, and he was eating well when I left. Whether the movement of his arm will be affected we don't know . . . Demelza . . .'

'Yes?'

Ross listened to the complaints of Jeremy, who had just been carried off. Clowance slept peacefully through it all.

'I have been thinking of Drake.'

'Oh?'

'D'you know, my dear, I don't believe I have sufficiently esteemed him. On this expedition he behaved with courage. I'll tell you of that later. But it seems to me that we should try to set him up in some way. We have money now. He is excessive young – that is a great disadvantage – but it is a disadvantage that time will take care of. I do not know whether it would be better to set him up on his own – perhaps in some small engineering or tool-making way – or whether he might be better engaged with Blewett at ship-building in Looe, with a view to an eventual partnership. In two years he will be twenty-one and will be capable of taking over my interest there then.'

Demelza studied Ross's expression. 'Judas, this is a change-around. I thought you looked on my brothers like the plagues of Egypt.'

Ross laughed. 'Drake – Drake is so much like you that I have found myself resenting it. But in spite of the unfortunate involvement with Trenwith he has become a greater concern of mine. Indeed, on the way home, I have been thinking of that too.'

Demelza said: 'My love . . .'

'If we can establish Drake in some position where he can afford a respectable marriage, and if the Chynoweth girl stays faithful to him for a couple of years, as seems likely enough, why should we not contrive a match between them – right outside the orbit of the Warleggan household? She will be in Bodmin, and if he were in Looe –'

Demelza said: 'My love. I have to tell you that that is no longer possible.'

'Why not?'

'Because Morwenna was married to Osborne Whitworth in Sawle Church a week ago.'

CHAPTER TWELVE

It had all happened to Morwenna very quickly. Or it seemed very quickly to her. A landslide of pressure and emotion and panic and duty may move slowly to carry someone away, but the person so carried feels as if in the grip of an avalanche.

The news that Drake had been freed had brought such relief to her that for a while nothing else seemed to matter; and she was reconciled to a return home and all that that entailed. A disappointed mother, curious and inquisitive sisters, an attempt to pick up a routine she had now outgrown. Geoffrey Charles was still at Cardew, and she did not expect to see him again before she left. But Drake was free and unharmed – that was the one vital concern. Everything else could be forgotten now, and time – for everyone but her – would see that it eventually was. The eighteen months she had spent in the Warleggan household would become just an episode in the life of a young woman who had made a rather foolish and injudicious friendship. Bodmin was far away. News of her indiscretion might travel – vastly exaggerated no doubt – but it could be lived down. She did not want to go home; her life with Geoffrey Charles had been too pleasant for her not to know that she was returning to a narrower and poorer existence. But she accepted that and was only waiting for her mother to come and fetch her.

Even this seemed a far from necessary journey for a delicate and overburdened lady; but George and Elizabeth had insisted that it should be so.

In the interval of waiting she spent more time with Agatha, whose needs increased as her day neared. Remarkably in so old a woman, Agatha drew on fresh reserves of interest and energy and concern the more she found to do and to think about. 'Doing' meant in the main getting someone to do for her, and now that Geoffrey Charles was no longer in Morwenna's charge, and now that Morwenna sought to be as little as possible in the company of the other members of the household, she spent several hours a day with the old woman, mainly in her room, but usually accompanying her on her forays downstairs. In Agatha's company she was protected against the raising of matters to do with her own life. And her attendance was not without an element of penance. The horrid atmosphere of the old woman's room was a sort of hair-shirt she drew on to counteract the prickings of her own thoughts.

One Sunday it had been morning service, and she came home to find all the old people down together. This was something she knew would keep George away, so she sat with them sharing a pot of tea and trying to listen to their desultory conversation.

On this came Elizabeth, smiling at them all, coolly pleasant, refusing the tea, which she thought should not be drunk at this time of day, and saying that she wanted a word with Morwenna. So Morwenna rose and went with her, and Elizabeth said she thought she should tell Morwenna to change her frock after dinner for the Whitworths were expected about seven.

Morwenna felt a constriction round her heart. 'But – why are they coming, Elizabeth? You should have told me – I could have gone before they came!'

'No . . . they are coming to see you. Mr Whitworth has been very good, very patient with you. Osborne Whitworth knows nothing of the trouble we have had here.'

'But . . . Mr Warleggan said he had written!'

'So he did. But after he had released that man – that young man – he decided not to send the letter. Lady Whitworth and Mr Osborne Whitworth were due in any case to come to stay with us, and so we have said nothing to dissuade them.'

'And – how can I greet them? How can you –.'

'As if nothing had happened.'

'But much, so much, has happened! It's not possible to pretend – '

'There is no need to pretend anything. Be your normal, natural self. What is there to be afraid of?'

'But, Elizabeth . . . How can this be? . . .'

Elizabeth smiled. 'How can what be? All that has occurred is that Mr Warleggan and I have talked together and we have decided that the incident of your infatuation with this young man was too trivial to be allowed to wreck your life. It need never be mentioned among us again. After all, who knows of it?'

'Many – many people. Even here – even in this house! Your own father and mother and – and – '

'My father and mother are aware that something happened, but they are not really very interested. You only have to look at them to know that. Aunt Agatha knows nothing. Geoffrey Charles will spend the rest of the summer away. As for the rest – a few village folk, who can be ignored.' Elizabeth stopped at the door and looked out. 'It is a fine day, and I trust the way will not be too rough for their journey. Lady Whitworth is getting up in years and Mr Whitworth did not wish to leave until he had read prayers and preached.'

'Elizabeth! . . . I – it has come as such a great shock! I do not know how I can possibly face them at such short notice!'

'There's time enough. We considered it better and kinder to arrange it thus. I know it has startled you, given you a small shock to begin. But I believe when you have thought a few minutes and realize that now you have lost nothing at all of what you thought you had lost, you will be very happy to greet them.'

'I cannot see how that can be!'

Elizabeth's face hardened. The delicate beauty of her cheek and chin seldom moved into harder lines, but when it did the change was noticeable. 'Morwenna, pray, pray count your blessings. That young man has been spared the prosecution and punishment which would have ruined *his* life. When Mr Warleggan decided to withdraw the charge against him, it was a very compassionate and kindly thing to do. I'm sure you appreciate that.'

'Oh, indeed I do! All I ever – '

'Well, from it stemmed our other wish. If the young man was not to suffer for his indiscretion, why should you? This is the moment to be grateful, not one to renew your obduracy.'

They walked down the steps and out into the garden. A gardener touched his cap to them and Elizabeth spoke to him about the roses. When she had rejoined Morwenna she said: 'I'm sure your mother will give you good advice, my dear.'

'Yes, I know she will! When will she be coming?'

'She sleeps in Truro tonight, and if the weather is good should be with us for dinner tomorrow. I know how much you are looking forward to seeing her again.'

'Elizabeth, could it not be arranged for me not to meet Mr Whitworth again until after I have seen her? I so badly want her aid and advice.'

'It is hardly possible. You cannot absent yourself for a whole day. But nothing need be decided in the first day. You only have to be welcoming and polite, as you so well know how to be.'

'But if – How *can* it be kept secret, what has happened? I have told my mother everything and she will most certainly have said something to my sisters. Perhaps others too . . .'

'She does not know yet.'

'But I *wrote* to her – six pages last week. It will certainly have reached her before this and – '

'I did not have it posted,' Elizabeth said. 'It is upstairs now. It has not been opened. Nothing that you wrote has been read. Oh, you may think it was a liberty on my part to withhold it. But if so, it was only done with the kindest of intentions.'

Morwenna bit at her lip to keep back the protest.

'With this – this new accommodation in mind,' Elizabeth said, 'we thought it better that your mother should know nothing of your association with this young miner until you met her. Then you can tell her what you choose to tell her in your own words. We cannot stop you, my dear, nor would we attempt to! But when you meet her you will be in a cooler and more reflective mood. She arrives tomorrow knowing only of your earlier proposal of marriage from Mr Osborne Whitworth and whatever you may have written to her about that.'

Lady Whitworth did not seem to Morwenna to be the delicate elderly flower Elizabeth's words had suggested. She was a tall, strong-built woman with tough but sagging cheeks, a masculine voice and button-bold eyes. She would never for a moment have thought this modest quiet girl suitable for Osborne in her own right; but the connection with Mr Warleggan's money made it something she would welcome from a practical point of view. She constantly wielded a fan, indoors and out, barely relinquishing it to eat; and her harsh strong aristocratic voice filled every room she entered.

Her son topped her by a couple of inches and his voice joined with hers in dominating the conversation. Aunt Agatha, who had known Lady Whitworth's mother and thought little of the daughter, had not included them in her birthday invitation.

Ossie's attitude towards Morwenna was reserved, and a little more haughty than hitherto. He knew he had been rejected in Truro and, while he took small account of this – many girls thought it their duty to refuse a man a couple of times as part of the game – the rejection rankled. He needed the marriage dowry, which was much the best in sight – and he needed the girl's body, which was so incapable of being hidden even in those dowdy clothes – but he had a grudge against the personality behind those shy sleepy brown eyes. He was prepared to overlook it for the gains which would accrue but it left him a little stiff and constrained.

That first evening he did have a few moments alone with her but he did not stoop to press his suit. Instead he told her the text of the sermon he had preached that morning and the effect his sermon had had on the congregation, and of the extreme difficulty he had had in getting away from his parish in order to pay this visit to Trenwith. It could not have been more cold or more formal. But all the time he was looking at her, and she knew he was looking at her.

Then the following day just before dinner – and really fatigued by the journey, not like Lady Whitworth ready for a strong rum and a game of quadrille – came her mother. So tired was she that they postponed the meal until three.

Amelia Chynoweth had been, and indeed still was, a very pretty woman. She had been born a Tregellas, daughter of Trelawney Tregellas, the notorious bankrupt. When he died in the Fleet, it was considered a good match for his only – legitimate – daughter that she should marry the Reverend Hubert Chynoweth, a man of unimpeachable family, a fine tenor voice, and a rising light in the church.

Well, he had risen; and propagated; and set too soon, leaving an impoverished widow of forty-two and a brood of children quite unprovided for. Amelia Chynoweth, perhaps because she came of a father who had always been out of step, first in the county of his birth and then in the metropolis that he sought to conquer, had herself hardly ever put a foot wrong. In voice, in bearing, in taste, in opinions, she conformed. Over the years it had ceased to be an anxious conformity and become a willing and instinctive one. So it was not surprising that she should look with some pleasure on the union of her eldest and first unprovided-for daughter with a man of superior family and another rising light in the church, however far his voice might fall short of tenor quality.

They talked of it for two hours the next morning, in the tiny dark panelled Tudor bedroom which was the only bedroom left for Mrs Chynoweth to occupy. Morwenna did not tell her all – Elizabeth's prophecy came true and somehow the whole story of her relationship, as she had told it in the letter, could not now come out – but she spoke of Drake as a young man in the district, a carpenter, related to the Poldarks by marriage, and a good-living, pure-hearted Christian, whom she loved devotedly and whom she would love to her dying day.

Her mother was not without sympathy and understanding. She knew something of Morwenna's sincerity and honesty and steadfastness in all things. When Hubert died she had been the greatest comfort. But Amelia lacked empathy, that ability to put oneself in another's place and to see the world through another's eyes. She had done this so much for the last twenty years on a superficial level that she had lost the ability to do it in depth. While Morwenna was talking she looked back into her own life and vaguely wondered – and could not remember – whether she had loved Hubert when she married him. Marrying him had been the culmination of a number of 'right' things to do. Since her marriage the 'right' things had been more clearly defined by her position and her responsibilities. Since she became a dean's wife, the responses had become automatic.

How, then, to deal with a daughter who was sorely troubled at heart because she loved a quite unsuitable man?

'Morwenna, my dear. To be sure, I understand how you feel. But I think you have to remember that you are still exceeding young.' Morwenna's heart sank at this, for she saw now, instantly saw, imminent defeat. Whenever anyone told her she was young . . . Her mother went on speaking for some minutes, and she scarcely listened, staring into an almost unfaceable future. It was an appreciable time before her mother's voice broke through the darkness and the bitterness and the fear. 'Of course, it could be said that you need not marry at all – at least, not yet. This young man whom you misfortunately and injudiciously met – such a marriage is hardly to be considered, is it? You don't even suggest it. I know you see that yourself. But the other choice, this Mr Whitworth. I think you must be very careful before you do anything which will discourage him. I quite see that your – your feeling for one young man will make it more difficult to entertain the same or a similar feeling for another. But I think you must take that into account and try to overcome it.'

'And if I fail, mama?'

Mrs Chynoweth kissed her daughter. 'Try not. For your own sake. And for all our sakes.'

'You ask me to do it for your sake?'

'No, no, not just for *my* sake. Though I should find much happiness in it – not just selfish happiness, I assure you. Take the widest view you can of this. Oh, I so wish I could put an old head on your shoulders so that you could consider it wisely and thoughtfully and from the experience which you cannot yet have had. I ask you to consider it for your own sake first: a better marriage than you could really ever hope to make again; an assured position in society; enough money; a personable young husband with great prospects in the church; *security* for the rest of your life; and a good religious life. It is what any girl would jump at. I know how much your father would have rejoiced at the thought of his daughter marrying into the church. Then, after you have thought of that, consider the great generosity of Mr Warleggan in making this marriage possible, and whether it is seemly that you should reject it. Finally, only then, spare a thought to my own pleasure at such a match. And relief, my dear – I have to confess it. Relief. Not that I wish to lose you or would not welcome you home with open arms, but there are three others, as you well know, all younger, and our means are small. You know how delicate I am and how much of a struggle it has been for us since your father died. Do not let this be of major concern to you –'

'Oh, but it is, it is!'

'Not of *major* concern, my child. It is your own future you must consider first and foremost. And it is because of your own future that I hope and pray you will make a wise decision. But I am sure Mr Whitworth will speak to you in the course of the next day or two. *Please* think carefully how you shall reply.'

Mr Whitworth spoke to her. He found her – not by chance left alone – in the garden in the late afternoon. She had been a walk with her mother almost as far as the cliffs, when they had carefully avoided the subject and talked about church happenings in the deanery of Bodmin; then when they returned her mother had had to go indoors to rest from the exertion, and Elizabeth, who had come to meet them, was mysteriously called away. So Mr Whitworth, seeing her alone, bore down on her and they walked round the garden together.

As has been said, Ossie's dealings with women in the main had been either on the superficial, drawing-room level or on that of passing over a couple of silver coins for an hour in an upstairs room. His courtship with his first wife had been brief and simple, for before their marriage she had adored him, a condition which he had thought very natural in a woman and one which had made formal words unnecessary. This slightly hostile young creature had been approached once and had met him with a half-rejection. It was off-putting, to have to say it all again, especially without the absolute certainty of success.

Nor was a garden quite the situation he would have chosen, but time pressed and his sense of *amour propre* would not let him shirk the opportunity.

He broke off from a remark about the failure of the summer crops and stiffly said:

'Miss Chynoweth – Morwenna . . . You will know of the further discussions which have taken place between your cousin Mr Warleggan and myself regarding our marriage, regarding this proposal of marriage which I have made, regarding this offer I have made for your hand. You may feel that in all this I have addressed myself too much to your guardian and too little to yourself. But when we last spoke I acquainted you with my feelings, and you gave me to understand that you required time to consider my offer, time to prepare yourself for so important a step. In the meantime, therefore, it seemed proper to me not to press my suit personally but to attempt to discover from your guardian from time to time what your sentiments were and how far they had progressed.'

He stopped and put a hand up to his stock, adjusted it, returned his hand to its customary place with the other behind his back. He flattered himself that so far he had not stammered or hesitated.

'Yes,' said Morwenna.

'Last night I spoke again to Mr Warleggan, and before dinner today I had some converse with your charming mother. They both told me what I wished to hear.'

'Did they?'

'They did. But . . . in order that my happiness should be complete, I need to receive the same information from your own lips.'

Morwenna looked down at a bed of Canterbury bells, nodding their heads gently in the breeze. Then she stared across the lawn to the old grey stone of the house. A little to the left of them was the ornamental pond where Drake had had his fun with the frogs. Beyond that and further to the left, just over the fold of the hill, was the coppice where Drake and she had first met. That window up on the first floor of the house was the one from which she had sometimes watched for his coming, and from which she had seen him leave for the last time, walking slowly down the drive, his figure dwindling until it disappeared beyond the gates. So had gone her love and her life.

'Mr Whitworth,' she said. 'I – '

'Osborne.'

'Osborne, I do not know what I can say . . .'

'You know what I want you to say.'

'Yes, yes, but . . . You see, forgive me; if you wish me to tell you that I love you, then I cannot do this. If – if that is what you need, what you mean you need to make your happiness complete, then – then I cannot supply it. I am deeply conscious of my failure.'

Osborne stared at her and swallowed and then stared away.

'I am told,' Morwenna said, 'that I . . .' She stopped.

'Pray go on. Pray speak plainly.'

'What may happen if we should marry I do not know. I am told such feelings grow . . .'

'You have been told aright.'

'But, Mr Whitworth, I would not – could not be honest with you if I pretended to – to feelings, emotions which I do not have. You tell me that you wish to marry me. If knowing what I have now told you, you *still* wish this, then I will marry you. Even though – '

'That is what I wished to hear! It is all I wished to hear!'

'All—'

'All for the present. Much will be added in marriage. Feelings that you are not yet aware of. You are too young to understand. You must believe me. I will guide you.' He took her hand, which was cold. Her hands were always cold. He hated that. 'I have no doubts at all. You shall be the mother to my daughters and in due course will have children of your own. The vicarage is ready. During the summer the necessary repairs have been completed, for the previous vicar allowed it to become run down. The chimney has been rebuilt and the dry rot taken out. It is a house you may enter into at once.'

'It is not that,' Morwenna murmured. 'The house, I am sure—'

'I wish to be back on Sunday, for I have made no arrangements for a locum to read the prayers. Being new in the district and having a number of distinguished parishioners who customarily attend, I would not wish to cancel the ordinary and prescribed Sunday service. We can be married on Friday and return the same day—'

Morwenna choked. 'Friday? *This* Friday? But it is impossible! How can that be? It is impossible, I tell you . . .' She stopped, realizing that if she were to go through with this and if she were to make any attempt to begin a new life such as had been dictated for her, she *must* keep the antagonism out of her voice. 'I'm sorry—but it *is* impossible isn't it? Arrangements could not be made in the time!'

'Venturing,' said Ossie, 'to build on the information I had received, and on my belief that time and reflection would override your hesitations, I did make some arrangements. Last week I obtained a licence from the bishop in Exeter, and we can be married in your own church before we return to Truro.'

Morwenna felt as if the last vestiges of hope were being stripped from her, as if every door of retreat, however temporary, was being slammed as she approached it.

'Mr Whitworth, please—'

'Osborne—'

'Osborne . . . I have no *clothes,* no bridal things! There is nothing ready! You *must* give me time, give me more time. . . .'

His face tautened. He was far more sure of himself now. 'My love, you have had six months to think of this. That is surely time enough. As for clothes . . . who is going to care? Your mother has no money for a bridal outfit,' he added with some contempt '– she has already told me so – but you have a white frock; Mrs Warleggan will have a veil; it will not be difficult to improvise. Then when we are married there will be provision made for your day and evening clothes. As my wife you will be properly and suitably dressed. A wedding should be a religious ceremony, not an occasion for vulgar display.'

'But Friday is but three days! Could it not be arranged for September? I have promised to stay here for old Miss Poldark's birthday. That is in two weeks' time. A little longer – '

Ossie would not release her hand. An urgency was creeping through him, as if the contact brought him a new contagion. 'No . . . It must be now. Morwenna, look at me.'

She glanced up, eyes smeared, looked away again. 'It must be now,' he said, and for the first time stumbled over his words. 'It must be this week. I need you. My – my children need you. Besides, when would there be another time when both your mother and mine were under the same roof? What better church to celebrate it in than the family church of the Warleggans who have so befriended you?'

So at about the time that Drake Carne was nursing his damaged arm in the wood above Quimper and trying not to ask for more water which he knew his friends must risk discovery to fetch, Morwenna Chynoweth was preparing to abandon her maiden name in the Gothic church of St Sawle. Elizabeth had done more than lend her a veil of old lace: she had produced her first wedding frock, twelve years old and never worn since; too short for Morwenna and too tight; but in three days of intensive sewing Elizabeth and Mrs Amelia Chynoweth had worked wonders so that on the day it fitted well enough, and no one unable to see beneath the surface could have guessed at the contrivances that had gone on.

There were only a dozen people in the church, and after it a quiet wedding breakfast at Trenwith; just the family; and Ossie and Morwenna in the centre of it all: Ossie looking at his most extreme in a new coat of ribbed orange velvet with double lapels – the inner ones green striped – and the palest lavender stock, all brought with him specially for the occasion; while Morwenna sat like a shy madonna, the whiteness of her clothes making her skin look dark but silky; smiling when expected to smile but with absent eyes, a shell from which the spirit had tried to fly but found itself chained.

And George watched it all with a composed, quietly satisfied manner. Defeat to him did not mean what it meant for most people: to him it was only an occasion for regrouping his pieces and shifting his ground. He had accepted and given way to Ross's threats after careful deliberation, having weighed the risks of defiance and calculated the advantages of a civilized, tactical withdrawal. He had not allowed hot blood to sway him. He had observed that by withdrawing the charge he could move back to his original position and bring the marriage with Osborne Whitworth into being after all. It had been a considerable gain for a small loss of face. On the whole he was content with the exchange.

After the breakfast a hurried farewell – with Agatha protesting like a wounded bat in the background and the rest of the family coming to the door to see them off in the coach that George had lent them. Thereafter three hours of lurching and bumping, during which Osborne never seemed for a second to cease to be touching her: her arm, her knee, her shoulder, her hand or her face; until at last they were descending the steep rutted hill into Truro. Then jogging over the cobbles, through the town to St Margaret's church on the other side, through gates and up a short muddy drive and they were entering the house; two servants bobbing curtsies and two tiny girls in the charge of a nursemaid, staring, staring, fingers in mouths, and up into a bedroom smelling of old wood and fresh paint. And after that one hour to herself and then supper, just the two of them waited on by a manservant, and some good food which she toyed with and some canary wine of which she drank enough to subdue the fit of shivering that had threatened to overtake her.

And all the time Osborne talking in a loud voice – a voice just like his mother's. All day he had been jolly, but it was as if his jollity were put on to hide his true feelings not to express them. Several times he rose from the table during supper to kiss her hand and once he kissed her neck, but a shrinking movement, however nearly controlled, prevented him from doing that again. But all the time his eyes were heavy on her. She looked for love in them but saw only lust, and a small measure of resentment. It was as if she had only just failed to escape him and he still bore a grudge against her for having tried.

So supper ended, and in a panic she complained of sickness after the ride and asked if tonight she might go early to bed. But the time of waiting, the time of delay was over; he had already waited too long. So he followed her up the stairs and into the bedroom smelling of old wood and new paint and there, after a few perfunctory caresses, he began carefully to undress her, discovering and removing each garment with the greatest of interest. Once she resisted and once he hit her, but after that she made no protest. So eventually he laid her naked on the bed, where she curled up like a frightened snail.

Then he knelt at the side of the bed and said a short prayer before he got up and began to tickle her bare feet before he raped her.

CHAPTER THIRTEEN

The fifth of August, which was a Wednesday, was an exceptional day in that cold and fitful summer. The sun rose in a sky barred with cloud like a Venetian blind, the wind dropped and the land drowsed under its first real heat.

With five days to go to her party Agatha was awake early and would have risen, tempted by the soft airs coming through her window and the drowsy twittering of birds; but, conscious always of the need to conserve her strength, she felt she would keep to her normal routine of the morning in bed, a light dinner at two, and then a forage downstairs of two or three hours around tea time.

The loss of Morwenna, gone now nearly two weeks had been a great disappointment to the old lady, for before she left she had become a tower of strength. Now it was back to dependence on Lucy Pipe and the fitful visits of Elizabeth. But somehow almost all was ready. Mrs Trelask had made the frock, of black Flemish lace with two white satin flowers at the bosom and a cape of black satin falling just to the waist. It was not at all to Agatha's liking, but the other women all thought it uncommon smart and quite the thing; and at least it was new and uncreased and had cost a fancy price, so she had reluctantly agreed it would do.

She had had her topaz ring stretched so that it would go over her knuckle, and in a wavering hand on the back of an old bill had written directions that after her death it was to go to Clowance Poldark. She had had a new wig made and fitted, of a specially good hair, almost white but with a few becoming streaks of grey, and had bought a new black lace cap to top it. She had ordered and had only received yesterday a new jet choker. She was angry about this because it had been made too big and fell round her tiny throat like a necklace, but she hoped Elizabeth would be able to shorten it in time.

The one thing she was still short of was new buckles for her slippers. Her feet were so shrunken and lumpy that it had been impossible to order new shoes, but her best slippers would have done well enough if they could have been brightened by two silver buckles. They had not come. Elizabeth swore that she had twice sent in to the sliversmith's in Truro, and that they were promised faithfully before Monday – but time was so short now. After all this waiting, all these months and months, all this preparation, time was now so short. In five days' time only. In five days' time.

Smollett stirred on the bed and stretched, so she leaned over to the side table and lifted his saucer of milk on the bed for him to take a lazy lick or two.

Thirty-eight guests had accepted – or was it forty-eight? Agatha could not quite remember. Once or twice she wondered why George Venables had not replied. He had been perhaps the nicest man she had ever known; they said he was too old for her, but he could not have been more than forty at the time. (Forty, a *child,* a veritable *child!*) But he had lost all his money in the South Sea Bubble and had gone abroad with the Duke of Portland (was it?) and she had never heard from him again. (But she had kept his address and had specially instructed that an invitation be sent. You couldn't trust the people in this house. They might well have lost the invitation or forgotten to post it.)

Then there was Laurence Trevemper. Gay and handsome. Captain (was he?) in one of the good regiments. How they had danced together! He had said: 'Miss Poldark, when I am on the floor with you, God's life, you give me wings!' Killed in some rash brave futile cavalry charge at a place called Pontenoy. Thirty five, that would be. (Or was it 'forty-five?) His wife had been a prodigious nuisance.

Before that there had been Randolph Pentire. A bit of a rascal, always fumbling at one's blouse. Eventually he had married that Kitty Something – Kitty Hawes – and had never had *any* children. After all that lubricity. She had not sent invitations to *them*.

Then there had been, oh, five or six others. She had not been wanting in suitors. Only, for one reason or another, none had ever quite *suited*. Or they had gone off like dear George. To hear the young talk today you would think no one had had any excitement in the past, any heartaches, any problems, any bitter frustrations or heady fulfilment. The young of today were more than a shade tedious; pompous, self-centred, so sure that their concerns were the first important ones that had ever happened. They had no *perspective,* no sense of proportion. Perhaps it was necessary to be old to acquire a true sense of proportion. It was small consolation but it was something.

On these quiet dreamy reflections, between one doze and the next, came another George than the one she was dreaming about – the one that she disliked so much.

One moment she had been gazing across at Lucy Pipe folding up her night shawl, then she opened her eyes and George Warleggan was there and Lucy Pipe was retreating through the door.

It was a rare event – a unique event – for him to come here. If he had ever been in this room before she could not recollect it. She did not like this: it disturbed her. She shrank more into herself and pulled her day shawl about her shoulders as if his presence were a cold draught she must guard against. Smollet, thus disturbed, arched his back and spat. It was a great satisfaction to Agatha that George was now the only person Smollett ever spat at.

Mr Warleggan was dressed as if for visitors, in a tight, buttoned, high-collared coat, cut away to show the tight breeches. The short double-breasted waistcoat was of crimson silk, with brass buttons. Her sharp, critical eyes noted his carefully controlled paunch, the cheeks and the shoulders growing heavier each year. Then they noticed he was smiling. It was unheard of. He was smiling at her. It was not a nice smile; but then no movement of his features would have been pleasant to her – unless they expressed pain. He was saying something. He had set down a book on the table beside her and was speaking to her in a voice he well knew she could not hear. Venom curled on her damp grey lips.

'Speak up! What is it you want?'

He came nearer to her and then raised his handkerchief fastidiously to his nose. It was a deliberate insult.

She said again: 'Speak up, George! Ye know I'm hard of hearing. To what do I owe this honour, eh? Eh? It's not me birthday till Monday.'

Smollett had upset some of the milk from his saucer and two white blobs like two white eyes stood on the counterpane. She brushed them away.

George came nearer to her than perhaps he had ever been before. He spoke loudly, close to the grey whiskery ear. 'Can you hear me now, old woman?'

'Aye. I can hear ye. And I'll have no more insults, or Elizabeth will learn of it.'

'I have bad news for you, old woman.'

'Eh? What is it? What is it? I knew ye'd not come with aught but bad news. Ye've got it writ all over ye, like blood on a carrion crow. Speak up.'

George looked at her and shook his head. His brief smile had gone. He was sober now, his manner grave and decisive.

'There will be no party on Monday.'

Agatha felt a surge of blood move through her old body. She must be careful. If he had come to taunt her into illness she must take great care.

'Nonsense. Ye could not stop it, George, though no doubt twould give ye great pleasure.'

'I must stop it, old woman. Otherwise you will be made out to be a liar.'

Agatha looked him up and down. An old adversary, this. She must beware his tricks.

'Leave me be. Leave me in peace.'

'Can you hear me? It is important you should hear me! When Morwenna was married to the Rev. Osborne Whitworth, I observed the church register and saw that its records went back a century and a half. Yesterday, as I was passing, I called on Mr Odgers and spent a half-hour reading through the register. It made interesting reading, for it was a history of the Poldarks and the Trenwiths, all in dry, old ink; nearly as old and faded as you, old woman.'

Agatha did not speak. She watched him out of small venomous eyes.

'I looked to a record of the baptisms, old woman. And I looked for yours in 1695. It was not there. Can you hear me? It was not there! You were baptized, the entry is there, for September 1697. What do you say to that?'

Agatha's heart was pumping. She felt it was pumping in her head. Keep calm. Keep calm. Don't let him triumph.

'Tis a lie! A scabby lie! There's no such—'

'Hark, old woman. Can you hear me still? I was not quite content with that, for baptisms do not always instantly follow births. So last afternoon and eve and all this morning I have had the servants turning the lumber out of the old room above the kitchens, where everything was thrown when the house was changed and repaired. Can you hear me? Let me come closer. Let me speak right into your ear. We found the old family bible which once used to be downstairs in the hall when Francis's father was alive, and behold I have found an entry in it. Let me read it to you. Or would you prefer to read it yourself? Here!'

He took up the book from the table and opened it. He offered it to her but she shrank away.

'Then let me read it. I dare suppose it is your father's handwriting; the ink is very faded. But very very clear, old woman. Very clear. It says: "Ye tenth day of August, 1697, born to us this wet summer morn eleven o'clock in ye forenoon, our first child, a daughter, Agatha Mary, Praise be to God." Can you hear me or shall I read it again?'

'I hear.'

'And then in the margin beside in another hand is written: "Christened third September." So you see, old woman, on Monday next you will be but ninety-eight.'

Agatha remained quite rigid. The black cat, unaware of her agitation, looked at her and yawned and tried to settle beside her. George turned and took the book to a table by the window and then came back and considered his victim. With this old woman he had carried on a bitter vendetta for years. It was too long ago to remember who had begun it, whether it had been a mutual antipathy from the start or had grown from some resented slight. But it was too late to heal it now, too late for half measures or for drawing back the knife.

'Can you hear me? I am going downstairs to instruct that letters shall be sent to all the people of the country who have accepted your invitation. It will inform them that you have made a mistake as to your age and that a new invitation will be issued in two years' time.'

'Ye would not dare! Elizabeth would ne'er—ne'er allow it! Nor would she! Nor would she!'

'She cannot stop me. I am the master of this house, and, although I would have permitted this celebration to take place in it, I will not be party to a flagrant deception. You are ninety-seven, old woman. On Monday you will be ninety-eight. Live two more years and you may invite your friends all over again.'

You tried to control yourself. All the iron discipline of determined old age told you what to do – close your eyes, breathe deeply, shut out the angry thoughts, remember only survival. It had been practised before in so many every-day affairs. Apparent temper, apparent furious scoldings were surface storms, creating no real disturbances, no disturbance in depth. You grew to know how . . . But sometimes the discipline does not, cannot work. The fury, the agony builds up until it bursts all controls, and you are defenceless against all the rushing, blood-surging, damaging emotions which sweep through you and over you and will eventually destroy you.

God in his heaven has no help.

George was going to the door. 'Wait!' she said. He turned politely back. He gave no outward sign of any triumph he might be feeling. Could she plead? Could she lower herself to plead with this man?

'All this prepared,' she said. 'All me clothes. Things got ready. In the kitchens. Food ordered.' She stopped and tried to get her breath. She could not. It had left her.

He said: 'A pity. It will all do again.'

She gasped, swallowed, took in air just in time. 'Send Elizabeth . . . Ask Elizabeth to come . . . Birthday on Monday whether or no. Party for me whether or no. Ninety-eight. Good old age . . . But I'll be a *hundred*. I know. I *know*. I've counted. How could I be wrong?'

'You're wrong, old woman, and there will be no party. It will be easy to cancel. And open your window more on such a fine day. This room stinks.'

'Stop!' He was going again. 'I'll not live two year more. Ye know that. Who'd know if ye said naught? I'll ne'er live another two year. I'll not cross ye again, George. I've been looking forward to this so long. Eh? Eh? I'll not cross ye again, George. Twill do ye no hurt. No harm will come of it. I'll make a new will – leave ye the money that I have in Consols. No one'd ever know.'

'I don't want your money, old woman!' George came back, book under his arm. 'Nor your goodwill. I'm sorry for you now, but I'll see you rot in this room before I'll be party to such a lie!'

Then the hatred was plain on both sides, on that of the normally cool, composed, dignified man, on that of the wisp of tattered humanity clutching and gasping in the bed. Tears were on her cheeks now, and they were not the perpetual tears of a watering eye.

'If ye do this to me,' she said, and choked and spat to get the words out, 'may ye rot too – and rot I know ye surely will. Aye, you and your clumsy father and your vulture uncle and your – your stupid clammy mother and your twisted son. Little Valentine! Born under a black moon and *twisted* already! He'll eat the worms of this world afore he's far gone! I *know*! I can tell! Born under a black moon! The last of the Warleggans!'

Although her life was far spent, she had sight enough to perceive that for the moment her puny shot was stinging him. She might be going down, but she would continue firing to the end. That shot had told. And one last shot remained.

'The last of the Warleggans, George! Or be he a Warleggan at all?'

George had gone to the door and had turned to watch her, this puny, smelly, shrivelled old woman. She was a pitiable sight, twisting and choking, her lips blue, some last flush of blood in her cheeks, eyes like slits, lips pendulous, struggling to shout, to bite, to inject him with a last venom.

She said: 'That wasn't no seven-month baby, George. Nor eight month neither, for the matter of that. I seen 'em seven month – I seen 'em eight month – many times and oft in my life. No nails they have, see. And skin wrinkled like a – like an apple kept too long and . . .' She choked and spat saliva on the sheet. '. . . and no cry, a poor weak cry like a meader, and – and no *hair*. *That* were a full term child! Your precious twisted Valentine were a *full term* child, I'll lay my oath! So . . .'

He stared at her, and it was as if he could well have spat back. But he did not. He stood there listening while the last shots were fired, the last injury attempted.

'Maybe ye didn't wait for the wedding ceremony, you and Elizabeth, eh? Maybe that was it. Was that it, eh? . . .' She showed her gums in a snarl. 'Or maybe someone else was riding she afore ever you was wed! Eh? Eh? *Your* precious Valentine!'

He left the room and the slam of the door shook the old house. Agatha Poldark sank back on her pillows. And the blackbird in the cage by the window twittered in fright,

And a gentle breeze lifted the curtains and told that a curre. of air had passed.

Four miles away Ross sat with Demelza and his two children on the lawn in front of their house. Except for the thump and rattle of a tin stamp, which somehow was absorbed and ignored by the ears, there was no untoward sound. On the upper ground of the valley the chimney of Wheal Grace emitted a trickle of cloudy smoke, and a few figures moved among the offices of the mine.

It was unusual for them to sit as a family like this, but the hot day had interfered with their normal intentions. Ross sat with Clowance on his knee and Garrick crunching a bone at his feet. Jeremy was sprawled on his stomach making a daisy chain, and Demelza was sprawled on her stomach helping him. A contentment marked them all. After the first shock of knowing that his best plans for Drake could now come to nothing, Ross had deliberately willed himself to think no more of it. Now and then in the night he woke up and remembered George and his rare and galling ability to turn a set-back into a victory, and all the incipient goodwill of the time of his homecoming was gone again. But he saw well enough that it would be irresponsible to allow this recurrent bitterness in one aspect only of his life to spoil the over-all contentment. Something must be done for Drake, and meantime he must *forget*. Forget George and forget Elizabeth and see only all that he had. For all that he had was all that he wanted. And the sun was shining; and Clowance was dozing gently on his knee, her small head suddenly top-heavy on its frail stalk; and on the grass beside him Demelza and Jeremy were making a daisy chain . . .

And a dozen miles away Caroline Penvenen was watching a groom help Dwight mount his first horse. He accomplished it like an old man, needing two hoists before his own muscles would take him up; and when he got there he seemed close to slipping off again. But having settled himself he grinned in triumph, a paper-white grin which a week's good food had not yet given enough red blood to, and Caroline smiling beside him was glad they had chosen her oldest and staidest mare. They had settled on an October wedding, though had not yet decided between Caroline's desire for a big one and Dwight's for a small. Much in his attitude, she suspected, would depend upon how quickly he

:covered his physical health . . .

And in Truro the Reverend Osborne Whitworth, restored to perfect mental health, was arguing in a loud voice with his warden about the contributions of the pew-owning families, while Morwenna Whitworth, holding the stocky hand of one of her little step-daughters, looked out across her garden to where the river had just gone down and wondered if it might be better to drown in mud, in real mud, rather than suffocate in the mud of physical revulsion . . .

And in Falmouth Drake Carne limped down the main street with Mrs Verity Blamey to meet her husband whose packet the *Caroline* had but an hour ago dropped anchor in the roads. His arm was still in a sling but his shoulder was much better, and his hands had completely healed. He was eating enormously, he felt well, and some of the pleasures of life were returning. This was more particularly because Ross, before he left, had let drop that Morwenna was not now to marry the parson from Truro after all. Even if Morwenna were not for him, this made so much difference to his feelings, for he knew she had no liking for Whitworth. His days were no longer tortured. By now, he thought, she would be in Bodmin. Who knew but that sometime he might walk to Bodmin to see her? Just the sight of her now and again would be enough. He looked no further than that. He asked no more . . .

And in Trenwith George walked slowly through the house, with no expression on his face but something in his mien which made servants shrink away from him as he passed. It was such a beautiful day that all the family were out of doors, even the two old Chynoweths.

He had killed his viper. He had given it, he knew, a mortal wound. But as he took his foot from its neck it had turned and bitten him in the heel. And the venom it had left behind was working. After he had completed two circuits of the house he slowly mounted the stairs and went into his study. He locked the door and took a seat in his favourite chair. For once in his life he felt ill and unsure of himself. The spread of the poison was slow but steady. He did not know if he could shake it off.

It might be that he would die of it. It might be that others would die of it. He did not know and only time would reveal the extent of the poison . . .

And at the other end of the house Agatha was fighting for her life. She was quite alone. Lucy Pipe had settled in the

382

kitchen and would certainly not stir again until the bell jangled. Only the blackbird twittered in its cage and Smollett, having been disturbed by all the commotion on the bed, had dropped to the floor and was licking one of his back legs near the door.

In spite of years of bible reading, Agatha had little convinced belief in a future life, so she clung to this one with a rare tenacity, trying to marshal the last ebbing forces and see perhaps tomorrow. With age one never looked far ahead. The marathon horizons of youth narrowed and shortened into the hurdles of age. If she could see tomorrow she would have made the next objective. Control was everything; quiet the heart, regulate the breathing, relax the mind. Forget the anger, ignore the disappointment, concentrate on only one thing, the necessity of the next breath, of simple survival.

But this time she had gone too far. The shock of the disclosure, the overwhelming fury which had possessed her, had in a few minutes consumed the last fuel in her old body. This was not faintness; she knew it was something more. It would not do to be taken ill now, for in a few minutes her father would be here to take her to the party. There would be some dancing later on, and a few tables of whist. She must subdue this nervous stomach; her mother said it was time she grew out of it at seventeen. She must get up. She tried to move her legs and could not. The sensation had gone out of them. She whimpered with fright and moved a hand. That at least was still hers.

A coffin was in the room. That sick-sweet smell of decay and flowers. She had seen so many such. Whose was this? They had all looked so composed but so small in death, each one before the lid was screwed down. They had fallen about her all these years.

She lifted her hand up to her eyes and wiped the mist and the coffin away. The warm sunlight flooded in to the room, the life-giving sunlight that had no life to give back to her. The gentle scented breeze, the shadow of moving leaves, the flutter of birds; these might all have helped her at another time. Five more days until she was twenty-one, and they were disappointed with her that she had not turned out more pretty. Someone, too, an aunt, had told her she was lacking in vivacity. But that wasn't what George Venables had said. George Venables had said many beautiful things. But why wouldn't he let her have her birthday party?

Death came like a rising tide, inch by inch, putting her

body to sleep. Soon there was no stomach, then there was no breathing left. She did not gasp for breath for she no longer needed air. For the last time, seeing its approaching extinction, her brain came clear again. What had she said? What trouble had she started, and for whom? She had not meant to injure Elizabeth. What had she said?

The bed shook as Smollett jumped on it again. Her head was sinking sideways on the pillow. With a great effort she straightened it. For a moment that was better. But then the light began to go, the warm, milk yellow sunlight of a summer day. The beamed ceiling smeared and blurred. She could not close her mouth. She tried to close her mouth and failed. Her tongue stopped. But one hand still slowly moved. Smollett nudged up to it and licked it with his rough tongue. The sensation of that roughness made its way from her fingers to her brain. It was the last feeling left. The fingers moved a moment on the cat's fur. Hold me, hold me, they said. Then quietly, peacefully at the last, submissively, beaten by a stronger will than her own, her eyes opened and she left the world behind.

The water wa... [barcode] her skin. The s... surface like a million diamonds.

She looked around. The small boat they'd used to get away from the dock and *Cassandra* bobbed several hundred yards away.

"I can swim back. I'm fine now that I have my breath back." Without her volition, her fingers began rubbing small patterns on his smooth skin. She could feel the muscles contract beneath her as he kept them both above water. Did she have her breath back? Being so close to Nikos was robbing her of air again. Her legs tangled with his as they lazily kicked to keep upright. Her left side was pressed against him.

"You look lovely."

"You've got to be kidding," she said. "My hair is hanging in strings. I have no makeup on and I'm covered in salt water."

Nikos's eyes took on a distinctive gleam. "You look beautiful," he said in that low, sexy voice.

Dear Reader,

Come with me on an adventure in the beautiful land of Greece. It has long been a place of fascination for me, and I dream about going there one day to soak up the sunshine and the beauty of the landscape; to lie on pristine beaches and tour historic sites. Until that time, I use the places I've visited around the Mediterranean to picture how sailing the Aegean would be, how the breezes would feel and how the dynamic and gorgeous Greek men would look. What would be more fun than to travel the Aegean in a luxury yacht, visiting quaint isles for their history, or colorful markets with fabulous bargains? All on the arm of a sexy Greek man, of course. As a vacation locale, could we find a better spot? So come visit Greece with Sara and Nikos, and be swept away on a mini vacation that will give you the feel of an exotic land we may all one day see.

Love,

Barbara

BARBARA McMAHON

Greek Boss, Dream Proposal

TORONTO • NEW YORK • LONDON
AMSTERDAM • PARIS • SYDNEY • HAMBURG
STOCKHOLM • ATHENS • TOKYO • MILAN • MADRID
PRAGUE • WARSAW • BUDAPEST • AUCKLAND

Recycling programs
for this product may
not exist in your area.

ISBN-13: 978-0-373-17603-8

GREEK BOSS, DREAM PROPOSAL

First North American Publication 2009.

www.eHarlequin.com

Printed in U.S.A.

Barbara McMahon was born and raised in the U.S. South, but settled in California after spending a year flying around the world for an international airline. After settling down to raise a family and work for a computer firm, she began writing when her children started school. Now, feeling fortunate in being able to realize the long-held dream of quitting her day job and writing full-time, she and her husband have moved to the Sierra Nevada mountains of California, where she finds her desire to write is stronger than ever. With the beauty of the mountains visible from her windows, and the pace of life slower than that of the hectic San Francisco Bay Area, where they previously resided, she finds more time than ever to think up stories and characters and share them with others through writing. Barbara loves to hear from readers. You can reach her at P.O. Box 977, Pioneer, CA 95666-0977, U.S.A. Readers can also contact Barbara at her Web site, www.barbaramcmahon.com.

CHAPTER ONE

SARA ANDROPOLOUS leaned over to view the pastry from all angles. It looked perfect. Satisfied, she slid it onto one of the delicate china plates and drizzled a bit of honey on top. Two mint leaves completed the presentation and she smiled. One down, five more to do in less than five minutes.

Working swiftly, she finished the last in less than the allotted time. Perfection.

She'd been on her feet for five hours, yet she felt as fresh as if she'd just started. She loved creating works of art for consumption. Time flew, and she was absorbed in her work to the exclusion of all else.

"See how this pleases your guests," she murmured in a one-sided imaginary conversation with Nikos Konstantinos.

When Sara had first arrived in Greece four months ago, her temporary assignment at the τραγο´υϖδι αο´ερα, Windsong Hotel, several miles from Thessalonika had seemed like an answer to prayer. She'd been trying to find a way to get a toehold in Greece for so long, it was amazing to her how swiftly things had fallen into place. No one suspected her real intent. The sudden opportunity to move to Greece had been impossible to refuse. She'd left her friends, sublet her flat, and headed for the Aegean with one thought in mind—find a way to make contact with her grandmother, Eleani Konstantinos.

As the yacht gently bobbed on the sea, Sara wondered for the nth time if she were really any closer to her goal. It had seemed meant to be when her friend Stacy had discovered that Sara's grandmother had remarried and found where she had been living all these years. When Stacy had then told her five months ago about an opening at the exclusive Greek resort owned by the grandson of the man her grandmother had married, Sara had applied instantly for the job. Amazingly, she'd been hired within two weeks of her first interview. Being Greek herself and knowing the language had been a big plus. But she also liked to think her accomplishments had commanded the attention of the interviewer. The lavish salary she was getting indicated they expected no less than outstanding work.

So far things had progressed better than she'd expected. After only four months in Greece, it was nothing short of miraculous that she'd been promoted to temporary chef on Nikos Konstantinos's luxury yacht. With any luck, at some point, they would put in at the island his family owned—the key to getting to her grandmother. How she was to accomplish the next step was beyond her at the moment. Still, she was closer than ever. Time would present the opportunity she needed.

Stretching her muscles, she placed the desserts on the elegant silver tray and put it on the open area of the counter where the steward would pick it up to deliver to the guests in the main dining salon. It was after nine and she was just about finished for the day. She felt revved up, wide-awake and not at all ready to go to bed, though she'd been up before six every morning to prepare breakfast.

The chef on the yacht *Cassandra* had become suddenly ill with appendicitis, and she'd been selected to fill the role until he recovered. As the chief chef at the resort had explained when selecting her for the assignment, their boss, resort owner Nikos Konstantinos, had guests expected for a week's cruise around the Aegean and needed someone versatile enough for all meals and desserts. The chief chef had recommended her even though she was the newest member of the kitchen staff. She still couldn't believe her luck. At this rate she'd finally meet her grandmother before the month was out!

Her intelligence unit, as she called her friends in London who had rallied round to help her get to Greece once they'd learned of her goal, were certain her mother's mother was living on the Konstantinos family island in the Aegean. Strategically isolated for privacy, the island offered no way to gain access unless a family member brought guests. Since her letter had been returned unopened, her phone call refused and no e-mail address available, she knew no one would vouch for her. To the contrary, she suspected if she petitioned Nikos Konstantinos directly, he'd have her fired on the spot and erect even stronger barriers between her and her grandmother. She was not going to put that to the test. She'd find a way onto the island on her own.

If she could just meet the woman, maybe she could ignore some of that stiff Greek pride that apparently ran rampant in her mother's family and tell Eleani Konstantinos about her daughter's death, and the last words her mother had said— how she wished she could have reconciled with her parents. It had been too late by the time Damaris Andropolous had uttered those words. She had died two days later.

Sara wanted to carry them back, heal a breach that had split the family for almost thirty years. She had been working more than a year to achieve that aim to fulfill the promise she had made to her mother just before she died.

Was the end really in sight?

Looking back, the best thing her mother had ever done was insist Sara learn Greek. Most of their family friends in London had been of Greek descent, a close-knit community of Greek expats who had loved to celebrate special occasions together. Her friend Stacy swore she loved the English lifestyle more than anything, yet she, too, had studied their ancestors' language. Sara knew her fluency in Greek had landed her this job, she was sure of it. She had had no difficulty in adapting to life at the resort. It was a delightful change from the rainy weather she'd left in London and she'd thrown herself into her job with determination that had obviously paid off.

As she put the pots and bowls she'd used to prepare the evening meal in the sink to soak, Sara thought about how she'd approach her grandmother—if she got the chance. Stacy had been a font of information, relying on the gossip of her own cousins who still lived in Greece. Sara's grandfather had died several years ago, and Eleani had remarried Spiros Konstantinos, head of the legendary Konstantinos Shipping empire. Sara had scrambled to find out as much information as she could about the family, only to come up with very little.

They obviously used a good deal of the money they made ensuring privacy.

"I'm late. Sorry. Won't happen again," Stefano said as he swooped up the tray of desserts. The steward was late at least once a day—and always claiming it wouldn't happen again. She had gotten used to it and if Nikos Konstantinos didn't care, she certainly didn't.

"Looks delicious, as usual. I'll get it up to the guests." He talked so fast Sara sometimes had trouble understanding him. She made sure he had all he needed for the guests, then began preparing a tray for the crew.

When Stefano returned, he leaned against the door and let out a long breath. "So the daughter is turning up her charm. I suspect this is a cruise to ensure the lovely Gina Fregulia and Nikos have a chance to get to know each other better. Her father is hinting for marriage, you know. And it doesn't seem as if Nikos is resisting at all."

"Now how would you know that?" Sara asked as she worked. She silently urged him to continue. The more she knew about the Konstantinos family, the better able she'd be to deal with them, she thought.

"It's no secret. The man's thirty-four years old. Past time to marry and start a family, else who will inherit all the money?"

Sara looked up at that. "You're thirty-five. Are you married?"

Stefano laughed. "It's different for me. I get to see beautiful women every day. Sail the Aegean on every cruise. Maybe I will settle down one day. But I don't have two fortunes to leave when I die."

"Two?"

"Nikos didn't follow his father and grandfather into shipping. But he's still the sole heir after his father. He's making a small fortune in his own right with the resort and all the collateral businesses. Wish I had some of that money."

"I'm sure we all do. Actually, we get some by doing our work properly," Sara said mischievously, smiling at the steward.

"I meant, have it to spend without working. It'll be interesting to see how the relationship between Miss Fregulia and the boss pans out."

"Do you think it won't?" Sara asked, curious. She longed to ask a dozen questions, but didn't want to give rise to suspicion.

Stefano gave a shrug. "The way I hear it, Nikos loved his first fiancée. I never knew the full story of the breakup, but for a long time, he had the temper of a bear. Arranged marriages are a bit passé for those of us in the regular world, but in the world of huge fortunes, not so uncommon. I think Nikos Konstantinos will marry for the good of the resort, and to provide heirs for the fortunes. The Fregulias are big in wine in Italy. Their fortunes surely match those of Nikos. At least he doesn't worry about being married for his money. I predict a match made in business."

"An oracle," Sara said, finishing the last touch on the desserts for the crew. "I wish them happy." A happy Nikos meant a more amiable man if she ever had to call on him for access to her grandmother.

"I expect Gina Fregulia will be happy if she gets her hands on Nikos's millions."

"Thought you said she was wealthy."

"Her father is, subtle difference. Nikos will be the prize," Stefano said.

Sara shook her head. Stefano called their boss by his first name around the staff, but she knew he'd have infinitely more respect when in the presence of Nikos Konstantinos. At least she thought he would. She had yet to meet the man. Didn't care much one way or another if she ever met him, as long as his yacht docked on the family island at some time while she was still aboard.

"The captain won't be having dessert. He's returned to the helm to relieve the mate. This looks nice for the crew," Stefano said as he lifted the second, less elaborate, tray full of delicious pastries.

"We should have our food as nicely presented as the guests," Sara said, putting the finishing garnishment on the last plate.

Sara followed Stefano to the aft deck where a table had been set up for the crew to use. Those already seated had left her a place at the end since she didn't normally join them until dessert. Except for Stefano, the rest of the men were around her mother's age. They had probably sailed on the Konstantinos yacht for years.

Sara relaxed slightly. Her duties for the day were completed. The gentle breeze that swept by as the yacht plowed through the sea made it most pleasant to be outside. It was a cool relief from the hot kitchen. The stars were growing brilliant against the darkening sky. Only the running lights from the yacht and the illumination spilling from the salon disturbed the velvet darkness.

Once she'd finished eating, she considered relaxing on one of the loungers and just studying the sky. With little ambient light, the stars seemed to multiply. She saw more each night than she'd ever seen in London.

They'd be stopping at anchor soon. The Aegean rocked the boat gently each night. She loved it. Maybe she should consider looking for a permanent berth on some ship once her task had been completed.

"Thank you," one of the crew said as he rose. "It's good."

One by one the others rose and thanked her. Sara was beaming when Stefano left to clean the kitchen. He'd removed all the dishes and utensils, leaving the table bare, except for her glass of water.

One of the men went to sit near the aft rail, gazing out across the sea. The others left, presumably to other tasks or for an early bedtime.

Sara enjoyed the night air for a short time, then went back to the galley to check on preparations for breakfast. Once she had that done, she'd call it a night.

She had been longer on the aft deck than she thought. The galley was gleaming. Stefano had finished and vanished. She would have enjoyed some company in the quiet space while she mentally reviewed the checklist for the ingredients she would need to bake individual quiches for breakfast. She'd make a pan of sweet rolls and cut up fresh fruit. The larder of the galley was bigger than the pantry she had in her flat. The yacht was spacious and outfitted to suit the most discriminating tastes.

Humming as she double-checked everything, Sara was startled when she heard the door open behind her. Turning, she stopped in surprise. No doubt about it, Nikos Konstantinos had come to the galley.

In a land where all men seemed to be handsome, she was momentarily taken aback. Feeling tongue-tied like an idiot schoolgirl, she could only stare for a long moment, feeling every sense come to attention as she gazed at him. He had wavy black hair and a tan that spoke of hours in the Aegean sun. Dark eyes gravely regarded her. He seemed to fill the doorway, his head barely clearing the lintel. He was over six feet, with broad shoulders and a trim physique. The white dinner jacket he wore seemed out of place on a ship, yet suited him to perfection. Bemused, Sara wished her friend Stacy could see how the rich dressed for dinner—even on a private yacht. This man would take the crown for good looks. She felt a frisson of attraction, and the surprise shocked her out of her stupor. He'd think she was an idiot if she didn't say something.

"Can I help you?" she asked. For a moment she felt a pull like a magnet's force field, drawing her closer. Looking away for a scant second, she was vaguely pleased to note her feet were still where they had been. She hadn't made a fool of herself by closing the gap between them.

"You are the chef replacing Paul?" he asked in disbelief.

Sara almost groaned in delight at the husky, sexy tone of

his deep voice. She wanted to close her eyes and ask him to recite some lengthy passage just to hear him speak. But Sara Andropolous was made of sterner stuff. Tilting her head slightly, she gave a polite smile, ignoring her racing heart and replied, "I am."

Be very wary, she warned herself. This man held the key to the Konstantinos family island. She dared not do anything to jeopardize that. But for an instant she forgot all of that as she took in his stunning good looks. The tingling awareness seemed to grow with each tick of the clock.

He narrowed his eyes slightly. "I had not expected a woman so young," he said softly.

"Age has little to do with accomplishments," Sara replied, her back up now. What, a woman still in her twenties, though barely, couldn't be as great a chef as one in her fifties? So much for instant attraction. Reality slapped her in the face. He came from the same world that had ended so cruelly for her mother thirty years ago. What did he know of deprivation, hardship, heartache? Or working one's butt off to get ahead? She'd fought long and hard to achieve the level she had attained. Age had nothing to do with it. Sheer dog-headed determination and drive had.

While not precisely the enemy, Nikos Konstantinos was, nevertheless, not a friend either.

"My apologies, I didn't mean to imply it was. You caught me by surprise, that's all. I came to compliment you on tonight's meal. My guests were most pleased. The lamb almost melted in our mouths."

Sara was pleased with the compliment and equally surprised her new boss had taken time to come to tell the chef in person.

"I am Nikos Konstantinos," he said. As if she wouldn't know.

"I am Sara Andropolous," she replied. Would he recognize

the name from the one letter she'd sent months and months ago? Or had he not been the one to refuse it and have it returned to sender?

"You are finding everything you need?" he asked.

"Yes. The galley is perfect."

"As are the meals you are preparing. I am pleased."

She felt a warm glow. She had worked hard to achieve her goals. She would fight tooth and nail to keep her position. But not, it seemed, today. The man she now worked for was satisfied.

"I believe in passing along compliments so people know their work is appreciated," he commented.

She studied him a moment longer not knowing what to say. He nodded his head once and left.

Nikos Konstantinos had not followed in his father's and grandfather's footsteps, but had made his mark in the hotel industry. Since building the Windsong, his impact on Greek tourism had been assured, Sara had been told more than once. The employees of the hotel bragged about its success, and with good reason. The excellent staff had had a lot to do with it, after all. The resort was rumored to have a waiting list of more than a year for a reservation. Guests not staying in the hotel could sail into the wide harbor, rent a slip at the lavish marina and use all amenities of the resort—including dining in one of the six fine restaurants. Those staying at the resort could choose which restaurant in which to dine each evening or arrange for room service to deliver and serve a meal as elegantly on a private terrace or balcony as in any of the five-star restaurants.

She was surprised he was as young as he was to have accomplished all he had. Maybe she should have returned the compliment. But then, he had started with a wealthy family backing him; he had probably leapfrogged over growth pains others had to endure.

She returned to her task. Their backgrounds couldn't be more different. Sara had been raised without a twopence to spare. Fighting her way above the poverty level, she'd put herself through culinary school by working endless hours in kitchen sculleries to afford the training needed to rise above the level of short-order cook. Perseverance, determination— and yes, even some of that stiff-necked pride from her mother—had pushed her through and to success.

Whereas Nikos had probably merely spent one month's allowance and had the Windsong built with a snap of his fingers. Nikos, she thought, like they were friends or something. Mr. Konstantinos, she corrected herself silently. If his guests continued to be pleased, he would be, as well. Which meant he'd keep her on board longer. Fingers crossed it was long enough to visit the family island.

Heading for her tiny cabin a short time later, Sara grew optimistic. She'd met the owner and he was satisfied with her work. Surely that meant things were still looking up for her plan.

Sara knew she'd been unbelievably fortunate that the chief chef had recommended her for this cushy spot. There were five other crew members in addition to herself. With the guests and Nikos, that made twelve. Nothing like the number of dishes she had to prepare in one of the resort kitchens each evening.

Her first sight of the yacht had inspired a touch of awe. It was beautiful—sleek, gleaming white and riding with a high bow off the water. The main body looked to be longer than her apartment in London and the aft deck could have easily hosted a party for fifty. That's where she and the other crew could spend off hours. At least the owner was generous with his staff.

Sara frowned. She wasn't sure she wanted to list admirable

attributes. Nikos Konstantinos might be one of the sexiest men she'd ever met, but he was no more than a means to an end for her. She had better not forget that. Besides, Stefano had said this was almost an engagement cruise—a chance for Nikos to decide whether to marry the daughter of a business associate. Sounded cold to her. It also mirrored the same circumstances her mother had been in years ago—an arranged marriage. At least this time it sounded as if the prospective participants were not averse to the plan.

She was astonished to find herself attracted to the man. For a second she had almost forgotten what she was doing and been tempted to flirt. A handsome man, a lonely woman, the perfect romantic setting.

How dumb would that have been?

CHAPTER TWO

NIKOS left the galley to return to the suite that served as both office and bedroom when on board. His chef had been a surprise. Her dark wavy hair had been tied back, with tendrils escaping to frame her face. Her large brown eyes had revealed a wariness that had surprised him. He was used to the awe in which some held him. This was somehow different. Yet her manner had been professional. He'd detected a note of annoyance with the comment about her age. Nikos almost smiled. Touchy—weren't all great chefs? Though the only ones he'd ever met before had been male. A female chef was a novelty. At least she had not instantly tried to flirt and garner more interest.

He had grown weary of the flirtatious ways of the women he met. If he thought a single one would be interested in him if he had not a dime to spare, he might feel differently. But he'd learned early on that most women wanted one thing— to live a life of luxury—preferably off the proceeds of a susceptible male. His own aborted engagement proved that.

It was as if life were a lottery and he one of the prizes. Nikos did not like to consider himself conceited, but maybe he had grown so with the attention of so many lovely women over the past ten years.

He found Sara's totally professional attitude refreshing. What would it be like to have people judge him on his own merits? To have a friend who wanted nothing but him as he was?

George Wilson and Marc Swindard were the only two friends to come to mind. Perhaps because they'd shared so many holidays at school when it was too inconvenient for each of them to be flown home. He would send them both e-mails and catch up. Maybe they could get together soon. The demands of business could be consuming. He was guilty of not making more of an effort to get away. But a short trip to New York or London in the near future could be arranged.

Of course, if the idea of marrying Gina Fregulia grew, maybe he'd be contacting his friends to announce his engagement. This time the engagement would be more likely to endure—no lies of love and passion to cloud the issue. He found Gina attractive. She certainly knew how to entertain and moved in the same social circles he did. She'd be a definite asset to the restaurant side of the resort with her knowledge of excellent wines and the contacts her family had.

Nikos pushed open the door to the suite and loosened his tie. He had a little time to catch up on business before he retired for the night.

When Stefano brought his breakfast promptly at seven the next morning, Nikos had been working for almost an hour. The yacht rode at anchor during the night and Nikos had taken advantage of that to have a quick swim in the sea at dawn before showering and dressing for the day. Satellite connections kept him in constant touch with the resort and anyone else who wished to contact him—such as his father, who called just as Stefano put the tray on the desk.

"Have you checked on your grandfather lately?" Andrus asked when Nikos answered the phone.

"Is there a problem?" Nikos asked. It was rare his father spoke of family matters. The shipping business was even more consuming than hotels, especially to Andrus. He had lived for the family shipping company as long as Nikos could remember—to the exclusion of everything else.

"He has some idea about buying another boat to use to get from the island to the mainland. He says the old one is too decrepit."

"It's in perfect running order," Nikos said. He made sure maintenance was always current on all the family's watercrafts.

"I think he wants a new one, smaller, that he can drive himself. But he's eighty-two years old. Too old to be jaunting all over the Aegean by himself," Andrus said in disgust.

"Did you tell him that?" Nikos asked, already knowing the answer.

"Do you think I'm crazy? I thought you could visit, convince him to keep the ship's crew and make sure he doesn't do something foolish."

"My grandfather is not a foolish man," Nikos said mildly. His father asked him to act as intermediary between them from time to time. It was the closest to familial affection his father got.

"When were you there last?"

"A month ago," Nikos replied.

"Can you get away soon?" his father asked.

Nikos gazed out of the wide window at the sparkling sea. "I could when my guests leave. I'm entertaining the Fregulias and Onetas right now."

"Next week, then. Let me know." His father hung up.

"Want to know how my own business is going?" Nikos said

as he hung up the phone. To his father, if one wasn't in shipping, it was of no account. "Or how about my plans to ask Gina to marry me?" He knew the answer to that one, as well: do as you please. Nikos didn't mind anymore. His father wasn't going to change—any more than his grandfather would. If the old man wanted a powerboat so he could operate it himself, he'd get one. Nikos wasn't going to try to talk him out of it. More power to him. He hoped *he* was as active when he was eighty-two.

Nikos poured a cup of coffee, surveying the meal. An individual portioned quiche lorraine centered the plate. A fresh fruit compote accompanied it, as well as two slices of a rich walnut bread. How early had Sara risen to have this prepared by seven, he wondered?

He knew so little about his temporary chef. He admitted to being a bit intrigued by a woman who had risen so fast in a field dominated by men. Yet the chief chef had recommended her. That spoke volumes. The fact that she was pretty didn't hurt, either.

He shook his head and picked up the reservation schedule for the next month. He had other things to do besides think about his temporary chef.

At noon Nikos consulted with the captain and arranged for the ship to stop on one of the smaller islands not too far distant. It would offer his guests a chance to visit the local market and see some of what the Aegean islands had to offer.

Nikos instructed the captain to give the crew the afternoon off and then set sail again at seven. That would allow for dinner on board and some after-dinner conversation before going to his suite for the night.

Shortly after the island came into view, Nikos received a communiqué from the resort. He went to take the call, only to be told his assistant was busy trying to deal with a power outage at the sprawling resort—no power to rooms, pools, common areas or kitchens. When they docked at the island, Nikos sent word to Gina he would be tied up for a little while but urged the Fregulias to go on ahead and he'd catch up, if the situation could be resolved soon. Tapping his fingertips on the desk, he chafed at the distance between him and the resort. He wanted to be right there finding out what had gone wrong, handling the emergency. With the portable phone held to his ear, he went to the cabin's wide windows.

It was market day on the island. Colorful canopies lined the streets, fluttering in the breeze, shading the wares and goods for sale. The small population seemed to turn out in force to see what bargains they could get, and he watched as Gina happily went down the gangway with her parents and the Onetas, the other couple cruising with them. Soon they were lost from sight as they began exploring the market.

Fifteen minutes later he'd been briefed on the cause of the outage—a power cable severed by road construction near the outer perimeter of the resort. Nothing to be done except wait. The generators had been started and for the most part the resort was operating as usual. Nikos instructed his assistant to keep him informed and hung up. Nothing he could do from the ship.

He started to leave to find his guests when he realized he hadn't seen any of the crew disembark when he'd been at the window. He'd given instructions they were to have the afternoon off. Glancing at the bridge, he saw it was empty. He went to the kitchen to see if any were there. Pausing at the doorway, Nikos's gaze went straight to Sara. She was even prettier in daylight. He frowned. He had no business thinking about her at all.

She was wrapping a platter while Stefano lounged against

one of the counters chatting. When he saw Nikos, he straightened up, almost coming to attention.

"Did you need something, Mr. Konstantinos?" he asked.

Sara looked at him. "Did you want lunch? I had it nearly prepared when I heard the change in plans. Are you hungry?"

He looked at the sandwich wraps artistically arranged on a platter. Stepping closer, he reached beneath the plastic wrap and took one. Biting into it, he recognized good Greek cheese and olives. And a hint of some spice he wasn't familiar with. It was delicious.

"As it happens, I have not eaten. There was a minor crisis at the resort, so I sent my guests ahead. Perhaps you could prepare me a plate and bring it up." He'd eat lunch before leaving the ship. No sense in wasting food, or her efforts.

"Yes, sir, right away, sir," Stefano said.

Nikos's eyes met Sara's. "Actually, I thought Miss Andropolous could bring it up. It would give her a chance to see more of the yacht. The captain has also gone ashore, so I could show you the bridge, as well."

She glanced at Stefano and shared his look of surprise.

"Thank you, I would love to see the rest of the ship. I can bring you a plate in ten minutes," she replied. "The crew decided to eat on board and then we're all going exploring."

Nikos nodded once and then left. He wasn't sure why he'd made the offer. He'd never done so before. But then, he'd never had a woman chef before, either. For a moment Nikos wondered if he'd lost his mind. He was considering marriage to Gina Fregulia. He's spent less than a total of ten minutes with Sara Andropolous. Yet he could postpone finding Gina to show a stranger his ship? Maybe the sun was getting to him. To single out a crew member went against everything he normally did. Yet there was something fascinating about the woman. And she was only bringing his lunch.

Sara knocked on the door in exactly ten minutes. He heard her say something and wondered if she'd needed Stefano to guide her to the suite.

He opened the door and caught a glimpse of Stefano disappearing around the bend.

"Come in." He stood aside as she entered, carrying a tray with his lunch—a plate piled high with delicacies and an iced beverage.

She looked around and headed for the low table in front of the sofa. Placing the tray carefully, she straightened and smiled in delight as she walked straight to the windows. "Wow, this is fabulous. You are so much higher than our quarters. What a great view of the harbor. What island is this?"

"Theotasaia, a small island whose inhabitants depend upon fishing for a living. Today is market day. The perfect entertainment for my guests."

"They like to shop?" she asked, still looking from the window.

Nikos crossed to stand beside her. The colorful market was spread out before them, the canopies still fluttering in the breeze.

"I do not know them well," he said. "They seemed content enough with the suggestion."

Sara looked at him. "You did not go with them."

"I was needed here. There was a power outage at the resort." He briefly told her the situation. He turned back to the plate she'd prepared. There was plenty of food.

"Did you eat?" he asked.

"I nibbled as I was preparing lunch. May I go out to the upper deck? I'll wait there until you eat—for the tour."

"I'll be along in a few minutes."

Sara let herself out of the stateroom and hurried to the

upper forward deck. Being around Nikos Konstantinos was
unnerving. She couldn't forget she was hoping he'd get her
access to her grandmother. But he disturbed her equilibrium.
She vacillated between wanting to stay away, lest she let
something slip, and getting to know him better. On the surface
he was just the kind of man her mother had run away from—
wealthy, self-assured and maybe a touch arrogant. And in the
midst of arranging a marriage to a woman who matched his
fortune. Did Gina Fregulia really want a marriage like that?

Stepping out onto the deck, Sara immediately felt the warm
breeze blowing from the sea. The sun was almost directly
overhead, the sky a cloudless blue. She went to the railing and
looked down. It was quite a distance to the sea's surface.
Gazing around, she looked behind her at the wide windows
of the bridge.

If her mother had married the man her father had picked
out for her, would she have enjoyed luxurious yachts and
visits to Aegean Islands? The reality had turned out far differently from what her mother had once envisioned when she'd
run away with Sara's father. But her pride had kept her from
admitting a mistake and returning home to seek forgiveness.

Sara still hadn't come to any conclusion when Nikos joined
her a short time later.

"Come, the captain is not on the bridge. We can see everything and he'll never know," he said with a hint of amusement
in his voice.

She laughed, intrigued by the hint of mischief in her boss.
"You're not afraid of your captain, are you?" she asked as she
followed him to the side door and stepped inside.

"He does not consider the bridge a sightseeing stop for
guests. I do what I can to keep him happy," Nikos replied.

She couldn't imagine the man afraid of anything. He

carried himself with such an air of competence and assurance, she knew he could do anything he wanted. Interesting that he humored the captain.

The bridge had a 360-degree view. The wide windows had been tinted slightly to keep off the glare from the sea. The wheel was more like an automobile's than the wooden spoke-handled ones of old. With all the gadgets, dials and computer equipment, she marveled at how the captain managed all with only one mate to back him up. Or maybe that was why—everything that could be automated had been.

"Wow, this is fantastic," she said, enjoying the view. "Surely the captain wouldn't mind showing this to guests."

"He is an excellent man and I don't want to jeopardize his staying."

"Like he's about to quit," she murmured. From what she'd learned from the rest of the crew at meals, this was a cushy assignment, and every one of them was grateful for their position.

"If he does, it won't be because I ruffled any feathers," Nikos said, coming to stand closer to Sara and pointing to the west.

"Thessalonika is that way." He swung his arm a bit more. "Thessaly is almost due west of us." Another swing. "And Athens is that way."

"But not close," she said, feeling the heat from his body as he stood so casually near. She could smell his aftershave, a woodsy scent that had her senses fluttering. She wanted to step closer. See if there was some special chemistry between them.

Appalled at her thoughts, she moved away. She would be the most foolish woman on the planet if she thought anything would ever come between her and the fabulously wealthy heir to the Konstantinos shipping fortune. Not to mention Nikos's own fortune from the resort.

"Tell me more about this little island," she said, looking over the rugged terrain. The only flat ground seemed to be where the town had been built. White homes with red tiled roofs filled the small valley. A few had been built at the lower levels of the hills. Several weathered fishing boats bobbed nearby. Probably the majority were out working.

"It only recently became a place for ships to stop. Ten years ago their docks couldn't service a ship with a deep draft. It was suitable only for the smaller fishing boats, but nothing like the *Cassandra*. Now I bring friends here from time to time. I thought my guests would enjoy it."

"Did you get the crisis resolved?" she asked.

"For the time being. We await repair of the main cable, but the generators will suffice until then."

"So now you can join your guests onshore. I shouldn't hold you up," she said, turning a little. He'd stepped closer, and she almost bumped into him. Her senses went on high alert. Her awareness gauge shot up. He was too close; she felt as if he were taking the air and leaving her breathless again.

"Come and I'll also show you the main square of the town. Time enough to find my guests. We're not leaving until seven this evening."

Sara blinked at that. Was he serious? The host of the yacht going off for an afternoon with the hired help? What was wrong with this picture?

"Do you think that wise?" she asked in a husky voice. Her heart was tripping so fast she thought he must hear it, or at least see it pounding in her chest.

"Why wouldn't it be?"

"Maybe because I'm your chef?" she asked. Hadn't Stefano said he expected to hear of an engagement between Nikos and Gina? What kind of man would spend the afternoon with another woman if his almost-fiancée was nearby? Her instincts rose. He was the kind of man she wanted to stay away from.

"It is only an afternoon in a market square. Come if you like. Or say no."

She nodded, looking away. She was not responsible for how Nikos Konstantinos behaved. She needed more information if she wanted to get on the family island. Maybe this was the chance to find out more about his family—and satisfy some of the curiosity she had about him.

"I'd love to see the square. I'll need to be back around five to have dinner ready by eight. But until then I'm game."

If the crew on the yacht thought it odd the owner was escorting the new chef when he had guests visiting from Italy, no one said a word. Ari had drawn guard duty, and he was at the gangway to make sure no unauthorized person came aboard. He gave a two-finger salute to Nikos and grinned at Sara.

In only moments they were in the midst of the crowd that clogged the streets where the market was set up. Old women all in black carried string sacks in which they put the produce they bought. A small boy walked beside his mother carefully carrying a fresh loaf of bread wrapped in paper. Children's laughter rang out, mingled with the rise and fall of bargaining debates and the spiel of those with less popular items trying to entice buyers.

It was more fun than she'd had in a while, Sara thought. Her mother would have loved it. She felt a pang when she remembered how her mother had spoken so fondly of her childhood memories. Sara nodded to the vendors, sampled one of the sweets—walnuts and honey—and danced out of the way of several children running through the marketplace.

Nikos caught her arm to steady her. She felt the touch all the way to her toes. Catching her breath, she looked at him. "Thanks."

Oh, goodness, those dark eyes looked fathomless. His face was angular and masculine. His hair was tousled just a bit from the breeze. She wished they could have met under other circumstances.

But what other circumstances? If not for her needing access to his family island, they would never have met in a thousand years. Their lifestyles were too distant.

"Why, Nikos, you took care of the emergency already?" A tall dark-haired woman seem to spring up from the ground beside Sara. As she looked at the woman, Nikos released his hold.

"Gina." For a moment he said nothing. Sara wondered if that was resignation in his eyes, but it couldn't be. Wasn't this the next Mrs. Nikos Konstantinos? Or was she a friend from Thessalonika?

The woman slipped her arm between his and his chest and leaned against him slightly. "I lost Mama and Papa. I knew the yacht was the best place to go if I got lost. But now I have you to show me the sights. I saw the cutest church on the town square. I would love to see inside."

Sara watched her for a moment, wishing Stacy could be here. She'd make some snide comment, which would have both of them laughing at the obvious ploys of this Gina. Yet the woman had to know she was special to Nikos. Sara mentally sighed. She had known spending the afternoon with a fabulously wealthy man was beyond her reality.

"Sara, may I introduce Gina Fregulia, one of my guests for the cruise. Sara is responsible for the wonderful meals we are enjoying."

"Oh, the quiche this morning was just delicious. I couldn't eat it all, of course, I do have to watch my figure. But what I sampled was simply divine. You're so clever. I can't cook."

She glanced up at Nikos with a simpering smile. "But I don't need to. We have a cook for that. I do have other talents."

"I'm sure you do," Sara said softly in English, just imagining what talents the voluptuous Italian woman had.

Nikos caught her eye, amusement evident in his. She must have misread the earlier emotion.

"Well, I'm looking for fresh produce to enhance tonight's meal. Enjoy visiting the church," she said briskly and turned.

"Sara," Nikos called.

She turned.

He hesitated a moment as Gina clung. "Tell them to charge it to the yacht, they will know how to collect."

For a split second she had hoped he was calling to reissue his invitation to see the town square together. To dump his guest and spend the afternoon with his chef. Ha. Gina was much more his type. He had been kind to offer to show her around. She relieved him of his impetuous offer.

Waving gaily, she turned and plunged into the crowd, hoping to lose herself quickly before the false smile plastered on her face dissolved and her disappointment showed. She would have liked to explore the island with someone who knew it. That was all.

Sara ended her afternoon at a small taverna near the docks. Fishing boats arrived every few minutes and she watched as the catch of the day was handed from the smaller crafts to a large ship that had tied up only moments before the fishermen returned. Most of the fish went into cold storage in the ship that probably took it straight to the mainland. Some fishermen carried their catch straight to a series of tables with running water to clean the fish and pass it along to one of the booths at the market.

Giving in to impulse, she went to buy some fresh catch to

serve for dinner. She could rearrange her menu and knew the fresh fish would be excellent.

When she returned to the ship, she saw Nikos standing near the rails, talking with his guests. They were seated on the cushioned chairs dotting the upper forward deck.

Just before she looked away, he glanced around, his gaze catching hers. For a long moment he merely stared at her. Then slowly he raised his glass in silent toast.

Someone—probably Gina—said something and he looked back. Sara hurried on board, her nerves tingling. Would he seek her out again before the trip was over?

Why would he? she silently asked.

CHAPTER THREE

ONCE the yacht stopped for its nightly anchorage, Sara felt an unexpected rise in anticipation. She and several of the other crew members were lounging on the aft deck, enjoying the evening. It was much cooler tonight. She'd brought a sweatshirt. The breeze that blew constantly was refreshing but chilly. She listened to the conversation more than contributed. Now that the ship had dropped anchor, she wondered if Nikos would come again to thank her for the meal. She'd taken extra pains with tonight's dish, broiling the succulent fish to perfection.

Probably not. He'd merely been kind to a new employee last night. He expected good work; she delivered. And he'd also been hospitable when he'd offered to show her around the upper deck of the yacht. She didn't think he was the type to mingle with his employees on a routine basis. With the rest of the crew lingering on the aft deck, even if he wanted to speak to her again, she doubted he'd do so in such a public place.

And why would he want to? She wasn't a regular member of the crew. Once the chef with the ruptured appendix recovered, he'd be back in his galley and she'd be back at the resort looking for another way to contact her grandmother.

Unless she could somehow get to the family island before that.

One by one the crew members rose to depart to their quarters. When only Sara and the captain remained, she changed seats to be closer so she could ask him some questions. She wanted to be able to turn the conversation to access to the island.

"Have you been in charge of this ship long?" she began.

"Since it was commissioned. Before that, I was captain of a ship for Mr. Andrus Konstantinos, Mr. Nikos's father. I have served the family for almost twenty years."

"An ideal job, I'd say, sailing around the Aegean all the time."

"Ah, but sometimes we go further—into the Med and to ports west of Greece. One summer I took the patriarch and his new bride to Spain and Morocco. It was a beautiful summer sail."

That had to be her grandmother he was talking about. The senior Konstantinos was now married to Eleani. "How long ago was that?" she asked.

"Many years now. More recently we have sailed to Egypt and to Italy."

"Do you have any family?" she asked, wondering how they managed his being from home for long voyages.

"Only a brother and his children. His wife died two years ago. They are mostly grown, but I see them at holidays if not required on board. Have you sailed a lot?"

"No, this is my first trip."

"Lucky for you seasickness is not a problem."

"If she'd gotten sick, she'd have been in a real pickle," Nikos said from the shadows.

The captain turned his head and nodded a greeting. "Mr. Nikos. Did you require something?"

"Just a brief break from the work that never ends. I came

to check up on my chef and compliment her on the excellent dinner tonight. The presentation added to the delicious taste of the fresh fish."

Sara surreptitiously wiped her damp palms on her slacks and tried to keep her breathing under control. "I'm pleased you and your guests enjoyed the meal."

"As did we all," the captain added. "Aeneas did well in recommending Sara. We all enjoy Paul's food, but Sara has brought new dishes to the table that the entire crew appreciates."

Nikos walked to a side railing. The ship bobbed gently on the sea, the breeze blowing from the bow. "Tomorrow I think we should find another island for our guests to visit. They seem to grow bored easily," Nikos said.

"I can't understand it myself," the captain said. He rose. "If we are to depart early, I will retire now."

"After seven. I want a swim first," Nikos said.

"Absolutely." He bade them both good-night.

Sara was the only one left on the aft deck with him. She should say something. Or maybe he wanted to be alone and knew his guests wouldn't intrude in this area.

"So you swim each morning before we weigh anchor?" she asked, gazing over the starlit surface of the Aegean. The water was dark and smooth, almost like a mirror to the stars.

"If time and weather permit."

She smiled. She couldn't picture herself swimming each day before starting work.

"Would you care to join me?" He half turned to look at her.

Sara was startled at the invitation. She thought about it for a moment. It was hard to be swimming when she should be preparing a meal. "I'd better not. I have omelets planned for tomorrow and fresh walnut bread again. I'll need time to have it all ready for your guests."

"Come for fifteen minutes. You can work around that," Nikos urged. "Besides, I'm the one who eats early, and the crew. My guests haven't had breakfast before nine since they've been on board."

"Okay. No, wait. I did not expect to swim. I didn't bring a suit." She would love a chance to swim in the sea to start the day. It had never crossed her mind that she'd actually have an opportunity to do so or she would have packed a swimsuit.

"We have extra suits on board. Sometimes guests don't plan to swim, either, and then change their minds. I'll have Stefano bring you one."

"Thank you," she said. She hoped Stefano would not suspect there was more to the invitation than there really was—merely a time to go swimming before beginning the day's work. She didn't want to give rise to gossip that could harm her chances of staying on board.

"I usually start around six, swim a half hour, shower and dress to be ready to work at seven," he said.

"Early," she murmured. It was already close to midnight.

"It's a routine that suits me well."

"So you swim mornings at the resort, as well?" she asked.

"Weather permitting. Sometimes in the sea, sometimes in one of the pools."

She tucked that piece of information away. Maybe she'd get up early once in a while for a swim herself, instead of swimming in the pool at midnight after her work was finished each day.

He studied her in the faint illumination of the anchor light. "How are you adjusting to being on the sea? You did say you weren't seasick."

"It's challenging to cook in such a small space, but the captain keeps the boat on an even plane so I don't have spills or liquids sloshing over. Stefano keeps it clean once I'm

finished preparing the meal. Actually, I'm enjoying myself."
She was surprised to say it, but it was true. She'd been so
focused on trying to find her grandmother, she had overlooked how much she was enjoying the experience of working
in this situation.

"I'm glad," he said.

She glanced away, feeling the attraction that flared whenever
he was near. She knew it was only a part of her visit to Greece
in which she didn't have to calculate ways to get to the island.
Sooner or later Nikos would return to his family home. With
any luck, she'd still be aboard when he did. She should make
the most of this opportunity, but couldn't think of a thing to say
to ingratiate herself with him. She so wanted to get to the
island—just for an afternoon. That's all she'd need.

"It's late. I'll see you at six," Nikos said.

"Good night," Sara replied. She'd see him again in a few
hours. They'd swim together and then she'd be back in the
galley. Wait until Stacy heard.

Sara had spent her time while preparing this evening's
meal imaging Nikos enjoying every bite. She'd also thought
about when he'd offered to play guide and the anticipation she
had felt. She hoped his guests enjoyed the food, as well. But
the reality was she was cooking for him. Wasn't the old adage
something about the way to a man's heart was through his
stomach? She didn't want to get to his heart—just his island.

Sleep proved difficult. She knew she had to trust in luck to
get her what she wanted. And so far her luck had been spotty.
None in trying to contact Eleani Konstantinos, good luck in
landing a job at the resort. No luck in finding a way to the
Konstantinos's island on her own. Amazing luck in getting a
berth on the ship. Now could she hope that luck held? Or was
there something she could do to press it?

By six-fifteen the next morning Sara still didn't have a swimsuit. She debated forgetting the entire idea and dressing in her regular resort uniform of khaki slacks and navy shirt with the resort's logo on the left side then heading for the galley. In the light of dawn, maybe Nikos had a change of heart.

The soft knock went almost unheard. She crossed to the door. Stefano grinned at her when she opened it, holding out a small box. "Compliments of Mr. Konstantinos. He said to meet him at the aft deck when you're ready."

She took the box, thanked him and shut the door. The swimsuit was a brand-new one-piece in a lovely teal color. She pulled it on. It fit perfectly. Tying her hair back, she slipped on her robe, not having any other swimsuit cover-up, and headed for the aft deck, her heart pounding. Would the other crew members resent her swimming with the boss? Or was this a common practice that she was making more of than it warranted?

Nikos stood by the back railing. He turned when he heard her and watched as she crossed the space in her bare feet. Without her working shoes, which gave some elevation, she was more conscious than ever of his height.

Sara tried not to be intrigued by the broad shoulders and well-developed muscular chest. It was hard not to imagine herself drawn against him, feeling those muscles hold her close. She longed to trail her fingertips across his tanned skin, to feel the texture, the warmth and strength.

Then the reality slapped her. He was someone she needed in order to accomplish her goal. That was it. Otherwise he lived the kind of lifestyle she was wary of. She should never forget that.

"Ready?" he asked.

"Yes." The air was cool. Would the water also be? She

slipped off her robe and walked to the railing, peering over. "Do we just jump in?" she asked. They were still eight feet or more above the water.

"No." He flipped open a section of railing, indicating ladder steps built into the boat. "We climb down to that swim board. It's a platform to get on and off the ship."

It was not wide, maybe eighteen inches out, running the width of the ship. Nikos showed her how to use the ladder and in only a couple of moments they stood side by side on the platform.

"Now," he said, diving into the blue water.

Sara took a breath and followed.

It was heavenly. The water was cool but not cold. The faint pink still showing in the wispy clouds in the sky was the first thing she saw when she surfaced. Turning, she saw the boat not far away. Looking around, she saw nothing but sky and sea and ship.

Nikos broke the surface a dozen yards ahead of her and began swimming away. Sara smiled at the pure sensual enjoyment of the moment and began to swim after him. She loved the water, and one of the perks of working at the resort was the swimming she could enjoy during her time off. Very different from her life in London.

She was beginning to wonder if she should turn back when she saw Nikos had stopped and was treading water. Catching up with him, she grinned in delight.

"This is fabulous. What are your guests doing still asleep? They should be out enjoying a swim."

Nikos stared at her for a moment, then glanced back at the yacht. "I think Senora Fregulia is not so fond of a swimsuit. Senor Fregulia is too focused on business, and getting her hair mussed is not Gina's thing. The Onetas take their lead from the Fregulias.

It is of no matter. I hope my guests are enjoying themselves, even if we do not share liking of the same activities."

"What about the crew? Surely some of them would like to swim."

"Occasionally when we are at anchor they do. Mostly not." Nikos shrugged. He didn't much care about the other crew members at this particular moment. He was enjoying the obvious pleasure Sara derived from the early-morning swim. She was open in sharing in her emotions. No guile. No flirtation. Was it the novelty that intrigued him? Or the mysterious chef herself who had come to work for him?

She obviously liked her position and had given no hints she wanted more. She didn't pester him with dozens of questions about his life, about his likes and dislikes. Sara took each moment as it came. She was enjoying the water and it showed. Definitely a novelty after the jaded women he usually met at receptions and parties.

She wore her femininity unselfconsciously, moving with grace whether walking across the deck or touring the bridge. She was comfortable with who she was. Witness the wet stringy hair that had escaped her tieback. She merely swept it away from her face and gazed around in delight.

Nikos didn't mix business with pleasure. No matter how much he enjoyed being with her, he would never overstep the bounds of employer-employee. He still didn't understand the impulse that had caused him to issue the invitation. He was glad he had, however. If only to enjoy her pleasure in the simple exercise.

"I'd say I'd race you back to the boat, but you're a stronger swimmer than I am," she said. "This is so lovely. Can I swim every morning?"

"If you wish," he said, beginning to lazily swim back.

"Not when we are in port, however. The water near marinas is not so fresh."

She wrinkled her nose, keeping up with his slower pace. "Too many oil spots. I've seen the rainbow colors floating on the surface."

"We'll be stopping at another island today. The ladies loved shopping yesterday. Today's island won't have a market, but there are shops and cafés. There is even an old fort sitting on a bluff with a terrific view. Maybe you can tour that."

"We'll stop before lunch?"

"You get another free pass. I'll take my guests to lunch at one of the waterfront cafés. No lunch preparations needed."

For a moment Sara looked wistful. Was she wishing she could join him? Suddenly Nikos wondered what it would be like to take a few days off. Get away from work, from duty, and just enjoy Sara's company. Maybe when this cruise was finished he'd find out. Unless he became engaged to Gina by then. The thought surprised him. He'd started the cruise with that intent. Was he having second thoughts? The alliance would work to the benefit of both. Yet momentarily he'd forgotten his intent, his interest in Sara overriding his common sense.

"We're going to have a lot of food left over if you keep changing the meals," she commented.

The ship was getting closer every moment. When they reached it, she'd disappear to change and get to work. Nikos knew he'd not see her again today—unless she lingered on the aft deck after dinner. He could tell her again how much his guests enjoyed her cooking.

When Nikos was dressed for the day, he went to his desk and powered up his laptop. First order of business, catch up on e-mail and check in with his assistant at the resort. By now the power should have been fully restored. But there would be other minor crises to deal with. While he worked, Stefano brought his breakfast. An omelet as light as air, loaded with mushrooms, onions, spinach and green peppers was the first thing he saw. The walnut bread on a separate plate was still warm. The coffee was strong and hot. As he ate, he tried to visualize Sara preparing the meal. He frowned. He had no idea how cooks worked. His education was sadly lacking. One day he should check out the galley and see her in action.

When his cell phone rang, he answered.

"Nikos, it is your grandfather," the familiar voice said.

"I know. I recognize your voice." Nikos smiled. He had spent many summers on the island while his parents traveled. It still remained his favorite place.

"Your assistant tells me you are on another cruise. Where this time?"

Nikos filled him in and waited. There was usually a reason his grandfather called at this early hour. Informal family chats were unheard of.

"I'm thinking about buying another boat," he finally said.

"Oh?" Nikos suspected his grandfather knew his son had called Nikos.

"I wanted you to vet it for me. And don't be telling me I'm too old to buy a new boat. This one is for Eleani and me to go out together. No privacy otherwise."

Nikos shook his head. The *Cassandra* offered plenty of privacy and was available whenever his grandfather wished. But he understood the older man's reasoning. Last night he'd been very aware that he and Sara hadn't been alone.

"I am committed for another three days, then must return my guests to the resort and await their departure before I can come home," Nikos said, glancing at his calendar. He had no important meetings or commitments the following week. "I'll come after that."

Nikos always found it easy to relax on the family island. It had been a while since he'd visited. He could enjoy his grand-parents' company and really take a few days away from work.

"Good, plan to stay awhile. We have not seen you in a long time."

"I will stay a few days. Give my regards to Eleani."

He hung up, his mind already returning to the situation at hand. Why shouldn't his grandfather and his wife enjoy a small boat? They might be older, but they were both perfectly capable of running their own lives. His own grandmother had died when Nikos had been a boy. When Spiros had remarried, to a widow, Eleani, Nikos and his family had accepted her as Spiros's wife. She'd had no one. That had been almost ten years ago. She had easily become a vital part of their family and had been the best thing for his grandfather. Nikos liked her warmth and devotion to Spiros. And she'd shared that warmth with the rest of the family when they'd let her.

Nikos hoped he was as active when he was in his eighties. Hard to imagine now reaching that age. He could not picture himself married, much less very much in love with a wife in fifty years.

It was stupid to cast all women in the same light as Ariana, but he had a tendency to do just that. She'd professed undying love when they'd been engaged. But once he'd caught her with another man in bed, he'd had trouble believing it. The truth had been that she'd wanted the lifestyle Nikos could offer. She didn't love him; she loved being with men—rich, poor, young, old. Ariana hadn't been too particular.

To a young man who had been in love, it had been a double blow. First, that she hadn't loved him and second, that he hadn't been wise enough to realize that before finding proof. He'd learned the lesson well, however. Unless a woman had a fortune to match his, he would never consider her in the matrimony stakes.

Gina would make a perfect businessman's wife. She was polished, aware of the demands of work and brought a wealth of contacts with the wine industry in Italy.

Yet still he hesitated. If left to him, he probably would not marry. Families were overrated. He knew from his own experiences and shattered expectations that it was an institution best handled carefully. Currently he set his own goals and had no one to blame except himself if things didn't go as he wanted. A wife would be an additional responsibility. Still, he did want children, some boy or girl to leave the resort to. To teach the ways his forefathers had lived for generations. Would Gina be that wife?

He didn't have to decide on this cruise, but he wasn't getting any younger.

He quickly scanned his messages, replying to two that were urgent. Shutting off his laptop, he rose, ready to face his guests and offer some of the hospitality of the small island they were heading for.

The ruins were spectacular. He'd taken other guests on a tour of them in the past and everyone had raved about the antiquity of the stones and the view of the sea that seemed endless.

He hoped the Fregulias and Onetas would like it, as well.

Four hours later Nikos knew this particular outing hadn't met with the same success as the visit to the market had the day before. The three couples had walked around the cobblestone streets of the old town, stopping in several shops but purchasing nothing. The morning was winding down. There was time for a quick visit to the ruins before a late lunch, but his guests seemed disinclined to continue.

Senor Fregulia wanted to visit a taverna. His wife wanted out of the sun. Nikos knew what Gina wanted but the more she seemed interested in him, the less he felt interested in her. Was it just the normal reluctance of a man to commit to one woman?

"It is so hot," she complained for the tenth time.

"Perhaps we should return to the boat and continue the sail," he suggested.

"No, I wish to visit the taverna. A drink of fine wine while sitting in the shade and watching people would suit me better than the boat. I seem to be prone to a touch of seasickness," Senor Fregulia said, heading in the direction of an outdoor café.

"I wish to see into some more of the shops," Senora Fregulia said, looking at her friend. An instant later Senora Oneta agreed.

Gina was pouting. Nikos wanted to shake the lot of them, but his duties as host prevented that. How had the outing turned out to be so annoying?

"Gina?" A young man dashed over and began talking with her in rapid Italian. His speech was too fast for Nikos to follow with the limited Italian he spoke, but the gist seemed to be they had been friends who hadn't seen each other in a long time.

"Excuse my manners," Gina said at one point, linking arms with the young man. "Pietro, this is our host, Nikos Konstantinos. Nikos, my friend Pietro from Rome."

Once introductions had been completed, Gina flirted with Pietro, keeping a careful eye on her father and on Nikos.

"Come, we will all enjoy some wine and watch the boats in the harbor," she suggested, drawing Pietro toward the taverna. "Nikos can tell us all about this quaint little island and the people who live here."

It was obvious to him what she was doing and he had no intention of playing her game of pitting one man against another. If she thought that would spark his interest, she would be very surprised to know his thoughts, which of course he would never voice.

Senor Fregulia waved Nikos over.

"I know you are a busy man. We can entertain ourselves this afternoon. Go, do what you need to do. What time shall we return to the yacht?"

"By six." Would it be this easy? To have the rest of the day to himself?

"We will return by then." The older man turned to his wife and urged her down the sidewalk with an admonition that she could shop after they'd had some refreshments.

For a moment Nikos watched the group walk away. Duty required he be a good host; good business sense dictated he not alienate a man whose business he wanted. Prudent planning for the future indicated he should get to know Gina better. The truth was he wanted to be on his own—just for the rest of the day.

Turning, he walked back to the harbor. He could call his assistant, get up to speed on the various projects in the works and maybe even respond to some mail if anything crucial was pending.

Just as he reached the wide dock, Nikos saw Sara walking toward him. She was wearing a floppy hat to keep the sun from her face. Her arms were bare and lightly tanned. She was looking around as she walked. He noted the instant she recognized him. For a moment her smile lit up the harbor, then was replaced with a frown and a wary look.

"Hi. Did you forget something?" she asked as she walked closer.

"No. Where are you going?"

"Sightseeing. The captain said we were all free until six. Was that right?"

"Yes. We will not sail until after that. Dinner at eight."

"Then I'll be back by six, no problem."

She stepped by him.

Before she'd gone three feet, he said impulsively, "Would you like to see the ruins on the mountaintop?"

Nikos wasn't sure who was more surprised—Sara or himself. Vanished was the idea of working. Gone was the concern for his guests. He had enjoyed swimming with her; now he wanted to show her some of the island. See how she related to the history that was so much a part of their culture. Spend some time with someone who didn't expect him to propose in the next minute.

"I would love to see the ruins. Can you spare the time?" she asked. The wariness had not left her eyes.

"The afternoon is free, it turns out. I would like to see them again myself." With a sweep of his hand indicating she should precede him, they walked down the dock to the street. Two cabs were parked nearby, their drivers leaning against the side of one, talking.

Nikos summoned one and in seconds he and Sara were on their way through the town and beyond. The mountain was not very high, sloping gently up from the sea. The lush vegetation that grew along the side of the road served as a green backdrop to the incredible blues of the sea and sky.

Nikos watched Sara as she gazed out of the side window.

"This is beautiful. At times like this I wish I was a photographer or painter and could capture the scene forever."

"You'll have to remember it."

She nodded. "I shall! Thank you for bringing me along. It's fantastic."

Sara felt her heart turn over when Nikos smiled at her comment. She quickly looked back out the window. With butterflies dancing inside, it was safer to feast her gaze on the view of the sea rather than drown herself in Nikos's eyes. She felt that growing sense of awareness sweep through, though she kept her gaze firmly on the distant horizon. She felt tongue-tied. What could she say? Nikos was the type of man her mother had fled Greece to avoid. Surely her daughter wouldn't be so foolish as to fall for him? He was so out of her league.

Yet the trip to the ruins was an unexpected treat. Why had he invited her along?

"Your guests didn't wish to come?" she asked.

"No. They were content to sit in town and watch the inhabitants."

"That sounds nice," she replied politely. In some circumstances maybe. For her the chance to see more of the island beat sitting in one spot all day.

The road wound up the hillside until the vegetation grew thin. Rocky expanses dotted the land, giving way to a deteriorating wall that outlined where the ancient Roman garrison had once stood. When the cab stopped at the graveled parking lot, Sara was delighted with the setting. There were few other cars. With several acres of ruins to view, there weren't enough people to make it crowded.

Nikos held out his hand to assist her from the cab. His fingers were warm and strong as they wrapped around hers. She shivered slightly in response, though the day was quite warm. Pulling away quickly, she walked toward the ruins feeling fluttery and excited and foolish all at once.

He spoke to the taxi driver as he paid him off. The cab turned toward the town.

"So tell me about this place. It certainly has a commanding view of the sea," she said when he joined her, walking toward the walled expanse.

"It was a Roman outpost before the time of Christ. Not a strategic one. Archaeologists have suggested it might have been an outpost for rest and relaxation. The stones that comprised the fort remain, if in some disrepair."

They were a warm pinkish color, huge in size and placed without mortar. The sheer size ensured they did not topple over. Sara regarded them with awe, wondering how men two thousand years ago could have moved them to the summit.

They walked to the parapet, and Sara caught her breath at the beauty of the island and sea.

"If I'd been a Roman soldier stationed far from home, I'd love to have come here for R & R," she said. "Do you ever wonder what it would have been like?"

"More often when I was a child than now," Nikos said. "All of Greece is steeped in ancient history. I wanted to be a Spartan when I was younger."

She glanced at him. "You'd have made a good one, I'm sure."

"Based on?" he asked, amusement evident in his eyes.

"Just a hunch. Of course, I guess I'd really need to see your skill with a spear before passing judgment."

Nikos laughed. "A skill not fully developed, I fear."

Sara smiled and returned her gaze to the sea, feeling the pull of attraction strengthen toward the man standing beside her. He rested a foot on the low wall and gazed out, as well. She could feel the warmth of his body near hers and was torn between moving away or moving closer. She did neither, just savored the day and the company and tried to keep a perspective on things.

A group of young children ran across the ruins, yelling and laughing. Sara turned to watch. They were having the time of their lives. Behind them a couple stood side by side and watched indulgently. Sara felt a tug of nostalgia. Her mother used to take her places, usually with one of her friends, and would watch as Sara and her friend ran and jumped and laughed. The excursions had been limited to the parks and gardens they'd been able to afford on her mother's meager salary. But they'd been outings of fun and joy.

She missed her mother. For a moment sadness threatened to overrule her pleasure in the day. Her mother had turned her back on all this at eighteen. Even years later when Sara knew she'd yearned to return home, Damaris had refused. Her pride had not let her return home in disgrace, as she so often said. Her pride had kept her from the one thing she'd longed for. Sara knew about pride, but she was a touch more practical than her mother. If she wanted something, she'd go after it.

"Noisy," Nikos said, stepping away from the low wall and watching the children.

"They're having fun!" she said. "It's what makes wonderful memories of family outings. Would you not have them here?"

Nikos watched silently for a moment, then turned away. "It's hard to take in the grandeur of the place with children running around."

"One day you'll bring your own children to run around here. Don't you have happy memories of similar expeditions?" she asked, walking along the wall, heading for the other side. The fort had been situated on the highest point in the island, commanding a 360-degree view. Perfect for watching from all aspects. And the view of the green of the island, the white strip of beach and the azure of the Aegean had to have made it an ideal family spot.

"No," he murmured.

Sara looked at him in surprise. "Why not?"

"Not everyone associates families with happy children and holidays together," he said.

Sara blinked. "What does that mean?"

"Nothing. Have you seen enough?"

"Not nearly. After we walk the perimeter, I want to explore that curious building in the center."

"Probably where the troops slept. The view is the same from all sides."

"No, it's not. If you are tired of showing me around, feel free to leave. I'm sure I can get a cab back to town." Sara was surprised with Nikos's attitude change. He suddenly seemed to close off and distance himself. Had she said something to offend him? Trying to remember every word she'd just said, she couldn't find anything wrong.

"No, I brought you, I'll stay."

"Gee, what enthusiasm. Go. I'll be fine." Now she felt like an unwelcome burden.

She walked to the far parapet and looked at the view, not seeing a thing. A flare of anger burst forth. She'd been having fun. Maybe she wasn't supposed to have fun with the keeper of the key, as she thought of Nikos Konstantinos. He was the only way to get in to see her grandmother. She needed to remember that.

"Rome lies in that direction," his deep voice said in her left ear. She turned and almost bumped noses with Nikos.

"I used to wonder if soldiers longed for home or were satisfied serving the emperor wherever he sent them. Even in antiquity, this was a small island, isolated from all the grandeur of Rome, from the excitement the big city held. Were they lonely?" he continued.

"Probably—and missing families and all."

She felt him move away. Aha, *families* was definitely the key.

Sara turned. Nikos hadn't moved that far. Her shoulder brushed his chest. "Don't you like families?" she asked bluntly.

"I have nothing against families," he said evenly.

"You're lucky, you still have your parents and grandparents. I have no one. That's why when I marry, I will fall madly in love with the man. I want us to have lots of children. I want to marry into a large family so my children will have huge celebrations at holidays and birthdays. Lots of cousins, aunts and uncles and loads of love."

"Not everyone is cut out to marry and start a family. Though most do it from duty."

"I agree not everyone is cut out to be a parent, but I think life is enriched by children. For most people anyway," she said, thinking of her own father. He'd abandoned her mother when Sara had been two months old. He couldn't take the interrupted nights of a newborn baby. He resented not having his friends over whenever he wanted. He hadn't liked being a father. And the consequences were ones Sara and her mother had lived with for the rest of her mother's life. Had he ever regretted leaving? She'd never know. She didn't even know if he was still living.

"Families aren't always like you imagine. I often wonder why my parents had a child," Nikos said.

"So, no brothers or sisters?"

He shook his head. "Probably a good thing in the face of things. There were no other children to be ignored and brought out only on occasion to show off." He shook off the memories from his youth. He'd made his way in the business he wanted. As an adult, he could far better understand his parents.

"You're young to be alone in the world. No other relatives?" he asked.

She shrugged. "No one I know. So it's just me, until I find that special man to fall in love with and marry."

"I wonder if marriage is for me," he said.

Nikos took a breath. He usually had more finesse when warning a woman off who might have any matrimonial intentions. Not that he thought Sara was contemplating such a move. She had shown none of the flirting that he was used to. He was thinking of Gina. The trip was proving more important than he'd anticipated. The more he was around Gina, the more doubts crept in.

He knew his duty to his family was to provide heirs. He would need to hand down his grandfather and father's shipping business. Maybe he'd have several children and they could each decide what to do with their lives. He would not force any along career paths they disliked. But was Gina the right woman?

"Everyone has to decide that for himself. If you fall in love one day, you might change your mind," she said.

If she only knew.

"On the other hand, I suspect love is overrated. Good for some, disastrous for others," she added, nodding.

Nikos suddenly wanted to know why she said that. Had she fallen in love and been hurt as he had? If so, she had rebounded with optimism.

"It does work for some," he admitted reluctantly. "My grandfather and Eleani are a perfect example."

"Oh?" she said.

"They married about ten years ago and are blissfully happy together. In fact, my father wishes me to check up on them soon." He frowned, studying the horizon, and wondered why he'd thought to bring that up. He hadn't even told Gina.

"Is there a problem?"

"No. But my grandfather has a crazy idea that my father wants me to talk him out of. If you ever saw my father and grandfather together, you'd understand why I act as a buffer between them. But it gets tiresome." He stopped talking. It was not like him to share any family business with a stranger. Much less an employee. He didn't know what kind of gossip Sara might be.

Sara looked at him oddly, then turned away.

"I know a path that leads to one of the beach villages if you're up for such an adventure," he said. She had no interest in his family situation. The sun was high overhead, and despite the breeze, the air was growing uncomfortably warm with the heat reflected from the stones. They could enjoy the walk and then find a taxi to return to the dock.

"It's mostly shady," he added. "Or I can arrange for the taxi to return here to pick us up."

"Sounds more like an adventure to walk back down. Do you want some water before we start? I brought a couple of bottles," she said, rummaging in the small tote she'd slung over her shoulder. She handed him a bottle and opened the second one, taking a long drink.

"Warm but wet," she said with a grin.

Nikos drank the entire bottle, wondering what Gina would have made of the situation. She would have complained the ground wasn't suitable for her shoes. The water was warm and not cool. The sun was too glaring.

But he was not interested in taking her to ruins. Yet, as he watched the children running and shouting and obviously having the time of their lives, he knew he'd want to bring his own children if he ever had any. He'd want them to know and love their country's history as he did.

Try as he might, he couldn't picture Gina with them.

Sara, yes.

The thought startled him. Sara still had that starry-eyed wonder as she took in everything. She'd urge the children on and demand to know every aspect of the history of a place to share with them. And probably make up stories about where the men had been from, or what they had left behind.

The trail to the village was well marked and wide enough to walk two abreast. Just a few yards from the ruins, trees began. The leafy canopy soon dappled the path in shade, lowering the temperature significantly.

"Lovely," she said as they walked in the quiet. The noise from other visitors at the ruins faded completely when they made a sharp turn. The trail made a series of switchbacks to enable the path to be easily navigated while ascending or descending the steep hill. "I imagine this dates from the Roman times. Soldiers probably used this very path to go to the village for supplies," Sara said, envisioning men traveling up and down the trail.

"Maybe. Would you have liked cooking for the garrison?"

"Most men seem to appreciate good cooking. I'd make the best dishes in the Empire, and soldiers would long for this duty station," she said, falling into the fantasy.

"I'd improve my spear prowess to get the duty assignment."

Sara laughed. "No need. I'm happy to cook for you aboard the *Cassandra*."

"And I'm happy to eat your meals."

"Ah, how gallant. If I served oatmeal for breakfast, would you say the same?"

"Depends. I suspect your oatmeal would far surpass that which I ate at school in America."

"Ah, so that's the trace of accent I hear when you speak English," Sara said. They'd spoken Greek most of the time, but she'd heard him once or twice speak in English and been intrigued by the faint accentuation on some words.

"I went to university there for two years for postgraduate work. Stayed in a variety of hotels to get an idea of what I liked and wanted for my resort."

"I've never been. Maybe one day," Sara said.

It was after two by the time they arrived at the fishing village. Sara was ravenous and uncertain how to respond when Nikos suggested they stop for lunch at one of the tavernas lining the small fishing harbor. She agreed and then had second thoughts.

Colorful umbrellas shaded the tables. The food was plain but delicious—fresh fish, grapes and some local wine. Conversation was awkward.

"Is your Italian supplier's wine better than this?" Sara asked as she sipped the delicate white wine, casting about in her mind for other topics. The one in the forefront was too dangerous.

"This is excellent. Perhaps I should explore having more Greek wines," Nikos said, as he sipped from his glass.

"Do you make all those decisions?" Sara asked. "Seems like you would have hired others to do that."

"For the most part I delegate to the different departments of the resort. But I do like to keep an eye on every section. I shall suggest this to the sommeliers of two of our restaurants. Are you also a wine connoisseur?"

"Nope, not at all. But I know what I like," Sara said. She smiled as she gazed around. Her milieu wasn't small cafés with plain fare. She loved cooking meals with drama and flair. But that didn't mean she couldn't appreciate the appeal of a quiet place, and good basic food.

"Thank you for today. It's been a treat," she said.

"I'm pleased you've enjoyed it."

"In Spain they have siesta after lunch. Eating makes me sleepy," she commented, finishing the last of the food on her plate. Maybe she'd return to the ship and lounge on the aft deck, dozing a bit.

"In half an hour, you could swim again. Care to join me on a short swim? I have some diving equipment on board."

"I thought you said swimming near docks wasn't a good idea."

"The yacht has a small runabout. We'll go out into the sea a distance, away from the shore."

Once again Nikos had surprised her. Warily she examined the pros and cons of another swim. The pros would obviously be the joy of swimming in the sea. And maybe getting more information from the man. Opposed to that was the proximity to Nikos. She was drawn to him each time they were together. The last thing she wanted was some kind of connection that would hinder her goal. She had nothing in common with the man. In fact, she wasn't sure she even liked him. But her body seemed to have other ideas.

"Very well, I'll go swimming. I'm not sure about the diving," she said at last. And hoped she wasn't making a mistake. But she was only in Greece for a short time. Why not make the most of unexpected chances?

Two hours later Sara and Nikos had changed, commandeered the small runabout from the yacht and set out. He'd convinced her to try diving. After donning the cumbersome scuba gear, Nikos and Sara slipped into the sea. The water was like silk against her skin. The sun sparkled on the surface like a million diamonds. Sara was treading water, feeling awkward with the air tanks strapped to her back, while Nikos once again explained the rudimentary aspects of scuba diving. She pulled down the face mask and stuck the mouthpiece in her mouth. Taking a breath, she found the air was cool and a bit dry, but she filled her lungs, excited about this adventure. It struck her as a bit odd that the man she was using to find her grandmother was willing to teach her how to dive. To even spend time with her. She would not look a gift horse in the mouth.

His hand grabbed hers. "Once we're under the water, if you feel any discomfort or become nervous, squeeze my hand and we'll surface immediately. We are not going deep."

She nodded. He put his mouthpiece in and motioned with his free hand to begin.

She took a deep breath and held it as they slipped beneath the water. She'd done a little snorkeling on a vacation in Spain a couple of years ago, so expected the crystal clarity of the sea. A moment later she let her breath escape and breathed again. It was magical, being beneath the water's surface and still breathing. She felt an affinity with the fish.

Nikos began swimming slowly, his hand tugging her along. She kicked her flippers and soon was swimming beside him. His fingers linked with hers and he matched his own pace to hers so they were in sync. Sara kept her eyes forward, resisting the urge to watch Nikos swimming. His body was honed from exercise and swimming. His broad shoulders and tight stomach muscles made her own heart flip over. She'd much rather watch him than look for any fish, but peripheral vision was severely limited with the face mask and it would be too obvious if she turned her head.

Nikos swam in a large circle, not wanting to be beneath the water too long on Sara's first time. She seemed like a natural. Surfacing at one point, he asked her how she was doing.

"This is the greatest thing in the world," she said once she removed her mouthpiece.

"Good." He released her hand. "Try it on your own."

She nodded, her eyes sparkling behind the glass. She repositioned her mouthpiece and dove beneath the water. He remembered that first rush when he'd started many years ago. Lately he'd been too busy to go diving. Maybe he'd take a few days at the island. There were several coves where colorful fish proliferated. Maybe Sara would like to see them.

He trod water for another moment. When he went to the island, he wouldn't need Sara. She could resume her work at the resort restaurant. He'd have only the captain, the mate and Stefano as minimum crew for the short distance between the resort and island.

Unless he decided differently. Replacing his own mouthpiece, he dove after her.

She wasn't where he expected. He swam faster. Had she run into trouble? Then he felt a tug on his ankle. Flipping over, he bumped into Sara. From the laughter in her eyes, he knew she was all right and playing. She kicked away, on her back, watching him as she moved through the water. He surged after her.

Suddenly she was gasping. He caught her under her arms and swam swiftly to the surface. Pulling the mouthpiece from her mouth, he held her above the water while she coughed.

She pushed back the face mask and gasped for air. A moment later she looked at him ruefully.

"First rule of scuba diving—don't laugh," she said. She coughed again and drew in a deep breath.

"Is that what caused this?"

She nodded, her hand resting on his shoulder. "You looked so surprised when you saw me, I couldn't help it. I forgot about being underwater. When I laughed, water came in my mouth. Thanks for the rescue."

"Enough for today."

She looked around. The small boat they'd used to get away from the dock and *Cassandra* bobbed several hundred feet away.

"I can swim back. I'm fine now that I have my breath back." Without volition, her fingers began rubbing small patterns on his smooth skin. She could feel the muscles contract beneath her as he kept them both above water. Did she have her breath back? Being so close to Nikos was robbing her of air again. Her legs tangled with his as they lazily kicked to keep upright. Her left side was pressed against him.

He swept back his own face mask and gazed into her eyes, his gaze then dropping to her lips. Sara licked them. Salty. She wrinkled her nose.

Nikos's eyes took on a distinctive gleam. "You look delectable," he said in that low, sexy voice.

"You've got to be kidding," she said. "My hair is hanging in strings. I have no makeup on and I'm covered in salt water."

He leaned forward the scant inches separating them and kissed her.

CHAPTER FOUR

SARA kissed him back. Her tongue met his. His slow kicking kept them upright while the kiss went on and on. She hugged him, her hand brushing against the top of his tanks, the breathing hose and straps separating her from his skin. She wanted to be closer, impatient to drop the tanks and have nothing between them.

Then reason returned. Slowly she pulled back, her eyes wide as she gazed at him. He looked at her lips again, then into her eyes.

"This is *so* not a good idea," she said. For a gazillion reasons. Yet she couldn't move.

"Why is that?" he asked.

"Relationships between boss and employee always end badly—usually for the employee." It was not her first reason, but one that would suffice.

He released her and swam back a foot or so. "This was merely a kiss. You are correct, relationships between working people don't end well."

Sara sank to her chin, turning to swim toward the runabout. He'd shown pity on a lonesome crew member and with his free afternoon offered to show her how to dive. He'd probably wanted to go alone. She was not reading anything into their afternoon. Not even the kiss. People kissed others for various reasons.

She refused to explore why she'd kissed him back. Enough to have enjoyed the afternoon. She didn't need anything further from Nikos Konstantinos.

The kiss had surprised her. But she'd not been able to help herself and had returned the kiss. Magical—like the entire cruise. The sooner she had her wits about her, the better.

Sara reached the boat first. She tried to pull herself in, but the weight of the tanks offset her balance too much. Rats, now she'd have to rely on his help, and that was the last thing she wanted. If she could levitate herself in, she'd do so.

Nikos pulled himself easily into the small craft, shrugged out of his tanks and went to the side to assist Sara, lifting her without difficulty. Once standing on the rocking boat, she unfastened her own straps. Before the tanks could slide off, he lifted them from her shoulders, carefully placing them in the rack built into the back of the boat.

"Thank you again, I enjoyed the diving," she said politely, refusing to meet his eyes. If the yacht hadn't been so far away, she would have struck out swimming to avoid this awkwardness.

"My pleasure." His deep voice sent shivers down her spine. Could they recapture the ease they'd enjoyed before? Did she want to?

He pulled up the anchor and started the motor. Sara sat in the seat next to his and gazed straight ahead. The day had been magical. She would ignore the change after the kiss and remember the good part. Her friends would want to hear every detail when she returned. And she'd tell all—except about the kiss. Some things were too private to share.

It took less than ten minutes to return to the *Cassandra*. One of the crew heard the motor and was there to take the lines and secure the small boat when Nikos stopped. He turned and offered his hand.

She smiled politely and took it to step to the swim platform and then up the ladder to the aft deck.

"Oh, Nikos, where have you been?" Gina leaned over the side, eyeing Sara as she climbed swiftly up.

"Took advantage of the time for some diving," he said. "What are you doing here?"

"The captain said you'd be returning on the aft of the boat, so I came to wait. You should have told me you wanted to go swimming."

Gina continued to watch Sara ascend. When she reached the deck, Gina walked over. "Aren't you the cook?"

"Chef," Sara corrected, walking back down the deck toward the door to the lower decks.

"We didn't go swimming, Gina," Nikos said as he reached the deck. "We went diving. You said you didn't know how or I would have invited you."

"I could have gone swimming," Gina was saying to Nikos as Sara walked through the door and headed for her cabin. Let him explain to his guests why he'd taken the hired help diving and ignored his invited guests.

As Sara stood beneath the minuscule shower a few moments later, she wondered why herself. He certainly had the choice of a wide variety of women. She knew a half dozen who would love to trade places with her. So why had he spent the day with her? Was it because he recognized a kindred spirit who also loved antiquities? She hardly thought so.

By the time Sara had the evening meal prepared, she had regained her equanimity. The duck *à l'orange* was perfection. The lightly steamed vegetables *al dente* and nutritious. Once the dishes were served, she'd send the crew's meals out and begin to work on the dessert. Not that all the delicacies were consumed each evening. She had her suspicions about which guests did not eat the sweets. Their loss. The triple-chocolate mousse cake tonight would melt in their mouths, the bitter chocolate flakes on the frosting a contrast to the sweetness of the mousse. It was one of her favorite desserts. She'd made a double batch to make sure the crew had enough. And she could indulge, as well. Nothing like chocolate to set things right.

Stefano returned for the desserts a short time later, and Sara took her own dinner to the aft deck. Those crewmen off duty were lounging in contentment.

"The dinner was great," one called when she stepped out.

"I'd have more dessert if there is any," another said, holding up his empty plate.

Sara smiled; she loved it when people appreciated her efforts.

"There's more. Help yourselves, or ask Stefano to get you another piece." She sat at the end of the long table, eating while she listened to their desultory conversation. The gentle rocking of the boat was soothing. The air was cooler than earlier, but quite pleasant enough to sit outside. If she were in London now she'd be slogging away in some hot kitchen, making dishes to order and dashing around to find everything she needed with other chefs working at frantic speed, as well. Maybe after she found her grandmother she'd consider working for a private club or household or yacht. She enjoyed planning the meals and preparing them at a more leisurely pace.

That day was still a long way off.

Sara didn't leave the aft deck when she finished eating. Stefano cleared the dishes. One by one the rest of the crew bade her good-night and left. Soon darkness fell and she felt alone standing by the railing as she gazed over the sea. The surface was calm, almost glassy, reflecting the stars that

pierced the night sky. When the moon began to rise, its sliver
of light cast a delicate pale yellow trail across the sea. She felt
almost as if she could step out and walk along it all the way
to the moon.

Nikos watched Sara from the bridge. She stood so still as she
gazed across the sea. He wondered what she was thinking
about. The captain looked up from the chart he was reviewing by the small lamp.

"Is everything all right?" he asked.

"Yes. The cruise is going well," Nikos replied, still watching Sara. He wanted to go down to the aft deck and steal a
few minutes of peace. Today's kiss had shown him how dangerous that would be. It had just been a kiss. And if he had
resisted that impulse, their time together could have continued. Now he had to distance himself before she thought there
was more to his wanting to spend time with her than an escape
from the duties of work.

That thought firmly in mind, he'd refrained from going down
to the aft deck tonight. But it didn't stop the desire to do so.

"We head for Mazure tomorrow?" the captain asked.

Nikos swung around. "No, head for home. I'm cutting this
cruise short. I'll explain to my guests tomorrow." With a nod
he left. The sooner he got his guests on their way, the sooner
he could head for the family island. The return was only one
day ahead of schedule. He'd treat them to a lavish suite at the
resort to make up for it. And he'd head for his grandfather's.
He still had not asked Gina to marry him. After today he
wasn't sure he wanted marriage. He would bide his time a bit
longer, bid the Fregulias farewell and think about the future
when he was on the island.

And say goodbye to Sara.

In his office a few moments later, he was churning with frustration. He'd only been with the woman a few times. Once back into the swing of things, he would forget her soon enough. She'd be cooking in the kitchen of the farthest restaurant at the resort; he'd be at the other end in his offices and suite of rooms.

"Blast it!" he rasped out, slamming his palm against his desk. She was pretty, talented and content with her life. She had not made a single overture that could be misconstrued. Unlike him.

He sat in his chair, leaned back and gazed out of the darkened window.

What if he continued to see Sara for a while? The novelty would wear off and he'd be on to the next woman on the horizon. Maybe marriage wasn't for him. At least his father had settled on one woman.

Sara's appeal was her unique spin on things, which made her intriguing. Once back in his normal routine, he'd soon miss the witty repartee of women of his own social set. He'd miss the gala dinners, the receptions. He'd find her enthusiasm and wonder boring after a while and begin to long for the more sophisticated, cynical women he knew.

But until then, could he continue to see Sara?

Why not take her to the island? The thought came unbidden.

Why not, indeed. She seemed content to be on the boat. He knew she liked swimming, standing in the dark watching the stars, diving.

Would she be equally content going to formal receptions, meeting dignitaries and businessmen who played an important role in developing Greece? Wearing designer dresses and expensive jewelry? Any woman he developed a relationship with needed the sophistication to move in his world.

He knew how to play the game. He wanted his resort to

become world renowned and knew what it took to get there. But sometimes he longed for quiet, tranquility and genuine people. Like Spiros and Eleani. They were content on the island, or traveling when the mood suited them. They entertained and also spent time alone enjoying their own company.

He could find that tranquillity at the family island. His father wanted him to stop in. His grandfather had invited him. He'd go.

And he'd take Sara with him.

The next morning Nikos rose early. Ignoring his computer and the work that awaited, he donned his swimming trunks and grabbed a towel. In less than ten minutes, he was on the aft deck, contemplating the sea. He'd had all night to think about his plan. If Sara kept her distance as she had yesterday on the runabout, he'd have a harder sell. If she showed some sign of interest, he'd move ahead.

"Good morning," she said from behind him.

Nikos let out a breath he hadn't known he'd been holding as he turned slowly around.

Sara dropped her own towel and cover-up on one of the chairs. Her hair was bound back in a ponytail. She didn't look directly at him, but he didn't care. She'd come to swim. He would take that as the sign he wanted.

"Good morning. I hoped you would come to swim."

She looked at him in surprise. "You did?"

"You seemed to enjoy it. Why not take advantage of the opportunities?" He thought that sounded reasonable. Which was not at all the feeling he had seeing her again this morning. He felt a most unreasonable attraction.

"My thoughts exactly."

He wished she'd smile. Her eyes lit up when she did. But her expression remained solemn.

He opened the railing gate and gestured for her to go first. She descended the steps quickly and without a word dove into the sea. He followed. She was ahead of him, swimming leisurely. She didn't seem angry or upset. Just distant.

She bobbed up and trod water, looking around. The sun was rising, the air crisp and clear.

"Is it always this beautiful?" she asked when he stopped next to her.

"Always."

She grinned at that and shook her head. "What about the storms? Wasn't one of Shakespeare's plays based on a severe storm in the Med?"

"Ah, but this is the Aegean, always perfect." He relished her grin. What could he do to keep it there?

"And never any storms?" Her doubt was obvious.

He shrugged. "Only if nature's awesome power can be described as beautiful."

She rolled her eyes at his attempt to describe the storms that sometimes erupted without warning and were the bane of sailors. No body of water ever escaped storms.

"Today will be clear, however," he reassured her.

"And duty calls," she said, turning to swim back to the *Cassandra*. "I need to get breakfast ready for your guests."

"And for today's meal?"

"Eggs Benedict."

"A favorite of mine," he said, keeping pace with her.

She frowned. "I didn't know that."

"Now you do." He would not let her retreat.

"So tomorrow will be oatmeal," she retorted. Reaching the swimming board at the back of the yacht, she held on while kicking her legs lazily in the silken water.

"No oatmeal."

She grinned again. "We don't have any on board anyway. But it's good and nourishing."

"Fine for a cold winter's morning."

"So should I wait for such a cold snap?"

He felt foolish talking about oatmeal, but at least Sara hadn't scurried up the ladder and disappeared into the galley. Twice she'd grinned at him. Could he go for three?

"I'll come up with something different tomorrow," she promised.

"Actually, there will be no need."

"What do you mean?"

"We're returning to the resort this afternoon. I'm cutting the cruise short."

"Why?"

Nikos hesitated. "Family business," he said.

"Oh." She grabbed hold of the support and lifted herself onto the swim board and then scrambled up the steps to the deck. "I'll make today's breakfast special, then," she said, leaning over the rail to see him. "And lunch on board?"

He nodded.

She disappeared from view.

Sara's heart pounded. Family business. Did that mean something was wrong? Not with her grandmother, she hoped. While she had no warm feelings for the woman, she desperately wanted her to read her daughter's last letter. It meant so much to Sara that her mother's mother knew how much her daughter had loved her and wanted to return to Greece. How much she regretted her impetuous marriage and asked for forgiveness.

All through breakfast Sara speculated on what Nikos had meant. Would he be going to the family island? Would he take the *Cassandra* and its crew? Even if he did, she'd learned it was less than a three-hour cruise to the island. There was a chef in residence on the island, so he undoubtedly would feed the smaller crew. A ship's chef would not be needed.

And she had no other incentive to offer. She couldn't hope that the chef fell ill like the ship's chef she was substituting for had.

Could she smuggle herself on board? Hide in the stateroom? Or did the crew sweep through before sailing to verify no stowaways? Just her luck to be found. Then what would she say?

The word about the change in plans swept through the crew quickly. Stefano told Sara and she pretended she didn't know and asked what he'd heard. "Why the change, do you know?"

"He is probably tired of his guests," Stefano said as he waited for the plates for breakfast.

"He would cut the trip short for that? I thought he was interested in Miss Fregulia."

Stefano shook his head. "He never has cut short a cruise before and sometimes he can get some very demanding guests. But it's only a day early. The captain said we were returning, no reason given. I'm not privy to the captain's orders. Nor the path of true love—or at least the proposed walk down the aisle."

"Nor am I. Just curious." Raging with curiosity, was more like it. "What happens with the *Cassandra*? Do we stay aboard?"

Stefano shrugged. "I also work at the resort. If he does not plan another trip soon, I would resume my duties there. As you would, I'm guessing."

"Probably." At least she had the job at the resort. And if Nikos took another cruise, maybe he'd ask for her. Oh, no—wait. The regular cook for the yacht would be ready to sail again in only a few weeks. If the ship didn't go out before that, she would not be included on the next trip.

It had seemed destined when she'd landed this berth. Now without ever getting close to the family island, she was going to miss the opportunity. She would not wish sickness on anyone, so she couldn't keep hoping the regular chef would not be able to go the next time. But one quick trip before he was well would suffice.

"I'll return as soon as they finish lunch to clear the galley and stow any nonperishables. The rest will be taken to one of the restaurants," Stefano said as he hoisted the tray laden with breakfast plates. "We'll wait until the guests take off before leaving—just in case they want any last-minute assistance."

"I'll make sure my cabin is clean," she said, wiping off one of the counters.

Sara packed quickly. It didn't take long. She'd only been aboard a few days and her clothing was almost entirely resort uniforms. Suitcase by the door, she went to the porthole in her wall and gazed out. She could see land in the distance. They'd be back at the resort soon. And she'd accomplished nothing.

Sara went up on the aft deck as the resort came closer and closer. The wind blew her hair back when she leaned over to look toward the direction they were heading. Shading her eyes with her hand, she looked up to the bridge. Nikos stared down at her. She caught her breath and looked away. For his sake she hoped the family situation was not an emergency.

Leaning over the railing, she watched as the yacht was tied to the dock, the gangplank lowered and the passengers disembarked. Gina held on to Nikos's arm as if she'd fall without his support. Senor and Senora Fregulia followed with their friends behind. No one seemed particularly upset, Sara thought. Maybe the family situation was a happy event—like a new baby born or someone got engaged.

"We're leaving," Stefano said from the doorway. "The

Cassandra sails again this afternoon. Captain wants to talk to you on the bridge."

"I'll go straightaway, then pick up my bag." She walked over and offered her hand. "It's been a pleasure, Stefano."

"It was mine," he said as he shook her hand. "I hope we sail again together," he said formally. "I'm sure to see you around the resort." With a slight nod of his head he turned and walked back down the short corridor.

Sara climbed up to the bridge, loving the view of the resort from this height.

"You wanted to see me?" she asked the captain when she entered the pilot house.

He looked up from some papers he was reading. "Ah, Sara Andropolous. Mr. Konstantinos would like you to remain on board. We sail again in a few hours and he has requested you sail with us."

"I'm happy to stay," she said, thinking what an understatement that was. "To where do we sail next?" she asked, almost crossing her fingers and toes.

"To the Konstantinos family island."

Sara almost jumped with joy at the news. But conscious that all things could change, she merely nodded and smiled. "I like sailing on the *Cassandra*. I look forward to extending my time on board."

"Your meals are excellent. It's no wonder Nikos wishes you to remain. I've enjoyed each one you've made."

She smiled in delight. "Always words to warm a cook's heart. Thank you."

She did a little skip as she headed out. Walking down carefully to the main deck, she went to the railing and looked around. There were several luxury yachts moored in the resort's marina. Three smaller boats were also tied up.

The activity on the docks seemed lively and she enjoyed people watching.

There was one person she was especially watching for.

CHAPTER FIVE

SARA sat in the shade of the aft deck writing to her friend Stacy when Nikos appeared. She had not left the ship, not knowing when it might sail and not wanting to miss her only chance.

"I brought your mail," Nikos said, handing her a slim stack of envelopes.

"Thank you." She glanced at them—all from friends at home. She smiled, looking forward to catching up on all the news. She had pretty much brought Stacy up to date in her letter and asked her to tell all their friends the situation.

He sat on the side of the chaise next to hers. "The captain spoke to you?"

"About staying aboard? He said we would be going to your family's island. I've never known anyone to own an island."

"It's small, been in my grandfather's family for generations."

"Descendant from the Roman times?" she asked, thinking of their trip to the ruins.

"Hardly. It's not strategic at all. In fact, the only way in and out is by sea or helicopter. No roads. And only one stretch of really usable beach. The rest is rocky."

"Sounds private."

"For various reasons it suits the family."

"So this is your vacation after your cruise?"

"No, family business. We'll only be gone a few days, once we leave port. However, bad weather threatens for the next couple of days. Just as well we brought the Fregulias and Onetas back when we did."

"What—storms in your perfect Aegean Sea?" she asked with a smile.

He nodded, amusement in his eyes. "So we'll make a run for the island when the captain thinks there's a window of opportunity. In the meantime, since we'll be leaving on short notice, I appreciate your staying close."

She lifted her tablet. "I have letters to write. More, I'm sure, once I read those from my friends."

He glanced at them, then at her.

"One from a special friend?"

She fanned them out and nodded. "Stacy and I have been friends since starting school. From the thickness of the envelope she's written a lot."

"I was wondering about a particular male friend."

She looked again, then caught his meaning. Meeting his eyes she narrowed hers.

"That's really none of your business, is it?" He may hold the key to getting to her grandmother, but he didn't run her life.

He looked away, studying the masts of a large sailboat tied up nearby. "I was taking a friendly interest in an employee."

"I prefer to keep my private life just that—private." Plus she hated to admit to this dynamic man that there was no one special in her life.

He nodded and rose. "As do I as a general rule. Someone will let you know when we get under way. If you'll excuse me, I have work to do. We will run with a minimum crew."

Sara stared after him when he left, wondering what kind of

complex she'd developed because of her background. The man had been cordial to her and she'd just about bit his head off. She didn't want to give herself any ideas, so had nipped any personal talk. She couldn't get past the man's background, so different from her own. Yet had her mother not stood up to her own father and refused to marry the man he had chosen for her, Sara would have had a very similar background to Nikos's.

Instead, her childhood had been a struggle. With no father in the picture, and a mother scarcely trained for work, money had always been tight. But her mother had made the best of things. Sara remembered happy evenings with only grilled cheese sandwiches for dinner. It hadn't mattered, her mother had made it fun.

She leaned back, lost in thought. She missed her mother so much. Damaris Andropolous had had a hard life, nothing like what she had once expected. Sara wished she'd lived to enjoy some of the fruits of Sara's work. By the time Sara was earning enough money for a lovely flat, nice secondhand furniture and friendly neighbors, her mother had been too ill to enjoy it.

Life wasn't always the way one wanted, she knew. Sara was alone in the world—save the grandmother she'd never met. She had no illusions the woman would embrace her with delight. She'd hand her the letter and that would be that. Sara had a full life in London. Her visit to Greece made for a nice change, but it was not permanent. She longed for the familiarity of home.

Stefano arrived with another crew member in tow, each carrying bags of groceries. Sara went to put things away, chatting amicably with Stefano as he helped.

"We will likely eat breakfast on board and the rest of our meals with the staff at the island," he said. "That's the way it's been in the past."

"Tell me what you know about this family island," she said, hoping to glean some more information about the Konstantinos family.

"It's pretty. The house is huge. The servant quarters are quite spacious, and we can use the beach unless there's a house party, when it's reserved for guests. I like making the trip. For the duration of Nikos's visits, we're on call, but never needed. Lots of downtime—and we get paid."

"Sounds good. Will they need my help in the kitchen?" she asked, wondering how to ask the questions she really wanted to know—when and where might she see Eleani Konstantinos.

"No need," Nikos said from the doorway.

She spun around, surprised to find him at the galley entrance.

"We have a fine chef who cooks to suit my grandfather. As Stefano says, you have the days to yourself. Will you get bored?"

"I doubt it. If there's a beach, I'll go swimming."

"There are some coves around from the main dock that offer a variety of colorful fish if you care to go diving."

Stefano kept stowing the groceries, but Sara knew he was listening avidly. Had he known Nikos had taken her diving? She felt her face grow warm remembering that dive—and the kiss that followed. Surely they'd been too far from the boat for anyone to see.

"Sounds like something to think about," she said, conscious of Stefano's presence. Did Nikos mean to go with her? Or after only one short lesson, would he trust her on her own? Did others of the crew dive? She didn't want to go with anyone else.

Nikos didn't seem in a hurry to leave. He leaned against the doorjamb and watched as she checked off the ingredients and Stefano stowed them. What was he doing?

"Did you need something?" she asked.

"No. Just wondered what was for dinner. It's supposed to storm through the evening so we will stay put for the night. The aft deck isn't protected. No need to cook if you don't wish to. We can take our meals at the resort."

"Or we take our meals in our rooms in inclement weather," Stefano said.

"Then if you wouldn't mind cooking, it would save the crew going out into the bad weather," Nikos said.

"So individual trays," Sara murmured, wondering if Nikos sat in solitary splendor in the dining salon or invited the captain to join him.

"Perhaps you'd care to join me this evening once the meal is prepared."

Sara stopped and stared at Nikos.

Stefano stopped and stared at both of them, his head turning like a spectator's at a tennis match.

Sara's heart rate doubled. She studied him for a moment. "Why not? Thank you for asking. When I have everything ready, I'll ask Stefano to bring up the tray."

Nikos glanced at Stefano. The steward stared back, obviously at a loss for words. "If that suits you, Stefano."

"Of course."

Nikos nodded and turned to leave.

Sara looked at the steward. "Something tells me he doesn't often ask the chef I'm replacing to eat with him."

"Never. But then, Paul is not a beautiful woman."

Sara laughed nervously. What had she just agreed to? "Neither am I, but thank you. I think I'll prepare lamb with mint jelly. He liked it last time I made that."

"As far as I know he has never been a picky eater," Stefano said, busying himself with the last of the grocery placement.

"How long have you known him?" she asked.

"I've worked for the resort for six years. And been steward on the *Cassandra* for almost five. I wouldn't say I know him, precisely."

And never been asked to eat with him, Sara guessed. She didn't know whether to be wary he had asked for her company or annoyed at the barrier it might raise with other crew members. She had to work with these people. She didn't want any resentment.

Nikos wondered if he was making a mistake. He stood near the tall windows of the dining salon awaiting dinner. Stefano would bring it up in only moments. And Sara would come up, as well. It was unheard of for him to invite a crew member to dine with him. Though he and the captain had shared many meals on the bridge, he'd never shared one in the main salon unless guests were present and they wished the captain to share in the festivities. As to the rest of the crew, Nikos occasionally ate on the aft deck with them, but none had ever eaten in the salon when he was aboard.

The trip to the island would of necessity be brief. He had already been several days from the resort. But he hadn't seen his grandfather in several weeks and wanted to spend a few days with him. He and his wife always made Nikos feel at home and urged him to stay as long as he could. The island held the best memories of Nikos's childhood. He remembered exploring, learning to dive, learning to pilot the yacht. And his grandmother's loving smile. Spiros's second wife, Eleani, was as loving as his first. What was his secret to finding women to love him and for him to love?

He'd thought Ariana would be someone to grow old with. That relationship had proved false and left him wary of women and their motives. While he'd dated over the years, it wasn't until he began to consider Gina as wife material that he'd grown serious. Until he met Sara.

She was nothing like the woman he wanted for a wife. She lacked...what? The cosmopolitan veneer he was used to? That made him feel cynical. Yet he was just as skeptical of her own delight in all things. How long would it take to find the key to Sara? Did she long for fame as a chef? For a high-prestige job? Or just pots of money and the lifestyle that went with it?

"Dinner, sir," Stefano said, arriving with the tray. The table had been set a half hour ago. The steward placed the tray on the stand and began serving.

Sara entered, her cheeks rosy from heat in the kitchen. She'd obviously changed for the meal, wearing a simple dress instead of the resort uniform.

When they'd been seated, served and Stefano had left, Nikos poured a bit of wine in her glass. "A bottle from our own islands."

She took a sip. "Lovely. So have you rethought Greek wines?"

"The resort has always served local wines, but perhaps we'll expand the offerings. In addition, I have a new agreement for the next three years with Senor Fregulia. After that time I'll review the consumption rate of both and make a decision."

Sara longed to ask about Gina. But since Nikos had never brought up the subject, she couldn't. But it seemed odd that he would dine with her if he were on the brink of asking another woman to marry him.

"Maybe the head chef at the resort will think up a special dish to go with the island wine and when ordered the somme-lier can suggest this variety," she said, nervous. Now that it was the two of them, it felt like a date. What would they talk about? Diving? The resort? Or could she steer the conversa-tion to families and Eleani Konstantinos in particular?

She glanced at the windows on which rivulets of water ran

down. The rain had started shortly after the groceries had arrived and not let up since. The ship bobbed by the dock, obviously impacted by the winds accompanying the storm. It had grown dark early with the storm.

"So it's a good thing we didn't head out," she said, tasting the lamb. It was delicious. If nothing else, she'd fall back on describing how she had prepared the meal.

"We would have had a rough ride, but the *Cassandra* is very seaworthy, and this storm would have been a mere inconvenience, not a threat."

"I wonder if I would have been seasick," she said, watching him take a bite of the lamb.

"Delicious," he said as he savored the flavors.

Sara smiled, relaxing a tiny bit. "Thank you."

Talk revolved around the ship as they ate the meal. Sara asked how often he sailed, where he had been, what his favorite places were. By the time they finished, Sara was feeling much more at ease. And knew more about her boss. His experiences far surpassed hers in travel. This was her first extended stay anywhere outside of England. She loved listening to him talk about America and even his few months in the UK.

When they were finished Stefano quickly dispatched the dinner dishes and brought the trifle Sara had prepared. He also brought a bottle of brandy from the sideboard and two snifters. Pouring hot coffee from a silver pot, he stepped back and eyed the table, then looked at Nikos.

"Thank you, Stefano. You can clear the rest in the morning."

Stefano bowed slightly, set the coffeepot on the table and left.

As soon as Sara finished her trifle, she folded her napkin and looked at Nikos.

"Thank you for inviting me to eat with you. I think I'll return to my cabin now."

"So soon?" Nikos asked. "It is still early. What would you do in your cabin?"

"Read, make plans for the next few days' breakfasts." She felt her nerves stretched taut. She resisted drawing closer to the man, yet every minute she spent with him was making it harder to resist. She tried to remember all her mother had said about the strong Greek men who rode right over women and their interests. So far she had seen no evidence of that, but she scarcely knew the man.

"Stay. The night is young. If you like, we can take our brandy up on the bridge. It's dry under the shelter, yet we'll be able to see the resort lights through the rain."

She placed her glass carefully on the table. "What do you expect from me? If I didn't know better, I'd think you're flirting. I'm confused. I thought rumors said you were on the verge of marriage with Gina Fregulia."

Her question caught him off guard. What did he expect? She worked for him, which precluded any close tie. Was he just fighting against tying himself down with one woman when he married? Or did he really want to know more about this particular woman?

"I want nothing except a pleasant evening. And perhaps a diving partner when we reach the island. The only family members there right now are my grandparents, who are not quite up to the activities I enjoy. Consider this a perk of the job. Beyond that, I expect nothing. And for the record, I did not ask Gina to marry me."

"A diving partner," she clarified, confused.

He shrugged. He was surprised that she knew of his earlier plan. Yet it was no secret. Gina had not given any evidence of being upset when she had left, but he knew she too had expected a proposal on the cruise.

She dropped her gaze to her brandy.

"Still, if you are close to becoming engaged, it wouldn't do to spend much time with another woman. It might give rise to the wrong impression." She looked up at him thoughtfully and added, "Even if it might be more of a business arrangement than a love match."

He laughed softly, amazed at her daring.

"Don't you believe in love?" she asked.

He took a breath. Talking about his family didn't come easily. His roommates at school had heard the complaints, the frustration and then the resignation. Usually he maintained a careful facade that revealed nothing of his true feelings. Sara wanted to know more. Did he wish to tell her? Where to start and where to stop? Should he share the history of him and Ariana as well?

"Never mind," she said. "I changed my mind. You keep your secrets and we'll see how it works to be diving partners." She poured cream into her coffee and sipped, her brandy only half-gone.

Her disinterest acted as a goad. "It's no great secret. I don't want a marriage that would end up like my parents'. They had one child—me, but I didn't fit into their plans or lifestyle. Nannies, tutors and boarding school made up my childhood. The few times I returned home for summer holidays or Christmas, I was lucky to find them at home one night to catch up on my life before they were off to another function or short trip abroad. If it hadn't been for the island and the time my grandparents took to be with me, I might as well have lived my entire childhood in a boarding school."

She stared at him. "Not much of a family life for a child,"

she said slowly. "So different from mine. It was just my mother and me. My father vanished shortly after I was born. She gave me the best home in the world, despite our financial difficulties. I always thought if we'd just had a bit more money, things would have been perfect. Maybe I was viewing things wrong. Time and love are far more important than all the money in the world." As her mother knew when she'd lost both her parents' love and their money. It had been the loss of family she mourned.

"My parents are too wrapped up in themselves to care for a child. I feel the same way about the resort. It is very demanding. It would be a mistake to marry, father a child and then ignore him or her while putting the resort first."

She tilted her head slightly, thinking. "I don't believe you would do that. Firstly, you know what it's like and would cherish your child too much to put him through what you experienced."

He shook his head. "How can anyone be sure?"

Sara bit back her comment. She thought his view of marriage and families was sad. He'd obviously never experienced the close tie that love brought. Was that the Greek way? Marry for business or convenience, not for love.

Not that she had fallen in love, but she knew what it was like from observing her married friends. And one day she hoped she'd discover it for herself. She wanted an emotional tie as well as the legal one. As had her mother. Only, she hoped her marriage, should she ever have one, would end up much happier than her mother's.

She drank the last of her coffee. She liked being around Nikos too much even when their opinions differed. He kept her guessing where he would lead the conversation next.

Time to leave, however. She dare not risk her emotions on a man who would do perfectly well without her.

She rose. "I really am retiring now," she said.

He rose and bade her good-night.

She turned toward the door feeling just a twinge of disappointment that they hadn't connected on a basic level.

"Sara," he said softly.

When she turned, his eyes were focused on her.

She licked her lips, her heart racing. Butterflies had a field day in her stomach, and Sara felt as if time stood still. She recognized desire. That much was clear. She yearned for another kiss, but hesitated. It would only make her compare him to every man she kissed after Nikos; what if she became spoiled by his kisses and never found another to measure up?

Granted, she'd only been kissed in the sea, hardly the stuff of romance. Yet she had dwelt on that experience more than any other in her life.

"Sara?" he said again, stepping around the table and walking directly to her.

She stepped closer and lifted her face, her gaze fastened on his.

He closed the distance and cupped her face in his hands and kissed her.

CHAPTER SIX

His lips were warm as they pressed against hers. Slowly he swept his tongue against her lips, seeking entrance to her mouth. Sara complied, stepping closer, longing for him to wrap her in his arms and keep the kiss going forever.

He must have read her mind as his hands moved to lift her hair, then slide down her back and pull her into closer contact. The kiss deepened, and Sara felt like she was floating. Desire flared. She actively kissed him back, her tongue dancing with his, her arms holding him as tightly as he held her. Only the lack of breath caused her to pull back eventually, gasping.

He continued to kiss her—first her cheek, then along her jaw, then a long slow slide down her throat to the rapid pulse point at the base. Then back up the other side.

She stood still as if afraid the slightest movement would end the magic. When he covered her lips again she responded. It was glorious. She could fall for this man. If he kissed her once a day, she'd probably be content to stay forever in Greece.

The thought filtered in, then struck with clarity.

She pulled back slightly, feeling dazed and confused. And guilty. She had no business becoming involved with Nikos Konstantinos. He was practically engaged to another woman.

And she was trying to use him to gain access to her grandmother. Nothing was working in her favor. She suspected he would be a dangerous enemy. She dared not provoke him or lead him on. He would feel betrayed once he knew the truth. She could not aggravate the situation by sending false messages.

He opened his eyes and looked at her.

"I need to go to my cabin," she said quietly, disentangling herself from his embrace.

He started to say something but Sara held up her hand. "No, don't say a thing. This was not *just a kiss*. I can't do this."

She fled from the salon. Once she reached her small cabin, she shut the door softly and leaned against it. Blowing out a puff of air, she tried to get her roiling senses under control. She could feel the blood pounding through her. She was still breathing faster than normal. Good grief, she was attracted to Nikos as she'd never been to anyone else. And falling for the man was a guaranteed heartache.

She pushed away and went to the small porthole to gaze out at the rainy night. It was too dark to see much; only the dock lights cast faint illumination on the ship. The resort glowed in the wet evening. Had everyone else aboard gone to bed? She checked her watch. It was after ten. Early yet.

You're stalling, Sara, she admonished herself. She could not get sidetracked by an attraction to Nikos. Granted he was gorgeous and successful. He had been more than kind in showing her around the island, teaching her to dive. But she knew he had no intention of becoming involved with her. Was this just a fling before settling down? The thought made her sick—and did not jibe with what she knew of Nikos. He was too honorable. So…maybe the lovely Gina was out of the running. That still didn't give her a chance.

"Darn it," she said aloud. The first man she'd met she

really felt an attraction to, and he was off-limits. She knew he would end up disliking her once he knew she'd used him. Was there any way to keep a relationship?

Friendship—she didn't want that, she wanted more.

She lay back on her bunk and relived the kiss. Magical, no other word. Did he know he could melt her insides with a sexy look? Did he care? He probably had women falling all over themselves to impress him.

To fulfill the promise made to her mother, she had to focus on her goal—give the last letter to her grandmother.

But she wished she could dally a bit with Nikos Konstantinos. It would make her Greek trip the ultimate fantasy.

The next morning Sara rose early. She'd slept fitfully during the night, soothed by the sound of the rain, waking as each dream cast her into Nikos's arms. She was glad for the dreary morning sky. Working would help.

She prepared an omelet again for breakfast, with an assortment of fresh fruits and a delicious coffee blend she hadn't tried before. She nibbled as she worked.

With only a minimum crew and Nikos, the workload was easy. Would she need to prepare any other meals besides breakfast? That would depend on the weather. It took less than a half day to reach the island. Once there another chef would be in charge. Maybe she could offer her assistance.

"I'll take up the captain's plate. He says we're leaving this morning," Stefano said.

"It's still raining," Sara said with another quick glance out the window.

"But not windy, which is the bad part of a storm. Rain can't hurt the boat."

She nodded. "There, take it away. That's for Nikos, that's

for the captain," she said pointing out the two plates. "Do we eat in our rooms for breakfast, too?"

"We'll stand around the counter for breakfast. We don't have a lot of rainy days on the ship."

After breakfast Sara stepped out on the aft deck, keeping beneath the small overhang to stay dry. The air was humid, the rain warm to the touch when she extended her hand. If they hadn't been in the marina, could she have gone swimming? What a novelty—to swim in the rain. At home it was usually too cold in rainy weather to swim.

She stayed awhile enjoying the change in weather, then turned to return to the galley. Stefano was about through with the dishes. He glanced up.

"The captain asked if you'd like to come to the bridge to watch as the yacht left the marina. I've done it a few times. Gives a different perspective to things," he said.

"I'd love to." She'd relish a chance to see how the yacht was actually operated.

"Take a fresh pot of coffee. It's cool up there and the captain commented he especially liked today's blend," he added.

Fifteen minutes later Sara entered the bridge, two coffee mugs and a coffeepot in hand. She stopped when she saw Nikos standing at the high chart table, reviewing the charts with the captain. Heat washed through her.

He looked up casually and nodded. "Good, you brought more coffee."

The captain smiled. "Come in. We'll be pushing off in a few minutes. I thought you'd like to watch. Without much of a crew to cook for, you will have more free time."

"Thank you. I brewed a fresh pot," she said, walking over and placing the two mugs on the flat surface near the charts.

Pouring the coffee carefully, she refused to allow even one drop to spill on a chart. But it took all her concentration. Her instinct was to watch Nikos.

She handed one mug to Nikos and one to the captain.

"You didn't bring a mug for yourself," Nikos commented, taking a sip and watching her over the rim of the cup.

"I didn't know you were here or I would have brought another."

He offered her his.

Sara drew in a sharp breath, hesitated, then slowly reached out and took it. The coffee was hot and fragrant. She took a couple of swallows then returned the mug, feeling an intimacy at the gesture. Moving to the wide windows, she looked at the activity on the dock. Despite the rain, men were working, wearing bright yellow slickers.

"So the storm won't affect our trip," she said.

"Not unless the wind kicks up again," Nikos replied. "And we're hoping it won't."

"The last weather report indicated the worst had passed," the captain murmured, checking a list as he flipped switches and checked gauges.

She watched another minute, then made up her mind. She could act like an idiot and avoid the man as much as possible or take advantage of the invitation to the bridge and learn all she could.

She spun around and almost marched to the high table with the charts. "So what are we looking at?" she asked, peering at the yellow page with blue lines swirling around.

"A depth chart of the sea between here and the island. We are looking for deeper water, which will minimize some of the wave action. We want as smooth a journey as possible," Nikos said, moving slightly so she could see better.

He put his arm over her shoulder and pointed to a series of irregular circles. "This shows the topography of the sea floor. Here are depth indicators." She watched as he pointed out aspects of the chart and the route they were planning.

"How will you know where these are from up here?" she asked.

Nikos removed his arm and looked at the captain. The older man gave a concise explanation of the depth sounder and GPS positioning to which Sara was able to listen and understand without Nikos's touch rocketing her senses.

"I thought you just hopped aboard and took off," she said at the end of the explanation.

"More or less if we use the heliport. My father usually uses that as it's faster than ship, but I prefer the *Cassandra*. Since the weather has kicked up a bit, we're looking for a smoother passage than the usual route we take. We'll be there by lunchtime."

"So if it takes you hours to get there, I bet shopping is a two-day affair."

"There are islands nearby which offer shopping and other amenities. My grandfather wants a new runabout to get to the nearest one. Takes about forty minutes in a smaller boat."

"Your grandparents are there now?" she asked. She couldn't be this close and bear to learn her grandmother was elsewhere.

"Of course, they're who I'm going to see."

She nodded and looked back out of the window.

Sara enjoyed watching the men on the dock cast off the lines. She marveled at how the captain could maneuver such a large ship away without a scrape anywhere. The rain had not abated. The large wipers on the front windows kept the glass clear. She smiled as she felt the power of the engine when they went to cruising speed sometime later.

Turning, she met Nikos's eyes. He was standing on the far side of the bridge, leaning against the glass watching her. He raised an eyebrow in silent question.

"This is fantastic. Do you ever drive the yacht?" she asked.

"Sometimes."

"He is as proficient as I am," the captain commented. "Perhaps with not as much practice, though."

"Who has time to command a yacht when a resort needs a firm hand?" Nikos asked.

"So who is running the resort while you are away?" Sara asked.

"I am. The marvels of modern electronics. I have a laptop here that connects to the main computer at the resort. My assistant can manage the day-to-day activities. I am always available if he needs me."

"Will I meet your grandparents?" Sara asked. She might as well find out from the get-go.

"Do you wish to?" he asked.

She shrugged, trying to show a casual demeanor. What would another crew member do? She didn't even try to guess—none of them had been invited to the bridge since she'd been on board.

"Just wondered."

"My grandfather knows all the crew—except you. He'll want to meet you. In the meantime, you can swim in the sea, enjoy the island. We have some beautiful flowering gardens. A nice gazebo near the beach. I'll take you to one of the coves to dive—there are some amazing sponges and fish there."

"Sounds like a vacation, not work," she said. He still hadn't answered her question. It looked as if it would be up to her to find a way to meet Eleani Konstantinos.

Once the ship was under way, Sara grew bored with watching the rain on the windows and the gray sea that stretched out to the horizon. It would have been lovely had the weather been good. She gathered up the mugs and the coffeepot and thanked the captain for the time on the bridge.

Nikos opened the door for her and followed her into the narrow passageway.

"Thanks for the chance on the bridge. I'll get these back to the galley and see about what to prepare for lunch."

"We'll be at the island by lunch," he said. "And the crew eats with the island staff. You're done for the day."

"Oh."

"Dump the cups and come to the aft deck. We can sit in the lee of the wind and stay dry."

"I'm not sure that's a good idea," she said slowly. Her first inclination was to say yes. Yet, after his explosive kiss last night, the last thing she should do is place herself in the path of temptation.

He stopped her and swung her partway around. "Come for a little while," he coaxed softly, his eyes warm and dark.

Her heart skipped a beat. This was *so* not a good idea.

"Okay. Unless it gets too wet."

"It won't."

She went first to the galley, then stopped in her cabin for a sweatshirt. It was part of the uniform, with the logo of the resort clearly embroidered over her heart. She stared at herself in the mirror. "Do not forget this is only a means to an end. You are not going to get any more attached to the man!"

Sara had a feeling she was lying to herself. The attraction she felt for Nikos was not something she controlled. Maybe her tactics were wrong. Maybe she should be around him as much as possible—to see if once she saw the flaws he was bound to have, it would lessen the pull.

Nikos was already on the aft deck when she stepped out. The overhang had kept the three feet of deck closest to the main structure dry. The wind hadn't touched it. The air was cooler than she expected. The wake was white against the steely gray of the water.

She shut the door and walked to stand beside him. Nikos had pulled two chairs over and dried them. The towel was on the floor.

Sitting, she looked at him.

"So, what shall we talk about?"

He groaned softly. "If we have to talk about what to talk about, we have nothing to say."

"Do we?"

"You mean after last night?"

"Of course."

"You mean a chance to kiss a beautiful woman after a pleasant evening together?"

"Good line. I think I've heard it before."

He shrugged. "So I need to polish my technique."

"I don't think you need to change a thing. It's clear you like your lifestyle and I live a very different one. I told you."

He tilted his chair back, resting against the wall. "And if I don't see them as that different?"

"Trust me, there's a world of difference between us. You are rich, I'm not. You evidently were neglected as a child. I was not."

"Not neglect. My parents gave me the best that money could buy."

"Neglected by them, however. The greatest gift parents can give their children is their attention. My mother and I did so much together. Even when I was a rebellious teenager. She loved me. There was never any question."

"Some people are not meant for marriage. My parents aren't the only reason."

"So what else? Burned at love?"

"You might say so. Now I wonder if I really loved Ariana at all. It was an advantageous match."

"What are you talking about?"

"My engagement—surely you've heard the tale."

She shook her head. "I thought you didn't ask Gina Fregulia. So there was another engagement that ended. Were you heartbroken?" she asked sympathetically.

He gave a harsh laugh. "Hardly. Mad as hell. Ariana was beautiful and pleasing and professed to love me. Our relationship was meant to be, she said a hundred times."

"Uh-oh, I think I've heard this tale before," she murmured.

"Do you want to hear it or not?" he asked.

"Yes." She closed her mouth tightly and looked at him.

He looked away. "Damn, I don't want to explain. Sufficient to say my loving, meant-to-be fiancée found our own relationship wasn't quite enough, so she found other meaningful relationships with as many men as she could."

"Ouch," Sara said. "Tacky."

He looked at her in surprise. "Tacky? Is that all you have to say?"

"Well, you said your heart wasn't broken. So then it was probably embarrassing to end the engagement if others knew why. But her behavior definitely was tacky. You're well rid of her."

He nodded. "Well rid of any suggestions for future alliances as well—unless the rules are clearly defined. In the meantime I'm content with the way my life is going."

Sara thought about what he said. She felt the tension in his words. Maybe he had been hit harder by the betrayal than he wanted to admit, even to himself. And for a moment her heart softened. No one should be in love and have that love thrown back into their face by such wanton betrayal.

She had a hard time picturing Nikos Konstantinos heart-broken, but he might have been and hidden it from the world. She wanted to reach out and touch him with sympathy but refrained. She didn't know how that would be received.

She began to relax. Hearing he had problems with life like anyone else made him seem more normal or approachable. Not the mighty millionaire resort owner living in an ivy-covered tower. Did she dare spend time with him? They'd never have to be alone—except when diving. He had never made an untoward comment or move on her. And she'd be leaving soon. Putting distance between them would be the best solution in the end. Despite her love of what she'd seen of Greece so far, her home was in London. Her friends were there. Her memories. Her mother was buried there.

She had a few days. She dared not reveal that being with him rocked her emotions. That kissing him was the most glorious feeling ever. That she longed for more when reality kept slapping her back. They had no future. She should adopt that as her mantra.

She dared not give voice even to herself of what she feared might happen—that she'd fall madly in love with him and end up going home with the world's biggest heartbreak. He might like to kiss her, but his barriers were well established. She was not some femme fatale that men fell for. He'd already set his course—marriage to Gina, business arrangement. She shivered. It sounded so cold and sterile. She wanted love, heat, passion and loyalty that lasted a lifetime.

Take the time on the island as a gift. One day she could look back on her great adventure in Greece. Were all Greek women destined to heartbreak? Her mother had been betrayed yet had loved the man she gave up her family for. She had never found another to love after he had left. And her pride had kept her from admitting she'd made a mistake and returning home. Sara dearly hoped she would not follow in her footsteps. Pride was well and good in its place. But not to the detriment of love and family.

Nikos shifted his focus to the sky. "I think this storm will last all day. Not the best way to see the island when we arrive. It's quite beautiful with all the flowers in the garden."

"So are the gardens at the resort," she said, feeling oddly adrift now that her goal was drawing closer. She had not thought beyond handing her grandmother the letter. What next?

"I took the advice of grandmother Eleani for the gardens. She loves flowers and worked with a landscape architect to design the gardens at the resort."

"That's what you call your grandmother," she asked.

"My real grandmother died when I was a teenager. About ten or eleven years ago my grandfather married a widow— Eleani. She is a delightful person, warm and friendly and openly adores my grandfather. I can't help but love her because of that. As you may have gathered, my family is not very demonstrative. Except for Eleani."

Sara was hungry for any information about Elcani. But would it appear odd if she questioned Nikos? She was wary of getting to know too much about him. Wouldn't that lead to expectations that she couldn't fulfill? Once he knew he'd been the reason for her presence, as a key to the island, he would be furious.

Again she bemoaned that she'd met him only as a means to an end, and then had become attracted to him. Why couldn't life be easy for once?

"So tell me why you know as much about running this boat as the captain," she said, deliberately changing the topic.

"I love the sea. When I was younger I was always after the captain to show me how, so he convinced my grandfather to let him give me a crash course of several weeks. We loaded up on supplies and set off. It was one of the best summers of my life. I learned about charting, learned how to read the weather, how to sound for depth. How to dive. We were gone eight weeks and it flew by like the wind. By the end of the summer, I could pilot the boat as well as the captain. I had grown proficient in diving and received a good overview of the Aegean, to boot."

Nikos told her of the villages and cities they'd visited. How he had crashed into more than one dock and had been the despair of the captain whenever he turned the yacht into a port. Sara laughed more than once, as she knew he wanted. He was a natural storyteller and she listened avidly to every word, relishing the deep tone of his voice and the fluttering inside that occurred whenever she was near him. She was growing used to being in constant turmoil around him.

When he wound down, he asked her about her favorite summer. She told him about the trek through Scotland she and her mother had made—despite the rain and cold weather. How they ate at pubs each night and tried to like haggis, but gave up midway through their trek and switched to porridge.

At Nikos's expression, she laughed, remembering he didn't like oatmeal.

"So how did you end up a chef?" he asked.

"I like to cook. My mother quoted that saying 'Do what you love and you'll never work a day in your life' to me from when I was a little girl. I learned to prepare simple Greek dishes at her side when I was quite small. It seemed like a logical career for me."

"And it's worked out?"

"There's a bit of a bias against female chefs. Especially in some of the more posh restaurants in London—the ones where I could really explore all kinds of exotic dishes. But I'm still young. I'll keep pushing ahead. The fact I've worked for your resort will add a fillip to my résumé. Maybe I'll have better luck when I return to London."

"And must you return?"

"It's my home." Now they were getting close to her secret.

"But not too soon," he said.

Sara shrugged. She knew she would not have a job once Nikos discovered why she'd been working at his resort. Yet he'd been the one to ask her to accompany him to the family island. In a way, he'd facilitated part of her quest. Would he see it that way? Would he understand why she'd had to resort to subterfuge to reach her goal?

She wanted to forget about seeing her grandmother. The thought shocked her. Ever since her mother had gotten sick, Sara had wanted to reach Eleani. Two years and counting. How could she even for a moment consider coming this far and not contacting her?

Yet being with Nikos had made her more interested in this exciting man than in seeking some unknown woman who had let her only child leave and never resumed contact. What good was any of it going to do at this late date? Her mother was dead. She had tried to heal the breach and been rebuffed. Why should Sara try?

Because of a promise.

She had made her mother a promise, and Sara would stand by her word.

No matter who got hurt? a small voice inside whispered. No matter that her mother would never know one way or the other?

A promise was a promise. She had to keep hers to her dying mother.

Nikos looked at a seagull gliding on the wind.

"We're getting close," he said.

Sara looked around. "How can you tell? It all looks the same as it's been since we left the resort."

"Birds live on land. This one is either from our island or Patricia, the nearest island where you can shop." He glanced at his watch. "Besides, we've been traveling long enough."

So their time together was ending. Maybe it was for the best.

"Despite what you say about your family, you're happy to be going home, aren't you?" she asked.

He nodded. "The island is special. The best place for our family—when we all gather together. I won't see my parents this visit, but my grandfather holds a special place in my heart. I owe him more than most grandchildren owe their grandfathers."

"Family ties are the hardest ones to break. They are strong no matter what the circumstances," Sara said slowly.

"True. I'd do anything for him."

She nodded, studying him gravely. "No matter what he asked?"

Nikos shrugged. "I can't imagine him asking anything I would not be willing to do."

"Even if it were hard or seemed pointless at some stage?"

"Even then. If it meant enough for him to ask me, it would mean enough for me to do it."

Sara looked away. Nikos had reaffirmed her own beliefs. At least they had that in common—not that he'd ever know it.

"Did I miss something?" he asked.

"What?"

"The conversation turned very solemn all of a sudden."

"I was just asking about commitment and family ties. Sometimes things happen. Promises are made. Remember that."

"I think I can remember that—things happen, promises are made."

She laughed, forcing away her dismay and focusing on the moment. She'd caught a glimpse of Nikos's attachment to his family's island. She suddenly yearned to see it—through his eyes if possible.

Before long he rose and peered over the railing toward the bow.

"There it is." The excitement in his tone had Sara jumping up and going to stand beside him. He drew her in front of him, holding her steady against the motion of the yacht. She peered around until she could see ahead. Rain hit her in the face, but she could see the silhouette of an island dead ahead.

Sara leaned back against Nikos's chest. She felt the shelter of his arms as he steadied them on the railing of the ship as it rose and fell meeting the waves head-on. She could stay here forever—though they'd be soaking wet in a few minutes

"It doesn't look like much today, but see it in the sunshine," he said by her left ear. "When we get closer, you'll see the house on the highest point, with gardens surrounding it like a beautiful, colorful skirt. The beach is pristine and we work to keep all oil and waste from the yacht away from the sand. The cove I told you about is around the leeward side."

"It's larger than I thought it would be," she said, as the island seemed to gain in size every bit closer they came.

"A few square miles. There is a small compound behind the house where the servants have their homes. Even a guest house, which my parents use when they visit."

Even more important than finding her grandmother, Sara would find out where Nikos called home. See what kind of place he loved. Find out more about boyhood escapades. While he sounded as if he'd led a solitary life, he'd also had this glorious place to explore. Despite what he felt as a lack of parental involvement, they had done a fine job in giving him a safe place to live as a child that he still cherished today.

Sara definitely didn't feel that way about the flat she'd grown up in. The best thing said for it was its proximity to the public gardens.

A deckhand was on the dock waiting to tie up the *Cassandra*. Other than that, no one was in sight.

Sara and Nikos had returned to the bridge to watch the docking procedure. Now the captain turned off the engines and snapped up his chart portfolio. "So we are here. Sailing again when?" he asked Nikos.

"A few days at least. You're free to do whatever you wish here. I'll contact you in plenty of time to prepare for our return trip. It will undoubtedly be after the weekend."

Since it was Tuesday, Sara could look forward to at least five days to see over the island. She hoped the weather would clear so she could go diving again. And see the flowers in the garden. Her heart pounded—and find her grandmother. But she was trying not to think about that step now that it was here.

"You will all take your meals at the main house as usual," he continued. Looking at Sara he said, "A respite from your duties. Feel free to visit the house kitchen if you wish, but Dimitri and his staff will prepare our family meals."

She nodded. They were to stay aboard during the visit. No need to have employee quarters prepared when their cabins suited. She was glad she'd brought along a couple of mystery books. Without reading to look forward to, she'd be bored to tears with the inactivity in the rain.

An older man walked down to the dock, an umbrella carefully sheltering him from the rain. He had a furled umbrella in one hand.

"I see your grandfather," the captain said.

"I'd better go." He hesitated a moment, looking at Sara, then nodded and left the bridge.

Sara moved to the window closest to the pathway and tried to get a good glimpse of her grandmother's second husband. He was as tall as Nikos, she thought. Perhaps Nikos would look like him when he was old.

A feeling of regret swept through. She would not get to see him grow old. Their paths would have diverged long before either of them was old. She wished for him a happy life. Maybe Gina, or someone like her, would change his warped views of family and would love him forever.

She hoped she'd find a man like that, who could make her forget the past and sweep her away into a future of love and happiness. She sighed softly and watched as Nikos met the older man on the dock and they hugged. He took the umbrella his grandfather offered, and in only moments the two of them disappeared from view as they went up to the house.

CHAPTER SEVEN

SARA didn't see Nikos the rest of Tuesday. She took one of her books to the aft deck, pulled over one of the chaises and dried it off to sit in the fresh air and read. When the wind shifted, she felt the drizzle and gave up and went below. She could have joined the men in the salon, free for their use while on the island. But she didn't relish the card game they were playing and couldn't concentrate on her book with the noise of their conversation.

Not that she was exactly engrossed in the story. She kept wondering when Nikos was coming back.

Sara fell asleep in her cabin with the book across her chest. Sometime later she woke when there was a knock on her door.

She jumped up and tried to become fully awake. Opening the door, she saw Stefano.

"We're going up to the house for dinner now. Want to walk up with us?"

"Yes. Just let me run a brush through my hair."

"We'll wait at the gangway," he said, turning away.

The rain had stopped, but every shrub and tree between the dock and the house dripped. The late-afternoon sun shone beneath the lingering clouds, making the drops of water sparkle like jewels.

"Tomorrow should be a good day," the captain said on the walk. "You can go swimming if you like."

"I would like. The cabin is a bit small for being stuck inside all day," she said.

He laughed. "You should have come to the salon."

"I had a book to read."

"Stefano said you were napping. The book not compelling enough?"

"Guess not," she replied, smiling up at the older man. "But if I am ever troubled with insomnia, I'll know what to read."

Dinner was quite festive with the boat crew greeting staff members of the house like old friends. Sara was the odd person out but was quickly introduced to the others.

When the captain complimented her to the chef on her desserts, the chef's eyes took on a speculative gleam.

"Perhaps you could spare some time to work with me while you are here."

"I'd be very delighted," she said. It would fill the days, which now seemed to stretch out endlessly. Nikos would make a difference—if he had time for her. In the meantime, she'd never been so conscious of their situation as now, when he was upstairs with the person she had come to Greece to see, and she was so close but still a floor away with no clear-cut way to meet Eleani.

Soon after the meal ended, Sara returned to the yacht. She watched the house for a while, the lights shining like a beacon on the hilltop. She couldn't hear any sounds, but could imagine the talk and laughter. For the first time, she felt like an outsider. Eleani was her grandmother just like Spiros was Nikos's grandfather. She had as much right to be there as he did. Yet no one knew that, and she doubted she'd be welcomed once the facts were revealed.

* * *

Waking early the next morning, Sara debated going swimming. With only one ship tied up, surely the water would be clean enough near the dock. Going around to the beach might be risky. She dressed in her swimsuit, pulled on shorts and a shirt and went topside to determine if she dare risk it.

"I was hoping you'd get up early," Nikos said when she stepped out on the aft deck.

He sat in a chair near the rail, relaxed and wearing swim togs and a shirt.

"Want to go for a swim before breakfast?"

"Is the water clean enough here?" she asked. Had he been waiting for her?

"Sure, but I was thinking of a cove around the lee side of the island. It's sheltered and has very colorful fish. We could snorkel until hunger drives us back."

"Sounds great."

He motioned her to the side and pointed down at a small runabout tied to the dock. "I had one of the men pull it out of the boathouse. Perfect for putting around the island."

Sara was soon riding in the small boat, watching Nikos as he skillfully maneuvered it around the yacht and, keeping close to shore, began to go around the island. The sun was just above the horizon, not yet as burning hot as it would become later. The air was soft against her skin as they skimmed across the water.

When he turned into a small cove, Sara looked around with interest. Foliage grew to the water's edge on most of the horseshoe-shaped cove, flowers blossomed in profusion. The tiny sandy beach, almost in the center of the cove, was pristine.

The water was crystal clear. She could see every aspect of the sandy bottom and the colorful fish that swam lazily around when the boat stopped and was carried forward by momentum. He lowered an anchor and soon they were stopped.

Nikos pulled snorkeling gear from the small locker. Sara took off her shirt and shorts and accepted the mask and breathing tube. Donning the mask and flippers, she stepped off the boat into the silken water. It was cooler than a bath, but not cold like the water off the English shore.

They swam for more than an hour, Nikos leading the way and pointing out things as they went. When they kept still, fish would swim within touching distance. A kick of a flipper would send them darting away.

Breaking the surface at last, Sara pushed her mask up on top of her head and shook off some of the water. Nikos surfaced beside her.

"This is a wonderful spot," she said, treading water.

"My favorite on the island."

"Can you get to it over land?" she asked, studying the unending greenery that lined the shore.

"There's a path, if it hasn't gotten overgrown. But it's easier and cooler to come by boat."

"Time for me to head back for breakfast?"

He glanced at his waterproof watch. "The kitchen staff will have it set out by now. We can eat on the terrace. I told the captain you were not going to cook this morning and that they should avail themselves of the house's breakfast buffet."

She nodded, suddenly aware that she and Nikos were in a similar situation to one before—when he'd kissed her in the sea. She felt anticipation rise with nerves and tension. Would he kiss her again?

Not wanting to tempt fate, she turned and began to swim to the boat. Nikos passed her and reached the craft first. He drew himself up and over the side with his strong arms, then turned to offer a hand to Sara, easily pulling her from the water in one swoop.

She stumbled a bit on the rocking boat and fell against Nikos. His skin was cool from the water, but warmed instantly where she pushed against him. Sara felt the water dripping down her back from her wet hair, felt the heat rise between them and wondered whimsically if there was steam evident from the heat she generated. But she would not be accused of flirting.

Had the trip been her subconscious at work? She loved the feel of the man, the energy and desire he evoked while kissing her. Just being near him was extraordinary. But she never wanted him to suspect. How horrible if he thought she came swimming just so they would end up kissing.

So much for her resistance. He followed her and drew her into his arms. Despite her own thoughts only seconds ago, she didn't resist. When his mouth covered hers, she put her arms around him. Dimly aware she was being reckless, she didn't let that stop her. She'd tried; her resistance wasn't strong enough. There would be little likelihood of Nikos giving her the time of day after she revealed who she was and that she'd deliberately sought out a position at his resort in hopes of gaining access to the island. But until then, she wished every moment to be as special as this one.

He broke away a few moments later, resting his forehead against hers and staring into her eyes. "Hungry?"

For you, was the unbidden thought that popped into her mind. But she knew he meant food. "Yes. A bit."

"Time for a quick shower before breakfast," he said, stowing their gear and pulling in the small anchor. Once under way, Sara felt cool as the water evaporated from her skin. And itchy from the salt. She glanced at Nikos as he handled the boat with assurance. She didn't get it. The more she was around him, the more he puzzled her. The scuttlebutt from the ship was that he was on the verge of getting engaged. He so did not act like a man almost committed to one special woman. He said he wasn't engaged, but he'd never said he wouldn't be one day.

From what her mother had told her about the wealthy families of Greece, Nikos didn't fit the mould. Granted, if he proceeded with a business marriage, it would be similar to her mother's situation. Yet the antagonism she expected against such a man and arrangement vanished. For a few moments she wished she had the chance of an arranged marriage—if the groom was Nikos.

"So we all eat up at the house this morning?" she asked.

He nodded. "It's buffet style, to allow for different times people wish to eat. Lunch will be at one and dinner at seven. But breakfast is from eight until ten."

"Sounds like a hotel," she commented, wondering how many people were around to need such a big window of time for the first meal.

He shrugged.

"Your grandparents are well?" she asked a few minutes later. So far she wasn't sure how to proceed. She couldn't just march in and demand her grandmother's presence.

"In top form. Today I'm going with my grandfather to see the new boat he's buying. To appease my father."

"Why can't your father check it out?" Sara asked. If Nikos's father was so concerned, shouldn't he be the one here?

"Business before family," Nikos said. He chuckled mirthlessly. "Speaking of which, much as I have deplored my father's focus on business, I find I follow in his path. With my absence from the resort last week for the cruise and now being here for a few days, I'm going to have to work when I return from the boat shopping expedition."

"On the *Cassandra*?" she asked.

"I have an office in the main house that ties directly into the one at the resort."

Sara thought he worked hard enough, but didn't feel she could offer that observation. She wondered if she dared explore the grounds while he was tied up. And if her grandmother just happened to be in the garden, wouldn't a meeting be completely acceptable?

Sara showered quickly, towel dried her hair and pulled it back. Before she left her cabin, she pulled the letter from her bag and folded it over, tucking it in one of the pockets of her shorts. Just in case.

Breakfast was on the terrace that overlooked the sea. Sara suspected every terrace around the mansion overlooked some portion of the sea, since the island wasn't that large. Two of the crew were talking as they drank coffee. Their empty plates showed they'd already enjoyed a large breakfast.

The buffet would do the resort proud. Silver chafing dishes gleamed in the sunshine. Eggs, bacon, sausage, breads, sweet rolls and fresh fruit lined up ready to tempt everyone who walked by. Fragrant coffee brewed at the edge of the buffet table. Sara piled her plate high. Swimming before breakfast gave her a big appetite.

"Do enjoy the chef's offerings. He gets very annoyed with guests who nibble at a token amount and then leave most of it on their plates," Nikos said as he stepped behind her and began placing food on his own plate.

Sara glanced at him in surprise. Looking around the terrace, she saw only members of the crew and the members of the household staff she'd met. Should he be eating with them?

"I can sympathize. Don't worry, I like food. The eggs look light and fluffy even after steaming in the chafing dish for a while. And the fruit is icy cold. You're fortunate in your chef."

"I know that and he knows that. Luckily he and my grandfather came to an agreement that makes them both happy, so there is no fear he'd leave for a better post."

"Wise man, your grandfather. A truly gifted chef is in high demand."

"And you, are you in high demand?" he asked as they moved along the buffet.

"I'm getting there. Every job I've had is moving me along. One day I'd like to be able to set my own salary. And pick exactly where I'd like to work."

"And that would be?" he asked, gesturing to an empty table near the edge of the terrace, an umbrella tilted to shade it from the early sun.

"I used to think London. Now, maybe the Greek Isles," she said with a smile. "Or a ship that sails the world."

"It's nice to see the world. I enjoyed my two years in the United States and the various hotels and resorts I visited on my summer school holidays."

Nikos watched as Sara began to eat. Her comment about settling in the Greek islands had surprised him. And instantly had him raising barriers. She'd never tried to coax him into giving her something she wanted. Even a job recommendation. Nor had she ever flirted. She was totally unlike the other women he knew. Yet once she'd made that comment, he felt as if the balance between them had shifted. She worked for him. He was merely enjoying swimming and snorkeling with someone with similar interests.

If she thought staying would allow for more involvement, she was mistaken.

Yet the thought of her leaving also filled him with disquiet. Sara was refreshing to be around. She was totally content with her own accomplishments and goals. She didn't try to pretend she was anyone else.

He'd surprised his grandparents last night when he'd mentioned one of his crew was interested in diving and he planned to spend some time enjoying that activity.

They didn't say anything, but Eleani had smiled and suggested he have her come to meet them. His grandfather had echoed that, saying he wanted to meet the newest member of the *Cassandra*'s crew. He already knew all the others.

It was one thing to enjoy diving with Sara and another to give rise to any speculation on her part that he was looking for more. He'd made it as clear as possible he was not in the marriage field. He knew she'd heard about Gina and his tentative plans. As long as she knew the rules, she'd have no reason to expect more from him than he could deliver.

That wasn't why he'd brought her to the island.

He didn't wish to examine too closely exactly why he had. He only knew the more he grew to know her, the more she intrigued him.

He stood when she rose and watched as she left the terrace and headed back to the ship. For the first time ever, Nikos regretted having the strong sense of duty he'd had ground into him. He'd much rather go after Sara, pack a picnic lunch and return to the cove—just the two of them.

Duty called, however.

Once he'd finished his coffee, he went to his office, called his assistant and became engrossed in the daily challenge of running a world-class resort. When his grandfather was ready, they'd go check out the boat he was interested in buying.

* * *

Sara watched the clock. She'd been told lunch would be at one and hoped Nikos would take a break to eat when she did. The yacht's galley had been designed by a professional. She had no trouble inventorying supplies, especially the spices and herbs. They were an important part of any dish, so it was crucial these were kept fresh and fragrant. She made a list of ones that needed to be replaced. The rest of the staples were sufficient for the next few meals she'd planned. Had they been departing on a cruise, she would have shopping to do. By the time that happened again, Nikos's regular chef would be recovered and ready to return to work.

She sat on the high stool at the counter and gazed out the porthole. Would she like being a chef for one family? She thought of the captain and his years of service for the Konstantinos family. She enjoyed working in different environments, but the benefits and security of a long-term assignment like he had did hold a certain appeal.

Especially if she ever married.

She began to think again of home. Once back, she'd try to find a position that would offer career potential. She'd have the lovely memories of her Aegean adventure to remember— especially how a dynamic Greek millionaire had kissed her in the warm waters of the sea.

Stefano stepped inside. "We're going up to the house for luncheon."

Sara smiled and hopped off the stool. "I'm more than ready. I can't believe after the humongous breakfast I ate that I'm hungry again, but I am. And I want to see what Dimitri has done this time."

"One chef taking ideas from another?" he joked.

"Only with permission. I am learning more and more about Greek food. My mother was not much of a cook, so we were limited in what we ate. Now I'm having such fun discovering new recipes and taste sensations."

As Sara approached the big house, her anticipation grew. Would Nikos share his meal with her again? Or was breakfast the only meal he'd have until dinner? She knew he had enjoyed all the meals she'd prepared for him and his guests on the cruise, but did he keep different hours when he wasn't entertaining guests?

The lower terrace was again set with two large tables and a long buffet table near the house. The grapevines winding around the arbor provided shade from the noontime sun. The table where she'd shared breakfast with Nikos looked forlorn when the other tables were obviously set for the meal.

The higher terrace was set with one small table. A silver-haired man sat watching the group as Sara and the others approached the lower terrace. The captain waved in greeting and the man nodded in reply.

Sara knew that was Spiros Konstantinos, Nikos's grandfather. She wished they were closer so she could get a better look. Then she was distracted by the greetings of the household staff.

Sara sat between Stefano and Ari. The captain sat at the head of their table. A silver-haired butler sat at the head of the table where the household staff sat. He could also see the family's terrace and how the waiter was doing there.

From her vantage point, Sara could barely see the table on the other terrace. There were flowers growing in large containers, softening the angles of the house, almost enclosing the terrace. A large trellis shaded that terrace, as well, thick with grapevines offering a green canopy overhead.

She could smell the delicious aromas from the buffet table and glanced around. No one was serving themselves yet.

"We wait for Mr. Konstantinos to be first," Stefano said, leaning close. "Once the family has been served, we are free to enjoy ourselves."

Nikos came out onto the terrace then, escorting an older woman. Sara felt her breath catch as she knew she was looking at her grandmother for the first time.

The woman was as tall as Sara, slender and walked with a regal bearing. Her hair was dark, threaded through with silver. She smiled and waved at the crew and staff, then greeted her husband. Nikos pulled back the chair to seat her, then took a seat to his grandfather's right.

Nikos glanced around and looked at Sara. She felt the connection almost like a touch. A second later he turned slightly toward her grandmother, obviously in response to a question the woman posed.

The Konstantinoses were soon served their meal, and the staff then was free to partake of the lavish buffet the chef had created. She loved the spinach, feta cheese and walnut salad that she'd had before. In one of the hot chafing dishes was fresh lamb, grilled to perfection. In another a chicken dish. Another held fish. Sara sampled everything. She had to ask if the chef would share some of his recipes. The food was delicious.

As before, she ate quietly, listening to the conversation flow around her. She knew most of the staff had worked together for years, and she was definitely the newest member.

Lunch was followed by freshly brewed coffee and tea. Sara sipped some of the sweet tea that smelled so much like passion flower. She missed being on the aft deck of the boat, bobbing gently in the water. But this was the next best thing. She'd have to remember every detail to share with Stacy and her other friends.

Nikos approached their table when the meal was over. Several people looked up in surprise. Stefano jumped to his feet.

"Do you need something, sir?" he asked.

"No. Finish your coffee. My grandfather wishes to meet the newest member of the crew," he said.

Sara nodded slowly and rose. She felt odd ever since seeing her grandmother for the first time. Now Nikos was inviting her to meet her—unbelievable. Should she take advantage of this opportunity and give Eleani the letter? Or wait and hope for a more private moment? The envelope suddenly felt as if it was bulging out her pocket.

"Should I be meeting them at the luncheon table? Not the office? Is that proper?" she asked softly.

Nikos laughed. "Entirely proper. We'll talk diving and boats and maybe you can offer some insights to my grandfather about my resort, which he and my father think is a waste of time when I could be working in shipping."

"You love the resort," she said without thinking.

"I do. And I find the stringent regulations and many requirements necessary in shipping to be very dull. But my grandfather and father are convinced one day I'll get my priorities straight and quit the resort."

"I can't ever see that happening." How could they be talking about such mundane topics when she was about to meet her grandmother for the first time?

As they approached the table on the upper terrace, Sara had eyes only for the woman seated there. As they drew closer, she searched for any resemblance to her mother, but found little. Maybe in the way she held her head. In her eyes? Her mother should have been the one walking across the terrace. How could this gentle-looking woman have been so hard-hearted as to reject her only child?

"Grandfather, this is Sara. Temporary chef aboard the *Cassandra*. Sara, Spiros Konstantinos, my grandfather, and Eleani, my grandmother."

"How do you do?" Sara said, remembering to smile at the older man. Her muscles felt strained. Now that she was face-to-face with her grandmother, she wanted to dash away.

"Do sit with us. It's lovely for Nikos to find someone to join him on his diving forays. It's too dangerous to dive alone. I'm afraid my diving days are behind me. Though I do love a nice paddle in the sea," Eleani said, smiling.

Nikos held the chair for Sara, who was glad to sit down. Her knees felt definitely wobbly.

"Who doesn't like swimming in the sea?" Spiros Konstantinos asked. "Where are you from, Sara?"

"I've been working at the resort in Thessalonika. When the chef on the *Cassandra* got sick, I was tapped as his replacement."

Spiros looked at Nikos. "Interesting. How did you know she liked to dive? Was it something you asked the chief chef to check into?"

Nikos leaned back in his chair, completely at ease. Sara thought she'd shatter if anyone touched her, every nerve in her body was so keyed up. She looked at her grandmother again. So close. Should she hand her the letter?

"She likes the sea. We went swimming and I asked if she'd like to try diving. She takes to it like a natural. And no, I had no inkling of that before we sailed."

"Nothing very deep yet, though," she said, wanting to make a contribution to the conversation and not sit like a star-struck groupie doing nothing but stare at Eleani. "I love it. Seeing the colorful fish, the contour of the bottom of the sea—it's all so different from swimming on the surface."

"Has Nikos taken you around to the cove?" Eleani asked.

"We went snorkeling for a while this morning. Maybe tomorrow we'll dive," he said.

Sara wondered when she and Eleani would ever have a moment alone. That's all she would need.

"Sounds like a good plan. Have you and Spiros settled on the boat?" Eleani asked Nikos.

"Nikos thinks it's fine," Spiros answered testily.

"And is not putting up roadblocks like Andrus?" she asked with a fond smile at her husband.

"He has more sense than that." Spiros glared at his grandson as if challenging him to deny the statement.

Nikos laughed softly. "You say that because I'm agreeing with you."

Spiros nodded, his eyes suddenly twinkling as he studied Sara. "I think you and your diving friend should spend the afternoon exploring the coves. Maybe tonight you can take her to Patricia."

"Spiros," Eleani said. "Nikos has made plans." She gave him a very meaningful look.

"Actually, I've put some plans on hold," Nikos said. He looked at Sara. "Would you like to go to dinner at a favorite spot of mine on the nearby island?" he asked her.

"I never turn down a chance to try new places," she said. If his grandparents didn't find it odd he'd invite her out, she wouldn't refuse. "Good Greek food?"

"The best," he replied.

There was a small sound from Eleani. Everyone looked at her. She stared at Sara.

"For a moment you reminded me of someone," she said slowly.

Sara wondered if it was her mother Eleani had seen. She

glanced at Spiros and Nikos. They didn't seem to find anything suspicious.

"I understand you're buying a new boat. To get to Patricia," Sara said to Spiros, hoping to distract Eleani from further speculation.

"I'll finalize the deal soon. Nikos tested it, checked the specs and said it looked fine to him. The captain of the *Cassandra* has vetted it as well. I take delivery soon. Are you a boating enthusiast?"

"Actually my first time on a large boat was when I started working on the *Cassandra*. I enjoyed the cruise very much. It was a bit tricky at first, learning how to prepare meals when the floor beneath my feet didn't remain level and still."

"Try preparing food in a gale," Eleani said with a smile. "Remember that trip to Sardinia, Spiros, when it was so stormy, and then Paul got seasick and I tried to prepare a simple meal? We ended up eating cheese and bread and drinking wine from a coffee cup with a lid so it wouldn't splash everywhere."

"We made it through and with perhaps a better understanding of the travails of our cook," he said with a fond look at his wife.

The conversation stayed on extraordinary experiences on boats over the years. Sara laughed at some of the stories, and her eyes widened a time or two when the outcome could have been drastically different. She was charmed by Spiros Konstantinos. And she was puzzled by her grandmother. She didn't seem the kind of woman her mother had made her out to be. Eleani came across as a warm and loving woman. She obviously adored her husband and was fond of Nikos. This played so differently from Sara's expectation. Where was the hard-hearted woman she'd thought to find?

The letter burned against Sara's leg. For a moment she considered standing, handing it to Eleani and returning to the yacht. Something held her back. It would be better to be alone with the woman, not have her surrounded by the men of her family.

Nikos glanced at his watch. "I hate to break this up, but I have an important call coming in about five minutes."

Sara stood up. "It was nice meeting you both," she said. If they only knew.

"I'll be down at the ship by six," Nikos said, also standing.

She nodded and walked away, longing to turn and question her grandmother without delay.

But, selfishly, she wanted an evening with Nikos. That would really be a date. She might as well make her last day at the island memorable.

It was shortly before six when Nikos boarded the *Cassandra*. He'd worked straight through after leaving the lunch table.

He looked forward to showing Sara the neighboring island of Patricia. While not large, it was considerably larger than the family one. The main center had many shops and cafés. The seaside town still had a definite charm that appealed to visitors. And the food was excellent. They'd take the runabout. No need to take the yacht.

He checked the galley on the way to the aft deck. It was pristine but empty. Stepping out on the deck, Nikos hoped she was there. He didn't want to have to figure out which cabin was hers.

Sara sat in the shade, reading. Two of the crew were also on the deck, one sleeping in a chaise, the other with a fishing line tossed over the side of the yacht. For a second Nikos wondered what he'd do if he caught a fish. Who was going to prepare it if the chef was dining on Patricia that evening?

Sara looked up. "Hi." She wore the same dress she'd worn when they'd dined in the salon. He hadn't thought about it, but she'd hardly had time to pack another since she didn't leave the ship during the few hours they had at the resort.

The fishing crewman turned to see who she was talking to. Seeing Nikos, he started to get up, but Nikos shook his head.

"Ready?" he asked Sara.

"Yes," she said, rising swiftly.

In less than ten minutes they were in the runabout heading around a point of the island. When they reached the open water, the wind kicked up. Nikos looked at her.

"Not too much?"

"It's wonderful," she said, raising her face to the setting sun. "Business satisfactorily completed for the day?" she asked. Nikos loved the way the wind blew her hair back. He remembered the silky feel and couldn't wait to touch it again. Concentrating on driving the boat, he tried to ignore the rising desire for Sara.

"Yes. The evening is mine."

"Your family island is lovely. You're lucky to have such a place to visit. Will it be yours one day?"

He glanced at her and nodded. "But not for a long time, I hope."

"So you need to get married and have children to leave it to," she commented, her eyes shut.

Who would he pass it on to? The thought surprised him. For the first time he thought about the future in terms of family. His grandfather was growing old. Already in his eighties, he wouldn't be around forever. There were few bonds as strong as those between Spiros and Nikos. He had never felt the same love from his own father. When Spiros died, it would leave a huge gap in Nikos's life.

And what would fill that gap? Work at the resort? To what end?

After the cruise, he wasn't sure he was ready to ask Gina to be his wife. He wasn't looking for the love his grandfather had found twice. Some men were luckier than others.

But he realized he had no one to teach to dive, to share the beauties beneath the sea with—except friends. No child to instill with family history and to leave his life's work to. What happened when he grew older?

His grandfather was proud of Nikos's accomplishments. He knew his father respected what he'd accomplished, even if it wasn't in shipping. But he wanted more than respect. Nikos realized he wanted love. He'd thought he'd found it with Ariana, only to be shown how false that had been.

Could he find it elsewhere? Did it even exist?

"Thank you for bringing me today. It's another memory to add to my Aegean summer memories," she said.

Summer memories. Nikos had a few special ones himself. Was that what Sara thought of this, a memory of a summer spent in Greece? Would she really return to London after a while? He expected her to resume her job at the resort when Paul was well enough to rejoin the *Cassandra*. Would she stay a year, maybe two or three and then return home?

He wasn't sure he wanted Sara to leave.

CHAPTER EIGHT

SARA loved Patricia. From the first moment she stepped from the dock area onto the old cobblestone streets she was enchanted. White buildings almost touching, red tiled roofs peaked, flowers everywhere, it was a dazzling town. The sidewalks were narrow, scarcely giving room for them to walk side by side. Twice when they met others, Nikos pulled her close with an arm around her shoulders, to allow the others to pass.

"I want to see everything," she exclaimed.

"Fortunately, that won't take long. It's a small town," Nikos replied.

He steered her to the town square where the old church dominated one side. The other sides were crowded with shops and small cafés. Sara was tempted to stop at one of the tavernas for a drink but didn't want to spend the time sitting when there was more to see before it got dark.

"Come, I think you'll like this one," he said as they rambled around the old square. Entering one of the specialty shops, Sara stood transfixed for a moment. It appeared the shop had all the spices in the world. She drew a deep breath, savoring all the different aromas she could detect.

"Wow, I could spend an entire day here!" She began

walking up one aisle and down another, stopping from time to time to sniff a special spice or herb. Gathering small bottles of different spices as she walked, she glanced at Nikos from time to time, worried he'd be bored and anxious to leave.

He patiently walked beside her, looking around with interest.

"This will have to do," she said, her hands full of small bottles. "I can't wait to use them in special dishes. Fresh spices and herbs make all the difference."

Nikos insisted on carrying the shopping bag when they left.

"I called for reservations at seven," he said. "We don't want to be too late returning to the island. Another shop or two, then we must head for the restaurant."

"I'm ready now if you want to head that way," she said. "Tomorrow maybe I can try a dish or two with the spices. Do you think Dimitri would let me use his kitchen?"

"Yes. As long as you let him assist. He's always looking for new food to please my grandfather."

"Then I'll ask him. I can't wait."

They walked along the sidewalk, gazing into the windows, stopping once or twice to discuss something they saw.

As they approached the restaurant, Sara was struck with how ordinary it looked. She'd expected a man like Nikos to go for an upscale place like the restaurants at his resort. This looked homey and friendly—almost like a family place.

Which it proved to be when they entered.

Instead of some elegant, quiet, dignified restaurant, this one was huge, boisterous and loud. Families and couples vied for room at the many trestle-style tables. The food was served family style—huge bowls and platters set in the midst of every table from which customers helped themselves.

They squeezed into a spot near the door and introductions were hastily made, first names only. Two of the men at the table knew Nikos and asked after Spiros. The conversation was lively, the food plain but marvelous. Sara ate her fill in record time. The lamb was tender and flavorful. The vegetables were prepared exactly as she enjoyed. And the crusty Greek bread was delicious. The wine was plentiful, as well, poured from a pitcher.

"Nothing pretentious here," she murmured at one point.

"No. Do you mind?" Nikos asked, leaning closer to better hear her.

"I'm having the time of my life. This is great." She almost had to shout to be heard, but she didn't mind. The lively atmosphere was infectious. She wasn't sure why his grandfather had urged him to bring her to Patricia, but she was glad they'd come. This was the kind of gathering she and her mother had attended in London whenever there was a celebration. She almost expected to look around and see her mother or one of her friends.

At nine, several musicians filed onto the small raised platform at the back of the large room and began to play. Immediately couples left the tables for the dance floor to join in the traditional Greek dances. Sara was enchanted. "I didn't expect this," she said.

"It's a local place, not for tourists. Do you dance?"

"Some. We had lots of Greek friends in London. Our parents made very sure none of us forgot our heritage. This is a kind of line dance, right?"

"Right. After this comes a *ballos*, a couples' dance."

"Ah." She looked at him with a challenge. "So you do that one?"

"We do," he said, holding her gaze.

Sara could feel the anticipation rise as she stared back. The *ballos* was a romantic dance—definitely for couples. Had he danced it with Gina? Being Italian, she probably did not know the traditional Greek dances. Whereas Sara, on the other hand, had been schooled well.

She tore her gaze away and looked at the dancers on the floor. The music made her blood pound—or was it the proximity of Nikos Konstantinos?

When the next dance began, the crowd greeted the music with a roar of approval. Sara clapped her hands and rose when Nikos did, pleased to show him she knew as much about their heritage as someone raised in Greece.

The dance was fast and fun. It followed the age-old romance tradition—flirtatious and sassy. Definitely masculine versus feminine role playing. As they whirled and stamped and came together, then parted, Sara laughed in sheer joy. She had loved going to celebrations in the neighborhood. The expatriate Greek community in London had been closely knit. Engagements, weddings, christenings and funerals had brought the entire community together. Of course, there was no dancing at funerals, but other causes to celebrate were embraced with enthusiasm and traditional music and dance.

When the dance ended, the musicians moved on to another, this one a traditional line dance, with one of the older men from town leading. She and Nikos laughed, danced and shared in the delight of the night.

It was late when Nikos said it was time to leave. Sara was tired but buoyed up by the exuberant dancing and the friendly locals who had included her as if she'd been born there. Being with Nikos had a lot to do with it, she was sure. They still had the boat ride back to the island.

The moon had risen, a silvery crescent high in the sky. Once on the boat and heading away from Patricia into the night, Sara glanced around, not seeing anything but stars, moon and sea. She hoped Nikos knew where they were going.

He piloted the craft with confidence. She was content to sit back and remember the evening's frivolity. She glanced at Nikos. This was a side of him she'd never expected—steeped in tradition, reveling in neighbors and casual dining. And dancing with the best of them.

"I could tell you enjoyed yourself," he said, once they were on the open sea.

"It was great fun. I hadn't expected dancing."

"And I didn't expect you knew our dances."

"Why not? I'm as Greek as you. Of course I know them. And more."

"Usually we learn them as children."

"As did I," she said, remembering some of the events she and her mother had attended. Then an old memory flashed into her mind. They'd been at a wedding of a friend of her mother's. When almost the entire group of guests rose to dance, her mother had looked sad, commenting that no one had danced at her wedding.

Sara gazed across the sea. How much had her mother missed by her impetuous marriage? If her parents had helped her instead of repudiating her, would she have found happiness with another man and married him? She could have had more children, followed a traditional Greek woman's life. Maybe not lived any longer, but she would have been happier.

"I've dated Greek women who don't know the dances," Nikos said.

She shrugged. Her happiness had faded as she thought about Nikos seeing other women. Yet what would she expect, that he was celibate? He was too dynamic and involved with life not to date and enjoy the companionship of others. It wasn't as if she had any special claim.

* * *

Nikos guided the boat by rote. He'd traveled from Patricia to the island many times and could probably find his way home blindfolded. He felt wide-awake after the dancing. Sara's expertise had surprised him. Ariana had not enjoyed dancing—at least not their traditional Greek dances, which were fast and strenuous. She had preferred going to modern nightclubs.

He no longer cared about Ariana. She'd made sure of that when he'd discovered her lies. Any feelings he'd felt for her had shattered. Trust was too fragile to repair once it had been broken. So why did he use her to compare other women to? As a reminder of treachery and betrayal? Or as a barrier against falling for someone else? Love made a man foolish. He was beyond that time of his youth, though seeing his grandparents again had him wishing for more in life than the suitable marriage to someone like Gina Fregulia. Was he in danger of changing his views on marriage?

He glanced at Sara. She seemed pensive.

"What are you thinking?" he asked. He expected tiredness, but at least a happier face as she remembered the evening.

"Sad thoughts," she said, turning toward him. The faint light from the control panel didn't illuminate her face at this angle. She was in shadow, with only the light of the moon showing her silhouette.

"After the dancing we did? Impossible." Unless she regretted the evening coming to an end. He did. He could dance with Sara all night.

"I was thinking of one of the wedding festivities we attended when I was younger. My mother had almost cried when she spoke of no one dancing at her wedding."

"Didn't she have a traditional Greek wedding?"

Sara shook her head. Nikos wondered why she hadn't.

Sara didn't speak much about her family. Only to say that her father had left them when she was very young and her mother had died last year. What had it been like growing up in London? She spoke perfect Greek, knew their dances, the food. Obviously, her mother had wanted to maintain the connection. Yet she had no other relatives. Why had her parents moved to England? Why not stay in Greece and forge ties with neighbors to aid the small family?

Sara had started out intriguing him. The more time they spent together, the more she fascinated him. It wasn't only the physical attraction, though he enjoyed kissing her, touching her, feeling her warmth against him. He wouldn't mind a closer connection, but she'd never given any sign she'd be interested.

Except for her kisses. Maybe he should push the issue and see where they went.

She was unlike most of the women he associated with. She reminded him a little of Eleani—Sara was warm and friendly and kind. Maybe that was what set her apart. She was kinder than Ariana had been, that was certain. Gina last week had been catty in some of her remarks. He never remembered Sara saying anything unkind.

They arrived at the dock with no problem. He tied the lines to the cleats and helped Sara from the boat. They walked silently to the gangway for the yacht. He escorted her up and stopped on the forward deck.

"I'll say good-night."

"Thank you for dinner and the evening. I had a wonderful time," she said politely.

"Everyone is probably asleep, but I feel as if we are on display. Who knows who can be watching," he said, leaning over and brushing his lips against hers.

He turned her around and gave her a gentle push. "Go to bed, Sara. I'll see you tomorrow."

He turned and left the yacht, wishing the evening could have ended with Sara in his bed. The thought surprised him. He wasn't thinking just tonight, either. What would it be like to wake up with her each morning? Spend time together when he wasn't working? She liked to dive, to swim. She was a terrific dancer. And she cooked like a dream. What was not to like about Sara Andropolous?

As he walked up to the house, he idly considered a life with a woman like Sara. He knew love existed. Spiros had loved his first wife and was devoted to his second. A man could learn a lot about marriage studying his grandfather.

Intellectually Nikos understood people could fall in love and share their lives happily and with true contentment. He'd asked Ariana to marry him thinking they'd have the perfect modern marriage—similar interests and friends that would enable them to have the kind of life both enjoyed. He had loved her only to be disillusioned with her betrayal.

She had wanted more than his love—more men and more money. Would things have been different had he already achieved the success he now enjoyed? No—love would overlook finances. She had not loved him, not the way he wanted.

Reaching the house, Nikos turned and looked at the yacht, almost invisible against the dark sea. For a moment he debated returning, going to her cabin, asking her to stay a while longer. Common sense took over. If she was amenable, she would be as keen tomorrow as tonight. And if she shot down the idea, he'd rather it be later.

The next morning Nikos rose early and went for a morning swim at the beach. The sand was being raked by one of the groundskeepers. The yacht showed no activity. He dropped his towel, pulled off his shirt and plunged into the sea. The water felt cool and invigorating.

He swam some distance out and then floated for a little while. Hearing splashing, he looked at the shore. Sara was swimming out toward him, still some distance away.

Treading water as she approached, he ignored the feeling of satisfaction that blossomed. Her coming out this morning had to mean she enjoyed the early-morning swims as much as he did.

"Hi," she said a moment later. She shook her head and water drops splayed all around.

"I thought you'd sleep in," he commented. She was beautiful in the soft morning light, even with her hair wet and hanging around her face. Her eyes sparkled with enjoyment.

"Couldn't sleep in. Not in the habit. With no meals to plan or prepare, I have a lot of time on my hands. Maybe I should return to the resort. I'm sure not earning my salary here."

"Aren't you enjoying being here?"

"Too much. I'll get spoiled," she said with a grin.

He wanted to spoil her, give her jewels and dresses and make sure she never lacked for anything.

"Except before I do return, I want a couple of recipes from Dimitri. That salad the other day was delicious. I figured out all the ingredients except one. Which is the one that makes it so special. Do you think he'll share?"

"I expect so. If not, tell him I said he should."

She laughed. "If he does not wish to share, I certainly wouldn't threaten him with you."

"Why not?" The more he knew her, the more she puzzled him. Wasn't that the way of the world? Get what you want no matter how it's accomplished?

Ariana would have used every bit of power she had to

obtain her own ends. He looked away. He must stop comparing Ariana to every other woman he met. Sara was nothing like her. End of comparison.

"You're up as early as I," she said, lazily dog-paddling around. "Why not take advantage of this brief holiday and sleep in?"

"Feels too much like I'm sleeping the day away."

"What do you have to do today?" she asked.

"Work, what else."

She splashed water on him. "Play is what else," she said before diving beneath the water before he could retaliate by splashing her.

The chase was on. Nikos knew he was the stronger swimmer, but he let her get ahead before giving chase. When he tagged her, she came to the surface and laughed.

"You need to watch that laughter," he warned, coming closer. "You're going to drown one day if you're not careful."

She laughed again and nodded. "I'll try not to laugh underwater. Now I'm it." And she surged toward him. He'd been expecting it and swam to one side, diving deep and moving parallel to the shore.

They played until both were breathless. Then Nikos took her hand and drew her closer.

"I didn't get a proper good-night kiss last night."

"No one was awake on the yacht," she said, entwining her legs with his, encircling his neck with her arms, pressing against the length of him.

"It felt like prying eyes were watching from every porthole."

He felt her laughter as she kissed his jaw.

"So?"

"So I don't want to put a burden on you by being seen with me."

"Everyone on board knows your grandparents asked to

meet me. What's to know? It's not as if we have a torrid affair going."

"It's not as if I don't want one," he said.

Her start of surprise showed him she'd never considered it. Damn. Surely she didn't think he kissed every woman he knew like he kissed her.

Maybe he should show her what they could have together.

He pulled her close and kissed her with all the pent-up desire that consumed him. She kissed him back, her mouth sweet and hot, her arms holding him closer as the kiss went on until he forgot where they were. The water closing over their heads was unexpected. Breaking the kiss, he kicked up and when they bobbed to the surface, he released her.

"You're too dangerous in the water," he said. He released her and began swimming toward the shore.

Sara swam beside him.

"So?" he asked when their feet touched bottom and they walked the short distance to shore. He saw her towel beside his on the pristine beach. The groundskeeper had left. They were alone.

"So what? Breakfast? I'm starving, how about you? I'll whip something up in the galley just for you," she said.

He ignored her attempt to change the subject. When she picked up her towel, he followed suit, drying his chest as he watched her watch him. "I meant an affair and you know it."

She shook her head sadly. "Sorry, Nikos, I'm not into affairs. Tempting though this would be, I want something special when I marry."

"What if you don't marry?" he asked, annoyed at her statement.

"Don't say that. I want to marry for love and be loved forever. I want kids and ties and a feeling of belonging. If I don't get them, I'll feel life has cheated me. I'm holding out for what I want."

"Until then, we could have fun."

"Sure. What happens if I fall in love with you?"

He stepped back involuntarily. "I told you I'm not looking for love."

"Just a suitable marriage, allying two business families."

"There is something wrong with that?" he asked stiffly.

"Not if that's what you want. But what about love? Don't you think that would make a marriage so much better? Look at your grandparents—they obviously adore each other."

"My parents made a suitable marriage."

"Oh, and from what you've said, that's been a success for the two of them—but not the kind of family I want."

"It works."

"Don't you want more for yourself and your children if you have any?"

He hesitated a moment.

Her comment bothered him—especially in light of his thoughts from yesterday about who he had to leave his life's work to, who was there to share the cove with. Who could he teach to dance the traditional dances?

What would it be like to have children with Sara? She'd spoil them to death. But she'd love them to pieces. And her husband—would she also love him to pieces?

"You have to be the world's biggest idiot," Sara told her reflection after her shower ten minutes later. She still had wet hair, was wrapped in a clean towel and had wiped off the small mirror in the minuscule bathroom adjacent to her cabin. "Looking the way you do, he asked you to have an affair, and you go all high-and-mighty and say no."

She sighed and turned. She could never have taken Nikos up on his suggestion knowing he would find out soon enough who she really was and her reasons for wanting to visit his island. She couldn't add further betrayal to that by becoming intimate with him if she wasn't being totally honest.

She knew he wasn't in love with her, but obviously the attraction she felt was met by his own desire. How fabulous it would be to make love with Nikos. They could find seclusion at the cove, enjoy each other's bodies, then go swimming. She loved to swim, and her newly acquired basic skill in diving. Would she ever get another chance?

Taking a determined breath, she donned her clothes. Not likely after today. She was going to find Eleani and give her the letter. After that, the entire Konstantinos family would likely expect her to swim to the next island to get off this one as soon as possible.

It couldn't be helped. Long before she met Nikos she'd made her mother a promise. She was honor-bound to keep it, no matter what it did to her tentative relationship with Nikos Konstantinos.

Sara prepared a light breakfast. Her nerves were growing taut with the concern about meeting Eleani. Sipping hot tea, she remembered all her mother had told her about her life before running away to marry Sara's father. Nothing could hurt her mother now. Sara could fulfill her last wish and move on.

At ten o'clock, Sara left the yacht and walked up to the gardens surrounding the house. She felt much the way she thought a condemned prisoner must feel. It was fate, nothing more, but she wished she could predict the outcome.

Stepping onto one of the flagstone pathways, she wandered around the gardens. Normally their beauty and tranquillity would prove soothing. Today she only saw opulent luxury that had been denied her mother. The pots of flowers they had sometimes been able to afford for their windowsill had been all her mother had. She'd talked often of the lovely gardens at her childhood home. She would have loved the gardens here on the island.

Turning a corner, she stopped. Eleani Konstantinos sat on a wooden bench in a clearing, gazing at a basket of cut flowers. She looked up and smiled.

"Sara. What a pleasant surprise. Come sit by me. Where is Nikos?"

"Working." She stepped closer, her eyes never leaving Eleani's.

"He works too hard. He gets that from his grandfather and father, I expect. Will you two be going diving later?" She patted the bench beside her in invitation. Slowly Sara walked over and sat on the edge.

"No, I don't believe we'll go diving again," she said slowly. Reaching into her pocket, she pulled out the letter and handed it to the older woman.

"What's this?" Eleani asked, reading her name on the envelope.

"A letter I was asked to deliver," Sara said, watching, noting the faint lines around her grandmother's eyes, the soft tones of her skin, the silver in her hair.

Eleani studied the handwriting for a long moment, then slid her finger beneath the flap and tore open the envelope. She withdrew the two pages. Catching her breath, she began to read.

Sara watched her. She felt the hot sun beating down on her head, but didn't seek shade. The play of emotions across Eleani's face had her wondering exactly what her mother had written. All she'd told Sara was that she had a letter for her mother, for Sara to promise she'd get it to her.

She'd fulfilled her mother's last wish. Sara rose and turned away. She could go home now.

"Wait!" Eleani said. "Sit back down."

Sara turned and looked at her. "I've done what I came to do."

Tears spilled from Eleani's eyes. "My daughter is dead," she said brokenly.

Sara nodded. "She died more than a year ago."

Eleani shook her head, crushing the letter against her breasts. "My baby, my poor, poor baby. How could she die? She was too young to die. Ah, my beautiful Damaris. My precious baby girl," she said, leaning over and sobbing.

Sara was totally taken aback. This was not the reaction she had expected.

Sara looked away. "I'm sorry this is unexpected news."

"Unexpected? I never thought to hear from her again. But at least I had the consolation of knowing she was happy in England. I have missed her every day since she left."

Sara whipped around and stared at her. "She was not happy. My father deserted us weeks after I was born. Mum had no skills for work, she'd been raised as a pampered daughter of a wealthy family. Do you know she scrubbed floors because that was a skill she could quickly acquire? We had the help of friends, handouts, Mum used to call them. They seared her soul. She hated that." But not as much as she hated the thought of returning to her parents' home and admitting she'd been wrong.

"I didn't know," Eleani whispered, "The one time we tried to contact her, she refused. Her father said to leave her to her life. We did the best we could. Now she's gone. I'll never see her again."

Eleani covered her face and cried.

Sara frowned. This was not going the way she thought it would. It distressed her to see anyone so distraught. Awkwardly she patted her shoulder, wishing now that she'd just left the letter on a table to be discovered.

She didn't know how long she sat there, staring across the garden toward the sea, seeing in her mind the small, old apartment she and her mother had shared until Sara had begun earning enough money to help pay for a better place. She saw her mother's looks fade as poor nutrition and the stress of her life wore away her youth and health.

She glanced around the beautifully landscaped setting. The money used for just one season of gardening would have changed her mother's life drastically. She felt numb. She missed her mother. She wasn't sure bringing the letter had been wise, now that the deed was done.

What had her mother written? To take care of Sara? She had said she wanted to make sure her daughter was taken care of.

Sara was a grown woman with an excellent career ahead of her. She didn't need someone to take her in at this stage of her life.

She heard the steps and turned to watch as Nikos stormed toward her.

"What the hell have you done to my grandmother?" he asked in a low growl.

CHAPTER NINE

SARA watched him approach. She could almost feel the waves of suspicion pouring off him.

She rose and faced him. "I was asked to deliver a letter and I did."

"Eleani, what is it?" Nikos asked, sitting beside the woman and drawing her into his arms. He rubbed her back, glaring at Sara.

"What was in the letter?"

"I don't know. It was sealed."

"Who is it from?"

"My mother."

Nikos frowned, saying soothing words to Eleani.

"I'm Sara Andropolous, Eleani's grandchild."

The statement stopped Nikos cold. He stared for a long moment. Giving way to anger, he bit out an epithet. His gentle hands soothed his grandmother.

"I didn't know she had a child, much less a grandchild," he said a minute later.

"My mother ran off to get married when she was eighteen. Her parents cut her off because she chose to find her own husband. I find the entire situation sordid and inexcusable."

He swung back at that. "You find it inexcusable. What about lying and cheating to gain access to my grandparents' home? Wreaking who knows what havoc? I find that inexcusable!"

"I never lied to you nor cheated. I was hired to work in the kitchen at the resort. I used my skill and experience, which would be hard to cheat with. You're the one who allowed me to work on the *Cassandra*. You're the one who insisted I stay on board when you came to your family's island. You are the one who introduced me to them the other day."

"Stop it, both of you. I can hear your voices from the house." Spiros rounded the corner and took in the scene. "Eleani, my love, what is wrong?" He immediately went to his wife. In the confusion of Eleani telling her side and Nikos telling what he knew, Sara spun around to leave.

Guessing her intent, Nikos moved swiftly to her side.

"You can't waltz in here and cause this uproar and think you get to leave without further explanation."

"What further explanation do you need? I gave her the letter. There's nothing more," Sara said, starting to feel again. She wanted to weep, knowing she'd damaged whatever had been building between Nikos and herself. Still, honor had demanded she carry out her mother's last wish. Which she had—at a personal loss. Now she just wanted to leave. She felt nothing but resignation and regret.

Spiros sat beside his wife. Eleani had stopped crying and leaned against him tiredly. His face was set in anger. His eyes flashed when he looked at Sara. Saying nothing, he reached for a handkerchief to dry Eleani's eyes.

"I would like an explanation, young lady," he said sternly.

At that, Eleani looked up and saw Sara and Nikos.

Sara felt a spurt of anger. "Didn't your wife tell you she had a daughter in England? She was my mother. Before she died Mum asked me to deliver a letter to her mother. I've done just that."

"I know about Damaris," Spiros said slowly. "It saddens me to learn she is dead. We had hoped at some time she'd return to Greece to see Eleani."

Sara frowned. This didn't make sense.

"She couldn't come home. Her parents had told her if she left she would not be welcome to return," she said. "How could you? She was a teenager, sheltered and protected. Her one fling ended disastrously, but did her parents come to her aid? Did they forgive a youthful indiscretion and take her back home to help? No! Her father said he would disown her. How true that was."

"It wasn't like that," Eleani said sadly. She struggled to sit up.

"Now you wait until your mother is dead and come to disturb my wife?" Spiros asked.

"My mother asked only that I deliver a letter she wrote to her mother. I never knew the details of the letter. I do know she refused to return home until she was too sick to make the trip. As soon as I can get off this island, I plan to get as far away from here as I can. I'm sorry to have been the cause of such upset."

Eleani began crying again. "Don't go," she said forlornly.

"Where would you go?" Spiros asked.

"London, where I belong. Away from people like all of you."

Nikos made a sound of surprise. "People like us?"

"Uncaring, unfeeling, sanctimonious rich people who only want things to go their own way and never mind family members who don't fit in with the path you decide they should take. Like my mother. Like you yourself, Nikos."

Spiros turned in surprised to look at his grandson. "What has Nikos to do with this?"

"You and his father pressured him to join the family shipping firm. Pressured him for marriage with a 'suitable' woman—translated to mean 'equally wealthy'. What about what he wants?"

Nikos shrugged when his grandfather looked at him.

Sara wasn't finished. "Instead of following your dictates he made his own way. Do you ever really see what he's done? Ever give him praise for fighting against the current and still coming out with something marvelous?" she continued, impassioned.

Spiros looked back and forth between Sara and Nikos. "It is true I wished for Nikos to join our shipping firm. But I see now it would have been a mistake. It was hard enough to let go the reins when Andrus took over. Two strong personalities are more than the company can bear. Nikos added to the mixture would have been a mistake. He was wise to go into a field he chose."

"And to have done so well," she added.

Spiros's features softened a fraction. "So you stand up for Nikos?"

"I'm not standing up for anyone but me. I'm stating facts."

"Then listen to this fact," Eleani said. "Damaris ran out on her wedding. We were the ones who had to tell Alexis she wasn't coming. We had to face our friends, business acquaintances, family and say our daughter had shamed us in front of everyone. She ignored all we had done for her and ran off with an irresponsible man who wanted access to our money. Your grandfather was heartsick. It pained him greatly, and he refused to have any more to do with her while she was with your father. But had she left him, we would have welcomed her home—despite the shame she brought to our family. Even now, when I see Alexis, I am embarrassed. He is such a nice young man. She would have done so well to marry him. He says he has no hard feelings, but she had to have hurt his pride if nothing else. He loved her, you know."

Sara stared first at Eleani then at Spiros. She was taken aback by the revelation. Had her mother lied all these years? Or merely glossed over the details of the truth? Either way, she had painted an entirely different picture in Sara's mind.

"Come, sit down and tell us about Eleani's only child," Spiros said gently.

Sara was very aware that Nikos was standing at her side. She went to a chair and sat gingerly on the edge. He moved to stand farther away, gazing out to the sea.

"You need to stop crying now, Eleani. Listen to what Sara tells us," he said gently.

Eleani nodded, blotted her eyes again and leaned against Spiros as if for strength.

Sara didn't know where to begin. She ached for the difficulty of her mother's life. And from Eleani's reaction, she had believed her daughter had led an entirely different life.

"I only know the past from what I was told. My mother had hardly been in England six weeks before she knew her parents had been correct about the man she'd run off with. It had been romance, pure and simple, that had persuaded her to leave her family home. She had believed herself to be in love. She railed against the intractable demands her father had made—marrying to ensure the family coffers. She had believed my father to be different from who he truly was. She did not have the wisdom to see reality. She was eighteen for heaven's sake."

"She wasn't forced to wed Alexis. We thought she was captivated by him. He was only six years older, and very much in love with Damaris," Eleani said. "We were pleased. His family is very respected."

"So why did your mother not return home once she realized her mistake?" Nikos asked.

"No money. No welcome." Sara hesitated a moment. "Pride. And she was pregnant with me. She said she wrote to her father asking for help. He refused. She swore over and over she would never ask again."

Eleani gave a small sound. "Ah, that stubborn pride of the Marcopusoses. Always I had to fight against it. For years I asked him to find our daughter. He finally gave in and said he'd have a private detective locate her. Weeks later he said Damaris was happy with her life and that was the end of it. He must have approached her and been rebuffed and rather than tell me, he concocted such a story."

Sara shook her head, frowning. "When my father vanished, she was not yet twenty, a single parent with no skills. One of her friends helped by watching me nights after her own day of work so Mum could go and clean offices. That was the best job she could get for a long time."

Eleani groaned softly. "My precious baby girl," she whispered.

"Go on," Nikos said.

Sara turned to look at him. "I'm telling this."

"Not fast enough."

"Let her proceed at her own pace," Spiros said.

"We lived in a section of London with a large group of Greek expats. It was the best thing on one hand—everyone knew everybody else. We shared the language, the food. But it constantly reminded my mother of all she'd lost."

Slowly, as if viewing the scene for the first time, Sara continued. "It was only after she was diagnosed with cancer that she began to talk about contacting you. We learned from mutual friends of her father's death and your remarriage. My mother wrote a letter and mailed it. It was returned. By then she was really ill. She wrote the one I brought today. After her death, I tried contacting you. I ended up here."

"I thought she was happy," Eleani repeated. "Stanos told me that."

Had her mother's stiff-necked pride kept her from her home? Sara remembered some of the pretending they had done when she was younger—to preserve her mother's standing with her friends. Excess pride. None of it mattered anymore. She'd fulfilled her promise. "That's it. May I go now?"

"No. Stay. I want to hear all about Damaris and you," Eleani said. She lifted the letter. "Damaris asked me to watch out for you."

"I don't need watching out for." She had her own share of the family pride.

"Bad choice of words. How about having close contact with your grandmother," Nikos said.

Sara flashed him a look and then returned her gaze to Eleani. "What do you want to know about Mum?"

"Nikos has raved about your cooking. How did you choose that profession? Did Damaris ever learn to cook? We had a chef at home so she never learned as a child," Eleani said.

Sara smiled in memory. "Mum was okay as a cook, at least by the time I noticed such things. But nothing special. She loved the big gatherings best when everyone brought something. Authentic Greek food was what she craved, but we also ate English. I think some of my reasons for going into food preparation was to explore new dishes in self defense against Mum's limited choices."

Talking helped show Sara she no longer felt the burning

ache of loss after all the months. She could remember her mother with pride and happiness, not overwhelming grief.

"I'll have Marsa bring you some refreshments. Talk as long as you wish," Spiros said gently, standing and motioning to Nikos.

Nikos watched for a moment. Sara was like a stranger to him. For days he'd been intrigued by her—now he knew the reason she behaved so differently from others. She genuinely did not want anything from him but transportation to the island. Now that she'd achieved that, what?

Would she try to worm her way into her grandmother's affections—become her only heir? Eleani was wealthy enough Sara could quit her job and live the life her mother should have enjoyed.

"Do you know more?" he asked his grandfather when they left the women behind and were alone.

"No. Eleani told me long ago that she had a daughter she hadn't seen in years. I only knew Stanos by reputation. He was a hardliner—had his own rules and stiff-necked pride. I think I can see him in a temper, cutting off his only child."

"He had a private detective look into her life. He would have reported that Damaris was a single parent, that there was a little girl."

Spiros nodded, studying his grandson. "What of you, Nikos?"

"What about me?"

"Sara isn't the person we thought her to be. She's more than a crew member of the *Cassandra*. I will welcome her into our family as I would any relative of Eleani's."

"It's your home, do as you wish. I'm returning to the resort as soon as the captain can get the *Cassandra* under way," Nikos said. He'd return to work and forget about the pretty chef. There'd no longer be a need for Sara to continue to work. He'd instruct his human resources office to begin a search to fill her position.

The sooner he was consumed with business, the better.

"Don't leave before Monday. That's when you originally planned, right? Stay and visit with your grandfather a little longer. Give her a few days to visit with Eleani."

Nikos hesitated, then nodded once. He'd stay for his grandfather's sake.

"Sara's right, you know. I never told you how proud of your accomplishments I am. You have made a major contribution with the resort. I am proud of you and so is your father."

Nikos smiled slightly. "That's stretching it, don't you think?"

Spiros shrugged. "I'm sure if he thought about it, he'd be proud of you."

"You seem to be taking Sara's revelation in your stride," Nikos said.

"I was shocked when Eleani first told me she had a daughter. Hard as it is to hear the truth, it is best to find out. Too many lies have gone by in that family. Maybe Eleani will gain some peace knowing Sara. And I hope neither makes the same mistake Damaris and her father made."

"Not likely," Nikos said, looking back out the window. "Sara is no naive eighteen-year-old. She's almost thirty, has worked her way up in a grueling profession. Been on her own for a while. And definitely wasn't born with a silver spoon in her mouth."

"You're angry with her. I know. It's understandable."

"She used me to get to Eleani. I don't like being used."

"That's not all," his grandfather said.

"That's all I'm focused on now," Nikos said. "I'll tell the captain we leave at first light on Monday." He left before his grandfather could say any more.

Nikos went to the room he used as an office. He sat and turned on his computer. But when the screen came on, he didn't see it. He heard Sara telling him she had no family. She'd lied.

Or did she truly believe that? Eleani seemed more than willing to accept Sara.

She'd used him. Had all their time together been with the sole aim of getting to the island? The mutual interests? The kisses? What was truth, what false?

Thank God he'd never pushed for more.

So he'd wait for Monday. Escort Sara back to the mainland and wash his hands of her. Blast it!

By lunchtime, Sara's nerves were stretched tight. She'd spent the morning talking with her grandmother. She'd finally come to believe the woman had had no inkling of the dire straits they had sometimes lived through. She began to soften the stories, glossing over the hardships Damaris had faced, trying to put a happier note on everything. She didn't want to cause Eleani any more distress than she already felt. Again and again she looked at the letter and then at Sara.

By the time Marsa announced lunch, all Sara wanted to do was flee to the yacht and see if the captain would take her to the next island.

But she rose when Eleani did, used the proffered powder room to freshen up and went bravely to the terrace where lunch was being served.

Today she was escorted to the family table. She saw the crew's table on the lower terrace and wished she was going there instead.

Spiros joined them a moment later.

"Nikos has work to do. He's eating inside," he explained to Eleani.

Sara knew the truth. He couldn't even stand to be around her for the length of a meal. She was surprised at how much that hurt. For a few magical days she'd enjoyed herself. It was time to pay the piper. She was not some glamorous socialite like the ones Nikos was used to. She'd used him to get to Eleani. But she'd lost a lot along the way.

After an awkward lunch, Sara excused herself and headed for the boat. The first person she saw was Stefano who asked her if the rumors were true—was she Eleani Konstantinos's granddaughter?

"Stefano, do not listen to rumors," she said, brushing past him and going to her cabin. She pulled on her swimsuit, covered it with shorts and a top and grabbed a towel. She wanted to be alone, to think and to swim and to find some peace.

She approached the captain about taking the runabout.

"Where are you going?" he asked, not saying no. He'd also probably heard the rumor.

"Around to the cove Nikos took me to. I'll stick close to the island and anchor on the beach."

"Do you know how to run the boat?"

She nodded. She'd watched Nikos. It didn't look hard.

The captain inclined his head. "Take drinking water and don't swim deeper than where you can stand."

Sara smiled, warmed he was concerned enough to lecture her on swimming safety. And smart enough to know she needed to be alone.

"I'll be careful," she promised.

She banged the dock twice trying to get the runabout away, but once she had it pointed in the direction she wished to go, she was set. In only moments Sara felt as alone as anyone could. There was only sky and sea and a bit of an island. And heartache.

When she reached the cove, she nosed the boat to the beach. Holding the anchor and line, she jumped out and dragged it up on the shore. Satisfied the boat wasn't going anywhere, she waded back for her towel. She swam first, staying close to the shore, back and forth as if swimming laps. When she was almost too tired to lift her arms again, she waded ashore and moved her towel to a spot of shade where she lay down and tried to keep her mind empty.

But scenes from the day replayed. Nikos's anger. His aloof stance by the window. His hard eyes. She couldn't get any of them to vanish and wondered if she'd be doomed to repeat those scenes over and over all her life.

Finally the soothing warmth of the breeze and the gentle lap of the sea lulled her into the welcomed oblivion of sleep.

When Sara awoke, she was not alone. Nikos sat not five feet away. She sat up slowly, glancing around. There was no other boat.

"You came by the path?" she asked.

"You took the boat."

"I thought you had work to do."

"I finished and thought I'd take a swim."

She gestured to the water. "Have at it."

"You should not have gone swimming alone. It can be dangerous."

"As if you care," she replied petulantly. She wished she could recapture the feelings she'd had when they'd been here before. Blinking her eyes to keep tears at bay, she stared across the sea. Why had doing the right thing for her mother ended so badly for her?

"I do not wish an accident to befall anyone," Nikos said.

After a moment he spoke again, "Why didn't you tell me? We talked about family. Why not say you were estranged from your grandmother?"

"I was afraid you'd know instantly I was trying to reach Eleani and stop me."

"Things might have been better if left as they were."

"I promised my mother I would do my best to see her letter reached her mother. Would you have me renege?"

"Your mother is dead. She would not have known."

"But I would have known I hadn't kept a promise. Would you have broken a promise, Nikos?"

He was silent for a moment. Then reluctantly he said, "No, I would have honored my promise as you did. I think there might have been a better way to handle things."

"I tried the normal means. I could not make contact. It seemed like an act of fate when I got the job at the resort. I was so close. And when I was chosen to work on the *Cassandra*, I knew it was right. I'm sorry you feel I used you. In a way I guess I did, but I never lied to you about anything."

He didn't say anything, just stood and walked to the water. Sara watched as he dove in and swam away. He turned when he was some yards off shore and began to swim parallel to the beach. The cove was not wide. He swam laps. Sara watched every stroke, wishing he'd asked her to join him.

She rose and picked up her towel, shaking off the sand. She waded to the boat and tossed in her towel, then plunged into the silken water. Keeping out of Nikos's way, she swam hard, trying to tire herself out so she could sleep tonight. If he didn't arrange transportation for her soon, she'd have to stay through the weekend. How awkward that would be. She'd have to explain things to the crew—not that it was any of their business, but they had befriended her when she joined on and it was the right thing to do. If it fed gossip, so be it. Better than rampant speculation.

Sara lost track of time. She plowed through the water, growing tired but pushing on. Zoning out while swimming helped her forget everything. There was only the water and the sky. Finally almost too tired to move, she stopped to tread water for a moment. Looking around, she spotted Nikos in the boat. For a second her heart skipped a beat. Would he leave her here? She'd never find the pathway back.

Unlikely. He sat in the boat, watching her. She began to swim slowly back. Her arms and legs felt like limp spaghetti. Her breathing was still hard. But she also felt at peace for the first time since she walked up to the house that morning.

"Need a hand?" he asked when she reached the boat.

She shook her head, standing in the shallow water.

"Then push the boat off and get in. It's time to go back."

She went to get the anchor. Nikos coiled the line as she brought the anchor to the boat. She pushed the bow away from the beach, facing it seaward. Then she scrambled aboard. Taking her towel, she dried her face and arms. Tying it around her, sarong fashion, she sat in the copilot's chair. Nikos had started the engine as soon as she boarded, and once she was seated he opened the throttle until Sara felt as if they were flying.

Before long they were tied up behind the looming back of the *Cassandra*.

He turned off the engine and looked at her.

"Now what?" she asked.

"My grandfather would like you to join us for dinner," he said evenly.

She thought about it for a moment. "Okay, I guess."

"I thought you'd say that," he replied.

She looked at him. "What do you mean by that?"

"It seems likely that having made your presence known to Eleani, you'd expect to enjoy the benefits of being her granddaughter."

"You think that's why I told her? I don't know her at all. I don't consider I'm due any benefits of being her granddaughter. She owes me nothing. I owe her nothing."

"You're wrong. If what she says is true, and I believe it is, she didn't know about you."

"She should have taken the time to find out," Sara grumbled.

"Women of her generation usually bend to their husband's dictates. Her husband told her Damaris was fine. What was Eleani to think—that he lied?"

"He did lie."

"But she would not have thought that. If anyone is at fault or to blame about anything, it's Stanos. He's dead, so can't be held accountable. She should have known, and maybe she should have tried herself to find Damaris—especially after he died. But she didn't. She thought everything was the way it was to be. Now she knows the truth. Give her a chance."

"So which side are you on? You practically accuse me of kissing up to her for the so-called benefits—which you don't think I'm entitled to. Then you defend her actions and suggest I get to know her better."

"The relationship between you and your grandmother is not my business. You two have to find your own way."

"And the relationship between us?" she asked challengingly.

"There is no relationship between us." Nikos stood and stepped to the open part of the boat.

"There is. Or was. Even though you don't want to call it that, we had the beginning of a relationship," she said, standing and balancing herself against the rocking.

"You may think so."

"Come off it, Nikos. I know you don't want to be burned again like with Ariana. But every woman on the planet isn't after your money. I liked being with *you*. Except for dinner last night, I haven't cost you anything but your time. Admit it, we were becoming friends. And it sure seemed like you were pushing for more with those hot kisses."

"Hot kisses," he repeated.

She felt herself grow warm as she glared at him. He knew they were hot. And as much as he denied it now, she knew there had been a spark of something between them.

She also knew that spark would never have a chance to become a full-blown conflagration. She had put paid to that notion with her actions.

"What time is dinner?" she asked.

"Seven."

"I only brought my uniforms and the one dress I wore last night."

"I'll take care of that."

By the time Sara reached her cabin a few moments later she longed for a hot shower. She'd really love to soak in a tub, but that kind of luxury wasn't available aboard the *Cassandra*— at least not in the crew quarters.

The shower did a lot to refresh. Drained after this morning's confrontation and the swimming she'd done, Sara lay down for a nap.

At six-thirty there was a knock on her door. Opening it, Sara was surprised to find one of the maids from the house. She held a box out for Sara.

"For you. A dress for tonight," she said. Smiling briefly, she turned and fled as soon as Sara took the box.

Sara closed the door and placed the box on the narrow
bunk. Opening it, she stared for a long moment. The dark
burgundy color was rich and perfect for her coloring.
Lifting it, she stared. It was formal enough for dinner and
beautiful enough to make anyone wearing it feel like a
princess. Slipping it on a few moments later, Sara wished
she had a full-length mirror. She studied as much of herself
as she could. The dress fit like a dream. She liked the way
it brought out her coloring. Her dark hair gleamed. Her
cheeks were pink with anticipation. She felt very special.
How nice of her grandmother to send her the dress to wear
with dinner.

Or had it been Nikos? His words echoed. Heat washed
through her. Had he bought the dress? Where? Unless he'd
gone to Patricia. Not a short hop in a car, but at least two hours
of his time.

Not likely. But what was the likelihood of such a beautiful dress just lying around the house waiting for someone her
size and coloring to show up to wear it?

At five minutes to seven Sara walked up to the house. She
could see the lower terrace was already set for the staff's
dinner. The table on the upper terrace was bare. Going to the
front of the house, she knocked on the door. A moment later
Nikos opened it. He was wearing a dark suit, white shirt and
maroon tie—almost the color of her dress.

"You are family, Sara, no need to knock. Come in. My
grandfather thought it best if we eat inside tonight. Not so
many distractions."

Like the crew watching their every move, Sara thought.
"Fine." She stepped inside, looking around with interest. The
high ceiling and white walls gave the illusion of coolness
even in the warmth of the evening. Wide windows in the salon

were open to catch the breeze. The furnishings were a bit heavy for her tastes, but obviously old and much loved if the patina was any indication.

"You look lovely," he said.

She looked at him. "Did you buy this dress?"

He looked thoughtful for a long moment, then inclined his head. "I thought it was the perfect dress for you."

"It is. Thank you." She didn't want to tell him how special it made her feel. Now, knowing he'd bought it for her alone made it even more special.

"Sara, you are here. Welcome," Eleani said. "We are ready to go in to dinner." She seemed nervous. Nikos offered an arm to each and escorted them into the lavishly appointed dining room. Eleani smiled when she saw Spiros. The connection was obvious—she relied on him.

Sara felt a touch of envy. With her mother dead, she had no one to rely on. She so longed for a close connection with someone—a person she could trust with anything and know he would always be there for her.

Involuntarily her gaze flicked to Nikos. He had seated her and was talking with his grandfather. His manners had been exquisite. His demeanor all that anyone could expect. But the ease between them was gone.

"Welcome, Sara," Spiros said.

Nikos's dark eyes were unreadable.

Dinner was awkward. Eleani tried to carry on a normal conversation, but kept looking nervously at Sara. Nikos said little, eating and watching Sara. She felt as nervous as Eleani obviously was, with his gaze constantly on her. At one point she almost told him to look away.

As soon as dinner was finished, Sara hoped she could escape. Despite the lovely dress and all the discussion she and

Eleani had shared that morning, she was out of place. She did not belong.

"Shall we move to the salon? It's more comfortable there," Eleani said.

"Perhaps I'm needed on the ship." She looked at Nikos. "Will I be taken back to the resort in the morning?"

"No, we sail as scheduled on Monday."

"Very well." So he didn't wish to get rid of her instantly. She wanted to bring up the situation about her job. So far at least he hadn't told her there was no job waiting at the resort. Yet, it would be too awkward for her to stay. She wanted the comfort of familiar things and friends. She'd return to London as soon as she could.

"I'll escort you back to the ship, if you wish to leave now," he said, rising.

"I can manage."

He didn't reply, just came around to pull her chair back and gently take her arm.

"Dinner was delicious, Eleani," he said.

"I'll tell Dimitri you said so." Her smile was wobbly. "Good night, Sara. Perhaps you'd like to have breakfast with me in the morning—just the two of us on my balcony."

Sara was surprised at the invitation. "Thank you. What time should I be here?"

"Around eight," Eleani said, her smile growing warmer.

Once Sara and Nikos left the house, she said, "I'm surprised you didn't have me shipped off already. Why wait until Monday?"

"It's only a couple of days. Time for you to get to know Eleani."

"Your idea or your grandfather's?"

"It was his idea but I agree with him. You may think I'm

without feelings, but Eleani has always been very kind toward me. I think she deserves a chance."

Sara mulled that over.

"And I think you do, too," he said after a moment.

"A chance for what?"

"To build family ties."

"Oh." Sara tried to see his expression, but it was too dark.

"So we call a temporary truce?" she asked.

"We are not at war," he replied.

"You're angry."

He walked along for a few seconds, then said slowly, "Would you expect me not to be?"

CHAPTER TEN

OVER the next two days Sara spent more time with Eleani than alone. She saw Nikos only at dinner. Breakfasts were spent with her grandmother on her private balcony. Lunches were often shared with Spiros and Eleani. She answered endless questions and asked many herself about her mother as a young child and then as a teenager. It was a bittersweet time. The easy acceptance that Eleani showed should have been for her mother. And the awkwardness she felt now around Nikos tore at her heart. They'd meshed so well once upon a time.

She knew she never should have had secret thoughts about them developing some kind of relationship, but she had. Stupidly, she'd fallen in love with the man. Now he ignored her. He used work as an excuse, but she knew he had time enough to spend hours with his grandfather. Doing right should bring a reward, not sever something special. Though she was fooling herself if she thought Nikos would ever consider her as more than an employee who liked learning to dive. Still, her heart ached when she saw him.

On Sunday afternoon she sat with her grandmother on the large upper terrace, enjoying the serenity of the gardens and the view of the Aegean. Clouds built on the horizon, but seemed too distant to take seriously. The breeze from the sea was pleasant and fragrant after skimming across the blossoms.

"Sara," Eleani said after a quiet lull in conversation. "Spiros and I want you to move here with us."

Sara turned to look at her in surprise. "I can't do that," she said.

"Please. Think about it at least. I missed so much of Damaris's life. I can never make up for that. But you can have a different life than you've known. Stanos left a small fortune. I have more money than I can ever spend, so you would never be a burden. Please. It would mean so much to me to have you here."

Sara shook her head slowly. "Thank you. I appreciate the gesture. But my home is in London. My friends are there." Her mother was there as well. Somehow Sara had never thought of leaving London permanently.

"Don't say no right away. Think about it," Eleani urged.

"I'll think about it but don't believe I'll change my mind. Perhaps I could come to visit from time to time. We hardly have had time to catch up on everything." Maybe a holiday, a few months away would give time for Nikos to get over his initial anger. Maybe they'd be able to be friends of a kind again.

She pushed away the thought that by the next time she came to visit, he might be married to Gina. How would she deal with that?

"Of course you must spend holidays here. But think about living here—if only for a year or so. We know lots of people, have visitors frequently. You can go to Thessalonika, Athens, I could show you where Damaris grew up. There is so much to see in Greece. It's your heritage, after all."

"I know. I'll think about it." Sara was starting to feel pressured. This was not something she wanted. Especially with

Nikos already angry at her. He would think she'd planned it all along. Ariana had wanted money; he'd think she did as well.

It was *family* Sara wanted. Could she turn down Eleani's offer? She was growing fond of the older woman. Instant love had not sprung forth. But the more she knew about her, the more Sara could see her as a victim of circumstances and her upbringing. Maybe she could not have done things differently regarding her daughter. Sara would never know.

And as Nikos had suggested, she was giving Eleani a chance.

After lunch, at which Spiros also had extended an invitation for Sara to stay, she decided she needed some time to herself. She said she wanted to swim before the clouds developed into rain, and went back to the yacht.

She donned her swimsuit and gathered her things and a book to read on the beach, then went to find the captain to see if she could use the runabout again. He was on the bridge reviewing charts.

Nikos was with him, dressed in shorts and a T-shirt. She stopped short at the doorway, thrilled as always to see him. The T-shirt hugged his muscles lovingly. She swallowed, wishing things were the way they once had been.

"Do you want something?" he asked, catching sight of her.

"I wanted to use the runabout if that's okay. I wanted to go swimming once more before leaving tomorrow."

He raised an eyebrow. "I thought you'd be staying."

She frowned and slowly shook her head. "I'm not staying."

Nikos glanced at the captain and then moved around the high table. "I'll take you to the cove. You shouldn't swim alone."

"I was planning to stay close to the shore."

"I'll take you," he repeated.

The ride in the runabout was in silence. Sara didn't have anything to say and Nikos was obviously still angry.

Anchoring on the beach, Nikos shut down the engine and looked at her.

"My grandfather said you were invited to remain here with them."

She pulled her top over her head and shimmied out of her shorts. "Eleani invited me. I said no."

That surprised Nikos, she could see.

"Why? Isn't that the entire goal? Get to know your grandmother, spin her a sad tale and end up living the life of luxury? The island has to be several steps up from the flat you shared with your mother in London."

She wanted to knock him overboard. "That's your style of thinking, not mine. My goal as you call it was to deliver the letter my mother wrote just before she died. I thought you'd kick me off the island that same day. I have no plans to stay here."

He looked skeptical. She gave a sound of disgust and stepped over the side of the boat. How dare he think she was looking for an easy berth. She realized then and there he had not really learned anything about her in the days they'd spent together. How could she even think herself in love with such a man? Unfortunately, the heart had its own reasons.

Nikos watched Sara swim away from the boat as if being pursued. Was she spinning another tale, or had she really refused to stay? Was it temporary until she could make arrangements at home or was she seriously not planning to move to the island?

It made sense that his grandfather's wife would want Sara living with her—Sara was her only grandchild. Eleani was a woman full of love and devotion to her family. She would love to have Sara to spoil and be with. Especially after having missed her entire life up to this point.

Nikos tried to think of other women he knew who would refuse such an offer. Carte blanche on anything. Never having to work again. Shopping, luncheons, parties—who would prefer to work in a hot kitchen?

No, Sara had to be holding out for higher stakes. Maybe she wanted a share from Stanos's estate that should have gone to her mother.

He frowned, watching her as she swam. That didn't fit with what he knew about Sara.

They had talked. In-depth discussions of things like families—and promises. He remembered her comment about doing the right thing no matter what. She evidenced a strong sense of honor.

If that carried through, she would not stay. Her quest had been completed.

Did that mean she'd return to London?

Nikos refused to examine why that thought rankled. He had already decided to dismiss her from the job at the restaurant. Now he wondered if that would be wise.

No sense alienating his grandparents. She'd either give it up herself and return to London or change her mind and accept Eleani's offer.

He stepped off the boat and began swimming after her.

As Sara drew near the curve of the cove, she turned and began swimming back toward him.

When they met, they both stopped swimming.

"Want to go diving?" he asked. Seeing her so close, hair wet around her face, eyes sparkling with the delight she found swimming, he had the urge to kiss her again. How dumb was that?

"I'd love to." She looked at the sky. "Will the storm hit soon?"

He glanced around, studying the growing gray clouds, still

far enough away to be safe. "I think we'll have an hour or so and still have a margin of safety to get back to the dock."

"Then I'd love to."

They donned the scuba gear from the runabout and were back in the water in less than ten minutes, exploring beneath the surface.

Nikos swam a bit behind Sara, to better keep an eye on her. He could tell she continued to find delight in the beauty beneath the sea. She chased fish, explored encrusted rocks on the sea bed and swam near one arm of the cove then pointed up. Surfacing, he followed her up.

She raised her face plate and took out her mouthpiece.

"Can we go a little around the side, to see the rocks?"

"The current's a bit tricky there. You have to watch for surges. Are you sure you're up to that?"

She thought about it for a moment. "Have you done it?"

"Many times. Some of the rock formations are amazing. It's not very dangerous, just be cautious."

"You lead, I'll follow you."

"I'd rather be able to see you."

"Then side by side?"

"You stay on the sea side, let me be closer to the rocks." If a surge came, he would be able to manage things better than she would.

"Thanks." Pulling down the face mask and popping the mouthpiece back in, she dove beneath the surface.

The exploration was fascinating. It had been a while since Nikos had been over this section and seeing it anew as if through Sara's eyes had him appreciating the beauty even more. He should take time to enjoy pursuits he enjoyed—like diving. He may not like what Sara had done, but he was suddenly grateful to her for rejuvenating his love for diving.

They turned just as a wave surge hit. For a moment Nikos was slammed against a rock, Sara bumping into him. He caught her before she could be swept to the rocks and held her close. The pressure abated and he kicked away, giving a wider berth to the rocky shore than before.

She pointed upward, but he shook his head and pointed back toward the cove and the boat.

In only a few moments they reached the boat.

When they surfaced and Sara took off her face mask and mouthpiece, she looked at him. "That was wild. Are you okay?"

"Fine." His left shoulder and part of his back burned like fire. He knew he'd scraped the skin, and probably bruised some muscles with the impact. At least it had been him and not Sara.

"You must have hurt something. My bumping into you wasn't a light tap."

"I've had worse." He looked at the clouds, now moving swiftly across the sky, some early fingers already overhead. "I say we get aboard and back to the dock."

She looked up and quickly nodded. "It looks like it's getting darker by the minute."

Nikos levered himself out of the water and into the boat, pulling Sara in a moment later. Divesting himself of the air tanks, he winced when the strap rubbed against his shoulder.

"Let me see," she said, half turning him. "Oh, oh, it's bleeding. Do you have a first-aid kit aboard? You don't want that blood getting all over you and everything else."

"No first-aid kit. It'll be okay." It was starting to burn. The sooner they got back, the sooner he could take care of it.

"Wait." She picked up her shirt, and before Nikos guessed what she was doing, she tore off a strip from the hem. Folding the rest into a large pad, she formed a makeshift bandage and covered the bleeding skin. "I'm not sure this will hold," she said, trying to tie it on with the strip. "Put your shirt on over it, it'll help hold it in place," she said.

Helping him pull on the shirt, her hands brushed against his chest, against his back. Nikos drew in a sharp breath, her touch doing nothing to alleviate the pain of the scrape but raising his blood heat by several degrees. Finally she was satisfied.

"That'll hold until we get back," she said. "I think you need to see a doctor."

"I'll be fine. Let's go." He began to pull the anchor in. It dragged across the sandy beach but came readily. In less than five minutes he had the motor going and was backing away from the beach. The sea was running higher than when they started. Once out of the shelter of the cove, they felt the force of the wind. The water was choppy with large swells breaking every few moments.

He kept the boat on course and they made the dock safely. Two crewmen were there to help tie up. Bumpers had been placed between the *Cassandra* and the dock as the force of the wind bumped it into the floating dock.

"Brewing up quite a storm," one of the men said.

"You're bleeding through the shirt," Sara said.

"I'll be okay once I get into the house." His shoulder was stinging. Still, once he washed off the salt water, he'd have a better idea of how bad it was.

"Go in and get changed," he said as they walked along the dock.

"Are you going to be all right?" she asked.

He didn't want her worried, but it was nice to have her so concerned. "I'll be fine."

He waited until she hurried up the dock and then headed for the house.

Once under the shower, Nikos knew the injuries were more

than superficial scrapes. He'd need help with taking care of them. He dried off, donned a pair of khaki pants and then tried to see what he could do. He saw the blood oozing from a couple of deep cuts. The rocks had been irregular and sharp. If he'd been at the resort, he could have called upon the nurse he'd hired in case guests needed anything.

Sara was wet by the time she reached the house before dinner. The rain had started shortly after she and Nikos returned. She'd showered, dressed and then watched the rain the rest of the afternoon as it poured down. She hoped Nikos wasn't as injured as he looked. With all the blood smeared around, it was hard to tell.

She'd donned a windbreaker and scarf to try to protect herself from the weather, but it proved futile as the rain was relentless. An umbrella would have been useless with the gusting wind. Finally she reached the front door and was sheltered by the portico. Knocking, she waited impatiently for it to open.

"Miss." One of the maids opened the door wide and urged her in. "Let me take your wet things. I will bring you a hair dryer," she said, as Sara took off the windbreaker. Her shoulders were damp, but would soon dry. Her hair was dripping, however.

"I'd appreciate it," she said.

The maid hurried away just as Eleani came down the stairs.

"Goodness, Sara, you are soaked."

"The maid is getting me a hair dryer. The rest of me isn't as wet and will dry soon. It's really raining hard. How is Nikos?"

"Men! They think they're above being injured just by thinking that. Two of the cuts are deep. But there was nothing to be done but use adhesive to tape them together. I have some antibiotic ointment so I used that and bandaged the area. He should know better."

"We didn't expect the surge in the water."

"A storm was brewing, anyone could see that," Eleani said with exasperation.

Sara nodded, feeling guilty that her desire for swimming had cause havoc.

The maid returned holding a hair dryer. "If you wish, you can use this powder room," she said.

"I can get you some dry clothes," Eleani said.

"I'm fine. If I can dry my hair, the rest will dry soon. It's not that cold."

Shortly, Sara joined Eleani and Spiros in the main salon. He expressed concern about their diving and Sara explained how they'd left the cove. It was at her request, yet Nikos was the one who had suffered.

"Dinner," one of the servants announced.

"Shall we?" Spiros offered his arm to Eleani.

Sara rose. When she entered the dining room, she did not see Nikos.

"Is Nikos joining us for dinner?" she asked.

"He should be here by now. Probably got tied up on some call." Spiros turned to the man waiting to serve them. "Check on Nikos for me, would you?"

"At once."

Taking their seats, they talked desultorily for a few moments until the man returned.

"He's asleep on his bed. Should I waken him?" he asked.

"No, let him sleep, Spiros," Eleani said, placing her hand on her husband's. "It will help the healing. We can send up a tray after we eat."

"Fine."

Sara missed Nikos being there, even though the last couple of meals had been uncomfortable with him glaring at her. At least she knew him, they'd shared parts of their lives with each other. It was not the same with the two older people she scarcely knew, and one of whom she still had mixed feelings about. Sara still couldn't reconcile her grandmother's actions or lack thereof. Yet the more they talked, the more she grew to know the woman. Eleani had loved Damaris. That much was clear.

After dinner Sara offered to take up a tray for Nikos. Spiros agreed and soon one was brought from the kitchen. She followed the older man's directions and turned left at the top of the stairs. The house was large, with seven bedrooms, she'd been told. The flat she and her mother had shared would fit in the main salon and leave room to spare.

The door was slightly ajar when she approached. Balancing the tray, she knocked. There was no answer. Pushing the door, she saw Nikos was sprawled across his bed, on his stomach, asleep. She opened the door enough to enter. Setting the tray down on a small table near one of the tall windows, she crossed to the edge of the bed.

"Nikos?" she said softly.

He looked just as formidable asleep as he did when awake. His hair was tousled. He was bare from the waist up and the white bandage was a stark contrast to his tanned skin.

She felt odd watching him as he slept—as if she were intruding. She was also fascinated. Glancing around, she saw a straight chair, which she brought over so she could wait for him to waken. The dishes were covered; they'd keep the food warm for a little while. She wanted to reach out and touch him, feel the warmth of his skin, maybe even lean over and kiss him as if she had the right.

She sat and waited, watching him sleep and thinking of

how she might have done things differently. Perhaps it would have resulted in a different outcome. Maybe she could have salvaged their growing friendship, if nothing more.

Sara lost track of time. She was about to leave when he stirred.

"Nikos?" she said softly.

He opened his eyes and looked at her. For a moment she felt cherished. Then his awareness kicked in and his gaze grew hard. "What are you doing here?" He rolled over, groaned softly and sat up. Reaching out, he switched on a bedside lamp.

"Damn, this shoulder hurts more than I expected," he said, rotating it a bit.

"Don't start it bleeding again. Eleani said two of the cuts were deep." She jumped to her feet and reached out as if to stop him. She pulled back her hands when she realized what she was doing.

"I brought you some dinner, but didn't waken you as I thought you'd need the sleep. It's probably cold by now," she said, going to the table and lifting one of the plate covers. Steam rose. "Maybe not."

He rose and crossed the room. He reminded her of a panther on the prowl. Barefoot and bare-chested, he moved with elegant grace. The play of light and shadows on his skin had her fascinated.

When he reached the table, he took a fork, cut a small portion and popped it into his mouth. Shrugging, he pulled a chair closer. "It's warm enough and I'm hungry enough to eat anything."

"I'm sure Dimitri would be happy to warm it up or prepare you something else," she said.

"Don't hover. Sit." He pointed to a chair and took another bite. "It's fine. I've had worse." He looked at her. "And better."

"Will we still leave in the morning?" she asked, pulling the straight chair closer to him and sitting.

He nodded. "This storm will blow out by then."

It was already dark outside. Rain coated the windows.

Sara was content to watch him eat, as she had been to watch him sleep. She was storing memories to last a lifetime. She'd already decided that once she returned to the resort, she'd turn in her resignation and return to England. Her task was done. She wanted familiar people, places. She wanted the love of her friends and the trust she couldn't have with people who suspected her motives for everything.

So this might be the last time she'd be with Nikos. She treasured every moment.

"Did you eat?" he asked.

"With your grandfather and Eleani," she said.

"She's your grandmother, you can call her that," he said slowly.

She shrugged.

"You know." He took another bite, ate it slowly then looked at her. "Your mother could have come back and confronted her parents. She didn't need to try to reconcile by mail. Did you ever think of that?"

"Of course I did. I even asked her several times why she didn't. It was the family pride. She had as much as her father, I think. And I truly thought she was content enough with life in England. Her getting sick showed me how much she had missed Greece all her life. Even if she hadn't reconciled with her parents, she could have made a good life for us among her friends and in familiar settings of her former home in Greece. But she refused to even visit."

"Don't tell me you never had a vacation or went on a trip," he said.

"We took lots of trips, to the north of England, to Scotland, Wales."

"That money could have been spent on airfare to Greece. So since she didn't, how important was it to her to return to her parents? Maybe her death was just the excuse you needed to come here and meet Eleani and worm your way in."

Sara took a breath with the shock. She thought they'd gotten past this with the dive and all. Nikos still thought she was after money and nothing else.

Slowly she rose, replaced the chair where she'd found it.

"Good night," she said with dignity and left the room.

"Sara, wait," he called, coming after her.

He caught up with her at the top of the stairs, reached out to take her arm to stop her from descending.

"Let me go. You've made your position clear over and over. I don't know why I ever thought you were someone special. You are cynical and jaded and haven't a trusting bone in your body. You should spend your life alone so you never have to wonder if anyone loves you or only your money. At least your parents have a life that they want—even if it didn't include you. At least they reached out and tried. You do nothing but hide away in your resort and spurn anyone who tries to get close to you." She yanked free and almost ran down the stairs.

"Sara, wait," he called.

She threw open the front door and dashed out, but pulled it shut carefully behind her so no one else in the house would know how angry she was. It was hard to see the wide path in the dark, rainy night, but she could see lights on board the *Cassandra* and took off almost at a run.

Tomorrow they'd return to Thessalonika and the next day she'd be back home in London. She could hang on that long. She had to. What choice did she have?

CHAPTER ELEVEN

"Nikos?" Spiros said behind him.

Nikos slowly closed the front door he'd wrenched open after Sara had fled. Turning, he looked at his grandfather.

"Is something wrong?"

"No. Sara and I argued. She left for the boat. She'll get soaked."

"She can dry off there. Eleani had hoped she'd stay the night. I'll have to tell her Sara has already left. What I won't tell her is that she left so precipitously."

Nikos headed back to the stairs.

"Are you all right?" his grandfather asked.

"I'm always all right."

But it was a lie. Nikos realized that when he stepped back into his bedroom. His lonely bedroom. When he'd been younger, he'd been so full of hopes and dreams. He would not have a marriage like his parents'. He would find a beautiful woman who would love him. Who would want to have all the closeness of family he saw with his grandparents and that his own parents had spurned.

Ariana was that woman, he'd once believed. She had proved false and it had changed him. Now for the first time in years, he thought about his old dreams. A home, family, children. The insight that had shocked him before returned. Who would he teach about the island's history and special places? Who would he regale with family stories, from the war to the rebuilding, to the exploits of his grandfather and father? If he did not marry, did not have children, the family ended with him.

But he needed more than children. He wanted someone who came to a marriage with dreams similar to his own. Was someone out there—waiting for him?

What if Sara's dreams matched his? He could get past the way she'd used him if they did. Had the way she'd been with him only been talk? What if she'd been that way to gain his sympathy in case things didn't work out as she'd planned, and she needed to enlist his help?

He looked at the bed, remembering that first moment when he'd awoken and had seen Sara. For a split second it had felt absolutely right. As if he expected her there, and there she was.

She'd never once asked for anything—unlike other women who wanted trinkets or wanted to be seen in nightclubs, not spend quiet evenings on the aft deck of a yacht.

Damn, if he could just trust his own feelings.

He had once before and had been proved wrong. Dare he risk it again?

The sun rose the next morning in a cloudless sky. Sara had her things packed before the *Cassandra* began its engines. She had sent a message to the house thanking them for their kindness and saying goodbye. She knew they might be up already, but she had no desire to speak to anyone.

Stefano brought her some breakfast, croissants and rolls, freshly baked by Dimitri. She hadn't got the recipes she'd wanted. So be it.

She knelt on her bunk and looked out of the small porthole as they pulled away, watching as the house on the hill grew smaller until the *Cassandra* swung round and the house was lost from view.

She felt numb again. They would reach the resort before lunch. She'd contact the travel desk and see what the earliest flight to London was. She didn't need to worry about leaving anyone in the lurch by her departure. The kitchen at the resort had made arrangements when she'd been chosen to serve on the *Cassandra*. The yacht wasn't scheduled for another cruise that she knew of. By the time it was, its regular chef would be ready to come back.

It wouldn't take her long to clear out her room at the resort. Maybe there'd even be a flight out today.

As far as her relationship with Eleani was concerned, she'd write. They could gradually build up a connection. Or maybe not. Sara had done as her mother had asked. Her life was not her mother's. Eleani was a relative, but there was only a tiny bond between them. It might grow or not. Sara didn't care at the moment.

She refused to think about Nikos. He'd made his position clear numerous times. She had been dumb in the extreme to even hope for a difference in him. She refused to admit she loved him. He would never love her in return, and she did not want to end up like her mother, always pining for a man who had left and would never be back.

The knock on her door later had Sara's heart leaping in expectation. She opened it, disappointed to see Stefano there.

"The captain asks if you'd like to watch our arrival from the bridge."

She considered it. But shook her head. "Please tell him thank you, but I'll stay here. I'll be ready to leave when we dock."

She closed the door, knowing she was closing off her last chance to spend some time with Nikos. It was not worth the pain of saying goodbye again for a few moments in his company. She preferred to make the break clean and final.

When they docked at the resort she was ready. She watched from her porthole until she saw Nikos striding away from the ship. Then she went to find out how soon she could be on her way to England.

Luck was with her. She booked a seat on a 7:00 p.m. flight to London. Packing the things in her room swiftly, she arranged to have her bags picked up and delivered to the taxi she'd take to the airport.

She went to the kitchen to tell the chief chef she would not be coming back to work. It was hard. She'd enjoyed the weeks she'd spent in the kitchen and all she'd learned about genuine Greek cuisine. She vowed she'd keep it up when she returned home.

It was time to leave.

She looked neither left nor right but went straight to where the taxis picked up and delivered guests. Pointing out her bags, Sara was on her way. She gazed unseeingly out the windows as they sped through the traffic and on to the airport. Despite her best efforts, her heart was aching. Tears flooded her eyes and she brushed them impatiently away. She'd learned about doing without her heart's desire from her mother. Maybe the Andropolous women were destined not to find happiness with the first man they fell in love with. It didn't mean she had to settle for anything but the best. Someone who was above all the other someones in the world. Would she ever find it again?

She loved Nikos Konstantinos. The admission hurt. She rubbed her chest and tried to shake off the ache. She hardly knew him. She'd forget about him within weeks of getting back home.

Liar, an inner voice said.

Sara knew she'd never forget Nikos.

She paid for her ticket, checked her luggage and made her way to the concourse to await the flight. She couldn't wait to see Stacy and tell her everything. Or almost everything. Sara wondered how long it would be before she could talk about Nikos without revealing how she felt.

The preliminary boarding began. She'd be home in a few hours.

"Sara," Nikos said.

She looked up. "What are you doing here?" she asked, astonished to see him.

"I want to talk."

"You can't be here. Only people with tickets can be here. Besides, they've called my flight."

"I bought a ticket. It was the only way. But I don't want to use it. I don't want you to use yours. I want to talk."

"We have nothing to say. You've made that perfectly clear—especially the part where you think I'm angling for money, no matter who gets in my way."

"I think I was wrong about that."

"What? You *think* you were wrong about that. You were totally wrong!"

People began to watch them. Sara glanced around, seeing the curiosity on their faces.

"Go away," she said, looking anywhere but at Nikos.

"If I go anywhere, it'll be to London. If we have to sit side by side on the plane and hash this all out, I'm good to go."

"We are not sitting together on the plane."

He held out his boarding pass. The seat number was adjacent to hers.

"How did you manage that?" she asked suspiciously.

"Money has its uses. I bribed the ticket agent."

"That's just wrong."

"Not as wrong as your leaving before we have a chance to talk—really talk. Sara, don't go. Stay here in Greece. Get to know Eleani. Get to know me."

"You? What do you have to do with my relationship with my grandmother?"

"Nothing. Do what you want with her. Stay for me."

She didn't understand. "I'm going home."

"Make Greece your home. You speak the language, know the food, the traditions—the dances. Stay, make your life here—with me."

Now Sara knew she was confused. Nikos wanted an arranged business marriage. He couldn't be proposing.

"Exactly what are you talking about?" she asked.

It was his turn to look around at the avid audience they had. Frowning, he held out his hand for hers. "Come with me. I'd prefer some privacy."

"Nothing you have to say requires privacy, unless you plan to blast me for using you to reach my grandmother."

"Dammit, I want to ask you to marry me, but not in front of a hundred strangers," he snapped.

Sara blinked. "Marry?" she squeaked. Had she heard him correctly? The man who thought all women were after his money and couldn't love him. The man who wanted a business marriage with a woman of equal fortune was proposing to her? Poor, working woman Sara Andropolous?

No, she had not heard him correctly.

Someone in the group of passengers clapped. Soon dozens took up the applause.

Sara felt the heat rise in her cheeks. "Did you just propose?" she asked. How dare he propose in front of a hundred strangers.

"I did. You have enough witnesses."

"You don't want to marry me."

"If you would come with me as I asked, I would explain."

She rose and picked up her tote. Turning to face the majority of the passengers, she shrugged. "Looks like I'm not going to London after all." With a smile she turned back to Nikos. "This had better be good. If you have me miss my flight for anything less than perfection, I'm not going to be happy."

He reached out and took her hand, lacing his fingers with hers, raising them to his lips for a brief kiss.

"If you would just say yes, it would make everything easier."

"And why do I want to make things easier for you?" she asked, feeling daring. Her heart sang. He had proposed and she had no intention of refusing. But if he didn't know that yet, it wouldn't hurt to draw this out a bit.

He began striding down the concourse. Sara had to run a couple of steps to catch up.

"How did you find me?" she asked.

"I called your room and you didn't answer. It didn't take long to discover you had booked a flight out tonight. My fear was the traffic, that I wouldn't make it before you left. Which means I would have had to follow you to England."

"You could have said something before," she grumbled. "We were on the boat for three hours."

"I wanted more privacy than can be found on *Cassandra*," he said, heading back to the terminal. In less than five minutes they were in the back of his limousine. He flipped a switch, closing the window to the driver's section. He pulled Sara into his arms and kissed her. Thoroughly.

Breathlessly she pulled back a few moments later and gazed up into his warm brown eyes.

"Is that a yes?" he asked.

"I thought you were going to explain things," she countered, stalling. She still wasn't sure he knew what he was doing. He really wanted to marry her?

"Time enough for all the explanations in the world once you tell me you'll marry me. I love you, Sara. I never thought I'd say those words again. I never thought I'd truly feel the emotion again. But I do—when I'm with you. When I think about you. When I dream about you.

"I want to spend my life with you, and have you with me every day. Maybe we'll have some babies together—children we can love together, raise together, and who will give us grandchildren that will delight our souls. Or if we don't, you will always be enough for me. Say you love me. Tell me you didn't just use me to get to Eleani. That our time meant something special to you—as it did to me."

"It did. *Of course it did!* I fell in love with you, too. I was thrilled when you visited me on the aft deck. But your story about Ariana scared me. I knew you were planning to ask Gina to marry you—rumors like that don't stay quiet long. I didn't want to repeat the mistake my mother made. I didn't want to hold on to hope that you would learn to love me. She never stopped hoping my father would return."

"She loved him that much?"

Sara shook her head slowly. "I'm not sure. Sometimes, and especially after talking with Eleani, I wondered if it was just her pride. She'd given up so much for him, she wanted it to come right. Only, for her it never did."

"We won't be like your parents. Nor mine, come to that. I

don't mind entertaining or going to parties, but it's you I want
to be with. Sailing in the *Cassandra*, swimming in the sea."

"Working at the resort. I can still cook there, right?"

"If you want. Or not, if you don't."

"I do. I love my job. And there's so much more I can learn
about Greek foods. If you adjust your hours, we'll be together
when we're not working."

"So you have it figured out?"

She smiled and touched his cheek. "It just came to me. It
would be the perfect life."

She couldn't believe Nikos Konstantinos was proposing to
her. Afraid to pinch herself lest she wake up, she continued
to gaze into his warm eyes, brimming with love—for her.

"If we have any children, I want us to raise them, not a
series of nannies and tutors. No boarding school."

"But we will show them the island."

"Of course. We can teach them to dive in the cove, swim in
the sea," he affirmed. "And explore historic places. Together."

"You're serious about this, aren't you?" she asked with
wonder. Who would have expected Nikos to marry a Greek
woman who had no money and a job as a chef?

"You still haven't said you will," he reminded her.

"Yes! Of course I'll marry you. I love you, Nikos. Please
love me forever."

"I know how you view promises made. I share the solem-
nity of a vow. I promise I will always love you," he said with
a kiss that had Sara convinced of his love.

She had the happy ending her mother had missed. She would
embrace it with both hands and never take it for granted. Their
love would last forever, of that she was sure. Nikos had promised.

* * * * *

RICK'S APPOINTMENT with his attorney early Wednesday morning went only moderately better than his meeting with social services the day before. The prognosis wasn't great— but at least his attorney was going to file a motion for DNA testing. Just so Rick could petition to see the child...his sister's baby. The sister he didn't know he had until it was too late.

The rest of what his attorney said had been downhill from there.

Cell phone in hand before he'd even reached his Nitro, Rick punched in the speed dial number he'd programmed the day before.

Maybe foster parent Sue Bookman hadn't received his message. Or had lost his number. Maybe she didn't want to talk to him. At this point he didn't much care what she wanted.

"Hello?" She answered before the first ring was complete. And sounded breathless.

Young and breathless.

"Ms. Bookman?"

"Yes. This is Rick Kraynick, right?"

"Yes, ma'am."

"I recognized your number on caller ID," she said, her

voice uneven, as though she was still engaged in whatever physical activity had her so breathless to begin with. "I'm sorry I didn't get back to you. I've been a little…distracted."

The words came in more disjointed spurts. Was she jogging?

"No problem," he said, when, in fact, he'd spent the better part of the night before watching his phone. And fretting. "Did I get you at a bad time?"

"No worse than usual," she said, adding, "Better than some. So, how can I help?"

God, if only this could be so easy. He'd ask. She'd help. And life could go well. At least for one little person in his family.

It would be a first.

"Mr. Kraynick?"

"Yes. Sorry. I was…are you sure there isn't a better time to call?"

"I'm bouncing a baby, Mr. Kraynick. It's what I do."

"Is it Carrie?" he asked quickly, his pulse racing.

"How do you know Carrie?" She sounded defensive, which wouldn't do him any good.

"I'm her uncle," he explained, "her mother's—Christy's—older brother, and I know you have her."

"I can neither confirm nor deny your allegations, Mr. Kraynick. Please call social services." She rattled off the number.

"Wait!" he said, unable to hide his urgency. "Please," he said more calmly. "Just hear me out."

"How did you find me?"

"A friend of Christy's."

"I'm sorry I can't help you, Mr. Kraynick," she said softly. "This conversation is over."

"I grew up in foster care," he said, as though that gave him some special privilege. Some insider's edge.

"Then you know you shouldn't be calling me at all."

"Yes… But Carrie is my niece," he said. "I need to see her. To know that she's okay."

"You'll have to go through social services to arrange that."

"I'm sure you know it's not as easy as it sounds. I'm a single man with no real ties and I've no intention of petitioning for custody. They aren't real eager to give me the time of day. I never even knew Carrie's mother. For all intents and purposes, our mother didn't raise either one of us. All I have going for me is half a set of genes. My lawyer's on it, but it could be weeks—months—before this is sorted out. Carrie could be adopted by then. Which would be fine, great for her, but then I'd have lost my chance. I don't want to take her. I won't hurt her. I just have to see her."

"I'm sorry, Mr. Kraynick, but…"

* * * * *

*Find out if Rick Kraynick will ever have a chance
to meet his niece.
Look for A DAUGHTER'S TRUST
by Tara Taylor Quinn,
available in September 2009.*

**We'll be spotlighting a different series
every month throughout 2009
to celebrate our 60th anniversary.**

**Look for Harlequin® Superromance®
in September!**

*Celebrate with
The Diamond Legacy
miniseries!*

Follow the stories of four cousins as they come to terms
with the complications of love and what it means to
be a family. Discover with them the sixty-year-old secret
that rocks not one but two families.

A DAUGHTER'S TRUST by *Tara Taylor Quinn*
September

FOR THE LOVE OF FAMILY by *Kathleen O'Brien*
October

LIKE FATHER, LIKE SON by *Karina Bliss*
November

A MOTHER'S SECRET by *Janice Kay Johnson*
December

Available wherever books are sold.

You're invited to join our Tell Harlequin Reader Panel!

By joining our new reader panel you will:

- Receive Harlequin® books—they are FREE and yours to keep with no obligation to purchase anything!
- Participate in fun online surveys
- Exchange opinions and ideas with women just like you
- Have a say in our new book ideas and help us publish the best in women's fiction

In addition, you will have a chance to win great prizes and receive special gifts!
See Web site for details. Some conditions apply.
Space is limited.

To join, visit us at
www.TellHarlequin.com.

REQUEST YOUR FREE BOOKS!
2 FREE NOVELS PLUS 2
FREE GIFTS!

HARLEQUIN®

Romance

From the Heart, For the Heart

YES! Please send me 2 FREE Harlequin® Romance novels and my 2 FREE gifts (gifts are worth about $10). After receiving them, if I don't wish to receive any more books, I can return the shipping statement marked "cancel". If I don't cancel, I will receive 4 brand-new novels every month and be billed just $3.84 per book in the U.S. or $4.24 per book in Canada. That's a savings of at least 15% off the cover price! It's quite a bargain! Shipping and handling is just 50¢ per book.* I understand that accepting the 2 free books and gifts places me under no obligation to buy anything. I can always return a shipment and cancel at any time. Even if I never buy another book, the two free books and gifts are mine to keep forever.

114 HDN EYU3   314 HDN EYKG

Name	(PLEASE PRINT)

Address	Apt. #

City	State/Prov.	Zip/Postal Code

Signature (if under 18, a parent or guardian must sign)

Mail to the **Harlequin Reader Service:**
IN U.S.A.: P.O. Box 1867, Buffalo, NY 14240-1867
IN CANADA: P.O. Box 609, Fort Erie, Ontario L2A 5X3

Not valid to current subscribers of Harlequin Romance books.

**Are you a subscriber of Harlequin Romance books
and want to receive the larger-print edition?
Call 1-800-873-8635 today!**

* Terms and prices subject to change without notice. Prices do not include applicable taxes. Sales tax applicable in N.Y. Canadian residents will be charged applicable provincial taxes and GST. Offer not valid in Quebec. This offer is limited to one order per household. All orders subject to approval. Credit or debit balances in a customer's account(s) may be offset by any other outstanding balance owed by or to the customer. Please allow 4 to 6 weeks for delivery. Offer available while quantities last.

Your Privacy: Harlequin Books is committed to protecting your privacy. Our Privacy Policy is available online at www.eHarlequin.com or upon request from the Reader Service. From time to time we make our lists of customers available to reputable third parties who may have a product or service of interest to you. If you would prefer we not share your name and address, please check here. ☐

HR09R

Coming Next Month

Available September 8, 2009

This fall, curl up and relax with a Harlequin Romance® novel!

#4117 KEEPING HER BABY'S SECRET Raye Morgan
Baby on Board

Cameron's from the richest family in town. Diana's pregnant, unwed and definitely unsuitable. But will it stop these old friends from falling in love?

#4118 CLAIMED: SECRET ROYAL SON Marion Lennox
Marrying His Majesty

A year ago, Lily accidentally became pregnant with Prince Alexandros's baby. Now Alex wants to claim his son. Will Lily agree to *Marrying His Majesty?* Find out in the first book of this new trilogy!

#4119 EXPECTING MIRACLE TWINS Barbara Hannay

Follow surrogate mom Mattie's *Baby Steps to Marriage...*in the first of a new duet by Barbara Hannay. How can Mattie begin a relationship with gorgeous Jake when she's expecting twin trouble?

#4120 MEMO: THE BILLIONAIRE'S PROPOSAL Melissa McClone
9 to 5

When Chaney finds herself back working with billionaire playboy Drake, she must remember how he broke her heart, *not* his devastating charm... Oops!

#4121 A TRIP WITH THE TYCOON Nicola Marsh
Escape Around the World

Join Tamara as she travels through India on a trip of a lifetime, and catch the fireworks when she bumps into a blast from her past, maverick entrepreneur Ethan.

#4122 INVITATION TO THE BOSS'S BALL Fiona Harper
In Her Shoes...

Watch in wonder as this plain Jane is transformed from pumpkin to princess when she's hired to organize her boss's company ball...and dance in his oh-so-delicious arms!

HRCNMBPA0809